COLLECTING THE NEW NATURALISTS

This striking linocut by Robert Gillmor was commissioned by the New Naturalist Collectors' Club as the main artwork for the 2nd symposium in 2011. The linocut is based on the dust wrapper design for *British Warblers* (1985). This was originally created using four separate line drawings in black Indian ink on clear acetate, which made the four colour blocks. (The New Naturalist Collectors' Club/Robert Gillmor)

COLLECTING
THE
NEW NATURALISTS

TIM BERNHARD & TIMOTHY LOE

WILLIAM
COLLINS

William Collins
An imprint of HarperCollins Publishers
1 London Bridge Street
London SE1 9GF

WilliamCollinsBooks.com

First published in Great Britain by
William Collins in 2015

20 19 18 17 16 15
10 9 8 7 6 5 4 3 2 1

A catalogue record for this book is available
from the British Library.

ISBN 978–0–00–736715–3

Publishing Director: Myles Archibald
Senior Editor: Julia Koppitz
Design and Art Direction: Rob Payne
Layout and corrections: Tom Cabot/ketchup
Production: Anna Mitchelmore and Chris Wright

Colour reproduction by FMG
Printed and bound in Hong Kong by
Printing Express

Contents

Tim Bernhard

This book is dedicated to William (Billy) Collins who
instigated and inspired an unparalleled series of
British natural history books.

Also to the various members of the Editorial Board
(particularly James Fisher), who, for 70 years, through
their combined knowledge, enthusiasm
and dynamism, have ensured the continued success
of the New Naturalist library.

Timothy Loe

To Imogen and Harriet, that one day they might
love books as much as their father.

Preface

MY LIFE IN NATURAL HISTORY has been peppered with New Naturalist moments – The original *Broads* and *British Birds of Prey* were part of my early years, Imms' *Insect Natural History* was bedside reading at university, and Harris' *Angler's Entomology* and the Boyd's *The Hebrides* are required reading – then and now. Little did I know the importance of walking into George's (as it then was) on Park Street in Bristol and buying one of only 650 of the first-edition, first state *British Warblers* for the cover price. Just over 12 months later I was employed by Collins to help Crispin Fisher run the series, at what was its nadir. In the 28 years and 56 volumes since, the series has gone from strength to strength. The rebuilding of the series depended on the support of a core of enthusiasts and collectors – notably by the redoubtable Bob Burrow, who started the New Naturalist Collectors' Club and then by his even more notable successor, Tim Bernhard. They both taught me of the passion that the enthusiasts had for the series and their huge desire for every last tiny piece of information that was available. It is thus with huge pleasure that we bring together the combined knowledge of Tim Bernhard and Timothy Loe, who seem to know more about the idiosyncrasies of the books than anyone. It is a joy to read their encyclopaedic knowledge in one place and I can think of no better book to celebrate the 70th Anniversary of the publication of the first New Naturalist volume. In the meantime, the Editorial Board and I will continue to make plans for further titles in the series – only another 870 volumes to go!

Myles Archibald, London, November 2014

Foreword

Book collecting, someone said, is the gentlest form of madness. It grips you with an intensity beyond rational explanation, and quite possibly beyond words. Only fellow addicts understand the inner world of the serious collector: the faraway places of the imagination, the unexpected new interests it opens up, such as printing, design and publishing, the pleasures of communicating with the similarly addicted. We are masters of recondite collector's jargon with its 'tipped in', 'first thus' and 'very good' (meaning 'not very good'). We are bargain hunters and slippery sellers. We habituate second-hand shops and book fairs, and we know almost by instinct where to find boxes of books in the backstreets. Collecting may look like madness to some (partners and spouses, for instance) but we know better. Books enhance life and bring enormous comfort and pleasure. We are *literati* united by a love of books, and if we love something, why not collect it?

I am, I admit, not a proper book collector. I *am* a bibliophile, that is, someone who loves books, but I rarely amass them for the sake of it; for one thing I don't have room. As a book reviewer and a writer of books about books I have developed a thick skin. I give, throw away or flog most review copies and keep only a minority of them. The available book-space in my modest home (plus home from home, plus attic) has reached saturation. To make space for a new book I have to throw an old one away – pitiful, isn't it? Most of my books, in theory at least, are working tools or current reading. But in certain cases they are also very, very special.

The New Naturalists are special. We all know that. They are beautiful and distinctive, and they are designed to be seen together, as a library. Each volume is pretty well the last word on the subject – outside an academic library anyway. They are the right size (why aren't more books the right size?), their famous jackets are, I think, one of the minor miracles of our age. Who,

apart from perhaps Billy Collins, would have hit on the idea of wrapping works of cutting-edge popular science in 'art' covers? Who, apart from the Ellises and Robert Gillmor, would have dedicated so much of their time and talent on what is generally considered to be one of the minor arts? Neither the jackets nor the books inside them were the product of some plan of transcendent genius, made at the very start. Rather, they have evolved, like, say, an elephant. Like that great and wonderful mammal, these books embody a whole set of good ideas, honed and perfected by experience.

When I wrote *The New Naturalists*, long ago, back in 1994, the books were not collected quite as eagerly as today, judging from their original prices. Everyone I knew who owned a good set of them was a fellow naturalist, not a book collector as such (and so not fussy about editions). Quite a few dealers specialised in them and the series was often on prominent show at book fairs and second-hand shops – more so perhaps than today. But the 'New Nats' were not yet part of the book-collecting mainstream. You could find second-hand copies of most titles for less than thirty, sometimes less than twenty, quid, and even the scarcest were still just about affordable. I remember that mint, 'first-state' copy of *Warblers* I saw on sale in 1992 at £200! Outrageous! Who would possibly pay that sort of money? I wish I had.

Although I came to own a complete set, I did not specifically set out to buy every title. I grew up with the series at school and university, when most of those I bought with pocket money and college grants were the old Fontana paperbacks (the exceptions were the flower books – *Chalk & Limestone*, *Wild Orchids* and *Mountain Flowers*, which I used to plan botanical journeys). Later on, I replaced them with hardbacks, generally those from the 1960s with a sometimes updated text and, I think, the nicest typography (they even smelt nice – I loved that New Naturalist scent of new-mown hay). After the calamity of *Orkney/Warblers* I bought each new title as it came out, and so acquired what became known as the Golden Thirteen at cost. I wasn't going to bother with the monographs, until I bought *The Redstart* simply because it is such an adorable book. Then, a few weeks later, I spotted *Ants* at a bargain price and, well, you know how it is... Then a dealer saw me eying *Measles, Mumps and Mosaics* at a book fair and whispered in my ear, like Mephistopheles: 'You may never find another one, you know'. In life, as in stories, one thing leads to another, and after another couple of years I had collected all the monographs too. Oh, and the short-lived *New Naturalist* magazine.

For most of that time I had no particular plans to write up my research, though I did dream about it. It seems to be in my genes to want to find out about things and write about them afterwards. I knew some of the authors, and enough about the scientific background to see the possibilities of an original kind of natural history viewed through the prism of a set of books. I did write a short article-cum-bibliography for *Book and Magazine Collector* and later for *British Wildlife*, but that, I thought, was probably that.

What turned it into a book, *The New Naturalists*, was a series of lucky chances. My friend and former senior colleague Derek Ratcliffe had joined the board of Editors and the rather diffuse plan to publish a book to celebrate the 50th birthday of the series fell into his lap. He knew about my interest in the series since we had talked about it during a long walk, and in the bar afterwards. As a result I had been, unknown to me, penciled in as a possible author. By the time I got to hear about it, they were pretty desperate. If the celebratory volume was to appear in time, it would have to be researched and written in little more than a year. Luckily for them I was willing and able to drop everything to do it. At that time I could live cheaply, which was just as well because the offered terms were, as my brisk and friendly Collins editor, Isobel Smales, put it, 'a pittance'.

I did not have much trouble persuading them to let me write the book as I wanted to do it, at least not after the patriarch of the series, Max Walters, lent me his confidence and enthusiastic support. It was more a question of whether writing such a history was even possible. Very little about the series had been digested and written down, and the job would have to be done mainly through documents and interviews. I borrowed every file and minute from the Collins office in Fulham, and for six months my spare bedroom was piled up with them. I made detailed notes on the publishing history of each title in a large red notebook – 'the red book' – and it was just as well that I did. When Collins became a paper-free office all these records were put into storage in Glasgow. And then, as sometimes happens to goods in storage, a disaster happened. There was a flood and the whole archive – files, artwork, letters, everything – turned to papier-mâché in the waters of the Clyde. My handwritten notes have become, in précis form, the raw history of the series.

I traced and corresponded with most of the authors still living. I remember lunches and winter afternoons spent in the company of Rosemary Ellis, Max Walters, Morton Boyd, Richard Fitter, Eric Simms, Max Nicholson and, of course, Derek Ratcliffe, none of whom are now among the living. Each was unfailingly generous with their replies to my questions and demands for cvs. One sensed a kindred spirit among New Naturalist writers – that, be their academic standing ever so high, they were true naturalists, people with a heightened sensibility to nature. They were, in the main, modest and approachable, and in many cases were great talkers. My only regret was to have missed the opportunity to meet some of the great men of the series: William Collins, James Fisher, E. B. Ford, Harrison Matthews, Sir Maurice Yonge, Sir Alister Hardy, Gordon Manley ... Fortunately in many cases their papers and the testimony of friends and relatives provided a vivid glimpse of the men behind the books.

In hindsight, *The New Naturalists* came out at a fortunate time for the series. Its fortunes were then at a low ebb and sales were rock bottom. The book, and the jolly party held in April 1995 to celebrate the half-centenary, created new interest in the series, although recovery was slow. Recruitment of new titles had slowed to a trickle and it was not until 1999 that the series began to expand again.

It has never looked back: thirty new titles in the past decade, lately three per year. Confidence has bred a distinct whiff of commercialism (what are those 'leatherbounds' *for*?). One sign of a reviving interest was the spiraling prices of the thirteen titles that preceded *The New Naturalists*, something that I had not foreseen. Evidently many people who had stopped collecting the books had started again and were looking to fill the gaps. I regret the price hike but I feel proud of my contribution to the fortunes of the series. It was all amateur dabbling but I like to think my book told a coherent story and generated this new interest.

Not that the story ended there, of course. So much has happened in the New Naturalist world since 1995. As a recent article in *Book and Magazine Collector* pointed out, the series has become a virtual sub-genre of book-collecting, with a host of new words – leatherbounds, PODs, belly bands, Bloomsburys, blogs, repro-jackets. For those who have collected everything and want to go on collecting there are foreign editions, author biographies, allied series and so on, perhaps *ad infinitum*. Then there is the phenomenon of New Naturalist ephemera, such as catalogues and fliers, calendars, Christmas cards and even mugs. Gentle madness indeed! Is it wise to throw anything away? Did anyone keep the chocolate bar that was, rather weirdly, included in the goody-bag handed to guests at the 60th anniversary party in 2005? Although proving provenance might be difficult, a chocolate wrapper signed by, say, all the New Naturalist editors might be worth a bob or two.

And so to the latest milestone in the story and a major one: *Collecting the New Naturalists*. Tim Bernhard is the best friend a book series could ever have. He is a natural history artist with design experience, and his creative side will ensure that this is a beautiful book. He is also a delver *extraordinaire*. Who else but someone with the most remarkable focus and persistence could have rounded up images of every single one of the New Naturalist authors, plus all their signatures! Who else would have even thought of collecting their bookplates! Tim is the keeper of the jewel house. He has compiled a large collection of New Naturalist memorabilia and minutiae in what amounts to an alternate archive. One day, we hope, it will form the heart of a curated collection on the series that will be consulted by scholars and admirers. What would I not have given for such a thing when I was researching the series!

Timothy Loe of Loe Books who has perhaps the largest stock of New Naturalists in existence has taken the next logical step in the story by entering the world of the collector full on (I always tended to skirt round it). He has put the series under the microscope, sorting out small but telling differences in editions and impressions as well as cataloguing the full range of alternate versions of the books which have sprung up over time: bookclubs, paperbacks, leatherbacks, Bloomsbury imprints, Folios, PODS, reprints, foreign editions …. What is more they have persuaded the likes of Alan Titchmarsh and Nick Baker to sing the praises of the series.

This book is the best compliment the New Naturalist library could have, and the best kind of treat for the seriously addicted. It is a minutely researched cornucopia of delights that will surely form the standard reference work on the series for a long time to come. Great credit is also due to the long-serving series editor Myles Archibald, assisted by Julia Koppitz, for publishing the book, and to the highest standards. It will, I hope, look particularly nice when placed next to *Art of the New Naturalists* by Marren & Gillmor, and that copy of the bound New Naturalist magazine you found in a junk shop thirty years ago.

Relax, peruse and enjoy!

Peter Marren, Wiltshire, February 2014

Natural History Publishing, the Genesis of the New Naturalist Library and Some Collecting Issues

A HISTORY OF NATURAL HISTORY BOOKS IN BRITAIN AND IRELAND

The story of natural history books in the British Isles begins well over a hundred years before the printed book arrived from Europe, with the early Christian monks who filled their manuscripts with gorgeously coloured depictions of the wonders of Creation: birds, plants and animals. Ever since, natural history books have served as decorative objects and collectors' items, as well as scientific guides and absorbing reads.

One of the earliest named writers to deal specifically with observations of wildlife was Gerald de Barri. A high-born cleric, courtier and writer, Gerald recorded the names of fishes and birds he studied, and included observations of beavers on the River Teifi in his *Journey Through Wales* in the early thirteenth century. The real driver of medieval natural history writing was not academic curiosity but medical need. Works like those of the Dominican friar Henry Daniel pioneered the study of botany as a branch of medicine. Herbals, as these botanical reference works were called, were being printed in England just a few decades after the arrival of the printing press from Germany. The first, *Banckes's Herbal* (1525), had no illustrations, yet was found useful enough to be reissued in many editions. It was followed a year later by *The Grete Herball*, the first printed herbal to include illustrations.

As the study of nature developed, so less obviously functional works, catering to curiosity about the natural world, were printed. The religious upheavals of the sixteenth century prompted scholars to look more carefully at scripture, and at the same time they began to scrutinise God's works as they saw them in the natural world and to branch out from the mainly medicinal study of plants. William Turner was a major figure in early modern herbalism, but he also wrote one of the first books on ornithology, filled with stories of his own lifetime of observation. Thomas Penny, similarly, came to the study of insects through his medicinal study of plants and wrote the first book on entomology printed in England; however Penny died in 1589 before the book's completion and it was taken on by his younger friend and colleague, Thomas Moffet. Finally published in 1634 after Moffet, too, had died, *Insectorum sive minimorum animalium theatrum* contained detailed descriptions and woodcuts, including field notes on nineteen species of British butterfly. Books on snakes and animals also joined the ever-popular herbals on the shelves of the seventeenth-century collector.

Works on flora and fauna became much more detailed and systematic in this period, with a greater emphasis on fieldwork. The partnership between John Ray, a botanist, and Francis Willughby, a zoologist, produced *Systema naturae*. After Willughby's death *Ornithologia* was published in 1676 from a mass of notes left to Ray. This book described about 190 species of British bird that the two of them had personally observed. *Ornithologia* was to remain the standard book on the subject for many years and contained engravings instead of the more usual woodcuts.

Ray's final work, *Historia insectorum*, was published posthumously by the Royal Society in 1710. Although incomplete, it described 47 species of butterfly, more than twice the number listed by Thomas Penny. One of Ray's travel companions, Martin Lister, became a Fellow of the Royal Society in its early years and alongside contributions to the Society's Transactions, published pioneering works on molluscs and spiders. His comprehensive work on shells was used in the cataloguing of the Royal Society's vast collections.

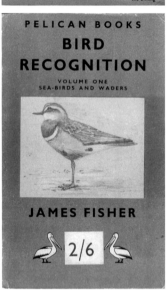

James Fisher's well known *Watching Birds* published by Pelican Books in 1941. The book became an instant success amongst war-time Britain and was followed by a series of further paperbacks on 'Bird Recognition'.

This was the era of the 'cabinet of curiosities'; of collections kept by the wealthy both for display and for learning. The urge to classify demanded a number of specialist works on particular species, such as Johann Dillenius' work on mosses and liverworts, and James Petiver's *Papilionum Britanniae icones* (1717), the first printed book devoted entirely to British butterflies. The aesthetic appeal of the new fad for butterfly collecting was emphasised by the first ever book on British natural history to be illustrated in colour: Eleazar Albin's *A Natural History of English Insects*, first published in 1720. Containing 100 copperplates which Albin had hand-painted himself, this was the first of many imitators. Albin went on to produce a three-volume work on birds (1731–38), also with colour illustrations, and *A Natural History of Spiders and other Curious Insects* (1736). Other naturalist-artists followed, such as the talented engraver Moses Harris with his work *The Aurelian* (1766). A few years later, William Withering became the first botanist to list all British flora, in English, according to the Linnaean system.

The collecting and classificatory mania went beyond botany. Inspired to his love of nature as a small boy by a present of a copy of *Willoughby's Ornithology*, Thomas Pennant became best known as a key correspondent of Gilbert White's during the composition of White's *The Natural History and Antiquities of Selborne, in the County of Southampton* (1788). Pennant also produced his own famous work, *British Zoology* (1761). Written in English and covering mammals, birds, reptiles, amphibians and fishes, this was among the first popular books on general natural history.

The burgeoning Georgian interest in natural history was catered to by some spectacularly beautiful works, such as James Sowerby's *English Botany* (1791–1814) which was packed with 2,592 hand-coloured plates by the artist William Curtis. With such desirable books available, gentlemen's collections extended to books as well as to specimens. Publishers catered for the upper classes' passions for shooting and fishing, with impressive and expensive works such as *The Fresh Water Fishes of Great Britain* by Sarah Bowdich (1828–38) and *The Birds of Great Britain* by John Gould (1862–73). But coloured plates were expensive to produce, and there was a limited market of collectors who could afford lavishly illustrated volumes. One solution for publishers was to reduce costs, as Thomas Bewick did with his editions filled with exquisitely carved woodcuts, including *A General History of British Quadrupeds* in 1781 and the two volumes of the *History of British Birds* a few years later. It also made sound business sense for publishers to issue books in parts, to spread the costs of producing plates over a longer period.

Technology was to provide the great breakthrough to mass-market publications. Steam power brought mechanical cast-iron printing presses, which made large print runs possible at a much reduced cost. And by the 1830s, copper-plate engraving was being replaced by lithography which offered more detailed illustrations at a third of the cost of the older technique. Letterpress text and mass-produced cloth bindings also drove down costs. The ever-increasing railway network ensured faster and cheaper distribution of books, and measures like the price-protecting Booksellers' Regulations and surplus trade stock (remainders) enabled publishers to reach new markets and to produce journals and magazines, such as *The Zoologist*, cheaply.

In the midst of all these dynamic changes to publishing, Edinburgh printer William Home Lizars decided in 1832 to produce the first major series of natural history books: The Naturalists Library. Together with his editor and brother-in-law, Sir William Jardine, Lizars saw that there was a general thirst for information and illustrations on the wonders of the natural world. Their plan was for a series of books to be made to a uniform size, compact for easy handling and available individually. They were to include volumes on flora and fauna from around the world, more than half covering exotic species, and would contain as many coloured illustrations as possible. Importantly, with cheap techniques and with the advantage of Edinburgh's comparatively low printing costs, they would be affordable to the middle classes. Beginning in 1833 with a book on hummingbirds, 40 titles were published over ten years. They were a huge success. Individual titles sold as many as 10,000 copies and were re-issued around the country. A little over a hundred years later, the New Naturalist library would be the brainchild of Billy Collins, who as a boy in early twentieth-century Scotland would most likely have been familiar with the previous Naturalists library and may have named his series with Lizars' in mind.

The new technologies, combined with increased literacy and demand, encouraged a flourishing in natural history publishing. Publishers like Longman, Orme, Brown and Green, the Ray Society, John Van Voorst, Lovell Reeve and Robert Hardwicke began to specialise in natural history. In the late nineteenth century a new generation of hobbyist naturalist, armed with improved field equipment and more leisure time, demanded not just detailed guides to the flora and fauna of Britain but also reminiscence books, more relaxed writings on travels and anecdotes from the field. William Henry Hudson's classics *Birds in a Village* (Chapman & Hall, 1893), *British Birds* (Longman, 1895), *Nature in Downland* (1900) and *Hampshire Days* (1903) tapped into the British public's enthusiasm for their native wildlife, and more libraries of cheap classics were published in the opening years of the twentieth century, including J. M. Dent's Everyman's Library and similar enterprises by Nelson and Collins.

Photography offered exciting new possibilities for nineteenth-century illustrated natural history books, although early photographic equipment was prohibitively cumbersome for use in the field. Technological advances from 1879 made things a little easier, but it was still only the most intrepid naturalist who would lug negatives and lumière plates around to distant parts of the country. The first major work to successfully use photography was *British Birds' Nests: how, where and when to find and identify them*, published by Cassell & Co in 1895. Thanks to the introduction of offset lithography using revolving cylinders, by the 1910s sharper photographs and print were possible. The first true use of colour photographs in natural history publishing was by Dent in 1910. Cassell followed, producing *Wild Flowers As They Grow* a year later, as part of a series of books using high-quality colour photographs.

Series like Frederick Warne's, beginning with works such as Edward Step's *Wayside and Woodland Blossoms* in 1895 and *The Birds of the British Isles* by T. A. Coward in 1920, were successful popular reference works before the days of the field guide. With his Observer Books, Warne offered a true pocket guide. By the 1940s they had sold over 200,000 copies, and soon afterwards they expanded their subject matter beyond natural history. Other publishers, such as Oxford University Press, Hutchinson and A&C Black, all launched similar publishing ventures, but it was Penguin Books, launched in 1935, that stole the limelight. Although not especially concerned with natural history, the imprint Pelican published the classic *Watching Birds* by James Fisher. Around the same time, Penguin published its edition of the hugely popular classic book by Henry Williamson, *Tarka the Otter*, which was a pioneering animal biography – fictional, yet based on detailed observation. It also marked the return of beautiful illustrations, in Tarka's case drawn by Charles Tunnicliffe. The interwar interest in animal ecology and conservation was also reflected in non-fiction works like Charles Elton's *Animal Ecology*, published by Sidgwick & Jackson in 1927. Whether for entertainment, aesthetic pleasure or scientific interest, by the Second World War the British public's love of natural history books was established.

THE STORY OF COLLINS

The Collins family's entrance into publishing began in Glasgow, where William Collins started his career as a weaver at the turn of the nineteenth century. He soon progressed to the position of clerk, and began teaching Sunday school as well as giving lessons in the 3 'R's to mill workers at night. After opening a successful private school in Glasgow, Collins founded two businesses in 1819: a printing outfit under his own name and Chalmers & Collins, Booksellers and Stationers, in partnership with Thomas Chalmers. Their publications were evangelically religious and educational. In 1821, Collins issued his first schoolbook, *A System of Commercial Arithmetic for Use in Schools and Private Families*, and soon afterwards made his first trip to London where he added to his growing distribution network. His energy brought him rapid success: in 1823 Collins published his first bestseller, *The Christian Philosopher* by Thomas Dick, and by 1826 he was able to buy Chalmers out and became the sole owner of the business. Collins' Glasgow presses ran continuously, selling not just at home but also in the United States through the New York agents Leavitt, Lord and Company. By the time Collins died in 1853, he had established a prosperous publishing firm including printing, binding and stationery, with a list which by this point included the beginnings of Collins' famous series of illustrated dictionaries.

William Collins' son, William Collins II, was to prove a shrewd and ambitious heir to the business who shared his father's passion for moral causes such as temperance. Upgrading the

William Alexander Roy (Billy) Collins in his office at the elegant eighteenth-century buildings of 14 St James's Place, London. These were the main London offices used by Collins from 1945 until 1981. (National Portrait Gallery, London)

company's printing works with steam presses, the younger Collins fed the rising demand for educational books in Britain's expanding school system. He published a number of travel books including *The Pacific, North Africa, Greece* and *Palestine*. He also ventured into geology and astronomy, publishing titles including *Celestial Scenery* by Thomas Dicks as well as bibles, dictionaries and cheap editions of books such as *The Pilgrim's Progress* and *Holy War*. Joined by his two sons Alexander and William III, the company continued to flourish, particularly with greater bible sales. William took an interest in mechanics and the technique of manufacture and invented a machine to fold, gum and dry envelopes to keep pace with the ever-increasing demand for stationery.

After Sir William Collins II's death in 1895, his son William Collins III expanded the printing works and bindery and also added to Collins' rather worthy list of many entertaining books for children, both classics and newly commissioned stories. In 1900, William Collins V was born in London and was to become the Billy Collins responsible for the New Naturalist library. Six years later, Billy's grandfather died in a tragic accident, falling down the lift-shaft in his apartment building. The firm then passed to his son, William Alexander Collins, who ran the company together with his brother Godfrey and cousin William Collins Dickson. Around the core base of bibles, schoolbooks, reference books, childrens' books and stationery, they published award-winning novels and phenomenally successful detective stories.

Billy Collins took over the day-to-day running of the company after Sir Godfrey's death in 1936, and soon found himself contending with the challenges of wartime, including severe cutbacks on imports such as paper, production and transport delays as well as the enormous amount of destruction due to bombing raids in the major cities. Collins found itself bombed out of its Pall Mall offices in 1945, when it moved to its famous location in elegant eighteenth-century houses in St James's Place. This became the main London offices until 1981, when the company moved to Grafton Street.

The war brought opportunities for publishers too. During the dark days of war, with regular black-outs and reduced opportunities for evening entertainment, and also among the many thousands of off-duty service men and women, there was a huge demand for books. One of the publications helping to boost national morale was the Britain in Pictures series (see page 18). This series of books contained many colourful illustrations. Although there were 132 titles in the series, as well as several omnibus editions, only a handful were devoted to natural history. This included volume number 36 of *The Birds of Britain* by James Fisher, which sold nearly 100,000 copies up until 1952 in over four editions. The success of James Fisher's *Watching Birds* in 1940 had shown that natural history was a popular topic in troubled times.

The beginnings of the New Naturalist library
Wildlife was a personal interest of Billy Collins'. An avid collector of beautiful antiquarian books on the subject, he had an ambition to publish a quality series of natural history books. Even in wartime, Billy Collins saw his opportunity. Thanks to high sales in the late 1930s, the company had been allocated a higher paper ration than most, and they were also fortunate in that their main printing works were in Glasgow, away from the bombing raids in London. They also had access to large-format Kodachrome film through Wolfgang Foges and his company Adprint, who had worked with Collins on the Britain in Pictures series. In the spring of 1942, Collins and Foges approached the prominent zoologist, writer and broadcaster Julian Huxley to discuss the proposal of a series of books on British natural history.

They met at Au Jardin des Gourmets in Soho, and Huxley brought with him James Fisher, an ex-student of his and an enthusiastic and dynamic naturalist and writer. The lunch meeting was very productive, with Huxley showing great interest in Collins' proposal. Huxley and Fisher were to form the nucleus of the Editorial Board and to match subjects with authors, seeing each book through to publication. Adprint were to take care of the production of illustrative material, and the books would be printed by Collins in Glasgow.

The following January the Editorial Board had their first meeting. Joining Huxley and Fisher were L. Dudley Stamp to cover earth sciences, John Gilmour, a botanist, and Eric Hosking, who would take the role as photographic editor. Eventually, with all the frustrations and obstructions of wartime, by the end of 1945 the first of the books was being printed.

The New Naturalist series was one of the most outstanding success stories of post-war British publishing. The timing of the books could not have been better. After the long drawn-out dark days of war, suddenly these bright new books appeared, striking in appearance, with numerous colour plates, and at a reasonable price. But much more importantly, the books also coincided with the increasing popularity of the new science of ecology. The authors were skilled field naturalists, trained in traditional sciences and writing with passion and with great ease of communication. The publishers were in a perfect position to take advantage of the combination of plentiful paper, production facilities and promotional power. With colour film and Billy Collins' determination to see the project through, it was destined to be a success.

Post-war natural history publishing

Apart from the bold New Naturalist series from Collins, the years following the war were an uncertain time for the publishing industry in Britain. Rising production costs made many publishers careful with new endeavours. There were one or two grand offerings, such as *The Birds of the British Isles* published by Oliver & Boyd (1953–63), which was written by David Bannerman and illustrated by George Lodge and ran into 12 volumes. Great advances in photography were overshadowing finely printed paintings, especially with the high-speed photography. Nocturnal habits of mammals could now be photographed in the wild; and at around the same time, in 1954, the Mammal Society of the British Isles was formed, and ten years later the *Handbook of British Mammals* was published. As in the 1830s, there was a great resurgence of specialist societies including the Herpetological Society in 1947 and the British Lichen Society in 1954.

Although there were a string of serious books on nature conservation, it was the identification guides which were to steal the limelight during the 1950s. Penguin had started the ball rolling with James Fisher's *Watching Birds* in 1940, but the first of the field guides appeared in the United States with Houghton Mifflin publishing *A Field Guide to the Birds* by Roger Tory Peterson. It was designed to be used in the field and to make identification as quick as possible, with principal visual characteristics illustrated. The book was a huge success; 2,000 copies were sold in the first week of publication alone.

It was Collins who published the first British field guide in 1954. *A Field Guide to the Birds of Britain and Europe* was written by Roger Tory Peterson, Guy Mountfort and P. A. D. Hollom. Collins also produced a number of pocket guides and so began a seemingly unstoppable flow of related books. Richard Fitter wrote many of these, including the popular *Pocket Guide to Wild Flowers*, which he co-wrote with David McClintock and which Collins published in 1956. Another classic book on botany was *The Wild Flower Key* by Francis Rose, published by Warne in 1981. Although plants and birds undoubtedly held the centre stage for many years, with butterflies not far behind, in recent times there has been a good deal of interest in other insect orders, with the

publication of field guides to grasshoppers and crickets, among others.

British publishers also produced impressive publications on foreign wildlife, including *Flora Europaea*, eventually published in five volumes by Cambridge University Press (1964–80), and the nine-volume *The Birds of the Western Palaearctic*, published by Oxford University Press, 1977–94. T. & A. D. Poyser and Christopher Helm filled the gap left by Witherby and produced a large number of exceptional books on birds and bird ecology, and Blandford Press and David & Charles also published an impressive selection of natural history books. But with leaner times in the 1970s, a number of well-established publishers were either swallowed up by other companies or disappeared completely. Amongst these was Warne, which was taken over by Penguin Books in 1981.

Another publisher that has produced some outstanding natural history publications in recent years is Harley Books. Beginning life as Curwen Press, the printing firm was eventually taken over by Basil Harley in 1983, from which point the company specialised in natural history books. On retirement Harley sold the stock and copyright of some of his ongoing series to Apollo Books, based in Denmark, who continue to publish entomological books.

The 1990s were another troubled period, which saw high inflation and the demise of the Net Book Agreement in 1995 – which stripped publishers of their control over the prices paid for their books. As a result, there is now much more competition in the sale of books, away from the traditional book shops to supermarkets and the ever-increasing use of the internet. The publishing industry is set to face many more changes in the future as the book-reading market changes and embraces new

The New Naturalist Editorial Board meeting at St James's Place in June 1966. Standing (left to right): James Fisher, Sir Dudley Stamp and Eric Hosking. Seated: John Gilmour and Sir Julian Huxley. (Eric Hosking)

technology, but as long as there are collectors of natural history and countryside books and demand for field guides, at least a few natural history publishers will survive.

The New Naturalist library today

On the face of it the New Naturalist series would appear to be in the very best of health. Up to four titles a year were published from 2007, illustrated in full colour throughout and with striking dust jacket designs by Robert Gillmor. These included some superb additions to the library which have been very well reviewed. In 2009 Collins introduced the print-on-demand service through their website, making all the earlier main-series volumes available for the first time, and in hardback. This catalogue was extended to include the full set of Monographs in 2011. There are other changes too, such as the development of electronic books, which are now available for each new publication as well as, increasingly, older titles in the series. Whatever the future brings for the ways in which books are presented to us, past writers, illustrators and publishers have left us a fine library of books to collect, read and enjoy.

In February 2013, a new William Collins imprint was established to bring together the former HarperPress imprint and elements of Collins publications including history, biography, science, politics, natural history, reference, business, philosophy and religion. William Collins' vision in 1819 was to publish books of the highest quality, available to every home in the land. The new William Collins imprint draws on his original values of integrity, authority and clarity and HarperCollins hope that this new imprint will help to engage with a broader audience through events and digital platforms. These developments are deemed a very good move for natural history publications and will help to reinforce the future of the New Naturalist library.

James Fisher

James Fisher was an authority on sea-birds and instigated the British Trust for Ornithology's nest-record scheme. His wartime Pelican paperback, *Watching Birds*, still in print after thirty years, introduced thousands of wartime Brits to the joys of birdwatching (some say it invented that word). He was a media star and author of a string of well-read books, many of which found their way into the hands of bird enthusiasts, such as *Thorburn's Birds*, which married Archibald Thorburn's pictures with Fisher's dense notes on distribution and breeding. His *Shell Bird Book* was a kind of birder's Bible, an extraordinary *vade mecum* of ornithological topics from birding personalities to fossil birds, which revealed the unusual range of Fisher's interests and the depth of his scholarship (he had even found the first birder: not St Francis but the sixth-century St Serf of Fife who had tamed a robin). Those that met Fisher found him charming, affable, enthusiastic and, above all, effortlessly knowledgeable.

Peter Scott would have been the first to agree that Fisher had made a greater contribution to bird study than he. Once, when a boy came up to him to ask him for his autograph, Scott indicated Fisher, who was standing by, and murmured: 'His is the one you should be getting, not mine.' The two had known each other since their school days – Peter Scott was a pupil at Oundle School where Fisher's father was headmaster. On their 'wild goose chase' together to Iceland, in 1952, to discover where Britain's wintering pinkfoot geese nested in the summer, Scott found Fisher an 'excellent companion, good-humoured, witty, practical and erudite'. Niall Campbell, who once shared a convivial evening with Fisher on a cruise ship off St Kilda, recalled that 'at the end of our cheerful evening I had to be lowered like a sack of potatoes into an inflatable and taken ashore … I wish that I had met him more often'.

Perhaps Fisher comes alive most vividly in *Wild America*, the record of a 100-day journey he made in spring 1953 with another lifelong friend, the American artist and naturalist Roger Tory Peterson. The inevitable frustrations and longeurs of long-distance travel were surmounted by their shared, unquenchable love of birds. Fisher and Peterson talked about birds the whole time (Peterson, at least, rarely talked about anything else). 'Birds-birds-birds!' wrote Fisher. 'Roger showed me more birds today than I have ever seen in one day before'. Every time Fisher spotted a new bird he would whisper (or shout) 'tally-ho', a pun on 'tally' or list. A Californian condor, America's mightiest and rarest raptor, met with a 'Tally most incredibly ho!' as I ticked it off my checklist.' 'Quite a bird', murmured Peterson, 'Exhibit A.' – 'Worth seeing actually.' They had travelled ten thousand miles to see it. Fisher was a great list maker. The *Shell Bird Book* contains 120 pages of them. The bibliography he wanted to add to the already oversized *Fulmar* ran to nearly 2,300 references. To write that book, aptly called 'an extraordinary accumulation of knowledge' by one reviewer, Fisher had managed to visit nearly every substantial island in the North Atlantic. It might have been necessary for censusing the bird, but, one suspects, Fisher had a psychological need to tick off sea-bird islands. He loved islands, boats and the open sea. He visited the remote archipelago of St Kilda at least nine times, and was a member of the intrepid expedition that raised the Union Jack on the remote Atlantic rock of Rockall in 1955. He often remarked that he had set foot on more British islands than anyone else. He was also a great mapper. Often with his son Crispin's help, Fisher devised special maps for his New Naturalists and other books and, like many a tick-using naturalist, fixed each locality with a dot. A dot was a fact of distribution; like a list, it was a concise way of summarising knowledge. Wearing his scientific hat, Fisher knew how to be thorough.

Fisher was at the forefront of a new generation of ornithologists who, realising that there was already far too much accumulated knowledge for anyone to master the whole field, became specialists. In effect they adopted a species to study, which is, of course, why there was a readymade queue of authors to write the New Naturalist monographs (and why most of the books were about birds). Fisher's birds were the gannet, the rook and the fulmar. He had worked on gannets before and after the war, and on rooks during it, but the bird he loved to the point of obsession was the fulmar. He found bottomless fascination not only in its lonely nesting grounds but in the way the bird had spread around the British coast from its remote former stronghold at St Kilda. The colonial nesting habits of rooks and sea-birds lend themselves to censusing; and Fisher's two New Naturalist bird books are

Above left: James Maxwell McConnell Fisher in the field, 1939 (Clem Fisher). **Above right:** James Fisher and Eric Hosking, photographed at the International Ornithological Congress, The Hague in the Netherlands, September 1970. This was perhaps the last photograph taken of James Fisher as he died in a car crash shortly afterwards. (Robert Gillmor)

concerned above all with populations and numbers. Once he had got *The Fulmar* and *Sea-Birds* out of the way, Fisher asked the New Naturalist Board which topic he should cover next: the gannet, the rook or moorland birds? His preference was for the rook, but all three were listed as forthcoming 'special volumes'. Fisher's enthusiasm had a tendency to run ahead of practical realities. None of these titles were completed – or at least not by him.

Fisher's most lasting achievement, though, is surely as a populariser. He might have had a blue chip education – Eton and Oxford – but Fisher was interested in the Mass-Observation movement of the 1930s, went on at least one protest march and was active in his local Labour party. His credo is stated in his book, *Watching Birds*, the cheap Pelican paperback that came out in the year of the Battle of Britain (and took him, he claimed, only two weeks to write or dictate):

'Birds are part of the heritage we are fighting for. After this war ordinary people are going to have a better time than they have had; they are going to get about more … many will get the opportunity, hitherto sought in vain, of watching wild creatures and making discoveries about them. It is for these men and women, and not for the privileged few to whom ornithology has been an indulgence, that I have written this little book.'

Later on, he reminded his readers how right he had been: 'In the first paragraph of my first preface I was rash enough to make some prognostications. As far as I can make out, these have come quite true.'

Fisher wrote fast, though, as his daughter Clemency told me, after much prevarication: 'the long morning baths, the thus-dampened newspaper, the tv, the bird table, polyhedral origami, etc'. His versatile mind transferred seamlessly to his speech, and he became a first-rate broadcaster and public speaker.

He was also a popular journalist, writing articles for *Punch and Woman*, as well as *Bird Study*. He had the capacity, wrote Elspeth Huxley, 'to cast a spell over vast audiences while still remaining charming to the least of individuals. In conversation he was quick and sympathetic, widely read and learned, with an easy command of facts'. He brought this 'people-skill' to the New Naturalist Board. The basic idea was partly his, and it was almost certainly his energy and commitment that sustained the series after the initial impetus of large sales had worn off. Of all Fisher's achievements, the New Naturalist series is, arguably, the most enduring.

James Fisher crammed a lot into a life robbed of its older years. His thousand-odd radio broadcasts, most notably *Children's Hour*'s Nature Parliament, made him among the best known naturalists of the 1950s and 60s. He was a loving husband and father of six children, all of whom made names for themselves in different fields. He spent a lot of time on the groups and committees of the bird and conservation world, including his local Northamptonshire Wildlife Trust, and was latterly a kind of troubleshooter and Deputy Chair of the Countryside Commission. He is the only person to have received all three of the top birding awards: the BOU's (British Ornithologists' Union) Union Medal, the RSPB's (Royal Society for the Protection of Birds) Gold medal and the BTO's (British Trust for Ornithology) Tucker Medal.

How much of all this still reverberates today? What is the standing of James Fisher among today's younger birders? All his books are out of print (though they are certainly still read), and his style, like that of most of his contemporaries, is no longer in fashion. He believed that the bird was the subject, and that the author must keep himself in the background as much as possible. His Uncle Arnold (A.W. Boyd) would have agreed in disliking 'nature-dramatisers … who proffered peeps at their powerful personalities in the guise of facts about their feathered friends' (though that did not prevent him from writing a popular and long-running column in the *Manchester Guardian*). Most of the first generation of New Naturalist books share the same modest credo: that personal experiences should give way to objective facts.

During the past ten years, nature writing has become far more confessional in style, with the authors setting themselves firmly in the foreground. At its best, the new writing has introduced a lyricism and insight into our individual relationships with nature. James Fisher's engagement with the fulmar, that 'ghost-grey bird' on 'green islands in grey seas' was deep and genuine, but his expression of personal feeling is confined to the foreword.

That is why the popular natural history writers of the 1940s and 1950s seem so different from their descendents today. The contemporary writer Tim Dee detected what he saw as 'loftiness and patrician hauteur' in some of James Fisher's writing, picking on the densely-packed *Shell Bird Book* as an example: 'He marshals his chapters for our benefit like a headmaster and writes with the slightly bored swagger of imperious certainty'. Dee is more drawn to John Buxton's New Naturalist Monograph, *The Redstart*, where the author is less inclined to sift through scientific papers for the facts, preferring to concentrate on his own thoughts and experiences. Tellingly, this approach led to a good-humoured clash of cultures between the 'amateur' Buxton and the 'professional' Fisher. 'You have definitely overdone the "mere naturalist and not a scientist" attitude', smiled Fisher, 'Can you please do something mildly about it?' Yet some would say that it is the 'mere naturalist' in John Buxton that makes him so readable now: the romance of an educated man shut up in a prisoner-of-war camp for years who found consolation and intellectual stimulation by watching familiar birds going about their daily business. He was entranced by the bird's 'grace and beauty, and for the sweet gentle charm of its song'.

Equally telling is Elspeth Huxley's comparison between James Fisher and Peter Scott in her biography of the latter. To Scott, bird migration was a 'mystery', while to Fisher it was a 'puzzle' A mystery admits non-rational forces, something partly beyond human reason, but a puzzle has a solution, and when that is found out it is no longer puzzling. Sooner or later, implied Fisher, ornithologists would discover exactly how birds migrate, and that would be that. Another key difference was that Scott had the ability, rare among naturalists, to boil things down and get to the point quickly. To Fisher, the point was sometimes lost in the detail. As Roger Tory Peterson said of him, 'James has almost too much factual information'.

James Fisher's life, with its combination of action and reflection, would make a good biography. There is tragedy there too. Apart from Fisher himself, his talented children, Edmund, Crispin and Selina all died before their time. Fisher's biographer would not lack materials. His vast personal archive was sold after the death of Fisher's widow, Margery, in December 1992 and the subsequent sale of Ashton Manor. Fortunately his papers were saved by the intervention of Bruce Coleman and John Burton and are now in the library of the Natural History Museum – an indication of Fisher's enduring high standing at least among scholars.

— James Maxwell McConnell Fisher, 1912–1970

Britain in Pictures

The revolutionary use of colour in publishing during the 1940s had a huge impact on natural history books. Wildlife and landscapes depicted in glorious colour were to become a trademark of the New Naturalist library but their origins lay in an earlier collaboration between Collins and Adprint. Just before the outbreak of the Second World War, Collins and Adprint produced a series of garden books called The Garden in Colour, which was remarkable for being illustrated exclusively by colour photography by John Hinde, who was working for Adprint at the time. These books were very successful and proved to be a useful demonstration of what could be achieved using photography and letterpress printing.

The Collins-Adprint partnership continued with a now-famous series of books known as Britain in Pictures. The original idea for a series of short illustrated books about Britain came from Hilda Matheson, who at the time was engaged on propaganda work for the new Ministry of Information. Together with Walter Turner and Dorothy Wellesley, they formed the first editorial committee and would meet monthly with Billy Collins (who would take the chair), and two other Collins representatives: F. T. Smith (editorial) and Sidney Goldsack (finance). The design of the books was influenced by Wolfgang Foges and his team at Adprint. These books were produced in octavo size and were all very similar in appearance, covering every aspect of British life. They were hugely successful and sold in their thousands. The first of these books was published in March 1941 and was regarded with a great deal of national pride. The bright jackets of the book would have made a colourful display presesnted en masse in bookshop windows in the dark days of wartime Britain.

Although each book in the series was well illustrated in colour, colour photography did not feature and instead Adprint borrowed from the vast collections of old colour engravings and paintings. Although the books were quite slim they were well printed and attractive to look at, particularly with the Fontana typeface which Collins created in 1935.

Britain in Pictures is perhaps best remembered today for its wide selection of authors, including well-known novelists, dramatists, poets, artists and historians. These included Graham Greene and George Orwell, whose books in the series are particularly sought after. Of the ten books which covered various aspects of British natural history, seven were written by future New Naturalist authors. The most successful title in the entire series was *The Birds of Britain* by James Fisher, which had a total edition of 95,534 copies over four impressions. Six of these natural history books were later bound in a larger omnibus edition titled *Nature in Britain*, which can be found with two different jacket designs, including one by Charles Tunnicliffe.

Altogether 132 books were published in the Britain in Pictures series between 1941 and 1950. The books were bold and colourful and hugely successful, so much so that in 1951 Collins advertised that nearly three million copies had been sold since 1941. Numbered at the head of the spine, they were very much in the spirit of the forthcoming New Naturalist library. With Collins' large paper allowance and with Adprint's experience with colour

TABLE 1: Britain in Pictures titles written by New Naturalist authors

No.	Title	Author	Year of pub./Edition	No. of copies sold
16	*English Farming*	Sir E. John Russell	1941/4	41,108
21	*The Story of Scotland*	F. Fraser Darling	1942/4	57,647
36	*The Birds of Britain*	James Fisher	1942/4	95,534
52	*Wild Life of Britain*	F. Fraser Darling	1943/3	79,024
70	*British Marine Life*	C. M. Yonge	1944/–	15,939
79	*British Botanists*	John Gilmour	1944/2	29,207
85	*Islands Round Britain*	R. M. Lockley	1945/2	29,492

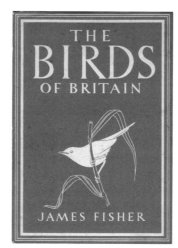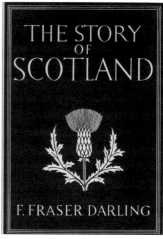

photography and printing, they were all set to start work on Billy Collins' next idea of producing a ground-breaking series of books on British natural history.

SOME COLLECTING ISSUES

A note on the name: The New Naturalist or New Naturalists?
In the minds of those who created 'The New Naturalist' it was clear that the term was a collective noun, an umbrella term to cover a concept, a general title for a library of books on British wildlife. This is explained in Stamp's preface to No. 49 *Nature Conservation* in which he writes '… after much discussion [we] coined the general title "The New Naturalist" toward the end of a long meeting'. It is not until comparatively recently that the title has been, one might argue erroneously, 'pluralised' to the 'The New Naturalists'. The jacket blurb for the first edition of *Insect Natural History* (1947) includes '…there are several excellent books on these insects that are readily accessible, including Dr. Ford's volume on *Butterflies* in the New Naturalist.' Not 'in The New Naturalists', or even 'in The New Naturalist Series', but just simply 'in The New Naturalist'. A 1947 advert states 'The New Naturalist A survey of British Natural History… The New Naturalist is edited by James Fisher, John Gilmour, Julian Huxley…' and a 1949 advert 'The New Naturalist A series for the General Reader covering all aspects of Natural History in Great Britain… A Library that will exceed 100 volumes'. And the jacket blurb for *The Weald* 'In the New Naturalist project…'. The New Naturalist is complete in itself: it is a series, a library, a survey, a project, a concept, a publishing venture; even a creed – and to some an institution! Having said that, all things change and evolve and 'New Naturalists' tends to be used to describe the books themselves, rather than the project or library, and perhaps it is useful to draw a distinction between the library – without the 's' and the books themselves – with the 's'. Hence the title of this book, and accordingly I have tried, in my text, to use the two variants to draw this distinction, but I may not have achieved absolute consistency, even being the pedant that I am.

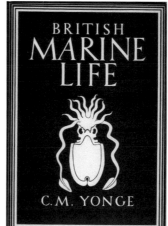

Collecting the New Naturalists
The New Naturalist library consists of two series, the first commonly referred to as the *Main Series,* in octavo format, and the other, *The Monographs,* which was (generally) in the smaller duodecimo format. Additionally there are a few ancillary

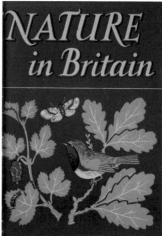

A selection of volumes in the famous Britain in Pictures series, including James Fisher's *The Birds of Britain*, which sold over 95,000 copies. Six titles in the series were bound under the title of *Nature in Britain* (1946). This book is found with two different jacket designs, the scarcer of the two featuring a watercolour painting of a wheatear by Charles Tunnicliffe.

productions such as the journals, the *Art of the New Naturalists* and this book.

The main series now numbers 125, of which the first 120 are examined in this book, but the second editions of NN6 *Highlands and Islands* and NN82 *The New Naturalists* were so comprehensively revised that they are usually considered separate books. The monograph series has 22 titles, and so therefore this bibliography examines in detail 144 titles and, additionally, in a slightly less detailed manner, the supplementary titles.

The first book in the main series was published on 12 November 1945 with new titles still being published today; the first monograph *The Badger* was published 7 February 1949, but the last M22 *The Mole* was published 42 years ago on 1 November 1971.

There is no intention to terminate the main series, and books will continue to be published into the foreseeable future, at around three per year. Conversely, there is no intention of resurrecting the monographs, but important monographic subjects will be included within the main series, e.g. NN114 *Badger*.

From NN70 *Orkney*, all titles were also published concomitantly in paperback format. Additionally some titles have been subsequently reprinted as paperbacks, or published under license by other imprints, occasionally in foreign languages. A recent innovation has been the introduction of a print-on-demand service, where all titles are available to order as digital copies.

All jackets in the main series up to and including NN70 were designed by Clifford and Rosemary Ellis, with the exception of NN14, 46 and 47, as were all the monographs with the exception of M7, M10 and M14. From NN71 until the present all jackets in the main series have been designed by Robert Gillmor.

The rarest books in the series, published from the mid-1980s to the mid-1990s, are often referred to as the *Golden 13*, which is somewhat of a misnomer in that that they are not golden from the collector's perspective (although perhaps they are from the seller's perspective), but rather infamous. Furthermore, there are in fact 14 and these are NN70–83. The *gang of 14* might be a more appropriate term, but whether this or the *Golden 14*, 'G14' is the term generally used in this book.

Why collect the New Naturalists?

The New Naturalist series is outstandingly collectable. A truism perhaps, but for the reader who is unfamiliar with the beguiling ways of the series, here is a brief analysis.

Firstly, the New Naturalist is well defined. It is a known entity, a constant; it knows what it is about and so does the collector. It has its own credo, which clearly states its objectives:

> The aim of this series is to interest the general reader in the wildlife of Britain by recapturing the enquiring spirit of the old naturalists. The Editors believe that the natural pride of the British public in the native flora and fauna, to which must be added concern for their conservation, is best fostered by maintaining a high standard of accuracy combined with clarity of exposition in presenting the results of modern scientific research. The plants and animals are described in

relation to their home and habitats and are portrayed in the full beauty of their natural colours, by the latest methods of colour photography and reproduction.

This credo appears in the front of virtually every book, (albeit abridged post *c.* 1973), and while this might appear to be a matter of small importance, it is a significant factor in the success of the NN phenomenon. It serves as a constant reminder of the principles on which the series was founded and weaves a unifying thread through its history. If the New Naturalist was to depart from these principles it would soon lose its identity, and thereby much of its appeal.

It is these principles, based on the vision of the founding Editors, that has ensured that many NN titles are outstanding books presenting the latest findings in an accessible manner, often supported with fine illustrations. The books are also well-made and pleasing physical objects that stand apart from the average modern book.

At its best, the New Naturalist is a brilliant synthesis of science, nature writing and art; the latter manifested in the form of the dust jackets. Individually they are often outstanding, but all conform to the same graphic framework, which ensures aesthetic cohesion when viewed together on the shelf. There are few sights in any library as striking as a fine New Naturalist set, and indeed for many the jackets must be the principal trigger for collecting the series.

Importantly, it is a numbered series. As irrational as it might be, the simple addition of numbers to a group of like items fundamentally and irrevocably changes the complexion of that group – at least to anyone with the slightest inclination to collect. And so it is with the New Naturalist. We must order them by their prescribed series numbers, not by subject or chronology; gaps must be filled, the next number purchased.

Finally there is the history and longevity of the series, which features many of the most eminent British naturalists of the last 100 years, and this has its own romance. The collector is not only buying a book or a series but is 'buying into' the history of British natural history.

All these factors taken together render the series an irresistible proposition to any naturalist and bibliophile with the slightest inclination to collect.

How many collectors?

The number of collectors will always be in a state of flux, and this number will vary depending on the definition of collector used. For the purposes of this exercise, a collector is: '*someone who is interested in the series beyond individual titles and who actively adds to their collection*'. So how many such collectors are there?

The New Naturalist Collectors' Club (run by Tim Bernhard) currently has approximately 450 members, of whom at least 90 per cent will be collectors. But, if my experience of talking to various collectors is in any way representative, then I would estimate that significantly less than half of collectors are members. That being the case, our figure rises well above 1,000.

The number of copies of new titles sold within the first six months of publication is also a useful indicator of the size of the collectors' market. Over the last five years or so this has averaged around 3,000 copies. Of course, many copies will also sell to non-collectors and libraries, but nevertheless from this we can extrapolate an upper figure of say 2,500. NN85 *Plant Disease* (1999) is perhaps a good indicator, as it is not a book with 'title appeal', but the NN collector will usually purchase the latest hardback irrespective of subject. Approximately 2,000 copies each of the paperback and hardback editions were printed of which around 1,800 hardback copies sold within the first six months, whereas only around 600 paperback copies sold in the same period. Undoubtedly the number of collectors has grown since *Plant Disease* was published. Another helpful, more recent indicator, is *Art of the New Naturalists,* as this is directly concerned with one of the most important elements of NN collecting – the jackets: around 2,500 copies sold within the first six months of publication.

On 6 February 2013 the Collins website the *New Naturalists Online* recorded its 3,000th member; though gauging by the paucity of members who actually post on the (now defunct) forum, one has to conclude that many of these are casual observers. Nevertheless, all must have or have had a passing interest in NNs to have bothered registering.

Unfortunately none of this is conclusive but it gives an idea, which leads to a speculative answer to the question how many collectors are there? Probably around 1,800.

How many complete sets?

Considering the main series, only 725 first-state copies of *Warblers* and *Orkney* were printed so there can never be more than that number of 'first-state sets'. But some of those copies were sold to libraries and non-collectors so the number is probably nearer 500,

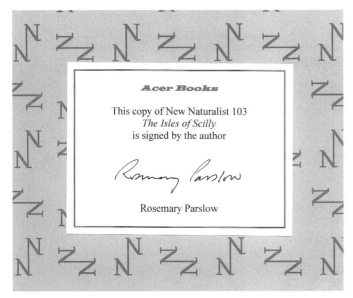

Books signed to plates or slips pasted or tipped in, are less desirable to the collector than copies signed directly to the book (flat signed). In this example the signed plate is poorly designed and aesthetically compromises the decorative endpaper. Such 'subtleties' are not overlooked by the discerning collector.

possibly less. Then there are the sets made up with second-state books, of which 500 were produced, so that's probably another 350 sets or so. Therefore it is unlikely that there could be more than 850 complete main series sets in existence, but I would suggest a number nearer 600 might be likely. In addition there will also be sets completed with the odd paperback or facsimile copy, and then other sets actively being built. There are a number of collectors with two or even three complete sets, justified on the basis that one is a fine 'collecting' set and one for reading. As for the third set? That's difficult to justify, but understandable.

Who are the collectors?

Most collectors of the NN series are interested in natural history – but certainly not all. As has been previously mentioned, the eye-catching jackets are one of the main reasons for collecting, and some collect for this reason only and make no bones about it.

Most collectors are British, and while collecting may not be a solely British preserve it is certainly a strong national trait. The Victorians were the master collectors, as attested by the cornucopian wealth of our regional and national museums. The study of natural history in the 19th century was inextricably linked with the collecting of specimens and it is out of this tradition that the New Naturalist was born; so it is perhaps therefore not surprising that we want to collect them! There appear to be only a few overseas collectors but, as is to be expected, there are more in the Republic of Ireland.

The majority of collectors are men, mostly middle-aged, who come from all walks of life, but there are also a surprising number of younger collectors. All these people have one factor in common: they have the 'collecting gene' and more than likely they will collect other things too. A friend with a fine set has an important collection of early Zeiss binoculars; another collects mineral and fossils. For some inexplicable reason there is a preponderance of collectors with a passion for butterflies, many of whom keep their store boxes and cabinets in close proximity to their New Naturalist collection.

To those without the requisite gene, the habits of the collector are unfathomable. A nonsense, and a profligate nonsense at that. If you have the collecting gene, don't attempt to defend your ways to anyone who hasn't: you are sure to fail because the collector's ways are fundamentally indefensible. Remember that. Accept your affliction and accept you are irredeemably subject to the beguiling allure of New Naturalists, binoculars, trilobites and whatever else besides – and be grateful that there are not more like sufferers, as that would only serve to push up prices...!

Braggers, birds' eggs and inventories

Courteous, gracious and highly knowledgeable would describe the average book collector, but beyond this circle of normality reside a few other types, two in particular worth mentioning. The first, 'the bragger', delights in showing off his collection and every time a new nugget is acquired, it is announced to the world. While his exhibitionist traits might be somewhat irksome, he is essentially a good man simply following his instinct, as a member of a gregarious race, to share his pleasure with others. The second, what we might call 'the bird-egg collector', is intent on keeping his collection under wraps: he has no desire or need to tell of it, or share his pleasure with anyone. He is a sole operator. Whether osprey eggs or stolen masterpieces, ownership is, to him, an end in itself. Beware the man who will not disclose his collection.

Ideally an inventory should be made of all collections, where accession details are also noted. Not only is this a useful record for future reference but one that can be copied to researchers and other collectors. An inventory is invaluable when the collection is to be sold off or disbanded, especially if the owner is no longer around to oversee it!

What to collect?

The majority of collectors will want first editions in fine, bright, unclipped dust jackets, preferably without any internal inscriptions or foxing. A general principle of second-hand book collecting – of all collecting, for that matter – is to purchase the best you can afford and so it is with New Naturalists. There is no doubt that fine first-edition copies always hold their value better than inferior fare and will be easier to sell too. That said, if the principal reasons for establishing a collection are for its contents and aesthetic appeal, it really should not matter if the books, of which it is composed, are reprints. If dust-jacket art is the single most important trigger for starting a collection, it is somewhat paradoxical that so many collectors place such emphasis on collecting first editions. Most titles have been reprinted, and the reprints are always much cheaper than first editions and often significantly cheaper than POD copies. Their content is the same, and if they have been updated, sometimes superior, and most, barring a few 1970s reprints look equally good on the shelf. For those without the means to afford fine first editions, fine reprints are much better option than an affordable but tatty first. But, as already established, the ways of the collector are unfathomable.

It is generally recognised that the reprints of NN6 *Highlands and Islands* and NN82 *The New Naturalists* are so different that they are in essence different books and therefore a complete collection should include both 6A and 6B and 82A and 82B. Some may also want to have both states of *Orkney* and *Warblers* in their collections and other more obvious binding variants, e.g. *The Hawfinch* with the plain green jacket, or may wish to include important revisions such as the 1970 revised edition of *A Natural History of Man in Britain*. Additionally, most will also want *The New Naturalist: A Journal* (hardback and paperback issues) and *Art of the New Naturalists*.

Then there are the monographs, but many will not actively pursue them until they have completed the main series. Beyond that, what to collect? Unlike the *Wayside and Woodland* series and *Observer* books, few NN collectors are interested in binding and jacket variants. This is probably because there tends to be less variation in NN books than those other series and also because to do so would require many metres of shelf space (about 24 metres so far). There are two fools that I know of who have attempted to collect every known edition (British and Foreign), reprint and variant: the authors of this book.

Signed copies are a far more reasonable pursuit; preferably first edition *association copies* (a book signed or annotated by the author and belonging to someone connected to the author); and if the author has added a doodle, even better (see page 47). There appears to be a growing number of collectors pursuing signed copies, a few with the avowed intention of assembling, as near as practicable, a complete set of signed books. As several authors died before the publication of their books (Hewer – *British Seals*, Ratcliffe – *Galloway*, etc.) a full signed set is an impossibilty, unless earlier signatures are tipped in. Signed NN books are scarce, particularly the earlier titles, and are rarely offered on the open market: when they do appear, they sell quickly.

Additionally, NN ephemera (prospectuses, review slips, author's letters and so on), as well as any associated artwork are now eagerly collected. Increasing the scope of a collection to include such items, and additionally any other associated areas that might whet the acquisitive appetite, for instance foreign editions (many of the US variants are scarce and virtually unobtainable) or non-NN books wearing Ellis jackets, will ensure the collecting challenge is kept alive indefinitely.

Collecting is not unlike hunting or modelling: with hunting it is the chase that thrills, not the kill; with modelling it is the challenge of the making that entertains, not the display of the completed model. And so it is with collecting: *the joy is in the collecting, not in the completing.*

Provenance

Many collectors of modern first editions, including NN collectors, have a disproportionate aversion to bookplates and inscriptions. Regularly fine books are rejected due to their presence, even if the bookplate is small and well-designed and the inscription neat and tidy. Conversely, to the antiquarian book collector inscriptions and bookplates are an enhancing feature as they often cast light upon the specific history and previous owners of a particular book. A book's pedigree or, in collecting parlance, its *provenance*, is an important additional dimension which might influence value significantly.

The first New Naturalist was published a little less than 70 years ago, so whether we like it or not, the majority of early titles in the majority of collections will have been pre-owned, so perhaps it is time to embrace copies enriched with signatures and bookplates rather than search for the antiseptic perfection of the uninscribed and the plate-free.

The future

Like all collectables, New Naturalist prices wax and wane, and currently, in these straitened times, values are lower than they have been for some years. And supply is undoubtedly greater too, which has lead some to suggest that the NN collector is a dying breed. However, New Naturalist books are fundamentally and inherently attractive. Their appeal is timeless and as we, all of us level-headed, intelligent and discerning people, have been captivated by them, so others will be in the future. All the time there is a 'collecting gene', New Naturalists will be collected.

Collecting signed or inscribed books is something of an acquired taste. Many collectors are not at all bothered by signatures, whilst others make it their quest to find as many signed books as possible. If interested in signed books, collectors may only look for a full, clean and undedicated signature, perhaps on the title page, or they may be less fastidious and accept any form of autographed item.

There are four main categories of books with signatures. The first is an association copy. This applies to a book which once belonged to, or was annotated by, the author. Association copies can also have belonged to someone connected with the author or the contents of the book. Secondly, a presentation copy is usually a book which is presented by the author. It will probably be inscribed in the author's hand to a named recipient and dated on or near publication. Examples may be found where a book is inscribed with the recipient's name, but having 'from the author' or 'with the author's compliments' instead of a signature. In cases where the recipient is well known to the author, the signature may comprise of only a forename or merely an initial or two. Sometimes the book itself may not be signed but will contain a loosely inserted note or compliments slip from the author or publisher. The third kind is an inscribed copy. This means that the book has been autographed or signed by the author, but unlike a presentation copy, an inscribed copy is signed some time after publication, perhaps in response to an owner's request. The inscription will usually be dedicated to a particular person, often accompanied by some kind of sentiment. When searching for signed copies from booksellers it is worth noting that an inscribed copy may simply mean that a previous owner has written his name and perhaps the date, usually on the front endpaper. Finally, listing a book as a signed copy usually implies that the book is autographed without a dedication or inscription.

The signatures themselves also fall into three categories. A book which has been signed on one of its pages, most likely to be either on the title-page, half-title page or front free endpaper, is known as flat signed. Many books will also be found which have an author's signature cut from another source, perhaps from a letter, and lightly attached by gum or paste. This is known as tipped-in and can also refer to errata slips, newspaper cuttings, letters and other documents. If these items are not actually attached to the book, they are described as laid-in or loosely inserted.

Finding signed copies of the older New Naturalists is remarkably difficult. There are some authors who were prolific writers and signed their publications regularly. Books signed by such authors as James Fisher, Richard Fitter, Alister Hardy and Ernest Neal turn up fairly frequently, whilst other authors do not seem to have signed their books at all. In the case of *British Seals*, the book was published after the author's death so any signed copies offered would be dubious to say the least. Individual authors tend to sign in the same place and very often in the same coloured ink. For example, signed copies of *A Country Parish*

invariably bear A. W. Boyd's very neat signature in dark blue or black ink under the names of the Editors opposite the title page.

Perhaps the most prized of all New Naturalist-related signatures are those that are inscribed from one author to another or, even better, to or from a member of the Editorial Board. Eric Hosking, the photographic editor, was a great collector of natural history books and a number of copies amongst his complete collection of New Naturalists were inscribed to him. Hosking also took great care of the books themselves. A New Naturalist volume, such as one of these, in near fine condition and inscribed from an author to a member of the legendary Editorial Board is just about as good as it could possibly get, and would be quite valuable.

Multi-signed books, perhaps where there is more than one author or contributor, can be particularly difficult to find. It may be that the authors rarely sign together and the more signatures to add, the more difficult it becomes. The monograph *The Birds of the London Area* was produced by a Committee of the London Natural History Society of which R. C. Homes was the chairman. To find a copy signed by all seven members would be a very rare discovery indeed.

Certain booksellers specialise in signed copies. For a while the bookseller Ron Norman, with his business The Book Squirrel, provided a limited number of signed New Naturalists. This seems to have begun with *Mammals in the British Isles*, signed on the front free endpaper by Leo Harrison Matthews. The following book, *Reptiles and Amphibians in Britain*, was also signed similarly by Deryk Frazer, and so too was *The Natural History of Orkney*. Eric Simms signed his name on the title page of British Warblers as he did for the following two books, *Heathlands* and *The New Forest*. It seems that 100 of each were signed and when they turn up they are always very similar. It is not known why these signed editions discontinued, possibly it was just too difficult to arrange. Another bookseller who has supplied signed copies to collectors is Acer Books. Some of these editions, such as *British Bats*, had cards tipped in which were signed and dated and included the edition number. Other books, such as *A History of Ornithology* and *The Isles of Scilly*, were signed and numbered on the title page. All of Acer Books' signed New Naturalists seem to have been editions of 50 copies. Since 2008, HarperCollins have made signed copies of each hardback available as part of their website service and 100 copies of each new title are signed by the author, usually on the title page.

Whether it is a signed copy of one of the classic books or part of the recent signed limited editions, a signature will add value and interest to a book. Association and inscribed books will always be scarce and sought after and therefore particularly valuable.

Annotated and corrected copies
Very occasionally, an author's personal copy may be found. This may be identified by a signature, bookplate or ownership stamp, all of which make the book special. Even more scarce are copies which have been annotated and corrected by the author, perhaps for a reprint or new edition. The marks are usually written in pencil and frequently in the page margins, making the book a unique item. Because these are working copies, they are often in

well-used condition; however, such books are extremely rare and are undoubtedly even more valuable than a copy that is merely signed, even when in poor condition.

Correspondence from authors

From time to time a New Naturalist volume may be discovered which contains a letter or postcard from the author. This may be loosely inserted or, perhaps more frequently, glued or taped onto the front past-down endpaper. Tape marks can be removed with care (see page 32 for restoration techniques), and it is probably safer to either leave the item loose or place it in an archival clear envelope, enabling it to be read without actually handling it and therefore avoiding the risk of damage. These items of correspondence will often be directly associated with the book's subject matter, which will make them of particular interest and will enhance the value of the book. The book may also contain the owner's name or bookplate and if the letter is addressed to that same person, the provenance becomes apparent and therefore significant, providing an insight into the history of the book beyond the added value a simple signature can offer.

CONDITION AND COMMON FAULTS

Condition

Condition, second to general rarity, has the greatest influence on value. We all want fine books with bright crisp pages, the boards to still creak when opened, dust jackets that are bright without blemish. In fact, seeking out such copies of early titles is perhaps the most pleasurable of the various challenges facing the New Naturalist collector. *Butterflies* first edition is a common book, but find one in a truly fine dust jacket – well, that's a rare thing. So many New Naturalists suffer from fading: try finding a first-edition copy of *Birds of Prey* that has not suffered the attentions of the blighting sun. I've never seen one; more persecuted than a harrier on a grouse moor.

Most have to put up with less and 'upgrade' as opportunities present themselves – and expect to pay significantly more for a genuinely fine first edition. (See table 2 on pages 36–7 for suggested values.)

Standardised terms of condition

Within the second-hand book trade there are standardised terms to describe condition – although the interpretation and use of them is often far from standard! This set of terms uses the familiar grades of fine, very good, good, and so on, and was first proposed in 1949 by *AB Bookman's Weekly*, a US magazine for booksellers and collectors. Many books are now purchased online and The Independent Online Booksellers' Association (IOBA) and AbeBooks both advocate the use of these standard terms, but offer slightly different definitions. To compound matters, Amazon has its own condition categories but these tend to be less exacting – as one might expect. Notwithstanding this subjectivity, these standardised terms are a very useful tool for the collector and bookseller alike. Here is a suggested, hopefully objective, interpretation:

1. **As New:** self-explanatory: applied only to a book which is in the same immaculate condition as when it was first published.
2. **Fine:** approaches the condition of As New, but without being crisp. It has lost that new feel, but without any apparent defects.
3. **Near Fine:** really a sub-category, though often used. As Fine but with minor faults such as price-clipping, minimal fading to the spine, perhaps a signature. All faults must be mentioned.
4. **Very Good:** a used book that displays minor evidence of wear. Dust jacket a little rubbed with perhaps a few short tears, slightly soiled, possibly with a little fading and possibly price-clipped. The book itself with some general wear and rubbing, but without tears or chipping to the cloth. Internally some foxing may be present along with a signature or two, but the binding will be tight. It shouldn't have any significant faults. Any defects must be noted.
5. **Good:** supposedly this describes the average used and worn book, but in reality it means not good! The dust jacket, if present, will be worn with tears and chipping. The binding will have some wear, possibly with bumped corners and perhaps the odd short split or tear to the cloth – it could be stained. Internally, with obvious reading wear, the page edges no longer crisp, the binding may be slack, an inscription and foxing may be present. But the book will be complete and readable.
6. **Fair:** a worn book that has complete text pages (including those with maps or plates) but may lack endpapers, half-title, etc. The binding may have splits to the cloth and may be stained. The jacket (if extant) will also be worn, probably soiled with chunks missing.
7. **Poor:** you really don't want to go here! Fortunately, New Naturalist books are very well made, so it is unlikely you will have to, but for the record here it is. On the plus side, the text should be complete but endpapers, title pages and plates might be missing. The binding might be broken and the backstrip and/or boards detached or missing. Soiling, scuffing, staining, tearing, foxing should all be expected as should loose joints, hinges and pages. Generally rough.

Other terms are also used: a reading or reference copy – a euphemism for fair or poor, meaning a copy that can be read, though it might take some effort to do so; gift quality – supposedly a book in such fine condition that it would be suitable as a gift (though I would be pleased to receive an indifferent first-state *Orkney*); mint – self-explanatory, but a term not liked by purists as in reality few books are ever mint – most copies sitting on bookshop shelves are not mint, not to mention that books are not 'minted' but are printed; acceptable – a term introduced by Amazon and paraphrased as a readable copy, complete but possibly with considerable notes and the dust jacket may be missing. Probably best avoided. Impossibly good is the term used by one New Naturalist collector to describe books of suitable condition for his collection – he still has a number of gaps.

Digital images

Ideally, in addition to these categories, all faults should be mentioned, but cataloguing books is a tedious task and it is much easier for booksellers to use these generic terms, without mentioning specific defects. However hard the industry attempts to standardise terms, there will always be a large degree of subjectivity surrounding the condition of books. One man's very good is another man's fine. And there will always be those who will apply these terms in a loose and casual way.

This being the case, the condition of a book must be seen to be realised (Michael Sadler). If purchasing a book blind, ask for a digital image, and make sure the image shows clearly the spine of the dust jacket in relation to the front panel. It is the spine that is always the most subject to wear, so seeing this in association with the front panel will also enable you to determine if there is any fading. In our digital age this is not an unreasonable request and if a bookseller is unwilling to provide an image or two, go to someone who will.

Most booksellers will also be happy to send books on approval, i.e. if you don't like it you send it back for a full refund. The book trade has been doing business this way for centuries so don't hesitate to request this service.

Common faults

Faults fall into two categories – those due to manufacturing defects and those brought about as a consequence of wear. The former can throw up some interesting aberrations and in this sense may not necessarily be faults in the eye of the collector.

Damp

The greatest enemy of books, less because of its direct detrimental effects but more because it creates the correct environmental conditions for the highly deleterious effects of moulds, not to mention silverfish and bookworm.

A direct consequence of damp is waviness of pages, or as it is often referred to in the book trade: 'cockling'. Damp stains or water stains are a common fault of older books and show as a tide mark, usually along the edge of the page. Not infrequently they occur in association with mould, though very rarely are New Naturalists blighted in this way.

Although in modern centrally heated houses the direct and indirect affects of damp are not usually an issue, ventilation is always essential.

Foxing

Foxing, or more euphemistically, spotting, affects many copies of early titles in the series – particularly those printed on paper with an acid reaction. It manifests itself as disfiguring brownish or yellowish blotches or small spots. Its causes are not fully understood but it is often attributed to moulds and iron particles in the paper; it is also associated with specks of dust and other contaminants, which explains why page edges are commonly

Always request an image showing the spine of the jacket in association with the front panel. This first edition copy of *Dartmoor* has a perfect front panel but the spine is faded, tanned and chipped: it is the spine of the jacket that is always the most subject to wear.

An otherwise perfect copy of *The Salmon* jacket marred by foxing.

A copy of NN68 *Mammals* with mouse damage to lower edge.

spotted. Foxing is usually more prevalent at the front and rear of the book, perhaps suggesting that impurities in the casing and associated glues are also involved. Undoubtedly damp conditions and a lack of ventilation are important factors in the development of foxing. While unsightly, it does not appear to have any long-term detrimental effects on paper, but for aesthetic reasons prints and documents are often 'washed' by paper conservators using weak solutions of various chemicals including Calcium hydroxide, Calcium hypochlorite and ChloromineT (less in favour now) which will remove or mitigate the effects of foxing. Once treated, the paper is thoroughly washed and deacidified. With a book it is a more difficult task to treat foxing in situ, but endpapers can be quite easily treated.

Museum beetle and bookworm

This is hardly of concern to the New Naturalist collector as they are rarely encountered in the modern library. Their presence is obvious. The best way of treatment is to place the book in a plastic bag and leave it in the freezer for a few days.

Silverfish

The familiar Silverfish (*Lepisma saccharina*), one of the bristletails, lives almost exclusively in human dwellings and is a much more serious pest of books. They enjoy damp conditions and prefer a starchy diet but are able to digest cellulose. 'Silverfish grazing' is comparatively common, where the surface layer of a binding material or paper is grazed. Rarely does this affect the integrity of a book, but it can be disfiguring. Silverfish can be very selective in their grazing and I have seen a number of NN jackets with the printed text left perfectly intact but with the surrounding blank areas eaten. The best method of control is to reduce humidity levels, but check your books regularly.

Rodent damage

Damage caused to books by mice is much more common than generally appreciated, especially for books stored in cardboard boxes. Scalloped areas of loss with telltale teeth marks are instantly recognizable as being caused by rodents. But a little vigilance, a good cat and the odd *Little Nipper* trap will soon resolve the problem.

Ex-library books

There are two types of person to whom books should never be entrusted: children and librarians. The former usually work on a fairly small scale, but the latter are responsible for countless crimes against books.

The term 'ex-lib' conjures up all sorts of abhorrent images in the mind of the serious book collector and is the death knell of many a book. Ex-library books are usually obvious and their telltale signs of stamps, pockets, index and lending cards, plates and Dewey numbers need no elaboration here. If a book is not obviously ex-library then it should not be stigmatized by this previous life but assessed on its merits. In fact, some ex-lib books, kept in warm institutional libraries, out of direct sunshine and infrequently, if ever, borrowed, can be in

exceptional condition. Often dust jackets are protected at purchase and if unmarked can be outstanding examples. At the other end of the scale are copies rebound in library bindings, often cut down, practical perhaps but utterly inelegant, though with New Naturalists, which are so well made, it is difficult to see what is to be gained by rebinding.

Missing plates, pages and errata slips

Occasionally New Naturalists are found with missing or loose plates and pages, however it is relatively simple to tip these back in. Occasionally a series of pages (a gathering) might be duplicated as a binding error, usually with the correct gathering missing, in which case little can be done. Plates found in antiquarian books are often purposefully removed for their decorative qualities – the sum of the parts being greater than the whole, but we need not worry about this here. If you are able to do so, try to collate the book before purchasing by scanning the pagination and comparing the plates with the list of illustrations at the front of the book.

It is common practice in the publishing industry to remove the title pages of damaged books, however small the defect. Theoretically this is to prevent them being resold, but in the case of valuable rarities, sellers will go to considerable trouble to insert facsimile title pages and I have seen two such copies of first-state *Warblers*. So do check!

A number of first edition New Naturalist titles were supplied with tipped-in errata slips and these are an integral part of the book and should be present but, not irregularly, they are missing.

Inscriptions, annotations and highlighting

The purist collector may find such markings intolerable, and there are even a few who look upon an author's signature as a disfiguring blight, *singed* rather than *signed*. There is fine line between value-enhancing association and disfigurement. Ted Ellis's personal copy of *The Broads*, battered and stained, but with his diminutive handwritten notes throughout the text would be seen as a great treasure, conversely the observational notes of a keen but 'unknown' botanist in a copy of *Flowers of Chalk and Limestone* would be a defect, yet both add interest to the book.

Otherwise it is about degree, neatness and personal preference, but generally books with inscriptions are less valuable and less in demand.

Bookplates, prize-plates and booksellers' labels

These all add provenance and unless exceptionally crude (and some undoubtedly are – see below), ideally should be left in place. It is often relatively straightforward to remove such plates (as described on page 31).

Ghosting and tanning

Ghosting is a term sometimes used to refer to the 'shadow' left on the free endpaper as a result of contact with the flap of the dust jacket. In fact the flap protects part of the endpaper from tanning or browning and appears as a brighter section. Newspaper clippings and other inserts can all cause ghosting.

Tanning and browning of endpapers, pages and dust jackets is seemingly brought about by the interaction of air, humidity and the cellulose in the paper. Atmospheric pollution and the acidity of the paper are other major contributing factors. However, it does not necessarily follow that books with browned pages will also be foxed or spotted.

Tanning is a little disfiguring but not necessary detrimental, although it can indicate acidity. Paper that is highly acidic becomes brittle and if the book is valuable, deacidification of the paper is required. Fortunately, New Naturalists do not suffer unduly in this regard and we need not concern ourselves with such problems. Tanning or browning of endpapers can be removed by washing, but this is best left to a paper conservator.

Replacement endpapers

Not uncommonly, NNs have had their front endpaper replaced, occasionally the rear one, too. This has usually been done to remove some ill, a library stamp or ugly inscription. If done very well they can be difficult to detect but they can always be found out. If suspicious of your endpapers, firstly compare the front endpaper with the rear endpaper and if they are obviously different, one has been replaced. Next, check to see if they are correctly trimmed and when the book is closed the edges are in line with the other pages. Look, too, for the impression of the original paste-down under the new endpaper; (very rarely is the original paste-down part removed). If these checks fail to produce conclusive results, compare with other NN titles published at the same time.

Dust jackets

Originally produced, as the name implies, to protect the cloth from dust and other potential harms en route to the final customer. Originally they were utilitarian and ephemeral, designed to be thrown away once the book was in the hands of the reader, but in the 1920s they started to be used as a marketing tool, often eye-catching with striking graphic designs. Today, the book jacket is considered an essential bibliographical component and consequently most collectors will pay a significant premium for a book in a fine dust jacket.

New Naturalist jackets are of immense importance – and without them the series would not enjoy its elevated status. They are bright, sophisticated and unifying. A complete set of New Naturalists in bright jackets is one of the finest sights on a library shelf, but these copies are also the most vulnerable, and therefore fine jackets are much rarer than fine books. For early titles in the series, a fine jacket can be worth five-fold the value of the book itself.

The wrong jacket

Commonly books are found with incorrect jackets – and as one might imagine it is usually a first edition in a fine later edition jacket. Rarely is it the other way round. These are usually second marriages arranged by collectors and dealers, but occasionally these are instigated by the publisher as an expedient. They are often declared in bookseller's descriptions, but not always. Be

warned. Generally for first editions the New Naturalist table to the rear panel will not list titles beyond the current one, but there are a number of exceptions. The catalogue and tables detail the salient features of all jackets and it should be easy enough to determine the edition, independent of the book.

Jacket spines – fading, chipping, browning and smoke damage

The spine is the most important part of the dust jacket as this is the portion that is seen on the shelf, and probably the single most important element when considering book condition. It is this part that is exposed to light, handling and other ills; if the spine is in fine condition then it is likely that the jacket and book will follow suit and be in similar condition.

The head and tail areas are particularly prone to chipping where they are carelessly pulled off the shelf, but archival sleeves will prevent this.

Direct sunlight is quick to fade many titles, particularly colours in the yellow to red spectrum; the number 24 on the spine of *Flowers of the Coast* is notorious for fading and is often illegible (all titles prone to fading are discussed individually under their catalogue entries). Faded jackets detract from a collection, are less desirable and are worth significantly less than unfaded copies and, moreover, they cannot be restored. For further details of fading see page 29.

Tanning or browning is another common fault that manifests itself more on the spine than on other parts of the jacket, again this is because this part is the most exposed to the interaction of air, atmospheric humidity and pollution. Tobacco smoke is a major culprit in this respect, and it would seem that many New

Another example of a personalised bookplate of the sort that most would rather do without.

Naturalist collectors were pipe smokers, though these are now a rare breed. In the early days of the series, open coal fires were commonplace, and their corrosive smoke would, over time, tan dust jackets and in the severest cases cause the paper to become brittle. However, browning can often be successfully removed by washing (see page 33).

Dust jacket trimming and positioning on the spine

Dust jackets are trimmed to the correct size and occasionally they are irregularly trimmed, i.e. more is trimmed from the bottom than the top and vice versa, and in the worst cases the number roundel or imprint is truncated.

Dust jackets are not always correctly folded onto the book – the number roundel should be positioned in the middle of the spine. The current jacket designs only wrap round the book onto the rear panel by one or two millimetres, and where they are folded off-centre a blank white line will be evident on the left shoulder. These are not serious defects but if they can be avoided, so much the better.

Tears, chips, creases and other faults

All are unwanted, but often these are common features of jackets. Rubbing, browning, foxing, old Sellotape marks, sticky-backed plastic, etc. are frequently present too, but all these faults are dealt with in the care and repair section. New Naturalist jackets are rarely inscribed, but it is not unusual for the table on the rear panel to be ticked off.

Duraseal – remove or retain?

A proprietary name for a clear plastic (polypropylene) protective covering. There are a number of concerns regarding *Duraseal*. Firstly and most seriously the glue used to adhere it to the jacket can discolour and stain the underlying paper; secondly, if applied too tightly it causes the edges of the jacket to curl; thirdly, it has a tendency to ripple. It can also become browned, especially when exposed to tobacco smoke. These are all good reasons to remove it, however from a collector's perspective it is an integral part of the jacket and should be retained. Certainly jackets which are missing their *Duraseal* are not as collectable as those with it and recently a fine first-state copy of *British Warblers* was rejected by a collector on the grounds that the *Duraseal* was missing. When *Duraseal* has been removed there are always the telltale marks left by the glue and invariably some surface damage to the underside of the jacket.

Price-clipping

To some, a significant shortcoming, to others, inconsequential. The price is an integral part of the jacket and therefore it must be better to have it present than not. Certainly, a price-clipped jacket will be less valuable (jackets complete with their price are commonly described as being entire). In an ascending hierarchy of detrimental attributes, for most collectors price-clipping rates above a neat inscription, but there are some who will take a price-clipped book but certainly not one defaced with an inscription. Some New Naturalist titles, often reprints, appear to have a preponderance of clipped jackets and it is likely that these copies were sold through the bookclubs at prices significantly less than the net book price, therefore rendering the printed price both obsolete and potentially confusing.

It must also be remembered that price-clipping was often undertaken by the publisher when re-pricing stock and, in this case, provided that the replacement price-sticker is extant, such copies should be seen as legitimate variants and not reviled. Though of course whilst they may be of first edition stock, they will have been sold subsequently and so will not be as valuable as an entire jacket.

CARE, CLEANING AND REPAIR

Conservation and Repair

In conservation circles it is generally held that intervention should be kept to a minimum and then only justified if it prolongs the life of the item in question and is reversible. In reality a rather more pragmatic approach is adopted and many paper conservators earn their keep washing and bleaching and repairing drawings, prints and documents, to bring them up to an aesthetically acceptable or, more to the point, a saleable standard. There is of course a balance to be struck, but where exactly is determined by personal and often differing opinion.

New Naturalist collectors want their books to look as bright and as unblemished as the day they were made. Tears, chipping, browning, foxing all detract from this ambition, but simple procedures can often significantly enhance the aesthetic appeal of a less than perfect volume.

There is a good deal of mystery and intrigue surrounding paper conservation, and there is no single book or manual that explains in a straightforward manner the principal methods employed. Undoubtedly a good proportion of paper conservation is concerned with mitigating the consequences of acidic papers. New Naturalists are no different in this respect, as most books in the series and their jackets, prior to around 1977, were printed on acidic paper, which explains why in these books there is a greater preponderance of tanning and foxing.

Below is a short guide – and that is all that it is. It is certainly not definitive and paper conservators will employ a raft of different techniques beyond the scope of this book. It must also be noted that with some techniques, incorrect procedure can lead to the destruction of paper and the reader must proceed at his risk. Always err on the cautious side and practise on something worthless first. Additionally, the prices charged by most professional conservators are very reasonable: expect to pay around £15 for the washing and cleaning (and transformation) of an octavo format dust jacket.

But care comes before repair...

Care

Library Conditions and Bookcases

Damp is the greatest enemy of books and it is essential that they are kept in well-ventilated dry conditions. Try to maintain a temperature within the range of 15°C to 20°C (59–68°F) and relative humidity (RH) should be kept as constant as possible, within the range of 45 per cent to 60 per cent (at RH greater than 65 per cent moulds and staining are likely to occur). Never store books next to radiators or other heat sources.

It is thoroughly good practice to place spacers (lengths of clean timber or plastic) at the rear of the shelf so that a gap is created between the back of the bookcase and the book. This will increase airflow and will help protect against the affects of damp should the bookcase be positioned against a damp wall. Additionally, the correct width of spacer will ensure the books line up with the front edge of the shelf, which, aesthetically, is a superior arrangement.

Regularly spaced, close-fitting shelves will further improve the presentation of your collection and will reduce the incidence of dust on the books' top edges.

Guarding Against Fading

The problem of fading or photodegradation is multi-faceted and more complicated than generally realised. Exposure to ultra-violet light is undoubtedly the greatest cause of fading, but it is certainly not the only factor: heat, light in the visible spectrum, artificial indoor lighting and humidity all play a part. It is perhaps well to remember though, that whatever measures we take, it is probably impossible to prevent fading completely.

A few collectors have taken the somewhat extreme measure of storing their books the wrong way around, that is, with the spine to the back of the shelf so the jacket is never or rarely exposed to light. While this will go a long way to prevent fading, it is surely self-defeating with a series that looks so well en masse. One of the pleasures of owning a set is to enjoy it – and to show it off!

Other collectors purchase facsimile sleeves and wrap these round the original jackets, not as extreme as the above and clearly an effective way to protect the original (is the facsimile printed on acid free paper?) but the cynic might question 'why bother with the original'?

Books should never be subject to direct sunlight or bright light at any time. A bookcase on a north wall in a darkish room is ideal and probably adequate. Further protection can be afforded by adding doors or roll-down blinds to the bookcase, which will also keep out dust.

UV filters are an effective weapon in the fight against fading. Jackets are available for fluorescent lighting and fit neatly over standard tubes; UV filter film is also available for glass; but of most interest to the collector is UV Light Filter Polyester Film, which can be cut to size and folded round jackets. It is not particularly cheap, and supplied in large rolls, but its benefits are sufficiently great to render these inconveniences inconsequential.

Dust jacket protectors

Dust jackets, as already identified, are the most vulnerable part of the book and a simple non-adhesive proprietary jacket protector is an excellent investment and will prevent further damage, particularly to non-laminated jackets. They are essentially an open sleeve with one side clear and the other paper; the jacket is inserted between the two. They are variously referred to as archival sleeves, jacket covers, *Mylar* protectors, archival *Mylar* and so on. (*Mylar* is often used generically to refer to polyester film or plastic sheet, however, it is a registered trademark owned by Dupont.)

The most significant disadvantage of these protectors is that they add a gloss or sheen to jackets intended to be matt, but if all books in a collection are protected in the same type then at least uniformity is achieved.

There are a range of different types and makes available, perhaps the best known being *Adaptaroll*, which is manufactured from 70 micron polypropylene with a self-adhesive strip. It is easy to apply, but it is better to use a product without integral glue as there is a possibility that over time this could degenerate and stain the underlying jacket. I prefer *Paperfold*, which is manufactured from 38 micron polyester (because polyester is inert it is favoured by conservators, the paper-backing should also be acid-free) and is crisp and sharp and simply folds round the jacket without the need for adhesive or tape. It also has the added attraction of also being about the cheapest paper-backed protector available!

Clear polyester, also referred to by the trade names *Polymex* or *Melinex* or Gresswell's product *Polyester Book Cover* (38 micron polyester) is even cheaper, as it has no backing. This is available in rolls and can be cut to size and folded round the jacket (it can also be folded round books without jackets), but as it does not encase the jacket it does not offer quite the same level of protection as archival sleeves.

Cleaning

Many books can be significantly enhanced by simple, non-invasive cleaning techniques: all that is required is the right equipment and a little patience. For instance, it is often a straightforward matter to lift surface dirt from a jacket using an appropriate rubber. It must also be remembered that dust and other contaminants are often acidic and contain chemicals that will, over time, have a deleterious affect on your books, so removing them goes beyond the aesthetic.

Common Equipment

Before embarking on any repair or enhancing procedures it is helpful to have all necessary equipment to hand:

1. Dusting brushes. Soft brushes for gently removing rubbings, dust and so on.
2. Lint-free cloths for applying various cleaning agents.
3. Fine artists' brushes for applying thin beads of glue or working solvent under tapes and labels, they need only be synthetic, and sizes 000–5 in variety are ideal, depending on the job.

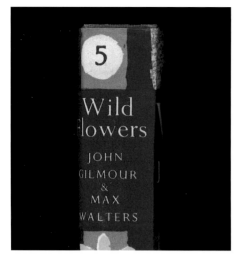

The jacket of this 1978 reprint of *Wildflowers* has been badly folded and the series numeral is off-centre.

A 1976 reprint of *The World of the Honeybee*, where the Duraseal protector has been applied too tightly causing the top edge to ruck and crease.

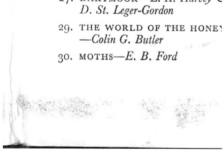

A first edition of *The Lake District*, with staining along the bottom edge caused by the adhesive used to secure the Duraseal covering.

4. Blotting paper is essential to protect and shield underlying and adjacent areas and pages and to absorb any free liquids. It should be as heavy as possible – at least 300 gsm and, of course, acid-free.
5. Sheets of stiff acetate to isolate the working area and to protect underlying pages – even if they get just a little damp they are liable to cockle.
6. Kitchen paper is ideal for mopping up any excess liquids and cleaning off tools.
7. Bone-folder, for burnishing paper and conservation tapes.
8. Fine flat pallet knife for teasing off labels and scraping off glue.
9. Scalpel or craft knife.
10. Very soft toothbrush. Ideal for cleaning cloth and gently working solvents into glues.
11. An eraser or two.

A note on erasers

Erasers, or rubbers if you prefer, are both ubiquitous and utilitarian but it would be a mistake to think that they all do the same job and all are equally effective. A quick internet search will reveal a bewildering cornucopia of erasers, some of which are designed for specific tasks and some for general use and many more of undetermined purpose. Choosing the correct eraser for the task in hand will produce a better result and mitigate potential damage to the underlying paper, but a favourite is a foam eraser manufactured for PEL (Preservation Equipment Limited) though, it has the texture of an ordinary rubber rather than that usually associated with foam. A superb eraser, which removes dirt better than any other, creating long beads of 'rubber' as it is used. A very close second is the Japanese Pilot Foam Eraser. For an environmentally friendly alternative the polyvinyl chloride free Pilot Clean Eraser is very good, though not quite as efficacious as the above.

In addition to pencil erasers, there is a bewildering range of ink erasers, but generally none is worth bothering with; essentially they work by abrading the surface of the paper and once the ink has been removed so has most of the paper.

Dust soiling

Unless books are kept in enclosed bookcases dust will collect along exposed edges, particularly the top of the book-block and will in time stain surfaces upon which it collects. Cordless handheld vacuums (*Dustbusters*) with a soft brush attachment are an excellent starting point. Next use *Groom Stick*, (a natural rubber, kneadable 'molecular' trap of neutral pH), which will pick up and carry away a wide array of foreign matter. It is particularly good for getting into corners and the area immediately underneath the head/band. Try removing more stubborn marks with a soft rubber, but when cleaning the book-block, ensure that the book is well clamped in one hand, otherwise page edges are easily damaged. Dust will also penetrate into endpapers or other parts which are slightly open and this is easily removed using the *Groom Stick* and a foam rubber used to finish off.

Removing surface dirt from dust jackets
Many dust jackets (not laminated) can be significantly improved by simply removing surface dirt with appropriate erasers and dry cleaning pads. Take particular care when cleaning edges as these are vulnerable to rucking and tearing if not firmly held down. Always remove the jacket from the book before commencing.

It is worth mentioning doughy white bread, as it is often advocated for cleaning paper. I have experimented with it on several occasions and never found it satisfactory, and also as the bread contains moisture and a little fat, it must be used with great care to prevent surface damage.

Much preferable to bread are dry cleaning pads of neutral pH, filled with powdered rubber or fractice (also know as draft cleaning pads). The pad is gently twisted and squeezed, sprinkling fine rubber granules over the surface to be cleaned, and these are then rolled around like breadcrumbs under your fingers, or the pad gently rubbed over the surface. They are then removed using a fine brush (these powdered rubber granules or equivalent are also available loose and generically known as draft cleaning powder). The dry cleaning pad can be used in conjunction with *Groom Stick*.

Once general cleaning has been completed, areas of more intense soiling can be worked on with a foam eraser, but over-enthusiastic rubbing can remove surface colour.

Laminated jackets can be carefully cleaned with a little moisture – general household or baby wipes containing mild cleansing agents are ideal. For stubborn marks try a little lighter fuel on a soft cloth (as modern laminated jackets are coated with a fine plastic film the solvent should not affect the underlying inks – but always experiment first on an inconspicuous area).

Cleaning casing fabrics
Due to the quality and close-weave nature of the buckrams used in New Naturalists, it is rare that the bindings need cleaning, but for those rare occasions that cleaning is required, here are some suggestions.

Before commencing work on bindings, isolate the book-block by wrapping it in paper or placing acetate sheets under the boards. Always do a trial run before committing to a full-scale clean.

Bachus Bookcloth Cleaner: an industry standard and part of the booksellers'/restorers' armoury for many years, but unpopular with some on the basis that supposedly books cleaned with it quickly become dirty again. This, however, has not been my experience and if used correctly it can remove deep-seated dirt and revive old cloths. Apply with a soft cotton cloth, lightly rubbing in all directions until the surface is revived; it can also be worked into the weave using a very soft toothbrush and the dirty liquid then removed with a cloth or kitchen paper. With severe cases it will be necessary to apply the cleaner several times, removing the dirt each time. Finish with a clean soft cloth, gently buffing as it dries to ensure the original lustre is restored.

Repair
Health and Safety
Most of the procedures listed below are perfectly safe, but a few include the use of solvents that are potentially harmful and must be used responsibly. Always follow the precautions printed on the container and use in a well-ventilated space and do not mix chemicals.

Removing bookplates
For the purposes of removal, bookplates can be divided into two categories: those that use traditional starch- and animal-based glues (bioadhesives) and those that use synthetic or pressure sensitive adhesives (PSAs). Most bookplates found in NNs are applied with bioadhesives including the 'lick-and-stick' variety. Conversely, later bookplates are often of the peel-off variety, which use PSAs. All are generally straightforward to remove (there is always the exception), but require different methods: essentially a water-based solution is used for bioadhesives and a solvent for synthetic adhesives. By simply looking at the bookplate it is usually straightforward to tell which type it is.

Bookplates are often signed or stamped and it is essential to test for fastness before applying solutions – to remove a disfiguring bookplate but create a stain in the process would be self-defeating.

Ink can easily be removed from a label or bookplate by sanding with fine (micro-grit) emery paper or with an abrasive ink eraser; it is often possible to delaminate the surface of the label and this is ideal as it both removes the ink and enables the solution to reach the adhesive more quickly.

The easiest way of removing traditional bookplates is to use hot water, but adding a detergent will improve its efficaciousness hugely; a concentrated washing-up liquid is about the best. Before starting work, mask off the rest of the book-block with a sheet of stiff acetate and on top of this lay a sheet of thick blotting paper. The blotting paper will absorb any free moisture and the acetate will prevent any dampness working through to the adjacent leaves. Also ensure that the bookplate is flat so any applied moisture does not run off.

Bookplates on paste-downs (bioadhesives)
Gently apply the water/detergent mixture to the surface of the bookplate with a soft brush, letting the moisture soak into the plate. Keep applying the liquid until the plate is thoroughly saturated (it has to work its way through the paper to the glue underneath). Gently test the edge of the plate with a brush and if it starts to lift, carefully peal off. You may have to peel off in strips, in which case keep applying the liquid to the remaining parts. Once the label has been removed, using your brush in conjunction with a clean cloth and more of the liquid if necessary, remove any glue residue still on the paper. You will be left with a damp rectangle in the middle of paste-down and it is now essential to dampen evenly, the rest of the paste-down, to avoid tide marks forming as it dries. Place a sheet of blotting paper on top of the damp endpaper, then a sheet of acetate, and close the

book. Place weights (other books are fine) on top of the closed book to ensure that the paste-down/board dry flat.

Alternatively, cut a piece of strong kitchen paper to approximately the same size as the bookplate, impregnate it with the hot water/detergent mix and place it over the bookplate; place a piece of acetate over the top and then a sheet of thick blotting paper. Close the book and apply some weights; 15–20 minutes later the bookplate should peel off, clean and finish as above.

Bookplates on free endpapers
Essentially the same technique is used to remove plates from free pages as that for paste-downs, but the whole leaf must be dampened at the beginning of the procedure, otherwise rucking and creasing of the paper will occur as a result of uneven tension, caused by partial wetting. The underside of the paper can also now be wetted to allow the soapy mixture to work through to the glue from both sides. The rest is the same as above but dry under weight in a sandwich of blotting paper and acetate to both sides.

A note on pre-wetting
Thick non-absorbent papers might require hours of soaking to allow the moisture to work through to the underlying glue, which is often not practicable. In such cases it is necessary to 'pre-wet' with a solution of alcohol (ethanol, denatured alcohol, methylated spirits, iso-propanol) and water mixed at an approximate ratio of 1:1. The paper should 'wet' within a few seconds of being placed in such a solution.

If the above techniques do not work on bioadhesive bookplates, try to the proprietary products *Label Lifter* or *Stamp Lifter*. Though in my experience, if hot water, detergent and pre-wetting do not work, then neither will these.

Removal of synthetic adhesives (pressure sensitive tapes, sticky-backed plastic, stickers, bookplates)
Pressure-sensitive tape, so-called because light pressure causes it to stick readily to most surfaces, is the bane of the bibliophile, but most types can readily be removed. Often transparent and traditionally cellulose-based, these tapes are better known by their generic trademarks *Sellotape* (Europe) or *Scotch Tape* (USA). Self-adhesive labels, stickers, plastic barcodes, sticky-backed plastic are all variations of this undesirable theme with adhesives composed of synthetic or natural rubber and more recently of an acrylic polymer. Unlike gummed bookplates discussed above, they can only be removed with solvents, but once *Sellotape* has degraded and stained the underlying paper brown, there is no way of removing this staining.

There is an array of proprietary solvents available but the following do not stain, are cheap and readily available:
1. Lighter Fluid. Most Sellotapes and similar products can easily be removed using standard lighter fluid, which contains Naphtha and sold under various trade names, e.g. *Newport*, *Ronson* and *Zippo*. Lighter fluid is an industry standard, undeniably good, but not as efficacious as the following product.

2. *Evo-Stik* Adhesive Cleaner & Remover. This product contains both Heptane and Naphtha and in that sense is the best of both worlds. It evaporates extremely quickly, so has the advantage of being in contact with the underlying paper for only very short periods. It is often necessary to use it under acetate sheets to slow down the rate of evaporation.

As with bookplates, the ink on the label may run as soon as contact is made with the solvent and this will quickly stain the page. Remove the ink as described above.

Isolate the page concerned as described in the method for removing bookplates and with sheets of blotting paper and acetate, mask off the area around the article to be removed. With a fine artist's brush (the sort that might be used for fine illustration – sizes 1–3 would be ideal), work the solvent under the edges and gently probe away, lifting the label/tape as you work. Always have a piece of kitchen paper to hand to mop up any free solvent or dissolved glue. Remember, you need to get the solvent to the adhesive, and if removing plastic tape or labels, these will act as a barrier so as well as applying the solvent to the edges, apply it to the underside of the paper, so it can work through to the adhesive. Put a sheet of acetate under the page you are working on; this will protect neighbouring pages, but importantly it will also prevent the solvent from evaporating too quickly.

Once the offending article has been removed, wipe the area with solvent and if only a small page, apply a minimal amount to the whole leaf to ensure that as it dries no 'tidemarks' are left; alternatively feather out the solvent around the edges with the cloth. Simply leave the book in a well-ventilated place to allow the solvent to evaporate off. (Tidemarks are very rarely a problem with fast-evaporating solvents such as *Evo-Stik* Adhesive Cleaner.)

A word of warning: unpleasant, clear sticky-backed plastic, so loved by librarians, so hated by booklovers is virtually impossible to remove successfully and best left well alone.

Tears in paper
Unsightly tears in dust jackets and pages can be inconspicuously repaired using a few simple procedures. It should go without saying that sellotape and the like should never be used, but the simplest way is in fact to use a pressure sensitive tape. The conservation industry's standard is *Filmoplast P*, a wood-free, transparent, wafer thin, self-adhesive tape, non-ageing, non-yellowing, which is designed to protect cellulose fibres. Both the paper base and acrylic adhesive have a pH of 8.5 and buffered with $CaCO_3$. Once in place it should be burnished with a bone folder and this will render it almost invisible; cutting the tape longitudinally in half will also help to conceal its presence. Apply to the least conspicuous side of the tear. Theoretically it should be possible to remove it with water, but in my experience this is only possible for a short period after application, otherwise a solvent such a lighter fluid must be used.

Tears, where the edges overlap are, euphemistically referred to as 'closed tears', but are in fact straightforward to repair using a very fine layer of conservation PVA (pH neutral and fully reversible by rewetting with water) that can be applied to the torn surface using a extremely fine OO brush and the edges carefully pressed together. Remove any surplus glue with a damp cloth; while PVA is transparent when dry, it is also slightly shiny and therefore must be used sparingly. Ensure that all brushes, cloths and edges are clean as the glue will absorb any dirt and announce your repair to the world.

For more extensive tears and areas of paper that are weak and torn, hand-made Japanese tissues should be used. These very fine papers are alkaline, extremely strong and almost transparent when used correctly. The edges of the repair patch must always be torn, exposing the fibres and then applied with a methylcellulose paste. When dry or nearly dry, burnish with a bone folder. With a little bit of practice it is possible to repair tears so that they are almost impossible to detect. For larger tears, once repaired it may be necessary to 'touch in', as described below.

Repairing worn edges and chips to dust jackets

Jacket edges, particularly to the head/tail of the spine, are the most vulnerable to wear and are the most likely to be torn, chipped and creased. Start as always by assessing the problem, and using a fine but stiff artist's brush, tease out creased and torn sections. Older New Naturalist jackets will often delaminate at points of wear, where the upper printed surface becomes separated from the lower surface. These are easily glued back together. It is a sensible precaution to reinforce fragile and worn edges by gluing a strip of fine acid-free paper behind. This will prevent further damage but, provided conservation PVA is used, is a fully reversible process. In the same way glue appropriately shaped pieces of acid free paper to the rear of chips and small areas of loss. Ensure that the paper used is the same colour as the paper of the jacket and be careful not to get any glue on edges or upper surfaces to be touched in, as dried glue will not take colour.

Touching in

Creases, chips, tears and rubbed areas, often stand out because they are a different colour to the surrounding design. By using a fine brush and appropriate (acid-free) watercolour they can easily be touched-in to match the surrounding design. This simple technique can markedly and quickly improve the visual quality of a jacket, and render small tears virtually impossible to detect, but if the book is to be passed on, all such repairs should be declared.

With large areas of loss, photocopied portions can be inserted, but in my experience it is virtually impossible to match colours satisfactorily, in which case a facsimile jacket is probably a better option.

Creased pages and jackets

It is impossible to remove heavy creases completely but they can be mitigated, through wetting and subsequent drying under weight. Best to use a paper conservator for this.

Washing and bleaching

It might come as a surprise to some readers that dust jackets, prints and many works on paper can be cleaned simply by washing. Furthermore, washing is fundamentally a straightforward procedure, but yet one that can transform the appearance of a print or dust jacket. It also has the very welcome benefit of removing potentially corrosive contaminants from the paper and, if rinsed/cleaned in an appropriate alkaline solution, of deacidifying the paper. Deacidification neutralizes acid in paper, while depositing an alkaline buffer to arrest further degradation.

Washing and deacidification is often carried out as part of the process of 'bleaching'. Within paper conservation circles, bleaching generates more debate and controversy than any other area and acres of paper (probably acid-free) have been expended on the subject, yet conservators across the world continue to bleach paper on a daily basis. That it is taken seriously is indeed important, as incorrect methodology can irretrievably damage paper, but if done correctly it should cause no long-term damage; remember that most paper has been bleached in the first instance!

While both washing and bleaching can be undertaken on the kitchen table; it is far easier (and probably safer) to employ the services of a paper conservator, who, for a few pounds, will improve the aesthetics of your browned and stained jackets immeasurably – and deacidify them in the process.

Common and general repairs

Cracked book-blocks

The book-blocks of many old books become slack with gaps developing between the gatherings, exposing the mull behind the spine, though New Naturalists are so well made that this is rarely a problem. If not too far gone, it is easily remedied by brushing a bead of conservation PVA in the crack, realigning the adjacent gatherings and closing the book. The mull can then be pushed back into place and into contact with the glue by applying pressure on the spine. Glue each crack separately, allowing the PVA to set before starting on the next. As always, use the minimum glue required to do the job properly and avoid getting it onto the pages themselves.

Replacing endpapers

My preference would always be to retain original endpapers wherever possible, even if marked. Not uncommonly, however, the free section has been deliberately excised, usually to remove an inscription, or has become detached and lost as a result of a cracked hinge. The free section can be replaced with matching paper cut to size and pasted on at the hinge or if the hinge has also been repaired overlapped onto the paste-down. Alternatively the whole endpaper can be replaced. The latter will look better but again it is better to see as much of the original fabric of the book retained as possible. If the whole endpaper is to be replaced, ideally the originally paste-down should be removed (use the same techniques as advocated by bookplate removal above) but it is much easier simply to paste the new endpaper on top of the old. Use a prepared starch paste mixed with conservation PVA. When cutting the new endpaper to size, remember to take account of the depth of the hinge.

Removal of ink inscriptions, library stamps and other marks
The point of ink is that it is not supposed to be removed, and in this respect it is highly successful. There are two broad approaches to its removal, chemical and mechanical. Neither work well, though, and more often than not you will end up with a greater mess than that with which you started. Is that stamp or inscription really so disfiguring that it must be removed? If it is, seek the help of a paper conservator, but don't expect miracles.

Stamps and remainder marks on the edge of the text-block, i.e. stamped to the edges of the pages, can be removed using very fine microgrit emery papers; grades P320 to P500 are ideal. Carefully fold the boards back, clamping the text block tight between two rigid boards. The offending mark can be safely sanded off, assuming of course that the ink has not penetrated too deeply. This can be a laborious process, but make sure that the whole of the edge is evenly sanded to ensure a uniform finish.

Dewey and other library numbers written directly onto the buckram of the spine are much easier to remove as the binding fabric is not as absorbent as paper. Alchohol (methylated spirits etc.) will often remove white library numbers, otherwise try *Tippex* thinners or various liquid stain removers. Work the liquid into the ink using a rag or soft toothbrush (always experiment before applying solvents to ensure they will not stain).

Removing Duraseal
To retain or not to retain *Duraseal* has already been discussed at some length. However, even if you wish to retain it, it is sometimes necessary to remove temporarily to enable repairs and cleaning.

It is easily removed either by applying heat with a hairdryer or by using a solvent, but the use of heat will distort the plastic and if the intention is to reuse it, a solvent must be used. The heat or solvent is applied only to the two beads of glue that run parallel with the long edges, on the underside of the jacket. If using a hairdryer, the *Duraseal* will come away much more easily and quickly, if it can be lifted while the heat is still being applied. If using a solvent, my preferred choice is *Evo-Stik* Adhesive Cleaner and Remover, as its rapid evaporation means that it is unlikely to stain the jacket. As the original adhesive used for fixing the *Duraseal* is known to stain the paper, it is better removed in its entirety and conservation PVA used to refix the *Duraseal*.

Smoky and musty books
There is a great divide between an old book with the gentle and warm smell of antiquity and one that is musty or smells strongly of stale tobacco smoke. One is a pleasure to handle, the other is certainly not, but such unpleasant odours are surprisingly easy to

eliminate. Simply place the offending book in an airtight plastic container with Book Deoderizer (highly absorbent treated granules that inert, natural and non-toxic) and leave for around two weeks. A cheaper alternative is to use cat litter.

Cocked or leaning spines
The long-term success of treatment to cure this problem is very dependent on the underlying causes (sometimes slanting spines are caused by incorrect binding techniques), but as treatment is so simple, little is lost if it does not work. Gently manipulate the book so it is again square and place in a book press. Failing that, it is easy enough to use a makeshift clamp or secure the book in position with multiple elastic bands running top to bottom (not round the spine), ensuring that the corners of the boards are well protected with card. After a week or so remove the book from its clamp and all being well it will remain good and square.

Tipping in loose pages and plates
Very easily done. Gently open up the book as far as it will go without exerting undue pressure on the binding, with a fine artist's brush run a fine bead of conservation PVA inside the gutter margin. Line up the loose page or plate with the fore-edge and gentle push the opposite edge into the margin. When correctly aligned shut the book and apply a few weights. It is important to restrict the glue to the gutter only, otherwise the replaced page will not open freely.

SUPPLY, DEMAND AND VALUE

The value of a New Naturalist, like any other commodity, is determined by the dynamic law of *supply and demand:* everybody knows that. However, it is the factors that determine supply and determine demand that are probably less familiar, but altogether much more interesting.

Initial supply
Print quantities
A p/o (print-order) is sent to the printers, which specifies the print quantity or print run, and this is usually a round number, e.g. 8,000. However, the printer is governed by factors outside his control: minimum material quantities, setting up a printing machine ready to run the job (*make-ready*), breakdowns, damaged materials, etc., and in reality it is impossible for him to print, as in this case, exactly 8,000 copies. In recognition of this, the industry usually works on a tolerance of ± 5 per cent (sometimes ± 10 per cent) and the printer will 'manufacture to materials', which might mean a few less copies than ordered but it usually results in an overrun (overs), for which the customer must pay – assuming of course it is within the agreed tolerance. For example, this could represent an additional 400 copies.

This leads to rather bizarre quantities; e.g. *Bird Migration:* 4,000 copies ordered, 4,032 delivered, but often the overrun is much greater than this. The number of books actually printed is known as the *out-turn* (a Collins-specific term) and the sales-sheet, dated February 1960, includes the following note: '*Out-turn figs. before No. 31 not available. In some cases out-turn less or more than edition quoted*'. In other words, it is only the quantity ordered that is known and not the actual number printed. This is generally the case, but often the *print-order* is confused with either the *out-turn* or the number of books sold and can be misleading.

Discrepancy between the number of books printed and books sold
Firstly (and obviously) the number of books sold is closely linked to the number of books printed, but it would be a mistake to think that the two are the same: they are not. The number of books sold is always lower, and often significantly lower, a figure 15 per cent less than the quantity printed would not be unusual. This is an important point to the collector as it has a significant bearing on rarity. This discrepancy, or 'natural wastage' as it is sometimes referred to, is the norm within the publishing industry: it is accepted as being an operational expedient and is costed for accordingly. An NN sales report dated September 1958 includes the following caveat: 'Figs. take into account review and travellers copies, wastage, etc.' There are a number of reasons for it, which are examined below – with specific regard to Collins and the New Naturalist series.

Binding up in batches
Binding represents a considerable proportion (30–50 per cent) of the cost of physically manufacturing a book; consequently publishers are reluctant to commit to binding-up large quantities of a new title before it has been tested on the market. Conversely, adding 1,000 or 2,000 copies to an existing print-order increases the cost by a disproportionately small amount. Publishers aware of this dichotomy will commonly order a much greater number of books to be printed than they intend to bind up and will store the unbound copies either as sets of printer's sheets or *quires* (that is, sheets folded and gathered into sets) to be bound up at a later time should demand require it. This practice is of considerable interest to the bibliophile, firstly because it spawns binding variants (the series is often enriched in this way) and secondly, because it has a significant impact on quantities: inevitably the logistics of multiple binding operations will result in greater wastage than a single operation, also unbound stock is more vulnerable in the warehouse. Additionally, significant delays between binding operations will potentially lead to confusion over numbers printed.

Logistics, pulping and warehouse chaos
For a start, large publishers such as Collins are looking to the bigger picture: they will have dozens of titles in print at any one time, amounting to millions of units and they are not, unlike the niche specialist publisher, set up to deal with books trickling out in ones and twos over a protracted period: it is just not worth their while maintaining stocks of slow-selling titles.

Consequently, many titles are remaindered or pulped a few years after publication; an employee of Collins in the late 1970s describes how he was responsible for pulping five or six million paperback units a year! However, the New Naturalist series was Billy Collins's baby and his personal involvement ensured that stocks were retained in the Glasgow warehouse, probably many years after it made economic good sense to do so. But keeping stocks of books for many years will inevitably lead to damage and wastage. Small quantities of NN books, stored indefinitely, must have been an annoying irritant to the storeman responsible for the logistics of storing and despatching tens of thousands of Enid Blytons, Agatha Christies *et al*! He couldn't afford to lose sleep over the odd box or pallet of NN books that went missing. For us collectors, who revere our single copies, this is difficult to comprehend. (The move from Cathedral Street in the centre of Glasgow to the vast Bishopbriggs warehouse in the north of the city was a huge logistics operations and must have accounted for the 'loss' of numerous books.)

Gratis copies
Traditionally there were many 'freebies' – copies for the chairman and management, reps and miscellaneous employees; copies for the author/s and Editors and others associated with the book; sample and quality control copies, review copies (which alone, could be dozens for a good title). In the mid-seventies, senior staff could fill out a 'BS2 requisition form' and request multiple copies as required. Whilst the odd book might have been stolen, most of this 'wastage' was legitimate and part and parcel of the culture of publishing. More recently, the standard number of gratis copies costed for was 250 (including other wastage), which for many titles represented a sizeable percentage of the whole. It is worth noting that, for obvious reasons, the incidence of gratis copies is much more prevalent in first editions than in reprints.

Distribution and returns
Another important element to be considered is the way books were traditionally distributed and sold. Before the demise of the Net Book Agreement in 1995, and the advent of the internet, bookshop chains and supermarkets, most books were sold by small independent bookshops, and to these shops an army of publishers' reps peddled their tomes. In the early days of the series these reps were referred to as *travellers*, and each one would have had a sample copy or two of the latest New Naturalist. Books were often supplied to bookshops on a sale-or-return basis; the publisher adopting a 'see you right' policy with the bookseller. Inevitably many books did not sell, but they were well-thumbed by the time they were returned to the publisher and were no longer saleable. Either the title pages was removed and they went for pulping, or they were stamped 'damaged' and sold off cheaply. Now that many potential purchasers peruse online, less books are compromised in this way, but instead it seems a good number are damaged while in the post, due, primarily, to inadequate packing.

TABLE 2: **Availability of first editions
on AbeBooks during the second week of May
2011.** Only first edition copies were included
in this survey. The price range is for jacketed
non ex-library books, but no account was
taken of jacket condition. Quantities for
titles marked * may be distorted upwards by
bookclub editions not distinguished by sellers.

No.	Title	Green-back	Ex-lib	With DJ	Total No.	Price range (with DJS)
1	Butterflies	25	7	15	47	£5–50
2	British Game	24	4	23	51	£7–55
3	London's Nat. History	27	4	18	45	£10–54
4	Structure and Scenery	37	6	22	65	£5–42
5	Wild Flowers	4	5	22	31	£8–22
6a	Highlands & Islands	55	10	45	110	£5–58
6b	Highlands & Islands	–	3	14	17	£8–80
7	Mushrooms	5	1	22	28	£20–60
8	Insect Natural History	57	5	44	106	£5–46
9	A Country Parish	4	-	16	20	£60–250
10	British Plant Life	35	7	50	92	£5–50
11	Mountains & Moorlands	31	10	43	84	£6–54
12	The Sea Shore	44	9	46	99	£5–75
13	Snowdonia	44	6	26	76	£12–80
14	Art Botanical	12	2	19	33	£20–135
15	Life in Lakes and Rivers	25	7	27	59	£10–50
16	Wild Flowers of Chalk	14	3	30	47	£6–58
17	Birds and Men	22	8	36	66	£7–60
18	Man in Britain	19	9	21	49	£5–90
19	Wild Orchids of Britain	10	1	35	46	£10–98
20	Amphibians & Reptiles	5	1	12	18	£18–81
21	British Mammals	15	4	22	51	£5–70
22	Climate & British Scene	8	3	13	24	£20–55
23	An Angler's Entomology	11	–	6	17	£27–80
24	Flowers of the Coast	2	2	17	21	£20–75
25	The Sea Coast	8	6	9	23	£15–50
26	The Weald	2	2	10	14	£24–63
27	Dartmoor	3	4	12	19	£20–70
28	Sea Birds	12	6	17	35	£40–95
29	World of the Honeybee	1	1	6	8	£20–69
30	Moths	2	6	18	25	£20–72
31	Man & The Land	11	5	14	30	£12–50
32	Trees, Woods and Man	2	3	13	18	£25–75
33	Mountain Flowers	4	1	17	22	£20–100
4	The Open Sea I	3	3	9	15	£30–75
35	The World of the Soil	4	2	9	15	£25–125
36	Insect Migration	4	2	3	9	£66–250
37	The Open Sea II	3	3	10	16	£30–75
38	The World of Spiders	6	2	18	27	£45–160
39	The Folklore of Birds	1	2	13	16	£120–340
40	Bumblebees	1	4	15	20	£80–400
41	Dragonflies	–	3	13	16	£240–500
42	Fossils	3	3	9	15	£30–140
43	Weeds and Aliens	1	0	10	11	£45–175
44	The Peak District	11	4	4	19	£33–80
45	Common Lands	–	2	10	12	£60–220
46	The Broads	1	6	22	29	£50–175
47	Snowdonia	28	2	18	48	£12–80
48	Grass and Grasslands	3	2	16	21	£60–126
49	Nature Conservation	4	5	9	18	£25–84
50	Pesticides and Pollution	–	2	12	14	£40–112
54	Pollination of Flowers	1	1	9	11	£75–210
55	Finches	–	–	10	10	£30–110
56	Pedigree Words	–	–	17	17	£75–210
57	British Seals	–	1	19	20	£60–162
58	Hedges	–	7	9	16	£35–150
59	Ants	1	6	15	22	£95–225
60	British Birds of Prey*	–	–	12	12	£20–47
61	Inheritance*	–	6	9	15	£40–100
62	British Tits*	1	1	45	47	£12–90
63	British Thrushes*	–	2	60	62	£15–80

No.	Title	Green-back	Ex-Lib	With DJ	Total No.	Price range (with DJS)
64	Natural History Shetland	1	1	13	15	£115–288
65	Waders*	–	–	16	16	£40–125
66	Wales	–	–	12	12	£60–200
67	Farming and Wildlife*	–	1	8	9	£60–110
68	Mammals	–	–	19	19	£75–180
69	Reptiles & Amphibians	–	2	18	20	£140–350
70	Orkney 1st state	–	–	–	–	–
70	Orkney 2nd state	–	–	7	7	£700–1125
71	Warblers 1st state	–	–	1	1	£1850
71	Warblers 2nd state	–	–	3	3	£595–700
72	Heathlands*	–	–	10	10	£180–400
73	The New Forest*	–	–	13	13	£221–325
74	Ferns	–	–	15	15	£500–807
75	Freshwater Fish	–	–	6	6	£525–850
76	The Hebrides	–	–	8	8	£825–1500
77	The Soil	–	–	5	5	£440–635
78	Larks, Pipits & Wagtails	–	–	9	9	£450–750
79	Caves and Cave Life	–	1	12	13	£450–1200
80	Wild & Garden Plants	–	–	5	5	£500–800
81	Ladybirds	–	–	8	8	£500–950
82A	The New Naturalists 1995	–	–	4	4	£245–390
82B	The New Naturalists 2005	–	–	14	14	£45–72
83	Pollination*	–	–	11	11	£150–350
84	Ireland	–	–	21	21	£90–160
85	Plant Disease	–	2	14	16	£90–240
86	Lichens	–	–	13	13	£125–250
87	Amphibians & Reptiles	–	–	11	11	£75–215
88	Loch Lomondside	–	–	14	14	£75–154
89	The Broads	–	–	20	20	£75–220
90	Moths	–	2	14	16	£85–160
91	Nature Conservation	–	–	15	15	£50–135
92	Lakeland	–	–	10	10	£100–135
93	British Bats	–	1	13	14	£180–250
94	Seashore	–	–	25	25	£60–110
95	Northumberland	–	–	11	11	£65–200
96	Fungi	–	–	19	19	£65–125
97	Mosses and Liverworts	–	–	23	23	£31–110
98	Bumblebees	–	–	16	16	£75–150
99	Gower	–	–	20	20	£33–90
100	Woodlands	–	–	12	12	£60–120
101	Galloway	too recent for meaningful results				
102	Garden Natural History	too recent for meaningful results				
103	Isles of Scilly	too recent for meaningful results				
104	History of Ornithology	too recent for meaningful results				
105	Wye Valley	too recent for meaningful results				
106	Dragonflies	too recent for meaningful results				
107	Grouse	too recent for meaningful results				
108	Southern England	too recent for meaningful results				
109	Islands	too recent for meaningful results				
110	Wildfowl	too recent for meaningful results				
111	Dartmoor	too recent for meaningful results				
112	Books and Naturalists	too recent for meaningful results				
113	Bird Migration	too recent for meaningful results				
114	Badger	too recent for meaningful results				
115	Climate and Weather	too recent for meaningful results				
M1	Badger	20	8	20	48	£12–60
M2	The Redstart	1	–	6	7	£47–140
M3	The Wren	1	2	6	9	£168–275
M4	The Yellow Wagtail	–	1	19	20	£20–100
M5	The Greenshank	2	1	13	16	£73–203
M6	The Fulmar	2	1	4	7	£160–300

No.	Title	Green-back	Ex-Lib	With DJ	Total No.	Price range (with DJS)
M7	Fleas, Flukes & Cuckoos	–	–	9	9	£33–150
M8	Ants	4	3	5	12	£75–173
M9	Herring Gull's World	4	–	18	22	£28–93
M10	Mumps	–	3	7	10	£180–577
M11	The Heron	–	1	11	12	£90–300
M12	Squirrels	–	1	12	13	£50–180
M13	The Rabbit	2	2	6	10	£50–180
M14	Birds London Area	1	3	9	13	£26–240
M15	The Hawfinch	–	1	2	3	£270–300
M16	The Salmon	6	3	18	27	£15–65
M17	Lords and Ladies	–	–	15	15	£120–339
M18	Oysters	–	4	7	11	£85–180
M19	The House Sparrow	–	–	11	11	£45–156
M20	The Wood Pigeon	–	3	16	19	£30–100
M21	The Trout	3	6	21	30	£34–100
M22	The Mole	–	2	15	17	£40–90

Number of books circulated
It has been established that there is often a sizeable discrepancy between the number of books printed and actually sold, and whilst both figures are of interest to the collector, the quantity sold is of greater significance, as this is likely to be closer to the number of books circulated. Of course the number of books actually circulated is impossible to determine, but will be a figure somewhere between the number printed and the number sold.

Factors influencing the supply of 'collectable' books to the second-hand collectors' market
Finite quantities
Assuming that there is no intention to reprint a title, and disregarding print-on-demands, the supply to the second-hand market is finite. Clearly, many copies originally circulated will have suffered over the years and will no longer be in 'collectable' condition, i.e. in the categories of very good, near fine and fine. Some of the more significant causes of degradation are considered below, along with other factors that limit supply.

Library books
It is impossible to estimate accurately the percentage of NN books that end up in libraries, and to some degree the number must be influenced by title. Additionally, some libraries will prefer the cheaper paperbacks and others the harder-wearing hardbacks. The Publishers Association's statistics state that in 2007 the value of UK-published books sold in home territories was £1,915 million and that for the same period the total expenditure on books by libraries (excluding specialist libraries) was around £150 million, which represents around 8 per cent of the total. With more specialist books such as the New Naturalist, it is not unreasonable to assume that the percentage purchased by libraries is higher – say 10 to 15 per cent, and these copies, once 'tagged' with stamps, barcodes and other defacing paraphernalia, are effectively removed from the collectors' market.

The influence of title on condition
Some titles have greater appeal than others and are consequently well read; perversely, the poorer books in the series are often easier to find in fine condition as few have bothered reading them! Other titles might be on university reading lists and, conversely, become well-thumbed; some appeal to a wider audience and others were marketed overseas.

The influence of physical qualities on condition
New Naturalist books are generally well made and durable – far better than many, or even most, contemporary books. But they are not standard and, simply, some are better-built than others; this is particularly so with regard to the quality of the jackets. For instance, NN4 *Structure and Scenery* is printed on thin, acidic paper and table 2 on page 36 shows that the majority (57 per cent) of first edition copies offered are missing their jackets, whereas NN19 *Wild Orchids of Britain* has a much tougher jacket, and the

same table demonstrates that the majority (76 per cent) of first editions have their jackets. All books before *c.* 1975 were printed on acid paper, which has a greater susceptibility to tanning and foxing. The inks used on some jackets are not colourfast, and in the case of infamous titles such NN75 *Fishes*, virtually every title will be faded to a lesser or greater extent. Before the advent of centrally heated houses, foxing and browning and the attentions of silverfish were all common problems, often exacerbated by corrosive smoke that escaped coal fires. (For a more extensive account of common book faults, see pages 24–28.)

Customs, clipping and consignment
Dust jackets are such an iconic part of the New Naturalist series that it would today be considered sacrilege to remove them, but early in the twentieth century it was customary to do so, and this unfortunate habit occasionally lingered on into the early days of the series – sometimes longer.

In more decorous times, it would have been unthinkable to make a gift of a New Naturalist without clipping off the price – and probably without adding a sizeable inscription too. Today we are not squeamish about such things, and has anybody noticed that the price is now printed to the rear panel of the jacket as well as the front flap? A fair amount of butchering is now required to remove the price (but the modern-day recipient of the book in its Amazon box will know that the printed price is an irrelevance anyway).

No doubt a sizeable number of NN books, in the 67-year course of the series, have been consigned to the rubbish heap, or in more recent times recycled. This is particularly so with paperbacks, such as the Fontanas, which were printed in very large numbers, for instance 13,000 copies of *The Open Sea, The World of Plankton* were printed, but paradoxically are now virtually unobtainable.

Overall supply
The above factors conspire to reduce the number of extant collectable copies. Quite to what degree is impossible to determine with any accuracy, and will vary from title to title. But having accepted that, it would be useful to have an understanding of the potential number of extant collectable copies, even if it is a few hundred.

Let us assume that we are dealing with a hypothetical New Naturalist title – *The Natural History of Conjecture*, dating from the 1950s with a first edition print run of, say, 5,000. Numbers/percentages can be partially informed by an analysis of the breakdown of copies currently offered on the internet (see table 2 on page 36) and can be quantified as follows:

TABLE 3 *The Natural History of Conjecture*, published 1955; number printed: 5,000.

Depreciating factor	Quantity	Leaving…
Natural wastage	–400 (8% of 5,000)	4,600 copies
Library copies	–460 (10% of 4,600)	4,140 copies
Copies subsequently disposed of	–210 (5% of 4,140)	3,930 copies
Copies missing jackets	–1,180 (30% of 3,930)	2,750 jacketed copies
Copies with very worn jackets	–1,100 (40% of 2,750)	1,650 good/very good/ fine copies
Copies rated as good only	–740 (45% of 1,650)	910 very good/ fine copies
Copies rated as very good	–500 (55% of 910)	410 fine copies

From an initial print run of 5,000 copies, 55 years later we are left with 410 fine copies and 500 very good copies. Over the last seven years or so I have had the privilege to inspect hundreds of NN books and believe these figures appear to be a reasonable reflection of the actual position – given, of course, the caveats already mentioned above.

Availability
We have explored the initial supply of books and the potential number of extant collectable copies, but this is very different from availability at any given moment. However, it is important to remember that while the supply of out of print New Naturalists is finite (disregarding POD copies) and more or less static, availability is not. It is fluid and changes on a day-to-day basis, but also in the longer-term in response to shifting collecting trends and economic conditions.

The advent of the internet has brought hundreds of bookshops worldwide simultaneously into the living rooms of collectors and there is now greater choice than ever before. This has had the effect of making books previously perceived as being rare, common, but equally has underlined and emphasised the truly rare – often conspicuous by their absence on the internet, e.g. first-state *Orkney*.

In 1977 J. Richard Shelton, a US Professor of Biology, commented that it took him five months to track down a copy of *Lords and Ladies*, and in 2006 it took me several months to find a copy for a customer. However, table 4 demonstrates that at the time of writing 15 copies with jackets were being offered on one internet site!

In reality it is the knowledge of availability, rather than availability itself, that has significantly changed and it is now comparatively easy for a collector to assemble a set quickly, albeit perhaps of indifferent quality. It is worth noting that among the thousands of copies of pre-1970s books offered on the internet very few will be genuinely fine copies: to build a collection of such books remains a painstaking task.

AbeBooks is the principal internet book site and is used by most mainstream second-hand booksellers. It therefore gives us a very good window on current availability, trends and prices.

table 2 is an analysis of the current position on AbeBooks (May 2011), and while it is true that many other books are offered via shops, catalogues, auctions, eBay and elsewhere, this internet site is so universally used that we can be confident that it is representative of the wider picture.

Table 4 below demonstrates that the number of books offered at one particular moment on AbeBooks is a very small percentage of the original number printed. It is a percentage far smaller than the average used title, which underlines what we all already know: the New Naturalist series is strongly collected. It is also interesting that there is not a huge variation in percentages, which suggests that price as determined by the supply versus demand dynamic is working well.

TABLE 4 The number of books offered on AbeBooks on 05/05/2011 in relation to the number originally printed.

No.	Title	1st eds. Printed	All 1st editions offered on 05/05/2011		Jacketed 1st editions offered on 05/05/2011	
			Qty.	% of no. printed	Qty.	% of no. printed
1	*Butterflies*	20,000	47	0.0024	15	0.0008
10	*British Plant Life*	22,000	92	0.0042	50	0.0023
20	*Amphibians & Reptiles*	6,500	18	0.0028	12	0.0018
30	*Moths*	8,500	25	0.0029	18	0.0021
40	*Bumblebees*	5,000	20	0.0040	15	0.0030
50	*Pesticides*	6,500	14	0.0022	12	0.0018
60	*Birds of Prey*	4,250	12	0.0028	12	0.0028
70	*Orkney* 1st state	7,250	0	–	0	–
80	*Wild and Garden Plants*	1,500	5	0.0030	5	0.0030
90	*Moths*	3,000	16	0.0050	14	0.0047
100	*Woodlands*	4,200	12	0.0029	12	0.0029

Speculative buying
An additional factor influencing availability is speculative buying by dealers and to a lesser extent by collectors. Bob Burrow, the founder of the New Naturalist Book Club (now the New Naturalist Collectors' Club), regularly advised members of the investment potential of new titles, and no doubt many acted on these tips and *laid-down* new copies. I suspect that many NN titles printed in the last ten years or so, offered on eBay and elsewhere, are in fact new books that have never been previously owned. Most dealers are coy when it comes to this subject, but a conservative estimate would be that at least 10 per cent of NNs sold (at the time of writing in early 2011), in the first instance, are speculative purchases to be withheld from resale until the book goes out of print; perhaps less now that print runs are generally larger.

Rarity

General rarity

Firstly, let us consider unqualified rarity, in respect of availability in *isolation* of condition. These rankings (first editions) are subject to opinion, and the situation is undeniably an ever-changing state of affairs. Also remember that this is not a table of value, though there is a close correlation.

First-state *Orkney* and *Warblers* are of course the two rarest and most valuable titles, and undoubtedly *Orkney* is the rarer of the two, which is inexplicable as the number printed was the same for both titles, especially considering that there is such an interest in ornithological titles. In third place is *Hebrides* with *Wild and Garden Plants* in fourth spot; *Ladybirds* and *Freshwater Fishes* share fifth. Seventh place is shared between *Caves and Cave Life* and the 1995 edition of *The New Naturalists*, though the former usually costs about twice as much. Ninth place is a toss up between *British Larks* and *The Soil* (NN77), though *The Soil* probably shaves it. Eleventh place would now be *Ferns* – puzzlingly it appears to have become considerably more common in the last couple of years; previously it would have been in the top five. The remainder are all much more obtainable, though the genuine first edition *Heathlands* with Collins printed on the base of the jacket spine is a rare thing; in fact in terms of print run, the rarest after *Orkney* and *Warblers* with just 1,000 copies printed, but the price tag does not reflect this, presumably because most collectors are happy with the almost identical bookclub edition. Of the early titles there are the three high flyers which in descending order are *Dragonflies*, *Folklore of Birds* and *Bumblebees*.

The monographs are generally rarer than the main series. In the number one spot is *The Hawfinch* – in any of its guises, though the green-jacketed variant is the rarest by a long chalk. Second is *Mumps, Measles and Mosaics*, but it has become much easier to find in the last few years. The first edition of *Fleas, Flukes and Cuckoos* finds its way into third place, but in point of fact has a smaller print run than both of the above. Flying into equal fourth are *The Wren* and *The Fulmar*, with *The Heron* perched in sixth place. *Birds of the London Area* sits in seventh. *Lords and Ladies* follows in eighth position, with first edition *Oysters* in ninth, and *Ants* at number ten. *The Greenshank* is at eleventh with *The Rabbit* holed-up in twelfth; we need go no lower than that, but it's worth pointing out that *The Redstart* is a considerably rarer bird than its price belies.

Conditional rarity

Considering general rarity in isolation of condition only tells part of the story, especially when condition is such an important element of collecting. It has a direct bearing on both value and aesthetics. When evaluating condition, this is mainly in reference to the jacket. Very rarely is a rough book found in a fine jacket, but the reverse is common. Perhaps the real challenge to the collector is tracking down genuinely fine copies of the early titles and in real terms such copies are rarer than most of the titles appearing in table 5. This may seem to be a rather exaggerated claim considering that most of these early titles were printed in very large numbers, but it's not without foundation, especially if a distinction is drawn between scarcity and value. If you can afford them, at any one time most of the so-called *Golden 13* (more accurately the G14) are available on the internet (see table 2). But try to find a fine first edition copy of *Butterflies* in a bright jacket that isn't browned, faded or chipped and that's another thing altogether. While you're about it, try to scout out a copy of *The Seashore* without any fading to the pink on the dust jacket spine or a copy of *Structure and Scenery* in a jacket that isn't browned or rubbed to the joints. *Flowers of the Coast* and first edition *Bumblebees* (NN40) are always faded on the spine – or is there an unfaded copy or two lurking at the bottom of a dark drawer awaiting discovery? Probably not. One could add many other titles to this list of 'impossibles'. Table 4 shows that twelve copies of *British Birds of Prey* and six copies of *Freshwater Fishes* respectively are available with dust jackets on AbeBooks, yet every one of these is faded on the spine. But a pleasant paradox of New Naturalist collecting is that, if you are lucky enough to hunt a fine early title to ground, you will never pay as much for it as one of the acknowledged rare titles.

TABLE 5 General rarity of first editions – in descending order.

The Main Series by ranking

1	*Orkney* (first state)
2	*Warblers* (first state)
3	*Hebrides*
4	*Ladybirds*
4	*Wild and Garden Plants*
4	*Freshwater Fishes*
7	*Caves and Cave Life*
7	*The New Naturalists* (1995 1st.ed.)
9	*The Soil* (NN77)
10	*British Larks, Pipits and Wagtails*
11	*Ferns*
12	*Heathlands* (genuine Collins 1st. ed.)
13	*Natural History of Pollination* (1st ed – £30)
14	*New Forest* (genuine Collins ed.)
15	*Dragonflies* (NN41)
16	*Folklore of Birds*
17	*Bumblebees* (NN40)
18	*British Bats*
19	*Lichens*
20	*Insect Migration*

The Monographs by ranking

1	*The Hawfinch* (any variant)
2	*Mumps, Measles, & Mosaics*
3	*Fleas, Flukes & Cuckoos*
4	*The Wren*
4	*The Fulmar*
6	*The Heron*
7	*Birds of the London Area*
8	*Lords and Ladies*
9	*Oysters*
10	*Ants*
11	*The Greenshank*
12	*The Rabbit*

Paperbacks

Rarity cannot be discussed without mentioning the paperbacks, as many are considerably scarcer than their hardback cousins. Collectors have concentrated on the hardback editions and Collins, in response to this demand, has increased the print run of this format, but often with a reciprocal reduction in the print run of the paperback. Meanwhile the paperback has been bought by institutions, libraries and individuals who want the title primarily for studying purposes, so few of these appear to find their way onto the second-hand market. Consequently many paperback titles are now very difficult to obtain, particularly in fine condition – *Bats*, *Caves* and *Ferns* to cite but three and *Northumberland* (just 1,000 printed) and *The Natural History of Pollination* are almost unobtainable. In January 2010, six titles in paperback format were unavailable on AbeBooks, with only single copies offered of several other titles, whereas, at that time, only two titles in hardback format were unavailable.

Several of the Fontana paperbacks are also scarce, e.g. *The Open Sea: The World of Plantkon* and *Butterflies*. But no matter: very few collectors are interested in them and they can usually be picked up for just a few pounds.

us editions

Most us editions are scarce and there are several titles that are extremely difficult if not impossible to track down. Many were printed in very small numbers; often no more than a few hundred copies. Seemingly, the majority of these us editions were purchased by public and institutional libraries; never to grace a bookseller's shelves again. Despite their scarcity, when they are found, they are often very reasonably priced, so they are particularly attractive books to collect.

Demand

The New Naturalist series is outstandingly collectable, and therefore irrespective of title or contents, the dedicated collector will indiscriminately purchase each new title. Beyond that, if a new book is to be purchased by the non-collecting public or casual collector, it must have its own appeal and it is this, along with marketing, that generates demand.

The collector and non-collector

As inferred, demand can be broadly divided into two elements: demand from the collector and demand from the non-collector. The proportion will vary between titles and is impossible to determine with any accuracy, but if we assume that there are around 1,800 active collectors (see page 21) and modern hardback print runs are around 4,000, then it is 45/55 for a new title, and we know few collectors bother with the paperbacks.

As we go back in the series, so there is greater obsolescence of content and some titles will be less attractive to the non-collector, for instance, it is unlikely that the modern palaeontologist would be particularly interested in purchasing a copy of the out-dated *Fossils*, first published 51 years ago. For such titles demand will be almost entirely restricted to collectors.

TABLE 6 New Naturalist titles offered by Bob Burrow in the first New Naturalist Club newsletter in November 1998. (Presumably v/f is very fine.)

First editions v/f in v/f d/w. [November 1998]

No.	Title	Price
14	*The Art of Botanical Illustration*	£100
25	*The Sea Coast*	£50
26	*The Weald*	£60
27	*Dartmoor*	£55
30	*Moths*	£50
36	*Insect Migration*	£80
41	*Dragonflies*	£250
43	*Weeds and Aliens*	£100
48	*Grasslands*	£60
52	*Woodland Birds*	£55
53	*The Lake District*	£60
54	*The Pollination of Flowers*	£120
56	*Pedigree Words from Nature*	£95
57	*British Seals*	£65
58	*Hedges*	£55
59	*Ants*	£110
60	*British Birds of Prey*	£55
61	*Inheritance and Natural History*	£55
64	*The Natural History of Shetland*	£95
65	*Waders*	£35
66	*The Natural History of Wales*	£100
67	*Farming and Wildlife*	£75
68	*Mammals in the British Isles*	£50

It could reasonably be assumed that it is the average collector's goal to assemble a complete collection and therefore demand, from this quarter, will be the same for each title in the series. This extrapolation is, however, incorrect, as many never complete their collections and will purchase first those titles of greater personal appeal. And those favoured books will often coincide with other collectors' preferences, resulting in uneven demand.

Subject area and quality

Clearly some titles will generate greater general interest than others. The more esoteric the title, the less the appeal, and if confined to British wildlife then that is a further narrowing factor. *Bird Migration,* by definition, will be in demand beyond the shores of these islands, and as ornithology enjoys such a wide following, demand will be further increased. On the other hand, *Gower* covers a very small geographical region of Britain and therefore will be of limited general appeal. Some titles when published coincide with a resurgence of general interest in the subject and sell quickly, as was the case with *British Bats*, whereas demand for *Plant Disease* is slight, even considering a very low print run.

Let's be honest, not all nn titles are equal. Some are truly outstanding, superb exposés of their subject and brilliantly written, with fine accompanying illustrations to boot: Hardy's *Open Sea* duology immediately comes to mind. On the other hand, some are more ordinary, even indifferent – and there's no need to give examples.

TABLE 7 Retail prices for fine copies (in £s) of the G14 from 2004–2012. It can be seen that most prices peaked in 2008 following a substantial increase in the preceding few years (figures taken from Loe Books sales records, NNBC valuations and dealers' catalogues).

No.	Title	2004	2005	2006	2007	2008	2009	2010	2011	2012
70	*Orkney* (1st state)	1,300	1,400	1,500	2,100	2,400	2,500	2,600	2,500	2,300
70	*Orkney* (2nd state)	600	650	700	800	1,000	1,000	950	800	750
71	*Warblers* (1st state)	1200	1250	1300	1900	2,300	2,400	2,400	2,300	2,100
71	*Warblers* (2nd state)	500	550	600	700	750	700	650	650	600
72	*Heathlands* (Collins to spine)	200	250	320	450	480	400	400	380	350
73	*The New Forest* (Collins to spine)	240	250	280	350	420	350	320	300	300
74	*Ferns*	350	400	550	850	1,100	850	650	600	550
75	*Freshwater Fishes*	300	350	450	700	950	800	750	700	650
76	*The Hebrides*	650	750	850	1,400	1,450	1,300	1,200	1,100	900
77	*The Soil*	170	200	280	600	600	550	550	520	480
78	*Larks, Pipits & Wagtails*	250	300	350	550	620	600	550	520	480
79	*Caves and Cave Life*	200	250	350	800	950	800	700	550	550
80	*Wild & Garden Plants*	150	200	380	600	800	900	700	650	600
81	*Ladybirds*	350	400	500	850	1,200	1,100	850	800	750
82a	*The New Naturalists*	120	160	350	400	400	350	300	300	280
83	*Pollination*	60	80	100	250	300	300	280	250	220

Dust jackets and illustrations

Undoubtedly dust jackets have a significant influence on demand, which is why publishers go to so much trouble to ensure arresting designs. New Naturalist jackets are generally designed to a very high standard, exceptional in fact, and as asserted previously, they are one of the reasons, if not the principal reason, for collecting the series. But with 140+ different jackets to date there will be winners and losers, and inevitably collectors will concentrate on the better ones first. The jacket worn by Benton's *Bumblebees* is so outstanding that it has quickly become iconic and surely will be a priority for every new collector; conversely, if I dare mention it again, *Plant Disease* with its sophisticated but dull jacket, is not.

Modern New Naturalists are printed in full colour, but this hasn't always been the case and many titles have only black and white plates, which will have some influence on demand, particularly at the time of publishing. A few reviews criticised NN53 *The Lake District* when it was first published in 1973 for having no colour illustrations.

Advertising, reviews and exposure

Demand, like availability and unlike supply, is not static and there are many factors that influence its potency at any one time. *Woodlands*, the one-hundredth title, was a great milestone for the series and its publication was lauded with numerous articles in the press, many of which included order forms for the book. Consequently *Woodlands* was purchased by a wider section of the public than most NN titles, which is reflected in the fact that the first edition is a now a comparatively rare book and that it was reprinted five times. In the same way, enthusiastic reviews will have a positive influence on demand.

Occasionally books are mentioned on the radio or feature in articles, authors die and their obituaries appear in newspapers and other publications; all these factors serve to spike demand, at that particular time, but it may not be sustained.

Value

Recent historic position

The New Naturalists have been collected for many years, but at what point they became the collecting sensation that they are today is open to debate. Certainly, before the 1980s they were much more affordable – both as new books and as second-hand copies. It was not until the post-1985 *Orkney* and *Warblers* debacle that prices really took off.

In the first issue of The New Naturalist Book Club newsletter (November 1998 – when the club had less than twenty members) Bob Burrow, who did so much to promote the club and the New Naturalist series generally, had a lot to say about price and value, and 13 years on it is of particular interest. On the first page he says of *Ireland* '…but I [am] still of the considered opinion they will be changing hands at over £200 a copy in five years' time'. In this particular instance he was wrong, but Bob's predictions were often very accurate. He also states that 'NN81 *Ladybirds* and NN82 *The New Naturalists*, published in 1994 … are now selling at over £200 and £95 respectively'; 10 years later they were selling at four times these figures. Of the NN72–NN83 tranche, he was offering fine copies of: *The New Forest* for £260; *Ferns* for £350, *Freshwater Fishes* for £250; *The Soil* for £50, *Larks, Pipits and Wagtails* for £125; *Caves and Cave Life* for £75; *Wild and Garden Plants* for £95; *Ladybirds* for £250 and *The Natural History of Pollination* for £40. All have appreciated considerably, but it is interesting how *Ferns* has recently become so much more common than *Fishes*.

Additionally in the same November 1998 newsletter Bob

offered a selection of earlier titles as reproduced in table 6. Note that many of these prices are not dissimilar from today's prices – but Bob's prices were before the levelling effect of the internet.

Several years ago many of the G14 titles were simply not available and when they were offered, they sold almost immediately. Consequently prices rose quickly and half a dozen titles became £1000+ books: *Orkney* (in both states) and *Warblers* (1st state), *Ferns, Fishes, Hebrides, Ladybirds* with *Caves and Cave Life*, and *Wild and Garden Plants* very nearly reaching that figure.

Prices for most of the G14 reached a peak in 2008, as shown in table 7, but in the preceding year some remarkable prices had already been achieved on eBay: £820 for *The Soil* in April; £2,000 for *Hebrides* in August; £830 for *Wild and Garden Plants* in September; £1,729 for *Ladybirds* in October and £930 for *Caves and Cave Life*, also in October. All, admittedly, in fine condition. At a sale held by Keys Fine Art Auctions in Alysham on 20 June 2008, fine copies of *Ladybirds* (lot 65) and *Larks, Pipits and Wagtails* (lot 78) made £1,200 and £1,050 on the hammer respectively, to which 15 per cent commission was added! At this time there was such a contagious euphoria surrounding the series that it was difficult to believe that prices would not continue inexorably on their upward climb. But inexorable it was not and prices have since fallen off significantly, at least for most of the notorious G14, I hesitate to say, to more sensible levels (unlike, say, an original *Gould* or *Curtis's Botanical Magazine*, NNs do not have an underlying intrinsic value). Table 2 reveals that in May 2001 eight and fifteen copies of *Ladybirds* and *Larks, Pipits and Wagtails*, respectively were offered on one internet site with like copies costing, for a similar book, approximately half those 2008 auction figures.

Current position
Undoubtedly the economic recession is the principal cause of recent price erosion, but there is a little doubt that the internet has increased (knowledge of) availability and this has added to the downward pressure.

There is a general perception among collectors and particularly booksellers (though the latter are a pessimistic lot, anyway) that prices have come down significantly across the board, but I don't believe this to be the case. Indisputably, prices have stopped rising mesmerically, as they were a few years ago, and it is perhaps this which has led to the perception there has actually been a general and considerable erosion of value. Sure, prices for many later titles have stabilized and even fallen off a little, but this is not so for earlier first edition titles. Fine copies of titles pre-NN50 have been pretty much immune: they are just too scarce in this condition and demand remains high. Even among the G14 the decline in value has not been universal, with first-state *Orkney* and *Warblers* holding their own, the former even gaining. Simply, there are still not enough copies to go round, particularly of *Orkney* – even at a £2k+ price-tag.

The New Naturalist series is no different from anything else that is highly collectable: the better the condition, the higher the value. Moreover, first edition books in fine condition are not only much more likely to hold their value, but also to appreciate. For outstanding copies, especially of those 'difficult' early titles, expect to pay a significant premium and pay it happily – the greater challenge is finding them, not paying for them. Besides, in terms of scarcity they will still probably represent better value than later more expensive titles, as explained in the following paragraph. As the table suggests, expect to pay considerably less for 'very good' copies and just don't bother with anything less – unless of course you only want to read them!

Earlier in this chapter we looked at rarity and I suggested that a genuinely fine first edition copy of, say, *Butterflies* was, in real terms, rarer than most of the G14. However, it is unlikely that a collector, even though keen to secure such a copy, could be persuaded to part with a sum anywhere close to that demanded by any member of the G14. This phenomenon, based on perception and reputation might be called *perceived value* and there are many instances where it comes into play in New Naturalist pricings. Simply, a collector will not purchase a book if the price, however justified in terms of true scarcity, is above their perceived value of that book. Thus an exceedingly fine first edition copy of *Butterflies* will never be worth £500 (at 2011 prices).

When looking at the suggested values in table 8, it is well to remember that these are retail prices and if you are thinking of selling your books you are unlikely to receive these figures: if selling at auction, you will pay between 15 and 25 per cent in commission to the auctioneer and the purchaser will pay the same. Most booksellers are working on 60–100 per cent mark-up, depending on title and condition, and when selling on the internet, they will be paying around 15 per cent in fees and commissions to the hosting agent, e.g. AbeBooks or Amazon – which explains why many will offer a discount for direct purchase. Never hesitate to ask.

Signed and association copies, ephemera and art
The demand for signed and association copies and NN ephemera would appear to be increasing. Presumably, as collectors complete their collections they look to other areas, and as interest in the series grows generally, so signed copies, proof copies, author's letters, review slips, prospectuses and the like become more desirable.

A number of dealers have jumped onto the signed-book bandwagon and have arranged unofficial 'limited editions' of around 50 signed copies, often with slips tipped into the books. Of course books that are signed directly to the endpaper or title page, i.e. *flat signed*, are more desirable (and more valuable) than those signed to a tipped-in slip. One hundred flat-signed copies of each new title are now available directly from Collins (though it is a shame that they are not numbered) and are well worth the additional premium.

But more desirable still are association copies, books that have an inscription from the author to another well-known person, or say from one New Naturalist author to another. The figure on page 47 shows a copy of *The Herring Gull* with a doodle by the

TABLE 8 New Naturalist values, May 2011 (first editions with jackets, unless stated otherwise). Figures in bold reflect average collectable condition commensurate with the age of the book. From NN84–96, the distinction between 'near fine' and 'fine' is less valid so near fine values have been omitted. For the same reason, values in the 'fine' and 'very good' columns drop off as we come more up to date. For recent titles only the as-new value is given, as most copies are still in this condition. Note the significant difference in value between good and fine copies. Values marked * are copies with unfaded spines.

NOTE: Since compiling this list in 2011, values of most New Naturalists have come down further in value; very roughly assume 10 per cent for pre–no. 50 and the Monographs and 20–30 per cent post–no. 50.

No.	Title	As New	Fine	Near Fine	Very Good	Good
MAIN SERIES						
1	Butterflies	n/a	180	110	**60**	20
2	British Game	n/a	80	60	**40**	15
3	London's Natural History	n/a	80	60	**40**	15
4	Britain's Structure and Scenery	n/a	100	60	**40**	15
5	Wild Flowers	n/a	70	50	**30**	12
6a	Natural History in the Highlands and Islands (1947)	n/a	80	60	**40**	15
6b	The Highlands and Islands	n/a	70	60	**50**	18
7	Mushroom and Toadstools	n/a	80	60	**40**	15
8	Insect Natural History	n/a	70	50	**30**	12
9	A Country Parish	n/a	180	140	**100**	55
10	British Plant Life	n/a	70	50	**30**	12
11	Mountains and Moorlands	n/a	70	50	**30**	12
12	The Sea Shore	n/a	90	50	**30**	12
13	Snowdonia	n/a	80	60	**40**	15
14	The Art of Botanical Illustration	n/a	150	100	**60**	25
15	Life in Lakes and Rivers	n/a	70	50	**30**	12
16	Wild Flowers of Chalk and Limestone	n/a	70	50	**30**	12
17	Birds and Men	n/a	80	50	**30**	12
18	Natural History of Man in Britain	n/a	70	50	**30**	12
19	Wild Orchids of Britain	n/a	80	60	**35**	15
20	The British Amphibians and Reptiles	n/a	95	75	**45**	18
21	British Mammals	n/a	80	60	**40**	15
22	Climate and the British Scene	n/a	85	65	**40**	15
23	An Angler's Entomology	n/a	105	85	**60**	20
24	Flowers of the Coast	n/a	125	85	**50**	18
25	The Sea Coast	n/a	95	75	**45**	18
26	The Weald	n/a	95	75	**45**	18
27	Dartmoor	n/a	95	75	**45**	18
28	Sea Birds	n/a	140	110	**80**	32
29	The World of the Honeybee	n/a	120	90	**60**	25
30	Moths	n/a	110	80	**60**	20
31	Man and the Land	n/a	90	70	**40**	15
32	Trees, Woods and Man	n/a	110	80	**60**	20
33	Mountain Flowers	n/a	110	80	**60**	18
34	The Open Sea I	n/a	130	100	**60**	25
35	The World of the Soil	n/a	110	80	**60**	18
36	Insect Migration	n/a	150	120	**80**	32
37	The Open Sea II	n/a	130	100	**60**	25
38	The World of Spiders	n/a	150	120	**80**	32
39	The Folklore of Birds	n/a	400	300	**220**	120
40	Bumblebees	n/a	380	280	**200**	110
40	Bumblebees (1968 reprint)	n/a	180	160	**120**	70
41	Dragonflies	n/a	500	420	**320**	220
41	Dragonflies (1985 paperback reprint)	n/a	75	60	**50**	30
42	Fossils	n/a	140	100	**60**	25
43	Weeds and Aliens	n/a	150	120	**80**	32
44	The Peak District	n/a	95	75	**45**	18
45	Common Lands	n/a	200	160	**120**	70
46	The Broads	n/a	170	130	**80**	40
47	The Snowdonia National Park	n/a	110	80	**40**	15
48	Grass and Grasslands	n/a	140	110	**80**	32
49	Nature Conservation in Britain	n/a	90	70	**40**	15
50	Pesticides and Pollution	n/a	140	100	**60**	25
51	Man and Birds	n/a	110	**80**	40	20
52	Woodland Birds	n/a	120	80	40	18

No.	Title	As New	Fine	Near Fine	Very Good	Good
53	*The Lake District*	n/a	80	**60**	40	18
54	*The Pollination of Flowers*	n/a	180	**140**	100	55
55	*Finches*	n/a	90	**70**	40	–
56	*Pedigree Words from Nature*	n/a	130	**110**	90	–
57	*British Seals*	n/a	150	**110**	80	–
58	*Hedges*	n/a	120	**90**	60	–
59	*Ants*	n/a	150	**130**	100	–
60	*British Birds of Prey*	n/a	150*	**60**	40	–
61	*Inheritance and Natural History*	n/a	120	**100**	80	–
62	*British Tits*	n/a	70	**40**	25	–
63	*British Thrushes*	n/a	80	**40**	25	–
64	*Natural History of Shetland*	n/a	240	**170**	140	–
65	*Waders*	n/a	100	**70**	50	–
66	*Natural History of Wales*	n/a	140	**110**	80	–
67	*Farming and Wildlife*	n/a	140	**100**	70	–
68	*Mammals in the British Isles*	n/a	150	**120**	90	–
69	*Reptiles and Amphibians*	n/a	210	**180**	150	–
70	*Natural History of Orkney* first state	2800	2500	**2300**	2,000	–
70	*Natural History of Orkney* second state	950	850	**800**	680	–
70	*Natural History of Orkney* paperback	110	90	**80**	60	–
71	*British Warblers* first state	2500	2300	**2100**	1,700	–
71	*British Warblers* second state	880	780	**700**	650	–
71	*British Warblers* paperback	50	40	**30**	25	–
72	*Heathlands* (with Collins on jacket spine)	480*	420	**380**	320	–
72	*Heathlands* (1986 reprint)	300	260	**230**	200	–
72	*Heathlands* (BC – without Collins on jacket spine)	300	260	**230**	200	–
72	*Heathlands* paperback	90	70	**50**	40	–
73	*The New Forest* (with Collins on jacket spine)	450*	380	**320**	270	–
73	*The New Forest* (BC – without Collins on jacket spine)	380*	320	**250**	220	–
73	*The New Forest* paperback	90	70	**50**	40	–
74	*Ferns*	800*	680	**600**	520	–
74	*Ferns* paperback	130	110	**90**	70	
75	*Freshwater Fishes*	950*	820	**700**	650	–
75	*Freshwater Fishes* paperback	130	110	**90**	70	–
76	*The Hebrides*	1400*	1250	**1100**	920	–
76	*The Hebrides* paperback	140	120	**110**	90	–
77	*The Soil*	700*	560	**500**	450	–
78	*Larks, Pipits and Wagtails* paperback	100	80	**70**	60	–
79	*Caves and Cave Life*	700	620	**550**	490	–
79	*Caves and Cave Life* paperback	120	100	**90**	80	–
80	*Wild and Garden Plants*	850*	750	**650**	500	–
80	*Wild and Garden Plants* paperback	65	50	**40**	30	–
81	*Ladybirds*	900*	850	**800**	700	–
81	*Ladybirds* paperback	120	100	**90**	80	–
82	*The New Naturalists* (1995, with 50-year sticker)	420	350	**300**	260	–
82	*The New Naturalists* (1995) paperback	75	60	**50**	40	–
82	*The New Naturalists* 1996 reprint	180	150	**130**	100	
82	*The New Naturalists* 2005 new edition	65	55	**45**	35	–
82	*The New Naturalists* 2005 new edition paperback	65	**50**	–	40	–
83	*The Natural History of Pollination* (1st priced £30)	450*	320	**250**	200	–
83	*The Natural History of Pollination* (rep. priced £35)	280	240	**200**	150	–
83	*The Natural History of Pollination* paperback	120	**90**	–	70	–
84	*Ireland: A Natural History*	140	**120**	–	100	–
84	*Ireland: A Natural History* paperback	75	**60**	–	50	–
85	*Plant Disease*	180	**160**	–	120	–
85	*Plant Disease* paperback	30	**25**	–	20	–
86	*Lichens*	220	**180**	–	130	–
86	*Lichens* paperback	90	**80**	–	60	–
87	*Amphibians and Reptiles*	140	**120**	–	100	–
87	*Amphibians and Reptiles* paperback	90	**70**	–	60	–
88	*Loch Lomondside*	130	**110**	–	90	–
88	*Loch Lomondside* paperback	20	**15**	–	10	–
89	*The Broads*	140	**110**	–	90	–
89	*The Broads* paperback	60	**45**	–	35	–
90	*Moths*	140	**120**	–	100	–
90	*Moths* paperback	80	**60**	–	50	–
91	*Nature Conservation*	120	**100**	–	80	–
91	*Nature Conservation* paperback	70	**50**	–	40	–
92	*Lakeland*	140	**120**	–	100	–
92	*Lakeland* paperback	50	**35**	–	25	–
93	*British Bats*	250	**220**	–	180	–
93	*British Bats* paperback	120	**100**	–	75	–
94	*Seashore*	90	**80**	–	60	–
94	*Seashore* paperback	25	**20**	–	15	–
95	*Northumberland*	100	**90**	–	70	–
95	*Northumberland* paperback	90	**70**	–	60	–
96	*Fungi*	90	**80**	–	60	–
96	*Fungi* paperback	60	**50**	–	40	–
97	*Mosses and Liverworts*	70	**60**	–	–	–
97	*Mosses and Liverworts* paperback	50	**40**	–	–	–
98	*Bumblebees*	90	**80**	–	–	–
98	*Bumblebees* paperback	70	**60**	–	–	–
99	*Gower*	60	**50**	–	–	–
99	*Gower* paperback	30	**20**	–	–	–
100	*Woodlands* (patterned endpapers)	80	**70**	–	–	–
100	*Woodlands* (white endpapers)	100	**90**	–	–	–
100	*Woodlands* limited leather – bound edition of 100	**600**	–	–	–	–
100	*Woodlands* paperback	50	**40**			
101	*Galloway*	60	**50**	–	–	–
101	*Galloway* paperback	30	**20**	–	–	–
102	*Garden Natural History*	60	**50**	–	–	–
102	*Garden Natural History* paperback	25	**20**	–	–	–
103	*Isles of Scilly*	60	**50**	–	–	–
103	*Isles of Scilly* paperback	30	**25**	–	–	–
104	*History of Ornithology*	60	**50**	–	–	–
105	*Wye Valley*	60	**50**	–	–	–
105	*Wye Valley* paperback	25	–	–	–	–
106	*Dragonflies*	**50**	–	–	–	–
106	*Dragonflies* limited leather- bound edition of 250	**225**	–	–	–	–

No.	Title	As New	Fine	Near Fine	Very Good	Good
106	*Dragonflies* paperback	**30**				
107	*Grouse*	**50**	–	–	–	–
107	*Grouse* limited leather-bound edition of 250	**225**	–	–	–	–
107	*Grouse* paperback	**30**	–	–	–	–
108	*Southern England*	**50**	–	–	–	–
108	*Southern England* limited leatherbound edition of 150	**250**	–	–	–	–
108	*Southern England* paperback	**30**	–	–	–	–
109	*Islands*	**50**	–	–	–	–
109	*Islands* limited leather-bound edition of 150	**250**	–	–	–	–
109	*Islands* paperback	**30**	–	–	–	–
110	*Wildfowl*	**50**	–	–	–	–
110	*Wildfowl* limited leather-bound edition of 150	**250**	–	–	–	–
110	*Wildfowl* paperback	**30**				
111	*Dartmoor*	**50**	–	–	–	–
111	*Dartmoor* limited leather-bound edition of 100	**250**	–	–	–	–
111	*Dartmoor* paperback	**30**	–	–	–	–
112	*Books and Naturalists*	**50**	–	–	–	–
112	*Books and Naturalists* limited etherbound edition of 100	**250**	–	–	–	–
113	*Bird Migration*	**50**	–	–	–	–
113	*Bird Migration* limited leatherbound edition of 75	**250**	–	–	–	–
113	*Bird Migration* paperback	**30**	–	–	–	–
114	*Badger*	**50**	–	–	–	–
114	*Badger* limited leather-bound edition of 75	**250**	–	–	–	–
114	*Badger* paperback	**30**	–	–	–	–
115	*Climate and Weather*	**50**	–	–	–	–
115	*Climate and Weather* limited leatherbound edition of 50	**250**	–	–	–	–
115	*Climate and Weather* paperback	**30**	–	–	–	–

MONOGRAPHS

No.	Title	As New	Fine	Near Fine	Very Good	Good
M1	*The Badger*	n/a	80	50	**30**	15
M2	*The Redstart*	n/a	105	75	**45**	25
M3	*The Wren*	n/a	350	300	**240**	140
M4	*The Yellow Wagtail*	n/a	80	50	**30**	18
M5	*The Greenshank*	n/a	170	130	**90**	55
M1	*The Badger*	n/a	80	50	**30**	15
M2	*The Redstart*	n/a	105	75	**45**	25
M3	*The Wren*	n/a	350	300	**240**	140
M4	*The Yellow Wagtail*	n/a	80	50	**30**	18
M5	*The Greenshank*	n/a	170	130	**90**	55
M6	*The Fulmar*	n/a	360	300	**240**	130
M6	*The Fulmar* paperback reprint	n/a	75	55	**45**	30
M7	*Fleas, Flukes and Cuckoos*	n/a	250	180	**140**	65
M8	*Ants*	n/a	200	170	**130**	75
M9	*The Herring Gull's World*	n/a	90	70	**40**	25
M10	*Mumps, Measles and Mosaics*	n/a	450	370	**290**	170
M11	*The Heron*	n/a	330	280	**220**	112
M12	*Squirrels*	n/a	170	120	**95**	55
M13	*The Rabbit*	n/a	170	120	**95**	55
M14	*Birds of the London Area since 1900*	n/a	310	240	**190**	90
M15	*The Hawfinch* (Ellis jacket)	n/a	450	360	**280**	160

No.	Title	As New	Fine	Near Fine	Very Good	Good
M15	*The Hawfinch* (plain green jacket)	n/a	500	390	**300**	170
M16	*The Salmon*	n/a	80	60	**35**	20
M17	*Lords and Ladies*	n/a	300	240	**180**	95
M18	*Oysters*	n/a	250	180	**140**	70
M19	*The House Sparrow*	n/a	150	110	**85**	45
M19	*The House Sparrow* reprint 1967	n/a	105	75	**45**	25
M20	*The Wood Pigeon*	n/a	120	90	**60**	25
M21	*The Trout*	n/a	85	65	**40**	20
M22	*The Mole*	n/a	90	70	**40**	20

OTHERS

No.	Title	As New	Fine	Near Fine	Very Good	Good
–	*The New Naturalist: A Journal of British Natural History*	n/a	80	60	**40**	15
–	NN *Magazine No. 5: Birth Death and the Seasons*	n/a	150	120	**80**	60
–	NN *Magazine No. 6: East Anglia*	n/a	110	80	**60**	35

author to the title page, and such personalised copies are the holy grail of New Naturalist collecting.

Signed New Naturalists are scarce – surprisingly so – but signed early titles are even more elusive. Run a search on any internet site and you will be lucky to find a single signed book published before, say, NN90 *Moths*. However, not all signatures are of equal rarity and some titles are *comparatively* common as signed editions, e.g. *A Country Parish*, *Heathlands* and *Orkney*.

It is no surprise that signed books are worth considerably more than un-signed copies, probably at least a third of the price again in most cases, but a rare signature (flat-signed) or an association copy will enhance the value of a book by £100–£300, particularly if it is a first edition. Conversely, a modern signature by an author (still with us) might be worth only £10–£30. Ultimately the value of an author's autograph is impossible to quantify, and therefore the decision to buy, or not to buy, must be a personal one, but judging by the paucity of signed copies on the second-hand market, it would appear that most do not find it a difficult decision to make.

New Naturalist ephemera is even more difficult to value, principally because most of it is so rare, but it is all of interest and should you come across any, and the price seems reasonable to you, just buy it. I can't say more than that.

In October 2009 the Pinkfoot Gallery of Cley, in Norfolk, held an exhibition of Robert Gillmor's New Naturalist jacket artwork. Prior to that date virtually no artwork had been made available, of either the Ellis's or Gillmor's work, and it remained outside the realms of most collectors. Not surprisingly, the Pinkfoot exhibition was a great success: the total value of catalogued New Naturalist material was over £160,000 and a good proportion of it was sold – although there were a few linocuts left for anyone who missed out. Original Ellis jacket artwork remains unobtainable and all extant material is either in family collections or in the Collins archive, with a couple of exceptions. Should any of it ever make its way onto the open market, its value would be hard to quantify, but probably you would not get much change out of a family hatchback. Clifford Ellis paintings do occasionally appear at auction, usually fairly free watercolours and these make hundreds rather than thousands. His original lithographs are also offered from time to time and again make hundreds, though at an exhibition entitled *British Prints 1945–1970*, held by The Fine Art Society in Sept/Oct 2004, an original signed lithograph *Abstract Composition with Fish*, 1956, had a price tag of £1,800, as did an original signed Rosemary Ellis lithograph *Variations*, 1955. Perhaps some of the most exciting examples of the Rosemary and Clifford partnership are their posters, which do turn up sporadically at auction, and while the bidding is usually vigorous, the more common ones can be purchased for under £700. However, the London Transport designs are particularly sought after and a pair, *Down* and *River*, made £2,125 at a Christie's poster auction in London in November 2010.

More affordable are line drawings used in various books. Brin Edwards' superb pencil drawings for *Caves and Cave Life* were offered through the NNC for £100 each. An original drawing tipped onto the front endpaper of the book is particularly nice.

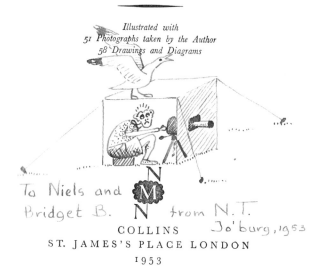

A superb doodle and dedication in *The Herring Gull's World* by the author (from the collection of John Cunningham). It would enhance the value of the book by £100–300.

Limited editions (leatherbound)

The first limited edition, *Woodlands*, published at £250 to commemorate the 100th title in the series, was met with great excitement and was subject to not insignificant speculation by collectors and a few dealers (not myself, I hasten to add) who cajoled relatives, neighbours, friends, the village bobby and the newspaper boy to subscribe on their behalf. Allegedly a few people acquired multiple copies this way. It came as no great surprise when, a week or two later, the first leatherbound *Woodlands* appeared on eBay – and sold for £2,000. More followed and all sold for an impressive profit – see table 9. But once the initial euphoria had faded away, prices started to drop.

Copy no. 32 (lot 700) sold for £600 on the hammer at an auction in Bloomsbury, London, in January 2009. In 2010 it was possible to pick up a copy on the second-hand market for around £1,000

TABLE 9 (information provided by David Kings)

Summary of leatherbound copies of NN100 *Woodlands* sold on eBay

No.	Date Sold	Price
31	26/11/2006	£2,000
23	15/12/2006	£1,391
47	16/12/2006	£1,562
61	13/01/2007	£1,750
28	15/03/2007	£1,510
5	16/12/2007	£2,402

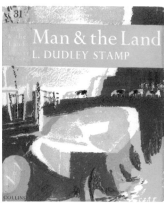

A selection of misprinted dust jackets. These may be quite subtle, such as where a colour printing has become misaligned, such as with *The British Amphibians and Reptiles* and *Man & the Land*. In extreme cases an entire colour plate may be absent. Examples above include *The Wren* and *Ants*, where the brown colour is missing, making the image incomplete.

and more recently copies have failed to sell on eBay for around half that figure.

Following the success of *Woodlands*, more titles followed in the same limited edition format, but demand for them has also dropped off significantly in the last couple of years. Titles such as *Dragonflies* or *Grouse* are now barely worth their original price of £250. In line with this diminishing demand, the number issued has steadily been reducing: 250, 150, 100, 75 and now just 50 copies. Surely at just 50 copies they must now represent a good investment?

Book Faults and Printing Errors

Serious collectors are often primarily interested in acquiring as perfect an example as possible of their chosen subject. But there are some collectors who are continually on a quest to find unusual or aberrant versions of whatever they collect. With books there is an important difference between errors of wording and errors of printing. First editions of books are likely to have more errors amongst the text and these are usually corrected in subsequent editions. Once the mistakes and misprints have been discovered after the book has been printed, an errata slip or leaf may be inserted into the book. This may be corrected with a second impression, where the whole book is put to press again. One interesting misprinted spine of a New Naturalist title was on the first edition of *Hedges*. On the buckram spine Max Hooper's name is misspelt Hopper, although it is spelled correctly on the dust jacket. This was corrected for the following reprint a year later.

Books may also be found which contain printing errors, although most of these errors do not make the books particularly collectable or sought after. Even more dramatic are entire books which have been bound upside down from the covers. With such a severe fault, these books would usually be returned to the publisher and destroyed. Occasionally these copies become available on the second-hand book market, but they are not regarded as being of any particular value and certainly not nearly as much as the correctly bound version. Examples have recently been found for *Seashore* and *Loch Lomondside*.

Much more interesting are misprinted dust jackets. If these were noticeably wrong they would have been discarded by the printers (such as Baynard Press and Odhams). However, occasionally jackets can be found which at first might seem a little odd or unusual. Examples have been found with an entire colour missing during the printing process. For instance, *The Wren* was printed with the brown-coloured ink missing and therefore much of the bird, including its leg, was absent. The second example is *Lords and Ladies*, on which the purple ink was missing, and a third example is for *Ants*. Here the entire golden-brown colour is missing from the print, which includes the number at the head of the spine. All of these examples are quite subtle and it is easy to miss the fact that they are different, unless they are closely compared with a standard example.

Other misprinted jackets, and probably more common than those with an entire colour missing, are examples where the inks are misaligned. This can be quite extreme, as in this example from *Man and the Land*. Here the light grey/green ink has shifted considerably to the left, creating the ghostly image of an extra cow on the horizon. In another example, from *The British Amphibians and Reptiles*, although less distinct, the deep brick-red colour has shifted slightly to the left. This is most obvious on the spine, where the number 20 is not lined up correctly within its circle.

There may well be more of these misprinted jackets sitting unnoticed on library shelves. As with any unusual collectable, such as a misprinted stamp, these aberrations are rare and unique.

New Naturalist ephemera

Collecting the books themselves is relatively straightforward, if potentially expensive. Finding New Naturalist ephemera is much more of a challenge.

Broadly speaking there are four different kinds of New Naturalist ephemera. The first of these includes official Collins documents and correspondence between the publishers, editors and authors. The second includes other items such as letters, postcards, booklets and published scientific papers written by a New Naturalist author but not directly associated with the New Naturalist library.

The third type of NN ephemera comprises official promotional and advertising material, such as catalogues, posters and promotional leaflets and postcards. This group also included pre-publication slips which were inserted into review copies of the books. Finally, the fourth kind consists of other material less directly associated with the publishers. This would include such items as sales and auction catalogues and also Collectors' Club newsletters and other collectable items.

While many collectors are not at all interested in these additions and are happy simply to collect the books themselves, the wide variety of ephemera appeals greatly to a growing number of New Naturalist collectors, especially to those who already possess a complete set of the books.

Official documents and other correspondence
Official letters and other correspondence are extremely difficult to come by. The most important collection of such items used to be held in the archives of Collins in London and latterly in Glasgow. Sadly much of this was lost when their files up to 1976 were gutted and now only legal documents remain, which continue to be held in the Glasgow archive. Other major collections are widespread and held in official institutions. These include the papers of John Morton Boyd which are kept in the archives of the University of St Andrews, the papers of John Buxton in the Alexander Library at the University of Oxford and the extensive papers of James Fisher at the Natural History Museum in London. These, together with a number of other important collections, are preserved and form an important part of our natural history heritage.

In the early days of the New Naturalist library, nearly all correspondence was sent by mail or telegram, with paper hardcopies filed away. Unfortunately, as many of the older authors are no longer with us, their papers have often been destroyed, very often at the time of their retirement from the various schools, universities and research stations. Apart from a few important collections, much of the official correspondence has been lost. Today, virtually all correspondence is dealt with via email and very few documents are archived or will ever become available to collectors.

Sometimes when looking though a book the reader can find correspondence loosely tucked inside. These may be letters or postcards from the author to the previous owner, or may include communications from the publisher, reviewer or others associated with the book.

On rare occasions Christmas cards from an NN author have been found within a copy of a New Naturalist volume. Most of these would not be particularly significant, apart from for the author's signature. In some cases NN authors illustrated their own cards, such as Norman Moore and Alister Hardy, making these considerably more interesting. James Fisher once had a fine Christmas card which featured the painting of Fulmars by Peter Scott, which was used as the frontispiece for his

monograph. This was probably cut from spare plates or damaged copies of the book.

More frequently found are newspaper cuttings; perhaps an author obituary or reviews of the title. As these books tended to be well used in the field by naturalists, it is also possible to find species lists either loosely inserted or actually written on the pages. An extreme example, recently discovered for *The Hawfinch*, had numerous newspaper and magazine articles pasted onto every available space within the book. Although interesting, such treatment seriously undermines the value of the book, particularly if it cannot easily be removed. To the serious collector most of these items are not particularly desirable, unless they are associated with the author or someone else connected with the book. An author-signed note, postcard or letter which may be part of the book's history, would certainly significantly increase its value, perhaps by a third.

As well as author and publisher correspondence, other documents did or perhaps still do exist. These might include contracts and manuscripts and, of particular interest, the minutes of the Editorial Board. The NN Editors used to meet almost monthly in the early days of the series. From the early 1950s this fell to about 5 times a year and by the mid-60s twice a year, which continues today. Minutes of the board meetings make fascinating reading and provide a real insight into the workings of the NN library, with detailed notes on proposed books and titles in preparation. These documents very rarely, if ever, come on to the market and are gold dust for collectors. More frequently found are lists of the New Naturalist library available at the time. These were sent out by Collins on request and often include details such as available, out of stock or out of print titles, and may also include information on reprints and prices.

Official promotional items
PRE-PUBLICATION SLIPS For many years, small slips of paper were inserted next to the title pages of books that were to be sent by

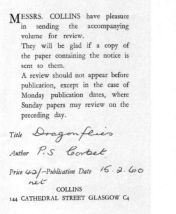 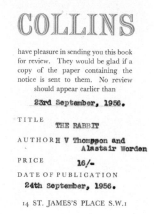

Pre-publication slips were usually loosely inserted into the title page of books sent out for review. They are now quite rare and interestingly record details of the book, including day of publication.

Collins for review. These are known as pre-publication slips. It is not known how many of each design were produced but it was probably a very low number. Generally they tend to be printed in green on thin white paper and measure about 102 × 140 mm. The title, author and publication date are typed into the space provided with the St James's Place address beneath. During the 1970s and 80s these became simple photocopies in black and white and not nearly so attractive. There are other examples where the text is printed in black and the details are handwritten in the spaces. In other versions the address is Cathedral Street, Glasgow. A third variant is a simple piece of plain white paper with 'Publishing Date' printed in red and the date itself stamped in blue or black ink. All of these items are scarce and are of particular interest because they show the exact date of publication.

NEW NATURALIST CATALOGUES   From the early days of the New Naturalist library, the publishers made a great effort to promote the books through advertising. Not only were the books listed on the backs of other natural history and countryside book jackets, but Collins also produced promotional leaflets and postcards. It is not clear how many different versions of these were distributed as no record seems to survive in the Collins archives. However, just occasionally a real gem will be discovered, perhaps when flicking through an old copy of an early NN in a second-hand bookshop or at a book fair. Few of these items seem to have survived and they are therefore scarce and collectable.

As well as catalogues which focused on the New Naturalist library, Collins also produced a number of more general catalogues, sometimes covering all subjects and occasionally just promoting natural history titles. An example of this was the *Natural History, Conservation Gardening and Wild Life* catalogue produced in 1972.

Two examples of early New Naturalist promotional catalogues. The 'coloured plate' catalogue (left) is very rare and is one of the first pieces of New Naturalist ephemera, dating from 1947. The 'Bookshelf-portrait' catalogue (right) was printed in 1953 and lists volumes up to *The Weald* with *Wild Flowers* and *Mushrooms and Toadstools* in preparation.

This brochure measured 185 × 215 mm and featured a gannet on the cover with nine pages devoted to the New Naturalist library.

Of particular interest are the little New Naturalist catalogues which can occasionally be found. There are several versions of these and the earliest ones were printed in black and white with a detachable order form. No record of the complete number of catalogues is known, but the following are examples of those which have been found.

1. Coloured plate – portrait: This is perhaps the first piece of New Naturalist printed ephemera. It measures 228 × 146 mm and consists of four pages with an introduction to the series and a quote from the *Sunday Times* by Professor A. G. Tansley congratulating 'the editors and publishers on the inauguration of this important series'. Interestingly, the third page describes it as 'A library that will reach at least 100 volumes', which is an indication of Collins' ambitions for the series. On this plate, too, *Butterflies, British Game, London's Natural History, Britain's Structure and Scenery, Insect Natural History* and *Natural History in the Highlands and Islands* are listed as already published. Titles to be published in 1948 include *British Plant Life, Mountains and Moorlands* and *The Sea Shore*. On the rear page the monographs are introduced along with a preview of forthcoming books on regions and national parks, plus a small order form for booksellers. The cover features a 'tipped-in' coloured plate and the only example seen uses a photograph of meadow cranesbill taken from the forthcoming *Wild Flowers*. It is possible that other copies of this promotional item may use different plates for the cover. This is a very rare item and dates from 1947.

2. Bookshelf – landscape: A black and white printed leaflet measuring 273 × 157 mm and including a detachable order form of 157 × 57 mm, advertising the latest volume of *British Amphibians and Reptiles*. Main series titles are listed up to *Wild Orchids of Britain* and special volumes consist of *The Badger, The Redstart* and *The Yellow Wagtail*. Titles listed as 'coming shortly' are *British Mammals, An Angler's Entomology* and *Climate and the British Scene*, with special volumes *The Greenshank* and *Fleas, Flukes and Cuckoos*. On the back of the leaflet is a paragraph describing the newly published *British Amphibians and Reptiles* volume. This catalogue probably dates from 1951.

3. Bookshelf – portrait: A black and white printed leaflet, folded twice, measuring 330 × 203 mm, with a detachable order form measuring 203 × 57 mm. Main series titles are listed up to NN26 *The Weald* with *Wild Flowers* and *Mushrooms and Toadstools* in preparation. Seven special volumes are listed up to M8 *Ants* with *The Wren, The Herring Gull's Word, Mumps, Measles and Mosaics* and *Herons* listed as in preparation. This catalogue probably dates from 1953.

4. Red squirrel: A leaflet measuring 162 × 517 mm and folded four

times, concertina-like. The reverse of the cover is an order form. The catalogue is printed in green and black and has a black and white photograph of a red squirrel and song thrush on the cover. NN titles are listed up to NN31 *Man and the Land* with *Trees, Woods and Man*, *Mountain Flowers* and *The Open Sea* in preparation. Special Volumes titles are listed up to M12 *Squirrels* with *The Salmon* in preparation. One of the panels features a map of the British Isles and lists the regional volumes both published and in preparation. This catalogue probably dates from 1954 or 1955.

5. Line drawings: A leaflet measuring 151 × 500 mm and folded three times. The reverse of the cover is an order form. This catalogue is printed in black and white and has a black band on the cover with various scraper-board-like natural history images, including an emperor moth and great crested grebe. NN titles are listed up to NN39 *The Folklore of Birds*, with *Dragonflies* listed as in preparation, although listed at NN40. Special volumes are up to M15 *The Hawfinch* and M16 is listed as *Bumblebees*, which was published in the main series as NN40. Five Collins pocket guides are also listed. This catalogue probably dates from 1958.

6. Oak leaf: A leaflet measuring 133 × 490 mm and folded five times, concertina-like. The reverse of the cover is an order form. The catalogue is printed in bright green and black and features a striking oak leaf motif on the cover. NN titles are listed up to NN46 *The Broads* with *Grass and Grasslands* in preparation. Interestingly, *Grass and Grasslands* is listed as NN47, which was to become *The Snowdonia National Park* in 1966. Special volumes are listed up to M21 *The Trout*. Ten Collins Pocket Guides are also listed. This catalogue probably dates from 1965 or 1966.

7. Royal blue: A leaflet measuring 125 × 597 mm and folded six times, concertina-like. The last panel, measuring 125 × 85 mm, consists of a detachable order form. This catalogue is printed in black and royal blue, with a royal blue cover. NN titles are listed up to NN50 *Pesticides and Pollution* and Special Volumes are listed up to M21 *The Trout*. Eleven Collins Pocket Guides are also listed. This catalogue probably dates from 1967.

8. Dark green: A leaflet measuring 125 × 597 mm and folded six times, concertina-like. The last panel, measuring 125 × 85 mm, consists of a detachable order form. This catalogue is printed in black and green, with a green cover. NN titles are listed up to NN50 *Pesticides and Pollution* and Special Volumes are listed up to M21 *The Trout*. Eleven Collins Pocket Guides are also listed.

A selection of promotional and sales catalogues featuring the New Naturalist library. These include the New Naturalist catalogue 'Red Squirrel' (top left) from 1954/5 and the 'Oak Leaf' catalogue from the mid-1960s. The plain-coloured portrait catalogues were printed with several different coloured covers. This royal blue example dates from 1969. Collins also produced general natural history catalogues which included the New Naturalist library, such as one with a gannet featured on the cover from 1972. Some booksellers produce catalogues devoted to the New Naturalist library such as this example by Henry Sotheran in 2007, a play on the jacket design for Peter Marren's *The New Naturalists* (1995). The foldout booklet (bottom) was produced to promote *The Badger* in 1948.

Very similar to the previous catalogue (no 6) but not listing NN2 *British Game*. This catalogue probably dates from 1969.

9. Dark blue: A leaflet measuring 125 × 597 mm and folded six times, concertina-like. The last panel, measuring 125 × 85 mm, consists of a detachable order form. This catalogue is printed in black and dark blue, with a dark blue cover. NN titles are listed up to NN50 *Pesticides and Pollution* and Special Volumes are listed up to M21 *The Trout*. Eleven Collins Pocket Guides are also listed. Very similar to the previous catalogue (no 7) but not listing NN21 *British Mammals* or NN12 *Squirrels*. This catalogue probably dates from 1970.

Most of the earlier catalogues are quite rare. When discovered, they will often be stamped in ink in a space provided for booksellers, so that customers can order their New Naturalist books from their local bookseller rather than directly from the publisher. Collins do not seem to have produced very much advertising material during the 1970s and 1980s, and if they did very little has survived. In 1995 HarperCollins produced a well-illustrated catalogue of the range of books available, from dictionaries to general reference. This included several pages of natural history publications and a page of New Naturalist titles.

The most recent New Naturalist catalogue was produced by HarperCollins in October 2009:

10. Fox poster: A leaflet measuring 384 × 590 mm, printed in full colour and opening up to form a poster featuring the unused artwork for *The Fox* by Clifford and Rosemary Ellis. The cover of this catalogue shows part of the cover for *Art of the New Naturalists*, which was published at the same time as this catalogue was issued. All NN titles up to NN111 *Dartmoor* are listed and illustrated with information on the history of the series, print-on-demand titles, leatherbound volumes and also an order form, which can be cut out without damaging the poster on the other side.

Fliers and other promotional items

It is not known exactly when Collins began producing promotional material as no record of this exists. Certainly there was a black and white photocopied leaflet for *Heathlands* in spring 1986 and probably others at around that time, although the New Naturalist brand does not seem to have been particularly marketed. During the 1990s Collins produced fliers which were sent out to a mailing list advertising each NN volume as it was published. These included an order form to buy the books directly from Collins in Glasgow. Some A5 leaflets were printed in black on coloured paper and examples certainly exist for *Wild and Garden Plants, Ladybirds, The New Naturalists* and *The Natural History of Pollination*. An A4 promotional leaflet was produced on bright green paper for *Ireland* in February 1999 and from then on for several years until the publication of *Dragonflies*, A4 leaflets were printed in full colour, often on heavy stock paper or card. For *Loch Lomondside* an A5 full-colour leaflet was produced in January 2001. The 60th

anniversary of the New Naturalist library and the publication of the second edition of *The New Naturalists* in 2005 was publicised with an A4 leaflet printed in full colour. This included the covers of all the recent books, a few paragraphs on the history of the series and an order form on the reverse. Over the following few years A4 photocopied letters were distributed, but these were eventually discontinued in November 2009. Announcements of the latest volumes are now mostly made through email from the HarperCollins marketing department in London (See Appendix 2 for a complete list of promotional leaflets issued by Collins).

For general publicity purposes, Collins have a generic A4 folder, the most recent of which is printed in dark blue with the HarperCollins logo in white on the cover. Press releases and information on forthcoming titles are photocopied or laser printed and inserted inside these folders. Today, catalogues are available online as PDFs and hard copies are rarely printed, except, perhaps, for special occasions such as the launch of the print-on-demand editions. The most recent example of a HarperCollins Natural History PDF catalogue was produced in 2011 and featured a *Pachygnatha degeeri* spider on the cover. A number of New Naturalist titles were listed but under individual subjects rather than in a section of their own.

An extreme example of New Naturalist ephemera is the paper wrap-around bands which were produced to promote the books in the shops. One example was printed in 1973 to promote *The Herring Gull's World* and to publicise the fact that the author Niko Tinbergen had won the Nobel Prize for Physiology or Medicine, jointly with Konrad Lorenz and Karl von Frisch. Another example was loosely wrapped around copies of the 1973 fifth edition of *Wild Flowers*. This band was printed in bright green with black and white text and announced 'The New Naturalist Library, A New Edition' with a quote from the *Times Literary Supplement* calling the New Naturalists 'a series which has set a new standard in natural history books'. It is likely that this band, which also featured the New Naturalist logo on the spine and the text 'new edition', was used on other new editions and reprints of the series at that time. Special offer price bands were also produced. One such price band was used for the reprint of *The Natural History of Shetland* in 1986. Very few of these have survived and they must now be exceptionally rare.

New Naturalist posters and showcards were produced at various times in the 1940s and 50s, particularly designed for shop window displays. One of these featured a fine painting of a heron by Clifford and Rosemary Ellis. More recently a poster was designed to promote Peter Marren's *The New Naturalists* in 1995, which also celebrated the 50th anniversary of the New Naturalist library. Show cards are still occasionally produced by the HarperCollins marketing department today. These are made in very small numbers, usually for a special event such as a book launch or signing and tend to consist of one or two copies of a cover, plus other information such as the price of the book. This is all mounted on strong black card with the HarperCollins logo in white at the base. As so few of these showcards are made, they are particularly rare.

Promotional postcards were also produced during the early days of the series. Once again, there seem to be no records of what cards were produced. We have seen examples for *The Redstart* and

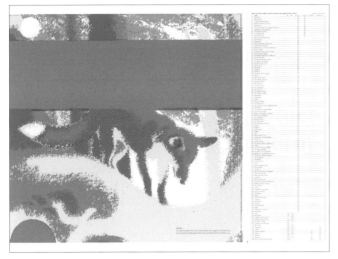
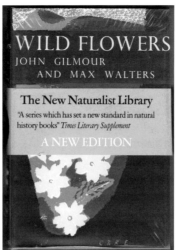

The 'Fox poster' catalogue (left) produced by Collins in 2009. The front of this catalogue featured the cover of *The Art of the New Naturalists*. Inside, all of the New Naturalist covers were illustrated up to Dartmoor (NN111). The leaflet opened out to reveal a rare and unused piece of artwork by Clifford and Rosemary Ellis for the monograph of *The Fox* which was never published. Examples of rare wrap-around bands (centre and right) produced by Collins to promote the books in shops. The 1973 fifth edition of *Wild Flowers* (centre) and the 1971 edition of *The Herring Gull's World* celebrating Niko Tinbergen as the Nobel prize winner in 1973 (right).

Mountains and Moorlands, both from 1950, and it is very likely that a number of others were also printed. The examples that are known to exist measure 138 × 115 mm and are printed in two colours with the words 'Just to let you know...' followed by details of the latest NN volume and its publication date. On the other side of the card is a paragraph about the book with details on the number of illustrations. These cards appear to be very rare but may turn up tucked inside a copy of one of the earlier volumes.

Other postcards and leaflets seem to have been issued by individual booksellers to promote a recent New Naturalist publication. One example of this was produced by E. W. Classey, the natural history bookseller, announcing the publication of *Moths* by E. B. Ford. This leaflet was printed in full colour on one side featuring a photograph of an Emperor moth, with black and blue text on the reverse, and measured 159 × 109 mm. Another example promoted *The World of the Soil* and was printed by Heffers booksellers in Cambridge. This leaflet measured 152 × 126 mm and was folded in half. It was printed in black on a pale blue card with information on the author, contents and illustrations, plus an order form on the back.

There are also picture postcards which exist featuring a coloured photograph by one of the series' photographers, such as John Markham. Although the text on the reverse of the card states that it is a New Naturalist photograph, there is no indication that these were officially produced by Collins.

Much more familiar are the general NN postcards printed by the publishers and inserted inside copies of the books. The idea was that if you were interested in collecting the series, you could be kept abreast of future publications by filling in a postcard with your contact address and returning it to the publishers. These postcards measure 150 × 109 mm. They are usually printed in dark green ink on a beige or yellowish card. On the reverse they advertise the *New Naturalist Journal*, which would date them from the late 1940s or early 1950s. More recently Collins have produced postcards printed

in black on white card which stated 'Thank you for purchasing this New Naturalist'. There was a space to complete your name and address and also information on how to order and pay for the books. There was also a general natural history postcard with the text: 'Thank you for purchasing this Collins Natural History Title'. In this case there was a quarterly £100 prize draw for anyone who completed their address details and returned the card to Collins.

The publishers also occasionally produced small booklets or pamphlets advertising a particular title. An example of one that we have seen is for *The Sea Shore*, published in 1949. The booklet measures 128 × 202 mm, with eight pages and stapled twice at the centre. It is printed in black and a dark grey-blue. The contents consist of general information on the book, the editors and the author plus a list of the contents and a selection of black-and-white photographs. Another example was produced for *Mountain Flowers* in 1956. This was a simple four-page leaflet which was printed in black and green and consisted of a brief synopsis of the book plus biographic details on the authors. On the back page was an order form by which books could be ordered through independent bookshops. These kinds of leaflets may have been printed by Collins with a blank area where the booksellers could place their details in the form of a stamp. Alternatively the leaflets may have been printed independently by the bookshops. Similar examples are known to exist for titles such as *An Anglers' Entomology* and *Fleas, Flukes and Cuckoos*, but it is not known how many of this kind of prospectus were produced and it is likely that several titles at this time were promoted in a similar way.

Another example of advertising material was a coloured plate from one of the books such as for *British Mammals*. The leaflet measured 153 × 222 mm and used the plate of a grey squirrel printed in full colour on one side with publication details on the reverse, including a small order form.

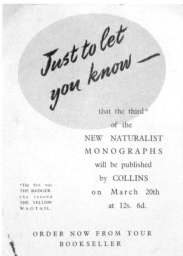

Two examples of rare promotional postcards, probably inserted into other New Naturalist volumes and promoting new titles in the series. These postcards were printed on both sides with information about the book on the reverse. The *Mountains & Moorlands* card was printed in green and black and landscape in layout (left). *The Redstart* (right) was designed in portrait layout and printed in red and black.

Other promotional items

HarperCollins have organised several New Naturalist parties over the years. The largest and most important of these celebrated the 50th anniversary of the series and Collins natural history publishing. The event coincided with the publication of *The New Naturalists* by Peter Marren. About 100 guests were invited and the party was held in the foyer of the HarperCollins offices in Hammersmith on 24 April 1995. The guest of honour was Sir David Attenborough and the party was attended by many of the New Naturalist authors. A fine invitation was printed featuring the '50 years' logo which appeared as a sticker on the cover of *The New Naturalists* and on Collins stationery at that time. There were also larger stickers used for display purposes. HarperCollins followed this with another similar party held on 5 April 2005, this time celebrating the 60th anniversary. A well-designed invitation incorporated eight dust jacket artworks by Robert Gillmor and a similar design was also printed onto a special celebratory mug which was handed out to guests as they left the party. The invitation itself is very rare and so too is the mug, of which 200 were produced. Very occasionally these turn up on internet auction sites.

HarperCollins produced the first New Naturalist calendar towards the end of 2010. Twelve designs by Clifford and Rosemary Ellis included a selection of unused colour sketches and final jacket artwork. The last two pages included an illustrated list of every volume in the series with an order form. A total of 2000 of these were printed by Forward Print in Essex, although it is unlikely that other NN calendars will be produced in the future.

Other collectables

Occasionally catalogues, booklets and leaflets can be found which, although they may not be directly associated with the series, provide an interesting link to some of the New Naturalist authors and editors, many of whom were well known and prolific writers. On rare occasions, tucked inside a copy of a New Naturalist may be an item connected to the book's launch. An example recently discovered was a luncheon menu card celebrating the publication of *The Broads* by E. A. Ellis, held at Jarrolds in Norwich. Ted Ellis

was an active member of the Norfolk and Norwich Naturalists Society and reprints from their journal can sometimes be found signed by him. Other booklets may pay tribute to a New Naturalist author, such as with the opening of the Pearsall Building at the Freshwater Biological Association, or they may be part of an exhibition. One such brochure was produced for an exhibition of bird photographs by Eric Hosking in 1957. The booklet 'Looking at Birds' included articles by James Fisher, Bruce Campbell and Peter Scott and several examples have been seen which were signed by all the contributors including Eric Hosking. Other pamphlets which may be loosely inserted are memorial service sheets associated with the author or perhaps a publicity and order form for the book. All of these items are significant additions and will add interest, individuality and potentially value to any book.

As well as official material produced by the publishers, there are also a number of other very collectable items which relate to the New Naturalist library. Perhaps the most accessible of these are auction catalogues and book dealer catalogues. Specialist natural history booksellers, both in new and old books, used to frequently print lavish catalogues and very often these would include long lists of New Naturalist books for sale. These, although not valuable, provide an interesting record of the prices individual titles have commanded over the years. Perhaps more collectable are catalogues which might be devoted entirely to the NN series. Henry Sotheran Ltd., in Piccadilly, have produced a number of beautiful natural history catalogues which are printed in very limited numbers. Some of these exclusively offer New Naturalist books for sale and feature a NN-themed cover. Auction sales sometimes also produce fine catalogues and although not usually devoted to the NN series, they often have large collections to be sold. Keys Auctions, in Norfolk, held an auction in May 2010 which consisted of the working library of Ted Ellis, author of *The Broads*. A well-printed catalogue was produced which illustrated a number of New Naturalist titles, many of which were inscribed and signed.

Robert Gillmor held a very exciting exhibition of his New Naturalist work at the Pinkfoot Gallery in Norfolk in October 2009. The private view was held on 24 October and there was a

Promotional prospectus booklets have occasionally been printed. These are very rare but occasionally turn up tucked within the pages of a New Naturalist. This example for *The Seas Shore* consists of 8 pages and was printed in two colours. Other New Naturalist related booklets turn up from time to time including *Looking at Birds*. This was produced for an exhibition of bird photographs by Eric Hosking in 1957. Another example was a booklet produced by the Freshwater Biological Association for the opening of the Pearsall Building in 1973.

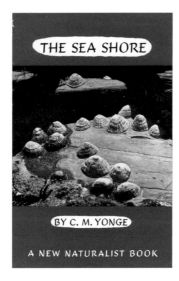

huge amount of interest in the original drawings and linocuts for many of the more recent jacket designs. A beautifully printed catalogue was available which illustrated most of the artwork for sale. Nearly everything sold out within hours. The event was also a second launch of *Art of the New Naturalists*, with both authors available to sign copies of the book, but with the reprinted blue band. Also available were two New Naturalist postcards, one reproducing the artwork for *Bumblebees* and the other for *Wildfowl*. A similar exhibition took place in November 2013, again at the Pinkfoot Gallery in Norfolk.

A major retrospective exhibition of Robert Gillmor's work was held at the John Madejski Art Gallery in Reading between October 2011 and April 2012. The original linocuts were on display from the four sets of post-and-go stamps that were commissioned by Royal Mail and a special booklet was also published by Two Rivers Press – 'Birds, Blocks & Stamps' – featuring the 24 designs along with a selection of preliminary sketches.

Another source of collectable material comes in the form of newspaper and magazine cuttings. Quite often a copy of a New Naturalist book will be found with cuttings loosely inserted into the front or back of the book. These are usually obituaries of the author that appeared in newspapers or cuttings relating to the subject of the book. These items do not add any real value to the copy but have a certain amount of charm and added interest. Perhaps more collectable are magazines with colour spreads on the NN series or such magazines as *Book and Magazine Collector* or *Books, Maps and Prints* which over the years have featured substantial reviews of the NN library.

The New Naturalist Collectors' Club is another major source of collectable New Naturalist-related material, particularly its newsletters. The New Naturalist Book Club was started on Jersey by Bob Burrow in 1998. Newsletters were photocopied in black and white to start with and by Newsletter no 9, April 2000, displayed a colourful design based on the spine of *The New Naturalists*. The newsletters contained articles on new publications and special offers, plus information on some of the older titles and books for sale. These continued to be produced in this way,

until Newsletter 39 in September 2007. Following the death of Bob Burrow in April 2006, Roger Long continued to edit the newsletter until the job was taken on by Tim Bernhard. The club was renamed The New Naturalist Collectors' Club and the first of the newly designed newsletters was issued at the end of 2007. To mark the re-launch of the club, a special Christmas card was printed which featured unused artwork for *Man and Birds* by Clifford and Rosemary Ellis. A special brightly coloured show card was also produced with information about the club. Since then other Christmas cards have been distributed to members of the club, with original artwork by Tim Bernhard based on the style of, and as a tribute to, the New Naturalist jackets. The first club event was organised for 24 October 2009 and was well attended by members of the club and authors of the series. The symposium included a day of lectures by NN authors and the launch of *Art of the New Naturalists*, which kept Peter Marren and Robert Gillmor busy signing copies. Interestingly, it was later revealed that the blue band which wrapped around the book had some textual errors and it had to be immediately withdrawn. Subsequently the blue band was reprinted and therefore true first-state copies of the book were only available on the day of the symposium. It is likely that about 250 copies of these exist. A brochure, ticket and special mug were also produced for those who attended the event and were strictly limited to 125 examples of each.

Following on from the success of the first symposium, a second, more ambitious, event was organised on 6 June 2011, again in the beautiful setting of Wallsworth Hall in Twigworth, Gloucester. As with the previous event, a limited edition mug was presented to each guest, along with a specially printed brochure. Robert Gillmor created a striking linocut based on his first New Naturalist jacket design (*British Warblers* – see frontispiece) and this was used as the main artwork for the 2nd Symposium, being featured on the limited edition mug, brochure cover and ticket. All of these items were made only for 150 guests, so consequently they are now quite scarce and rarely turn up on the collectors' market.

The third symposium was held at the University of Winchester on 7 September 2013. This was the largest and most successful

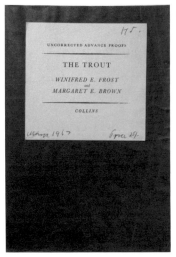
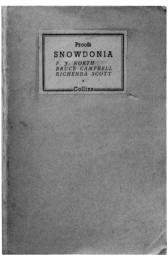

Three examples of bound New Naturalist proof copies. These usually have plain card covers with a typed label pasted onto the cover indicating the title and author(s). Occasionally proof copies turn up which also have a proof of the dust jacket. This example for *British Seals* only features the Ellis artwork with printers' registration and colour marks. The back cover is blank without any of the NN library details and other text.

symposium to date and included lectures by authors of the latest books. The day was superbly chaired by NN author Stefan Buczacki. Ian Nisbet flew in from the US especially for the event and joined David Cabot for an exclusive book signing of *Terns*, which had recently been published. The lunchtime signing session also included Ian Newton's third NN volume *Bird Populations*, which was the latest addition to the series. There were numerous stands displaying both new and second-hand natural history books and wildlife art. The day ended with a discussion panel which included Myles Archibald, David Streeter, Peter Marren and Robert Gillmor. Robert Gillmor was presented with a trophy by Stefan Buczacki for the most outstanding contribution to the New Naturalist series as voted by delegates during the day. Over 25 authors attended the symposium, making it a very special event. A limited edition mug, brochure and bookmark (featuring the artwork for *Terns*) were presented to each guest on arrival in a gift bag. As all these items were produced in very limited numbers, they are likely to become rare and sought after by New Naturalist collectors.

Proof copies

Printers' proofs date back to the 15th century. A single page, held in a tray, known as the galley, could be proofed on the press singly or in groups. The galley had three fixed sides with a fourth adjustable side known as a slice. Later, long continuous strips of lines would be proofed in wooden or metal trays which became known as long or column galleys. Proofs are prepared for the publisher and author to make any corrections and are rarely archived, which makes them highly prized by collectors.

A proof without any marginal corrections is known as an uncorrected proof and would include any of the printer's errors and misprints. Revised proofs are the intermediate stage to final proofs. Previously, final proofs were often stitched and bound with card wrappers by the publishers in very limited numbers. The stages of the production of a book fall into distinct areas: the work will start as a manuscript or typescript, followed by the printer's proof stages and, eventually, the first edition. So the proof stage is the halfway point between the author and the published book.

Two types of New Naturalist proofs are occasionally discovered.

The first is in the form of strips with the text printed continuously, without page breaks, onto thin proof paper. The sheets tend to measure 167 × 685 mm. A second type of proof is bound in paper or card wrappers. The earlier New Naturalist proofs were bound in plain brown card covers and those from the 1960s and 1970s were bound in red and occasionally blue card covers. Later copies had a printed label pasted onto the front cover with the title and the author/s of the book. From the 1970s these printed labels were replaced with a simple plain white label onto which were typed similar details. Occasionally a proof copy will also have a proof of the dust jacket wrapped around it. These artwork proofs do not usually have any text and often display the printers' registration and colour marks. Both types of proof copies may or may not contain any of the illustrations or plates. They are usually found uncorrected but it would be exciting to discover an advance proof actually marked and corrected by the author or the New Naturalist editor overseeing the publication of the book.

Even scarcer is what is known as a BLAD copy, or Basic Layout and Design copy. We have only seen one example of this, of *The Badger*. The book basically appears similar to a standard copy but on closer inspection it is much thinner. The dust jacket is the same as the standard first edition, and although bound in the usual green buckram, there is no text on the spine. Internally, there is the frontispiece, title page and other prelims but then the book launches straight into Chapter 3, a page of Chapter 4 and then back to Chapter 1, with all the plates bound together at the back of the book. These BLAD copies were designed to be shown to potential booksellers to demonstrate what the book would look like once published.

Bookplates and book stamps

Bookplates, also known as ex-libris, have largely gone out of fashion. They came into use in Germany in the 15th century, with the first known British example dating from 1574. Bookplates were placed inside books to declare ownership, particularly in the larger private libraries. They can be beautifully designed, sometimes by well-known artists such as William Hogarth, Aubrey Beardsley and John Piper, and many significant people such as Charles Dickens, Samuel Pepys and Rudyard Kipling have used them in their books.

They can also add to the provenance by identifying an earlier owner. There are collectors of bookplates and even a Bookplate Society, founded in 1972, which acts as a successor to the Ex Libris Society which flourished between 1891 and 1908.

Generally bookplates add interest to a book, although they can be unattractive. If this is so, in most cases they can be carefully removed. Of particular interest are bookplates which have a direct association with the author or the publishers. Most, if not all, of the early editors owned substantial libraries and both John Gilmour and Eric Hosking are known to have used bookplates. Some of the New Naturalist authors, such as David Cabot and Bill Hale, have collected large and important libraries and also have their own bookplates. Miriam Rothschild had a fine bookplate designed by the great typeface designer and printmaker Eric Gill. Bookplates belonging to the NN authors and editors are perhaps the most valuable and significant from the New Naturalist collector's point of view, however, a number of other important people in the world of natural history and conservation, such as David McClintock (co-author, with Richard Fitter, of the *Pocket Guide to Wild Flowers*) and Peter Conder (ornithologist and Director of the RSPB), also had bookplates. To find a New Naturalist book which includes the bookplate of such an influential person will almost certainly increase its interest and therefore value.

Some book collectors used ink stamps, usually on the front free endpaper. Many of these do not enhance the book but if they are from the library of a notable person they can significantly increase its value. Bruce Campbell's books were frequently stamped with his name in red ink and others may have marked done the same using a stamp made of their signature, including Ted Lousley. In a few cases, a stamp may not have actually been made by the owner. Richard Fitter's books were recently sold by a natural history bookseller and it was agreed with Richard Fitter's family that all of them would be stamped 'from the library of R. S. R. Fitter'. Similarly a recent sale of the working library of Ted Ellis featured a number of books stamped in ink with: 'Ex Libris – E. A. Ellis', which had been added by the Norwich Castle Museum while the books were in their care. Even though the original authors did not add these stamps themselves, they add provenance and significantly increase the values of the books. Other interesting stamps include those made by the publishers signifying a file copy, and are usually inked onto the front free endpaper. These may be stamped in red or black ink and often include a space for the publication date (added by hand) and other information such as the publishers' address and 'Not to be Removed'. Editorial file copies are very scarce but occasionally turn up. They do not really add any significant value to the book but have an interesting association with the publishers.

A selection of bookplates including those of New Naturalist editors and authors. Bookplates that have a direct association with the New Naturalist library are of great interest and will significantly increase the value of a book in which they are pasted. Bookplates which once belonged to other important and influential people such as Peter Conder will also increase interest and therefore value of a book.

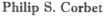

The New Naturalist: Bibliographic Features and Editions

CONVENTIONS AND CONSIDERATIONS

The printed book as we know it today dates to the 15th century. Until recently it has been the single most important medium for the transmission and dissemination of ideas, knowledge, opinions and, of course, entertainment. The medium itself has become an art form, and it is this, either in isolation or, coupled with the text, that makes certain books so collectable – the New Naturalist being a very good example. However, it must not be forgotten that books have been collected for nearly as long as they have been printed and, inevitably, a plethora of terms and jargon has evolved to satiate the curiosity of the collector and to explain and classify the cornucopian world of bindings, papers, printing and publishing.

The worlds of printing, publishing and bibliography coincide and many of the terms used by the different industries are the same, but it would be a mistake to believe that they mean the same thing! Even within the same industry a single term can have multiple meanings: folio to the printer might mean a format half that of the basic sheet, but it also might mean page number, whereas for the bibliographer it might mean the former, but never the latter and additionally might mean leaf, hence the abbreviations F., ff. referring to a single leaf or leaves. Quire is another potentially confusing homophone: the bibliographer understands it to mean a gathering or section and to a printer it might mean this or a one-twentieth of a ream of paper, but Collins, in their NN statements, used the term as a collective noun to mean a complete assembly of folded sheets, i.e. the unbound contents of a book.

Here we examine only those terms and conventions that apply to the New Naturalist series, but the terminology describing the physical elements of books is available online at www. newnaturalist.com; beyond this I refer you to the definitive book on the subject: *ABC for Book Collectors* by John Carter and Nicolas Barker (Oak Knoll Press and The British Library). Anybody with a vague interest in book collecting should not be without a copy on their shelves.

GENERIC BIBLIOGRAPHIC FEATURES

The New Naturalist monogram
The NN monogram is synonymous with the series and has appeared in every Collins hardback edition either on the dust jacket, title page or spine of the book – and usually on all three. It is an instantly recognisable trademark and an homogenising graphic element of the iconic New Naturalist jacket. One of the appeals of the series is this conformity of design, but a conformity always enriched with exceptions and anomalies, of which the monogram is an example. In fact there is much greater variation in the monogram than a cursory inspection would suggest.

The monogram, or NN symbol as *Marren* refers to it, is a simple but highly effective design of conjoined Ns one atop the other and originally designed by the Ellises. That used for the monographs includes a central M within a cloud motif, between the two Ns.

The monogram has been updated a number of times over the years, but the main element of two conjoined Ns remains; essentially all revisions are confined to changes in typeface and proportion. In the main series, seven different types have been used (Types A to F and K) and a further three types in the monogram series (Types G, H and J). Within these types there is a degree of variation. The use of these monograms may appear arbitrary and indeed it probably was, or at least expediential.

Embellished monograms and copyright

For the first 24 titles in the main series, a motif, or graphic emblem, was woven into the monogram. (This motif is often referred to in NN literature as a colophon, but bibliographically this term is generally used to refer to a printer's mark or device; what we might now call a trademark.) The motif was unique to each title and was inspired by the subject area of that title. NN28 *Sea Birds* (1954) was embellished with a bird's egg; but thereafter the use of this beguiling device was abandoned until it was revived for NN82 *The New Naturalists* (1995) and then again for NN96–101 (2005–2007), although only on the spine and jacket. Regrettably Collins had to drop the 'colophon artwork' when they trademarked the NN logo, as it had to be the exact same logo every time if the trademark was to be protected by the licence.

The monogram is also an important feature of the title page, but between 1978 and 1982 (NN64–69 and the 1978 *Wild Flowers* reprint NN5f) and between 1999 and 2002 (NN84–91) it was omitted, and these title pages look strangely bereft without it. It is also absent from the spines of a few Collins paperback editions (NN72–78 inclusively). NN66 *Wales* is unique in that this is the only title that omits the monogram from the spine of the casing.

Generally the monogram type used on the title page is replicated on both the casing and the jacket but there are exceptions, e.g. the 1st edition of NN62 *British Tits* has different types on the jacket, casing and title page. The embellished monograms of NN24 and 28, *Flowers of the Coast* and *Seabirds*, are reproduced in condensed form on the casings. The NMN monogram Type H always appears with a line around the perimeter of the 'cloud' on the casing, but never on the title page.

In the main series the monogram on the jacket is always in association with a graphic oval, with the exception of NN14 *Botanical Illustration*. The monogram and oval together are a powerful element of the jacket design format, and whilst varying in size and proportion, they are always situated above the tail of the spine. Of the 116 books in the main series, 108 have reversed-out white monograms on black or coloured backgrounds; four (NN13, 14, 17 and 22) are printed in black on white or coloured backgrounds; and four (NN49, 51, 53 and 55) are printed in colour on a coloured background.

The publication of NN100 *Woodlands* in 2006 saw the introduction of coloured endpapers with an attractive repeating pattern of Type F monograms; an excellent innovation which has been used for all books since.

Other monogram types

A distinctive variation of the monogram was used for *The New Naturalist Journal* with the two Ns arranged in the same format but separated in the middle and used to excellent effect as a bold graphic feature on the dust jacket. It was also used on the spine and in outline form with the date inserted between the Ns, on the title page (see below). The Bloomsbury facsimile editions with their new dust jackets departed from the usual format but retained the monogram and positioned it within a circle (see below).

Collins paperbacks

Because these are either facsimile copies (black paperbacks) or are bound up from the same sheets as the Collins hardbacks the monograms on the title pages show no variation. Those used on the spines of the black paperbacks are all Type E with the exception of *The Fulmar*, which is a reversed-out version of Type H. Monograms on the later paperbacks are identified in table 11.

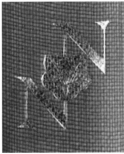

Fig. 1   Fig. 2

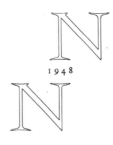

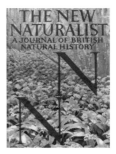

Fig. 3   Fig. 4

NN24 jacket monogram correctly proportioned on the jacket (left), and compressed on the case (right).

Other monogram types.

Monogram types: key features

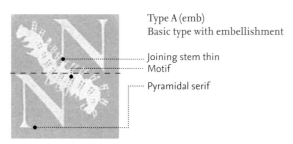

Type A (emb)
Basic type with embellishment

.... Joining stem thin
.... Motif
.... Pyramidal serif

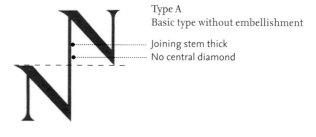

Type A
Basic type without embellishment

.... Joining stem thick
.... No central diamond

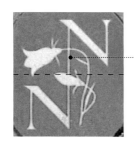

Type A (emb)
Note how it is now vertically stretched

.... Joining stem thin

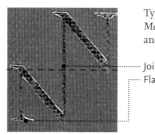

Type A variant
Man/Land 1st ed. (some), *Tits* rep.;
and *The Mole* 1st ed.

.... Joining stem thin
.... Flat serif

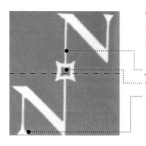

Type B
Basic type diamond centre (on DJ of NN51
stem bisects the diamond)

.... Joining stem thin
.... Central diamond
.... pyramidal serif

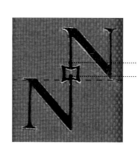

Type C
Condensed with diamond above centre

.... Joining stem thin
.... Diamond above centre

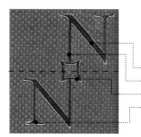

Type D
Tits, Thrushes, Waders and
Shetland casings only

.... Diagonal thinner
.... Joining stem thin
.... Large diamond
.... Flat serif

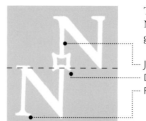

Type E
Note crooked joining stem and
generally poor articulation

.... Joining stem thick and crooked
.... Diamond above centre
.... Flat serif

Type A (emb) This is the archetype, and first appeared *embellished* with a motif. There is some variation and often it is vertically stretched to accommodate the graphic emblem. Gillmor used variants of it for his first three embellished monograms. It features from 1945–1952 and again in 1954, 1995 and 2005. (NN1–24, 28, 82, 96 and 97)

Type A In its unembellished form it appears in only four New Naturalists, spanning a 29-year period: NN14 *The Art of Botanical Illustration*, 1950 (DJ, casing and TP); NN31 *Man & the Land* (casing only of some 1st eds.); NN62 *British Tits*, 1979

(TP only); and M22 *The Mole*, 1971 We will probably never know why the use of this monogram was so erratic; there may be a very good reason for it, but more likely it was simply an expedient: deadlines looming – and it was to hand.

Type B Essentially a stretched form of Type A where the graphic emblem has been substituted by a central diamond. Perhaps the most elegant and proliferate form of the monogram, appearing on the jackets of 46 different titles, spanning a 34 year period. That for NN51 *Man and Birds* is unique in that the joining stem passes through the central diamond.

Type C A condensed form of Type B where the diamond is positioned more or less above the centre line, so that most is within the upper N. Used exclusively on casings, 1953–1977. Why it was felt necessary to use a condensed form on the casing is unknown but the proceeding embellished monograms NN24 and 28 were also condensed.

Type D An elongated and narrow form with a large central diamond, used on the casings only, of just four titles, 1978–1980: NN62–65, *British Tits* (not the 1980 reprint) *Thrushes, Shetland*, and *Waders*.

Type A variant (emb)
Note vertically stretched

Flat serif

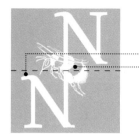

Type F (emb)
With embellishment

Serif decurved
Motif

Type F
Without embellishment

Type F (outline)

Type G

Type H no line
No line around edge of the cloud
(title pages only)

Type H with line
With line around edge of the cloud
(casings only)

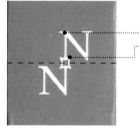

Type K

Long stem straight
Diamond in centre

Type E   A heavier and poorly executed form of Type C used from 1981–2006, in various combinations with other types, NN67–99. Note that the joining stem is inconsistent and crooked.

Type F   The most radical redesign of the monogram, incorporating spurs at the bottom of the diagonals designed by Martin Majoor. It first made its appearance on the jacket of NN98 *Bumblebees* but in embellished form and it was not until the publication of NN100 *Woodlands* in that it appeared in its outline form on the title page. NN101 *Galloway* was the last time it was

used, embellished with a symbol, but it has been used in plain and outline form ever since.

Type G   The 'prototype' for the monographs incorporating the word 'monograph' between the two Ns and it appears only on the title page of M1 *The Badger* (1948 1st ed. & 1962 2nd ed. only)

Type H   Used on the title page of all monograms excepting *The Badger* (above), and M22 *The Mole,* the letter M appearing within a cloud motif between the two Ns. This type was also used on the casings of all the monographs, excepting *The Mole,* but in a slightly different form with a line

around the periphery of the cloud, or is it a silver lining?

Type K   Essentially a refined form of Type E, the joining stem is straight and the diamond is centrally positioned. Used on just a few Colins paperbacks – NN79–84 (1993–1999).

Type J   Not a derivative of the iconic conjoined Ns but a simple typographical graphic consisting of NMN. This always features on the jackets of the monographs and there is a little variation as demonstrated in the examples shown at the bottom of page 63.

Title-page monogram types

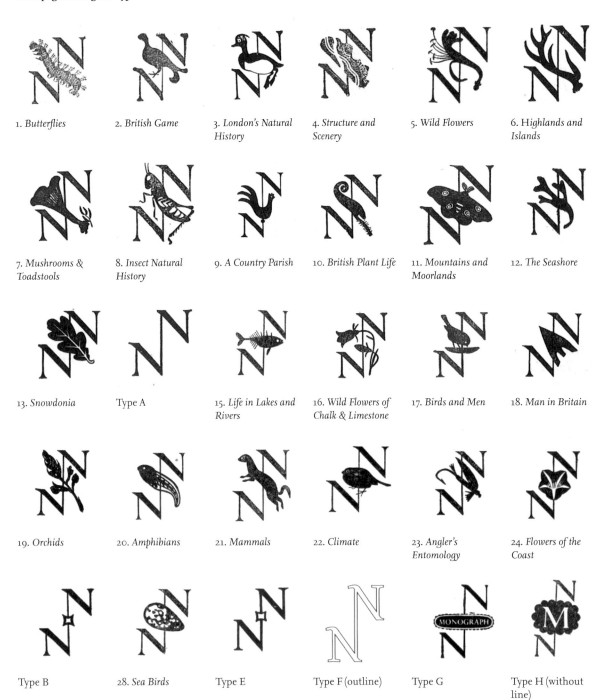

1. *Butterflies*	2. *British Game*	3. *London's Natural History*	4. *Structure and Scenery*	5. *Wild Flowers*	6. *Highlands and Islands*
7. *Mushrooms & Toadstools*	8. *Insect Natural History*	9. *A Country Parish*	10. *British Plant Life*	11. *Mountains and Moorlands*	12. *The Seashore*
13. *Snowdonia*	Type A	15. *Life in Lakes and Rivers*	16. *Wild Flowers of Chalk & Limestone*	17. *Birds and Men*	18. *Man in Britain*
19. *Orchids*	20. *Amphibians*	21. *Mammals*	22. *Climate*	23. *Angler's Entomology*	24. *Flowers of the Coast*
Type B	28. *Sea Birds*	Type E	Type F (outline)	Type G	Type H (without line)

Size Differential

The monogram blocked to the spine of the casings is often
smaller than that on the jacket or title page; if it is an embellished
monogram it may also be a little different, for instance NN7
Mushrooms & Toadstools.

Dust jacket main monogram types, including embellished forms

Monograms with a graphic emblem were printed in colour on the dust jackets. They are a particularly seductive feature of the series and it is regrettable that they have been discontinued.

1. *Butterflies*

2. *British Game*

3. *London's Natural History*

4. *Structure and Scenery*

5. *Wild Flowers*

6. *Highlands and Islands*

7. *Mushrooms and Toadstools*

8. *Insect Natural History*

9. *Country Parish*

10. *British Plant Life*

11. *Mountains and Moorlands*

12. *The Seashore*

13. *Snowdonia*

14. *Botanical Illustration* (Type A)

15. *Life in Lakes and Lakes*

16. *Wild Flowers of Chalk and Limestone*

17. *Birds and Men*

18. *Natural History of Man in Britain*

19. *Wild Orchids*

20. *British Ampibians and Reptiles*

21. *British Mammals*

22. *Climate and the British Scene*

23. *An Angler's Entomology*

24. *Flowers of the Coast*

28. *Sea Birds*

47. *Snowdonia*

51. *Man and Birds* (Type Ba)

54. *Pollination of Flowers* (Type B)

55. *Finches* (Type B)

82A. *The New Naturalists*

82B. *The New Naturalists*

84. *Ireland* (Type C)

91. *Nature Conservation*

96. *Fungi* (Type A variant)

97. *Mosses* (Type A variant)

98. *Bumblebees*

99. *Gower*

100. *Woodlands*

101. *Galloway*

102. *Garden Natural History*

M2. Type J variant

M5. Type J variant

M16. Type J variant

M21. Type J variant

No.	Title Jacket	Spine	Title	Page
1	*Butterflies*	A (emb)	A (emb)	A (emb)
2	*British Game*	A (emb)	A (emb)	A (emb)
3	*London's Nat. History*	A (emb)	A (emb)	A (emb)
4	*Structure and Scenery*	A (emb)	A (emb)	A (emb)
5	*Wild Flowers*	A (emb)	A (emb)	A (emb)
6a	*Highlands & Islands*	A (emb)	A (emb)	A (emb)
6b	*Highlands & Islands*	A (emb)	A (emb)	A (emb)
7	*Mushrooms*	A (emb)	A (emb)	A (emb)
8	*Insect Natural History*	A (emb)	A (emb)	A (emb)
9	*A Country Parish*	A (emb)	A (emb)	A (emb)
10	*British Plant Life*	A (emb)	A (emb)	A (emb)
11	*Mountains & Moorlands*	A (emb)	A (emb)	A (emb)
12	*The Sea Shore*	A (emb)	A (emb)	A (emb)
13	*Snowdonia*	A (emb)	A (emb)	A (emb)
14	*Art Botanical Illustration*	A	A	A
15	*Life in Lakes and Rivers*	A (emb)	A (emb)	A (emb)
16	*Wild Flowers of Chalk*	A (emb)	A (emb)	A (emb)
17	*Birds and Men*	A (emb)	A (emb)	A (emb)
18	*Man in Britain*	A (emb)	A (emb)	A (emb)
19	*Wild Orchids of Britain*	A (emb)	A (emb)	A (emb)
20	*Amphibians & Reptiles*	A (emb)	A (emb)	A (emb)
21	*British Mammals*	A (emb)	A (emb)	A (emb)
22	*Climate & British Scene*	A (emb)	A (emb)	A (emb)
23	*An Angler's Entomology*	A (emb)	A (emb)	A (emb)
24	*Flowers of the Coast*	A (emb) condensed	A (emb)	A (emb)
25	*The Sea Coast*	B	C	B
26	*The Weald*	B	C	B
27	*Dartmoor*	B	C	B
28	*Sea Birds*	A (emb) condensed	A (emb)	A (emb)
29	*World of the Honeybee*	B	C	B
30	*Moths*	B	C	B
31	*Man & Land* (BVAR1)	B	A	B
31	*Man & Land* (BVAR2)	B	C	B
32	*Trees Woods and Man*	B	C	B
33	*Mountain Flowers*	B	C	B
34	*The Open Sea I*	B	C	B
35	*The World of the Soil*	B	C	B
36	*Insect Migration*	B	C	B
37	*The Open Sea II*	B	C	B
38	*The World of Spiders*	B	C	B
39	*The Folklore of Birds*	B	C	B
40	*Bumblebees*	B	C	B
41	*Dragonflies*	B	C	B
42	*Fossils*	B	C	B
43	*Weeds and Aliens*	B	C	B
44	*The Peak District*	B	C	B
45	*Common Lands*	B	C	B
46	*The Broads*	B	C	B
47	*Snowdonia*	B	C	B
48	*Grass and Grasslands*	B	C	B
49	*Nature Conservation*	B	C	B
50	*Pesticides and Pollution*	B	C	B
51	*Man and Birds*	B (variant)	C	B
52	*Woodland Birds*	B	C	B
53	*The Lake District*	B	C	B
54	*Pollination of Flowers*	B	C	B
55	*Finches*	B	C	B
56	*Pedigree Words*	B	C	B
57	*British Seals*	B	C	B
58	*Hedges*	B	C	B
59	*Ants*	B	C	B
60	*British Birds of Prey*	B	C	B
61	*Inheritance*	B	C	none
62	*British Tits* (first ed.)	B	D	A
62	*British Tits* (1980 reprints)	B	A (variant)	A
63	*British Thrushes*	B	D	B
64	*Natural History Shetland*	B	D	none
65	*Waders* (1st ed. & 1981 rep.)	B	D	none
66	*Wales* (1st ed. & rep.)	B	none	none
67	*Farming and Wildlife*	B	E	none
68	*Mammals*	B	E	none
69	*Reptiles & Amphibians*	E	E	none
70	*Orkney* (1st & 2nd st.)	E	E	E
71	*Warblers* (1st & 2nd st.)	E	E	E
72	*Heathlands*	B	E	E
73	*The New Forest*	B	E	E
74	*Ferns*	E	E	E
75	*Freshwater Fish*	E	E	E
76	*The Hebrides*	E	E	E
77	*The Soil*	E	E	E
78	*Larks, Pipits & Wagtails*	E	E	E
79	*Caves and Cave Life*	E	E	E
80	*Wild & Garden Plants*	E	E	E
81	*Ladybirds*	E	E	E
82A	*The New Naturalists*	A (variant; emb)	E	E
82B	*The New Naturalists*	A (variant; emb)	A (variant; emb)	E
83	*Pollination*	E	E	E
84	*Ireland*	E	E	none
85	*Plant Disease*	E	E	none
86	*Lichens*	E	E	none
87	*Amphibians & Reptiles*	E	E	none
88	*Loch Lomondside*	E	E	none
89	*The Broads*	E	E	none
90	*Moths*	E	E	none
91	*Nature Conservation*	E	E	none
92	*Lakeland*	E	E	E
93	*British Bats*	E	E	E
94	*Seashore*	E	E	E
95	*Northumberland*	E	E	E
96	*Fungi*	A (variant; emb)	A (variant; emb)	E
97	*Mosses and Liverworts*	A (variant; emb)	A (variant; emb)	E
98	*Bumblebees*	F (emb)	A (variant; emb)	E
99	*Gower*	F (emb)	F (emb)	E
100	*Woodlands*	F (emb)	F (emb)	F (outline)
101	*Galloway*	F (emb)	F (emb)	F (outline)
102	*Garden Natural History*	F	F	F (outline)
103	*Isles of Scilly*	F	F	F (outline)
104	*History of Ornithology*	F	F	F (outline)
105	*Wye Valley*	F	F	F (outline)
106	*Dragonflies*	F	F	F (outline)
107	*Grouse*	F	F	F (outline)

TABLE 11 Monogram types appearing on the spines of the
paperbacks.

No.	Title	Jacket	Spine	Title	Page
108	*Southern England*		F	F	F (outline)
109	*Islands*		F	F	F (outline)
110	*Wildfowl*		F	F	F (outline)
111	*Dartmoor*		F	F	F (outline)
112	*Books and Naturalists*		F	F	F (outline)
113	*Bird Migration*		F	F	F (outline)
114	*Badger*		F	F	F (outline)
115	*Climate and Weather*		F	F	F (outline)

MONOGRAPHS

No.	Title		Spine	Title	Page
M1	*Badger* (1st & 2nd eds. only)		J	H (with line)	G
M2	*The Redstart*		J	H (with line)	H (no line)
M3	*The Wren*		J	H (with line)	H (no line)
M4	*The Yellow Wagtail*		J	H (with line)	H (no line)
M5	*The Greenshank*		J	H (with line)	H (no line)
M6	*The Fulmar*		J	H (with line)	H (no line)
M7	*Fleas, Flukes, Cuckoos*		J	H (with line)	H (no line)
M8	*Ants*		J	H (with line)	H (no line)
M9	*Herring Gull's World*		J	H (with line)	H (no line)
M10	*Mumps*		J	H (with line)	H (no line)
M11	*The Heron*		J	H (with line)	H (no line)
M12	*Squirrels*		J	H (with line)	H (no line)
M13	*The Rabbit*		J	H (with line)	H (no line)
M14	*Birds London Area*		J	H (with line)	H (no line)
M15	*The Hawfinch*		J	H (with line)	H (no line)
M16	*The Salmon*		J	H (with line)	H (no line)
M17	*Lords and Ladies*		J	H (with line)	H (no line)
M18	*Oysters*		J	H (with line)	H (no line)
M19	*The House Sparrow*		J	H (with line)	H (no line)
M20	*The Wood Pigeon*		J	H (with line)	H (no line)
M21	*The Trout*		J	H (with line)	H (no line)
M22	*The Mole* (first ed. only)		J	A	A

No.	Title	Spine
70	*Orkney*	E
71	*Warblers*	E
72	*Heathlands*	None
73	*The New Forest*	None
74	*Ferns*	None
75	*Freshwater Fish*	None
76	*The Hebrides*	None
77	*The Soil*	None
78	*Larks, Pipits & Wagtails*	none
79	*Caves and Cave Life*	K
80	*Wild & Garden Plants*	K
81	*Ladybirds*	K
82A	*The New Naturalists*	K
82B	*The New Naturalists*	A (variant; emb)
83	*Pollination*	K
84	*Ireland*	K
85	*Plant Disease*	E
86	*Lichens*	E
87	*Amphibians & Reptiles*	E
88	*Loch Lomondside*	E
89	*The Broads*	E
90	*Moths*	E
91	*Nature Conservation*	E
92	*Lakeland*	E
93	*British Bats*	E
94	*Seashore*	E
95	*Northumberland*	E
96	*Fungi*	E
97	*Mosses & Liverworts*	E
98	*Bumblebees*	F (emb)
99	*Gower*	F (emb)
100	*Woodlands*	F (emb)
101	*Galloway*	F (emb)
102	*Garden Natural History*	F
103	*Isles of Scilly*	F
104	*History of Ornithology*	F
105	*Wye Valley*	F
106	*Dragonflies*	F
107	*Grouse*	F
108	*Southern England*	F
109	*Islands*	F
110	*Waterfowl*	F
111	*Dartmoor*	F
112	*Books and Naturalists*	F
113	*Bird Migration*	F
114	*Badger*	F
115	*Climate and Weather*	F

TABLE 11A Imitation cloth types. * Still manufactured today in the UK
by FiberMark Red Bridge International of Bolton.

Fabric	Brand	Dates	Description	Type	Colour
A	Unknown Linson?	1976–82	The embossed pattern is slightly courser than Fabric C. The pattern in one direction has small wavy elements.	1	dark green
				2	dark green but a shade lighter than Type 1
				3	dark sea green
				4	light straw green
B	Unknown	1983	With pronounced lines	5	dark green – colour very similar to Type 1
C	Arlin*	1986	The embossed pattern finer than Fabric A, without any wavy elements	6	lime green
				7	dark sea green – almost identical to Type 3

With one exception, the casings of *all* Collins first editions in both series are covered in green or blue-green *buckram*, whereas most bookclub editions and a few Collins reprints are bound in green *imitation cloth* (embossed paper). The one exception is confined to a smooth, green cloth, variant binding of the first edition of *Woodland Birds*, but this is a rare aberrant and is dealt with under the entry for that title.

Clearly it is important to be able to tell true buckrams from imitation cloths, as this is one of the most reliable ways of distinguishing a Collins edition from an otherwise identical bookclub edition.

Buckrams

Buckram is a woven cotton cloth, starch filled, and now often with an acrylic coating which is durable and specifically designed for bookbinding. A number of different types have been used during the 65 years of the series, but the differences are often subtle and inconsistent. Early buckrams were of a much coarser weave and as such subject to considerable variation, with one batch of the same type differing from the next, rendering it difficult to categorise the various types used.

Broadly speaking, until the publication of NN71 *Warblers*, buckrams were smoother, slightly shiny with an almost waxy feel, the weave apparent, whereas those post-1985 are rougher to the touch and the weave is not obvious. The pre-*Warblers* buckrams divide roughly into two groups (though the distinctions are not always as clear as one might like), whereas those post are so similar that they warrant no further division and remain together as a third group.

GROUP 1 Until around 1955 the weave was coarser and more open, with one set of yarns, often wavy. For a few very early titles, including *Butterflies*, this was especially so, distinctly wavy and occasionally with small slubs. The buckram of these early titles is particularly prone to fading, often unevenly.

GROUP 2 From 1955 a finer material with a closer weave was used, characterised with lighter 'spots', almost like a lizard's skin but with less of a tendency to include wavy yarns. This type continued, in variation, until and including the publication of NN70 *Orkney* in 1983.

GROUP 3 Since and including the publication of NN71 *Warblers* in 1985, the buckram used is distinctly different from the types described above, but is very similar or identical to the synthetically coated buckram currently used (*Arbelave* 'Library' buckram 531); it is rougher to the touch, the weave not obvious, the colour consistent with minimal variation.

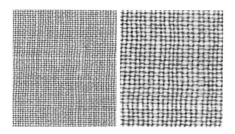

Group 1: Buckram typically faded
From *Butterflies*, 1945

Group 1: Buckram
From *Orchids*, 1951

Group 2: Buckram
From *Inheritance*, 1977

Buckram
Title specific *Wales* First Edition, 1971

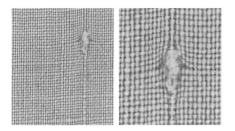

Group 1: Buckram, note slub
From *Butterflies*, 1945

Group 3: Buckram
From *Climate and Weather*, 2010

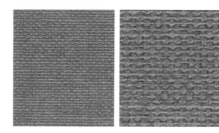

Imitation Cloth Type 1
From *Birds of Prey* BC edition, 1976

Group 2: Buckram
From *Man and the Land*, 1955

Imitation Cloth Type 2
From *British Tits* BC edition, 1979

Imitation Cloth Type 3
From *Waders* BC edition, 1981

Buckram
Title specific *Nature Conservation*
First Edition, 1969

Imitation Cloth Type 4
From *Waders* Collins reprint, 1982

Imitation Cloth Type 5
Farming & Wildlife Collins rep., 1983

Group 3: Buckram
From *Warblers* First State, 1985

Imitation Cloth Type 6
Shetland Collins reprint, 1986

Imitation Cloth Type 7
Orkney and *Warblers* Second State, 1986

TABLE 12 Titles and editions bound in imitation cloth.

Series No.	Cat. No.	Title & Type	Publisher	Date	Imitation Cloth Types						
					Type 1	Type 2	Type 3	Type 4	Type 5	Type 6	Type 7
M1	BCM1	*The Badger*	Book Club/Collins	1976	•						
30	BC30A	*Moths*	Book Club	1976	•						
52	BC52A	*Woodland Birds*	Book Club	1976	•						
60	BC60A	*Birds of Prey*	Book Club**	1976	•						
1	BC1B	*Butterflies*	Book Club	1977	•						
7	BC7B	*Mushrooms/Toadstools*	Book Club	1977	•						
11	BC11A	*Mountains & Moorlands*	Book Club	1977	•						
27	BC27A	*Dartmoor*	Book Club	1977	•						
29	BC29B	*Honeybee*	Book Club	1977	•						
53	BC53A	*Lake District*	Book Club	1977	•						
61	BC61A	*Inheritance*	Book Club**	1977	•						
5	BC5B	*Wild Flowers*	Book Club	1978	•						
32	BC32A	*Trees, Woods, Man*	Book Club	1978	•						
60	BC60B	*Birds of Prey*	Book Club	1978	•						
63	BC63A	*British Thrushes*	Book Club**	1978		•					
58	BC58D	*Hedges*	Book Club	1979		•					
60	BC60C	*Birds of Prey*	Book Club	1979		•					
62	BC62A	*British Tits*	Book Club**	1979		•					
62	BC62B	*British Tits*	Book Club	1980		•					
65	BC65A	*Waders*	Book Club**	1980			•				
65	BC65B	*Waders*	Book Club	1981			•				
60	NN60E	*Birds of Prey*	Collins rep.	1982				•			
65	NN65B	*Waders*	Collins rep.	1982				•			
66	NN66B	*Wales*	Collins rep.	1982				•			
67	NN67B	*Farming Wildlife*	Collins rep.	1983					•		
70	NN70B	*Orkney*	Collins 2nd State	1986*						•	
71	NN71B	*Warblers*	Collins 2nd State	1986*						•	
64	NN64B	*Shetland*	Collins rep.	1986							•

* Published in 1985, rebound in 1986.   ** Published concurrently with Collins first editions with which they are easily confused.

There are, of course, a few exceptions: most noticeably the first edition of *Wales*, which is bound in an unmistakable blue-green buckram (see page 66 for details). *Nature Conservation* has a particularly smooth buckram and the first edition variant of *Woodland Birds* with its silky-green variant binding has already been mentioned above. However, around 1968/69 a matt, brighter, bluer-green fabric appears on a number of reprints and seemingly always characterised by a poorly executed binding where the book-block is often slack and the fore-edge profile irregular – books include (some later-bound copies of) the 1966 revised edition of NN12 *The Seashore* NN12D, the 1968 second-edition of NN15 *Life in Lakes and Rivers* NN15D, the 1968 second edition of NN19 *Wild Orchids of Britain* NN19B, the later binding variant of the 1964 reprint of NN45 *Common Lands* NN45B (BVAR2) and the 1969 third edition of M1 *The Badger*. It would seem that despite earlier printing dates all these variants were bound up *c.* 1968.

Imitation cloths
Sometimes referred to by their trade names *Linson* or *Arlin*, but generically known as imitation cloths. Within the New Naturalist series their use often denotes bookclub editions, though they have also been used for a number of Collins reprints. Why inferior 'Arlins' were deemed acceptable for Collins reprints but not for first editions is unknown, but one can speculate: collectors would complain if their coveted first editions were cased in anything but the traditional buckram livery, but would be more or less indifferent to reprints. Or it could be simply and pragmatically that these reprints often doubled as bookclub editions.

Imitations cloths are lacklustre and on close inspection look more like paper than cloth, which, of course, is what they are. They are an inferior and cheaper product, not as hard-wearing as buckrams and where prone to rubbing, such as the head/tail of joints and corners, they become 'furry'; with the aid of a hand lens the broken fibres are easily observable. The swatches on page 67 should also help with identification.

Imitation cloths were only used for a 12-year period, 1976–1987. Three different fabrics (A, B and C) were used in a variety of colours, making a total of seven separately identifiable types. See Table 11A, page 65.

PRELIMINARIES

Generally, the preliminaries of New Naturalist books in both series are arranged in a standard sequence. Some titles diverge a little from this sequence and there have been the expected 'evolutionary changes' of a series that is nearly seventy years old.

Layout and sequence
The standard sequence for the main series is as follows:

Half-title THE NEW NATURALIST | A SURVEY OF BRITISH NATURAL HISTORY | BOOK TITLE. There is some variation – see details below.

Verso of half-title List of Editors and the New Naturalist credo (this is the page opposite the title page).

Title page Always includes three elements – firstly as the name implies this is where the *definitive title* is printed, usually in the format. THE NEW NATURALIST | TITLE; secondly the author's name and thirdly the imprint. The publication date (first editions) is also included on some title pages, as is an *illustrations blurb*.

Imprint page This is the verso of the title page and usually includes all or some of the following – publisher's details; printer's details; printing history with dates; ISBN, copyright, dedication (occasionally). Also referred to as the copyright page.

Contents Usually spread over one to three leaves.

Plates Occasionally with the heading 'illustrations'. Often divided into 'Colour Plates' and 'Plates in Black and White', and in which case usually accompanied by the following explanation 'It should be noted that throughout this book Plate numbers in Arabic figures refer to the Colour Plates, while roman numerals are used for Black-and-White Plates.' Earlier titles also listed 'Text Figures' and 'Maps' and 'Diagrams'. *Loch Lomondside* was the last title to include a list of plates. The list of plates for *The Herring Gull* is anomalously positioned at the rear.

Editors' preface Most titles carry a preface written by the NN Editorial panel, (Despite the fact that usually just one member of the Editorial Board is allocated to each title, this preface is always titled in the plural and never signed other than for Stamp's *Nature Conservation* – but in this case it doubled as an obituary for *Stamp*). But, of course there are exceptions, e.g. NN67 *Farming and Wildlife* does not have an Editors' preface and that for *British Warblers* is by the Collins editor *Crispin Fisher* rather than the NN Editorial Board.

Author's preface This follows the Editors' preface and up till around NN50 *Pesticides,* where present, was always titled thus (a few titles did not carry an Author's Preface e.g. NN12 *Sea Shore* and NN13 *Snowdonia*). In the early 1990s the Author's Preface

transmuted into the *Author's Foreword* and then a decade later into the *Author's Foreword and Acknowledgements*. Additionally, there are a few other nomenclatural variations.

Inevitably there are exceptions to this described layout: a separate acknowledgement page might be included, occasionally a quote or dedication leaf is slipped in (probably where the book designer had a spare page or two). The inclusion of additional material will usually necessitate a revision of the standard layout.

Key elements

New Naturalist Credo
'The aim of this series is to interest the general reader in the wild life of Britain by recapturing the inquiring spirit of the old naturalists. The Editors believe that the natural pride of the British public in the native flora and fauna to which must be added concern for their conservation, is best fostered by maintaining a high standard of accuracy combined with clarity of exposition in presenting the results of modern scientific research.'

This, in modern parlance if you like, is the New Naturalist 'mission statement' and, in its basic form, is included in nearly every title in the series with the exceptions of NN18, *Natural History of Man in Britain*; 26, *The Weald*; 50 *Pesticides and Pollution*; and M21 *The Mole*. First editions of early titles: NN1–17, 19–25, 28–33, 35, 36, 41 and 44 included the following supplementary sentence:

'The plants and animals are described in relation to their home and habitats and are portrayed in the full beauty of their natural colours, by the latest methods of colour photography and reproduction.'

From *c.*1973 this additional sentence is omitted from the reprints of these titles. NN34 *The Open Sea, Plankton* and NN37 *Open Sea, Fish and Fisheries* include only the first part of this sentence ending with *natural colours,* as is the case for NN38 *Spiders* and 42 *Fossils* but these two uniquely end with 'natural surroundings'.

The credo to the monographs is slightly different and begins 'The aim of THE NEW NATURALIST SERIES...' and is then supplemented with an explanation of the differences between the main series and the monographs:

'The volumes in the main series deal with large groups of animals and plants, with the natural history of particular areas of habitats in Britain, and with certain special subjects. THE NEW NATURALIST MONOGRAPHS, on the other hand, cover, in greater detail, a single species or a group of species. In both the main series and monographs the animals and plants are described in relation to their homes and habitats and are portrayed in their full beauty with the help of colour and monochrome photographs.'

Most of this supplement is also appended to the credo appearing in NN40 *Bumblebees* in the main series, providing further evidence of the original intention to include this title within the monographs.

In the main series the NN credo is always positioned below the list of Editors but it is reversed for the monograph series where it is always above the Editors.

In both series the NN credo is printed opposite the title page, but there are a few exceptions, usually as a consequence of this page being used for a frontispiece illustration. Therefore in such cases the NN credo (and the list of Editors) are either moved to the half-title page (*Caves and Cave Life, New Naturalists, Ireland, Loch Lomondside*) or the imprint page (*Hebrides* and *Seashore*). With M4 *The Yellow Wagtail*, the verso of the half-title is left blank and the credo and list of Editors are printed opposite the imprint page.

Editors

Every title with the exception of NN50 *Pesticides and Pollution* in both series includes a list of the members of the New Naturalist Editorial Board and this is usually printed in association with the NN credo, as described above. For a full list of Editors, their duration of service and the books they edited see Appendix 1, pages 309–12.

Half-title page (Main series)

Generally consistent but there have been some notable revisions to font, layout and nomenclature as the series has progressed; they can be divided into eight formats as identified in table 14.

The title and subtitle to the HT are often slightly different from that of the title page.

All books in the main series include three basic elements, each on a separate line:

1. The series title THE NEW NATURALIST or THE NEW NATURALIST LIBRARY
2. The generic title A SURVEY OF BRITISH NATURAL HISTORY
3. The book TITLE

The three elements are always arranged in this order; for the first 50 volumes in the series a ruled line was inserted between elements two and three, but thereafter was dropped.

Caves and Cave Life, The New Naturalists (both editions) *Ireland* and *Loch Lomondside* are the only four books in the series to include additional information on the half-title, namely the list of Editors and the NN credo. Conversely, the second printing of *The Natural History of Pollination* is the only book with just the book title.

In 1982 with the publication of *Orkney*, the series title changed from The New Naturalist to The New Naturalist library, though the original 'library-less' title made a few brief appearances after this date as identified in table 14.

A new layout was introduced with the publication of *Orkney*, left-justified and an abnormally small point size, though this format only managed six titles.

The publication of NN96 *Fungi* heralded the first use of colour on the half-title page and the distinctive FF Nexus typeface. For the first four volumes with coloured half-titles (NN96–99), the lettering was particularly large but from NN100 *Woodlands* onwards it was significantly reduced.

Half-title page (Monograph series)

There are four different formats as identified below. In the main series, all books include the generic title 'A Survey of British Natural History' on the half-title page, but this is absent from all monographs except for M22 *The Mole*.

Putting this exception on one side, there are just two elements: the book title and the series title, always in that order and on separate lines and always with a ruled line between, again accepting *The Mole*. (That for *The Greenshank* appears to have been drawn by a child using anything but a straight edge.)

We have come to know the smaller monographic series as 'The Monographs' but this has not always been the case. In fact only three of the twenty two books use the term 'monograph' (to both half-title and title pages). Three different generic series title were used as follows across the four layouts:

TABLE 13 Monograph series half-title types, identifying variation in title, layout and font.

Format 1) A NEW NATURALIST MONOGRAPH – M1, M2 & M4 (1949–1950)
Format 2) THE NEW NATURALIST – M3, M5–M8 (1951, '52, '53 & '55)
Format 3) A NEW NATURALIST SPECIAL VOLUME – M9–M21 (1953, '54, '56, '57, '59, '60, '63, '65 & '67)
Format 4) THE NEW NATURALIST – M22 (1971)

Frontispiece plates

In the main series there is a general paucity of frontispiece plates, while in the monograph series a little over half are so embellished. Titles in the main series with conventionally inserted frontispiece plates positioned opposite the title page include:

NN14 *Botanical Illustration* (colour)
NN28 *Sea Birds* (colour)
NN29 *Honeybee* (colour)
NN39 *Folklore of Birds* (colour)
NN40 *Bumblebees* (colour)
NN42 *Fossils* (colour)
NN43 *Weeds and Aliens* (colour)
NN46 *The Broads* (colour)
NN48 *Grass and Grassland* (colour)

Additionally, there are several examples where the frontispiece is not an inserted leaf or a bound-in plate printed on glossy paper, but an integral part of the first gathering and therefore included in the general pagination. These are therefore not plates *sensu stricto*, but are printed to the verso of the half-title leaf. They include:

TABLE 14 Main series half-title types, identifying variation in title, layout and font (capitals, lowercase, roman and italics). * = title in particularly large letters

Type	nos	Series title	Generic title	Book title	Alignment	Ruled line	Colour
1	1–50	THE NEW NATURALIST	A SURVEY OF BRITISH NATURAL HISTORY	U/c roman	centred	yes	no
2	51–69	THE NEW NATURALIST	A SURVEY OF BRITISH NATURAL HISTORY	U/c roman	centred	no	no
3	70, 72, 74, 76	The New Naturalist Library	A Survey of British Natural History	L/c roman	left	no	no
4	71, 73	The New Naturalist	A Survey of British Natural History	L/c roman	left	no	no
5	77, 78	*The New Naturalist*	A SURVEY OF BRITISH NATURAL HISTORY	U/c roman	centred	no	no
6	75, 79–95	*The New Naturalist Library*	A SURVEY OF BRITISH NATURAL HISTORY	U/c roman	centred	no	no
7	96–99	THE NEW NATURALIST LIBRARY	A SURVEY OF BRITISH NATURAL HISTORY	U/c roman*	centred	no	yes
8	100–120	THE NEW NATURALIST LIBRARY	A SURVEY OF BRITISH NATURAL HISTORY	U/c roman	centred	no	yes

TABLE 15 Main series title pages, identifying variations in the generic series title, and font (capitals, lowercase, roman and italics) * The subtitle for NN56 *Pedigree* includes both lowercase italics and capital roman.

Element	Wording	Capital roman	Capital italics	Lowercase roman	Lowercase italics
Generic Series Title	THE NEW NATURALIST	1–69			
Generic Series Title	The New Naturalist	70–74, 75 and 83			
Generic Series Title	*The New Naturalist*	75, 77–82A & 82B and 84–95			
Generic Series Title	THE NEW NATURALIST LIBRARY	96–120			
Book Title	–	1–120			
Subtitle	–	13, 56*, 87–89, 91, 92 and 95	9		5, 17–19, 28, 34, 37, 38, 53, 56*, 74, 107, 108 and 111
Author's name		40, 41, 44–49, 51–69 and 95–1	1–39, 42, 43	70–94, (inc. 82A & 82B)	50
Illustrations blurb		1–39, 41–48, 54, 57 and 61		64, 66, 69, 70, 72 and 75–95	40, 67, 73, 74, 76 and 106

TABLE 16 Monograph series title pages identifying variations in the generic series title and typography.

Element	Wording	Capital roman	Capital italics	Lowercase roman	Lowercase italics
Generic series title	NEW NATURALIST MONOGRAPH	M1, M2, M4			
Generic series title	THE NEW NATURALIST	M3, M5–M22			
Book title	–	M1–M22			
Subtitle	–	M7, M9, M10, M13			
Author's name		M1–M22			
Illustrations blurb				M1	M2–M22

TABLE 17 Analysis of the lettering elements to spines of NN first edition casings.

Lettering element to casing spine	Series numbers
Title in capitals	1–55, 57–63, 70–94 and M1–M22
Title in lowercase	56, 64–66, 67, 69 and 95–120
Title in capitals and lowercase	68
Diamond – solid	1–4 and 48
Diamond – in outline (in a variety of sizes and shapes)	5–12, 14–47, 49–55, 57–60, 62–65, 67–94 and M1–M19, M21, M22
No diamond	13, 56, 66, 95–120
Star (instead of a diamond)	61 and M20
Author/s in capitals	1–72, 87, 94, 96–120 and M1–M22
Author/s in lowercase	73–86, 88–93, 95
Authors' names omitted	13 (1st state)
Collins in capitals	1–94 and M1–M22
Collins in lowercase	95–120
With series number	66, 95

NN76 *The Hebrides* (b/w map)
NN79 *Caves and Cave Life* (b/w photograph)
NN82 *New Naturalists* (black and white, both 82A and 82B.)
NN84 *Ireland* (b/w map)
NN88 *Loch Lomondside* (b/w map)
NN94 *Seashore* (b/w photograph)

In the monograph series all frontispiece plates are true plates and not part of the general pagination. Those with frontispieces conventionally positioned opposite the title page include:

M1 *Badger* (colour)
M2 *Redstart* (colour)
M8 *Ants* (b/w)
M9 *Herring Gull* (b/w)
M10 *Mumps, Measles, Mosaics* (colour)
M11 *Heron* (colour)
M12 *Squirrels* (b/w)
M17 *Lords and Ladies*
M18 *Oysters* (b/w)
M19 *The House Sparrow* (colour)
M20 *The Wood Pigeon* (colour)

Additionally, a number of books have frontispiece plates positioned elsewhere within the prelims e.g. M6 *The Fulmar*, NN105 *Wye Valley* and NN112 *Books and Naturalists* (a fine line drawing by Tim Bernhard).

Title page (main series)

The format of title pages is very much a variation on a theme, but as identified all carry the book's title, author's name and imprint. For a 40-year period, from 1945–1985, they were centred and the layout reasonably consistent, but with an amount of variation to the various components as explained below. The first significant change was introduced in 1985 with the layout left-justified, but this only lasted for six titles and was abandoned in 1990 in favour of the traditional centred format. The next big change appeared in 2005 with the introduction of coloured titles and this was quickly supplemented with the new NN monogram (type F) a year later with the publication of NN100 *Woodlands*. Since then the layout has remained remarkably consistent.

Title Page Components
The title page components are as follows.

Generic series title From inception of the series in 1945 to 2004 (NN95 *Northumberland*) every book title was preceded with the generic series title THE NEW NATURALIST and then with the advent of NN96 *Fungi* it was changed to THE NEW NATURALIST LIBRARY and has remained so ever since. Why the change was introduced is unclear, as is how the series might have benefited from the change, other than once again being consistent with the nomenclature of the half-title page. The

font used for the generic series title has varied a little as identified in table 15.

Titles Always in capital roman and usually in bold, occasionally the letters widely spaced.

Authors' names Until 1958 (NN1–39) all authors' names were printed in capital italics. The convention was superceded with capital romans for the period 1959–1982. From 1983 to 2004 (NN70–94) the author's name was printed in lowercase romans, before switching back to capital roman for the period 2004 to 2013 (NN95–120), with a few exceptions identified in table 15; the most notable being NN50 *Pesticides*, where the author's name is uniquely printed in lowercase italics. For the first 48 titles, the author's name was always preceded with '*by*', thereafter the reader is left to assume that the book is *by* the person mentioned on the title page!

Subtitles Most New Naturalists do not have subtitles, but generally where present they are in lowercase italics, but there are exceptions as identified in table 15.

Dates From 1950 to 1971 all first editions carry a date at the base of the title page (NN5, 6b, 7, 9, 14–51). Prior to this, the date was not printed on the title page, only on the imprint page (NN1–4, 6a, 8, 10–13) as is the case from 1971–present (NN52–120).

Collins address Until 1981 (NN1–68) the address of *St. James Place, London* was printed to the base, but from 1950–1957, the building number was also added so reads *14 St. James Place*. From 1982–1990 (NN69–74, 76) Collins new address was featured – *Grafton, Street, London*. But since 1992 (NN75, 77–120) the address has been omitted altogether, in favour of a cleaner, more contemporary look.

Illustrations blurb With the exception of a dozen or so titles, all books published before 2004 included a blurb advertising the illustrations in the book. NN56 *Pedigree* is without illustrations, but, why the Collins editor decided to drop the picture blurb for a few well-illustrated titles in the 1970/80s is unknown. Modern printing, which enables illustrations to be cheaply reproduced, has rendered the illustrations blurb obsolete, as it should be 'taken as read' that any book of the calibre of a New Naturalist will be well-illustrated. For the first 38 titles (and NN54) the illustrations blurb is positioned within ruled lines, which are then subsequently abandoned. Generally printed in capital roman until NN61 and thereafter lowercase roman, but of course always with exceptions as identified in table 15.

Title page (Monograph series)

The title pages of the monograph series display very little variation in both general layout (all are centred) and in typography. Perhaps the most notable feature is the generic series title, which for M1 *The Badger*, M2 *The Redstart* and M4 *The Yellow Wagtail* is 'New Naturalist Monograph' whereas for all the others the generic title of the main series is used 'The New Naturalist'. The series title, book title, sub-title and author's name are always in Capital Roman; the illustrations blurb always in lowercase italics with the exception of M1 *The Badger* which is in lowercase roman. For M1–M13, M15, M16, M18, and M20 a horizontal 'diamond line' is used to separate the illustrations blurb from the author and title. All first editions with the exception of M22 *The Mole* are dated to the title page, and for the first 21 titles, the author's name was always preceded with '*by*', but again this was omitted for *The Mole* and in the case of this latter volume, inexplicably, the rare Type A monogram is used.

Collins, HarperCollins and logos to title pages

Before company logos were *de rigueur*, the imprint 'COLLINS' was simply printed in capitals at the base of the title page, usually in association with, and immediately beneath the NN monogram and remained so until 1990. In 1992 'HarperCollins*Publishers*' appeared on the title page and stayed until 2003, before reverting back to the 'Collins' imprint in 2004 and to 'WILLIAM COLLINS' in 2013.

The typefaces used for the imprint 'Collins' have changed a number of times during the course of the series, and one would imagine this was in line with revisions to the company's branding. It is therefore interesting to note that earlier in the series the typeface used on the title page was often different to that used on the dust jacket e.g. NN5 *Wild Flowers*, but in most cases, these differences are subtle with most typefaces being derivatives of *Baskerville*.

The *Baskerville* typeface was used almost exclusively for the 'Collins' imprint until and including the publication of NN69 *Reptiles* in 1983, with a few variations in point size and arrangement.

The typeface used for NN60 *Birds of Prey* in 1977 was unique for the series, but still in capitals.

For NN70–74 and 76 (1985–1990) the typeface *Erhart* was introduced, but still in capitals.

From 1992 to 2003 (NN75, 77–93) HarperCollins*Publishers* appears on the title page but in the period 1999–2002 (NN84–91) this was supplemented with the 'Fire and Water' logo – and no longer in association with the NN monogram which was temporarily abandoned.

The Seashore, NN94 (2004) is unique in displaying the Collins 'ripple' logo.

NN95 *Northumberland* in 2004 saw the inauguration of a new Collins typeface FF *Nexus* and this once again in association with the NN monogram.

The epochal *Woodlands* (NN100) heralded the introduction of the new 'ring' logo (sometimes referred to as the '*Croissant*') to supplement the new Collins typeface, and this arrangement remained in place until June 2013. Since then, the original fountain logo has been reintroduced as the 'new' William Collins logo.

Summary
1945–1990 (NN1–74 and 76): 'COLLINS' in capitals, principally using the *Baskerville* typeface.
1992–1993 (NN75 and 77–93): HarperCollins*Publishers* logo.

2004–present: Collins in lowercase, FF *Nexus* typeface.
2004 NN94: *Seashore* uniquely displays the Collins 'ripple' logo.
1999–2002 (NN84–91): 'Fire and Water' logo used.
2004–2013: Collins 'ring' logo used.
2013–present: William Collins fountain logo re-introduced.

Reprints

Preliminary pages to reprints frequently differ slightly from first editions with new prefaces or notes, which often necessitate a small revision to the layout e.g. NN49 *Nature Conservation* includes a 'Note on the Second Edition' in place of the author's preface; the new edition of NN82 *The New Naturalists* omits the original Editors' preface, but has a new foreword by *Stefan Buczacki* and the original author's forward is supplemented with an '*Author's Foreword to the Second Edition*'

SOME CASING CHARACTERISTICS

Rounding and backing

A good-quality hardback book will not only look and feel right with a pleasing convex spine and well-defined joints but, importantly, when opened it will lie flat – if not designed to be read in the hand. The operation required to achieve this is called *rounding and backing* (R&B). *Rounding* is the process of putting the round shape into the back of the book to help it open, whereas *backing*, a misleading term, is the process of creating a pronounced shoulder to the joint – sometimes known, more aptly, as rounding and jointing (R&J). Of course, R&B does not apply to paperbacks, but there is a progression of operations from the flat-backed paperback to the full rounding and backing of a hardback; it is not simply a question of either, or. With mass-produced books such as the modern New Naturalist, these operations are undertaken mechanically on a bindery line, and the resultant quality varies significantly – no doubt also influenced by the specification given to the binder. One has only to look at a few different NN titles published in the last 20 years to see the variation in the extent of rounding, joint definition, and the book's ability to lie flat when opened; ironically some of the most expensive titles, e.g. *Ladybirds*, have particularly flat spines, compare with *Northumberland*. This variation can also be to our advantage as it can be used diagnostically to differentiate one edition or variant from another, as is the case for a number of books in the series, for instance in distinguishing the reprint from the first edition of *The Isles of Scilly*.

Casing characteristics

The layout of New Naturalist bindings, or more accurately the casings, is remarkably consistent. Both boards are blank without any lettering or other features (excepting four 1953 RU editions, which are blocked 'Readers Union' to the rear board.) All lettering including the NN monogram is confined to the spine with the title always at the head, below which, traditionally separated by a diamond motif, is the author's name. At the tail of the spine is the Collins imprint with the NN monogram positioned immediately above. This sequence is *always* followed, with a few variations only to the individual elements as identified in table 17A (see page 346).

The lettering is always blocked in gilt with the exception of a few titles printed in 1971/72 that have silver-gilt lettering.

NN95 *Northumberland* deserves specific mention as it represents somewhat of a watershed in the series in terms of lettering to the casing. The Collins imprint and the title lettering change at this point from capitals to lowercase, conversely the author's name changes from lowercase to capitals. Additionally, from and including *Northumberland* the diamond motif is abandoned. *Northumberland* and the first edition of NN66 *Wales* are the only two books to include the series number on the spine casing.

There are a few notable aberrations: the first state of NN13 *Snowdonia* is the only book to omit the authors' names from the casing, and NN61 *Inheritance and Natural History* and M20 *The Wood Pigeon* use stars rather than diamonds. *The Mole* is the only monograph not to use the NMN monogram but instead uses either the rare type A or the more familiar type C monograms (see page 61). The monographs otherwise do not display any aberration in the lettering elements of their casings. (For an analysis of the NN monogram on the casing see page 60.)

The execution of the gilt blocking to the spines varies considerably but post NN70 *Orkney* is generally not as good, a few are particularly poorly executed with the author's name blocked in a minute font e.g. NN77 *The Soil* and 83 *The Natural History of Pollination*. On the spines of NN98 *Bumblebees* and 99 *Gower*, 'Collins' is positioned right on the bottom edge.

TABLE 18 The surface finishes of first edition dust jackets.

SERIES NO.	FIRST EDITION JACKET FINISHES
1–45	Matt
46, 47	Laminated, often prone to surface crackling
48–51	Matt (first edition, second state of NN51 *Man and Birds* has a *Duraseal* protector)
51–68	Matt finish but with clear plastic *Duraseal* protector
69	Upper side semi-glossy, underside matt
70, 71 1st States	Matt finish but with clear plastic *Duraseal* protector
70, 71 2nd States	Glossy laminated finish
72–95	Glossy laminated finish
96	Laminated, thick; matt finish to upper surface, underside glossy (some early prototype jackets with glossy finish to upperside)
98	Laminated, upper surface with a satin finish, underside glossy.
97, 99–120	Laminated, thick; matt finish to upper surface, underside glossy.

TABLE 19 Dust jacket series numbers and associated roundels.

white numeral	1, 22, 63, 69
coloured numeral	2–13, 15, 16, 18–21, 23–25, 27, 28, 30, 34, 35, 37–41, 44, 46, 48–51, 53, 55, 56, 58, 59, 68
black numeral	14, 17, 26, 29, 31–33, 36, 42, 43, 45, 47, 52, 54, 57, 60–62, 64–67, 70–99, 101–20
white roundel	2–11, 14–46, 48–50, 52–60, 62, 64–65, 67, 68, 70–85, 87–99, 101–20
coloured roundel	1 blue, 22 aqua, 47 red, 51 black, 61 russet, 63 orange, 69 black, 86 orange, 100 gold
no roundel	12, 66

DUST JACKETS

'It is surely Clifford and Rosemary Ellis, as much as anyone, who established the "brand image" of the New Naturalist series, and helped to make it the most long-running, and latterly also the most collectable, library of books in the natural history world', so eulogised Peter Marren in *Art of the New Naturalists*. In the same book the artistic qualities of the jacket designs have been expertly discussed and no further elaboration is required here, save to establish the key bibliographic features. But it might be of passing interest to note that there is generally more variation in these features, in the Ellises' designs than those of Gillmor. It is the flaps and rear panel of the jackets that are of most concern to us, as it is these elements that exhibit the greatest variation between editions and printings. Here the main series is examined in detail with a concluding note on the monographs. (All numbers cited in the following text and table refer to main series numbers unless otherwise stated.)

Paper and finishes
Through the history of the series a variety of different papers and finishes have been used for jackets. Those used on first editions

are summarised in table 18. The weight of paper and finish can occasionally be used diagnostic, for instance the first edition, first state of *Man and Birds* does not have a *Duraseal* protector but the second state does, and the first edition of the *Isles of Scilly* is printed on distinctly thicker paper than the reprint. These specific details are given under the dedicated catalogue entry for each title. Before about 1974 the paper used had an acid reaction and consequently these jackets often display a greater degree of browning and spotting than later jackets. From 1971 to 1985 all NN jackets produced for Collins were protected with *Duraseal*, a proprietary clear plastic (polypropylene) protector.

Front panel and spine
The jacket artwork always appears on the front panel and spine, and remains essentially unmodified for reprints and new editions (excepting NN82 *New Naturalists* which has a completely new design for the 2005 edition). There are occasionally variations of colour, scale and detail as a result of different printing techniques, but these are generally subtle and are highlighted under each title entry. The jacket artwork always includes the following unifying features:

1. A coloured title band (excepting NN14 *Botanical Illustration*): The photographic jackets of NN46 *The Broads* and 47 *Snowdonia National Park* have modified white title bands. The lettering on the title band is reversed out white with the exceptions of NN14, 18, 22, 26, 36, 46 and 120 where it is black, and NN47 and 51, red, and NN46, partly blue.
2. The NN monogram: Positioned at the base of the spine, it is usually in association with a graphic oval (see section on monograms on pages 60–65).
3. The series number: Positioned at the top of the spine, usually coloured or black within a white circle (roundel), but as usual, there are variations as identified in table 19. NN12 *Sea Shore* and NN66 *Wales* are unique in having no roundel as such, but the numbers are on white backgrounds and NN22 *Climate and the British Scene* has an additional circumferential white ring incorporated into the design. Various typefaces have been used and in a variety of point sizes.
4. The title: Always positioned above the author names on both the front panel and spine. (The jacket to NN13 *Snowdonia* is unique in not including the authors.) Generally for the Ellises' jackets the title is in lowercase (title-case) and the author in capitals, and for Gillmor's jackets both are in lowercase (title-case) but there are the inevitable exceptions, which are identified in table 20.
5. The imprint (Collins): Generally appears at the foot of the spine of the dust jacket (NN1–74, 76, 82B, 95–120), but between 1992 and 2004 (NN75, 77–81, 82A, 83–94) the imprint was omitted. Additionally in the case of NN72 *Heathlands* and NN73 *New Forest*

its absence denotes a bookclub edition – in the genuine Collins editions it is present.

Front flap
1. Blurb: This is the key feature of the front flap and for first editions it is always present in one form or another. It varies in length from a few lines to consuming the whole flap and in NN1, 3 and 8 it continues onto the back flap. In some of the early titles, the blurb included a mini biography of the author. Commonly the blurb is revised for subsequent printings; sometimes abridged or rewritten, or supplemented with press endorsements; often both. Occasionally it is omitted altogether in favour of a series of press reviews. Such revisions are identified in the catalogue entry for each title.
2. Jacket design credit (see table 21): Situated below the blurb, but not always, is the jacket design credit. Occasionally it is omitted and if there is insufficient space it is usurped to the rear flap, but it is interesting to note that for the first five books published (NN1–4 and 8) the Ellises went unacknowledged.

The Ellis credit is always in italics and usually takes the form '*Jacket design by Clifford and Rosemary Ellis*', occasionally 'designed'. It is often centred and on two lines. But there are anomalies. For a period roughly between 1947 and 1951, 'jacket' became 'wrapper', which is a dubious term because in bibliographical parlance it has nothing to do with dust jackets. Fortunately, it did not persist, but in recent times, since 2005 an equally incorrect term has been introduced: 'front cover'. Bibliographically, 'cover' means specifically the front and back

TABLE 20 Analysis of lettering used for the title and author/s on NN jackets. It can be seen that there was considerably more variation in the early days of the series.

	Caps front panel caps spine	Caps front panel lowercase spine	Mixed front panel caps spine	Mixed front panel mixed spine	Mixed front panel lowercase caps	Lc front panel caps spine	Lowercase front panel lowercase spine
Title lettering	38, 43, 46, 47	5, 17, 19, 26–28, 30, 32, 40–42	13	34, 37	3, 4, 8, 16, 24	35	1, 2, 6, 7, 9–12, 14, 15, 18, 20–23, 25, 29, 31, 33, 36, 39, 44, 45, 48–120
Author lettering	1, 3–12, 14–40, 42, 44, 45–69	82A, 82B				41, 96–120	2, 43, 70–81, 83–95

TABLE 21 Analysis of jacket design credits for first editions, unless otherwise stated. NN14, 46 and 47 with non-artwork jackets have been omitted from the table (* = designed).

JACKET DESIGN CREDIT WORDING	FRONT FLAP	REAR FLAP	OMITTED ALTOGETHER
Jacket design/ed by Clifford and Rosemary Ellis	5, 7, 17*, 18*, 19–21, 22*, 23, 24, 27–30, 31*, 32–36, 48–52, 56, 59–70	53, 54, 57, 58 (NN60B, NN54B, NN54C)	
Wrapper design/ed by Clifford and Rosemary Ellis	6*, 9*, 10–12, 15–16*	13*	
Jacket design by Rosemary and Clifford Ellis	34 reprints only		
No design credit			1–4, 8, (25 all eds.); 26, 54, (55 all eds)
Jacket design by Robert Gillmor	71–95 (71–87 in italics)		
Front cover design by Robert Gillmor	96–115		

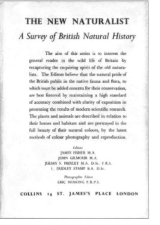

NN1 *Butterflies*, 1945 (and format for NN2–4 ,1945–1946)

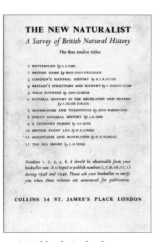

NN6 *Highlands & Islands*, 1947

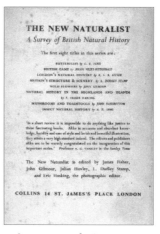

NN8 *Insect Natural History*, 1947

NN10 *British Plant Life*, 1948

NN12 *The Seashore*, 1949

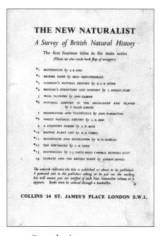

NN13 *Snowdonia*, 1949

NN11 *Mountains & Moorlands*, 1950

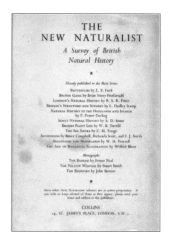

NN14 *Botanical Illustration*, 1950

Illustrated here (and overleaf) are all significant rear panel layout types that have appeared on main series first edition jackets, with several notable reprint layouts also shown. The rear panel is particularly interesting, as it demonstrates the progression of the series and an evolution of typographical design, and for these reasons the panels are arranged chronologically rather than in the usual series order. NN37 *Open Sea II Fish & Fisheries* (1959) was the first to have a coloured title band, a feature that persisted for nearly 40 years.

NN15 *Life in Lakes & Rivers*, 1951 (and format for NN16)

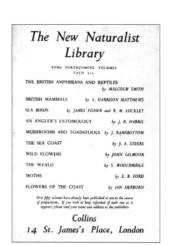

NN9 *Country Parish* 1951

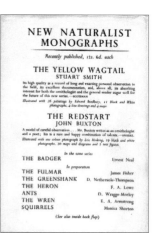

NN17 *Birds & Men*, 1951

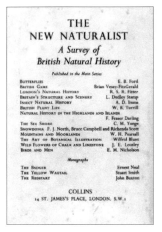

NN18 *Man in Britain*, 1951

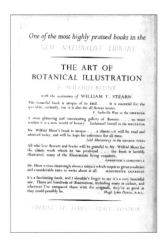

NN19 *Wild Orchids*, 1951

NN20 *Reptiles & Amphibians*, 1951

NN21 *Mammals*, 1952

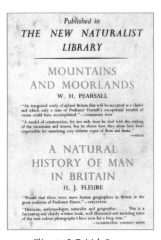

NN22 *Climate & British Scene*, 1952

NN23 *An Anglers' Entomology*, 1952

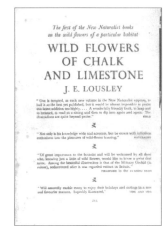

NN24 *Flowers of the Coast*, 1952

NN25 *The Sea Coast*, 1953

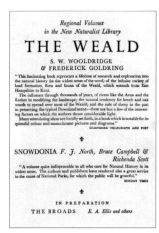

NN26 *The Weald*, 1953

NN7 *Mushrooms*, 1953

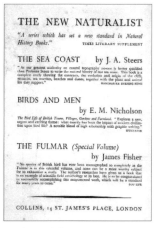

NN27 *Dartmoor*, 1953 (and format for NN32)

NN28 *Sea Birds*, 1954

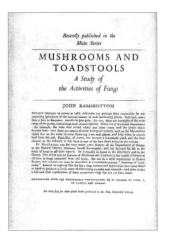

NN5 *Wild Flowers*, 1954

NN29 *Honey Bee*, 1954

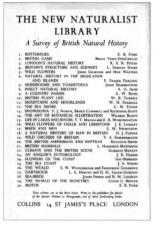

NN20 *Reptiles & Amphibians*, NN20B (DJ2), 1954

NN30 *Moths*, 1955

NN31 *Man & The Land*, 1955

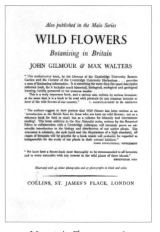

NN32 *Trees, Woods and Man*, 1956

NN33 *Mountain Flowers*, 1956

NN34 *The Open Sea I Plankton*, 1956

NN35 *The Soil*, 1957 (and format for NN12B)

(Type 36) NN36 *Insect Migration*, 1958 (and format for NN7C and NN15B)

(Type 38) NN38 *Spiders*, 1958 (and format for NN39 and NN34B)

(Type 37) NN37 *The Open Sea II Fish & Fisheries*, 1959 (format for NN40 and NN35B). First with a coloured title band. Note that it bleeds onto top edge.

(Type 41)
NN41 *Dragonflies*, 1960 (and format for NN31B). Very similar to Type 42 but a finer typeface used for the title.

(Type 41a)
1960 *Mountains & Moorlands* rep. NN11B and *British Mammals* 2nd ed. NN21B. Very similar to Type 42 but authors not italicised and typeface different.

(Type 42)
NN42 *Fossils*, 1960 (and format for NN43–68, i.e. 1961–1982). The most used of all NN library layouts.

Flowers of the Coast rep. NN24B 1962. For some unknown reason this reprint reverts to a style redolent of an earlier period but maintains double columns.

222AN
NN69 *Reptiles and Amphibians*, 1983 (and format for NN67B).

222AO
NN70 *Orkney*, 1985 (and format for NN71, 72, 73, and NN64B, i.e. 1985–86). Note: introduction of barcode.

222AP
NN74 *Ferns*, 1988. Title band 17 mm wide.

222AQ
NN75 *Fishes*, 1992 (and format for NN77–83, i.e. 1992–1996). Title band 12.5 mm wide.

222AR
NN76 *Hebrides*, 1990

222AS
NN84 *Ireland*, 1999 (and format for NN85–95, i.e. 1999–2004). Title band 10 mm wide and always black.

222AT
NN96 *Fungi* (and format for NN 97–101). 2005–2007. Title band now omitted.

222AU
(Type 102) NN102 *Garden Natural History*, 2007 (and format for NN 103–120, i.e. 2007–2012)

sides of the actual book, including the card covers of a paperback, but not the dust jacket; the term was probably introduced so that it could be used interchangeably for both paperbacks and hardbacks without the book designer having to change the terms of reference, but to the purists amongst us it grates. For the reprints of NN34 *The Open Sea*, somewhere, somebody took it upon themselves to change the order to Rosemary and Clifford – perhaps a sop to old-fashioned chivalry? But whoever it was overlooked the fact they always sign their work 'C & RE'.

3. Price: Always positioned over the lower corner. (This is the traditional location for books published in the UK, whereas for books published in the US, the price is positioned across the upper corner of the front flap – as in the Taplinger editions of NN54 *Pollination* and NN57 *Seals*). With the exceptions of NN84–91, which were priced at £34.99, NN hardback books have not been subject to 'psychological pricing' (concomitant paperback NN70–92 were priced psychologically). All titles before and including NN73 *New Forest* appended the word 'net' to the price. This was abandoned thereafter, but made a brief reappearance for NN79–81. For NN58 and 60–73 the price was diagonally printed across the corner with an associated dashed line indicating where it should be clipped (has this led to a greater proportion of clipped jackets?). Occasionally jackets are found without a printed price, but these are invariably bookclub editions (see page 88).

Rear flap

Generally the rear flap is used to advertise or list other books in the series: NN5–7, 9–101, 109 and 110. Often these adverts are for books of the same genera, e.g. the second edition of *Wild Flowers of Chalk and Limestone* (NN16B) carries adverts for three botanical titles: *Wild Flowers*; *Mountain Flowers* and *Flowers of the Coast*. Commercially, it is critical that adverts are current and therefore they are usually updated for each new printing. Today, books stay in print for such a short period of time that the use of dust jackets for adverts is less important; additionally now that the NN library is included within the book itself, the rear panel has been freed up for advertising. NN66 *Wales* is interesting in that six titles are listed by William Condry of which four were neither part of the NN series nor published by Collins.

Below the adverts a 'mailing list request' was included on many early titles, but by the mid-1950s its appearance was sporadic; this invited readers to write in with their details, and Collins would then notify them of each new title as it was released. The wording used took various forms.

Traditionally ISBNs have featured on the rear flap – for first editions these are NN51–69, 82B, 85–99; and for reprints published after 1970. Now that ISBNs are associated with barcodes it is more convenient for them to be positioned on the rear panel. Since NN72 *Heathlands* an author's biography has featured on the rear flap; the first two – NN72 and 73 included a small photograph of the author, but this personifying feature was abandoned

thereafter. NN102–108 and 111–120 have included only the author's biography. For NN82B and 85–99 the rear flap also carried a Collins logo or imprint and their website, and for NN100 *Woodlands*, just the logo.

Rear panel and the New Naturalist library

From the inception of the New Naturalist to the present, the rear panel has been used to advertise the series in one form or another and most notably by way of the NEW NATURALIST LIBRARY. The first four titles displayed the NN credo; NN8 *Insect Natural History* in 1947 was the first (in printing order) to display a list of titles, but the NN library did not become a standard feature until the publication of NN34 *Open Sea The World of Plankton* in 1956, though it had appeared erratically on a number of preceding titles. It remained an iconic element of the New Naturalist jacket for 52 years.

Before the NN library became the standard feature, the rear panel was often used to advertise like titles, e. g. first editions of *Birds and Men* advertised *The Yellow Wagtail* and *The Redstart*, and *Flowers of the Coast* advertised *Flowers of Chalk and Limestone*; and *Dartmoor* advertised *The Weald*. Additionally forthcoming titles were featured, e.g. *The Broads* was advertised on the jacket of *Snowdonia* in 1953, although in the event did not appear for another 12 years!

The Editorial Board meeting held on 27 November 1956 records that 'The editors considered it important that each book in the series should contain a list showing the whole series, with the volumes numbered' and accordingly the next title to be published, NN35 *The Soil*, in 1957 was the first book to display a numbered library.

When the NN library was introduced it was arranged in a single column, but by 1958 the list was too long and for NN38 *Spiders* it was arranged for the first time in double columns.

The library as it appears on the rear panel takes two forms: firstly, that which lists all titles published to date and, secondly, that which list only those titles that were contemporaneously available. At the meeting of 14 October 1959, 'Dr Stamp asked if a *complete* list of NN titles could be printed on the back of the wrappers of new volumes. At present when [a] title is o.p. it is omitted. Decided to print complete list in future, with the words "out of print" in brackets added where a title is o.p.' The first book to do so was *Fossils* in 1960, but the practice of listing all titles but identifying those out of print only lasted until 1966. Thereafter and until the publication of NN69 *Amphibians and Reptiles* in 1983, all books used the 'Type 42' library, which listed only those contemporaneously in print.

The 'Type 42' library is the most important to us as this format was used essentially unchanged for 23 years and appeared on numerous reprints as well as first editions. It was regularly updated. Table 33 (page 110) lists the variants and includes associated date ranges, which will quickly allow the era of the jacket to be established, irrespective of the book around which it is wrapped. The Editorial Board minutes of 16 February 1960 refer to a '… general policy of keeping all vols. in print where possible…' The

'Type 42' libraries give us a good indication of how many different titles were available at any one time (for most of the 1970s over 40 different titles were simultaneously available).

From NN70 *Orkney* to NN101 *Galloway* (2007) inclusively, the NN library included every title published in the series. The library expanded and *Orkney* was the first to have the now mandatory barcode and this also required space. Despite a reduction in point size, a narrowing of the title band and finally its abandonment altogether, it became impossible to shoe-horn the library onto the rear panel and from NN102 *Garden Natural History* the library has been inserted at the back of the book, with the rear panel once again used to advertise specific and forthcoming titles. The format used for the rear panel of NN102 has persisted to date and accordingly is referred to as 'Type 102'. A key feature of this format is the price, ISBN, barcode and website positioned within a box with a dotted border and rounded corners. Presumably, locating all this information together is a modern expedient, but inclusion of the price on the rear panel presents the would-be giver with a dilemma: should this be excised in addition to the corner of the front flap being clipped? For NN113–118 inclusively, the website was omitted from this box. For NN105–120 the rear panel also includes an advert for the New Naturalist website: 'Please visit the new New Naturalist website www.collins.co.uk/newnaturalists for more information and special offers'. For NN120 the price was additionally given in Canadian Dollars.

A note on the Monograph jackets

Unlike the main series the monograph jackets do not have a title band but instead the title on both spine and front panel is displayed within a rather loose, amorphous oval. There is less variation in the lettering than the main series: it is always either black or white with the title always in roman capitals to both spine and front panel; conversely the author is always in roman lower case to both spine and front panel. The one exception is the anomalous third state, plain green *Hawfinch* jacket (M15C) where the title to both front panel and spine is in italics, but lower case to the spine and upper case to the front panel. Three 'Special Volumes' have plain but sophisticated non-Ellis jackets, probably designed in-house. The front and rear flaps and rear panel are used essentially in the same way as those for the main series.

An important distinction with the monographs is that the series number is not a positive part of the design livery and appears to be very much an afterthought: in some titles, such as M12 *Squirrels* and even more so M3 *The Wren* it is so small that it is almost illegible, whereas with M19 *The House Sparrow*, it is overly large and dominates the title.

PRINT ON DEMAND

With the introduction of digital printing, it became economically possible to print very low numbers of books or even single copies, and therefore to make rare out of print books available once more.

Print-on-demand is a printing technology process in which new copies of a book are not printed until an order has been received. The use of POD means that many academic publishers and universities can maintain large backlists of titles, some of which may have been long out of print. Larger publishers such as HarperCollins can use POD in special circumstances, for example for reprinting older titles and books for specialist markets or perhaps for test marketing. HarperCollins were able to use this breakthrough in printing technology as a means to make every New Naturalist title available as a new book for the first time.

There will undoubtedly always be collectors who are only interested in the true first edition or perhaps another original reprint, but the POD editions are a simple way for collectors to fill a gap in their New Naturalist library without taking on a new mortgage. Print-on-demand books will also be invaluable to students who need to refer to some of the more expensive titles such as *British Bats*. This book went out of print very quickly and second-hand copies shot up in price, putting them beyond the reach of most students who want to use the book rather than collect the series. In this particular case, there are few books on the natural history of British bats and hence the book is very sought after by ecologists and naturalists as well as New Naturalist collectors. Even the paperback is a scarce item. By contrast the POD version is instantly accessible, reasonably affordable and has the added benefit of looking good on the bookshelf. Unlike some of the other editions, such as bookclub, paperback and Bloomsbury, the New Naturalist PODs look very similar to the genuine book and it is a challenge to spot one when it has filled a gap in a collection.

HarperCollins were delighted to announce the PODs towards the end of 2009, stating, 'We have been careful to ensure the quality is of the utmost standard and we're proud to have created the first ever hand-crafted, hardback, full-colour, print on demand series.'

Original copies of the books were gathered from a number of different sources and were not necessarily first editions. The pages of these original books were scanned and therefore do reproduce any printing flaws and errors. The books are manufactured by Martins the Printers at Berwick-upon-Tweed. Text pages are printed digitally on traditional cream Bookwove with colour and black-and-white plates printed digitally on gloss art paper. Once the contents are printed, the book is glued and lined, followed by trimming, adding the endpapers and the crepe lining which are glued onto the book-block to give strength to the book. The case material is similar to the green library buckram cloth used in the original series and this is cut to size, glued to the boards and sized to match the blook-block. The finished book is then assembled by pasting the endpapers and attaching the book-block inside the case. Once left in book clamp overnight for the glues to dry, the final process is the fitting of the dust jacket.

So as to avoid any confusion among collectors, it was important from the start to ensure that these POD editions of the New Naturalist library were clearly different from the genuine first editions. Although they appear quite similar at first, there are three main differences which set them apart.

1. The dust jackets are digitally printed on glossy laminated paper. They are also made up of two pieces of paper, joined to the left of the spine. The price on the inside flap of the jacket is £50. On the rear inside flap there is the official statement: 'This edition is a print on demand edition produced from an original copy by Collins. For further information go to www. newnaturalists.com'. The colours on the jackets tend to be slightly brighter than those on the originals and in some cases there have been some minor graphical changes to the text and NN logo on the spines.

2. At the foot of the imprint page, the official print-on-demand statement is repeated from the inside flap.

3. Although bound in the usual dark green buckram, there is no title or NN logo printed on the spines of the books.

All of the out of print titles available from NN1 *Butterflies* to NN100 *Woodlands* can be ordered on the HarperCollins website. Collins propose to gradually add other New Naturalist titles to the POD catalogue as they go out of print. Only in a few special cases will these books actually be reprinted. Although some collectors have taken the opportunity to purchase the full set, it is unlikely that these books will ever become particularly collectable as they are not printed in a defined edition. Providing Collins continue to offer them, an unlimited number can be ordered at any time. The success of these editions has prompted Collins to also make available the set of 22 Monographs from January 2011, expanding still further the range of NN titles now available to any reader or collector.

FACSIMILE EDITIONS

Early in 2008 the Folio Society in association with HarperCollins produced the first ten volumes in the New Naturalist series as facsimile editions. These were almost exact replicas to the originals with coloured plates, good reproductions of the Ellis dust jackets and bound in the familiar dark green buckram. Original books were scanned from copies in the Collins archive and the facsimile editions were printed and bound by Martins in Berwick-upon-Tweed. Unlike the print-on-demand books, which

state clearly that they are not the originals, these facsimile editions are not marked anywhere to betray the fact that they are not the genuine first edition; only their fresh new condition gives them away. It is an evocative sensation to leaf through one of these facsimile editions and to imagine what these early books might have looked like, gleaming in the bookshops when they were originally published in the 1940s.

The books were available either individually or as part of a rather elegant boxed set. The box itself was covered in dark green cloth with the New Naturalist logo printed in gold on the sides. 1004 sets were produced in the slip-case, with a run on of a further 150 of each individual title.

The facsimile volumes are pleasing objects. They are about the same weight and the reproduction of the plates is also very good, if not quite equal to those in the original book. The gold lettering and NN colophon on the spines is also not quite as sharp as the original but overall they are excellent reproductions. The greatest disappointment is the dust wrapper, not so much in its reproduction and printing but in the graphic art re-working which has been necessary to make them look like new books. It is clear that the original jackets which were scanned were perhaps not in the best of condition, and in most cases the designs, particularly on the spines, have been spruced up and the white areas brightened. The worst example is *Mushrooms and Toadstools,* where the text, colophon and circle containing the number at the head of the spine have been brightened, but the rest of the spine is a uniform muddy brown – quite unlike the original design, which would have been banded with white, greens and browns.

Initially the books were only available to members of the Folio Society, but it later became possible to purchase them from HarperCollins or booksellers such as the NHBS. The boxed set seems only to have been available from the Folio Society and this may well become a rare and sought-after item.

The books have only just begun to creep onto the second-hand market and it will be interesting to see how collectable they become. Perhaps they will mature to be even more valuable than the original first editions; certainly there are fewer of them. HarperCollins confirm that the books are now out of print and they do not have any plans to produce further facsimile editions.

THE LEATHERBOUND EDITIONS

To celebrate the 100th volume in the New Naturalist library, Myles Archibald had the inspired idea that HarperCollins would produce a special limited leatherbound edition of that title. For a while, as the fluid production schedules were taking shape, it was not clear which volume would be the 100th book. Once *Woodlands* by Oliver Rackham was set to be that special volume, a flier was produced by Collins advertising it. Only 100 copies were to be bound in leather, each one being numbered and signed by the author. The book was advertised as bound in dark brown Ross Napa leather, featuring gilt edges and raised bands on the

The first 10 New Naturalist volumes were re-issued as facsimile editions produced by the Folio Society in 2008. These excellent reproductions were available individually or as a boxed set (above).

spine and supplied in a buckram linen slipcase. In order to acquire one of these books, the application form had to be sent back to Collins in time for a ballot held on 21 August 2006. There was a huge amount of interest in this special edition and hundreds of application forms arrived at the HarperCollins offices in Hammersmith. Those lucky enough to be selected were then given the opportunity to buy one of these books for £250.

Originally the leatherbound version of *Woodlands* was to have been a 'one-off' but Collins were surprised by the great deal of interest in this book. After much discussion they decided to continue to produce further leatherbound titles in the series. The next one to be offered was *Dragonflies*, and once again a ballot was organised for 16 June 2008. Originally offered as a limited edition of 400, as a plate pasted onto the front free endpaper states, the run was in fact cut to 250. A replacement plate was soon sent out to all purchasers of the book to confirm the new and more exclusive shorter run. Similarly *Southern England* also had an extra erratum slip which was printed and distributed to all those who had purchased that edition. The original bookplate stated that 250 copies were available but the final figure was only 150.

Since *Dragonflies*, all New Naturalist titles have been available as a limited edition leatherbound cook, the print run slowly decreasing from 250, to 150, to 100, 75 and currently 50 copies of each title. There are also eight extra leatherbound copies distributed to the author(s) and members of the Editorial Board. Rather than being numbered, these copies are lettered with A (and sometimes B), going to the author(s), B/C to F/G are randomly distributed to the five members of the Editorial Board and the final two, G/H are for the Chief Executive Officer at HarperCollins and the Collins archive respectively.

Once the excitement over the *Woodlands* edition settled down, the other leatherbound editions have not attracted nearly so much interest and they are all relatively easy to acquire either through the HarperCollins website or on the second-hand market. *Woodlands* still has that legendary appeal and is probably the most valuable and sought-after leatherbound title.

These editions are bound and prepared in a series of 40 stages. This includes gilding on all three edges, binding in Nigerian goatskin leather, raised bands followed by blocking and embossing. The cover has the NN logo blind-embossed with gold blocking

TABLE 22

TITLE	LIMITED EDITION	RELEASE DATE
Woodlands	100	4 September 2006
Dragonflies	250 (400)	1 July 2008
Grouse	250	6 October 2008
Southern England	150 (250)	3 November 2008
Islands	150	5 February 2009
Wildfowl	150	10 June 2009
Dartmoor	100	8 October 2009
Books and Naturalists	75	26 February 2010
Bird Migration	75	29 April 2010
Badger	75	24 June 2010
Climate and Weather	75	14 October 2010
Plant Pests	50	17 February 2011
Plant Galls	50	12 May 2011
Marches	50	13 October 2011
Scotland	50	16 February 2012
Grasshoppers & Crickets	50	2 August 2012

applied to the spine. The leather binding is undoubtedly luxurious, but some collectors felt the lack of the cover art makes them less desirable than the main series. HarperCollins responded to this and from the publication of *Books and Naturalists* in February 2010, the leatherbound editions have been issued with dust jackets, which are also signed on the inside flap by Robert Gillmor.

BOOKCLUB EDITIONS

The bookclubs

Introduction

Before the dissolution of the Net Book Agreement in 1995, bookclubs were a major force within the new-book market, often working hand in hand with publishers. They are of particular interest to the New Naturalist collector as many NN titles were offered through the clubs, particularly the *Readers Union* (RU). In fact many more than commonly believed – probably around 50 titles, though it could well have been more. The relationship between the New Naturalist and the bookclubs was a long one, spanning a 43-year period: the first title to be published by the RU was *Butterflies* in 1953 and the last to be sold by *Book Club Associates* (BCA) was *The New Naturalists* in 1995.

In 1986 bookclub membership was about 2.5 million and book sales through the clubs was worth around £100 million. This represented around 20 per cent of the total value of all hardback sales to individuals, and as books sold through the clubs were on average 30 per cent below the publisher's net price, in quantity terms, the proportion was significantly larger.

The traditional bookclub was a mail-order operation through which selected books were sold direct to the public at a price significantly below the net book price, in return for a commitment to buy a particular number of books over a given period. Bookclubs, being mail order, were able to keep their

The leatherbound edition of *Woodlands* (left), which marked the 100th volume in the New Naturalist library. Although originally designed to be a one-off publication, leatherbound editions continue to be available, usually as a limited editions of 50 copies. The numbered plate pasted onto the front free endpaper and signed by the author (right).

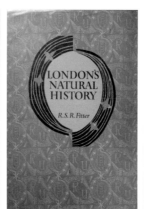

The two styles of Readers Union jacket were well designed in an understated manner, and were very much of their time: they sit well on the shelf together but not when in the company of the Ellis/Gillmor designs of the Collins edition.

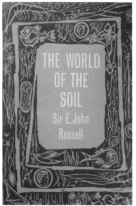
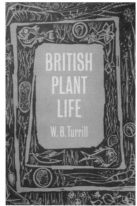
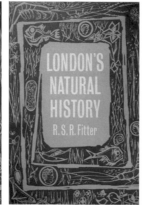
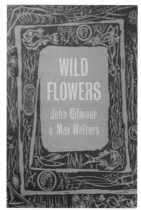

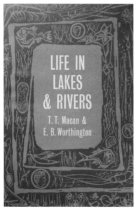
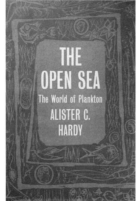
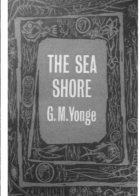
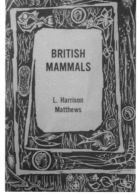

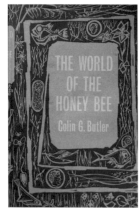

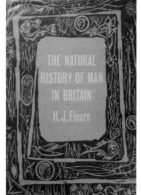

operational costs low and this, coupled with their buying power, meant they could pass on large saving to their customers. Bookclubs operated under the conditions of the Net Book Agreement and were administered by the Publishers' Association (PA). These conditions stated that membership was required for a period of not less than six months and that members must purchase within the first period of membership no fewer than three bookclub choices (excluding premiums). Premiums were titles offered to new members at a very large discount as an inducement to join. Under the regulations, net books could not be offered as premiums until at least six months after first publication as a trade edition. New books could be offered through the bookclubs at the same time they became available through the book trade (pre-1968 bookclubs had to wait at least nine months), but could only be offered to members as dedicated bookclub reprints six months after publication. These later reprints were often offered at even lower prices.

Members ordered books from catalogues issued on a monthly or quarterly basis. Bookclubs could not sell their books in shops, but paradoxically membership was often promoted through bookshops. Books produced for and by bookclubs are often without ISBNs, barcodes and printed prices, though this is not always the case, and with many NN titles it is impossible to distinguish a Collins edition from a bookclub issue. The dissolution of the Net Book Agreement allowed supermarkets, large bookshop chains and internet retailers such as Amazon to offer books at significantly discounted prices. This quickly undermined the traditional bookclub market, and most were soon marginalised.

The PA maintained a register of bookclubs and in 1986 there were around 70 listed, including 22 clubs owned by BCA and 18 owned by the RU. The largest player by far was BCA, who owned the very large general bookclubs, *Literary Guild* and *World Books*. *Leisure Circle* was in second place with the RU in third. Whilst the general bookclubs had memberships of hundreds of thousands, the average membership of BCA's 18 specialist clubs was 20,000 and RU's 16 specialist clubs under 10,000 with their smallest club having a membership of just 5,000. NN titles by

TABLE 23 Category 1: Bookclub editions with different jackets and dedicated title pages.

Class No	Title	Pub. date	Copy of:	Price	Title page	Casing	Dust jacket
BC1B	*Butterflies*	1953	1946 reprint	10s. 6d	RU imprint, cancel	Buckram, Collins to spine, Readers Union stamped in gilt to rear board	RU Jacket type 1 (repeating RU motifs)
BC2A	*British Game*	1953	1946 reprint	10s. 6d	RU imprint, cancel	Buckram, Collins to spine, Readers Union stamped in gilt to rear board	RU Jacket type 1 (repeating RU motifs)
BC2B	*British Game*	1959	1946 reprint	13s. 6d.	RU imprint, integral	Buckram, Collins to spine	RU Jacket type 2 (wildlife motifs)
BC3A	*London's Natural History*	1953	1946 reprint	10s. 6d	RU imprint, cancel	Buckram, Collins to spine, Readers Union stamped in gilt to rear board	RU Jacket type 1 (repeating RU motifs)
BC3B	*London's Natural History*	1959	1946 reprint	13s. 6d.	RU imprint, cancel	Buckram, Collins to spine	RU Jacket type 2 (wildlife motifs)
BC5A	*Wild Flowers*	1959	1955 new ed.	15s.	RU imprint, cancel	imitation cloth, RU to spine	RU Jacket type 2 (wildlife motifs)
BC7A	*Mushrooms*	1960	1959 3rd imp.	17s.	RU imprint, integral	imitation cloth , RU to spine	RU Jacket type 2 (wildlife motifs)
BC10A	*British Plant Life*	1953	1948 1st ed.	10s. 6d	RU imprint, cancel	Buckram, Collins to spine, Readers Union stamped in gilt to rear board	RU Jacket type 1 (repeating RU motifs)
BC10A	*British Plant Life*	1959	1958 end ed.	17s.	RU imprint, integral	imitation cloth, RU to spine	RU Jacket type 2 (wildlife motifs)
BC12A	*The Sea Shore*	1959	1958 reprint	15s.	RU imprint, integral	imitation cloth, RU to spine	RU Jacket type 2 (wildlife motifs)
BC15A	*Life, Lakes & Rivers*	1959	1959 reprint	17s.	RU imprint, integral	imitation cloth, RU to spine	RU Jacket type 2 (wildlife motifs)
BC18A	*Natural History Man*	1959	1959 reprint	15s.	RU imprint, cancel	imitation cloth, RU to spine	RU Jacket type 2 (wildlife motifs)
BC21A	*British Mammals*	1960	1960 2nd ed.	15s.	RU imprint, integral	Buckram, RU to spine	RU Jacket type 2 (wildlife motifs)
BC29A	*World Honeybee*	1959	1958 reprint	15s.	RU imprint, integral	imitation cloth, RU to spine	RU Jacket type 2 (wildlife motifs)
BC34A	*Open Sea 1 (Plankton)*	1959	1958 reprint	17s.	RU imprint, integral	imitation cloth, RU to spine	RU Jacket type 2 (wildlife motifs)
BC35A	*World of the Soil*	1959	1959 2nd ed.	15s.	RU imprint, integral	Imitation cloth, RU to spine	RU Jacket type 2 (wildlife motifs)
BC50A	*Pesticides and Pollution*	1967	1967 1st ed.	not stated	Scientific BC integral	Blue imitation cloth, black title to spine, no imprint	Brown and black featuring a tractor.
BCM7A	*Fleas, Flukes, Cuckoos*	1953	1952 rep.	10s. 6d	RU imprint, integral	Buckram, RU imprint to spine	RU Jacket type 1 (repeating RU motifs)
BCM22A	*The Mole*	1973	rep.	not stated	The Country BC, integral	Greyish imitation cloth, Country Book Club stamped to the spine	Same Ellis jacket with RU logo to spine.

their quasi-academic nature would have been sold via these small specialist clubs with their comparatively low memberships – even with the marketing clout of the bookclubs, the New Naturalist remained the preserve of an enlightened few.

BCA was founded in 1966 and dominated the bookclub market in the 1970s and 80s, but following this period of plenty, like all bookclubs, its fortunes tumbled. It switched emphasis to internet sales and was sold to the Webb Group in March 2011, but a year later Book Club Associates collapsed following the administration of the (new) parent company. However, few NN titles were sold through the BCA and these were mostly, if not always, unadulterated Collins editions, but perhaps with price-clipped jackets.

Originally established in 1937, *Readers Union* was the umbrella organisation for a group of specific subject area bookclubs – needlecraft, gardening, equestrian pursuits, photography etc. – but of most interest to us was their *Country Book Club*, through which numerous New Naturalist titles were sold. (This club appeared to change its name on a fairly regular basis and was also called the *Country Book Society* and *Country & Gardeners Book Society*; later it became the *Birds and Natural History Society*). In 1971, *David and Charles* (D&C) of Newton Abbot, Devon, bought *Readers Union* and the RU bookclubs flourished for the next 20 years. In 2000, D&C were acquired by the US publisher F+W Publications (now F+W Media), but by this time the bookclubs were beginning to fail. In 2008 D&C appointed their current managing director 'to see through the closure of our negative option bookclub business' and in July 2009 the clubs were closed. It marked the end of 72 years of the *Readers Union* bookclubs and an important chapter in the history of the New Naturalist.

The relationship between publisher and bookclub
Certainly an interesting one: on the face of it the publisher takes all the risks and makes the investment, and bookclubs are able to buy in without the risk or overheads. Essentially this is the case, but the bookclubs enable economies of scale and guarantee a significant sale, thereby underwriting the operation for the publisher. Where a bookclub run of between 4,000 and 10,000 copies was added to a publisher's run of a similar size, the unit costs of production could be reduced by between 30 and 50 per cent. New Naturalists were typically printed in this range and therefore deals with bookclubs were particularly attractive. (Economies of scale in production were largely exhausted at print runs over 15,000.) Additionally, the profit level per unit is much greater for the publisher than the bookclub.

Publishers may have been reticent to enter into an agreement with a bookclub for a new title, wishing to retain exclusivity, but once interest surrounding that title had waned, a deal with a bookclub became more attractive and might be the only way of ensuring the viability of a reprint. The minutes of the Editorial Board meeting of January 1958 record, 'The Editors were told of an offer from the Readers Union to take 2000 copies of nine New Naturalist titles for a special Readers Union edition. This offer would help considerably with reprints of books such as *The Weald*. The Editors welcomed the suggestion and gave their wholehearted agreement, so long as the New Naturalist is prominently mentioned in all Readers Union editions of these books.' (In the event, 12 NN titles were published by the RU during 1959 and 1960 – see table 23 on page 85).

Typically for 'whole deals' (printing plus royalty), bookclubs paid around 20 per cent of the net book price, i.e. an 80 per cent discount. Remember that the discount given to retailers was usually between 35 and 40 per cent, so bookclubs were paying significantly less but were purchasing hundreds or thousands of copies. The unit cost of producing extra copies for bookclubs was often as low as 5 per cent of the net book price, so the publisher still stood to make a profit from additional copies specifically manufactured for bookclubs. In an internal Collins memo dated 7 August 1986, BCA placed an order for 300 copies of *The New Forest*, but specified that the jacket be unpriced and without a bar code, plus 30 extra jackets (in the event the price was omitted but the barcode retained). £5 was paid per copy, which was made up from £1.34 manufacturing cost, 50 pence royalty (10 per cent of the price received – all to the author) and £3.16 mark-up. In another internal Collins memo, dated 5 April 1995, the deal was a lot less attractive: it was agreed to sell 250 copies from stock of *The New Naturalists* to BCA at £3.30 per copy made up from a £2.19 unit manufacturing cost, 33 pence royalty (10 per cent) and 78 pence mark-up.

Collins's relationship with the bookclubs was at times unquestionably expediential: that is, they used them as a quasi remaindering service. An internal memo dated 27 November 1978, which lists stock levels of titles in the series, finishes with the statement: 'Suggest we try to sell more stock to Readers Union …and possibly at even lower profit margins than usual to shift the stock'. Undoubtedly, during the 1970s and 80s many NN titles were sold off from stock in dribs and drabs to the RU, but such books were mostly reprints. These books are, of course, indistinguishable but for the fact that they were often price-clipped by the bookclubs, which explains why, with some titles, there appears to be a preponderance of clipped jackets, e.g. the reprint of the 1976 second edition of *Snowdonia National Park* (NN47C).

Rarely did bookclubs become involved directly in the content or layout of a book, leaving this to the publisher, but they might suggest subject areas of which they were short or felt would do well. Such involvement was usually confined to general bookclubs, though, and there is no evidence that Collins ever worked with a bookclub on a New Naturalist title at the inception or design stages. However, clearly discussions were taking place at the printing and binding stage, hence the existence of cheaper bookclub bindings. Often a bookclub ordered a new printing of a book already published and had it bound in their prescribed livery. A helpful feature of early Readers Union books was to include details of the font used on the imprint page, e.g. *The Sea Shore*, 1959: 'It is set in 11 pt Baskerville type leaded'.

An overview

The first New Naturalist titles to be offered to members of the Readers Union were *Butterflies, British Game, London's Natural History* and *British Plant Life*, all published in 1953. Collins held large stocks of these titles (around 6,000 each) but sales by this stage were comparatively slow so they agreed to sell 3,000 of each to the RU – at less than cost (in effect remaindering). The books for the first three titles were the Collins reprints of 1946, and in the case of *British Plant Life* the 1948 first edition; and were already bound in the traditional NN livery of green buckram, gilt-stamped with the Collins imprint and NN monogram to the spine; but to identify these copies as RU editions 'READERS UNION' was gilt-stamped to the bottom right-hand corner of the rear board. The existing title pages were excised and new title pages (cancels), displaying the Readers Union logo pasted in. The imprint page now stated: 'This edition has been made specially available to members of Readers Union. It was first published by William Collins and was printed and bound by them at the Clear-type Press, Glasgow'. *Fleas, Flukes and Cuckoos* was also published in 1953 by the RU, but this was specially printed as a 'run-on'.

Perhaps the most significant difference is the dust jacket, a bespoke Readers Union design of repeating RU and book motifs by Kenneth Lindley, printed in green and claret and used for all the 1953 titles. The title is situated within a central cartouche to the front panel, and the rear panel bears press endorsements and the statement: 'A Readers Union additional choice'. The front flap states: 'This volume must not be sold to the general public…' and diagonally across the bottom corner: 'for sale to Readers Union members only at 10s.6d net'. (The Collins editions at this time cost 21s.) The jackets were printed on thin, acidic paper and consequently are usually in poor condition or missing altogether.

In 1959/60 a further 12 NN titles were offered by the RU, but most of these had been specially printed for the RU, so had integral title pages and were bound in imitation cloth with the RU logo blocked to the spine. However, a couple of titles (*British Game* BC2B and *London's Natural History* BC3B) were sold to the RU from bound stock and so are characterised by Collins buckram casings and cancel title pages; seemingly *Wild Flowers* BC5A was sold to the RU from unbound stock and so has bookclub casings and cancel title pages. The jackets were changed to a more simplified and abstract design featuring an array of plants and animals, and printed in various shades of green and blue. The rear panel and flap are blank but for the solid ground colour and although printed on thin paper, they are better wearing than the 1953 jackets.

Pesticides and Pollution was published by the *Scientific Bookclub* (owned by the famous London bookshop, *Foyles*) in 1967, but in a slightly smaller format and without any photographic plates. It was bound in blue cloth and had an entirely different jacket. While a scarce book, there appears to be little demand for it, unlike its Collins sibling.

The Mole, in 1973, was the last New Naturalist to be offered by a bookclub (RU) in a bespoke binding: cream imitation cloth with a dedicated (integral) title page, though the dust jacket features the same Ellis design and is essentially a facsimile of the Collins jacket but with the RU logo on the spine.

From the mid-1970s NN titles continued to be available as bookclub editions but with minimal distinguishing characteristics. Indeed, some were identical and therefore cannot be separated as bookclub editions. Collins reprinted a number of earlier titles between 1976 and 1978 in part collaboration with the RU and consequently many of these reprints appear with the bookclub distinctions, albeit subtle. Collins agreed to a run-on of a few hundred extra copies for the RU, which subsidised the reprint costs for Collins. It would appear that the last title to be sold by a bookclub (BCA) was *The New Naturalists* in 1995 and was identical to the Collins edition.

The two styles of RU jackets used for their NN titles were well designed in an understated manner and were very much of their time; they sit well together on the shelf. However, bookclub editions are generally not regarded as being particularly desirable or collectable. Undoubtedly, some of the Readers Union 1976–1978 reprints are rare, having been printed in very small numbers – which underlines the fact that more than rarity alone is required to make a book valuable.

Identifying New Naturalist bookclub 'editions'

Unbeknown to their owners, it would appear that the ranks of many New Naturalist collections have been infiltrated by a bookclub impostor or two. As already identified, some books sold through the bookclubs were identical to the Collins editions, and therefore distinction is confined to provenance, which should be academic (although these copies were often price-clipped by the bookclubs). Other bookclub editions are so different that they could never masquerade as a Collins edition, but there are a good number which are very similar; the distinguishing features of which are particularly subtle. As a general rule of thumb a dust jacket without a printed price usually indicates that it is of bookclub origin, as does a jacket without a *Duraseal* protector printed between 1977 and 1982; imitation cloth is often another indicator. The situation is somewhat complicated by the fact that Collins occasionally 'borrowed' bookclub stock, to which they added their price stickers, once their own stock had run out.

As many collectors limit their attentions to first editions, it is bookclub editions which are ostensibly the same and have been issued concurrently with Collins first editions, that we have to be most wary of, but all such pretenders are identified in table 24. To aid identification, bookclub editions can be divided into three broad categories:

1. Books with a bookclub title page (either a cancel or integral), bookclub imprint stamped to the binding and with a bespoke jacket. These are all Readers Union books with the exception of *Pesticides*, published by Scientific Bookclub (Foyles).
2. Books that are textually identical to the Collins edition, with the same lettering stamped to the casing and the same

TABLE 24 Category 2: Bookclub editions ostensibly as Collins eds. but with distinguishing features. Titles highlighted in bold were issued concurrently with the Collins first edition, with which they are easily confused.

Code	No. Printed	Title	Date and Edition:	Distinguishing Features Dust Jacket	Distinguishing Features Binding Fabric
BC1B	??	*Butterflies*	1977 rep.	Unpriced, no *Duraseal*	Imitation cloth
BC5B	500	*Wild Flowers*	1978 rep.	Unpriced, no *Duraseal*	Imitation cloth
BC6BA	500	*The Highlands and Islands*	1977 rep.	Unpriced, no *Duraseal*	Imitation cloth
BC7B	unknown	*Mushrooms & Toadstools*	1977 rep.	Not Seen.	Imitation cloth
BC11A	500	*Mountains and Moorlands*	1977 rep.	Unpriced, no *Duraseal*	Imitation cloth
BC19A	500	*Wild Orchids of Britain*	1976 rep.	Price-clipped, with *Duraseal*	Imitation cloth
BC27A	500	*Dartmoor*	1977 rep.	Unpriced, no *Duraseal*	Imitation cloth
BC29B	500	*World of the Honeybee*	1977 rep.	Price-clipped, no *Duraseal*	Imitation cloth
BC30A	500	*Moths*	1976 rep.	Unpriced, with *Duraseal*	Imitation cloth
BC32A	350	*Trees, Woods, Man*	1978 rep.	Unpriced, no *Duraseal*	Imitation cloth
BC52A	1,000[?]	*Woodland Birds*	1976 rep.	Unpriced, no *Duraseal*	Imitation cloth
B53A	unknown	*The Lake District*	1977 rep.	Unpriced, no *Duraseal*	Imitation cloth
BC58A	3,850	*Hedges*	1975 rep.	Unpriced, no price sticker, with *Duraseal*	Identical – buckram
BC58B	Inc. above	*Hedges*	1977 rep.	Unpriced, no price sticker, with *Duraseal*	Identical – buckram
BC58C	Inc. above	*Hedges*	1979 rep.	Unpriced, no *Duraseal*	Imitation cloth
BC60A	**6,150**	***Birds of Prey***	**1976 1st ed.**	**Unpriced, with *Duraseal***	**Imitation cloth**
BC60B	Inc. above	*Birds of Prey*	1978 rep.	Unpriced, with *Duraseal*	Imitation cloth
BC60C	Inc. above	*Birds of Prey*	1979 rep.	Unpriced, no *Duraseal*	Imitation cloth
BC61A	**500[?]**	***Inheritance***	**1977 1st ed.**	**Unpriced, no *Duraseal***	**Imitation cloth**
BC62A	**9,262**	***British Tits***	**1979 1st ed.**	**Unpriced, no *Duraseal***	**Imitation cloth**
BC62B	Inc. above	*British Tits*	1980 rep.	Unpriced, no *Duraseal*	Imitation cloth
BC63A	**7,880**	***British Thrushes***	**1978 1st ed.**	**Price-clipped, no *Duraseal***	**Imitation cloth**
BC65A	**5,300**	***Waders***	**1980 1st ed.**	**Unpriced, no *Duraseal***	**Imitation cloth**
BC65B	Inc. above	*Waders*	1981 rep.	Unpriced, no *Duraseal*	Imitation cloth
BC65C	Inc. above	*Waders*	1982 rep.	Unpriced, no *Duraseal*	Imitation cloth
BC67A	**1,590[?]**	***Farming & Wildlife***	**1981 1st ed.**	**Unpriced, otherwise identical**	**Identical – buckram**
BC72A	**2,000**	***Heathlands***	**1986 1st ed.**	**Unpriced, Collins not printed to spine**	**Identical – buckram**
BC73A	**650**	***The New Forest***	**1986 1st ed.**	**Unpriced, Collins not printed to spine**	**Identical – buckram**
BCM1	??	*The Badger*	1976 rep.	Unpriced, no *Duraseal*	Imitation cloth

Collins dust jacket but with all or a combination of the following distinguishing features:

    i. cheaper imitation cloth binding,
    ii. dust jacket without *Duraseal*,
    iii. dust jacket without a printed price,
    iv. dust jacket without Collins printed to the spine.

In addition to the titles identified in table 24 there were a number of other titles reprinted in 1976/77 and these reprints may have been published by the RU with similar distinguishing features: NN12 *Seashore*, 1976; NN16 *Wild Flowers of Chalk*, 1976; NN37 *Open Sea II*, 1976; NN38 *Spiders*, 1976; NN47 *Snowdonia*, 1976; and NN23 *Angler's Entomology*, 1977. But to date hard copies have not come to light and there is no conclusive archival evidence available.

3. Books sold through the bookclubs with no distinguishing features, but dust jackets probably price-clipped. It is impossible physically to distinguish these books from ordinary Collins editions, so information must be gleaned from Collins sales statements and minutes, bookclub catalogues and the accounts of collectors, but the following

list is unlikely to be definitive: NN59 *Ants*; NN66 *Natural History of Wales* 1982 reprint (NN66B); NN68 *Mammals*; NN69 *Reptiles and Amphibians*; NN70 *Orkney* paperback (CPB70A); NN71 *Warblers* paperback (CPB71A); and NN82 *The New Naturalists* (NN82AA). Additionally, other titles were regularly 'remaindered' to the bookclubs.

THE NET BOOK AGREEMENT, REPRICING AND DECIMALISATION

The Net Book Agreement

The Net Book Agreement (NBA) was the principal foundation upon which the British publishing industry operated for almost the whole of the twentieth century. It prescribed the way books were sold and, by extension, published.

The NBA was an agreement between publishers and booksellers put in place in 1899 which set the prices at which books were to be sold to the public. A *net book* was a book published at a net price, i.e. at a price fixed by the publisher below which it shall not be sold to the public. It regulated profit margins to guarantee a reasonable income to both publisher and bookseller. Net books were supplied to booksellers at trade terms of between 30 and 40 per cent discount, subject to 'the standard conditions of sale of net books'. Publishers would refuse to stock any bookseller who broke these terms by offering books at prices lower than the *net published price*. However most retailers believed the arrangement worked in their favour too, so very rarely did this happen. Additionally, it was commonplace for booksellers to be supplied on a sale or return basis, so the need to discount was rarely an issue, though there was a clause which allowed old stock to be sold at reduced prices during the National Book Sale.

The NBA, through the National Book Sale, provided a mechanism for publishers and retailers to sell-off overstocks at discounted prices, and through the bookclubs (see page 83), also regulated by the NBA, publishers were able to remainder books and take advantages of economies of scale when printing.

In 1962 the Restrictive Practices Court examined the NBA, but declared that it was in the public interest as it enabled publishers to subsidise and promote works of less well-known authors or of an esoteric nature. But by the 1990s change was in the air, the free market was in full flow, competition was encouraged and *the public interest* was served by low prices and seemingly that alone. The NBA came under increasing pressure and in 1997 found itself again subject to the attention of the Restrictive Practices Court, but this time the court declared it illegal. The demise of the NBA triggered the mass closure of independent bookshops; by 1999, 500 had closed and figures from the Booksellers Association show that at the end of 2011 barely 1,000 independent booksellers were left.

While the NBA might have kept prices artificially inflated, it undoubtedly simplified matters for the purchaser as the price on the jacket was the price to be paid (and note how the printed price was usually appended with 'NET') and wherever a book was stocked, the price remained the same. There was no need for tedious internet searches to find the keenest price. Today the price on the jacket serves little more purpose than to determine the amount by which the book has been discounted, and certainly the price will vary from seller to seller.

Until the 1990s most New Naturalists were sold through independent booksellers, either directly or via mail-order subscription, and it was common practice for these bookshops to add their (usually discreet) label to the book (see above). While some collectors look upon these labels as blemishes, they do add a small layer of history. In the days of the NBA the relationship between publisher and bookseller was very much a symbiotic one; they were interdependent and regularly worked together on advertising, for instance the NN Board minutes for a meeting held on the 13 April 1961 record that special bookcases had been made up to hold 36 NN titles and were being lent to selected bookshops. Prospectuses for new titles were often undertaken by bookshops rather than the publisher, e.g. those for *Mountain Flowers* and *Angler's Entomology*. But in today's global market, such parochial relationships are all but obsolete. The majority of NN titles are now sold via mail-order and the internet.

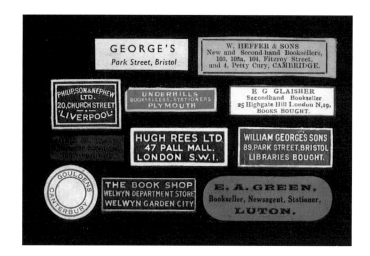

Traditional booksellers' labels add a small layer of history.

25^{s. net}

£1·80 net

£2.25 net
45s. net

It was not unusual to reprice books by clipping the original price and over-stamping with the new price. Books published around 1971, when the pound was decimalised, were printed with both pre- and decimal prices; the predecimal price was always printed nearer the corner, so later it could be clipped off leaving the decimal price (middle). At decimalisation, books already printed and in stock were clipped and over-printed with the decimal price; alternatively a price label was used as shown on the next page.

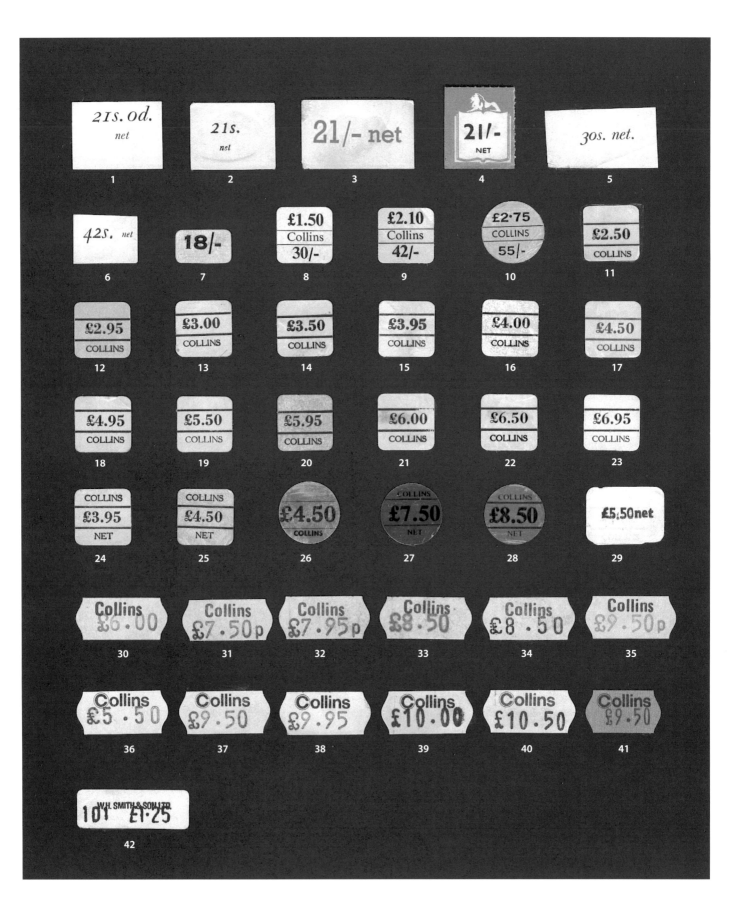

Comparative prices

The first New Naturalist *Butterflies* was sold in 1945 with a net price of 16 shillings, equivalent to around £29 at 2012 prices. However, by 1948 the net price had increased to 21 shillings and *Mushrooms and Toadstools*, published in 1953, was priced at 30s net; that is about £32 and £35 respectively at 2012 prices. A modern New Naturalist has a recommended retail price of £50, however that is misleading as, post the NBA, rarely would it be sold for that price: an average Amazon price for a new title would be between £30 and £35 pounds, with free postage. Therefore, in real terms, a NN at the inception of the series cost about the same as a new title today. But through the history of the series prices have fluctuated: at publication in 1952 *The Fulmar* cost the equivalent of £43, whereas *Squirrels* and *The Rabbit* cost around £17. Tellingly, perhaps, when the series was in crisis net prices increased significantly: *Orkney* and *Warblers* cost the equivalent of £51; *The New Forest* £56, and the most expensive of all *Ferns* was £68 – and when these titles were sold no discounts were available. (2012 values have been calculated using the Bank of England inflation calculator.)

Price labels

Nos 1, 2, 5 and 6 are hand cut and therefore often irregular; pasted on; no. 3 probably pasted on; no. 4 self-gummed (lick and stick); all the remaining are self-adhesive, sticker-type labels. No. 1–22 have printed prices, the remaining are machine priced on printed labels. The approximate dates when each price was used are shown in table 25.

Inflation, repricing and decimalisation

Today, books tend to remain in print for only a year or so, but this has not always been the case and it was commonplace for books including NN titles to be in print for many years, sometimes decades. Unless the net book price was periodically increased, inflation had the effect of reducing that price in real terms, sometimes significantly. *The Greenshank*, which stayed in print for 15 years without a price increase, at the end of this period cost in real terms about half that of when it was first published in 1951.

Unlike *The Greenshank*, the price of many NN titles was increased after a few years of being in print, as was the case in 1948. A contemporary flyer stated 'The price of New Naturalist volumes must regretfully be raised on July 1st, 1948, from 16s – 21s.' This entailed pasting a price label with the new price over the original printed price (see opposite). Later, books were repriced by clipping off the original price and over-printing with the revised price (see page 89); from around 1972 self-adhesive price stickers were generally used (see opposite).

During periods of high inflation, such as the 1970s and early 80s, publishers had to revise regularly, almost annually, the net prices of their stock (between 1972 and 1981 inflation averaged nearly 15 per cent a year). Considering the hundreds of titles across the Collins range that required re-pricing annually or bi-annually, this must have been both a logistically challenging and inexorably tedious task for the warehouse staff in Glasgow.

TABLE 25 Price labels: read in conjunction with image opposite.

No.	Price	Date	Notes
1–3	21s. net.	c. 1948–68	*Butterflies, British Game, London's Natural History*
4	21/- net	c. 1948–1952	'Book Production Economy Standard' *British Game, Insect Natural History* and probably others too
5	30s. net	c. 1962	*The Weald* reprint NN26c
6	42s. net	c. 1956–58	*The Fulmar*
7	18/-	c. 1960–70	From 1971–73 this was substituted with a 90p sticker
8–10	Dual-price stickers used at and a little after decimalisation in 1971		
11	£2.50	c. 1972–1974	
12	£2.95	c. 1975	
13	£3.00	c. 1975–76	
14	£3.50	c. 1975–76	
15	£3.95	c. 1976–77	
16	£4.00	c. 1975–76	
17	£4.50	c. 1976–77 (main series) c. 1978–79 (monographs)	
18	£4.95	c. 1976–78	
19	£5.50	c. 1977–79	
20	£5.95	c. 1977–78	
21	£6.00	c. 1976–1980	
22	£6.50	c. 1977–79	
23	£6.95	c. 1977–78	
24	£3.95	c. 1976–77	
25	£4.50	c. 1976–77	
26	£4.50	c. 1978–79	
27	£7.50	c. 1980–81	
28	£8.50	c. 1981	
29	£5.50	c. 1978–80	
30	£6.00	c. 1978–79	
31	£7.50p	c. 1980–81, 1984–85	
32	£7.95p	c. 1981	
33	£8.50	c. 1981	
34	£8.50	c. 1981	
35	£9.50p	c. 1981–84	
36	£5.50	c. 1978–1979	
37	£9.50	c. 1982–83	
39	£10.00	c. 1984–87	
40	£10.50	c. 1982	
41	£9.50	c. 1982–83 (atypical)	
42	W. H. Smith £1.25 sticker added to *The Salmon* 1968 third impression at decimalisation (jacket price 25/- net.)		

Opposite: Price labels associated with New Naturalist jackets (not all types and prices used are shown, but, for some unknown reason, books were never repriced at £5).

It is not that uncommon to see a price sticker placed over the top of an earlier one.

Decimalisation took place in 1971 and titles published around this time have both the old shilling price and the new decimal one printed on the jacket (see page 89). The old predecimal price was always positioned closest to the corner so it could be clipped off, leaving behind the decimal price. Books printed before 1971 but still on sale after decimalisation are frequently clipped and over-stamped with the new decimal price (see page 89).

Repriced jackets have a significant diagnostic role, as they allow us to determine, usually within 12 months or so, the year that that particular copy was sold (not printed). Additionally, they bear testimony to inflationary periods and perhaps most importantly from the collector's perspective they reduce the number of entire dust jackets available – and this can be considerable during periods of high inflation.

FOREIGN EDITIONS

In today's global economy, where books can be purchased online, from pretty much anywhere in the world, and English the established international language, the need for UK publishers to enter into publishing and distribution deals with overseas partners is no longer the necessity it once was. However, in the early days of the New Naturalist Collins worked hard to secure foreign interest, but there was (and remains) a fundamental stumbling block – The New Naturalist series is essentially concerned with British natural history and British geography, and as such does not export well. Of course, those titles that are not specific to the British Isles will have greater appeal to foreign publishers, and it is therefore not surprising that *The Art of Botanical Illustration*, *Insect Migration* and *The Folklore of Birds* all have multiple foreign editions. The monographs with their emphasis on a single subject, which may equally apply to other countries, have greater international appeal, as borne out by the preponderance published overseas; the record going to *The Herring Gull's World*, which has been translated into at least six foreign languages and has five US editions. To date over 60 foreign 'editions' have been discovered as identified in table 26,

though a good number of these are really no more than Collins editions, published or distributed by US publishers with perhaps a modified jacket and a cancel title page or distinguished by no more than an applied label.

Many foreign editions were printed in very small numbers and despite the concerted efforts of a number of collectors it has not been possible to track a few titles down, e.g. the US editions of *The World of the Honey Bee*. When a book is published in a language other than English, unless there is a reference to it in the Collins archive it will be very difficult to discover: to date the most obscure book to come to light is the Lithuanian translation of *The Herring Gull's World*, the dividends of many hours of internet investigation. Almost certainly there are others too awaiting discovery…

Inevitably, the US was the most important market outside Britain and well over half of all foreign editions are American; nearly every year during the 1950s, 60s and 70s a New Naturalist was published there, the first being *Insect Natural History* and *Botanical Illustration* in 1951 and finally *The Natural History of Pollination* in 1996. American books are often well made, in fact better made than their UK counterparts but not always elegantly so. US New Naturalists, which are ostensibly the same as the Collins edition, will frequently have slightly different specifications, for instance the boards may be thicker and jackets without *Duraseal*, and while we price our jackets to the lower corner of the front flap they price theirs to the top corner. During the 1970s, the American imprint Taplinger published a string of New Naturalist titles and contrary to the notion described above that country-specific titles do not have international appeal these books included *The Lake District* and *British Seals*, albeit in small numbers.

Japanese books have a justified reputation for being well produced, and the four Japanese NN titles (that we know of) are no exception, particularly *The Art of Botanical Illustration* housed in a slipcase.

Foreign New Naturalist books often have a modified suite of plates, or sometimes the plates may be the same but reversed. They are also apt to take greater liberties with the Ellises' jacket artwork, for instance the 1967 Anchor Books edition of *The Herring Gull* displays completely redrawn artwork that continues onto the rear cover; others sport newly commissioned jackets – varying in artistic accomplishment.

The New European Naturalist
At the Editorial Board meeting of 21st March 1949, under the heading 'The New European Naturalist' the subject of collaboration with overseas publishers was discussed and, sixty years later, offers a fascinating insight into the ambitions of the then Editors:

'The Chairman [James Fisher] read a letter which Mr Guest [Collins editorial staff] had received from Mr. Lars Holmberg of "Svensk Natur". In this letter it was suggested that the N.N.

A selection of foreign editions of New Naturalist volumes.

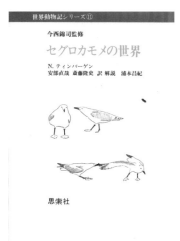

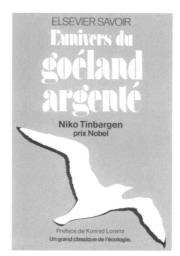

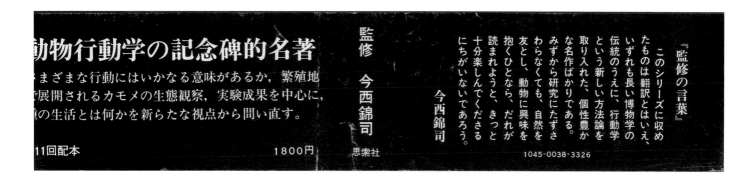

A selection of foreign editions of New Naturalist volumes, mostly of
Monograph titles such as the prolific *The Herring Gull's World*.

TABLE 26 Foreign editions of New Naturalist books. Over 60 are listed, but it is not unlikely that there are a few more still awaiting discovery. Many of those known, particularly the US editions are often little more than slightly modified versions of the Collins editions.

MAIN SERIES

Class no.	Title	Edition	Date	Publisher	Binding	Distinguishing features and notes	Print no.
US1A	Butterflies	US ed.	1957	Macmillan	h/b	as NN1C, casing and DJ with Macmillan	675
US1B	Butterflies	US ed., reprint	1962	Macmillan	h/b	unverified, presumed as NN1d but not seen	300
US7A	Mushrooms & Toadstools	US ed.	1954	Macmillan	h/b	exactly as NN7b with Macmillan label to DJ	850
US8A	Insect Natural History	US ed.	1951	Blakiston	h/b	as NN8A, cancel TP, bespoke binding; DJ not seen	1,000
US14A	Botanical Illustration	US ed.	1951	Scribner's	h/b		1,000
FOR14A	植物図譜の歴史 (Art of Botanical Illustration)	Japanese ed.	1986	Yasaka Shobo Inc.	h/b	not seen, in Japanese, h/b with DJ & slipcase; 4to format, extra clr illus.	?
US15A	Life in Lakes & Rivers	US ed.	1951	Macmillan?	h/b	not seen, presumed as NN15a with Macmillan label	100
US23A	An Angler's Entomology	US 1st ed.	1952	Praeger	h/b	as NN23A, with Praeger label to TP; DJ not seen	?
US23B	An Angler's Entomology	US 2nd ed.	1956	Countryman Press	h/b	as NN23B, integral TP, casing and DJ with Countryman	1,100
US23C	An Angler's Entomology	US 2nd ed., 1st rep.	1966	A. S. Barnes	h/b	as NN23C, integral TP, casing and DJ with Barnes	1,100
US23D	An Angler's Entomology	US 2nd ed., 2nd rep.	1973	A. S. Barnes	h/b	as NN23E, integral TP, casing and DJ with Barnes	1,000
US28A	Sea-Birds	US ed.	1954	Houghton Mifflin	h/b	as NN28A, integral TP, bespoke binding & DJ	2,500
US29A	World of the Honey Bee	US 1st ed.	1955	Macmillan	h/b	not seen, possibly no distinguishing marks	850
US29B	World of the Honey Bee	US 2nd rev. ed.	1975	Taplinger	h/b	not seen, possibly no distinguishing marks	500
FOR29B	Die Honigbiene (World of the Honey Bee)	German ed.	1957	Diederichs	h/b	in German, DJ, reduced no. plates	?
US30A	Moths	US ed.	1955	Macmillan	h/b	as NN30a with cancel TP; DJ not seen	1,000
US33A	Mountain Flowers	US ed.	1956	Macmillan	h/b	as NN33A, integral TP, casing with Macmillan	400
US34A	Open Sea: Plankton	US 1st ed.	1956	Houghton Mifflin	h/b	as NN34A, integral TP, bespoke binding & DJ	2,000
US34B	Open Sea: Plankton	US 1st reprint	1958	Houghton Mifflin	h/b	as NN34B, cancel TP, bespoke binding & DJ	1,600?
US34/37A	Open Sea (Plankton & Fish/Fisheries together)	US 1st one-volume ed.	1965	Houghton Mifflin	h/b	as NN34D/NN37B, integral TPs, bespoke binding & DJ	?
US34/37B	Open Sea (Plankton & Fish/Fisheries together)	US 1st one-volume ed., 1st reprint	1965	Houghton Mifflin	h/b	as above (US34/37A)	?
US34/37C	Open Sea (Plankton & Fish/Fisheries together)	US 1st one-volume ed., 2nd reprint	1970	Houghton Mifflin	h/b	as NN34E/NN37C, integral TPs, bespoke binding & DJ	?
US36A	Insect Migration	US ed.	1958	Macmillan	h/b	as NN36A, cancel TP, casing & DJ with Macmillan	500
FOR36A	Die Wanderflüge der Insekten (Insect Migration)	German ed.	1961	Paul Parey	h/b	in German, DJ, revised plates, no colour	?
FOR36B	昆虫の渡り (Insect Migration)	Japanese ed.	1986	Tsukiji Shokan	h/b	in Japanese, h/b with DJ, pp. 245, ISBN 4806722936	?
US37A	Open Sea: Fish & Fisheries	US 1st ed.	1959	Houghton Mifflin	h/b	as NN37A, integral TP, bespoke binding and DJ	2,500
US38A	World of Spiders	US ed.	1976	Taplinger	h/b	not seen, possibly no distinguishing marks	350
US39A	The Folklore of Birds	US 1st ed.	1959	Houghton Mifflin	h/b	as NN39A, integral TP, bespoke binding and DJ	990
US39B	The Folklore of Birds	US 2nd ed., revised and enlarged	1970	Dover	h/b	revised ed., bespoke binding & DJ	?
US40A	Bumblebees	US ed.	1959	Macmillan	h/b	as NN40A, cancel TP, casing & DJ with Macmillan	370
US43A	Weeds and Aliens	US ed.	1961	Macmillan	h/b		
US51A	Man and Birds	US ed.	1972	Taplinger	h/b	as NN51B, integral TP, casing & DJ with Macmillan	1,500
US53A	The Lake District	US ed.	1973	Taplinger	h/b	exactly as NN53A, with Taplinger label to DJ	350
US54A	Pollination of Flowers	US ed.	1972	Taplinger	h/b	as NN54A, integral TP, casing and DJ with Taplinger	1,500
US55A	Finches	US ed.	1973	Taplinger	h/b	as NN55A, integral TP, casing and DJ with Taplinger	1,540

Code	Title	Edition	Year	Publisher	Binding	Notes	No.
US56A	*Pedigree*	US ed.			h/b	bespoke binding and DJ	?
US57A	*British Seals*	US ed.	1974	Taplinger	h/b	as NN57A, integral TP, casing and DJ with Taplinger	1,500
US58A	*Hedges*	US ed.	1974	Taplinger	h/b	as NN58A, cancel TP, casing and DJ with Taplinger	540
US61A	*Inheritance & Natural History*	US ed.	1975	Taplinger	h/b	not seen, presumed as NN61A with Taplinger label?	350
US83A	*Natural History of Pollination*	US ed.	1978?	Taplinger	h/b	based on NN83b, bespoke binding and DJ	500
US83B	*Natural History of Pollination*	US ed.	1996	Timber Press	p/b	based on CPB83A	2,000

MONOGRAPHS

Code	Title	Edition	Year	Publisher	Binding	Notes	No.
FORM1A	ブナグマの森 (*The Badger*)	Japanese ed.	1974	Orion Press	h/b	in Japanese, h/b with DJ, pp. 241.	?
FORM1B	*Der Dachs* (*The Badger*)	German ed.	1975	Verlagsgesellschaft	h/b	in German, laminated boards, no DJ	?
FORM2A	*Rödstjärten* (*The Redstart*)	Swedish ed.	1953	Svensk Natur	h/b	in Swedish, h/b with DJ	?
FORM2B	*Rödstjärten* (*The Redstart*)	Swedish ed.	1953	Svensk Natur	p/b	in Swedish, as above but p/b	?
USM3A	*The Wren*	US ed.	1955	Macmillan	h/b	exactly as M3a with Macmillan label to DJ	250
USM7A	*Fleas, Flukes & Cuckoos*	US 1st ed.	1952	Philosophical Library	h/b	as M7a, cancel TP, casing and DJ with Philosophical L.	?
USM7B	*Fleas, Flukes & Cuckoos*	US 2nd ed.	1957	Macmillan	h/b	as M7C, integral TP, casing and DJ with Macmillan	250?
USM9A	*The Herring Gull's World*	US 1st ed.	1953	Praeger	h/b	not seen, but as M9A, Praeger label to TP?	400
USM9B	*The Herring Gull's World*	US 2nd ed.	1961	Basic Books	h/b	after M9B, integral TP, bespoke binding, rev. Ellis DJ	?
USM9C	*The Herring Gull's World*	US 3rd ed.	1961	Anchor Books	p/b	copy of 1961 USM9B, reduced format p/b	?
USM9D	*The Herring Gull's World*	US 4th ed.	1971	Harper Torchbooks	p/b	copy of 1961 USM9B, reduced format p/b	?
USM9E	*The Herring Gull's World*	US 5th ed.	1989	Lyons & Burford	p/b		?
FORM9A	*Grätruten* (*The Herring Gull's World*)	Swedish ed.	1956	Svensk Natur	p/b	in Swedish, p/b	?
FORM9B	*Die Welt der Silbermöwe* (*The Herring Gull's World*)	German ed.	1958	Musterschmidt	h/b	in German, h/b with DJ	?
FORM9C	(*The Herring Gull's World*) Russian ed.	1974	Mir, Moscow	p/b	in Russian, p/b		?
FORM9D	*L'Univers du Goéland Argenté* (*The Herring Gull's World*)	French ed.	1975	Elsevier Séquoia	p/b	in French, p/b	?
FORM9E	セグロカモメの世界 (*The Herring Gull's World*)	Japanese ed.	1975	Orion Press	h/b	in Japanese, h/b with DJ	?
FORM9F	*Sidabrinio Kiro Pasaulis* (*The Herring Gull's World*)	Lithuania ed.	1978	Mokslas, Vilnius	h/b	in Lithuanian, translated from Russian ed. h/b, no DJ	?
USM10A	*Mumps, Measles & Mosaics*	US ed.	1954	Praeger	h/b	as M10A, cancel TP, Praeger to casing, DJ not seen	250
USM16A	*The Salmon*	US ed.	1959	Harper & Brothers	h/b	as M16A, integral TP, Bespoke binding & DJ	1,000
USM18A	*Oysters*	US ed.	1960	Macmillan	h/b	Exactly as M18a with Macmillan label to DJ	1,000
FORM21A	*La Trucha* (*The Trout*)	Spanish ed.	1971	Editorial Academia	p/b	in Spanish, pb with DJ.	?
USM22A	*The Mole*	US ed.	1973	Taplinger	h/b	as M22A, cancel TP, Taplinger to casing and DJ	1,500

and this Swedish firm should co-operate in producing monographs. The Swedes were bringing out a monograph on the Red-backed Shrike and planned one on Seals. However when they saw the advertisement of Dr. Fraser Darling's forthcoming book on *The Seal* they thought it might be better to have his book translated rather than produce one themselves. They gave a list of 12 N.N. titles in which they were definitely interested, with a view to translating them into Swedish. It was unanimously agreed that this was an extremely interesting idea and should be extended to Switzerland and other European countries, and, in fact, that a New European Naturalist Series of Monographs might be started. Dr. Huxley thought that such titles as *Botanicals* [sic] *Illustrations* and *Animals in Art* would have a universal appeal also, and could very well be translated into French and Italian and other languages. Mr Fisher thought that the best plan would be to invite representatives from Sweden and Switzerland and any other countries that were agreed to come over in the Autumn and discuss the project.... After a short discussion it was decided that the first thing to do was to have this meeting with the foreign representatives.'

Whether this meeting did or did not take place is unknown, or at least is not mentioned in any of the minutes to which I was given access, but Svensk Natur did go on to publish Swedish editions of *The Redstart* and *The Herring Gull's World*.

BLOOMSBURY EDITIONS

In 1988 Crispin Fisher and the Editorial Board agreed that there was a need for reprinting some of the older titles in the series, most of which were long out of print. An application had been received from a reprints and remainders company to reprint 10–20 NN titles, to form a basic library of natural history, but this would not include any of the monographs. At that time it was not viable to print the books in-house and the remainder company with a much smaller profit margin would be able to retail them at between £10 and £15. They were to be published in hardback, with black and white plates and a new set of jacket designs but with a livery compatible with the main series. The plan was to market them through mail order and bookshops, reintroducing some of the old classic titles onto the market and generate much needed interest in the series.

At the editorial meeting on 20th April 1989, the board were shown proofs of the first six jackets by the wildlife artist Philip Snow (see page 283), and it was explained that 24 New Naturalist titles would be reprinted, in batches of 6 and that they were to be facsimiles of the first editions. The remainder company was to be Bloomsbury Books, an imprint of Godfrey Cave Associates Ltd. A maximum of 10,000 copies of each title were to be printed and if successful, a further 24 titles would be reprinted at a later date. As the books were facsimiles they were not actually new editions,

Above and opposite: A selection of Bloomsbury edition covers, featuring artwork by Philip Snow.

Collins provided file copies to copy from although these were not necessarily first editions as originally planned. 12 copies were printed in 1989 and a further 12 in 1990. The 24 titles chosen by Crispin Fisher did not include any of those recently reprinted in paperback, seriously out of date or regarded as not marketable.

The books themselves were printed on economical paper with the plates once beautifully coloured plates reduced to greyish images, lacking any contrast. They were bound in cream cloth with the title and NN logo in gilt on the spine. The contents were a direct copy from the original edition except that the title page included 'Bloomsbury Books, London' and the imprint page stated 'This edition published 1989/1990 by Bloomsbury Books an imprint of Godfrey Cave Associates Limited, 42 Bloomsbury Street, London WC1B 3QJ under licence from William Collins Sons' & Co. Ltd.' The dust jackets were printed on laminated paper and featured a new watercolour painting which continued

TABLE 27 The Bloomsbury facsimile editions.

Title	Year of publication	Edition copied from
Wild Flowers	1989	Reprint 1978
Mountains and Moorlands	1989	Reprint 1977
A Natural History of Man in Britain	1989	Revised edition 1970
British Mammals	1989	Second edition 1968
The Lake District	1989	Reprint 1977
British Birds of Prey	1989	Reprint 1982
Sea Birds	1989	First edition 1954
Fossils	1989	Reprint 1973
The Highlands and Islands	1989	Reprint 1973
Mushrooms and Toadstools	1990	Seventh impression 1977
Reptiles and Amphibians	1990	First edition 1983
British Plant Life	1990	First edition 1948
Woodland Birds	1990	First edition 1971
Life in Lakes and Rivers	1990	Third edition 1974
London's Natural History	1990	First edition 1945
Birds and Men	1990	First edition 1951
An Angler's Entomology	1990	Reprint 1966
Insect Natural History	1990	Reprint 1973
The Sea Shore	1990	Reprint 1971
The Peak District	1990	Second edition 1974
Wild Flowers of Chalk and Limestone	1990	Reprint 1976
Inheritance and Natural History	1990	First edition 1977
The Natural History of Wales	1990	First edition 1981
Butterflies	1990	Fourth edition 1977

all around the jacket, with a new version of the NN logo at the foot of the spine encircled in a black ring. Information about the book including a few reviews were printed on the front inside flap and on the rear flap was a note on the 'aim of the series' plus a list of other titles in this facsimile series. Interestingly the list omits some titles that were part of this series but included *The Art of Botanical Illustration*, which was never printed as a Bloomsbury edition.

In October 1989 the minutes record that 'the contract with Bloomsbury seems to have been a sad misjudgement; Collins would seek to discontinue it'. The books were remaindered very soon after they were released and stacks of them could be found in remainder book shops.

The Bloomsbury books are a little smaller than the main series and they do not sit well with them on a shelf, having very different jacket artwork and typography.

Today these books are a sort of forgotten cheap and cheerful second cousin of the main series and can still be acquired very reasonably on the second-hand book market. When found they will often be in perfect unread condition.

COLLINS PAPERBACKS

Paperbacks, or limpbacks, as they are also known, are now very much part of the NN brand, but this has not always been the case: they are in fact a comparatively recent introduction. The first New Naturalist title to appear in paperback was *The Badger,* published in 1958 by Penguin, quickly followed by others in the Fontana series (see page 102), but here we are only concerned with paperbacks that carry the Collins or HarperCollins imprint.

During 1984/1985 several old titles were reissued as 'affordable' paperback reprints, otherwise known as the *black paperbacks*. Since, and including the publication, in 1985, of NN70 *Orkney* and 71 *Warblers*, all NN titles have been concomitantly published in paperback and bound up from the same sheets as the hardbacks.

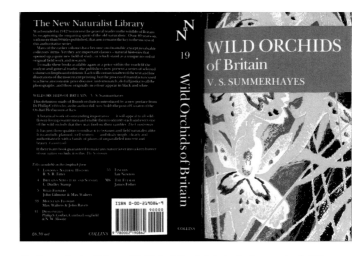

Black paperback edition of *Wild Orchids of Britain*: Each paperback follows a standard cover layout.

The black paperbacks

Eight Collins 'Limpback Reprints' were published in two tranches in 1984 and 1985 as identified in table 28, seven from the main series and one from the monograph series. They are b/w facsimile copies with the preliminary matter slightly revised, but the format, at 215 mm high, is identical to the height of the book-blocks of the originals.

The books are perfect bound, i.e. not stitched, with printed card covers; the front displaying the Ellises' jacket design but the rear cover and spine have a gloss black ground, hence *black paperbacks*. The title lettering on the spine is yellow, with the exception of the two ornithological titles – *Finches* and *The Fulmar* – where it is white; usefully, unlike the concomitant paperbacks, the series numbers are printed on the spines. The title lettering and band to the front cover have been reset.

The rear covers follow the same layout: the upper portion, a general blurb for the NN library; the middle section, the book blurb; the lower portion, a list of *'Titles available in this limpback*

TABLE 28 The Black Paperbacks. Note that the figure in the 'No. Sold' column includes remaindered books.

Class. No.	Series No.	Title	Copy of	ISBN	Pub. Date	Price	Print Order	No. Sold	No. Remaindered	Out of Print
BPB3a	3	*London's Natural History*	1946 rep. NN3b	0002190680	18/06/1984	£6.50	1,500	1,340	600 (1988)	1988
BPB4a	4	*Britain's Structure and Scenery*	1967 6th ed. NN4f	000219077X	16/07/1984	£6.50	1,500	1,390	500 (1988)	1988
BPB5a	5	*Wild Flowers*	1978 5th ed. rep. NN5f	0002193264	21/01/1985	£6.50	1,500	1,260	150 (1988)	1988
BPB19a	19	*Wild Orchids of Britain*	1976 2nd ed. rep. NN19d	0002190869	21/01/1985	£6.50	1,600	1,460	–	1988
BPB33a	33	*Mountain Flowers*	1965 1st rep. NN33b	0002190702	18/06/1984	£6.50	1,600	1,460	250 (1988)	1988
BPB41a	41	*Dragonflies*	only edition	0002190648	21/01/1985	£6.50	1,600	1,530	–	1985
BPB55a	55	*Finches*	1978 2nd rep. NN55c	0002190893	21/01/1985	£6.50	1,600	1,450	–	1989
BPBM6a	M6	*The Fulmar*	only edition	0002190656	18/06/1984	£7.50	1,600	1,200	–	1989

form'; with the ISBN, barcode, imprint and price positioned above the lower edge.

Each book includes a standardised introduction to the limpback reprints, which explains that '*the process of manufacture used to achieve an economic price does not, unfortunately, do full justice to all the photographs; and those originally in colour appear in black and white.*' The ISBN and publication information, including date and printer (all eight titles were printed and bound by Biddles Ltd, of Guildford and King's Lynn) is also given on the introduction page. Of more interest, a new preface by either author, editor or reviser as been added to each title.

Importantly, the cover designs of *The Fulmar* and *Britain's Structure and Scenery* were 'reorginated', i.e. copied from the Ellises' original (slightly soiled) artwork and, particularly in the case of the latter title, they are markedly different from the printed jackets, which, for this alone, makes them worth buying.

Commercially, the black paperbacks were not particularly successful and a number were remaindered, as identified in table 28, however *Dragonflies* purportedly sold out within a month of publication, though this is probably a little exaggerated. The print run of each title was around 1,600 copies and consequently these paperbacks are now much rarer than their price belies. They are difficult to find in fine condition – the surface colour along the joints and at the head/tail of the spine is apt to chip off, exposing the white card beneath.

The concomitant paperbacks

The *concomitant paperbacks* have been published simultaneously with the hardback editions since 1985 and at the time of writing 51 different titles have appeared, with *The New Naturalists* published twice. They are bound up from the same sheets as the hardbacks and, the height, at around 216 mm, is the same as the book-block of the hardbacks, but because the card covers are flush they are shorter in their bindings. For some unknown reason NN96 *Fungi* is shorter but not consistently so.

Importantly, because these paperbacks are bound up from the same sheets as the hardbacks, *they are true first editions*, unless of course they have been reprinted. Generally reprints of the paperbacks follow suit with the hardbacks, i.e. if the hardback is reprinted then so is the paperback, but inevitably there are exceptions: *The New Forest* reprint only appears in paperback format but reprints of *Heathlands* and *The New Naturalists* appear only in hardback.

The first two titles – NN70 *Orkney* and NN71 *Warblers* employed the same artwork for the front covers as the dust jackets, but for NN72–96 the front cover design was principally photographic, before switching back to the jacket artwork for NN97–120. During this period there have been a number of different cover layouts, as identified below, but since 2006 the style has been consistent, ensuring visual continuity on the shelf. At first the cover designs were particularly poor, visually muddled and in contrast with Gillmor's well-designed jackets.

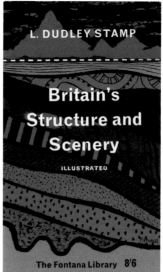

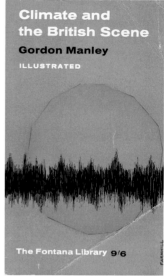

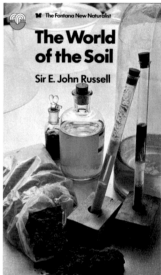

A selection of covers from the successful Fontana paperback editions, including the first New Naturalist title to be published as part of the Fontana library, *Britain's Structure and Scenery*, in 1960.

Paperback Design Type 1 (1985)
Used for NN70 *Orkney* and 71 *Warblers* and the only design to include the series number on the spine.

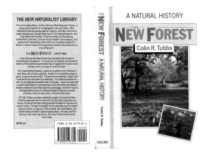

Paperback Design Type 2 (1986–1990)
Used for NN72 *Heathland*, NN73 *The New Forest*, NN74 *Ferns*, and NN76 *The Hebrides*. A graphically muddled design with too many elements and fonts – all on a marbled ground to add to the confusion! Pitiable: the lowest point of New Naturalist design. Fortunately this layout was only used for four titles – theEditors recognised that the paperback design was poor and resolved to improve it (minutes for 5 October 1989). Note the absence of the NN monogram (there is no external reference or visual clue to the New Naturalist on the front cover or spine).

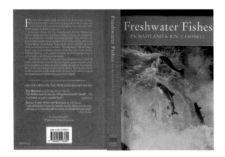

Paperback Design Type 3 (1992)
Used for NN75 *Freshwater Fishes*, NN77 *The Soil*, and NN78 *British Larks, Pipits and Wagtails*. A much crisper, more restrained design. Note the introduction of the HarperCollins imprint and the Fire and Water logo on the spine, but still no NN monogram and no external reference to being a New Naturalist.

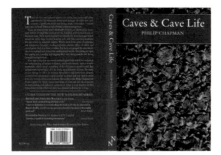

Paperback Design Type 4 (1993–2002)
Used for NN79 *Caves and Cave Life* through to NN92 *Lakeland*. Essentially as Type 3 but the Collins imprint has been omitted on the spine and the NN monogram introduced.

Paperback Design Type 5 (2003–04)
Used for NN93 *British Bats*, NN94 *Seashore* and NN95 *Northumberland*. Very similar to Types 3 and 4, still with a photographic front cover, but the most notable change is the introduction of the attractive colour 'thumbnails' of paperback titles under the heading 'Other titles in the New Naturalist series' printed to the rear cover. The Collins imprint has been introduced to the spine but the associated 'ripple logo' was used only on paperbacks NN93 *British Bats* and NN94 *Seashore* before being replaced with the Collins 'ring logo' on NN95 *Northumberland* and thereafter used consistently on all paperbacks at the base of the spine until the present.

Paperback Design Type 6 (2005)
Used only for NN96 *Fungi* and NN82B *The New Naturalists*. Essentially an intermediate between Type 5 and Type 7. The front cover remains photographic but the spines have evolved to layout of Type 7 – the NN monogram is now positioned at the head and the Collins ring logo and imprint at the tail.

Paperback Design Type 7 (2006–12)
Used for NN97 *Mosses and Liverworts* through to the present – NN115 *Climate and Weather*. This layout and design is, ironically, very similar to Type 1 used 21 years earlier. The dust jacket artwork has been reintroduced and the title band is without ruled borders; it is essentially a facsimile of the dust jacket front panel, but the title and authors' names are centred rather than left-justified. From NN98 *Bumblebees* onwards the monogram used has changed to the latest design by Martin Majoor, though for NN98–101 this was embellished with Gillmor's motifs.

TABLE 29 The Concomitant Paperbacks.

Cat. No.	Series No.	Title	Design Type	Dated	Pub. Date	Printed Price	Print Run	No. Sold	Remaindered	Out of Print
CPB70A	70	Natural History of Orkney	1	1985	11/11/1985	£9.95	3,700?	3,090 + 600 RU	Yes – qty?	1990
CPB71A	71	British Warblers	1	1985	11/11/1985	£9.95	5,300?	2,980+ 2,100 RU	Yes – qty?	1990
CPB72A	72	Heathlands	2	1986	21/07/1986	£9.95	2,000?	1,620	–	1989
CPB73A	73	The New Forest	2	1986	03/10/1986	£9.95	2,000?	2,630	–	1991
CPB74A	74	Ferns	2	1988	07/11/1988	£10.95	2,000	1,850	–	1993
CPB75A	75	Freshwater Fish	3	1992	23/07/1992	£14.99	2,460	1,610	?	1992
CPB76A	76	The Hebrides	2	1990	04/06/1990	£12.95	2,000	2,790	–	1993
CPB77A	77	The Soil	3	1992	13/02/1992	£12.99	2,078	1,310	–	1994
CPB78A	78	Larks, Pipits and Wagtails	3	1992	13/02/1992	£14.99	2,846	1,080	–	1993
CPB79A	79	Caves and Cave Life	4	1993	15/07/1993	£12.99	2,064	1,240	–	1998
CPB80A	80	Wild and Garden Plants	4	1993	11/11/1993	£12.99	3,040	1,350	1,000	1999
CPB81A	81	Ladybirds	4	1994	06/10/1994	£14.99	2,478	1,200	900	1996
CPB82A	82A	The New Naturalists	4	1995	06/04/1995	£14.99	1,751	1,110	–	1996
CPB82B	82B	The New Naturalists	6	2005	04/04/2005	£25.00	900	?	–	?
CPB83A	83	Natural History Pollination	4	1996	27/03/1996	£16.99	1,956	1,540	–	1999
CPB84A	84	Ireland: A Natural History	4	1999	01/03/1999	£17.99	3,053	2,520	–	2000
CPB85A	85	Plant Disease	4	1999	04/10/1999	£19.99	1,960	1,050	840	2004
CPB86A	86	Lichens	4	2000	06/03/2000	£19.99	1,978	1,780	–	2003
CPB87A	87	Amphibians and Reptiles	4	2000	02/10/2000	£19.99	2,050	1,690	–	2003
CPB88A	88	Loch Lomondside	4	2001	05/03/2001	£19.99	1,964	630	1,100	2004
CPB89A	89	The Broads	4	2001	05/11/2001	£19.99	1,981	1,180	600	2005
CPB90A	90	Moths	4	2002	04/02/2002	£19.99	1,944	–	–	?
CPB91A	91	Nature Conservation	4	2002	07/05/2002	£19.99	1,980	1,770	–	2003
CPB92A	92	Lakeland	4	2002	07/10/2002	£19.99	1,974	?	600	?
CPB93A	93	British Bats	5	2003	03/03/2003	£20.00	1,951	1,660	–	2004
CPB94A	94	Seashore	5	2004	05/04/2004	£25.00	2,250	?	964	2006
CPB95A	95	Northumberland	5	2004	04/10/2004	£25.00	1016	–	–	2005
CPB96A	96	Fungi	6	2005	03/05/2005	£25.00	1850	–	–	2007
CPB97A	97	Mosses & Liverworts	7	2005	05/09/2005	£25.00	1557	–	–	2008
CPB98A	98	Bumblebees	7	2006	07/03/2006	£25.00	1516	–	–	2009
CPB99A	99	Gower	7	2006	02/05/2006	£25.00	1,050	–	–	?
CPB99B	99	Gower (1st reprint)	7	2006	–	£25.00	550	–	–	?
CPB99C	99	Gower (2nd reprint)	7	2007	–	£25.00	780	–	–	2011
CPB100A	100	Woodlands (1st edition)	7	2006	14/09/2006	£25.00	2,524	–	–	?
CPB100B	100	Woodlands (1st reprint)	7	2006	–	£25.00	see note	–	–	?
CPB100C	100	Woodlands (2nd reprint)	7	2007	–	£25.00	see note	–	–	?
CPB100D	100	Woodlands (3rd reprint)	7	2007	–	£25.00	see note	–	–	?
CPB101A	101	Galloway (1st edition)	7	03/01/2007		£25.00	1,312	–	–	2011
CPB101B	101	Galloway (1st reprint – indistinguishable)	7	2007	2008?	£25.00	240	–	–	2011
CPB102A	102	Garden N. History (1st edition)	7	2007		£25.00	2,086	–	–	2011
CPB102B	102	Garden N. History (1st reprint – indistinguishable)	7	2007	2008?	£25.00	227	–	–	2011
CPB103A	103	Isles of Scilly	7	2007	06/08/2007	£25.00	2,580	–	–	2010
CPB104A	104	A History of Ornithology	7	2007	01/10/2007	£25.00	2,085	–	–	2009
CPB105A	105	Wye Valley	7	2008	04/02/2008	£25.00	2,100	–	–	2010
CPB106A	106	Dragonflies	7	2008	02/06/2008	£25.00	2,376	–	–	2014
CPB107A	107	Grouse	7	2008	01/09/2008	£30.00	2,100	–	–	2011
CPB108A	108	Southern England	7	2008	03/11/2008	£30.00	2,055	–	–	2011
CPB109A	109	Islands	7	2009	05/02/2009	£30.00	2,176	–	–	2011
CPB110A	110	Wildfowl	7	2009	29/05/2009	£30.00	1,700	–	–	2011
CPB111A	111	Dartmoor	7	2009	17/09/2009	£30.00	2,048	–	–	2011
CPB112A	112	Books and Naturalists	7	2010	04/–2/2010	£30.00	1,518	–	–	2011
CPB113A	113	Bird Migration	7	2010	01/04/2010	£30.00	3,012	–	–	2011
CPB114A	114	Badger	7	2010	27/05/2010	£30.00	2,048	–	–	2014
CPB115A	115	Climate and Weather	7	2010	02/09/2010	£30.00	1,534	–	–	in print
CPB116A	116	Plant Pests	7	2011	06/01/2011	£30.00	1,296	–	–	in print
CPB117A	117	Plant Galls	7	2011	28/04/2011	£30.00	1,001	–	–	2015
CPB118A	118	Marches	7	2011	01/09/2011	£30.00	1,004	–	–	in print
CPB119A	119	Scotland	7	2012	05/01/2012	£30.00	1,004	–	–	in print
CPB120A	120	Grasshoppers and Crickets	7	2012	05/07/2012	£30.00	1,004	–	–	2012

Notes: 1) the figure in the 'No. Sold' column does not include remaindered books. 2) NN100 *Woodlands* was reprinted five times but only three are distinguishable, for further details see bibliography.

A significant feature of the hardback jacket is the New Naturalist library listed on the rear panel, but this is omitted from the paperbacks, until NN102 *Garden Natural History* where, for both formats, the library is bound in at the rear of the book. The series numbers are also omitted from the spines of the paperbacks. These omitted features indicate that Collins was not aiming the softback format at the collectors' market.

From NN110 *Wildfowl* onwards, Gillmor's artwork is reproduced at a reduced scale, but inconsistently so. Presumably, this is to compensate for the slightly smaller format of paperback covers. At one extreme, NN111 *Dartmoor* is only 88.5 per cent of the original (dust jacket) artwork, whereas NN112 *Bird Migration* is reproduced at a scale of 99 per cent. The effect of these reductions can be to display a greater proportion of the original design that is trimmed off on the jacket; for instance the hedgerow at the base of the design for NN118 *Marches* is present in the paperback edition but mostly missing from the jacket – and this changes the balance of the design considerably.

FONTANA PAPERBACKS

The name Fontana was originally given to an exclusive new type face designed for Collins by Dr Hans Mardersteig in 1936. He worked for Collins in Glasgow and re-designed their 'classics'. Eric Gill also contributed to the new classics and designed the house colophon featuring an elegant fountain. The name was also given to the Collins in-house magazine which was launched in 1947. A few years later, in 1953, Collins marketed the first of their Fontana paperbacks, sporting full-colour varnished card covers. They are much smaller than a standard New Naturalist, what is known as A-format (110 × 178 mm) – the size of a regular mass-market paperback.

Originally 12 titles were published, which included bestselling novels by well-known authors such as Hammond Innes and Agatha Christie. This marked one of the biggest developments in the company's history and by the end of that year sales had reached the half-million mark. By 1960 Fontana sales totalled almost six million, and in the same year the Fontana Library of non-fiction was begun.

The first New Naturalist title to be published as part of the Fontana library was *Britain's Structure and Scenery* in 1960. This gave the main series a great boost and also enabled the authors to revise their text more substantially than would otherwise have been possible. The Fontana text could then be used in any new hardback editions. The covers of the first few titles did not match and used a rather basic FL logo at the foot of the spine. Sales seem to have been quite limited, as only a handful of titles were published under the Fontana imprint over the following few years. In 1968 the books were re-launched with colourful bright green spines and photographic covers. They also adopted a new colophon, which was an updated interpretation of the original Gill fountain. There was obviously an attempt to make the Fontanas seem more like a consistent library, and with their green spines they are quite distinctive. Although the original New Naturalist titles had never been written as text books, there was a growing demand for the Fontana versions from universities, particularly the Open University, which listed them as course reference books from about 1971. This was a turning point in the series' success, prompting Collins to issue a string of titles in quick succession, including some of the more popular volumes from the main series, such as *Mountains and Moorlands*, *Life in Lakes and Rivers* and *The Sea Shore*. Interestingly, only one monograph, *The Trout*, was included in the series, which seems strange as the paperback format would have been an ideal way of making the monographs much more accessible, especially to students.

Apart from the bright covers, the books were only illustrated in black and white. This was a particular disadvantage for titles such as *Butterflies*, sales of which were predictably low making it the final book to be published in the series in 1975. Overall 18 titles were printed as part of the Fontana New Naturalist library. This included *The Life of the Robin* by David Lack, which was never part of the main series and which featured illustrations by Robert Gillmor. The sales of these books continued to decline and most of them were out of print by the early 1980s. The last of the stock was remaindered in 1985.

Although not taken particularly seriously by collectors, the Fontana New Naturalist series is fun to search for and, unlike its cousins in the main series, very reasonably priced. The books are not numbered as in the main series, but when sitting in a row on a shelf their green spines combine to give the pleasing appearance of unity.

Boxed sets
Several boxed sets of Fontana paperbacks seem to have been available from the late 1960s or early 1970s. Four or five books were packaged in card boxes designed in bright colours and decorated with photographs, the title 'Fontana New Naturalist' and a butterfly logo. These sets appear to be quite scarce and when they do turn up, tend to be in fairly poor condition generally because the card box has weakened as the books have been removed and replaced.

OTHER NEW NATURALIST PAPERBACKS

As well as the Fontana editions, two other New Naturalist titles were also available in a similar paperback format. *The Badger* was published by Pelican Books in 1958 in their distinctive pale blue and white cover. *Fleas, Flukes and Cuckoos* was apparently also available as a Pelican paperback (1957), but we have never seen a copy. However, the book did appear as a Grey Arrow paperback, published by Arrow Books in 1961. Although hardbacks are more valuable for the average collector, the NN paperbacks testify to an important moment in the series' history and are therefore worthy of attention.

TABLE 30 The Country Naturalist

Code	Title and publication date	Author	Contents	Other details
CN1	*Birds of the Field*, 1952	James Fisher	36 pp, 16 colour plates 23 black and white plates.	Other: No. 1 printed on cover and spine 3/6 net on cover
CN2	*Butterflies of the Wood*, 1953	S. & E. M. Beaufoy	36 pp, 20 colour plates, 81 black and white plates	No 2 printed on cover and spine 3/6 net on cover
CN3	*Flowers of the Wood*, 1953	F. M. Day	36 pp, 17 colour plates, 19 black and white plates	3/6 net on cover
CN4	*Birds of Town and Village*, 1953	R. S. R. Fitter	36 pp, 20 colour plates, 22 black and white plates	3/6 net on cover
CN5	*Flowers of the Seaside*, 1954	Ian Hepburn	36 pp, 17 colour plates, 16 black and white plates	2/6 net on cover Advertises *Flowers of the Coast* on inside of back cover
CN6	*Beasts of the Field*, 1954	L. Harrison Matthews	36 pp, 8 colour plates, 26 black and white plates	2/6 net on cover Advertises *British Mammals* on inside of back cover

TABLE 31 The Countryside Series

Code	Title and publication date	Author	Contents	Other details
CS1	*Life on the Sea Shore*, 1974	John Barrett	160 pp, 24 black and white plates and line drawings by Geoffrey Potts	No. 1 printed on spine £1.95 on inside flap of dust jacket
CS2	*Birds*, 1974	Christopher Perrins	176 pp, 24 black and white plates, line drawings by Robert Gillmor	No 2 printed on spine £1.95 on inside flap of dust jacket
CS2A	*Birds*, 1976 Readers Union	Christopher Perrins	As above but plates bound together at centre of book	Dust jacket not priced
CS3	*Woodlands*, 1974	William Condry	176 pp, 24 black and white plates, line drawings by Denys Ovenden	No 3 printed on spine £1.95 on inside flap of dust jacket
CS3A	*Woodlands*, 1974	William Condry	As above but with reprinted dust jacket, black band and spine. Colour photograph.	No 3 printed on spine £2.25 on inside flap of dust jacket
CS3B	*Woodlands*, 1975 Readers Union	William Condry	As above but plates bound together at centre of book	Dust jacket not priced
CS4	*Plant Life*, 1977	C. T. Prime	160 pp, 24 black and white plates, line drawings by Marjorie Blamey	Laminated covers. No 4 at head of spine, not priced
CS4A	*Plant Life*, 1978 Readers Union	C. T. Prime	As above but plates bound together at centre of book	Dust jacket not priced
CS5	*Insect Life*, 1977	Michael Tweedie	192 pp, 24 black and white plates, line drawings by Denys Ovenden	Laminated covers. No 5 at head of spine, not priced
CS5A	*Insect Life*, 1978 Readers Union	Michael Tweedie	As above but plates bound together at centre of book	Dust jacket not priced
CS6	*Rocks*, 1976	David Dineley	160 pp, 22 black and white plates, line drawings by Alma Gregory	Laminated covers. No 6 at head of spine, not priced
CS7	*Fossils*, 1979	David Dineley	176 pp, 16 black and white plates, line drawings by Alma Gregory	Laminated covers. No 7 at head of spine, not priced
CS8	*Fungi*, 1981	Roderic Cooke	159 pp, 16 black and white plates, line drawings by Bob Parker	Laminated covers. No 8 at head of spine, not priced

RELATED BOOKS

Initially the New Naturalist library would appear to be fairly straightforward. Many collectors are only interested in first editions and would never contemplate adding a bookclub or Bloomsbury edition to their collection. For those intrepid collectors who are interested in widening their New Naturalist collection, there are a number of related books which are distant cousins of the main

library. Some of these, such as The Country Naturalist books and *The New Naturalist Journal*, are closely linked to the senior series, featuring some of the same authors and photographic illustrations. Other books, like The Countryside Series and particularly the Australian Naturalist Library, are quite different in appearance and do not at first seem related to the New Naturalist series at all. Most of these books are relatively easy to find and are usually inexpensive. For those collectors who thought they had every NN-related published book, the following few pages might come as

with an introduction by James Fisher. His introduction to each volume stated: 'Our British Islands, with their wonderfully varied geology and climate, present to the bird's eye an intricate patchwork of woods, fields, moors, mountains, towns and rivers, with a margin of sea coast of great length and complexity. Each of these types of country supports its own peculiar communities of plants and animals. The object of this series of illustrated popular nature books is to give the reader a first introduction to these members of Britain's living communities'.

The books were published between 1952 and 1954, each one being illustrated with 16 plates of 'full natural colour photography' and a further 16 plates in black and white. The covers proudly displayed one or two colour photographs. The series also had a logo or colophon, featuring a red squirrel, which was designed by Clifford and Rosemary Ellis.

Ultimately only six books in the series were produced. It is not evident why they were discontinued, though it may have been due to disappointing sales or perhaps the ever-rising costs of colour printing. The titles published included *Birds of the Field, Butterflies of the Wood, Flowers of the Wood, Birds of Town and Village, Flowers of the Seaside* and *Beasts of the Field.* The first two in the series, *Birds of the Field* and *Butterflies of the Wood*, were numbered on the front cover and also at the foot of the spine. Two other titles, *Birds of the Seaside* by James Fisher and *Butterflies of the Field* by S. and E. M. Beaufoy, were advertised as being in preparation on the backs of the covers but were never published. Each book was priced at 2/6 or 3/6 on the cover and occasionally examples are found with reduced price stickers placed over the printed price. Each title is thought to have had a print run of around 25,000, and although none of them were reprinted, they remained in print until the 1960s. Although these books were available as paperbacks, it is possible to find hardback versions, usually in dark green cloth and with the title printed in gold on the spine and cover. These were probably bound by libraries and will usually have the distinctive cancellation stamps. Due to the weak paperback binding it is quite difficult to find copies of the Country Naturalist in fine condition. They tend to have chipped spines or creased card covers, but this does make them very reasonably priced and it is well worth looking out for them.

Four examples of the Country Naturalist. Six titles were published between 1952 and 1954 under the editorship of James Fisher. Although well illustrated with colour plates, they were bound with card covers making them difficult to find in fine condition.

a surprise and will hopefully prove an interesting challenge.

The Country Naturalist

In November 1951, the New Naturalist Editorial Board met to discuss the idea of publishing a second, 'junior' series of books. The board members all agreed with this proposal, but felt that each new book should not be released until a year or two after the publication of the volume in the main series on which it was to be based. James Fisher was to be the overall editor and at that same meeting in St James's Place, he revealed to the board the forthcoming titles and asked for further suggestions for the series. The original idea was to re-use as many of the colour plates from the main library as possible and to publish them as a cheaper card-covered edition. The text would be written by the author of the parent main series volume and would be about 10,000 words,

The Countryside series

The idea of the 'Country Naturalist' series was picked up again in the 1970s, with the launch of the 'Countryside Series'. This series was regarded as a sort of junior version or 'cheap and cheerful second cousins' of the main New Naturalist library. Originally they were to be titled 'The Young Naturalist', although this was changed to The Countryside Series after some marketing issues. The books are much slimmer than volumes in the main New Naturalist library and were generally aimed at the younger reader, whilst still retaining a similar ecological pitch. Two of the authors, C. T. Prime and William Condry, had already written books in the senior series and Christopher Perrins was under contract to write *British Tits,* which was eventually published in 1979. Initially the books had striking jacket designs by Clifford and Rosemary Ellis with the artwork enclosed within a large CS logo printed against a strong primary colour, lending a bright and modern appearance to the books.

The first of the books, *Life on the Sea Shore*, was written by John Barrett and published in 1974. It was bound in a dark blue-grey cloth and priced at £1.95. As with the main-series New Naturalist volumes at that time, it was only illustrated with black and white photographs and line drawings by Geoffrey Potts. This was followed by *Birds* by Christopher Perrins and *Woodlands* by William Condry. These three books looked similar with bright, attractive dust jacket designs by Ellises. As with the main series, they were numbered at the head of the spine. Five more titles followed in the series but they were to change in appearance quite dramatically. From number 4, *Plant Life* by C. T. Prime, they were bound in a photographic laminated cloth without a dust wrapper. The spines were black with the number of the volume in the series in white at the head of the spine. They also had a black band running across the front cover, similar in position to that of the New Naturalist main series. Sadly, The Countryside Series was not as successful as Collins had hoped and it was discontinued in 1981. Several of the titles were also reprinted as bookclub editions from the Readers Union. These editions are not numbered and have dust wrappers with rather dull black and white photographs. All of the books in this series are easily found in second-hand book shops and on the internet and are usually very reasonably priced.

The New Naturalist Magazine

From early in 1946 there were plans to produce a New Naturalist magazine, and from the minutes of the Editorial Board of 14 August 1946, James Fisher reported that he had accepted the suggestion that he would take on the full-time responsibility for a year to investigate the possibilities of producing a New Naturalist magazine. This would lead to him producing a 'dummy' copy and also to eventually becoming the editor, using the office at 162a The Strand. It was agreed right from the start that this new magazine would deal only with British natural history. At that same meeting a selection of photographs were shown to the board which included one of a fritillary. James Fisher suggested using the photo on the cover of the magazine and went further to suggest that the magazine might be called 'Fritillary'. However, Dudley Stamp thought that 'New Naturalist' had become a kind of trademark and it was subsequently agreed by the board that the title should be simply 'The New Naturalist Magazine'. Wolfgang Foges, from Adprint, was also present at that meeting, and produced copies of a Swiss magazine called '*Du*' which was to be used as a model, although it was thought that the format was rather too large. The size proposed for the NN magazine was large quarto. James Fisher suggested that the magazine should be monthly and that every number should be a 'special' one, featuring one particular subject. There were other plans at this time to produce a series of NN postcards and also a calendar, but

none of these seem to have come to fruition.

By November 1946, James Fisher had compiled a series of contributions for two editions of the magazine, one on woodland and the other on the Western Isles. From the minutes of the Editorial Board for 13 March 1947, it is noted that James Fisher presented the 'dummy' copy of the *Woodlands* number, which included an excellent article by Sir Arthur Tansley. Due to currency restrictions at that time, the magazine could not be printed abroad and there was a possibility of bringing out the magazine in Britain twice yearly, using the very small paper allocation allowed for new magazines. Wolfgang Foges thought that the print run would be about 3,000 copies 'at the outside'. He also had the suggestion of

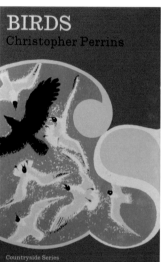
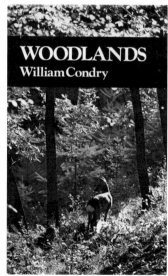

The Countryside Series ran for a number of years during the 1970s as a junior version of the main New Naturalist library. The first three titles had dust jacket designs by Clifford and Rosemary Ellis (top, left and right). Later additions to the series had photographic laminated covers with a black band and spine (above left) whilst book club editions had dust jackets illustrated with black and white photographs (above right).

producing the magazine as an annual. The first part of *Woodlands* was subsequently produced to canvas potential advertisers for what was intended to be a quarterly magazine and the first four parts would also be published together as an annual.

The first part of *The New Naturalist Magazine*, in quarto format (4to), was sent out in January 1948 together with a letter from James Fisher. The letter stated that this foretaste was not being published but was being circulated to those who contributed to it and to those who might be interested in it or likely to make useful comments on it. He went on to state that 'For the time being it is not possible to publish this magazine…' but went on to say that the annual would be published in the autumn of 1948. As a separate item, the first part is exceptionally scarce and only a handful of examples are known to survive. At that time it was hoped that publication of the magazine would be resumed at some stage and that the annual would continue to be available every autumn. Ultimately, only one annual was ever produced for

The scarce New Naturalist Magazine from January 1948 (top left). Entitled *Woodlands*, this was intended to be the first part of quarterly magazine. This was however later published as *The New Naturalist* journal, which consisted of the first four parts of the magazine (top right). Parts 5 and 6 (above, left and right) were published in 1949 and were the last editions of this short-lived venture.

which there are two very slightly different jackets. The first of these has the title text printed in dark green against a dark photograph featuring a woodland background. The title is very difficult to read and it is probably for this reason that a second version of the dust jacket was subsequently printed where the background is lightened behind the text, making it much more legible. The first version seems to be more scarce than the second. As well as the annual, two further magazines were also produced. Part 5, spring 1949, was titled *Birth, Death and the Seasons*, which was followed by the summer edition *East Anglia*. Although the annual is a relatively common book, and is frequently found in good condition, both of the magazines are quite rare. Sadly no other magazines were published and that became the end of the *New Naturalist Magazine*.

NNJ1 *The New Naturalist Magazine*. Number One, *Woodlands*, spring 1948. Issued in very limited numbers (probably less than 300), but not published. 64 pp, paper covers. 76 illustrations in black and white. Black and white photo of Bear's Garlic by John Markham on cover. Not priced. Published at 51a Rathbone Place, London, W1, jointly by Adprint and Collins, supervised by the Editorial Board responsible for the New Naturalist books (John Gilmour, Julian Huxley, L. Dudley Stamp, James Fisher (editor of the magazine), Eric Hosking (photographic editor) and produced with the help of Elisabeth Ullmann and Joan Ivimy. Printed by Jarrold and Sons Limited, Norwich.
  · The New Naturalist Editorial, James Fisher
  · *The Woodlands of England and Wales*, Jeanne Fitzpatrick
  · *This Woodland Number*
  · *British Woodlands*, A. G. Tansley
  · *British Forests in Prehistoric Times*, H. Goodwin
  · *Woodland Butterflies*, E. B. Ford
  · *Grey Squirrels in Britain*, Monica Shorten
  · *The British Elms*, R. Melville
  · *Woodland Bird Communities*, M. K. Colquhoun
  · *Woodland Tits*, Philip E. Brown
  · *Books and the Amateur Naturalist*, Stephen Potter

NNJ2A *The New Naturalist Magazine: A Journal of British Natural History*. Annual containing nos 1–4. Published autumn 1948. Editor: James Fisher. Assistant Editor: Elizabeth Ullmann. 216 pp, 12 colour plates, 175 illustrations in black and white. Black and white photo of Bear's Garlic by John Markham on cover. Bound in light brown cloth. Priced 21s net on inside flap of dust wrapper. Printed by Jarrold and Sons Limited, Norwich.
Spring, Woodlands:
  · The New Naturalist Editorial, James Fisher
  · *The Woodlands of England and Wales*, H. Godwin
  · *British Woodlands*, A. G. Tansley
  · *The British Elms*, R. Melville
  · *Grey Squirrels in Britain*, Monica Shorten
  · *Woodland Butterflies*, E. B. Ford
  · *Woodland Tits*, Philip E. Brown

- *Woodland Bird Communities*, M. K. Colquhoun
- *Books and the Amateur Naturalist*, Stephen Potter

Summer, The Western Isles of Scotland
- *Editorial*, James Fisher
- *The 'Outer Hebrides'*, Arthur Geddes
- *The Climate of the Hebrides*, Gordon Manley
- *The Passing of the Ice Age*, J. W. Heslop Harrison
- *St Kilda*, James Fisher
- *Leach's Petrel*, Robert Atkinson
- *The Natural History of Ailsa Craig*, H. G. Vevers
- *The Atlantic Seal* (pictorial)
- *Science or Skins?*, F. Fraser Darling

Autumn, Migration
- *Some Problems of Animal Migration*, C. B. Williams
- *Notes on British Immigrant Butterflies*, C. B. Williams
- *Bird Navigation*, G. V. T. Matthews
- *The Migration of Geese*, Peter Scott
- *The Problem of the Corn-crake*, K. B. Ashton
- *Bird Migration Stations in Britain*, R. M. Lockley
- *The Value of Bird-Ringing in the Study of Migration*,
  A. Landsborough Thomson
- *The Last Hundred Bird Books*, James Fisher

Winter, The Local Naturalist
- *On being a Local Naturalist*, Brian Vesey-Fitzgerald
- *A Directory of Natural History Societies*, J. S. Gilmour
- *The Natural History Societies of the British Isles*, H. K. Airy Shaw
- *School Natural History Societies*, David Stainer
- *Local Journals*, W. H. Pearsall
- *Naturalists on the Air*, L. C. Lloyd

NNJ2B As above with slightly different cover to dust jacket.
The area behind the title text has a graduated pale area which
improved the legibility of the title. Bound in green or blue-green
cloth. Contents identical to NNJ2A.

NNJ3 *The New Naturalist Magazine: A Journal of British Natural
History*. Number 5. Birth, Death and the Seasons. Published spring
1949. Editor: James Fisher. Assistant Editor: Elizabeth Ullmann.
52 pp, 40 illustrations in black and white. Card covers. Colour
photo of bluebells by Robert Atkinson on cover. Price on cover
of 6/. Printed by Clarke & Sherwell Limited, Northampton.
- The New Naturalist Editorial, James Fisher
- *The Biology of the Seasons*, C. B. Williams
- *The Breeding Seasons of Animals*, A. J. Marshall
- *Reproduction & Behaviour of the British Amphibia & Reptiles*,
  Malcolm Smith
- *The Spread of Plants in Britain*, Sir Edward Salisbury
- *Flowering*, P. J. Syrett
- *The Meaning of Bird Song*, E. M. Nicholson
- *The Death of Birds*, James Fisher
- *Insect Hibernation*, R. B. Freeman
- *The Hibernation of Mammals*, L. Harrison Matthews
- *Seasons in the Sea and on the Shore*, C. M. Yonge

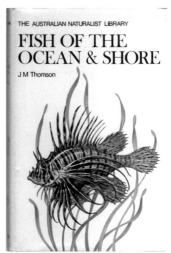 

 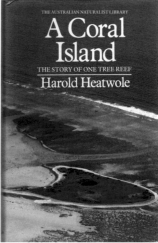

The Australian Naturalist Library was published by Collins in Sydney
between 1974 and 1981. Their content is fairly similar to volumes in the
main New Naturalist library, however their appearance is quite different.
Ultimately only six titles were ever published although they are not scarce
books, particularly in Australia.

The Australian Naturalist Library

During the mid-1970s, William Collins (Australia) Ltd, based in Sydney, published a series of books under the imprint of The Australian Naturalist Library. The content of these books is very similar to the New Naturalist main series but oriented to an Australian audience. However, the appearance of the books is quite different to the main library. None of the books are numbered and the dust jackets of all but the last volume are off-white with a painting on the front and spine of a species relevant to the book. They are quite similar to the other well-known natural history series of books published by T. and A. D. Poyser but are the same size (octavo) as the main NN series. The first five volumes in the Australian set are very similar in appearance and obviously form part of a series. The final book, *A Coral Island*, was published in 1981 and this, although similar in size, has a very different dust jacket based on a photograph. The first five books also have a distinctive logo at the foot of the spine,
again helping them to look like a series.

The Australian Naturalist Library were all printed in Hong Kong and bound in brown cloth (except for the final volume, which is bound in dark blue cloth) with gilt lettering. Internally the design and layout is quite similar to the main series, with text figures and colour plates. They appear to have been quite successful and well regarded by readers in Australia. In Britain the books appear on the market from time to time and there is a legendary tale of a huge remainder stock of *Living Insects* turning up at a shop in Hay-on-Wye some years ago. Although not directly part of the New Naturalist library, these six books form an interesting addition to any collection and may present a final challenge to anyone who has tracked down the main series, reprints and paperbacks.

Art of the New Naturalists

The idea of producing a large-format book to celebrate the New Naturalist jacket designs was first mooted in 2007. Myles Archibald contacted Peter Marren and Robert Gillmor to write a book which would reproduce the jackets at full size. At first Peter Marren was doubtful, for he felt that he had said everything he had to say in *The New Naturalists*. However there was a great opportunity for Robert Gillmor to comment on his own work and Peter was tempted by the idea of reviewing each of the Ellis designs. Peter also had the idea of commissioning guests to write about their favourite jackets. He also tried hard to find a new approach for each jacket, and to turn the progression of designs into a coherent narrative. In his own words, Peter 'wanted to say something about how a design develops from the complicated, and occasionally contradictory, triangle of editors, publishers and artists, and to show how the limitations of costs and print technology influenced the outcome'. There was also the chance to say more about the personal background and principles behind the art of Clifford and Rosemary Ellis, with considerable help from their surviving daughter, Penelope.

'The problems came with the printing,' Peter explained. 'Martin Charles had produced a terrific set of high-resolution

TABLE 32 The Australian Naturalist Library

Title	Author	Year of publication	Notes
Fish of the Ocean and Shore	J. M. Thompson	1974	208 pp, 16 pp colour plates, 4 pp b/w plates. Bookclub edition, Sydney 1975.
Living Insects	Richard D. Hughes	1975	304 pp, 60 colour and b/w plates, 69 text figures. Bookclub edition, Sydney 1974. US edition 1975.
Bird Life	Ian Rowley	1975	284 pp, colour and b/w plates, text illustrations and tables. Bookclub edition, Sydney 1975. US edition 1975. Paperback edition 1975.
Spiders of Australia	Barbara York Main	1976	296 pp, 44 colour illustrations, 12 b/w plates. Paperback edition 1984.
Frogs	Michael J. Tyler	1976	256 pp, 20 pp colour and b/w plates, text drawings. Paperback 1976, new paperback edition 1982.
A Coral Island	Harold Heatwole	1981	200 pp, 16 colour plates, text illustrations.

scans of the Ellis jackets, based on pristine proof copies, each of which was checked carefully. When the proofs arrived, the colours of some of the images had become badly distorted. When so much of the effect of these designs depends on exactness of colour, getting this right was essential.' Eventually, after much effort, most of these difficulties were overcome, but other problems came with the cover design. Peter felt it looked 'scruffy and cheap' and he was also disappointed by the blue title band. The authors would have preferred something matt and in a different colour, perhaps deep moss green, but it was not to be.

The first time the authors set eyes on the printed book was on the day of its launch at the New Naturalist Collectors' Club first symposium on 9 October 2009. But on the title band Clifford and Rosemary Ellis had been incorrectly credited as authors. The author blurb also contained some incorrect biographical details. The mistakes were acknowledged by HarperCollins and a new printing of the band with corrected wording was ordered immediately. Everyone who bought a copy that day will have the rare 'first state' title band, restricted to only about 250. From then on the band was replaced with a new version.

The first edition of 3,000 copies sold out very quickly, although only 2,875 were actually logged into the HarperCollins warehouse. These variations always occur with any large print run as the massive printing machines are not able to stop at an exact number of printed copies. This was followed by a second edition 'reprinted with corrections' of 2,000 (actually 2,191) copies which was still in print at the end of 2010. A limited edition of only 50 leather-bound copies of *Art of the New Naturalists* was also briefly available. This was published on 9th November 2009 and was completely sold out a few days later. This is by far the rarest of the leather-bound editions to date and although not strictly a NN volume, it is now probably one of the most collectable NN associated books so far produced.

Books that might have been
Reading through the minutes of the editorial committee meetings one comes across the ghosts of many books which were considered for inclusion in the ever-expanding New Naturalist library, but which never made it to publication. A list amongst those early files, dated March 1946, shows a list of 67 possible future titles and corresponding potential authors. Some of these were published in the NN library over the following decade or so, others took longer to find their way to publication, perhaps after extensive modifications and even changes of authorship. At that time *Woodland Birds* was listed as volume 22 in the series. James Fisher was down to write a book on moorland birds (number 35) and there were other titles such as *Fish* and *Ferns and Mosses* which for one reason or another did not make it into print for many years.

There are also a number of books which were listed as future New Naturalist titles but which were ultimately rejected. Some of these seem to have been in pre-production for quite a long time and it is interesting to read of their development, yet sad that they were destined never to be part of the series. In a few cases these works were published by Collins but not as part of the NN library. In other cases the authors were able to achieve publication elsewhere. Other books suggested over the years included a book on *Shore Birds* by the great bird artist Eric Ennion, *Whales and Whaling* by Leo Harrison Matthews, as well as better-documented books that nearly made it, such as *The Fox* and *Ponds, Pools and Puddles*. One or two other titles, such as *Bogs and Fens*, which was originally due to be published in 1981, may eventually still be published and would be a fitting addition to the series.

One little book which might have almost been one of the early monographs was *The Swallow*, written by Eric Hosking and Cyril Newberry, published by Collins in 1946. The design of the book is very much like that of a monograph but it is written in a more simple style and may have been primarily aimed at children. It is quite possible that this book helped to inspire the monographs which were established a couple of years later.

The Golden Eagle by Seton Gordon was mentioned in the minutes for September 1952 as a special volume, the manuscript of which was nearly finished. The artist J. C. Harrison even offered one of his paintings as a frontispiece. The following year it was decided that the book was not quite suitable for the NN series and it was eventually published by Collins outside of the series in 1955. The dust jacket featured the painting by J. C. Harrison and reading through the book it is quite easy to imagine it as one of the NN monographs.

Another book which nearly made it to the series was a new version of *The Broads*. Originally commissioned in 1977, this book was to be written by Martin George at the Nature Conservancy in Norwich. The book was completed in November 1982 but was found to be rather too long. By March 1984 the book was still being considered and in November 1986 the Board felt that, as remarkable a document as it was, it was not suitable for a New Naturalist. *The Land Use, Ecology and Conservation of Broadland* was eventually published by Packard, Chichester, in 1992, fifteen years after it was first thought of.

Today the New Naturalist library is as healthy as ever, with an excitingly broad range of titles scheduled for the future. Some of the new titles seem strangely familiar to one who has spent hours looking through Collins' old files, and it is gratifying to see them emerge from the long and unpredictable processes of publication. It will be good to see those titles eventually make it into the New Naturalist library, rather like a long-lost relative.

See www.newnaturalists.com for a complete list of books that were never published in the series.

E-books
To the committed bibliophile, the idea of replacing an entire bookshelf of beautiful New Naturalist volumes with digital files held on a handily portable e-reader would be anathema. But the development of the e-book is a major challenge and opportunity for the modern publisher.

Before the recent boom in online commercial e-book sales, an ecological puzzle prompted one New Naturalist author to issue his own e-book. When J. D. Summers-Smith's monograph *The House Sparrow* was first published in 1963, the house sparrow was such a common species that it was even considered a pest. But since the late 1970s the bird has been in dramatic decline not only in Britain but also in much of Western Europe. The urgent search for the reasons for this decline led to rising demand for copies of *The House Sparrow*. As a scarce collector's item the book was beyond the reach of the research community. The solution was to re-release the book in electronic format, as a PDF file on a CD-ROM which was distributed by Thersby Group, Stockton-on-Tees in 2004. The PDF is not a facsimile like print-on-demand books; instead, the text has been scanned with optical character recognition (OCR) technology. The pagination differs from the original and so page references in the text have also been corrected. Although not an official New Naturalist volume, the CD-ROM of *The House Sparrow* could be considered a collectable item with a place in the early twenty-first-century history of NN publishing.

Today, there are many kinds of file formats used for e-books, and an ever-expanding range of devices on which they can be read, from PCs to iPhones. Which of these formats and devices will last, and whether one particular standard will emerge, remains uncertain. But it is the development of dedicated e-readers, which use 'e-ink' technology to reduce the eyestrain associated with reading on conventional screens, which seems to be finally unlocking the potential of the e-book market. HarperCollins now issues many popular books directly to readers in the EPUB format, and its New Naturalist website offers sections of NN books for instant free download as PDFs. All forthcoming volumes in the NN series are now also available through Amazon to view on their Kindle e-reader, currently priced in between the paperback and hardcover editions although pricing, too, is liable to be fluid as the market develops. E-books can be downloaded to a computer, or directly to e-readers with wireless capability.

There are many points in favour of the e-book as a way of reading. The potential to make out of print titles widely and instantly available for download has already been mentioned. Fans enthuse about e-readers' portability, as a Kindle can hold over 200 non-illustrated titles and enable the reader to consult several NNs in the field or when travelling. One can also make notes in the text, highlight passages and add sticky bookmarks without defacing a precious book. And partially sighted readers can increase the font size, or even use 'text-to-speech' technology to turn a book into an audiobook.

Yet in spite of these advantages, it is hard to see as yet how e-books might fit in to a traditional book collection. The ease of instant downloads destroys the thrill of the chase which collectors enjoy while scouring bookshops, and all the problems of data corruptibility and obsolescence which hamper any digital archive will also apply to an e-book collection. Fundamentally, while a book collector may also enjoy reading e-books, they can never have the same appeal as a physical, paper-and-binding book. The tactile pleasure of leafing through a book and the enjoyment of the various smells of paper, ink and glue, will continue to entice bibliophiles whatever the technological alternatives on offer.

TABLE 33 Variants of 'Type 42' New Naturalist Library. A glance at this table will quickly allow the era of the jacket to be established, irrespective of the book around which it is wrapped.

Variant 1	NN1–41 inclusive (1960) but NN6, 9 & 13 stated as being out of print
Variant 2	NN1–43 inclusive (1961) but NN6, 9 & 13 stated as being out of print
Variant 3	NN1–44 inclusive (1962) but NN6, 9 & 13 stated as being out of print
Variant 3a	NN1–44 inclusive (1963) but NN9 & 13 stated as being out of print
Variant 4	NN1–45 inclusive (1962) but NN6, 9 & 13 stated as being out of print
Variant 4a	NN1–45 inclusive (1964) but NN9 & 13 stated as being out of print
Variant 5	NN1–46 inclusive (1965–66) but NN9 & 13 stated as being out of print
Variant 6	NN1–47; omitting NN13 (1966)
Variant 6a	NN1–48; omitting NN13 (1967)
Variant 7	NN1–49; omitting NN9 & 13 (1967)
Variant 8	NN1–50; omitting NN3, 9 & 13 (1967–71)
Variant 9	NN1–52; omitting NN3, 9 & 13 (1971–early)
Variant 9a	NN1–52; omitting NN2, 3, 9, 13, 28 & 39 (1971–late)
Variant 10	NN1–53; omitting NN2, 3, 9, 13, 17, 28 & 39 (1972)
Variant 11	NN1–54; omitting NN2, 3, 9, 13, 17, 28 & 39 (1972–73)
Variant 12	NN1–55; omitting NN2, 3, 9, 13, 17, 28 & 39 (1972–73)
Variant 13	NN1–56; omitting NN2, 3, 9, 13, 17, 28 & 39 (1973–74)
Variant 14	NN1–58; omitting NN2, 3, 9, 13, 17, 27, 28, 39, 40, 41 & 43 (1974–77)
Variant 15	NN1–60; omitting NN2, 3, 9, 13, 17, 27, 28, 39, 40, 41, 43 & 59 (1976–77)
Variant 16	NN1–61; omitting NN2, 3, 9, 13, 17, 28, 39, 40, 41 & 43 (1977–78)
Variant 17	NN1–61; omitting NN2, 3, 9, 13, 17, 27, 28, 39, 40, 41 & 43 (1977)
Variant 18	NN1–63; omitting NN2, 3, 9, 13, 17, 28, 39, 40, 41 & 43 (1978–79)
Variant 18a	NN1–63; omitting NN2, 3, 9, 13, 17, 21, 28, 39, 40, 41 & 43 (1979–80)
Variant 19	NN1–64; omitting NN2, 3, 9, 13, 17, 21, 28, 39, 40, 41, & 43 (1980)
Variant 20	NN1–64; omitting NN2, 3, 8, 9, 10, 13, 17, 21, 22, 24, 28, 36, 39, 40, 41 42, 43, 45, 46, 56, & 57 (1980)
Variant 21	NN1–65; omitting NN2, 3, 8, 9, 10, 13, 17, 21, 22, 24, 28, 36, 39, 40, 41 42, 43, 45, 46, 56, & 57 (1981)
Variant 22	NN1–66; omitting NN2, 3, 8, 9, 10, 13, 17, 21, 22, 24, 28, 36, 39, 40, 41 42, 43, 45, 46, 56, & 57 (1981)
Variant 23	NN1–67; omitting NN2, 3, 6, 8, 9, 10, 13, 17, 18, 20, 21, 22, 24, 26, 28, 31, 35, 36, 39, 40, 41, 42, 43, 45, 46, 50, 56, & 57 (1982)

THE BIBLIOGRAPHY

USING THE BIBLIOGRAPHY

Using the bibliography should be more or less self-explanatory, but a detailed interpretation is given below along with an explanation of the general methodology used.

Classification Codes
Each different generic type is assigned a unique classification code. These are always followed by the series number, so NN1 would be *Butterflies* and NN120 *Grasshoppers and Crickets* and, where M1 would be *The Badger* and M22 *The Mole*.

New Naturalist Books:
- NN — Collins New Naturalist main series (hardback).
- M — Collins New Naturalist monograph (hardback).
- CPB — Collins concomitant paperback.
- NNL — Collins leather-bound limited edition.
- COE — Collins other editions (hardback and paperback).
- BPB — Collins black paperback, main series.
- BPBM — Collins black paperback, monograph.
- BC — Bookclub main series.
- BCM — Bookclub monograph.
- POD — Collins print on demand digital copy.
- CFS — Collins/Folio Society facsimile edition.
- F — Fontana Paperback main series.
- FM — Fontana Paperback monograph.
- BL — Bloomsbury b/w facsimile edition.
- MIS — Miscellaneous UK edition, main series (p/b and h/b).
- MISM — Miscellaneous UK edition, monograph (p/b and h/b).
- US — Edition published in the United States, main series (h/b and p/b).
- USM — Edition published in the United States, monograph (h/b and p/b).
- FOR — Foreign language edition, main series (h/b and p/b).
- FORM — Foreign language edition, monograph (h/b and p/b).

Other associated books and series:
- NNJ — New Naturalist Journal.
- CS — The Countryside Series.
- CN — The Countryside Naturalist.

Regarding the two cases where essentially new books have been published but retain the same series number, NN6 *Highlands* and NN82 *New Naturalists*, the first edition is classified with a capital A epithet i.e. NN6A and the new edition NN6B.

Epithets
Each different edition, printing or state within each classification is assigned a letter, for example the first edition of *Mushrooms & Toadstools* would be NN7A, the second impression NN7B, the third impression NN7C and so on. To ensure consistency, the letter 'A' is always used for the first edition, regardless of whether there are further printings or not. In the same way the first printing will always be described as the first edition even if there are no further editions or reprints. Pre-publication editions are assigned a star e.g. NN2* – the very rare edition of *British Game* with the original title page dated 1945.

Additional Epithets:
- -VAR specific variant, other than binding and jacket variants (used only for patterned & plain endpaper variants of Woodlands).
- -B binding variant.
- -DJ dust jacket variant.
- -AP amended price: with specific reference to repriced dust jackets. (Note: 'rp' might appear to be a more appropriate code, but in bibliography 'rp' or 'rep' is an abbreviation for reprint.)

Therefore, for example, the code NN48A-B2-AP6 would be used for the second binding variant of NN48 *Grass and Grasslands* with a jacket repriced for the sixth time. In the bibliography all classifications are followed by a written summary of that classification, e.g. 'NN20E-AP1 1st Repriced DJ (1975–76), £4.00 sticker, *c.* 190 sold.' which, in this case, denotes that this is the first repriced jacket to appear on the fifth edition of NN20 *British Amphibians and Reptiles*, and that it was repriced with a £4.00 Collins sticker, of which *c.* 190 copies were sold thus.

Hierarchy
The order that books are catalogued within each individual title bibliography always follows the hierarchy of the above list. The main Collins editions are placed first, followed by Collins secondary editions; thereafter order is determined by the degree of physical separation from the Collins editions. Consequently books are not always catalogued in strict chronological order.

Standard information and layout
All NN first editions are presented in the same format as shown in the example below, which includes 13 separate elements, numbered here for clarity. However, in the individual bibliographies any element that does not apply to the title in question, or is unimportant diagnostically, is omitted.

The typography used in the bibliography is not an exact copy and does not replicate the original typeface, but it retains some elements of the original title page of each volume. The symbol '|' indicates a new line. An explanation of each element is given in the notes below.

1. NN30A   First Edition, 1955 (28 February 1955)
2. Title: 'The New Naturalist | Moths'
3. Author: 'by | E. B. Ford | F. R. S. | Genetic Laboratories | Zoology Department, Oxford'.
4. Illust: 'With 77 photographs in colour | 71 photographs in black and white | taken by S. Beaufoy | 19 maps and diagrams'.

5. Editors: James Fisher (JF), John Gilmour (JG), Julian Huxley (JH), L. Dudley Stamp (DS) & Eric Hosking (EH) (Photographic Editor)
6. Printer: Collins Clear-Type Press: London and Glasgow
7. ISBN: –
8. Collation: pp. xix, [1], 266, [2 NN adverts]; 16 leaves of colour plates printed to both sides; 12 leaves of b/w plates printed to both sides (18 × 16-page gatherings).
9. Casing: –
10. Dust Jacket:
    10a. Paper: acidic, matt.
    10b. Front panel: –
    10c. Front flap: blurb.
    10d. Rear panel: Advert for *The World of the Honeybee*.
    10e. Rear flap: Advert for *Butterflies* '*By the author of this Book*'. '*Also in the Library* Main Series' are listed *Insect Natural History* and *An Angler's Entomology* and as Special Volumes' *Fleas, Flukes & Cuckoos* and *Mumps, Measles & Mosaics*. Book details request.
11. Price: 35s. net
12. Print run: 8,500; total no. sold: *c.* 8,140; o/p: early 1966.
13. Notes: 1) the two pages of adverts at the rear include 'The New Naturalist A Survey of British Natural History'; main series and special vols. and an advert for *Butterflies*. 2) Book 27½ mm thick.

Notes:
1. The first date is the year of publication as printed in the book, the second date, in brackets, is the official date of publication.
2. The title is always taken from the title page and is always given in full including the generic series title and, where present, any subtitle.
3. The author's name is given as it appears on the title page, including all post-nominals.
4. Illust: this is a copy of the blurb advertising the illustrations that appear on the title page. Not all books advertise their illustrations, in which case this category will not appear in the table.
5. The list of Editors using their initials.
6. The printer and printer's location.
7. ISBN: this only appears in NN books from 1970/1971 onwards, and is therefore omitted for all books published before this date. For books published from 2006/2007 both the 10- and 13-digit ISBNs are given.
8. Collation: the measure of the book's physical composition, including the number of pages, plates and gatherings. Pagination is given by way of the usual formula where pp. = pages and square brackets indicate pages that are not physically numbered; plates and end papers, which are not part of the printed sheets, are excluded from the formula. Therefore, the above example 'pp. xix, [1], 266, [2 NN

adverts]' indicates that the last preliminary page is numbered xix, followed by a single unnumbered page and 266 text pages, with 2 unnumbered pages at the end of the text which, in this case, are used for NN advertisements. The total number of pages is therefore 19 + 1 + 266 + 2 = 288, which is made up from 18 × 16-page gatherings or sections. Added to this are 16 leaves of colour plates and 12 leaves of b/w plates.
9. Casing: this category is usually omitted as generally casings display minimal variation, but occasionally dissimilar cloths might be used or the lettering/monogram blocked differently e.g. '-B1' and '-B2' of *Man and the Land*. Occasionally casings will be of slightly different dimensions e.g. first and second state *Fungi*.
10. The dust jacket is subdivided into three/four elements that are important bibliographically.
    10a. Paper: The dust jacket paper and its finish is usually omitted as this is covered on pages 74–5; however where *Duraseal* should be present, this is always mentioned.
    10b. Front panel: With NN books the design to the front panel remains the same throughout printings with minimal variation and is therefore of little diagnostic interest. It is nearly always omitted but there is the odd exception such as *The Weald* where significant colour variation is displayed between printings.
    10c. Front flap: This element is not usually described as it generally follows the same format; that is, blurb for the book, with jacket design credit below. Where diagnostically significant it is included.
    10d. Rear panel: the rear panel carries greater variation and is more important bibliographically than any other part of the jacket and is therefore always described.
    10e. Rear flap: important bibliographically and likewise always described.
11. The price is replicated in the form that it appears on the jacket.
12. Print run: the number of books ordered to be printed i.e. the *print-order*. If the number is followed by '*(out-turn)*' this indicates the actual number of books produced. *Out-turn* is clearly more precise and therefore where known is always given priority. The sales history, when known, is additionally recorded in this category including the number of books sold and the date the book went out of print.
13. Notes: Key contributors such as artists and photographers and additional information not included in the above categories or in the introduction will be noted here.

Classification with respect to state and variant
State and *variant* are terms used to describe consistent variation within a group of books of the *same* printing. Usually they are prefixed with an ordinal number, i.e. first state, second state etc.

State is used here as a general term to describe significant variation, whereas *variant* is usually applied to a specific feature displaying subtle variation, i.e. variant binding or variant jacket. Therefore, with specific regard to this bibliography, state carries greater significance than *variant* and this is reflected in the assigned classification.

Using keys and tables

These have been used to highlight, in comparative form, the differences between states and variants, but only address variation that is both consistent and typical. However, anomalies and aberrations always exist and these will, either, not 'key-out' satisfactorily, or, be omitted altogether from the tables. Additionally it is well known that many NN titles were bound up in batches, often over a period of several years or more, but unless these different bindings display consistent and identifiable diagnostic features, they will inevitably have been overlooked. Then, there is, of course, the very real possibility that a recurrent variant or state with significant features has been missed altogether! The bibliography is not exhaustive. But hopefully the majority of significant states and variants will be included.

Generally I hope that these will be a useful tool to help determine the status of a book in hand.

Title priority Bibliographic convention states that the Author's name should come before the title, but in this bibliography the title comes first. This is because NN books are part of a numbered series and principally known by their title rather than their authors.

Publisher As all NN titles are published in the first instance by Collins/HarperCollins, publisher information is omitted from each catalogue entry; if a title is published under licence overseas, publisher information is given.

Publication dates and printing history The year given is as printed in the book, even though in the case of a few reprints and overseas editions it is incorrect. However, where known the correct or precise publication date is added within brackets. The printing histories given for reprints and subsequent editions always replicate the details given on the imprint page.

Out of print dates It has often been difficult or impossible to establish the date that many titles went out of print. Additionally the matter is complicated by a publisher's custom of retaining the last few books in store. In this book the out of print date given is essentially the date that the publisher sold the last of their commercially available stock, though it is likely that distributors and shops still had copies for sale beyond that date. Taking this into account, it is not unlikely that a few dates given are a little out; nevertheless most dates will be sufficiently accurate to give a fair indication of a book's shelf-life. If the out of print date is not known it is simply omitted.

Repriced jackets Books and specifically dust jackets repriced by Collins are individually catalogued. These are identifiable variants issued by the publisher and whilst, in themselves, inconsequential they are a part of a larger picture and tell us:

- When a particularly copy was on sale.
- How prices were increased in relation to inflation.
- The sales figures for a specific period. The number of books sold in entire jackets i.e. not price clipped (the difference between total number sold and the number of repriced-copies).

Repriced variants and the quantity sold of each are determined from the sales statements, but a number of variants have come to light which do not appear in these sales statements, and it must therefore be concluded that not all statements are entirely accurate. This being the case the quantity sold is generally rounded to the nearest 50.

Differences between editions Generally only differences are stated and similarities ignored; for instance if a reprint shares the same ISBN it will not generally be mentioned but if a different ISBN has been assigned then this will be stated.

Comparison The entries for each edition are always compared with the immediately preceding edition and not the first edition (unless expressly stated otherwise). This is simply for pragmatic reasons as there is generally a gradual evolutionary process in play and so to compare with the preceding entry requires a lot less ink than comparing with the original edition.

Adverts and listings 'Advert', as used in this bibliography, implies that the title in question will be accompanied by an endorsement, which will usually be one or more press reviews, whereas 'listing' implies that the title is given unsupported.
For instance the following statement – 'the rear flap advertises *The Sea Shore* and *The Sea Coast*' implies that these titles are accompanied by press endorsements, but the statement the rear flap lists '*The Sea Shore* and *The Sea Coast*' implies that they are unsupported listings.

The bibliography follows the classification status printed in the book It is not unusual for NN reprints to refer to themselves as editions, when, in fact, they are simply reprints. For instance the 1955 printing of *Wild Flowers* NN 5B is stated in the book as being a *new edition*, though it is no more than a straightforward reprint. The next printing is then stated as being the third edition when, correctly it is the first new edition i.e. the second edition. But in order to avoid further confusion, the bibliography follows the classification printed in the book, even though it might be technically incorrect. Occasionally the stated printing history of a title is so inconsistent that it is not possible to use the classification printed in the book, but the text will always elucidate such cases.

Dust jackets The photograph of the dust jacket featured at the beginning of each different book, is always taken from a first edition copy.

WRITING THE BIBLIOGRAPHY

Sources of information

The information, contained within the bibliographies has been assembled from a variety of sources, but there are two of particular importance: firstly, the books themselves and secondly, the Collins archive.

The books

Thorough comparison is the key to any bibliography and to this end every known NN variant, where available, has been collected together, a task that, before the advent of the internet, would have been virtually impossible. Through this process of assembly, many 'new' variants have been thrown up but, regularly within the New Naturalist series, there is variation within a single printing and therefore it is necessary to compare 'like' with 'like', and this is where the problems begin. Inevitably some variants, and these are likely to be binding variants, will have been missed, but fortunately I have been able to draw on the stocks of my book business, which amount to several thousand copies. When a new variant is discovered it is then necessary to establish that it is, in fact, that i.e. that it displays consistent features and is not just a one-off aberrant. This often requires correspondence with collectors and booksellers. Tim Bernhard and I have built up in parallel our own collections and this has enabled further comparison.

The process of comparison is time consuming and tedious! Quite simply multiple copies of the same title are compared, one alongside another, systematically checking jackets, casings, joints, hinges, stitching, title pages, plates, and so on. The bibliographic entry for the average New Naturalist has taken about two days to put together, but some titles, for example, *The Herring Gull's World* took over a week. However, when comparing the differences between very similar editions and reprints it was just not possible to check every single page; that is, if this book was to be completed within anything like a reasonable timeframe – and I suspect many might say that has already been grossly exceeded! Therefore some differences and features will have been overlooked, but hopefully nothing too significant.

The Collins archive: sales statements

The most important bibliographic information is contained with the New Naturalist sales statements as these usually give the number of books printed, the number sold, the sales period and the out of print date.

The majority of the sales statement from 1956 to the present are still extant (a total of over 60 statements), but there are a

number of gaps. I suspect that these missing statements exist somewhere: in some hidden recess of the Collins warehouse or indeed in various private archives – a few additional ones have come to light during the course of writing the bibliography. The earliest extant sales statement is dated 31 October 1956, none before this date has been found. The 1960s are reasonably well supplied, but the 1963 statements are missing as are all for 1968 and then the most significant gap of all, 1970–1973. Again, and perhaps surprisingly, the statements for the three-year period 1990–1992 were also unavailable.

Missing sales statements make it impossible, in some cases, to know the print run of titles printed during that period, but not infrequently, by looking at the total print figures before and after the missing period, it is possible to determine, with a fair degree of certainty, a print figure. For each individual title the relevant sales information from the 60 or so statements, has been extracted and added to a spreadsheet dedicated to that title: a time-consuming business, but one that enables a comparative overview and as such, an invaluable aid. These dedicated title spreadsheets have, on occasion, thrown up arithmetical errors and brought various discrepancies to light: in other words the sales/print information available is not always perfectly accurate. Neither are the sales statements always clear, for instance when stock is sold off to the Readers Union (or in some cases pulped) it is often not mentioned, and does not appear in the 'number sold' column but instead is simply recorded by a drop of equal quantity in both the 'stock' and 'number printed' figures. With these problems in mind, the figures given in the bibliographies are only as reliable as the information available but where a greater degree of uncertainty exists, figures are qualified thus '[?]'.

The Collins archive also contains individual book files and Editors' board minutes, a lot of which has been copied into my co-author's collection and from this material various bibliographic and anecdotal information has been gleaned.

Other sources of information

Peter Marren when writing *The New Naturalists* compiled hundreds of pages of immaculate handwritten notes and this has been an invaluable source of additional material. Author's biographies and autobiographies, notes and letters have also been plumbed and collectors with archives have been pummelled for information. The New Naturalist Collectors' Club newsletter, in the early days of the editor Bob Burrow, has been a useful source of additional snippets.

But despite these efforts, new information is frequently being uncovered and, with the NN library regularly being added to, this bibliography should not be viewed as anything other than a work-in-progress of which this present edition is the first of hopefully further more finely honed editions to follow.

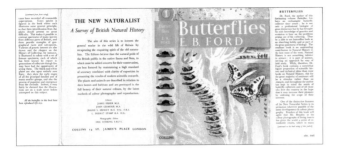

1 Butterflies

On the 12 November 1945 the New Naturalist was born and at its helm was the perfect book: *Butterflies*; for it is impossible to imagine any other being 'number 1'. *Butterflies,* with the Ellises' iconic jacket, set up the series brilliantly.

Butterflies; bejewelled denizens of the insect world, were the ideal subjects for an embryo series whose credo proclaimed to portray plants and animals 'in the full beauty of their natural colours by the latest methods of colour photography and reproduction.' *Butterflies* includes 48 colour and 24 b/w plates, more than any other early New Naturalist. In the words of the blurb: '…the illustrations are on a scale never before attempted on this subject.' This was echoed by Peter Marren, who felt the plates to be 'the most comprehensive and interesting collection of British butterfly pictures ever made.'

Butterflies was a landmark book not only because it was the first New Naturalist and because of its photographic plates, but also it was the first book in the literature of Lepidoptera to examine butterflies 'as part of the great panorama of biology'. Miriam Rothschild proclaimed Ford's book to be the best ever written about butterflies.

Clearly, then, *Butterflies* was an outstanding book and it is therefore not surprising that it sold prodigiously well, however there was another factor at play: *the war effect,* and it is this, rather than the book's exceptional qualities, that produced the unprecedented (and unexpected) sales figures. Bill Williams in 1946, then advisor to Allen Lane's Penguin, wrote: 'The fact is that poverty promotes serious reflection upon the less material values and therefore instigates an attention to serious books, music and the arts, which is absent in more prosperous times'. And so it was that during World War II the demand for books rose to an unprecedented level. Towards the end of the war, when victory seemed certain, books about the post-war world, particularly 'England's green and pleasant land' became ever more popular. BBC television was still off the air at that time and did not return until June 1946 (by 1951 over one million UK households held licences). Stanley Unwin observed that almost any book would succeed because demand far outstretched supply. This was the world into which the New Naturalist was born. *Butterflies* was published on the same day as NN3 *London's Natural History;* NN2 *British Game* and NN4 *Britain's Structure and Scenery* followed 9 months and 10 months later respectively. Tellingly, the early sales figures for each of these four titles were very similar and each was reprinted within a year.

If there is a criticism of *Butterflies,* it is its detachment, or rather the author's detachment (and this impassivity is a trait taken up by many NN authors that were to follow). Richard Mabey describes it as 'a peculiarly British attitude towards natural history – meticulous, obdurate and disengaged'. Considering the avowed aim of the New Naturalist was 'to interest the general reader in the wildlife of Britain by recapturing the enquiring spirit of the old naturalists' it is paradoxical that a preponderance of texts are written without recourse to personal experience, to the circumstances of discovery, to the excitement and rigours of fieldwork, or any other anecdotal information which might provide useful context – and enliven the text. Passion is never a substitute for knowledge but it can make that knowledge a lot easier to digest.

Butterflies ran to four editions and three reprints, though the first three editions were all very similar. These books also vary considerably in thickness, depending on the paper used and arrangement of plates. The 1977 edition was printed from blow-ups of the revised 1975 Fontana text and has no colour plates, but introduces ten new b/w plates of very good photographs by John S. Haywood. The printing is surprisingly crisp and quite different from previous editions, and despite the absence of the colour plates, it is sufficiently different to warrant having a copy.

The jackets of the various printings display significant colour variation. The 1967 reprint is dark and dingy and presumably the result of the reprographic technique used. There is one peculiarity regarding the jacket – the Ellises' monogram appears to be dated 1943, but as the prototype was not painted until September 1944 and the final artwork completed in February 1945, the '3' must actually be a '5'!

In addition to the Collins editions, *Butterflies* was published by the Readers Union in 1953; by Macmillan in the US in 1957 (and probably again in 1962); as a Fontana paperback in 1975; as a Bloomsbury facsimile edition in 1990; and as a Collins/Folio Society facsimile in 2008. The Collins edition remained in print until 1981, but was out of stock for *part* of 1956–57, 1961–62, 1965–67 and 1975–77.

The first edition jacket is difficult to find in anything other than indifferent condition; it is prone to browning and the blue to fading on the spine, the orange fades too but to a lesser extent, and being a popular book, more likely than not it will be ragged at the head and the tail of the spine. But a bright and fresh *Butterflies* jacket is a fine thing indeed and every New Naturalist collection should start with one.

NN1A	First Edition, 1945 (12 November 1945)
Title:	'The New Naturalist | Butterflies'
Author:	'by | E. B. Ford, M.A. D.Sc | Reader in Genetics, Lecturer and University Demonstrator in Zoology and Comparative Anatomy | A Hope Curator of Entomology Oxford'
Illust:	'All Known British Butterflies Shown Life- | size in Colour and 56 Colour Photographs | of Living Specimens by S. Beaufoy | 24 Plates in Black and White | 32 Distribution Maps and | 9 Other Diagrams'

TABLE NN1 Collins and Readers Union editions, showing print quantities and availability on the internet book site AbeBooks during the second week of March 2013. As might be expected, availability is roughly commensurate with the number of books printed, and the more recent the printing the greater proportion of jackets that have survived; when, in 1977, jackets were protected with *Duraseal*, all have survived. Since the second week of May 2011, when the availability of NN first editions on AbeBooks was first surveyed (table 2 on page 36), the number of first edition *Butterflies* has increased by 9 (i.e. 19 per cent), however not one copy, had then or has now a very good or better jacket.

Class	Year	Edition	Print run (print-orders)	No. offered on AbeBooks March 2013	
				Worldwide (inc. UK)	UK only
NN1A	1945	1	20,000	56 (20 with jackets)	47
NN1B	1946	2	17,000 (plus 3,000[?] sold off to the RU – BC1A)	36 (15 with jackets)	28
NN1C	1957	3	3,350 (of which 675 sold to the US – Macmillan)	4 (2 with jackets)	2
NN1D	1962	3, 1st rep.	2,200[?] (of which 300 sold to the US publisher)	4 (1 with a jacket)	2
NN1E	1967	3, 2nd rep.	3,500	6 (2 with jackets)	5
NN1F	1971	3, 3rd rep.	2,500	6 (5 with jackets)	5
NN1G	1977	4	2,500 (+ unknown no. of RU copies)	11 (all with jackets)	10
BC1A	1953	RU ed.	3,000[?]	10 (1 with a jacket)	6
Totals			**54,050**	**133**	**105**

Editors: JF, JG, JH, LDS and EH (Photographic Editor).

Printer: Collins Clear-Type Press: London and Glasgow (produced in conjunction with Adprint).

Collation: pp. xiv, 368, [2]; 24 leaves of colour plates printed to both sides; 12 leaves of b/w plates printed to both sides (24 × 16-page gatherings).

Jacket: [Rear panel] 'The New Naturalist | A Survey of British Natural History' under which is quoted the NN credo, followed by the list of Editors and the Collins address. [Rear flap] Continuation of the burb from the front flap (wing).

Price: 16s. net.

Print run: 20,000; o/p: 1946.

Notes: 1) Jacket blurb replicates sections of the Editors' preface. 2) Jacket design credit omitted from all editions. 3) Dedication below printing history on the imprint page. 4) Book 29 mm thick.

NN1B First Reprint (Second Edition), 1946. 'First published in September 1945… | …Reprinted, 1946'. As NN1A; possibly a few corrections. 'F.R.S' has been somewhat clumsily added to Ford's post nominals on the title page; imprint page reordered with dedication above printing history. Paper slightly rougher; boards thicker; book 31 mm thick. Jacket identical to first edition. Price: 16s net. Print run: 20,000 of which c. 3,000 sold to the RU in 1953. Notes: 1) The print histories to all succeeding printings refer to this 1946 edition as the 'second edition'. 2) In 1947 10,000 quires were waiting for binding so evidently there was more than one binding, though there do not appear to be any distinguishing features.

NN1B-AP1 Repriced Jacket (sold 1948–56). Label showing '21s. 0d.' or '21s. net' pasted over original price, or price-clipped, with 'Book Production Economy Standard' label of 21/- net (features a lion sitting above a book).

NN1C Third edition, 1957. 'First published in 1945… | … Second Edition, 1946 | Third Edition, 1957'. Minimal revisions, the most significant being the addition of a 22-line appendix to p. 327 concerning *Colias calida* – a new butterfly added to the British list. The title page has been reworded and reset – Ford with F. R. S. only and 'Genetic Laboratories Zoology Department, Oxford'; the illustrations blurb now reads: 'With 87 colour photographs, 89 in black and white. All known British Butterflies shown lifesize in colour. Living specimens by S. Beaufoy, 41 Maps and Diagrams'; the Collins address includes the street number. Text paper rougher, b/w plates on semi-glossy paper, printing of colour plates inferior. Book significantly thicker at 34 mm, with the jacket barely wide enough for the spine. Jacket identical to first edition but price: 30s net. Print run: 3,350 of which 675 sold to Macmillan in the US; o/p: 1961. Note: This edition characterised by very thick endpapers – about the heaviest of any NN book.

NN1D Third Edition, First Reprint, 1962 [early]. 'First published in 1945… | …Second Edition, 1946 | Third Edition, 1957 | Reprinted, 1962'. As NN1C with minimal revisions. Title page unchanged but Ford now 'Fellow of All Souls College and University Reader in Genetics, Oxford'. Editors: JH now Sir JH and JG now with VMH. Text paper smoother. Book 30 mm thick. The NN library to the jacket with green title band and listing NN1–44 (Type 42, variant 3); rear panel advertises Ford's *Moths*;

front flap with new short blurb that begins 'The author of this now famous work...', below which are two press commendations. Price: 35s. net. Print run: 2,200[?] of which 300 sold to US publisher; o/p: 1965. Note: The jacket flaps are particularly wide with the colour bar just evident to the front edge.

NN1E Third Edition Second Reprint, 1967 [early]. 'First Edition 1945 | Second Edition 1946 | Third Edition 1957 | Reprinted 1962 | Reprinted 1967'. Unrevised but for a few personnel details and imprint page reset. Ford to title page now 'Professor of Ecological Genetics and Fellow of All Souls College, Oxford'. Editors: JF, JG, JH and EH. b/w plates on glossy, thicker paper. Book 32 mm thick. The jacket printed, at a slightly smaller scale, using a new reprographic technique producing stronger colours and muddy-grey tones. The NN library to the jacket, with dark blue title band, lists NN 1–48 (Type 42, variant 6A); both flaps unchanged. Price: 45s. net. Print run: 3,500. (Occasionally found in a 1962 NN1D jacket).

NN1F Third Edition, Third Reprint, 1971. ISBN 0002130262 (to jacket only). 'First Edition 1945 | Second Edition 1946 | Third Edition 1957 | Reprinted 1962 | Reprinted 1967 | Reprinted 1971'. Minimal changes only. Ford to title page now 'Professor, and Fellow of All Souls College, Oxford'. Editors: JG, JH, MD, KM and EH. Colour plates on glossier, heavier paper. Book 31 mm thick. Jacket printing different again, with stronger colours, but without the muddy grey tones; the NN library lists NN1–52 (Type 42, variant 9); both flaps unchanged, but for addition of ISBN to rear. Price: £2.75. net. Print run: 2,500; o/p: 1975.

NN1G Fourth Edition, 1977. ISBN 0002193930. 'First Edition 1945 | Second Edition 1946 | Third Edition 1957 | Fourth Edition 1977'; pp. 352; 12 leaves of b/w plates printed to both sides (11 × 32-page gatherings). A new edition based on the Fontana revised edition of 1975 and printed from plates copied and enlarged from that edition, and consequently the setting is completely new; prelims inc. title and half-title page also reset. All colour images from the previous editions have been omitted, fourteen of the original b/w plates carried over to this edition and ten new plates of b/w photographs by J. S. Haywood incorporated (the page nos. for plates 20–24 on the list of plates are incorrect). The Editors' and Author's prefaces revised to reflect new plate arrangements. The text is ostensibly as the preceding editions, with some new information included and distribution maps updated, but according to the revised preface 'It should not be supposed, however, that the account given here is brought fully up to date...'. Somewhat contradictorily the jacket blurb states that the text has been extensively revised. Editors: MD, JG, KM and EH; last sentence of NN credo omitted. Book 27 mm thick. The colours of the *Durasealed* jacket are a little different still; the title has been 'reworked' resulting in a 'join' along the joint fold; and the title lettering slightly repositioned; the NN library to the jacket lists NN1–61 (Type 42, variant 17); rear flap advertises *Moths* as earlier jackets, but reset and press comments abridged; new blurb to front flap with *Yorkshire Post* endorsement beneath. Price: £8.00 net. Print run: 2,500; no. sold: *c.* 1,200 (inc. AP1) + probably *c.* 1,000 copies 'remaindered' to a bookclub; o/p: 1981.

NN1G-AP1 1st Repriced DJ (1981), £8.50 sticker, < 100 sold.

BC1A Readers Union Edition, 1953. As NN1B and from that printing, but with a cancel title page displaying the RU tree logo and dated 1953. Binding also identical, but stamped 'Readers Union' in gilt to the rear board. RU jacket 'Type 1'. Price: 10s. 6d net. No. sold to the RU: *c.* 3,000. Note: Supplied from the bound stock of NN1B.

BC1B Bookclub edition, 1977. (Probably Readers Union). Bound from the same sheets as the Collins fourth edition, NN1G and almost indistinguishable, but for following diagnostic features: casing of dark green imitation cloth; jacket identical but without a *Duraseal* protector and without a printed price. Print run: unknown but not particularly scarce. Note: It would seem that additionally 1,000 copies of the Collins 1977 fourth edition were 'remaindered' to a bookclub.

POD1A. **Print on demand** digital copy of 1945 first edition NN1A.

CFS1A Collins/Folio Society facsimile, 2008 (02 July 2008). ISBN-10: 0007278497, ISBN-13: 9780007278497. A facsimile copy with jacket of the first edition. Not declared as a facsimile edition. Cased in modern, dark green, *Arbelave* buckram. Elements of jacket spine digitally re-whitened. Print run: *c.* 1,000 (as part box-set of first ten) + *c.* 150 individual copies; o/p: Nov. 2010. (While not marked as a facsimile, the freshness of the paper, the casing fabric and digitally re-whitened jacket should not allow confusion with the genuine first ed. Copies sold individually by HarperCollins have a price sticker with ISBN, barcode and www.newnaturalists.com affixed to rear DJ panel.)

F1A Fontana Paperback Edition, 1975. ISBN: 0006334687; pp. 368; 12 leaves of b/w plates bound in three sections, printed on glossy paper, to both sides. 'A format', perfect bound paperback. A revised and reset edition, without colour and a reduced no. of b/w plates, but including ten new plates of b/w photographs by J. S. Haywood. The Editors' preface omitted and the author's preface revised to suit. Editors: JG, JH, MD, KM and EH. Adverts for Fontana Library titles at front. The cover photograph of a Red Admiral by John Haywood; rear cover with three press endorsements. Price: £1.50. Print run: 10,000; no. sold: *c.* 3,580, but all outstanding stock remaindered in 1979. (This Fontana edition was used for the Collins 1977 fourth edition.)

BL1A Bloomsbury edition, 1990 (31 December 1990). ISBN: 1870630491; pp. 352, [48 – b/w illustrations] (25 × 16-page gatherings). A b/w facsimile of the 1977 fourth edition NN1G. The jacket blurb is also as NN1G. Price: £12.95. Print run: unknown, but remaindered.

US1A US edition, 1957. Macmillan. The book is identical to the Collins 1957 third edition NN1C, including title and half-title pages, but the NN monogram has been omitted from the casing and 'Macmillan' has been blocked to the spine. The jacket exhibits greater differences: the same Ellis design with the same blurb that continues onto the back flap, but the rear panel is blank, and 'Macmillan' printed to the base of the spine. The price is printed to the top corner of the front flap (no price to the bottom corner), but is price-clipped. Print run (sold to Macmillan): 675.

US1B US edition reprint, 1962. Macmillan. Not Seen. Unverified. (July 1962 sales report mentions 300 copies sold to the USA). As the Collins 1962 third edition, first reprint NN1D, but presumably with similar distinctive features as the 1957 US edition 'US1A', but possibly exactly as the Collins ed. but with a 'Distributed By Macmillan' label to the jacket. Print run (sold to Macmillan): c. 300.

2 British Game

A fascinating book in terms of both its bibliography and, as far as the New Naturalist is concerned, its atypical style, but let us look at the former first, as that is of more interest to the collector.

British Game was published on Monday 19 August 1946, but it was written in the midst of WWII and was almost certainly the first New Naturalist title to be completed. The introduction to the reprint of the same year is initialled and dated 'B.V.-F. *Winchester 1943*' (the identical introduction to the first edition is undated). It might be unwise to read too much into the subsequent dating of the introduction, but it was obviously deliberate and probably pointed: there had been long delays, as explained below, which would have been irksome to the most phlegmatic of authors – and when reading *British Game* one does not get the impression that Brian Vesey-Fitzgerald was even vaguely phlegmatic!

Every title page of the 'first edition' is a cancel, i.e. it is a replacement: the original title leaf has been cut out and the new title leaf pasted to the stub of the excised leaf – if you look closely it is obvious enough, but it is so well done that, unless pointed out, it generally goes unnoticed. Considering this operation was done by hand and that 20,000 copies were printed, it must have represented more than a small distraction for the Glasgow bindery. But why all this trouble? Simply, the original title page was incorrect: the 'illustration blurb' referred to 20 distribution maps – there were none. Almost certainly, this cutting and pasting was done before the books were trimmed and cased, but a few copies of the original edition have survived – I know of just three. These were probably advance copies bound for editorial purposes and to enable 'travellers' to subscribe books to the trade. They are dated 1945 and it has been suggested that they are the true first edition, however, as *British Game* was not officially published until 19 August 1946, I have classified them here as a pre-publication variant with the reference 'NN2*'.

The title page debacle inevitably led to delays and this, coupled with the 'post-war effect', resulted in substantial subscription sales; so large in fact that the reprint was already underway before the first edition was published. Within a month of publication all but 1,000 of the 19,000 copies printed had sold. However, once the initial surge had abated, sales slowed considerably to the point where, in 1947, the editor James Fisher complained it was a slow seller! In fact the turnaround in the fortunes of *British Game* is quite remarkable: for the last ten years of its life sales averaged a little over 300 books per annum. By 1953, it was evident that the title was overstocked, so in response Collins sold around 3,000 copies, at 5s.3d. per unit, to the Country Book Club (Readers Union); this was at cost and essentially remaindering. These RU copies have cancel title pages and are blocked 'Readers Union' to the rear board of the Collins green buckram bindings; they were fitted with dedicated Readers Union jackets. In 1959 a further tranche was sold off to the RU and likewise these have cancel title pages, but this time the RU did not bother to add their imprint to the Collins casing.

The dust jacket of the first edition is always several millimetres too short for the book, though some collectors maintain that full-height copies do exist. The 1946 reprint jacket is textually and graphically identical but for one very obvious difference – the reverse has the same design boldly printed in a burnt orange-pink colour and, to my knowledge, all reprint copies are like this. It would appear that the background, which should have remained blank, was erroneously printed with one of the overlay colours, but rather than waste the stock (paper rationing still applied) the jackets were reprinted on the reverse. How such a conspicuous mistake came to be made, is not known; it is not at all unusual for jackets across publishers from this time, but particularly 1946, to be printed on the reverse of recycled jackets.

Alluded to, in the first sentence, is the quirky nature of *British Game* and it is, in many respects, a misfit within the New Naturalist: a goose amongst the swans, or perhaps that should be a swan amongst the geese? Just the title alone conjours up images of 'the glorious twelfth', gamekeepers and shooting, and not the science-based natural history that we expect of the New Naturalist. Brian Vesey-Fitzgerald is opinionated and certainly not detached, but his accounts reflect his personal observations and *British Game* is the richer for it. Richard Mabey describes it as the 'most vivid' New Naturalist. It contains some of the most compelling passages of all books published to date.

Additionally, there are no colour photographs, instead all colour plates are paintings or prints, after Henry Alken, Winifred Austen, Gould, J. C. Harrison, Seaby, Peter Scott, Thorburn, Joseph Wolf *et al.* (Tunnicliffe is the obvious name missing). With respect to the aims of the series, these reproduced paintings are anachronistic and certainly at odds with the newly conceived New Naturalist credo 'portrayed…by the latest methods of colour photography.' But more important than that, they are simply alien to the New Naturalist, and as Peter Marren has pointed out are much more akin to the wartime 'Britain in Picture' series.

The great number of books printed has not led to a munificent supply of fine jacketed copies: the acidic paper used for the jacket is weak and readily chips and browns. Genuine fine copies are rare, but when they do turn up they are never expensive; not, at least, in terms of *Orkney*, *Hebrides* or even *British Bats*, so patience will be rewarded.

NN2* Pre-publication variant, 1945. With the original title leaf that erroneously refers to 20 distribution maps; illustration blurb to title page states: 'With 24 Colour Plates | 81 Black and White Photographs | and 20 Distribution Maps'; the imprint page is dated 1945. No. bound up: unknown but probably just a handful. (The true first edition has a cancel TP that has been corrected. See intro. for a fuller explanation.)

NN2A	**First edition**, 1946 (19 August 1946).
Title:	'The New Naturalist | British Game'.
Author:	'by | Brian Vesey-FitzGerald | F.L.S. | Editor of "The Field"'.
Illust:	'With Twenty-Eight | Reproductions in Colour | and Eighty-One | Black and White Photographs'.
Editors:	JF, JG, JSH, LDS and EH.
Printer:	Collins Clear-Type Press, London and Glasgow (produced in conjunction with Adprint).
Collation:	pp. xv, [1], 240; 12 leaves of colour plates printed to both sides; 24 leaves of b/w plates printed to both sides (16 × 16-page gatherings).
Jacket:	[Rear panel] 'The New Naturalist A Survey of British Natural History', under which NN Credo given in full; Editors and Collins address. [Rear flap] 'The New Naturalist' listing 'The first four titles in the series'.
Price:	16s. net.
Print run:	20,000; o/p: 1946.
Notes:	1) The title leaf is a cancel (see intro.). 2) No author's preface but the intro. is initialled 'B'. 3) The list of plates in the preliminaries has an unusually generous spacing and uses eight pages. 4) Seven colour plates incorrectly orientated – see description for reprint. 5) Plate vb was the first published photograph of a British cock capercaillie. 6) Plate xxv captioned 'hare' is actually a rabbit. 7) written during the war – on p. 220, line 7 'The young men are at war now'. 8) Text to jacket printed in dark brown. 9) Jacket a few millimetres too short for the book.

NN2B Reprint, 1946. 'First published in 1945… | …Reprinted 1946'. As the first edition, but with a few corrections. Author to TP now noted as being 'Formerly Editor of "The Field"'; the intro. is initialled and dated 'B.V.-F. Winchester 1943'. Plates 2, 8, 10, 16, 18, 20, 24 now correctly orientated with caption to the gutter edge. The jacket is the correct height, unrevised, but all jackets are printed on the reverse with a burnt-orange version of the same jacket design. The price is unchanged at 16s. net. Print run: 20,000 inc. repriced variants below and both RU editions; o/p: 1968/69 (AP1). Notes: 1) The reprint was underway before the first edition

was published. 2) In 1947 there were still 10,000 unbound quires and therefore there are, at least, two bindings of the reprint, but no consistent variation has been detected. For further bibliographic details see intro. 3) The order of listing of the repriced jacket variants does not confer any priority, though probably sold at different times.

NN2B-AP1 Repriced DJ (1948? – 68/69) with label showing 21s. od., or 21s. net. or with 'Book Production Economy Standard' label of 21/- net (features a lion sitting above a book).

BC2A Readers Union Edition, First Issue, 1953. As NN2B and from that printing, but with a cancel title page displaying the RU tree logo and dated 1953. Binding also identical, but stamped 'Readers Union' in gilt to the rear board. RU jacket 'Type 1'. Price: 10s. 6d net. No. sold to the RU: 3,000.

BC2B Readers Union Edition, Second Issue, 1959. As BC2A; Part of the original Collins 1946 reprint NN2B printing, with a cancel title page, displaying the RU imprint and tree logo dated 1959; the green buckram casing carries the Collins imprint, and unlike BC2A not blocked 'Readers Union' to the rear cover. RU jacket 'Type 2'. Price: 13s. 6d. net. Note: This is not in the strict sense a second edition, nor a reprint, as it is from the same printing.

POD2A Print-on-demand digital copy of the first edition NN2A.

CFS2A Collins/Folio Society facsimile, 2008 (02 July 2008). ISBN-10: 0007278578. ISBN-13: 9780007278572. Published by Collins in association with the Folio Society; a facsimile copy with jacket of the first edition. Not declared as a facsimile edition. Cased in modern, dark green, *Arbelave* buckram. Elements of jacket spine digitally re-whitened. Print run: c. 1,000 (as part box-set of first ten) + c. 150 individual copies; o/p: Nov. 2010[?]. Note: While, not marked as a facsimile, the freshness of the paper, the casing fabric and the digitally re-whitened jacket should not allow confusion with the genuine first ed. Copies sold individually by HarperCollins have a price sticker with ISBN, barcode and www.newnaturalists.com affixed to rear DJ panel.

First reprint: the printed reverse-side of jacket.

3 London's Natural History

London's Natural History began life with the working title 'The Naturalist in London'. It is number 3 in the series but, in fact, was published on the same day as *Butterflies* and therefore should really be number 2. It, more than any other New Naturalist, evokes an age foreign to most of us and, doubtless, dim in the memory of the rest. Written during the Second World War, it includes many photographs of an urban environment, utterly different to the London we know today. But, historical document or otherwise, it remains eminently readable: a classic.

20,000 copies of *London's Natural History* were printed in 1945, with a reprint of the same number the following year; presumably therefore the best part of that figure had sold within a year. A prodigious number indeed; compare with, at the other extreme, *Ferns*, where less than 1,500 copies sold over a six-year period. *London's Natural History* stayed in print for 20 years, but by this time it was considered out of date and not reprinted. Fitter was too busy to rewrite it. It did however reappear later, in 1984, as a Collins 'black paperback', with a new preface by Fitter, and then again as a Bloomsbury facsimile in 1990 and finally as a Collins/Folio Society facsimile hardback edition in 2008.

London's Natural History does not include the customary *Author's preface*, but instead the *Author's acknowledgements* appear, in unconventional fashion, on the imprint page. It is recorded that this was because the acknowledgements were not received until after the book had been made up into pages and this was the only place left. As the acknowledgements are dated October 1945 and the book was published the second week of November, this is probably correct. Fitter requested that they be put in their proper place for the reprint but this did not happen. Fitter also asked for many corrections to be made to the reprint, but again these did not materialise, though it is recorded that Collins was to make up correction slips.

It would appear that the reprint was bound up in batches over a period of time (as is often the case with early title reprints) and different binding fabrics are evident, but in the absence of more telling diagnostic features, no attempt has been made to separate them out. However the earlier ones seem to be in the very open, wavy-grained buckram which is often characterised by uneven fading. While discussing variants, note that only some copies, of both the first edition and reprint, have a full stop after the NN credo (the RU editions have too). In itself it is a point of

superfluous detail, but what is the reason behind it? Was *London's Natural History* printed from more than one forme?

Despite the great number of books printed this is not a particularly easy title to find in fine condition, the jacket paper is soft and is liable to tanning, however the red does not fade half as readily as more recent titles. Strangely the boards are often quite floppy. Total print run: 40,000 (Collins and RU); o/p: 1965 (Collins hardback).

NN3A	**First edition**, 1945 (12 November 1945).
Title:	'The New Naturalist	London's	Natural History'.
Author:	'by	R. S. R. Fitter'.
Illust:	'With 52 Colour Photographs	by Eric Hosking and Others	41 Black and White Photographs	and 12 Maps and Diagrams'.
Editors:	JF, JG, JSH, LDS and EH (Photographic Editor).
Printer:	Collins Clear-Type Press: London and Glasgow (produced in conjunction with Adprint).
Collation:	pp. xii, 282, [2]; 20 leaves of colour plates printed to both sides; 16 leaves of b/w plates printed to both sides (18½ × 16-page gatherings).
Jacket:	[Rear panel] 'The New Naturalist A Survey of British Natural History', under which the NN Credo is given in full; list of Editors and the Collins address. [Rear flap] Continuation of the blurb from the front flap (referred to as the front wing) and 'The New Naturalist' listing 'The first four titles in the series'.
Price:	16s. net.
Print run:	20,000; o/p: 1946[?].
Notes:	1) The author's acknowledgements are 'signed' Highgate October, 1945. 2) The jacket text is printed in sepia rather than black.

NN3B First Reprint, 1946. 'First published in 1945... | ...Reprinted 1946'. As NN3A, seemingly without any revisions or corrections (see intro.). The jacket also identical to NN3A with same price. Print run: 20,000 including repriced variant below and both RU editions (BC3A and BC3B); o/p: 1965 (AP1).

NN3B-AP1 1st Repriced DJ (July 1948–65) 21s. net. label pasted over original price, no. sold: unknown.

BPB3A Collins Paperback Reprint, 1984 (18 June 1984). ISBN 0002190680; pp. [14], 282, [72 – b/w illustrations] (23 × 16-page gatherings). A b/w facsimile of NN3B with a few minor changes and revisions, the most notable being a new *Preface to the Limpback Edition* by R.S.R.F; the last line of the NN credo has been omitted and imprint page reordered. The Ellises' design to the front cover has been copied from a slightly soiled original, the red band superimposed, the edges now straight and the title lettering reset. Price: £6.50 net. Print run: *c.* 1,500; no. sold: *c.* 1,340 of which *c.* 600 remaindered in 1988; o/p: 1988.

BC3A Readers Union Edition, First Issue, 1953. As NN3B and from that printing, but with a *cancel* title page displaying the RU tree logo and dated 1953. The binding also identical, but stamped 'Readers Union' in gilt to the rear board. RU jacket 'type 1'. Price: 10s. 6d net. Print run: 3,000. (Due to overstocking Collins remaindered 3,000 bound copies of NN3B to the RU.)

BC3B Readers Union Edition, Second Issue, 1959. As BC3A; Part of the original Collins 1946 reprint NN3B printing, with a cancel title page, displaying the RU imprint and tree logo dated 1959; the green buckram casing carries the Collins imprint, and unlike BC3A not blocked 'Readers Union' to the rear cover. RU jacket 'type 2'. Price: 13s. 6d. net. (Most of the 1959 RU editions were specially printed for the bookclub but the cancel title leaf and the Collins casing indicate that this edition was made up from Collins's stock. Not in the strict sense a second edition, or a reprint as from the same printing.)

POD3A Print-on-demand digital copy of the first edition NN3A.

CFS3A Collins/Folio Society facsimile, 2008 (02 July 2008). ISBN-10: 0007278500, ISBN-13: 9780007278503. A facsimile copy with jacket of the first edition. Not declared as a facsimile edition. Cased in modern, dark green, *Arbelave* buckram. Elements of jacket spine digitally re-whitened. Print run: c. 1,000 (as part box-set of first ten) + c. 150 individual copies; o/p: Nov. 2010. (While not marked as a facsimile, the freshness of the paper, the casing fabric and the digitally re-whitened jacket should not allow confusion with the genuine first ed. Copies sold individually by HarperCollins have a price sticker with ISBN, barcode and www. newnaturalists.com affixed to rear DJ panel.

BL3A Bloomsbury Edition, 31 December 1990. ISBN: 1870630696; pp. [14], 282, [72 – b/w illustrations] (23 × 16-page gatherings). A b/w facsimile of NN3A, but with the new preface that appeared in the Collins paperback reprint BPB3A – contrary to the intro. which states 'with a new foreword by the author'. The blurb to the front flap is a précised form of the original jacket blurb. Price: £12.95. Remaindered.

4 Britain's Structure and Scenery

62,000 hardback copies were printed, making *Structure and Scenery* the most successful New Naturalist – at least in terms of numbers printed. If all other editions are included the number rises to c. 135,000 copies. It was reprinted six times, and, with the exception of the last, these are referred to in the print histories as editions even though revisions are generally minimal. An extensively revised edition was planned for publication in 1976–77, but a large order from the bookclub BCA did not materialise and the project was shelved.

After Stamp's death in 1966, Professor Clayton, and initially Prof. Funnell, of the University of East Anglia, were approached to revise the text. Originally the board wanted a rewrite but Clayton was clear that corrections only should be considered as this was a *classic text*. Over the next ten years the patient Clayton made repeated revisions on the invitation of Collins, including rewriting the sections on preglacial evolution and the Ice Age – the two areas where the book was most outdated. But none of these revisions was to come to fruition; all later reprints following the 1967 text and Clayton's contribution was limited to a short preface to the 1984 paperback edition (CPB4A).

The artwork on the jacket of *Britain's Structure and Scenery* exists in three different 'states', or at least in three distinct 'reprographic versions'. In each, the Ellises' monogram is slightly different and in the second the date is omitted. The subtle blue and grey areas of the first edition are characterised by a matrix of fine dots and dashes as if the printmaker has forced the colour pigment through a fine screen; a characteristic feature of 'reprographic version one', which was used for the first five editions. 'Reprographic version two' appears on the jackets of the 1967 sixth edition and 1971 sixth edition reprint; in this version the light colours appear more blotchy, but are in fact made up of even finer dots, and the light tan areas are now grey; the date has been omitted from the Ellises' monogram; the overall effect is less refined, bolder and more austere; this in fact is the version that is reproduced in *Art of The New Naturalists*. The third version, more distinct still, appears on the cover of the 1984 'black paperback' reprint and it would appear that this has been reoriginated, i.e. taken from the Ellises' original artwork, and reproduced using a photographic technique and is therefore more of a 'copy' than a 'print': the original paint (gouache?) is evident as is the texture of the paper, and a little 'dust soiling' of the original is also apparent (this edition is worth purchasing for the Ellises' artwork alone). This all goes to show how the techniques of the print/ block-maker and printing system used, combine to affect radically the end result.

To further complicate matters the first edition jacket reprographic version exists in two subtly different variants: in one the text and shadows on the rocks are printed in black; in the other, these elements are printed in a dark sepia; additionally the price is printed differently. It is difficult to determine a priority, but considering 20,000 jackets were required it is not unlikely that multiple production lines were used simultaneously; later-edition jackets were printed in black.

A note on a 1960s NN statement suggests that 1,500 copies of the 1960 reprint were sold to the Readers Union, but if so they were probably sold from stock as there appears to be no bookclub edition of this book. Despite 20,000 first edition copies, the jacket of *Britain's Structure and Scenery* is one of the most difficult to find in fine condition: it is prone to rubbing, particularly along the joints, is usually chipped to the head and the tail of the spine and the paper is susceptible to tanning. NN4A lets down many first edition collections. Later editions are easier to find in better condition.

NN4A | **First Edition**, 1946 (30 September 1946).
Title: | 'The New Naturalist | Britain's | Structure and Scenery'.
Author: | 'by | L. Dudley Stamp | C.B.E., B.A. D.Sc.'
Illust: | 'With 47 colour photographs | 40 photographs in black and white | 74 maps and diagrams'.
Editors: | JF, JG, JH, LDS, EH (Photographic Editor).
Printer: | Collins Clear-Type Press: London and Glasgow (produced in conjunction with Adprint).
Collation: | pp. xvi, 255, [1]; 16 leaves of colour plates printed to both sides; 16 leaves of b/w plates printed to both sides (17 × 16-page gatherings).
Jacket: | [Rear panel] 'The New Naturalist | A Survey of British Natural History' under which is quoted the NN credo, followed by the list of Editors and the Collins address. [Rear flap] 'The New Naturalist | The first four titles in this | series are' listing NN 1–4.
Price: | 16s. net.
Print run: | 20,000; o/p: 1947?
Notes: | 1) Two variants of the jacket exist as described below, both are however reproduced using the same reprographic technique. 2) C & RE 'signature' to DJ front panel dated '45. 3) Most photographs by Stamp, but James Fisher, Eric Hosking and others contributed. 4) *Britain's Structure and Scenery* is the title to the title page, half-title and casing, but to the jacket it appears as *Britain's Structure & Scenery*. 5) Book 24 mm thick. 6) Jacket design credit omitted from all editions.

NN4A-DJ1 First Edition, First Jacket Variant. Text and shadows on rocks printed in black (or what approximates to black); lettering finer and sharper, and blue brighter and colder than 'DJ2'; all digits of the printed price in line. No priority should be inferred – probably printed and issued concomitantly with 'DJ2'.

NN4A-DJ2 First Edition, Second Jacket Variant. Text and shadows on rocks printed in dark sepia; first digit 'I' of the printed price slightly subscribed; foot of the 'R' in Britain to the front panel with slight wobble. For other differences see 'DJ1'. This appears to be the rarer of the two jacket variants.

NN4B Second Edition, 1947 (Spring 1947). 'First published in September 1946… | …Second Edition 1947'. Essentially as NN4A. With a few minor changes including: 'Note to the second edition' dated December, 1946 added to p. xvi, which thanks correspondents for their 'helpful comments'; plates, as appropriate, now correctly acknowledged to M. Wight (though original errata note left in); several sentences to pp. 100–101 revised. Lettering and shadows to jacket printed in black; rear panel unchanged; rear flap lists first ten titles in the series pointing out that numbers 5, 6, 7, 9, 10 were not published at the time of going to press (March 1947); blurb to front flap unrevised but press endorsement from Ivor Brown in the *Observer* inserted below. Price: 16s net. Print run: 15,000. Note: It is not uncommon to find this edition in a first edition jacket; presumably some were left over from the earlier printing.

NN4C Third Edition, 1949. 'First published in September 1946… | …Second Edition 1947 | Third Edition 1949'. As NN4B with minimal revisions; errata note regarding incorrect acknowledgement of several plates excised; first line to p. 102 accidentally omits '…natural fertility and in their possible utilisation and it is for these…'. Paper smoother, creamier; book very slightly thinner. Lettering and shadows to jacket printed in black. Rear panel of the jacket advertises *Butterflies, London's Natural History* and *Natural History in the Highlands and Islands*; rear flap lists *Britain's Structure and Scenery, British Game, Insect Natural History, British Plant Life, The Sea Shore* and *The Badger* with request for details of other titles beneath; front flap textually identical but reset. Price: 21s net. Print run: 10,000.

NN4D-DJ1 Fourth Edition, 1955. 'First published in September 1947… | Third Edition 1949 | Fourth Edition 1955'. As NN4C with a few minor corrections and addition of 'some recent references'; 'Note to the fourth printing' dated October, 1954 added to p. xvi; omission in first line of p. 102 uncorrected. Book slightly thicker –27 mm. The jacket is exactly as that used for the 1949 third edition NN4C, but price-clipped and overprinted 25s net. Print run: 5,000[?]; o/p: 1960. It is unknown why a bespoke jacket was not printed for this edition, but presumably a significant batch was left over from the 1949 printing, and in the austere post-war 50s, it would have been natural to have used them; see also jacket variant 'DJ2' below.

NN4D-DJ2 Fourth Edition, Jacket Variant. In this variant the jacket reverts to that used on the 1947 second edition NN4B, i.e. rear flap lists first ten titles and the Ivor Brown press clipping inserted below the blurb, but the original price has been price clipped and the jacket overprinted 25s net. Again, it is not known why this old jacket was used, but, as above, probably a cost-saving expedient.

NN4E Fifth Edition, 1960. 'First published in September 1946… | … Second Edition 1947 | Third Edition 1949 | Fourth Edition 1955 | Fifth Edition 1960'. Essentially as NN4D with minimal changes. 'Note to the fifth edition' dated November, 1959, added to p. [xvi] in which the author thanks friends who have called his attention to misprints etc and states all changes of a minor character – though omission in first line of p. 102 still uncorrected. Title page slightly reset reflecting latest status of Dudley Stamp. Editors: JH now Sir JH, and LDS has additional post-nominals. The jacket rear panel displays the NN library in a single unnumbered column; a layout similar (but unique) to those of five years earlier and accordingly stops at *Moths* (1955) but starts with Stamp's other NN *Man and the Land*; the rear flap advertises *Man and the Land*; front flap reverts to that of NN4C. Price: 30s. net. Print run: 5,000; o/p: early 1966.

NN4F Sixth Edition, 1967. 'First published in September 1946… | … Second Edition 1947 | Third Edition 1949 | Fourth Edition 1955 | Fifth Edition 1960 | Sixth Edition 1967'. Essentially as NN4E. 'Note to the sixth edition' dated June 1966, added to p. [xvi]; this is identical to the note to the fifth edition, which it replaces. Omission in first line of p. 102 remains uncorrected. Editors: LDS now Sir DS. The jacket is printed using a different technique – 'the second version' described in the intro.; the NN library lists NN1–47 (Type 42, variant 6); both flaps unchanged. Price: 30s. *net*. Print run: 4,000.

NN4G Sixth Edition, First Reprint, 1970. ISBN 002130246 (to jacket only). 'Second Edition 1947 | Third Edition 1949 | Fourth Edition 1955 | Fifth Edition 1960 | Sixth Edition 1967 | Reprinted 1970 | First published in September 1946… '. As NN4F (p. 102 uncorrected). Editors: JF, JG, JH, MD and EH. NN library to the jacket lists NN1–50 (Type 42, variant 8); both flaps identical, but ISBN added to rear. Price: £2.25 net | 45s. net. Print run: *c.* 3,000; o/p: 1974.

BPB4A Collins Paperback Reprint, 1984 (21 January 1984). ISBN 000219077x; pp. xv, 255, [1], [64 – b/w illustrations]. A b/w copy of the 1967 sixth edition NN4F, though the imprint page has been taken from the 1960 fifth edition! A single page *Preface to the Limpback Edition* by Keith Clayton has been added. The cover design is a photographic copy of the Ellises' original artwork (reprographic version three), the bright, cold blue band superimposed and the title lettering reset. Price: £6.50 *net*. Print run: *c.* 1,500; no. sold: *c.* 1,390 of which *c.* 500 remaindered in 1988; o/p: 1988.

POD4A Print-on-demand digital copy of the 1946 first edition NN4A.

CFS4A Collins/Folio Society facsimile, 2008 (02 July 2008). ISBN-10: 0007278519, ISBN-13: 9780007278510. A facsimile copy with jacket of the first edition. Not declared as a facsimile edition. Cased in modern, dark green, *Arbelave* buckram. Elements of jacket spine digitally re-whitened. Print run: *c.* 1,000 (as part box-set of first ten) + *c.* 150 individual copies; o/p: Nov. 2010. (While not marked as a facsimile, the freshness of the paper, the casing fabric and digitally re-whitened jacket should not allow confusion with the genuine first ed. Copies sold individually by HarperCollins have a price sticker with ISBN, barcode and www.newnaturalists.com affixed to rear DJ panel.)

F4A Fontana Paperback First Edition, 1960. ISBN 0006322026 (ISBN appears only on 1975 11th imp.); pp. 317, [3]; 8 leaves of b/w plates bound in single section in centre, printed on glossy paper, to both sides (20 × 16-page gatherings). 'A format' paperback, stitched and glued. A reset copy of the Collins 1960 fifth edition NN4E, but without colour and a reduced no. of b/w plates. Adverts for Fontana Library titles at front and rear. The cover artwork by [Kenneth] Farnhill; rear cover with blurb and author's biography. Price: 7/6. Total print run including reprints below: 70,000. The following reprints exactly as preceding edition unless stated otherwise, changes to adverts ignored.

F4B Second Impression, April 1962. Book thinner, creamy better quality paper; not stitched. Price: 8/6.

F4C Third Impression, January 1965. As F4B.

F4D Fourth Impression, September 1967. 'Conditions of sale' added otherwise as F4c.

F4E Fifth Impression, October 1968. Cover changed to uncredited photograph of rocky cliffs (not seen).

F4F Sixth Impression, month? 1969. (not seen).

F4G Seventh Impression, July 1970. (not seen).

F4H Eight Impression, December 1970. Adverts at front/rear for NN Fontana. Price: 10/- (50p).

F4I Ninth Impression, date? (not seen).

F4J Tenth Impression, August 1972. Cheaper paper liable to tanning, thicker book. Price: 60p.

F4K Eleventh Impression, August 1975. ISBN: 0006322026. Editors added: JG, JH, MD, KM and EH. Price 80p.

5 Wild Flowers

'Enthusiasm is a quality that all true scientists possess, but not all express. Yet without the magic of enthusiasm the natural history movement could never have captured the heads of the British People – made scientists of amateurs and amateurs of scientists.' Thus begins the blurb for *Wild Flowers* and in these few words captures not only the qualities of this book but evokes the spirit of the New Naturalist. A spirit now sometimes seemingly lost in the rigours of modern scientific research.

Wild Flowers was due for publication in 1946 but in the event did not appear until 1954, and so chronologically should be 28th in the series.

Inevitably such a successful book ran to many editions, though none constitutes more than a fairly superficial revision of the first edition, but the bibliographies in later editions are more comprehensive. In a letter dated 20 April 1977, to John Gilmour, Robert MacDonald (of Collins) explained that the factory had lost the first colour plate (Goatsbeard) and neither could they find the original transparency, so requested a new photograph; accordingly plate 1 of the 1978 reprint is of plant communities rather than Goatsbeard.

Confusingly, some of the reprints are referred to as new editions, but to avoid compounding the confusion here they are referred to according to the designations printed in the books. Some of the 'editions' used distinctly different papers and consequently there is considerable variation in the thickness of these books – at the thinnest end about 22 mm and the fattest around 30 mm. This affects the way the jacket fits the book and its appearance on the shelf. The corrected fourth edition, the thickest, is perhaps the best due to the significantly superior paper used. The fifth edition of 1973 was fitted with a simple but stylish wrap-around advertising band, but few still exist (the generic nature of this advertising band would suggest that it was also intended for use on other titles, but its rarity indicates that this seldom happened).

A Readers Union edition was published concomitantly with the Collins 1985 reprint and shares the Collins livery and jacket but has the usual bookclub distinguishing features. A Fontana paperback appeared in 1972, followed by a Collins limpback edition in 1985 and finally in 1989, 35 years after its first publication, a Bloomsbury edition – though again all are essentially reprints. By the time these last two editions appeared, due to wholesale and rapid changes in agriculture, *Wild Flowers* had become an anachronism, albeit a thoroughly engaging one. Max Walters in the preface to the Collins paperback edition writes 'Formerly common plants are now rare…Our text predates these changes…' Neither of these last two editions was successful and both were remaindered.

Wild Flowers is one of the easier early titles to find in fine condition – perhaps because it is not as early as its series number suggests, though the jacket of the first edition is somewhat susceptible to browning.

NN5A   **First Edition**, 1954 (10 May 1954).

Title: 'The New Naturalist | Wild Flowers | Botanising in Britain'.

Authors: 'by | John Gilmour | M.A. | Director of the University Botanic Garden | and Fellow of Clare College, Cambridge | and | Max Walters | M.A., Ph.D. | Curator of the University Herbarium | Cambridge'.

Illust: 'With 45 colour photographs | 27 photographs in black and white | and 3 line drawings'.

Editors: JF, JG, JH, LDS and EH (Photographic Editor).

Printer: Collins Clear-Type Press: London and Glasgow.

Collation: pp. xiv, 242; 16 leaves of colour plates printed to both sides; 12 leaves of b/w plates printed to both sides (16 × 16-page gatherings).

Jacket: [Rear panel] Advert for *Mushrooms* under the heading 'Recently published in the Main Series'. [Rear flap] 'Other Plant Books in The New Naturalist Library' listing *Flowers of the Coast, Wild Orchids of Britain, British Plant Life, Wild Flowers of Chalk and Limestone* and 'Special Volume' *Mumps, Measles and Mosaics*; 'Write to Collins' for details of books in production.

Price: 25s. net.

Print run: 8,500.

Notes: 1) All text to jacket printed in green. 2) NN monogram to casing embellished with a honeysuckle motif. 3) Book 26 mm thick. 4) Date to title page.

NN5B New Edition, 1955 (October). 'First Edition: April 1954 | New Edition: October 1955'; no date to the title page. But appears identical to NN5A. The paper smoother, of better quality, but lighter weight resulting in a noticeably thinner book – 23.5 mm thick. The jacket unchanged and price remains at 25s. net. Print run: 5,000; o/p: end of 1961. Note: The print run almost certainly inc. *c.* 1,800 copies bound up later for the RU – see BC5A.

NN5B-AP1 First Repriced Jacket (1961). 30s. net; no. sold unknown, but scarce.

NN5C Third Edition, 1962. 'First Edition: 1954 | Second Edition: 1955 | Third Edition: 1962'. Minor corrections and updates to the text, with more significant revision to the bibliography and index; pagination and plates unaltered. Book only 22 mm thick. The NN library to the jacket lists NN1–45 inclusively (Type 42, variant 4), with the title box printed in bright lime green; rear flap as earlier jacket, but additionally includes *Weeds and Aliens, Mountain Flowers, Mushrooms and Toadstools, Lords and Ladies*, with *Mumps* omitted; blurb to front flap unaltered but two press commendations added – *V. Sackville-West, Observer* & *Percy Izzard, Daily Mail*. Price: 30s.net. Print run: 3,000; no. sold: *c.* 2,800; o/p: summer/autumn 1967. Note: Strictly speaking this is the second edition, as NN5B was in fact a reprint and not a new edition.

NN5D Fourth Edition, 1969 (June). 'First Edition: 1954 | Second Edition: 1955 | Third Edition: 1962 | Fourth Edition: 1969'. A 'Note on the Fourth Edition' has been added which states 'As far as is practicable without extensive re-setting, we have brought this edition up to date…', consequently revisions are inconsequential, but include many minor corrections. Pagination and plates unaltered. Max Walters acknowledged as being a Fellow of King's College, Cambridge, making the already busy title page busier. Editors: JF, JG, JH, MD and EH. Paper heavier; book noticeably thicker – 30 mm. Text to the jacket now printed in black; the NN library lists NN1–50, (Type 42, variant 8) with the title box changed to dark green, to match the title band to the front panel; blurb to front flap omitted and in its place five press endorsements; the jacket fails to credit the Ellises as designers. Price: 42s.net. Print run: 3,000; no. sold: *c.* 2,800; o/p: 1972[?]

NN5D-AP1 First Repriced Jacket (1971–1972). P. clipped, with Collins £2.75 – 55/- sticker; no. sold: unknown, but its rarity would suggest very few. (This round golden price sticker with dual display of pre-decimal and decimal currency would date this variant to around decimalisation in 1971. This is the only NN title I have seen with this dual sticker and a £2.75 variant is not mentioned in extant sales reports; odd too as it is more expensive than the later 1973 edition NN5E.)

NN5E Fifth Edition, 1973 (February). ISBN: 0002132516. 'First Edition: 1954 | Second Edition: 1955 | Third Edition: 1962 | Fourth Edition: 1969 | Fifth Edition: 1973'. Essentially as NN5D, with minor revisions only. The 'Editors' Preface' and the 'Authors' Preface' now include 'To the First Edition' and, a 'Note on the Fifth Edition' has been appended to the latter, which states 'In this edition we have, as far as practicable without complete re-setting, incorporated the alterations and additions included in the recently published Fontana paper-back edition…' The point size of the bibliography has been reduced, resulting in the last page [242] being blank. Plates unaltered. The book noticeably thinner – only 22 mm. The NN monogram to the casing unembellished – 'Type C'. The *Durasealed* jacket brighter, primroses green-yellow; the NN library lists NN1–55 (Type 42, variant 12); both flaps unchanged, but for addition of ISBN to the rear. Price: £2.50 net. Print run: 3,000; no. sold: *c.* 2,100 + repriced variants below. Notes: Some copies were fitted with an advertising band as illustrated on page 53. This edition is not a copy, blown up from the plates of the Fontana edition. From a bibliographical perspective, this is the fourth edition.

NN5E-AP1 1st Repriced DJ (1974–75), £3.00 sticker, no. sold unknown.

NN5E-AP2 2nd Repriced DJ (1975–76), £3.50 sticker, *c.* 280 sold.

NN5E-AP3 3rd Repriced DJ (1976), £4.50 sticker, *c.* 260 sold.

NN5E-AP4 4th Repriced DJ (1977), £7.50 sticker, *c.* 190 sold.

NN5F Fifth Edition, First Reprint, 1978. ISBN changed to 0002195437. 'First Edition: 1954 | Second Edition: 1955 | Third Edition: 1962 | Fourth Edition: 1969 | Fifth Edition: 1973 | Reprinted: 1973'. First colour plate changed (see intro.). The half-title, Editors', title and imprint pages all reset with revised layouts; the NN monogram omitted from the TP and the authors' post nominals revised. Editors: MD, JG, KM and EH. Last sentence of the NN credo omitted. Book 24 mm thick. The embellished monogram reinstated to casing. The NN library to the *Durasealed* jacket lists NN1–61 (Type 42, variant 16); both flaps identical, but for revised ISBN. Price: £8.50. Print run: 1,500; no. sold: *c.* 560 + repriced variants below + probably *c.* 550 sold to the RU from stock.

NN5F-AP1 1st Repriced DJ (1982–83), £9.50 sticker, *c.* 170 sold.

NN5F-AP2 2nd Repriced DJ (1984–85), £10.00 sticker; *c.* 100 sold.

BPB5A Collins Paperback Reprint, 1985 (21 January 1985). ISBN 0002193264; pp. [xx], 241, [3 blanks], [56 – b/w illustrations] (20 × 16-page gatherings). A b/w copy of NN5F with a few minor changes and revisions, the most notable being a new 'Preface to the Limpback Edition' by Dr Walters. The ISBN printed in the book is incomplete as the title specific part has accidentally been left off; that printed on the rear cover is however correct. Distinctly different colours to the Ellises' design, brighter, colder, the green band superimposed, the edges straight and the title lettering reset. Price: £6.50 net. Print run: *c.* 1,500; no. sold: *c.* 1,260 of which 150 remaindered in 1988; o/p: 1988.

BC5A First Readers Union Edition, 1959. Seemingly bound from the same sheets as Collins 1955 new edition NN5B, but with a cancel title page, displaying the RU imprint and tree logo, dated 1959. Bound in medium green imitation clock blocked with the RU tree logo to the spine. RU jacket 'Type 2'. Price: 15s. net. No. sold to RU:

c. 1,800[?]. Note: It is probable that Collins had stocks of unbound quires – the print run of their 1955 reprint was 5,000, and these were then specially bound by Collins for the RU, which explains the combination of cancel title page and bespoke RU casing.

BC5B Second Readers Union Edition, 1978. Bound from the same sheets as the Collins fifth edition, first reprint NN5F and almost indistinguishable, but for following diagnostic features: casing of dark green imitation cloth; jacket identical but without a *Duraseal* protector and without a printed price. Print run: 500.

F5A Fontana Paperback First Edition, 1972 (April). ISBN: 0006328903 (does not appear in the book); pp. 288; 8 leaves of b/w plates printed on glossy paper to both sides (18 × 16-page gatherings). A reprint but with the text and bibliography bought up to date as stated in the 'Note on the Paperback Edition' (these revisions were incorporated into the Collins 1973 hardback edition: NN5E). The photographic illustrations have been reduced to a 'selection of sixteen pages of black-and-white plates'. The subtitle to TP reads 'The Fontana New Naturalist'. Advert for the New Naturalist series at front listing 13 titles available in Fontana, inc. Lack's *The Life of the Robin*. Price: 60p. The photographic front cover is of a Welsh Poppy by John Markham. Reprinted as identified below. Print run: *c.* 17,500; no. sold: *c.* 16,850 (figures inc. reprints below); o/p: 1979[?].

The following reprints exactly as preceding edition unless stated otherwise.

F5B Fontana Paperback Second Impression, May 1972.

F5B-AP1 Fontana Paperback Second Impression Repriced. With black sticker to rear cover showing UK 75p etc.

F5C Fontana Paperback Third Impression, September 1972. Book thinner, smoother paper; covers lighter green.

F5B-AP1 Fontana Paperback Third Impression Repriced. With black sticker to rear cover showing UK 75p etc.

BL5A Bloomsbury Edition, 1989 (31 December 1989). ISBN: 1870630785; pp. xiv, 241, [1], [56 – b/w illustrations, integrated throughout] (19½ × 16-page gatherings). A facsimile of the fifth ed. reprint NN5F. Price £12.95. Print run: unknown, but a significant proportion remaindered.

CFS5A Collins/Folio Society facsimile, 2008 (02/07/2008). ISBN-10: 0007278527, ISBN-13: 9780007278527. Published by Collins in association with the Folio Society; a facsimile copy with jacket of the first edition. Not declared as a facsimile edition. Cased in modern dark green *Arbelave* buckram. Elements of jacket spine digitally re-whitened. Print run: *c.* 1,000 (as part box-set of first ten) + *c.* 150 individual copies; o/p: Nov. 2010[?]. Note: While not marked as a facsimile, the freshness of the paper, the casing fabric and the digitally re-whitened jacket should not allow confusion with the genuine first ed. Copies sold individually by HarperCollins have a price sticker with ISBN, barcode and www.newnaturalists.com affixed to rear DJ panel.

POD5A Print-on-demand digital copy of the first edition NN5A.

6A Natural History in the Highlands & Islands

'This work is not a handbook of natural history; that is why I have refused to call it 'The Natural History of the Highlands and Islands'; that would have been too presumptuous a title', so wrote Frank Fraser Darling in the author's preface. The board had wanted to call it simply 'The Highlands and Islands', but Darling was intransigent, though they got their way with the rewritten edition of 1964 – which was essentially a new book. The correct title of this book (6A), as appears on the title page is with an ampersand, whereas the correct title of the later book (6B) is with an 'and'. Because these are different books but have the same series number the designations '6A' and '6B' have been adopted.

The Natural History in the Highlands & Islands was not reprinted, principally because it received a damning review by Professor V. C. Wynne-Edwards in *The Scottish Naturalist*, whose criticisms while, undoubtedly, factually correct, perhaps failed to see the book for what it was: in the author's words 'the modern ecological view of wholeness and interdependence'. A case of not seeing the mountains for the *Diapensia*. The criticism was also aimed at the Editors' rather churlish disclaimer, which included the line: 'Every care has been take by the Editors to ensure scientific accurarcy'. Wynne-Edwards made it clear that he didn't think they had. It appears that publishers take negative reviews more seriously than anyone else, barring perhaps the author (how many of the buying public read *The Scottish Naturalist*?). This was not the only New Naturalist to receive a negative review – but in this case (and with *Man and Birds* and Wragge Morley's *Ants*) the decision was taken not to reprint. The Editors' disclaimer was axed too.

The Natural History in the Highlands & Islands was the first book to display the New Naturalist library to the dust jacket rear panel, though half of the twelve books listed were still to be published. The dust jacket is a little brittle and prone to chipping, but then it is 65 years old. When on the shelf, this title is easily confused with the new book of 1964, as it wears the same Ellis jacket, but the easiest way to distinguish it quickly is to look at the NN monogram: in this book the monogram is embellished with an antler, whereas the 1964 monogram is unadorned. The printing and sales history is incomplete, but it seems that around 30,000 copies were printed, with the book probably going out of print in 1954.

NN6AA   **First Edition**, 1947 (08 December 1947).
Title: 'The New Naturalist | Natural History | In The | Highlands & Islands'.
Author: 'by | F. Fraser Darling | D.Sc. F.R.S.E.'
Illust: 'With 46 colour photographs | by F. Fraser Darling, John Markham and others | 55 black-and-white photographs | and 24 maps and diagrams'.
Editors: JF, JG, JH, LDS and EH (Photographic Editor).
Printer: Collins Clear-Type Press: London and Glasgow.
Collation: pp. xv, [1], 303, [1]; 16 leaves of colour plates printed to both sides; 16 leaves of b/w plates printed to both sides (20 × 16-page gatherings).
Jacket: [Rear panel] 'The New Naturalist A Survey of British Natural History The first twelve titles' listing NN1–12, citing series numbers and titles, followed by 'Numbers 1, 2, 3, 4, 6, 8 should be obtainable from your bookseller now. It is hoped to publish numbers 5, 7, 9, 10, 11, 12 during 1948 and 1949' etc.; with Collins address above lower edge. [Rear flap] 'The New Naturalist A Survey of British Natural History' with short endorsing overview of the series by Professor A. G. Tansley in the *Sunday Times*; list of NN Editors; 'For a list of the first twelve titles in the New Naturalist series see the back of this wrapper'.
Price: 16s. net.
Print run: c. 30,000[?]; no. sold: c. 29,000; o/p: 1954[?] (AP1).
Notes: 1) The title to the half-title and title pages is with an ampersand, whereas that to the casing and jacket uses 'and' 2) Jacket rear panel: In the event only NN10 and 12 were published during 1948 and 1949. 3) The reproduction of many of the b/w photographs is poor – dirty tones with little definition.

NN6AA-AP1 1st Repriced DJ (1948–54?) with label showing *21s* net or 21s. 0d. net. pasted over original price.

POD6AA Print-on-demand digital copy.

CFS6AA Collins /Folio Society facsimile, 2008 (07 July 2008). ISBN-10: 0007278535, ISBN-13: 9780007278534. A facsimile copy with jacket of the first edition. Not declared as a facsimile edition. Cased in modern dark green *Arbelave* buckram. Elements of jacket spine digitally re-whitened. Print run: c. 1,000 (as part box-set of first ten) + c. 150 individual copies; o/p: Nov. 2010[?]. While not marked as a facsimile, the freshness of the paper, the casing fabric and digitally re-whitened jacket should not allow confusion with the genuine first ed. Copies sold individually by HarperCollins have a price sticker with ISBN, barcode and www.newnaturalists.com, affixed to rear DJ panel.

6B The Highlands & Islands

The Highlands & Islands is essentially a new book; and as the jacket blurb states 'an entirely revised and rewritten version of Dr Darling's *Natural History in the Highlands and Islands*'. It is also 32 pages longer than the foregoing title, but has fewer plates. It came about because the earlier title included a number of technical errors (which were somewhat of an embarrassment to the Editors), and it was unlikely that a revised edition would suffice. Fraser Darling was too busy to do it, so eventually Morton Boyd was drafted in to 'make good', and the new book was finally published 16 years after the first. The actual history of H*ighlands and Islands* is, of course, rather more complicated and convoluted than that. The minutes of the New Naturalist Editorial Board meetings, albeit incomplete, enable a thread to be traced through the evolution of this book as follows:

10th Mar. 1955: Mr Fisher reported that Fraser Darling had promised a rewritten book by 31st December 1955. The Editors agreed that this author should do the book, provided he submitted a satisfactory MS by the end of the year. The book should have an entirely new title. Some of the colour from the old edition would be used, but an entirely new collection of black and whites. Collins would make investigations to find out from booksellers and libraries in Scotland exactly what sort of book was needed. Mr Fisher to see the author.

6th May 1955: Dr Stamp said he was not at all in favour of this book being rewritten and issued under a new title as a new number in the series. If the book contained a large number of the colour plates from the present book the public would feel they had been cheated, even if the text had been almost completely rewritten. Mr Fisher suggested that the book might be called 'The Highlands and Islands Reviewed'. It might be numbered 6A in the series. The Editors agreed that only about half the original colour should be used, and a completely new set of black and whites. Mr Trevelyan to find out from the Scottish representatives what sort of book was needed.

27th July 1955: The Edinburgh representative had written to the effect that in his opinion the book should be issued under the same title, with a clear indication that it was a completely revised edition, but that it should carry the same series number as before. Dr. Huxley suggested that the representatives should be asked to consider whether the book might be called 'Natural History in The Highlands and Islands Reviewed', with a series number of 6A. Mr Trevelyan to follow up.

5th Jun. 1956: Mr Fisher said the author had not actually made a

start on the rewriting. No further action to be taken for the time being.

27th Nov. 1956: Demand is insufficient to warrant a reprint. The book to remain out of stock.

18th Jun. 1959: Dr Fraser Darling taking new post in America. Decided to consider new edition of *Highlands and Islands* for the future, to be worked on by some other Scottish naturalist, as Dr Darling will not be available. Mr Fisher to write to Dr Darling and see if he would be agreeable to this. Professor Stamp and Mr Fisher will make enquiries about possible author. Mr Fisher suggested J. Morton Boyd on the Nature Conservancy Board, also W. J. Eggeling. Thorough revision necessary but wish to use original book as basis and use all existing blocks.'

16th Feb. 1960: Mr Fisher seeing W. J. Eggeling this week to sound him on question of re-writing this volume.

18th Jan. 1961: Should be reprinted if largely rewritten and (?) with new title. Fraser Darling now wants to rewrite book himself. He wishes to devote less time to travelling and more to writing. Is coming in to see the Chairman middle of March to discuss whole situation…

5th Jul. 1961: Mr Collins has seen Fraser Darling who is very keen to rewrite book with the help of Morton Boyd…Only Fraser Darling's name to appear on new edition, but Morton Boyd will do research…have new title for new book?

14th Nov. 1961: Morton Boyd to send material to Fraser Darling. Boyd's name not be used, but he will have a percentage of the royalties. He hopes to finish his section by Christmas. To be a completely new book, with fresh photographs, which EH will collect; new title and wrapper. MAW to ask F. Darling about title.

15th Feb 1962: Morton Boyd still working on revisions.

18th Jul. 1962: (Revised edition). Morton Boyd is getting on well with revisions.

8th Jan 1963: (Revised edition). Boyd been working hard, written 12 chapters. To change title to the 'Scottish Highlands' by Darling & Boyd.

29th Oct 1963: (Darling and Morton Boyd) Corrections nearly done. Pictures being chosen. To come out next autumn or summer.

15th Oct 1964: (Darling and Morton Boyd). Finished copies will be through in a fortnight. To be published on November 23, 1964 @ 30/-.

These minutes partly explain why the new book was not given a completely different title, a new jacket and a new series number. But given the book was rewritten and the type completely reset, one can't help wondering if it would not have been more profitable for Collins to have marketed it as new book with a new livery. But a new book would have required a new suite of plates and, as it is, many are the same as the original book – and less of them too.

Only *c.* 5,000 first edition copies were printed, (commensurate with other titles published between 1959 and 1964) and, as such, it is considerably rarer than commonly believed. Additional printings followed in 1969, 1973 and 1977, bringing the total number of books printed to *c.* 12,000. In contrast to these modest numbers was the hugely successful Fontana paperback edition, of which 80,000 copies were printed; more than any other NN title in this format. It was first published in 1969 and was reprinted nine times over the following 10 years, finally going out of print in June 1981. The last hurrah for *The Highlands and Islands* was the 1990 Bloomsbury 'facsimile' edition: but not much of a hurrah. While the book is a copy of NN6B (the 1973 reprint), the jacket and casing uses the title of the preceding title NN6A 'Natural History in the Highlands and Islands'. Such shoddiness might aptly sum up the Bloomsbury editions but it's an unfitting end for an outstanding book. Neither has this book been published in POD format.

The jacket of the Collins edition is the same design as NN6A, but printed using a different technique, the title reset and Boyd's name added, the antler has been omitted from the NN monogram and the bird on the spine is blind; there are other more subtle differences described under 'Notes' below. *Highlands and Islands* wears well and is often in fine condition. Collins edition o/p: end of 1981/beginning of 1982.

NN6BA	**First Edition**, 1964 (23 November 1964).
Title:	'The New Naturalist	The Highlands and	Islands'.
Author:	'by	F. Fraser Darling	D.Sc., Ph.D., Ll.D. (Glasg.), F.R.S.E.	And	J. Morton Boyd	D.Sc. Ph.D.'
Illust:	'With 6 colour photographs and	50 photographs in black-and-white'.
Editors:	JF, JG, JH, LDS and EH (Photographic Editor).
Printer:	Collins Clear-Type Press: London and Glasgow.
Collation:	pp. xvi, 336; 2 leaves of colour plates printed to both sides; 12 leaves of b/w plates printed to both sides (22 × 16-page gatherings).
Jacket:	[Rear panel] The New Naturalist library listing NN 1–45 (Type 42, variant 4a). [Rear flap] Adverts for *The Peak District*, *Mountains and Moorlands* and *The Salmon*.
Price:	30s. net.
Print run:	c. 5,000; o/p: 1970[?].
Notes:	1) The colours and textures of the jacket are unmistakeably different; the greys are now buffs and the maroon band is decidedly darker, the edges sharper, with the black areas above extending over the edge of the band. 2) The title to the half-title and title pages, and casing is with an 'and', whereas that to the jacket is with an ampersand. 3) B/w plates printed on glossy paper, the quality of reproduction much better than those of NN6A. 4) W. J. Eggeling mentioned in the 1959/60 Board minutes as a possible candidate for rewriting the book, did in fact criticise the manuscript and corrected the proofs as mentioned in the Author's preface.

NN6BB Second Edition, 1969. 'First edition 1964 | Second edition 1969'; no date to title page. Minor revisions and corrections, but the bibliography has been revised and extended; the author's preface now starts 'It is nineteen years since the publication of this book in its first form' (the first edition, of 5 years earlier, read 'It is sixteen years' – either someone's maths was not very good or there was a significant delay between

revising the preface and publication.) Editors: JF, JG, JH, MD and E. H. Boyd now with F.R.S.E. to his name on TP. The NN library to the jacket lists NN1–50 (Type 42, variant 8); rear flap unchanged; first paragraph of blurb to front flap retained with four press endorsements inserted below. Price: 30s. net. Print run: 4,000 including repriced variant below; o/p: 1973.
NN6BB-AP1 1st Repriced DJ (1971–73) with Collins £1.50/30/– sticker, stuck over original price (in accordance with decimalisation).

NN6BC Second Edition, First Reprint, 1973 (Oct.). ISBN 0002130920. 'First edition 1964 | Second edition 1969 | Reprinted 1973'. As NN6BB. The NN library to the *Durasealed* jacket lists NN1–56 (Type 42, variant 13); both flaps unchanged but for the addition of the ISBN to the rear. Price: £2.50 net. Print run: 2,000 inc. repriced variants below; o/p: latter part 1977.
NN6BC-AP1 1st Repriced DJ (1975–1976), £3.50 sticker, c. 400 sold.
NN6BC-AP2 2nd Repriced DJ (1976), £4.50 sticker, c. 450 sold.
NN6BC-AP3 3rd Repriced DJ (1977), £7.50 sticker, c. 350 sold.

NN6BD Second Edition, Second Reprint, 1977 [after September]. ISBN changed to 0002194473. 'First edition 1964 | Second edition 1969 | Reprinted 1973 | Reprinted 1977'. As NN6BC. Editors: MD, JG, KM and EH. The NN library to the *Durasealed* jacket lists NN1–60 (Type 42, variant 15); both flaps unchanged but for the revised ISBN to the rear. Price: £7.50 net printed diagonally with a dashed line. Print run: 1,000; no. sold: c. 600 + probably c. 350 sold off, from stock, to the RU; o/p: end of 1981/beginning of 1982. Note: From c. 1973 the last sentence of the NN credo was omitted but it has been accidentally left in place in this edition.

BC6BA Readers Union Edition, 1977. Bound up from the same sheets as the Collins 1977 edition NN6BD, but cased in dark green imitation cloth. Jacket without *Duraseal* and without a printed price, otherwise identical. Print run: c. 500. A scarce edition.

BL6BA Bloomsbury Edition, 1989. ISBN: 187063098x; pp. xvi, 336, [28 – b/w illustrations, integrated thoughout] (22¾ × 16-page gatherings). A b/w facsimile of the 1973 reprint NN6BC. Price £12.95. Print run: unknown, but a significant proportion remaindered. Note: The dust jacket and the casing use the title of the preceding book NN6A *Natural History in the Highlands and Islands*, but yet the book itself is a facsimile of NN6B.

F6BA Fontana Paperback, First Edition, 1969. ISBN: 0006319556 (ISBN appears only after 1974); pp. [x], 405, [1]; 8 leaves of b/w plates bound in two sections of 4, printed on glossy paper, to both sides (13 × 32-page gatherings). A reset copy of the Collins 1969 second edition; no colour and a reduced no. of b/w plates. The subtitle to the front cover and TP reads the Fontana library. Adverts for NN series and Fontana NN series at front, listing 7 titles. Paper liable to tanning as usual. The photographic front cover of Ben More by National Guardian Publishing Co. Ltd.; rear cover carries 6 press clips for *The Highlands and Islands*. Price: 10/6. Total print run including reprints below: 80,000. In terms of print qty, the most successful of all NN Fontana editions.

The following reprints exactly as preceding edition unless stated otherwise.

F6BB Second Impression, July 1969. (not seen).

F6BC Third Impression, June 1970. Price: 12/– (60p). Advert for NN series with press clips introduced to last page.

F6BD Fourth Impression, August 1970. Adverts at front and rear revised.

F6BE Fifth Impression, May 1971. (not seen).

F6BF Sixth Impression, March 1972. Price: 60p.

F6BG Seventh Impression, September 1972.

F6BH Eighth Impression, April 1974. ISBN added to rear cover 0006319556. Adverts revised to rear with prices added. Price: £1.25.

F6BI Ninth Impression, May 1977. Adverts revised to front and rear, latter no longer priced. Editors added opposite TP: – JG, JH, MD, KM and EH. Price: £1.50.

F6BJ Tenth Impression, May 1979. Adverts revised to front and omitted from rear (most NN titles no longer in print in Fontana series). Price £1.95 ; o/p: June 1981.

7   Mushrooms & Toadstools

The Editors in their preface refer to Dr Ramsbottom as 'a sort of Robert Burton of the fungal world' and describe his book as 'something approaching a twentieth century "Anatomy of Toadstools"'. Robert Burton (1577–1640) is best known for his English classic *The Anatomy of Melancholy*, first published in 1621; a masterpiece famous for its eclectic mix of erudition, humour, linguistic skill and creative insights. According to Boswell, Dr Johnson said that it was 'the only book that ever took him out of bed two hours sooner than he wished to rise'. *Mushrooms* does have parallels with *Melancholy* – it is undoubtedly the product of a great mind with an encyclopaedic knowledge of the subject, written in a friendly discursive style, heightened with classical and literary references and leavened with humour, but nevertheless it was a bold comparison for the Editors to make. Fortunately the reviews for the book were universally eulogistic – look at the five examples cited on the front flap of the reprint jackets. It is perhaps fitting that a book that cites poetry associated with Fairy Rings should be one of the very few New Naturalist titles to conclude with the words 'THE END', as in fact did Burton's *Melancholy*, 332 years earlier.

While *Mushrooms & Toadstools* is number seven in the series, it was not published until after NN27 *Dartmoor*. It had been planned

The Ellises' monogram was doctored and the date removed from the original artwork and this version (far left) appeared on jackets published between 1953–69. The Ellises had originally dated their artwork 1945. The jacket used for the last two impressions of 1971 and 1977 (left) was 're-originated' i.e. reproduced from the original artwork

as a title for the series from the outset and was mentioned as early as 1943, before a single book had been published. The reasons for the delay were manifold but mainly due to Ramsbottom's interminable proscrastinations, as documented by Peter Marren in *Art of the New Naturalists*; however the issue of the dated jacket needs elaboration. The original artwork was indeed dated 1945, i.e. eight years before the book was published, but the signature to the first (and early) jackets was redone (it is quite different from the original), presumably by the 'blockmaster', and the date left out. The jacket for the last two impressions (1971 and 1977) was printed using a different technique, but 're-originated', i.e. reproduced, from the original artwork – which, of course, included the original undoctored signature and therefore includes the date.

Mushrooms & Toadstools ran to six impressions but without any revisions or new editions. A dedicated Readers Union edition was published in 1960 in an RU jacket. There is a bookclub version of the 1977 reprint but this is almost identical to the Collins edition. In addition, it appears that during the late 1970s the RU was regularly topped up with books from Collins stock; the sales report for 1983 gives a total of 4,408 books sold to the RU, but no indication is given as to how this total is made up. The ad hoc disposal of books to the Readers Union makes it impossible to determine accurately the quantities of each impression, printed and sold.

The early jackets have a tendency to brown, though they are colourfast. The third and fourth impression jackets (1959 and 1963) are much greener with stronger colours and, to my eye, the most attractive; the 1969 jacket has a blue hue. The 1970s jackets are crude and lack subtlety, are distinctly more yellow and the brown title band is 'remastered' with cold, straight edges. Total no. of books printed: c. 27,300 (including books supplied to the US and RU); o/p: 1978.

NN7A   **First Edition**, 1953 (26 October 1953).
Title: 'The New Naturalist | Mushrooms & | Toadstools | A Study of | The Activities of Fungi'.
Author: 'by | John Ramsbottom'.
Illust: 'With 84 colour photographs | by Paul L. de Laszlo and others | and 58 black and white photographs'
Editors: JF, JG, JH, LDS and EH (Photographic Editor).
Printer: Collins Clear-Type Press: London and Glasgow.
Collation: pp. xiv, 306; 1 colour frontispiece plate printed to

verso only; 23 leaves of colour plates printed to both sides; 12 leaves of b/w plates printed to both sides (20 × 16-page gatherings).

Jacket:	[Rear panel] 'Plant Books in The New Naturalist Library' advertising *Flowers of the Coast, Wild Orchids of Britain, British Plant Life* and *Wild Flowers of Chalk & Limestone*. [Rear flap] Advert for *Fleas, Flukes & Cuckoos*. 'Three 1954 Publications' under which listed *Wild Flowers, Mumps, Measles and Mosaics* and *The Wren*.
Price:	30s. net.
Print run:	7,800.
Notes:	1) Frontispiece and last colour plate tipped-in, otherwise colour plates in conjugate pairs, bound in. 2) Lettering to jacket printed in dark brown. 3) C & RE signature to DJ front panel not dated. 4) Dated 1953 to TP.

NN7B Second Impression (New Edition), 1954 (October). 'First Edition: October 1953 | New Edition: October 1954'. Date omitted from TP. As NN7A. Jacket identical too with same price: 30s net. Print run: *c.* 3,500 (of which *c.* 850 sold to us publisher – see US7A). Note: Month included in printing history on imprint page.

NN7C Third Impression, 1959 (June). 'First Impression October 1953 | Second Impression October 1954 | Third Impression June 1959'. As NN7B. Editors: JH now Sir JH. Paper smoother, creamier; book very slightly thinner. Jacket greener; NN library lists NN1–38, omitting NN6 and 26 (Type 36); rear flap advertises *Wild Flowers* and *Wild Orchids of Britain*; front flap unaltered, and price still 30s net: Print run: 3,000. Note: A few examples have been seen with the earlier NN7B jacket.

NN7D Fouth Impression, 1963. 'First Impression October 1953 | Second Impression October 1954 | Third Impression June 1959 | Fourth Impression October 1963'. As NN7C. The NN library to the jacket lists NN1–45 (Type 42, variant 4); rear flap advertises *Collins Guide to Mushrooms and Toadstools* with three press commendations; blurb to front flap replaced with 5 press endorsements, jacket design credit also omitted. Price: 35s. net. Print run: 3,000[?], o/p: early 1969. Note: One of just a handful of NN jackets that advertises a book other than a NN.

NN7E Fifth Impression, 1969 (end of year). 'First Impression 1953 | Second Impression 1954 | Third Impression 1959 | Fourth Impression 1963 | Fifth Impression 1969,'. As NN7D. Editors: JF, JG, JH, MD and EH. Green of jacket now blue-grey; NN library lists NN1–50 (Type 42, variant 8); both flaps unaltered. Price: 45s. net. Print run: 2,500 including 'AP1' below. Note: Month of publication dropped from printing history.
NN7E-AP1 1st Repriced DJ (1971), £2.25 sticker (decimalisation).

NN7F Sixth Impression, 1972. ISBN 0002131447 (to jacket only). 'First Impression 1953 | Second Impression 1954 | Third Impression 1959 | Fourth Impression 1963 | Fifth Impression 1969 | Sixth Impression 1972'. As NN7E. Editors: JG, JH, MD, KM and

EH. The jacket is a new printing taken from the original drawing; signature to front panel now dated 'C & RE 45'; edges to the brown title band straight and sharp, subtlety of design lost, colours distinctly more yellow; *Durasealed*, the NN library lists NN1–54 (Type 42, variant 11); both flaps identical, but ISBN added to rear. Price: £2.80 net. Print run: 3,000. Note: Lettering to casing silver-gilt, as often the case for 1971–72.
NN7F-AP1 1st Repriced DJ (1975), £3.50 sticker, no. sold unknown.
NN7F-AP2 2nd Repriced DJ (1975–76), £4.00 sticker, *c.* 500 sold.
NN7F-AP3 3rd Repriced DJ (1976), £4.50 sticker, *c.* 400 sold.
NN7F-AP4 4th Repriced DJ (1977), £7.50 sticker, *c.* 100 sold.

NN7G Seventh Impression, 1977. ISBN 0002194805 (changed from NN7E). 'First Impression 1953 | Second Impression 1954 | Third Impression 1959 | Fourth Impression 1963 | Fifth Impression 1969 | Sixth Impression 1972 | Seventh Impression 1977'. As NN7F. Editors: MD, JG, KM and EH. Last sentence of NN credo omitted. The NN library to the *Durasealed* jacket lists NN1–60 (Type 42, variant 15); both flaps identical. Price: £8.00 net, printed diagonally with dotted line. Print run: *c.* 2,500; o/p: 1981 –'AP1'.
NN7G-AP1 1st Repriced DJ (1981), £8.50 sticker, < 100 sold.

BC7A Readers Union Edition, 1960. Printed and bound by Collins at Clear-Type Press, Glasgow. As NN7C but specially printed for the RU; therefore with an integral title page displaying the RU imprint and tree logo, otherwise textually identical with the same composition of plates. The green imitation cloth casing, is blocked with the Readers Union tree logo to the spine, but the title lettering is the same as the Collins editions. Fitted with the RU jacket 'Type 2'. Price: 13s. 6d. net. Print run: *c.* 2,000[?]

BC7B Readers Union Later Edition, 1977. Bound up from the same sheets as the later 1977 Collins edition NN7G, but cased in dark green imitation cloth. 1977 jacket not seen – see note below. Print run: unknown but a scarce edition. Note: The only copy I have seen was with a 1972 Collins *Durasealed* jacket, price-clipped. This was probably an expedient: a few spare jackets of the earlier printing were available so were stuck on RU books. Additionally Collins kept the RU topped up from their own stock, but such copies are indistinguishable.

POD7A Print-on-demand digital copy of the 1953 first edition NN7A.

CFS7A Collins/Folio Society facsimile, 2008 (07 July 2008). ISBN-10: 0007278543, ISBN-13: 9780007278541. A facsimile copy with jacket of the first edition. Not declared as a facsimile edition. Cased in modern dark green *Arbelave* buckram. Elements of jacket spine digitally re-whitened. Print run: *c.* 1,000 (as part box-set of first ten) + *c.* 150 individual copies; o/p: Nov. 2010. Note: While not marked as a facsimile, the freshness of the paper, the casing fabric and digitally re-whitened jacket should not allow confusion with the genuine first ed. Copies sold individually by HarperCollins have a price sticker with ISBN, barcode and www.newnaturalists.com affixed to rear DJ panel.

BL7A Bloomsbury Edition, 1989. ISBN 1870630092; pp. [1], xiv, 306,

[71 – b/w illustrations] (24 ½ × 16-page gatherings). A b/w facsimile of the 1977 Seventh Impression NN7G. Price: £12.95. Print run: unknown, but a significant proportion remaindered.

US7A US Edition, 1954. Macmillan. Book and jacket exactly as the Collins second impression of 1954 NN7B but with a 'distributed by Macmillan' label to the jacket. Print run: probably c. 850.

8 Insect Natural History

In the early days of the New Naturalist the Editors struck upon a rich literary seam from which proceeded a flow of fine books, one of the best amongst them being *Insect Natural History*. It was universally well reviewed and *The Field* commented: 'Dr Imms cloaks great knowledge and experience with simplicity. Altogether the book is a triumph'. A synthesis of the inquiring spirit and the results of modern scientific research accurately presented in an accessible manner: the embodiment of the New Naturalist ethos.

Imms had wanted the title to be 'British Insect Life' but the Editors considered this to be too close to *British Plant Life,* so instead they decided on the title *Insect Natural History*. The sales history of *Insect Natural History* was one of prolonged periods of interruption and during its 31-year life was out of print for almost as long as it was in print; otherwise the total number of copies sold would have been much greater.

The first edition, published in 1947, of c. 30,000 copies sold out in 1952, but Imms had died three years earlier in April 1949. The book required updating and eventually, G. C. Varley and B. M. Hobby of the Hope Dept. of Entomology, University Museum, Oxford, were appointed, but it was not until 1956 that the second edition was published. However, the text remained substantially

as Dr Imms had written it. In early 1961 the book went out of print again, and the same problems were encountered in updating the book. Theodore Savory was considered as a suitable reviser, but his appointment did not materialise. Varley was contracted, but to the frustration of the Board, his progress was slow, and he struggled rewriting the chapter on flight. It eventually befell to Michael Tweedie to rewrite this chapter and the third edition was eventually published in 1971 following a hiatus of ten years.

A straight reprint followed in 1973, but with two distinct binding variants, and went out of print in 1978. A reprint was due for 1977 for which C & RE Ellis had produced a new jacket design and John Heath compiled a new bibliography, but it was decided to postpone this to let arrears build up. However the colour plant had been lost by the factory and the conversion to letterpress was prohibitively expensive, so it was decided to use just b/w illustrations. Eventually the project was abandoned due to soaring costs.

Insect Natural History was additionally published by Fontana in 1973, using the text of the Collins 1971 edition. At 10,000 copies, a small print run for a Fontana paperback, but the book remained in print for six years. The poor, dark and staged photograph used for the front cover was a particularly poor choice and could not have helped sales. 23 years later Bloomsbury published a utilitarian reprint, but this was commercially unsuccessful and was remaindered. There do not appear to be any foreign translations, but the book was also published in the US by Blakiston, in 1951, and bound up from sheets printed by Collins; now a rare edition.

Insect Natural History is not difficult to find in fine condition, though the jacket of the first edition is liable to brown. The 1973 jacket is distinctly more yellow. Total no. of Collins hardbacks printed: c. 38,500; o/p: 1978.

NN8A	**First Edition**, 1947 (05 October 1947).
Title:	'The New Naturalist	Insect	Natural History'.
Author:	'by	A. D. Imms	M.A. D.Sc. F.R.S.	Honorary Fellow of Downing College and Sometime Reader	in Entomology, Cambridge University'
Illust:	'With 99 colour photographs of living insects	and 7 colour photographs of preserved specimens	by S. Beaufoy, E. J. Hudson and others	104 photographs in black and white	8 distribution maps	and 40 diagrams'.
Editors:	JF, JG, JH, LDS and EH (Photographic Editor).

TABLE NN8 Diagnostic features of the two binding variants of the 1973 reprint NN8D.

Insect N. History 1973 reprint NN8D	NN Monogram to casing spine	Book thickness	Hinges (internal)	Jacket
1ST BINDING (B1)	Embellished with a a Grasshopper	28 mm	Mull evident under endpaper at hinges not extending to top/tail of EP.	Either 1971 jacket NN8c p. clipped and repriced or 1973 jacket at printed price or repriced at £4.00
2ND BINDING (B2)	'Type C' with central diamond	26 mm	Binding tape evident under EP at hinges which extends to top/tail of EP.	Almost without exception in p. clipped and repriced jackets

Printer: Collins Clear-Type Press, London and Glasgow
            (produced in conjuction with Adprint).
Collation: pp. xviii, 317, [1]; 20 leaves of colour plates printed
            to both sides; 16 leaves of b/w plates printed to both
            sides (21 × 16-page gatherings).
Jacket: [Rear panel] 'The New Naturalist | A Survey of British
            Natural History' listing the first eight titles in the
            series; New Naturalist Editors; Collins address. [Rear
            flap] Continuation of blurb from front wing [flap].
Price: 16s. net.
Print run: 30,000 of which c. 2,000 sold to the US publisher
            Blakiston; o/p: end of 1952.
Notes: 1) The position of 'Collins' in relation to the NN Oval
            on the spine is not constant, which suggests there
            were probably multiple printings of the jacket. 2)
            Book c. 28 mm thick. 3) Bound in 'Group 1' Buckram,
            open weave and always faded to a lesser or greater
            extent, often unevenly.

NN8A-AP1 1st Repriced DJ (1948{?}–52) with label either showing
21s. 0d. net or 'Book Production Economy Standard' (features a
lion sitting above a book) or 21/-net pasted over original price.
NN8A-AP2 2nd Repriced DJ (1948{?}–52), p. clipped, and
overprinted 21s. net to lower left corner.

NN8B Second (Revised) Edition, 1956. 'First published in 1947… |
…Second, revised, edition 1956'. Minor revisions by G. C. Varley
and B. M. Hobby: a number of small errors corrected, a few
nomenclatural updates in line with (the then) current practice;
bibliography and index enlarged and partially reset. The book
substantially as Dr Imms wrote it without the text reset, same
plates. 'Note to second edition' added to p. xiv and another 'Note'
added to p. xviii; the latter refers to (the addition of) a list of name
changes to p. 304, but this was accidentally omitted. Printing less
crisp, on rougher paper. Bound in later green 'Group 2' Buckram,
smoother with an even, almost dog-tooth weave, not liable to
fading; book appreciably thicker at c. 31 mm. The NN library to the
jacket is a unique layout and lists in a single column *Butterflies* to
The Open Sea, *The World of Plankton* (1–34), but omits *Highlands and
Islands*, *Insect Natural History* and *Trees Woods and Man*. Rear flap:
'Some Press Opinions of Insect Natural History'; the blurb has
been reset with a smaller typeface and does not now continue
onto rear flap. Price: 30s. net. Print run: 4,000 (of which c. 1,000
possibly sold to US publisher –see note accompanying US8A); o/p:
beginning 1961.
NN8B-DJ1 Repriced First Edition Jacket, 1956. Fitted with first
edition jacket NN8A. P. clipped and overprinted 30s. net.
(Presumably this variant with the 1st ed. DJ was sold before the
'dedicated' 2nd ed. jacket was printed.)

NN8C Third Edition, 1971. ISBN: 0002131021. 'First Edition 1947 |
Second Edition 1956 | Third Edition 1971'. Essentially as NN8B but
with Chapter 3 'On Wings and Flight' rewritten by Michael
Tweedie with 'note to third edition' added on p. xiv, to that effect.

This chapter was too long, so reset with smaller type (now 42
lines/page, previously 39). The bibliography and index also
enlarged and reset, the former in much smaller type. Otherwise
bulk of text unaltered and not reset, plates unaltered. Editors: MD,
JH, JG, KM and EH. Last sentence of NN Credo omitted. Paper
smoother and printing sharper. NN library to jacket lists NN1–50
(Type 42, variant 8); rear flap advertises *Angler's Entomology* and
Insect Migration with ISBN added; blurb completely omitted, in its
place seven press clips. Price: £2.50 net/50s. net. Print run: 3,500;
o/p: end 1973.

NN8D-B1 Third Edition, Reprinted, First Binding Variant, 1973
[January 1974]. ISBN unchanged. 'First Edition 1947 | Second
Edition 1956 | Third Edition 1971 | Reprinted 1973'.
A reprint of NN8C. For diagnostic binding features see table NN8
(opposite). Book thinner, 26 mm thick. The now *Durasealed* jacket
printed with different technique, some subtlety of line lost,
edges of the title band now straight and sharp, colours distinctly
more yellow; the New Naturalist library lists NN1–56 (Type 42,
variant 13); both flaps identical. Price: £3.50 net. Print run:
2,000 including 'B2' below; no. sold thus c. 800[?] including
variants below.
NN8D-B1-AP1 1st Repriced DJ (1975), £4.00 sticker.
NN8D-B1-DJ1 With 1971, NN8C, jacket, price clipped with Collins
£3.50 Sticker. (Presumably some jackets were left over from the
1971 printing.)
NN8D-B2 Third Edition, Reprinted, Second Binding Variant, 1973
[bound-up Dec 1974]. As B1 but without grasshopper
embellishment to the NN monogram, instead straightforward
'Type C' with central diamond; and different internal hinge
arrangement – see table NN8. With same jacket. No. bound thus:
c. 940. A very small number were sold in jackets with the original
price of £3.50, otherwise in repriced jackets as follows:
NN8D-B2-AP1 1st Repriced DJ (1975–76), £4.00 sticker, no. sold unknown.
NN8D-B2-AP2 2nd Repriced DJ (1976–77), £4.50 sticker, c. 500 sold.
NN8D-B2-AP3 3rd Repriced DJ (1978), £5.50 sticker, c. 150 sold.

POD8A Print-on-demand digital copy of the 1947 first edition
NN8A.

CFS8A Collins/Folio Society Facsimile, 2008 (07 July 2008).
ISBN-10: 0007278551, ISBN-13: 9780007278558. A facsimile copy
with jacket of the first edition. Not declared as a facsimile
edition. Cased in modern dark green *Arbelave* buckram.
Elements of jacket spine digitally re-whitened. Print run:
c. 1,000 (as part box-set of first ten) + c. 150 individual copies;
o/p: Nov. 2010[?]. Note: While, not marked as a facsimile, the
freshness of the paper, the casing fabric and digitally re-
whitened jacket should not allow confusion with the genuine
first ed. Copies sold individually by HarperCollins have a price
sticker with ISBN, barcode and www.newnaturalists.com affixed
to rear DJ panel.

F8A Fontana Paperback First Edition, 1973. ISBN: 0006331947
(ISBN appears only on repriced variant); pp. 348, [4 – adverts]; 8

leaves of b/w plates bound in two sections of 4, printed on glossy paper, to both sides (22 × 16-page gatherings). A reset copy of the Collins third edition of 1971 NN8C, but without colour plates and a reduced no. of b/w plates. The subtitle to the front cover and TP reads 'The Fontana New Naturalist'. Adverts for NN and Fontana Library titles at front and rear with order form also at rear. The front cover photograph of a dragonfly by Stephen Dalton; rear cover carries 2 press commendations for *Insect Natural History*. Price: 60p. Total print run: 10,000; total no. sold: 9,760 (all inc. repriced variant below). Note: A small print run for a Fontana p/b, but the book remained in print for six years.

F8A-AP1 First Repriced Variant With a black Collins sticker, applied over previous pricings to rear cover; on which printed, ISBN and UK and foreign prices; o/p: 1979.

BL8A Bloomsbury Edition, 1990 (31 December 1990). ISBN: 1870630394; pp. xviii, 317, [1], [72 – b/w illustrations] (25½ × 16-page gatherings). A b/w facsimile of the 1973 reprint NN8D. The jacket blurb is a copy of the first three paragraphs of that, that accompanied the Collins 1947 first edition. Price: £12.95. Print run: unknown, but remaindered.

US8A US Edition, 1951. Blakiston, New York, Philadelphia, Toronto. 'Printed in Great Britain | All rights reserved'. Hardback (with dust jacket?). From the same sheets as the 1947 first edition NN8A, same suite of plates. Title page is a cancel with 'The Blakiston Company' imprint and dated 1951, reference to the New Naturalist removed; half-title as Collins first edition with NN reference retained. The casing looks decidedly American and was almost certainly bound there. Print run: 1,000[?], but comparatively scarce particularly with an extant jacket. Note: The sales figures are ambiguous; either 1,000 or 2,000 copies were sold to the States of this edition. It might also be that an additional 1,000 copies of the 1956 second edition were sold to a US publisher, but to date no such copy has been located.

9 A Country Parish

In a letter to William Collins, written in October 1949, Boyd wrote 'I hope it will not severely let down the high standard of several of the earlier New Naturalist series; rather a fond wish, I fear.' But his fear was unwarranted for his contribution to the series was an exquisite albeit somewhat anomalous book. *A Country Parish* is an account of a rural England of a past age; as much a social history as a natural history. It remains as popular today as it ever was and is never the last volume to complete a collection.

Boyd commissioned an accomplished local photographer, C.W. Bradley, who was given a 25-gallon petrol allowance and is accordingly acknowledged on the title page. A few of these photographs appeared in later New Naturalist books: – The lime avenue at Aston Park in summer and in winter (plate 5 in *A Country Parish*; plate 15 in *Man and the Land*), and a black poplar at Arley Brook (plate 8 in *A Country Parish*; plate 16 in *Trees, Woods and Man*). Apparently a few also featured in a contemporary New Naturalist calendar.

Boyd was commissioned at the beginning of 1946 and completed the manuscript in early 1949, though the book was not released until August 1951. This slightly protracted period explains the adverts at the back of the book and why *A Country Parish* is NN9 in the series but was published after NN19 *Wild Orchids of Britain*.

According to the few sales statements that have survived from this period, 6,500 copies were printed, but total sales were 6,489 and so with natural wastage, the number printed must have been greater than stated; perhaps there was significant over-run? Other than this discrepancy, *A Country Parish* is pleasingly straightforward bibliographically: just one impression of a single edition, without any binding variants. It is the rarest of the early New Naturalists and the soft greys and blues of the jacket are prone to fading and browning, particularly on the spine, which, to boot, is usually a little chipped at the head and tail.

NN9a	**First Edition**, 1951 (13 August 1951).
Title:	'The New Naturalist	A Country Parish	Great Budsworth	in the County of Chester'.
Author:	'by	A.W. Boyd	MA., M.C.'
Illust:	'With 34 Colour Photographs	By C.W. Bradley and another	48 black-and-white photographs	and 9 text figures'.
Editors:	JF, JG, JH, LDS and EH (Photographic Editor).
Printer:	Collins Clear-Type Press, London and Glasgow (produced in conjunction with Adprint).
Collation:	pp. xvi, 278, [2 – NN adverts]; 16 leaves of colour plates printed to both sides; 16 leaves of b/w plates printed to both sides (18½ × 16-page gatherings).
Jacket:	[Rear panel] 'The New Naturalist Library some forthcoming volumes' under which 10 titles listed. [Rear flap] 'Recently published in the New Naturalist Library' under which 6 titles listed.
Price:	21s.net.
Print run:	> 6,500; no. sold: c. 6,490; o/p: 1959.
Notes:	The two pages of NN adverts at the rear, include a list of 32 titles 'Already published in the Main Series' and a list of 3 Monographs; adverts for specific titles: *Wild Flowers of Chalk & Limestone*, *Birds and Men* and *Life in Lakes and Rivers*.

CFS9A Collins/Folio Society facsimile A digital facsimile copy, with facsimile jacket of first edition. Published in 2008, but not dated in the book. Elements of jacket spine digitally re-whitened (number roundels, titling and monogram). Print run: *c.* 1,000 (as box-set of first ten) + *c.* 150 individual copies.

POD9A Print-on-demand digital copy.

10 British Plant Life

NN10 began life in 1943 with the working title 'Rare Wild Flowers' and then 'The Biology of the British Flora'. When in September 1946 Turrill completed the book (nine months ahead of schedule) he suggested the new title 'British Plant Life' with the subtitle: 'Its history, composition and behaviour'.

'The resulting story…is as exciting as a first-class detective novel', so extolled the jacket blurb to the first edition, but evidently the public was not convinced as *British Plant Life* was a slow seller. There were 10 years between the printings of the first two editions. The final printing was in 1972.

Despite being on sale over a 32-year period there were just four Collins printings, with minimal revisions; the 1971 printing being ostensibly the same as the 1948 first edition. Minutes of various Editorial Board meetings held in 1963 and 1964 record that it was recognised that the book needed updating and 'that at least four chapters needed extensive revision'. Max Walters and [David?] Briggs, both of Cambridge, were, at different times, suggested as potential candidates, but for unrecorded reasons a revised edition was never realised. *British Plant Life* appeared in Readers Union livery in 1953 and again in 1959, and then as a b/w facsimile edition published by Bloomsbury in 1989.

The print quantities of the first and second edition are impossible to determine accurately from the extant sales reports, and then exacerbated by Readers Union editions. It would appear that either 20,000 or 22,000 first edition copies were printed and either 2,000 or 4,000 second edition copies: the discrepancy in both cases, of 2,000, may represent RU copies.

The mauve tones of the first edition jacket are stronger than later jackets; the 1971 jacket is particularly washed out. Despite the very large number of first edition books available (table 2 on pages 36–7), *British Plant Life* is a very good example of 'conditional rarity'; the jacket is prone to tanning, rubbing on the joints and chipping to the edges: fine copies are scarce. o/p: 1980, but o/s for whole of 1971.

NN10A	**First Edition**, 1948 (04 October 1948).
Title:	'The New Naturalist | British Plant Life'.
Author:	'by W. B. Turrill | D.Sc. Lond., F.L.S. | Keeper of the Herbarium and Library | Royal Botanic Gardens, Kew'.
Illust:	'With 53 colour photographs | by John Markham, Brian Perkins | F. Ballard and others | 27 photographs in black and white | 8 maps and diagrams'.
Editors:	JF, JG, JH, LDS and EH (Photographic Editor).
Printer:	Collins Clear-Type Press, London and Glasgow (produced in conjunction with Adprint).
Collation:	pp. xvii, [1], 315, [3]; 24 leaves of colour plates printed to both sides; 12 leaves of b/w plates printed to both sides (21 × 16-page gatherings).
Jacket:	[Rear panel] Advert for *Snowdonia*; list of Editors and the Collins address above lower edge. [Rear flap] 'The New Naturalist A Survey of British Natural History' listing first 13 main-series titles, distinguishing those published.
Price:	21s. net. Print run: 20,000[?]; no. sold: *c.* 20,200[?]; o/p: 1957. (Figures include what was probably about 2,000 copies sold off to the Readers Union.)
Notes:	1) The Author's Preface is dated 8 August, 1946, two years before the book was published 2) Colour plates printed on semi-gloss paper and b/w plates printed on matt paper. 3) DJ design credit reads 'Wrapper design by…' 4) The jacket is trimmed off-centre, cutting in half the Ellises' monogram, at the lower edge. 5) Reference to the 'New Naturalist' series by Turrill is always in capitals. 6) A few copies appear to wear N10B jackets.

NN10B Second Edition, 1958 (after August). 'First published in 1948… \| Second Edition, 1958'. As NN10A, and despite being labelled the second edition, with minimal (if any) textual revisions. Title page: Turrill now 'formerly keeper' and 'V.M.H.' added. Editors: JH now Sir JH. The paper is rougher, less white. The reprographic technique used for colour plates changed, and now without the 'metallic' element of the 1st ed. plates and on glossier paper and b/w plates printed on semi-gloss paper. Jacket exactly as first ed. NN10A but price-clipped and overprinted 30s. net. Print run: 4,000[?]; o/p: summer 1962. Note: The sales statement for the period 1959–1960 refers to a price of 25s. net but this appears to be a mistake as all jackets seen have been overprinted 30s. net.

NN10C Third Edition, 1962. *'First published 1948 \| Second Edition 1958 \| Third Edition 1962'.* Essentially as NN10B: revisions restricted to the odd nomenclatural change e.g. on p. 45 *Anthriscus vulgaris* changed to *Anthriscus caucalis*, and the index slightly enlarged.

Title page: F.R.S. added after Turrill's name. Reprographic technique used for b/w plates changed (gravure to letterpress?) and now on glossy paper; some backgrounds a little marked, for instance top LH corner of plate IV. Text on slightly better paper. The jacket title band and campion foliage less blue, greener; the NN library lists NN1–45 (Type 42, variant 4); the rear flap advertises *Wild Flowers*, *Weeds & Aliens* and *Lords & Ladies*; front flap with extensive press comment from *Manchester Guardian*, below which is stated that the third edition has been revised and brought up to date; DJ design credit now '*Jacket design by…*' Price: 35s. net. Print run: 6,000; o/p: 1970.

NN10D-DJ1 Third Edition, Reprint, First Jacket Variant, 1971 [early 1972]. ISBN 000213022X (to DJ rear flap only). 'First published 1948 | Second Edition 1958 | Third Edition 1962 | Reprinted 1971' As NN10C. Editors: JG, JH, MD, KM and EH. The mauve tones of the *Durasealed* jacket lighter and greyer, the overall appearance somewhat washed-out, The NN library lists NN1–52 (Type 42, variant 9); rear flap advertises *Wild Flowers* and *Weeds & Aliens* with ISBN below; front flap features five press commendations (one unacknowledged). Price: £2.50 net. Print run: 3,000; o/p: officially June 1980, but effectively late 1979. Note: No books were recorded as sold during 1971 and therefore it is assumed that this reprint did not actually appear until early 1972.

NN10D-DJ1-AP1 1st Repriced DJ (1975), £3.00 sticker.

NN10D-DJ2 Third Edition, Reprint, Second Jacket Variant (printed 1972 or 73) Identical to DJ1 and *Durasealed* but NN library lists NN1–54 (Type 42, variant 11) Price: £2.50 net.

NN10D-DJ2-AP1 1st Repriced DJ (1980–81), £7.50 sticker, c. 150 sold.

NN10D-DJ2-AP2 2nd Repriced DJ (1981), £8.50 sticker, c. 80 sold.

NN10D-DJ2-AP3 3rd Repriced DJ (1982–83), £9.50 sticker, c. 350 sold.

NN10D-AP4 4th Repriced DJ (1985–early 1986), £10.00 sticker, c. 350 sold.

BC10A Readers Union Edition, First Edition, 1953. As NN10A and from that printing, but with a cancel title page displaying the RU tree logo and dated 1953. The binding also identical, but stamped 'Readers Union' in gilt to the rear board. RU jacket 'Type 1'. Price: 10s. 6d net. Print run: c. 2,000[?]. Note: It appears that Collins remaindered bound copies of NN10A to the RU; the cancel titles are crudely pasted in.

BC10B Readers Union Edition, Second Edition, 1959. As the Collins 1958 second edition NN10b and probably from that printing but with an integral title page, displaying the RU imprint and tree logo dated 1959. Imitation green cloth casing blocked with the RU logo to the spine. RU jacket 'Type 2'. Price: 15s. net. Print run: 2,000[?]

POD10A Print-on-demand digital copy of the first edition, NN10A.

CFS10A Collins/Folio Society facsimile, 2008 (02 July 2008). ISBN-10: 000727856X ISBN-13: 9780007278565. A facsimile copy with jacket of the first edition. Not declared as a facsimile edition. Cased in modern dark green *Arbelave* buckram. Elements of jacket

spine digitally re-whitened. Print run: c. 1,000 (as part box-set of first ten) + c. 150 individual copies; o/p: Nov. 2010. Note: While not marked as a facsimile, the freshness of the paper, the casing fabric and digitally re-whitened jacket should not allow confusion with the genuine first ed. Copies sold individually by HarperCollins have a price sticker with ISBN, barcode and www.newnaturalists.com affixed to rear DJ panel.

BL10A Bloomsbury Edition, 31 December 1989. ISBN 1870630831; pp. xvii, [1], 315, [3] [72 – b/w illustrations, integrated throughout] (25½ × 16-page gatherings). A b/w facsimile of the 1948 first edition NN10A. Price: £12.95. Print run: unknown, but a significant proportion remaindered.

11 Mountains and Moorlands

Mountains and Moorlands was a widely used student's textbook, in fact probably the mostly widely used New Naturalist text of all. The first edition was reprinted twice but in 1966 Winifred Pennington accepted the commission to revise the book (Professor Pearsall had died in October 1964). In her preface she writes '…it is a classic, and must not be touched by a lesser hand.' Accordingly she altered as little as was absolutely required in bringing the book up to date; in most chapters just a few sentences 'to conform with new discoveries' and 'the nomenclature of plants has been revised to conform with modern usage'. But Chapter 10 on ecological history was largely rewritten. This revised (second) edition was first published as a Fontana paperback in 1968, but did not appear as a New Naturalist hardback until 1971.

Despite the second edition being first published as a Fontana paperback it is incorrect to assume that the later Collins hardback edition was printed from blow ups of the Fontana plates, as has been suggested. It wasn't; most of the setting remains exactly as the first edition and was presumably printed from the original plates or at least copies of them. It is interesting to see many mistakes, admittedly mostly trivial, reappear uncorrected throughout the various Collins reprints and editions; e.g. on p. 72, line 17, 'media' is mispelt 'maedia' and on p. 73, line 22 'summarises' appears as 'summaries'. No doubt some of these mistakes were noticed but it was an expensive business to manufacture new plates – which could hardly be justified for something so inconsequential; but in the Fontana paperback where the text was completely reset many of these mistakes were corrected, including the above two examples.

The Readers Union ordered 500 copies of the Collins 1977 hardback reprint and these have the usual bookclub trademarks – imitation cloth casings; dust jackets without printed prices and without clear plastic *Duraseal* protectors. A particularly scarce edition though, no doubt, academic as few collectors want them.

The dust jackets of the early editions were printed on acidic paper and are particularly prone to tanning and foxing and, to a lesser extent, to chipping; but on the plus side, the colours of these early editions are comparatively colourfast, unlike the 1971 second edition and its reprint. Total print run: 27,000 (Collins) + 500 (Readers Union); total no. sold: *c.* 25,730 (Collins) + 500 (RU) + probably 700 from stock to RU; Collins h/b o/p: early 1986.

NN11A   **First Edition**, 1950 (17 April 1950).
Title: 'The New Naturalist | Mountains and | Moorlands'.
Author: 'by W. H. Pearsall | D.Sc. F.R.S. | Quain Professor of Botany | in the University of London | at University College'.
Illust: 'With 47 colour photographs | by John Markham, B. A. Crouch and others | 34 photographs in black and white | and 48 maps and diagrams'.
Editors: JF, JG, JH, LDS and EH (Photographic Editor).
Printer: Collins Clear-Type Press, London and Glasgow (produced in conjunction with Adprint).
Collation: pp. xv, [1], 312; 16 leaves of colour plates printed to both sides; 16 leaves of b/w plates printed to both sides (20½ × 16-page gatherings).
Jacket: [Rear panel] 'The New Naturalist A Survey of British Natural History' advertising 'The First Sixteen Titles in Main Series' (these are not numbered and do not reflect the first 16 books in the series, but those available or in preparation). 'A postcard send to the publishers…' with Collins's address at bottom. [Rear flap] Advert for 'New Naturalist Monographs' listing eight titles (see notes).
Price: 21s. net.
Print run: 15,500; no. sold: *c.* 14,600; o/p: Dec. 1959.
Notes: 1) An erratum is printed to p. x regarding the caption of Plate X. 2) The list of monographs to the rear flap includes: 'Amphibia and Reptiles' and 'Parasites of Birds', denoted as forthcoming titles: in the event the former was published in the main series as NN20 *The British Amphibians and Reptiles* and the latter as monograph no. 7 *Fleas, Flukes and Cuckoos*. 3) 'Collins' to DJ spine printed in black.

NN11B **First Reprint**, 1960 [latter part]. 'First published 1950 | Reprinted 1960'. As NN11A. The erratum to p. x is no longer present though the revision to the caption of Plate X does not follow the earlier erratum. NN library to jacket lists NN1–42 inclusively, but noting that NN6, 9 and 13 out of print (Type 41A;

rear flap carries adverts for *Mountain Flowers*, *Britain's Structure and Scenery* and *Fossils* with supporting press endorsements; front flap unchanged. Price: 30s. net. Print run: 2,500; no. sold: *c.* 2,370; o/p: end 1964.

NN11C **Second Reprint (Third Impression)**, 1965. 'First Impression 1950 | Second " 1960 | Third " 1965'. As NN11B. NN library to jacket rear panel lists NN1–46 (Type 42, variant 5); rear flap identical, but blurb to front flap has been précised allowing insertion of four press clips. Price: 30s. net. Print run: 4,000; no. sold: *c.* 4,340[?]; o/p: early 1969. Note: A few copies wear NN11B jackets – presumably there were some left over.

NN11D **Revised Edition** 1971. ISBN 0002131439 (to DJ rear flap only). 'First Edition 1950 | Reprinted, 1960 | Reprinted, 1965 | Revised Edition 1971'; pp: xvi, 312. The title page includes the statement 'With revisions by Winifred Pennington | (Mrs T. G. Tutin). A 'Preface to Revised Edition', signed 'W.P.' has been inserted below Pearsall's original preface; chapter 10 completely rewritten; bibliography extended otherwise revisions minor with most pages retaining original typesetting; plates unchanged. Editors: MD, JG, JH, KM and EH. 'Collins' to the jacket spine now printed in magenta. The NN library lists NN1–52 (Type 42, variant 9); the rear flap is unchanged, but for addition of ISBN; the blurb has been revised to advertise new edition with three press commendations below. Price: £3.15 net. Print run: 2,500; no. sold: *c.* 2,300; o/p: summer 1974. Notes: 1) This revised text first appeared in the 1968 Fontana edition. 2) Jacket prone to fading.

NN11E **Revised Edition, Reprint**, 1977. ISBN 0002194775 (changed from above and now printed to imprint page and DJ). 'First Edition 1950 | Reprinted, 1960 | Reprinted, 1965 | Revised Edition 1971 | Reprinted, 1977'. As NN11D. Editors: MD, JG, KM and EH; the last sentence of the NN credo omitted. The NN monogram to the spine casing now plain without the emperor moth embellishment i.e. 'Type C'. The jacket printed using different technique: less subtle with loss of definition, colours bolder and 'flatter', title band with crisp straight edges; 'Collins' still printed in magenta. Jacket *Durasealed*, the NN library lists NN1–60 (Type 42, variant 15); both flaps unchanged. Price: £6.95 net printed diagonally with dotted line. Print run: 3,000; no. sold: *c.* 1,200 + repriced variants below + probably 700 copies from stock to RU.
NN11E-AP1 **1st Repriced DJ** (1980–81), £7.50 sticker, *c.* 150 sold.
NN11E-AP2 **2nd Repriced DJ** (1981), £8.50 sticker, *c.* 100 sold.
NN11E-AP3 **3rd Repriced DJ** (1982–83), £9.50 sticker, *c.* 350 sold.
NN11E-AP4 **4th Repriced DJ** (1984–early 86), £10.00 sticker, *c.* 350 sold.

BC11A **Readers Union Edition**, 1977. Bound up from the same sheets as the 1977 Collins edition NN11E, but cased in dark green imitation cloth. Jacket without *Duraseal* and without a printed price, otherwise identical. The spine of the casing has been stamped with the NN monogram embellished with the emperor moth motif (the Collins edition used the unembellished monogram 'Type C'). Print run: *c.* 500. A scarce edition.

POD11A Print-on-demand digital copy of the 1977 reprint NN11E.

F11A Fontana Paperback First Edition, 1968. ISBN 006319440 (ISBN does not appear in any editions); pp. 415, [1]; 8 leaves of b/w plates bound in two sections of 4, printed on glossy paper to both sides (26 × 16-page gatherings). Title page states: 'revised by Winifred Pennington | (Mrs T. G. Tutin)' (see intro.). This edition used for the 1971 Collins hardback revised edition NN11D, but this Fontana ed. with no colour and reduced no. b/w plates. The subtitle to TP reads 'the Fontana Library'. Advert for 4 Fontana Library NN titles at front. The semi-wrap-around cover artwork uncredited but probably by Kenneth Farnhill, with New Naturalist square 'logo' to front cover; blurb to rear cover. Price: 12/6. Total print run including reprints: 27,000.
The following reprints exactly as preceding edition unless stated otherwise.

F11B Second Impression April, 1970. Later green livery with photographic front cover (uncredited) on which printed 'The Fontana New Naturalist'; rear cover has three press commendations. TP includes 'The Fontana New Naturalist'; NN adverts enlarged to front and added to rear. Price: 12/- (60p).

F11C Third Impression November, 1970. Creamy paper.

F11D Fourth Impression, October 1971. Price: 60p, adverts at rear revised, thicker book.

F11E Fifth Impression, October 1972. Slightly thinner.

BL11A Bloomsbury Edition, 1989 [31 December 1989]. ISBN 187063053x; pp. xvi, 312, [64 b/w illustrations, integrated throughout] (22½ × 16-page gatherings). A b/w facsimile of the 1977 reprint NN11e. Price £12.95. Print run: unknown, but a significant proportion remaindered.

12 The Sea Shore

'Your volume is one of our greatest successes and has done a great deal to establish the series.' So wrote the editor James Fisher to Colin Yonge on 27 August 1953. *The Sea Shore* is the second-best selling New Naturalist title, with over 100,000 copies sold in all formats (42,700 Collins hardbacks, 54,400 Fontana paperbacks, 2,000 RU hardbacks plus Bloomsbury hardback and US paperback editions). One of the reasons for this success was the outstanding and, at the time, cutting-edge photographs of D. P. Wilson, which appeared in colour and b/w throughout the book – wonderful, modern-day versions of those rich chromolithographic plates

that adorned the books of Philip Henry Gosse, of whom Yonge wrote so warmly in his introduction to *The Sea Shore*.

However, the colour plates, for the first edition, were at the centre of a printing debacle: a quick inspection will show that plates 17–36 have all been glued in (tipped-in) rather than bound in, as recorded in the Board minutes of 29 April 1949: 'The Chairman said that owing to some misunderstanding or carelessness the colour sheets had been folded wrongly at Glasgow. This necessitated tipping in all the colour illustrations which would delay the book about a month and increase costs. Miss Ulmann stated that she had taken special care to go and explain to Mr Delgado that the central sheets would have to be folded in eights instead of sixteens, and that even if he had not passed on the message the Glasgow House should have seen from her carefully made paste-up how it was to be done'. One can imagine the scene well: poor Miss Ullman trying to absolve herself of blame before the formidable New Naturalist board, but despite her protestations the plates had to be placed in the text opposite the plate-caption and this dictated that most central plates would need to be tipped in, whatever folding permutations of letterpress and plates were used. In short a monumental gaffe had been committed with far-reaching ramifications – all later reprints, even those in the 1970s, had a preponderance of stuck-in plates, which must have represented a significant additional cost.

The Sea Shore was reprinted five times and despite the 1996 reprint being referred to as a revised edition, the text was ostensibly unchanged. It remained in print over a 31-year period, though there was a hiatus of a couple of years during the period 1964–1966 when it was out of stock. The 1966 reprint had been repeatedly delayed – it was initially scheduled for 1964.

Apart from the customary changes to the New Naturalist library, the jacket was little revised over its life, so much so that the 1976 jacket was still advertising *Oysters*, even though it had gone out of print two years earlier.

The Sea Shore, around 1971, became a set book for the Open University and this helped sales of the Fontana paperback, which ran to 12 impressions, the last of which was printed in June 1979, finally going out of print in 1983. *The Sea Shore* was also published by the Readers Union in 1959 and by the US imprint Atheneum in 1963, the former as a hardback with jacket in typical RU livery, the latter as a paperback with the same cover art as the early Fontana editions (see Figure 12A).

Clearly not a rare book, but the pink to the first edition jacket is particularly fugitive, that on the spine should have the same richness of colour as that on the front cover, but it never does. I have yet to see a first edition copy that is even only slightly faded. However, later editions are often unfaded, which goes to show that the quality of ink used is all-important. The paper of the early edition jackets also suffers from tanning and, to a lesser extent, to chipping. These faults conspire to make a fine first edition jacket a thing of great rarity. If the aesthetics of your collection, on the shelf, is important to you I would suggest putting a fine later edition jacket over your fine faded first edition (the 1958, 1961 and 1966 reprints are the brightest).

Total print run of Collins hardbacks: *c.* 44,000; no. sold: *c.* 42,700; o/p: 1980.

NN12A   **First Edition**, 1949 (20 June 1949).
Title: 'The New Naturalist | The Sea Shore'.
Author: 'C. M. Yonge | D.Sc. F.R.S.E. F.R.S. | Regius Professor of Zoology in the | University of Glasgow | Chairman of Council, Scottish Marine | Biological Association'.
Illust: 'With 61 colour photographs | by D. P. Wilson and others | 62 black-and-white photographs | and 88 text figures'.
Editors: JF, JG, JH, LDS and EH (Photographic Editor).
Collation: pp. xvi, 311, [1]; 20 leaves of colour plates printed to both sides; 16 leaves of b/w plates printed to both sides (20½ × 16-page gatherings).
Jacket: [Rear panel] Advert for 'The New Naturalist | A Journal of British Natural History'. [Rear flap] Advert for The New Naturalist listing nine titles; details of further titles request.
Price: 21s. net.
Print run: 22,500; no. sold: *c.* 21,060; o/p: 1957.
Notes: 1) Errata slip tipped-in on p. [vi]. 2) Colour plates 17–36 inclusive, tipped-in. 3) No author's preface. 4) Dust jacket text printed in dark olive brown 5) Pink colour to jacket design fugitive.

NN12B **First Reprint**, 1958. 'First published in 1949... | ... Reprinted 1958'. Minimal revisions e.g. corrected photograph captions and footnote to p. [15]; JH now Sir JH, etc. Essentially an exact reprint. The NN library to the jacket lists NN 1–35 inclusively (the same layout as 1st ed. *Soil* NN35A); the rear flap features adverts for three other 'Marine' titles *The Open Sea*; *The Sea Coast* and *Sea-Birds*; the front flap has been reset with a smaller typeface allowing room for a press endorsement by the *Field*. Price: 25s.

FIG. 12A The cover design for later impressions of the Fontana edition. The design changed from that shown in figure 12c from around 1965.

net. Print run: 6,000; o/s: 1960. (The jacket is comparatively colourfast.)

NN12C **Second Reprint**, 1961. 'First published 1949 | reprinted 1958 | reprinted 1961'. Contents as NN12B; JH now Sir, etc. Jacket slightly revised: text now printed in black; NN library lists NN1–43 (Type 42, variant 2); rear flap advertises *Oysters* and *The Open Sea* (parts I and II); layout to front flap redesigned to enable insertion of three press reviews from *The Field*, the *Manchester Guardian* and *The Listener*, blurb unchanged. Price: 30s. net. Print run: 5,000[?]; o/p: end 1964/beginning 1965. Note: The jacket is comparatively colourfast.

NN12D **Third Reprint, Revised Edition**, 1966. 'First edition 1949 | reprinted 1958 | reprinted 1961 | revised edition 1966'. Notwithstanding, in essence a straight reprint with minimal revision, e.g. footnote added to p. 14; LDS now Sir. The New Naturalist library to the jacket lists NN1–46 (Type 42, variant 5); both flaps identical; price remains 30s. net. Print run: 5,000; o/p: 1970. Notes: 1) Some copies of this third edition are cased in a deeper matt-green buckram, characterised by poor, less well defined and slacker bindings. 2) The jacket is comparatively colourfast.

NN12E **Fourth Reprint**, 1971. ISBN: 0002132028 (imprint page) & 000213102 DJ rear flap. First edition 1949 | reprinted 1958 | reprinted 1961 | revised edition 1966 | reprinted 1971. A straight reprint with trifling changes e.g. footnote to p. 14 now removed; Editors: JF, JG, JH, MD & EH. The NN library to the jacket lists NN 1–52 (Type 42, variant 5); both flaps identical, but for addition or ISBN to rear. Price: £2.85 net. Print run: 3,500; no. sold: *c.* 2,700[?] + repriced variant below. Notes: 1) *c.* 1,400 copies were bound up later in 1974, but these appear to be indistinguishable 2) Jacket prone to fading.

NN12E-AP1 1st Repriced DJ (1975), £3.50 sticker, no. sold unknown.
NN12E-AP2 2nd Repriced DJ (1975–76), £4.00 sticker, *c.* 500 sold.

NN12F **Fifth Reprint**, 1976. ISBN 0002195194 (imprint page) & 2195194 (DJ rear flap). 'First edition 1949 | reprinted 1958, reprinted 1961, revised edition | 1966, reprinted 1971, reprinted 1976'. As NN12E with revisions restricted to prelims: Editors: MD, JG, KM & EH. Last part of credo omitted. The NN library to the *Durasealed* jacket lists NN1–60 (Type 42, variant 15), otherwise both flaps identical. Price: £6.50 net. Print run: 2,000; no. sold: *c.* 1,050 + repriced variant below + possible *c.* 750 copies 'remaindered' to a bookclub. Note: jacket prone to fading.

FIG. 12B From August 1971 (F12G) the Fontana paperback included The Open University symbol to the front cover, advertising it was a 'set book'.

NN12F-AP1 1st Repriced DJ (1980), £7.50 sticker, *c.* 120 sold.

BC12A Readers Union Edition, 1959. As NN12B. Specially printed for the RU with an integral title page displaying the RU imprint & tree logo, otherwise textually identical with the same composition of plates. Bound in dark green imitation cloth with the title & RU logo gilt-blocked to the spine. RU jacket Type 2. Price: 15/- net. Print run: 2,000[?].

POD12A Print-on-demand digital copy of the 1976 fifth reprint NN12F.

BL12A Bloomsbury Edition, 1990. ISBN 1870630246; pp. xvi, 311, [1], [72 – b/w illustrations] ((25 × 16-page gatherings). A b/w facsimile of the 1971 reprint NN12E. Price: £12.95. Print run: unknown, but a significant proportion remaindered.

F12A Fontana Paperback, First Edition, 1963. ISBN 0006322034 (ISBN appears only after 1975); pp. 350, 12 leaves of b/w plates bound in single section in centre, printed on glossy paper, to both sides (22 × 16-page gatherings). A reset copy of the original Collins edition, but without colour and a reduced no. of b/w plates. The sub-title to the front cover and TP reads 'The Fontana Library'. Adverts for NN & Fontana Library titles at front & rear. The wrap-around cover artwork by [Charles] Gorham (also used for US edition – see Figure 12A); rear cover carries 4 press reviews for The Sea Shore. Price: 10/6. Total print run including reprints below: 57,000.

F12B Second Impression, June 1965. (not seen)

F12C Third Impression, January 1968. (not seen)

F12D Fourth Impression, October 1969. Later green livery with uncredited photographic front cover of seashells on which now printed 'The Fontana New Naturalist'; rear cover has three press commendations. TP reset with 'The Fontana New Naturalist'. Creamy paper. Price: 12/-(60p).

F12E Fifth Impression, month? 1970. (not seen)

F12F Sixth Impression, Aug. 1970. Plates bound in three sections.

F12G Seventh Impression, Aug. 1971. 'Set Book The Open University' to front cover. Better paper. Price: 60p.

F12H Eighth Impression, April 1972. Poorer paper; thicker book.

F12I Ninth Impression, January 1973

F12J Tenth Impression, March 1975. (not seen)

F12K Eleventh Impression, June 1977. ISBN 0006322034. Editors added op. TP: – JG, JH, MD, KM and EH. Price: £1.25.

F12L Twelfth Impression, June 1979. (not seen)

FIG. 12C 1963 US paperback edition published by Atheneum. From the same printing as the 1963 Fontana edition with the same cover art by Charles Gorham.

US12A US Edition, 1963. Atheneum New York. 'Published by Atheneum | Reprinted by arrangement with | William Collins Sons & Co. Ltd., London'. From the same printing as the 1963 Fontana paperback first edition F12A and printed on the same paper, with same suite of plates. Title page with Atheneum imprint; half-title with biography of C. M. Yonge, but verso blank i.e. without references to the Fontana New Naturalist; adverts at rear list 31 Atheneum paperbacks. Printed card covers with same Gorham design and titling but with Atheneum imprint, and rear cover with single press commendation by *The Listener* (for additional details see entry for F12A). Price $1.95 (printed to front cover).

13 Snowdonia

Snowdonia, published in 1949, was only printed once, but NN collectors have known for a long time that the binding exists in two forms: one without the authors' names on the casing and one with. It is generally accepted that the variant without is the earlier of the two, and certainly all inscribed and dated copies I have seen support this assertion. The earlier type is the more common. The authors' names have also been omitted from the jacket, which was not updated. It is the only jacket in the series not to name the author/s.

Snowdonia was the first of the regional volumes and the first to cover a National Park (see Marren's *The New Naturalists*), though it was published two years before Snowdonia officially became a National Park. This might explain the range of titles that appear in the book: the title page includes the sub-heading 'The National Park of North Wales', whereas the sub-heading to the half-title reads 'In the National Park of North Wales'; the jacket and casing simply state *Snowdonia*. Collins was keen to promote the National Park theme and the rear jacket flap lists five titles under the heading 'The New Naturalist National Park Books': *Snowdonia* (published); *The Lake District* by Ernest Blezard and others; *The Broads* by E.A. Ellis, Robert Gurney and others; *Dartmoor* by L.A. Harvey and others; and 'Pembrokeshire' by R.M. Lockley and others. But Collins was again premature: *The Lake District* did not appear for a further 24 years and was, in the event, written by Pearsall and Pennington; *The Broads* was finally published 14 years later; and 'Pembrokeshire', as we know, never came to fruition. But the wait for *Dartmoor* was comparatively short at just four years!

15,000 copies of *Snowdonia* were sold in the first three years, but it remained in print until 1959. While the NN Editorial Board was keen to keep this title in print, the authors were not unanimous in their desire to see it reprinted. The book was essentially three books in one, hence its bulk and this, coupled with out of date sections and the authors' reluctance to undertake revisions, put it beyond the realms of a viable reprint. But in 1962, William Condry was commissioned to write a new, shorter book on the National Park, which appeared as NN47, in 1966, with the title *The Snowdonia National Park* (see page 186).

Despite the large number of books in circulation *Snowdonia* is not an easy title to find in fine or very good condition; the primary binding variant suffers from uneven fading and all jackets are prone to foxing, chipping and tanning, which is particularly evident giving the large areas of 'white' paper – it is the only NN jacket (artwork) without a coloured title band.

NN13A-B1 First Edition, Primary Binding Variant, 1949
(10 November 1949).

Title: 'The New Naturalist | Snowdonia | The National Park of | North Wales'.

Authors: 'by | F. J. North | D.Sc., F.G.S., F.S.A. | Keeper of the Department of Geology | National Museum of Wales | Bruce Campbell | PhD. | Secretary of the British Trust for Ornithology | Richenda Scott | Ph.D. (Econ.)'.

Illust: 'With 56 colour plates by John Markham and others | 48 black and white photographs | 6 maps and 26 diagrams'.

Editors: JF, JG, JH, LDS and EH (Photographic Editor).

Printer: Richmond Hill Printing Works Ltd, Bournemouth (produced in conjunction with Adprint).

Collation: pp. xviii, 469, [1]; double plate (2 leaves) colour map printed to one side only; 20 leaves of colour plates printed to both sides; 16 leaves of b/w plates printed to both sides (30½ × 16-page gatherings).

Casing: Early open-weave Buckram prone to fading; without authors' names to the spine.

Jacket: [Rear panel] New Naturalist library listing NN1–14 inclusively; the Collins address. [Rear flap] Five New Naturalist National Park Books (see intro.); four New Naturalist monographs: *The Badger, The Redstart, The Wren* and *The Yellow Wagtail*; The wrapper [jacket] design credit.

Price: 21s. net.

Print run: 20,000; no. sold: *c.* 18,760; o/p: 1959.

Notes: *Snowdonia* incorporates three double page maps, which are included within the general pagination: note how the book has been intelligently designed so these appear at the centre of gatherings (pp. 54–55, 214–215 and 310–311), ensuring that they are printed across the gutter and can easily be opened fully.

NN13A-B2 First Edition, Second Binding Variant, 1949 (1951?). Bound up from the same sheets but in a slightly later casing with the authors' names gilt blocked to the spine. The Buckram is either the early open-weave type as used in -B1, or a later closer-weave variant, less prone to fading.

POD13A Print-on-demand digital copy.

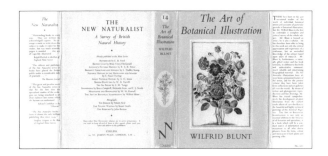

14 The Art of Botanical Illustration

'A glittering and intoxicating gallery of flowers… a new world of beauty' is how Sacheverell Sitwell described *The Art of Botanical Illustration* in *The Spectator,* and other reviewers were equally eulogistic (the 1967 reprint NN14D jacket quotes from 10 separate press reviews, a record for any New Naturalist). 'Botanical Illustration' soon became the definitive text on the subject; a New Naturalist staple that sold consistently well. Peter Marren writing in NN82 says of it that it is 'one of the few that sells readily *without* a jacket' and he is of course right, though perhaps now that the internet has increased availability, and the sumptuous Antique Collector's Club (ACC) new edition has been published, not quite as readily.

Given that *Botanical Illustration* was such a reliable seller, it is surprising that it was allowed to go out of print in 1976 when demand remained buoyant, but there is a story behind this missed opportunity. Firstly, in 1976 Dover Publications offered to reprint it (they had already published a new edition of *The Folklore of Birds* in 1970) but this was rejected by Michael Walters, the then Natural History Editor at Collins. Instead it was decided in 1978 to do a straight reprint, only to find that the original blocks (for the illustrations) had been misplaced. Blunt then set about tracing the original pictures so they could be re-originated, but still no reprint. By 1980 the new editor, Robert MacDonald, explained that time constraints and rising costs had prohibited a reprint and anyway Collins had decided that a substantial revision was needed. Blunt was too old and Stearn too busy so Sandra Raphael was commissioned to undertake the task, but for undisclosed reasons the revised manuscript was never delivered and by 1986 the project, effectively abandoned. Blunt was understandably nonplussed but perhaps it was for the better as eventually, William Stearn, the original co-author, thoroughly revised the work and it was published in large quarto by the ACC in 1994, a format far more suited to the reproduction of botanical illustrations than the smaller NN octavo format.

This work began life with the title *Botanical Illustrations* and that is how it appears in the early Editors' minutes. While on the subject of nomenclature, it is Wilfrid Blunt with an 'i' and not Wilfred with an 'e', but the latter incorrect spelling has crept into a not inconsiderable part of New Naturalist 'literature'.

Botanical Illustration is the first main series title not to sport an Ellis jacket; the front panel features a painting of roses by Johann Walther and the lily to the spine is by R. G. Hatton, but it also dispenses with the characteristic title band and as such is unique in the series, and lacks conformity with it neighbours, when on the shelf. It has a few other unusual features: most notably it uses the unembellished 'Type A' monogram for the jacket (see page 63), casing and title page, though for the 1967 and 1971 reprints the more traditional 'Type C' is used on the casing. It has a greater number of preliminary pages than any other title in the series, and the rear flap of the 1955 3rd edition NN14C jacket is unique in the NN library in that it is completely blank (notwithstanding a few US editions).

It is surprising that such a universal title has only been published twice overseas: a 1951 US edition and a very well produced Japanese edition with slipcase in 1986. *Botanical Illustration* was considered for both Bloomsbury and Fontana editions but as these formats lacked colour they were judged to be unsuitable, although jackets of the Bloomsbury New Naturalist books do erroneously refer to this title as being published in the Bloomsbury facsimile series. There are however completely unrelated books of the same title and Stearn writing in the introduction to the ACC revised edition says, 'There exists no copyright in book-titles and since 1950 two other books have used our title *The Art of Botanical Illustration*, a procedure both legal and confusing.'

The jacket of the first edition is particularly prone to tanning, chipping and rubbing and fine copies are scarce. Later editions are easier to find in 'collectable condition' though not being 'firsts', this is of little consolation to the collector! The absence of sales reports before 1956 makes it impossible to determine with certainty the number of first and second editions printed; the total for the two printings was 15,000. The total number of all Collins printings was 24,500, of which *c.* 1,000 were sold to the US imprint Charles Scribner's Sons. *Botanical Illustration* went out of print during the summer of 1976, but was out of stock for a period between 1965 and 1967 and for part of 1970/71.

NN14A   First Edition, 1950 (19/06/1950).
Title:	'The New Naturalist	The Art of	Botanical Illustration'.
Authors:	'by	Wilfrid Blunt	with the assistance of William T. Stearn'.
Illust:	'With 47 colour plates	30 black and white plates	and 75 figures in the text'.
Editors:	JF, JG, JH, LDS and EH (Photographic Editor).
Printer:	Collins Clear-Type Press, London and Glasgow (produced in conjunction with Adprint).
Collation:	pp. xxxi, [1], 304; colour frontispiece plate; 23 leaves of

colour plates printed to both sides; 16 leaves of b/w plates printed to both sides (21 × 16-page gatherings).

Jacket:	[Rear panel] The New Naturalist listing 12 titles 'Already published in the Main Series' and three Monographs; information request; Collins' address. [Rear flap] The New Naturalist with four endorsing press extracts.
Price:	21s. net.
Print run:	12,000[?] of which 1,040 sold to USA; o/p: 1951[?].
Notes:	1) The unembellished 'Type A' monogram is used for jacket, casing and title page. 2) b/w plates printed on matt paper. 3) The ground colour of the jacket is a soft putty grey. Book 29 mm thick.

NN14B Second Edition. 1951. 'First published in 1950... | ... Second Edition 1951'; no date to title page. Ostensibly as NN14A, but with several corrected errors and some additional information appended; all as listed in the new two-page 'Author's preface to Second Edition' signed W.J.W.B. and dated 6 Feb 1951. The pagination remains unaltered but in order to accommodate the new preface the dedication has been moved to the imprint page. The jacket is identical to NN14A and the price remains at 21s. net. Print run: 3,000[?].

NN14C Third Edition, 1955. 'First published in 1950... | ... Second Edition 1951 | Third Edition 1955'. As NN15A (pp. now xxxii, 304) with a few additional notes added to pp. xxxi and xxxii under the title 'Third Edition: Additional Notes', otherwise without any obvious revisions, but b/w plates printed on semi-glazed paper; text paper creamier and smoother to the touch, resulting a slightly thicker book – 32 mm. The ground colour of the jacket is a bluer, slightly darker grey; the NN library lists 29 titles in a single column but not numbered, in the same format as the first edition of NN32 *Trees, Woods and Man* (1956); rear flap blank (and accordingly unique in the NN library); front flap unchanged. Price: 25s. net. Print run: 4,000; o/p: early 1965.

NN14D Third Edition, First Reprint, 1967. 'First published 1951 | Reprinted 1967'. (Note: 2nd and 3rd eds. omitted from printing history.) As NN14C but with a few additional notes added to p. xxxii under the heading 'Fourth Edition: Additional Notes', (which commences with '*Redouté*' spelt '*Redout*') otherwise without notable revisions, but b/w plates printed on glazed paper; text paper not as good as previous edition with inferior reproduction of in-text figures; book thinner – 29 mm. Editors: JG now with a V.M.H.; JH and LDS now both Sir JH and Sir LDS, the latter with additional post nominals. The NN monogram to the casing reverts to the more familiar 'Type C'; i.e. with a central diamond, but the atypical 'Type A' remains to the TP and DJ. The ground colour of the jacket decidedly warmer, now a buff grey, the border to front panel illustration an even blue rather than blue and green of the earlier jackets, lettering to the front panel and spine denser and crisper; NN library lists NN1–50 (Type 42, variant 8); the rear flap given over to four press commendations; the blurb to the front flap has been replaced by six press endorsements. Price: 45s. net. Print run: 2,500; o/p: beginning 1970.

NN14E Third Edition, Second Reprint, 1971. ISBN: 0002130025. 'First Published 1950 | Reprinted 1967 | Reprinted 1971' (reference to 2nd and 3rd eds. still omitted). Exactly as NN14D. Editors: JF, JG, JH, MD and EH. The ground colour of the jacket is different still: a bluer colder light grey, that often fades to a soft duck-egg blue on the spine; the NN library lists NN1–52 (Type 42, variant 9A); both flaps unchanged, but for addition of ISBN to rear. Price: £3.00 net. Print run: 3,000; o/p: summer 1976.

NN14E-AP1 1st Repriced DJ (1975?), £3.50 sticker.
NN14E-AP2 2nd Repriced DJ (1975–76), £4.00 sticker, c. 650 sold.

POD14A Print-on-demand digital copy of the 1971 reprint NN14E.

MIS14A Antique Collectors' Club Revised Edition, 1994. ISBN 1851491775. Title page: 'The Art of | Botanical | Illustration | New Edition | revised and enlarged | Wilfrid Blunt | and | William T. Stearn. Antique Collectors' Club | in association with | The Royal Botanic Gardens, Kew'. 'This new edition revised by William T. Stearn' and 'Printed in England by the Antique Collectors' Club Ltd., Woodbridge, Suffolk, on Consort Royal Satin paper supplied by the Donside Paper Company, Aberdeen, Scotland. Typeset in Garamond' Hardback with dust jacket. Large quarto format 220 × 280 mm, i.e. significantly larger than the original Collins ed.; pp. x, 368, (23 × 16-page gatherings). Completely revised with colour and b/w illustrations, many of which new, integrated throughout the text, illustrative endpapers matching jacket front panel. Casing of fine sage green cloth with gilt lettering blocked to the spine and front board. The laminated jacket features a detail of *Paeonia officinalis* by Martin Schongauer to the front panel and *Gastavia augusta* by Margaret Mee to the rear panel. No printed price; print run: unknown, but not scarce. The jacket blurb includes the following synopsis 'Professor Stearn has revised and enlarged this classic work and greatly extended the chapter on the twentieth century. The new edition includes 126 colour plates (more than twice as many as the original edition) and 140 black and white illustrations, thus making available to the general public numerous examples of the work of great botanical illustrators past and present'. (Unfortunately the ACC were unable to provide print numbers or supply the official publication date, but did confirm the following two reprints.)

MIS14B Antique Collectors' Club Revised Edition, First Reprint, 1995. As MIS14A.

MIS14C Antique Collectors' Club Revised Edition, Second Reprint, 2000. As MIS14A.

US14A US Edition, 1951. Charles Scribner's Sons, New York. From the same printing as the Collins 1950 first edition NN14A (and not of the 1951 2nd ed. NN14B), but the title and half-title pages are cancels, the former carrying the Scribner imprint and both omitting all references to the New Naturalist, the NN credo is also omitted. The casing is of the same green buckram but omits the NN monogram and 'Scribners' has been blocked to the spine. The jacket is identical but overprinted 'Scribners' to the spine but not obliterating 'Collins'; the UK price has been clipped off and the US price overprinted to the top corner of the front flap. No. sold to Scribner's: 1,040.

FOR14A Japanese Edition, 1986. Hardback with dust jacket 190 × 264 mm; pp. (2), 344, + 13pp index. Based on the Collins second edition, 1951. Extended illustrations with 65 colour plates (the original edition had 47 colour plates) arranged in 6 sections of 4 leaves, printed on both sides. 150 black and white plates and other black and white illustrations within the text. Title page printed in black. Bound in grey imitation cloth, with a black embossed botanical motif on front cover and black lettering to spine. Bound-in ribbon bookmark. Silk laminated jacket printed in full colour with four of the coloured plates reproduced on the cover against a green ground, together with white, blue and black text. Supplied in a plain card slipcase, printed with black lettering, with a botanical motif on front. Print run unknown.

15 Life in Lakes and Rivers

James Fisher at the Editors' meeting of 21 March 1949 declared the manuscript 'an extremely good book' and *The Field* in their review said, 'Just about as perfect in its field as a book can be'. And, despite, being published less than six years after *Butterflies*, Collins, on the jacket was already advertising the New Naturalist as 'this famous series'. So heralded the publication of *Life in Lakes and Rivers*. The majority of the book was written by Macan (Worthington had been called back to Africa) as demonstrated by the royalties, which were divided 80 per cent Macan, 20 per cent Worthington.

Life in Lakes and Rivers, in its Collins NN guise, was printed six times and sold over a 32-year period, finally going out of print in 1983. It was, however, out of stock for part of 1962, and for the periods between 1966 and 1968, and the end of 1970 to the summer of 1974. By the time the third edition finally arrived in 1974, such a large number of backorders had built up that it was sold out within a couple of months. Another reprint was immediately ordered, and while this is also dated 1974, in point of fact it was not published until the spring of 1975.

During this long period there were inevitably changes and revisions, but Macan was clear with the 1962 second reprint that either the whole book had to be brought up to date or no corrections made at all: Collins went with the latter option. When it came to the 1968 second edition, the existing metal plates (from which the book was printed) made it impossible, without greatly increasing the price, to revise the text, so instead an additional section of 16 pages was added. This was originally to be an appendix but it ended up taking the form of a new preface which summarised recent discoveries and other revisions. It begins 'Sixteen years having passed since this book was written, there is now one page for each to bring it up-to-date' – though the preface itself was only 14 pages long.

The problem of revising the text was overcome for the 1974 third edition as it was printed from plates enlarged from the revised Fontana edition and consequently the typesetting is completely different from earlier Collins editions. However, it is crisply printed on creamy paper and hugely superior to the Fontana original. The printing of this edition is much sharper than the preceding Collins printings and, as the text incorporates many revisions, it is the best of the various editions. The dust jacket, however, is not.

The acidic paper of the first edition jacket is prone to tanning, but, oddly, not particularly to chipping. Total print run: 27,500[?]; o/p: 1983 (Collins editions).

NN15A   **First Edition**, 1951 (19 March 1951).
Title: 'The New Naturalist | Life in | Lakes and Rivers'.
Author: 'by | T. T. Macan | M.A., Ph. D. | and | E. B. Worthington M.A., Ph. D.'.
Illust: 'With 45 colour photographs | by John Markham and others | 68 photographs in black and white | 20 maps and 15 diagrams'.
Editors: JF, JG, JH, LDS and EH (Photographic Editor).
Printer: Collins Clear-Type Press, London and Glasgow (produced in conjunction with Adprint).
Collation: pp. xvi, 272; 20 leaves of colour plates printed to both sides; 16 leaves of b/w plates printed to both sides (18 × 16-page gatherings).
Jacket: [Rear panel] Adverts for *The Sea Shore*, *British Plant Life* and *The Badger*, under the strapline 'Some comments on this famous series'; Collins' address. [Rear flap] 11 titles listed in the main series; mailing list request below.
Price: 21s. net.
Print run: 12,000 of which 100 sold to USA; no. sold: c. 11,300; o/p: 1959.
Notes: 1) b/w plates printed on matt paper. 2) Book 25 mm thick.

NN15B First Reprint, 1959 (April). 'First edition 1951 | Reprinted 1959'; no date to title page. As NN15A, seemingly without any textual revisions; b/w plates now printed on semi-glazed paper. Editors: JH now Sir JH, etc. The NN library to the jacket lists NN1–38, omitting NN6 and 26 in a single column (Type 36); rear flap advertises *An Angler's Entomology*, *The Sea Shore* and *The Open Sea*; blurb to front flap unchanged but quote from *Field* inserted

below. Price: 30s. net. Print run: 1,500; o/p: beginning 1962. Note: This first reprint was printed with the 1959 RU edition, which explains the relatively short print run.

NN15B-DJ1 First Reprint, Jacket Variant. With a first edition jacket overprinted 30s. net.

NN15C Second Reprint, 1962 (late). 'First published 1951 | Reprinted 1959 | Reprinted 1962' As NN15B, without any obvious revisions, but b/w plates printed on glazed, shiny paper. Book 26 mm thick. The NN library to the jacket lists NN1–45 (Type 42 variant 4); rear flap identical but ISBN added; front flap unchanged. Price: 30s. net. Print run: 3,000; o/p: 1966.

NN15D Second Edition, 1968. 'First published 1951 | Reprinted 1959 | Reprinted 1962 | Second edition 1968'; pp. xxxii, 272 (19 × 16-page gatherings); suite of plates unaltered. The original 'Authors' preface' has been moved to its own leaf and a 'Preface to Second Edition' of 14 pages has been inserted (i.e. in total = one 16-page section). A conjugate pair of colour plate leaves (plates 10–13) has moved by four pages, with several b/w plates repositioned to suit, but the list of plates has not been revised to reflect these changes. Editors: JF, JG, JH, MD and EH; Last sentence of NN Credo omitted. Otherwise, all other text as NN15C (see intro.). Jacket printed using different technique; now composed of finely printed dots, rather than solid colour, much greyer, an appreciably different and inferior effect; NN library lists NN1–50 (Type 42, variant 8); the content of both flaps unchanged, but text reset. Price: 36s. net. Print run: unknown – see notes; o/p: late 1970. Notes: 1) The sales reports for this period are incomplete and those that are available are confusing: it might be that this edition was printed or at least bound up in two tranches of 3,000 and 2,000 copies, which might explain the following buckram variant. 2) Some copies of this edition, bound in atypical smooth bright green buckram of a fine weave; this unusual buckram was also used for the second binding variant of the 1964 reprint of *Common Lands* NN45B-B2. 3) The printing is not as crisp as earlier editions – presumably by this state the plates were worn. 4) While the second edition is dated 1968 the new 'preface to second edition' is dated September 1966.

NN15E Third Edition, 1974 (July). ISBN 0002131293 (to jacket only). 'First edition 1951 | Reprinted 1959 | Reprinted 1962 | Second edition 1968 | Third edition 1974'; pp. 320 (20 × 16-page gatherings), suite of plates unaltered. This edition taken from the Fontana revised edition of 1972 and printed from plates copied and enlarged from that edition, but with new contents and preliminary pages to reflect Collins format and contents. It is consequently completely different from the above editions and the revisions highlighted in the 'preface to the second edition', now incorporated into the text. Editors: MD, JH, JG, KM and EH. Bound in typical 'group 2' Buckram; 28 mm thick. The *Durasealed* jacket ostensibly as NN15D; the NN library lists NN 1–56 (Type 42, variant 13); both flaps unchanged, but for ISBN added to rear. Price: £4.00 net. Print run: 3,000; no. sold: c. 2,700; o/p: by end Aug. 1974.

NN15F Third Edition, Reprint, 1974 (But, 1975–April?). ISBN 0002194597 (to imprint page and jacket; changed to 'First edition 1951 | Reprinted 1959 | Reprinted 1962 | Second edition 1968 | Third edition 1974 | Reprinted 1974'. As NN15E. The printing of the *Durasealed* jacket is slightly different to NN15E with a thin white line introduced to the bottom edge of the title panel; the NN library lists NN1–58 (Type 42, variant 14); both flaps unchanged, but for ISBN to rear. Price: £4.00 net. Print run: 3,000; no. sold: *c.* 1,000[?] + repriced variants below + batches (probably) sold off to the RU.

NN15F-AP1 1st Repriced DJ (1976–77), £4.50 sticker, *c.* 400 sold.

NN15F-AP2 2nd Repriced DJ (1978–79), £5.50 sticker, *c.* 350 sold.

NN15F-AP3 3rd Repriced DJ (1979–80), £6.00 sticker, *c.* 250 sold.

NN15F-AP4 4th Repriced DJ (1980–81), £7.50 sticker, *c.* 100 sold.

NN15F-AP5 5th Repriced DJ (1981), £8.50 sticker, *c.* 100 sold.

NN15F-AP6 6th Repriced DJ (1982–83), £9.50 sticker, *c.* 150 sold.

BC15A Readers Union Edition, 1959. Printed and bound by Collins at Clear-Type Press, Glasgow. As NN15B and a run-on to that printing, but specially printed for the RU; therefore with an integral title page displaying the RU imprint and tree logo, otherwise textually identical with the same composition of plates. The green imitation cloth casing is blocked with the Readers Union tree logo to the spine, but the title lettering is the same as the Collins editions. Fitted with the RU jacket 'Type 2'. Price: 17/- net. Print run: *c.* 2,000[?].

POD15A Print-on-demand digital copy of the 1974 third edition NN15E.

F15A Fontana Paperback, First Edition, 1972. ISBN 0006329101 (ISBN appears only from 1973); pp. 320; 8 leaves of b/w plates bound in two sections of 4, printed on glossy paper, to both sides. Perfect bound. A revised edition (by Macan only) based on the second Collins 1968 second edition; no colour and a reduced no. of b/w plates. Editors: JG, JH, MD, KM and EH. Adverts for Fontana NNS at front, listing 12 titles. Paper liable to tanning as usual. The photographic front cover of an otter fishing by Geoffrey Kinns to which has been added 'Set Book The Open University' accompanied by the OU symbol.; rear cover carries 3 press clips for this title. Price: 60p. Print run including reprints below: 37,000; o/p: 1985. Notes: 1) Adopted by Open University – one of the lecturers who prescribed it was Margaret Brown co-author of *The Trout*. 2) The 1980 reprint has proved elusive: the sales reports indicate 4,000 copies were printed, so there should be a few copies around, but the ephemeral nature of these paperbacks makes them disproportionately scarce: supposedly the last 1,000 copies of Fontana stock were remaindered at 30p, but perhaps in the event there were no takers and they were pulped.

The following reprints exactly as preceding edition unless stated otherwise.

F15B Second Impression, May 1972.

F15C Third Impression, October 1973. Text revised to pp. 149–151. ISBN added to rear cover.

F15D Fourth Impression, March 1976. Adverts at front revised. Price: £1.25

F15E, Fifth Impression, June 1977. Price: £1.50

F15F Sixth Impression, 1980. Not seen. (this is the last of all Fontana New Naturalist printings).

BL15A Bloomsbury Edition, 1990 (31 December 1990). ISBN 1870630297; pp. 320, [72 – b/w illustrations] (24½ × 16-page gatherings). A b/w facsimile of the 1974 third edition NN15E. Price: £12.95. Print run: unknown; a significant proportion remaindered.

US15A US Edition 1951. Macmillan? *Unverified*. The sales reports consistently refer to 100 US copies. Presumably exactly as the Collins first edition of 1951 NN15A, perhaps with a cancel title page or with a 'Distributed by' label to the jacket. Print run: probably *c.* 100.

16 Wild Flowers of Chalk & Limestone

'It would be almost impossible to praise it too highly. This is a wonderfully friendly book, a book to keep and treasure, to read at a sitting and then dip into again and again. The illustrations are quite beyond praise.' So wrote *The Field,* and Marren, in *The New Naturalists,* describes it as 'the second best botanical travelogue ever written'. (His first is John Raven's *Mountain Flowers* – see NN82A, page 137, or NN82B, page 141.) Despite universal praise for the illustrations, they were all, apparently, printed from the wrong side of the transparencies and therefore all reversed, but the only one spotted by readers was plate 32 of Cheddar Gorge. The b/w plates of the first edition are printed on matt paper, whereas those of the 1969 second edition are printed on glazed (glossy) paper and are sharper, though they lack the period charm of the former. The dust jacket of the second edition is printed on whiter paper than the first edition and notes in the Collins archive suggest that it is now printed by letterpress, rather than the off-set litho technique of the first edition, but this is probably incorrect as they appear identical.

The first edition went out of print in 1964, but Lousley had submitted corrections for a new edition two years earlier. Collins dilly-dallied over the second edition, which did not appear until April 1969 – much to the embarrassment and annoyance of Lousley. Michael Walters, the then editor at Collins, blamed this on the 'factory' and certainly the 1966/7 sales reports make numerous references to the imminent appearance of the second edition. But despite this, it would appear that the delays were commercially driven (leaving a title out of print was a well-tested ploy to allow demand to build up). Certainly in the case of *Wild Flowers of Chalk and Limestone* it worked, as pre-orders were an excellent 1,500 copies – even at a price at over twice that of the first edition. The 1969 second edition sold well and was out of print by July 1971, but a reprint followed in the same year, this time without, or with just a brief, hiatus. It was printed once again by Collins in 1976 and finally as a Bloomsbury facsimile in 1990.

Wild Flowers of Chalk and Limestone is not a difficult title to find in very good or fine condition: the pink is colourfast, which goes to show that if the right inks are used, fading need not be a problem – compare with the similarly coloured *Heathlands*. The first edition casing is invariably, if not always, faded, but this is an inherent problem with the early buckram and, as nothing can be done about it, it's best ignored. The acidic paper of the first edition is prone to tanning, but not all copies are so. Total print run: 20,000[?]; total no. sold: *c.* 15,400; o/p: 1985.

NN16A	**First Edition**, 1950 (23 October 1950).
Title:	'The New Naturalist | Wild Flowers of | Chalk & Limestone'.
Author:	'by | J. E. Lousley'.
Illust:	'With 52 colour plates | by Robert Atkinson, John Markham, Brian Perkins and others | 29 photographs in black and white | 20 maps and 15 diagrams'.
Editors:	JF, JG, JH, LDS and EH (Photographic Editor).
Printer:	Collins Clear-Type Press, London and Glasgow (produced in conjunction with Adprint).
Collation:	pp. xvii, [1], 254; 24 leaves of colour plates printed to both sides; 12 leaves of b/w plates printed to both sides (17 × 16-page gatherings).
Jacket:	[Rear panel] Adverts for 'Two recent publications': *The Art of Botanical Illustration* and *Mountains and Moorlands*; Collins' address. [Rear flap] Advert for *British Plant Life*; mailing list request below.
Price:	21s. net.
Print run:	12,500[?]; no. sold: 13,500[?]; o/p: 1964.
Notes:	1) There is considerable ambiguity surrounding the number of books both printed and sold: the available figures are inconsistent and, on the face of it impossible, compounded by frustrating gaps in the extant sales reports. 2) It also appears some copies were bound up later.

NN16B Second Edition, 1969 (April). 'First edition 1950 \| Second edition 1969'; no date to title page. Text not reset, plates unchanged, but b/w plates now printed on glazed paper. A few nomenclatural revisions, otherwise text essentially unaltered. Several changes to distribution maps and a five-line 'Preface to the Second Edition' added. Editors: JF, JG, JH, MD and EH. The NN library to the jacket lists NN1–50. (Type 42, variant 8); rear flap includes adverts for: *Wild Flowers*; *Mountain Flowers* and *Flowers of the Coast*; the blurb précised, with three press comments inserted. Price: 45s. net. Print run: 2,500; o/p: July 1971.

NN16C Second Edition, First Reprint, 1971. ISBN 0002132583 (to jacket rear flap only). 'First edition 1950 \| Second edition 1969 \| Reprinted 1971', As NN16B. Editors: JG, JH, MD, KM and EH. The NN library to the *Durasealed* jacket lists NN 1–52 (Type 42, variant 9a); rear flap identical but ISBN added; front flap unchanged. Price: £2.75. Print run: 2,000 inc. repriced variants below; o/p: early 1976.

NN16C-AP1 1st Repriced DJ (1975), £3.00 sticker.

NN16C-AP2 2nd Repriced DJ (1975–76), £3.50 sticker, *c.* 320.

NN16D Second Edition, Second Reprint, 1976 (Summer). ISBN CHANGED TO 0002195615. 'First edition 1950 \| Second edition 1969 \| Reprinted 1976' (the 1971 reprint is omitted). As NN16C. Editors: MD, JG, KM and EH; Last sentence of NN Credo omitted. Jacket seemingly printed using different technique; colours stronger and brighter, *Durasealed*. NN library lists NN1–58 (Type 42, variant 14); rear flap unchanged but for new ISBN; front flap identical. Price: £7.00 net, printed diagonally with dotted line. Print run: 2,000; no. sold: *c.* 1,000 + repriced variants below; o/p: 1985.

NN16D-AP1 1st Repriced DJ (1980–81), £7.50 sticker, *c.* 190 sold.

NN16D-AP2 2nd Repriced DJ (1981), £8.50 sticker, *c.* 100 sold.

NN16D-AP3 3rd Repriced DJ (1982–83), £9.50 sticker, *c.* 330 sold.

NN16D-AP4 4th Repriced DJ (1984–85), £10.00 sticker *c.* 260 sold.

POD16A Print-on-demand digital copy of the 1971 reprint NN16C.

BL16A Bloomsbury Edition, 1990 (31 December 1990). ISBN 1870630548; pp. xvii, [1], 254, [72 – b/w illustrations] (21½ × 16-page gatherings). A b/w facsimile of the 1976 reprint NN16D. Price: £12.95. Print run: unknown; a significant proportion remaindered.

17 Birds & Men

A good review can make a book, as can a poor one destroy it; or at least cast a shadow sufficiently dark to taint it thereafter – look at Wragge Morley's *Ants*. It might be that a negative review is utterly unjustified, but it is a brave publisher who can dismiss it as such and forget it altogether. Most of the reviews for Nicholson's *Birds and Men* were thoroughly favourable, but seek out the one by 'P.H.T.H.' [Mr P. Hartley of Edward Grey Institute Department of Zoological Field Studies, Oxford] that appeared in the spring 1951 edition of *Bird Notes:* he starts: 'This is a disappointing book' and, of the 'life histories', he says '[they] contribute little or nothing that is new to our knowledge of birds.' Not a single good thing can he find to say about the book. E. M. Nicholson's acerbic response appeared in the summer 1951 issue of the same publication and his closing put-down is worth quoting in full: 'It has long been well known to authors and readers that some reviewers would have written any book quite differently from its author and far, far better, but it is unfortunately customary for this to be taken as read thus sparing the reader tedious details of the way in which the reviewer would have displayed his superior wisdom had he written it himself, and leaving some space to say what the book is actually about, which your reviewer successfully hides from your readers.' Nicholson was certainly right to be indignant, as *Birds and Men* was generously illustrated with colour and b/w plates, many of the photographs taken in the wild. In 1951 this was notable, yet Hartley failed to make a single reference to the illustrations.

Whether this disappointing review had any significant effect on the sales of *Birds and Men* is impossible to say, but it was not a particularly good seller. By 1964 it was going out of stock and the minutes of the October 1964 NN board meeting record that JH and JF felt it should be dropped, as 'it is not a very good book'. It was perhaps odd for Julian Huxley to have been associated with these comments as he had been influential in the book's creation – was he too influenced by that negative review? However, by this point, a new book on the same subject was already being discussed and by 1965 Murton had been contracted to write it, with the working title *Economic Ornithology*. It is principally for this reason, rather than any other, that *Birds and Men* was not reprinted. *Economic Ornithology* was finally published, in 1971, as NN51 *Man and Birds*, but Nicholson's *Birds and Men* did appear once more as a Bloomsbury facsimile in 1990. (*The New Naturalists* also mentions a 1959 Readers Union edition, but this does not appear to exist.)

Birds and Men would appear to have been bound up in batches at different times. The casing fabric used can be divided into two distinct types, with the odd copy displaying intermediate characteristics. The first is the classic early New Naturalist buckram, coarse weaved, distinctly wavy, prone to uneven fading; the second is a finer weave, waxier and not prone to uneven fading (see casing fabrics on page 66). The first is identical to that used in the very early NN titles and is presumed to be chronologically earlier, a presumption supported by copies with dated inscriptions. But beyond differences in fabric characteristics, there are no consistently reliable diagnostic features, and because of this and the presence of intermediate bindings, I have not attempted to catalogue them separately. Suffice it to say, that if your copy is bound in the same fabric as your first edition *Butterflies* then it is likely to be a first state binding!

Birds and Men is one of the easier NN titles to find in very good or fine condition: there were a lot of them printed. The jacket is a little prone to tanning as is usual for the acidic paper dating from this period.

NN17A   **First Edition**, 1951 (05 February 1951).
Title: 'The New Naturalist | Birds And Men | The Bird Life of British | Towns, Villages, Gardens & Farmland'.
Author: 'by | E. M. Nicholson'.

Illust: 'With 42 colour photographs | by Eric Hosking and others | and 41 black-and-white photographs'.
Editors: JF, JG, JH, LDS and EH (Photographic Editor).
Printer: Collins Clear-Type Press, London and Glasgow (produced in conjunction with Adprint).
Photo: Eric Hosking and Others.
Collation: pp. xvi, 256; 20 leaves of colour plates printed to both sides; 16 leaves of b/w plates printed to both sides (17 × 16-page gatherings).
Jacket: [Rear panel] 'New Naturalist Monographs' under which advertised *The Yellow Wagtail* and *The Redstart*, with *The Badger* listed 'In the same series' and *The Fulmar*, *The Greenshank*, *The Heron*, *Ants*, *The Wren* and *Squirrels* listed as being 'In preparation'. [Rear flap] 'The New Naturalist'; with press clip; 'To be published in 1951' listing: *A Natural History of Man in Britain*; *Life in Lakes and Rivers*, *A Country Parish*, *Wild Orchids of Britain* and *The British Amphibians and Reptiles*; 21s. each. Request for details of new NN publications.
Price: 21s. net.
Print run: 16,000; no. sold: *c.* 15,400; o/p: 1965.

POD17A Print-on-demand digital copy.

BL17A Bloomsbury Edition, 1990 (31 December 1990). ISBN: 1870630149; pp. xvi, 256, [72 – b/w illustrations] (21½ × 16-page gatherings). Price: £12.95. A b/w facsimile of NN17A. Remaindered.

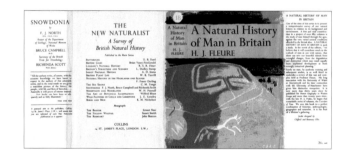

18 A Natural History of Man in Britain

A Natural History of Man in Britain, like NN6 *Natural History in the Highlands & Islands*, was thoroughly revised by a new co-author. The front flap to the new edition states 'Professor Fleure died in 1969 and his famous book has been revised and brought up to date by his old friend and one-time pupil, Dr. Margaret Davies – herself now a member of the New Naturalist Editorial Board'. But unlike NN6, the title of the 1970 new edition was not modified and Margaret Davies modestly suggested that Fleure's name alone should appear on the casing and jacket (though her name does appear on the title page), and therefore the new book looks no different from the original. The number of chapters and their headings are unaltered, however the total number of pages is nearly 50 fewer; there a few changes to orientation of plates and some of the b/w photographs are new, but the overall number remains the same; the line drawings are unrevised. The 1970 new edition is certainly sufficiently different to warrant having in addition to the first.

The revised edition appeared 20 years after the first but there was also a 1959 reprint, which incorporated a few revisions. The chairman had doubts about reprinting the book and in the event Fleure had to pay £10 for the cost of corrections. He was probably keen to remove references to Piltdown man, which included the statement: 'There is just a possibility that the skull may be that of a female, the jaw that of a male'; as is it turned out, the skull was that of a female – a mediaeval female, but the jaw – that of an orangutan.

Man in Britain is not a particularly popular title: are collectors subconsciously put off by the sombre earthy tones of the otherwise accomplished jacket? It is certainly not difficult to find fresh copies of both the first and new editions, though the paper of the former's jacket is liable to tanning. Total number of Collins copies printed: *c.* 18,500; total no. sold: *c.* 17,900; o/p: 1980, but o/s for around nine years before the new edition was published (late 1961 to 1970).

NN18A　　**First Edition**, 1951 (11 June 1951).

Title:	'The New Naturalist | A Natural History of | Man in Britain | Conceived as a study of changing relations | between Men and Environments'.
Author:	'by | H. J. FLeure'.
Illust:	'With 38 colour photographs by | Robert Atkinson, John Markham and others | 38 photographs in black and white | and 76 line drawings by Alison Birch'.
Editors:	JF, JG, JH, LDS and EH (Photographic Editor).
Printer:	Collins Clear-Type Press, London and Glasgow (produced in conjunction with Adprint).
Collation:	pp. xviii, 349, [1]; 16 leaves of colour plates printed to both sides; 16 leaves of b/w plates printed to both sides (23 × 16-page gatherings).
Jacket:	[Rear panel] 'The New Naturalist A Survey of British Natural History' under which 13 main series and 3 monographs are listed. Collins' address. [Rear flap] Advert for *Snowdonia*; mailing list request below.
Price:	21s. net.
Print run:	12,500; o/p: end 1957.
Notes:	1) Advert for the series on last page: 'The New Naturalist A Survey of British Natural History "One of the major publishing enterprises of the century"' listing 16 main series and 3 monograph titles; *Insect Natural History* is given simply as 'Insects'. 2) b/w plates on semi-matt paper.

NN18B Reprint, 1959 (April). 'Reprinted 1959… \| …First published in 1951'; no date to title page. As the first edition with a few minor corrections the most notable being to p. 28 where the previous references to Piltdown Man have been excised. Editors: JF now Sir

JH. Adverts omitted from the last page. The jacket rear panel displays 'The New Naturalist Library', listing in a numbered, single column NN1–38 but omitting NN6 and 26 (Type 36); rear flap still advertises *Snowdonia* but mailing list request inserted below; title to blurb to front flap omitted but blurb unaltered, two press reviews inserted below. Price: 30s. net[?]. Print run: 2,000; o/p: 1961. Note: This reprint is much rarer than the number printed would suggest; it is not unlikely that this figure includes books subsequently sold off to the RU.

NN18C Revised Edition, 1970. ISBN: 0002131536. 'First published 1951 \| Revised edition 1970'. A completely revised and reset edition; pp. 320; 16 leaves of colour plates printed to both sides; 16 leaves of b/w plates printed to both sides (20 × 16-page gatherings). Authors: H. J. Fleure and M. Davies (to title page only). Editors: JF, JG, JH, MD and EH. The suite of colour plates unchanged; the subjects of the b/w plates unchanged but many of the photographs are new; all plates now orientated vertically with the photographers acknowledged on the lists of plates rather than on the plates themselves; the b/w plates printed on glossy paper. The b/w line drawings unchanged though positioning and numbering of some revised; a list of the drawings has been added to the prelims. The title page is reset with both authors named but omits the 'illustrations blurb' and omits to acknowledge Alison Birch as artist of the text illustrations; the NN monogram is the plain 'Type D' with central diamond, i.e. without the arrowhead embellishment. The NN library to the jacket lists NN1–50 (Type 42, variant 8); rear flap advertises *Climate and the British Scene* and *The Seashore*; ISBN above lower edge; front flap with 6 press endorsements and new blurb. Price: £3.00 net \| 60s. net. Print run: 4,000; no. sold: *c.* 2,800 plus repriced variants below.

NN18C-AP1 1st Repriced DJ (1975–76), £3.50 sticker, *c.* 250 sold.
NN18C-AP2 2nd Repriced DJ (1976–77), £4.50 sticker, *c.* 350 sold.
NN18C-AP3 3rd Repriced DJ (1978–79), £5.50 sticker, *c.* 300 sold.
NN18C-AP4 4th Repriced DJ (1979–80), £6.00 sticker, *c.* 200 sold.
NN18C-AP5 5th Repriced DJ (1980), £7.50 sticker, < 50 sold.

BC18A Readers Union Edition, 1959. Printed and bound by Collins at Clear-Type Press, Glasgow. As NN18B and presumably a run-on to that printing, but with a cancel title page (i.e. pasted on to the stub of the original) displaying the RU imprint and tree logo, otherwise textually identical with the same composition of plates. The green imitation cloth casing, is blocked with the Readers Union tree logo to the spine, but the title lettering is the same as the Collins editions. Fitted with the RU jacket 'Type 2'. Price: 15/- net[?]. Print run: *c.* 2,000[?]. Note: It is unusual, for this period, for a RU New Naturalist to have a cancel title page, which might suggest fewer books than usual were purchased; additionally the sales statements indicate that the RU was also subsequently topped up with Collins own stock of the 1959 reprint.

POD18A Print-on-demand digital copy of 1970 revised ed. NN18C.

F18A Fontana Paperback Edition, 1971; pp. 336; 8 leaves of b/w plates bound in two sections of 4, printed on glossy paper, to both sides. Perfect bound. A reset copy of the 1970 revised edition NN18C, but with no colour and a reduced no. of b/w plates. The authors' names: H. J. Fleure and M. Davies appear on both title page and covers. 'Line drawings by Alison Birch to the title page'. Editors: JG, JH, MD, KM and EH. Adverts for Fontana NNs at front, listing 11 titles. The front depicts John Constable's painting 'Flatford Mill' and is thus atypical for a Fontana NN; rear cover carries 3 press clips. Price: 75p. Total print run: 15,000 inc. reprint below; o/p: 1976 latest.

F18B Second Impression, March 1972. (not seen)

BL18A Bloomsbury Edition, 1989 (31 December 1989). ISBN: 1870630734; pp. 320, [64 – b/w illustrations] (24 × 16-page gatherings). A b/w facsimile of the 1970 revised edition NN18C. Price: £12.95. Print run: unknown; a significant proportion remaindered.

19 Wild Orchids of Britain

Conceived in 1945, then with the working title *Orchids*, as a monograph with only eight colour plates, but Huxley made the case for its promotion to the main series and, in the event, a suite of 48 colour plates of every British species (excepting two) was included. Nearly all the colour photographs were taken especially for the book by Robert Atkinson during the summer of 1946 using locality notes provided by Francis Rose (is it possible to imagine a better summer assignment for the year following the end of the Second World War?). On the 28 October 1946 Summerhayes, with the help of J. E. Lousley, made his selection of Atkinson's photographs at the Collins office.

The scholarly and comprehensive text coupled with fine photographic plates rendered *Wild Orchids* a highly successful title, for which Summerhayes was awarded the Westonbirt Orchid Medal by the RHS. 'A botanical work of outstanding importance, likely to remain the standard text on its subject for many a long day' so acclaimed a contemporary, and prophetic, review in *The Countryman* magazine. And so it was. *Wild Orchids* was sold over a 37-year period though, admittedly, there were a few gaps in availability: it was out of print from 1964–1968 inclusively and again for a few months during the summer of 1969, and then in 1982–1984, before the paperback facsimile reprint appeared.

The second edition of c. 2,500 copies is dated 1968 but, in point of fact, did not appear until spring 1969 and promptly sold out within a couple of months, precipitating another reprint in 1969. The final hardback reprint appeared in 1976, of which five hundred copies were sold to the Readers Union, distinguished by their inferior imitation cloth bindings. In 1985 the Collins paperback facsimile reprint appeared.

Wild Orchids is never too difficult to find in very good or fine condition, but look out for the soft mauve on the jacket spine as this is apt to fade and, if the paper is in anyway tanned, the definition on the flower will be lost. Total no. of books printed: c. 19,500 (Collins h/b) + 500 (RU h/b) + 1,600 (Collins p/b reprint); o/p: 1982 (Colllins h/b); 1988 (Collins p/b).

NN19A   **First Edition**, 1951 (16 April 1951).
Title: 'The New Naturalist | Wild Orchids of | Britain | with a key to the series'.
Author: 'by | V. S. Summerhayes'.
Illust: 'With 61 photographs in colour | by Robert Atkinson and others | 39 photographs in black and white | 19 text figures and 43 distribution maps'.
Editors: JF, JG, JH, LDS and EH (Photographic Editor).
Printer: Collins Clear-Type Press, London and Glasgow (produced in conjunction with Adprint).
Collation: pp. xvii, [1], 366; 24 leaves of colour plates printed to both sides; 12 leaves of b/w plates printed to both sides (24 × 16-page gatherings).
Jacket: [Rear panel] 'One of the most highly praised books in the New Naturalist Library' featuring '*The Art of Botanical Illustration*'; Collins's address. [Rear flap] '*The New Naturalist Library*' listing five titles; mailing list request for new titles, below.
Price: 21s. net.
Print run: 12,000; no. sold: c. 11,700; o/p: early 1964.

NN19B Second Edition, 1968 [May 1969]. 'First Edition 1951 | Second Edition 1968'; no date to title page. Pagination and plates unaltered; text not reset with exception of preliminaries, which have been condensed to accommodate an eight page 'Preface to Second Edition', set in a smaller font. Revisions and corrections essentially restricted to the new preface, but bibliography extended and reset, and distribution maps substituted for those published in the 'Atlas of the British Flora' based on the survey by the Botanical Society of the British Isles. The quality of the paper and printing on a par with NN19A, but the distribution maps poorly printed, too small, and almost illegible. The jacket now printed using letterpress[?], cruder, bolder, without the subtlety and softness of the lithographed original, the green is yellower; 219 mm tall, several mm too short for book, trimmed losing most of the 'C' in 'C & RE'; the NN library lists NN1–50. (Type 42, variant 8), the rear flap advertises three botanical titles: *Wild Flowers of Chalk*, *Wild Flowers* and *Weeds and Aliens*; blurb to front flap rewritten, shortened with four press endorsements below. Price:

45s. net. Print run: 2,500; no. sold: *c.* 2,330; o/p: June 1969. Notes: 1) While dated 1968 to the imprint page, the second ed. was not actually published until May 1969. 2) Some copies are cased in an atypical brighter green cloth, characterised by a poorly executed binding.

NN19C Second Edition, First Reprint, 1969. 'First Edition 1951 | Second Edition 1968 | Reprinted 1969'. As second edition; also with same jacket as NN19B inc. trimming. The price remains at 45s. net. Print run: 3,000; no. sold: *c.* 2,850 including repriced and DJ variants below.

NN19C-AP1 1st Repriced DJ (1971–?), overprinted £2.25 adjacent to cut corner.

NN19C-DJ1 Second Edition, First Reprint, Reprinted Jacket. A new jacket printing using different technique, less subtle with loss of definition, colours less muted, green now emerald green; taller, only one 1 mm or so too short for book, trimmed to include most of the 'C' in 'C & RE'. Graphically and textually as NN19B, but without a printed price and now *Durasealed* (as *Duraseal* was not used in the NN series until late 1971, this printing must be around or after that date). All copies repriced as follows.

NN19C-DJ1-AP1 1st Repriced DJ (1972[?]–75), overprinted £2.25.

NN19C-DJ1-AP2 2nd Repriced DJ (1975), £3.50 sticker, *c.* 330 sold.

NN19C-DJ1-AP3 3rd Repriced DJ (1976), £4.00 sticker, *c.* 220 sold.

NN19D Second Edition, Second Reprint, 1976. ISBN 0002195496. 'First Edition 1951 | Second Edition 1968 | Reprinted 1969 | Reprinted 1976'. As NN19C. Editors: MD, JG, KM and EH; last sentence of NN credo omitted; imprint page reset and reordered. The *Durasealed* jacket 2 mm too short; the NN library lists NN1–58 (Type 42, variant 14); rear flap advertises *Wild Flowers of Chalk and Limestone* and *Wild Flowers* as NN19B, but *Weeds and Aliens* now omitted (out of print), ISBN; front flap identical. Price: £7.00 net printed diagonally with dotted line. Print run: 2,000; no. sold: *c.* 1,250 + repriced variants below.

NN19D-AP1 1st Repriced DJ (1980–81), £7.50 sticker, *c.* 220 sold.

NN19D-AP2 2nd Repriced DJ (1981), £8.50 sticker, *c.* 150 sold.

NN19D-AP3 3rd Repriced DJ (1982), £9.50 sticker, *c.* 200 sold.

BPB19A Collins Paperback Reprint, 1985 (21 January 1985). ISBN: 0002190869; pp. [26], 366, [72 – b/w illustrations] (29 × 16-page gatherings). A facsimile of NN19D, with an eight-page 'Preface to the Limpback Edition' by Philip Crib (successor to Summerhayes at Kew). Price: £6.50 net. Print run: *c.* 1,600; no. sold: *c.* 1,460; o/p: 1988. Note: The orchids to the Ellises' cover design are now a candyfloss pink and the title band a soft lilac, the font and setting of the title revised.

BC19A Readers Union Edition, 1976. Bound up from the same sheets as the 1976 Collins reprint NN19D but cased in dark green imitation cloth. However unlike usual bookclub editions the jacket is *Durasealed* and all examples price-clipped, so evidently from the same stock as NN19D. Print run: 500. (A scarce ed.)

POD19A Print-on-demand digital copy of the first edition.

20 The British Amphibians & Reptiles

The first of a trio of NN books on the British amphibians and reptiles and, from a sales perspective, the most successful of the three. It was printed five times and remained in print, for 27 years, though was out of stock during 1961 and 1962 and for a few months in 1973. It was the first authoritative book on the subject for many years and this, coupled with its readily readable style, ensured its success. It was much used as a textbook and consequently was considered for the Fontana paperback library, but this never came to fruition: perplexing, as surely its success was guaranteed in this affordable format?

From the very beginning, New Naturalist jackets have advertised other books in the series and this is a feature that will be familiar to all collectors, but the first edition jacket of *Amphibians and Reptiles* is the only book in the series to advertise the peripheral *New Naturalist Journal*, including the now scarce single paperback editions – parts 5 and 6.

The sales report dated December 1960 notes that 2,004 copies were sold to the RU, though does not clarify whether this was a contemporary or earlier sale. There does not appear to be a RU edition, so perhaps books were sold to the RU from stock or was this entry a mistake? Either way, this will remain a point of ambiguity until further information is forthcoming – and that's unlikely.

Amphibians and Reptiles wears well, and the book and jacket are often in very good condition. The jacket is a little apt to fade on the spine; not so much the early editions, but the last two editions were evidently printed with inferior inks and the terracotta colour on the spine soon mellows to a straw yellow.

Total print run: *c.* 18,000; total no. sold: *c.* 17,100; o/p: 1978.

NN20A	**First Edition**, 1951 (24 September 1951).
Title:	'The New Naturalist	The British	Amphibians & Reptiles'.
Author:	'by Malcolm Smith'.
Illust:	'With 18 colour photographs by W. S. Pitt	33 black and white photographs	5 drawings in monochrome	and 88 text figures'.
Editors:	JF, JG, JH, LDS and EH (Photographic Editor).
Printer:	Collins Clear-Type Press, London and Glasgow (produced in conjunction with Adprint).

Collation: pp. xiv, 318, [4 – NN adverts]; 8 leaves of colour plates printed to both sides; 8 leaves of b/w plates printed to both sides (21 × 16-page gatherings).

Jacket: [Rear panel] The New Naturalist library listing inclusively in a single column the first 22 titles in the series; the last two titles are noted as being in preparation. The price is quoted as 21s each. (Note: NN21 *British Mammals* and 22 *Climate* were published at 25s.) [Rear flap] Advert for New Naturalist Special Volumes with first 6 titles listed; below which an advert for the *New Naturalist Journal* (see intro.) and mailing list request.

Price: 21s. net.

Print run: 6,500; no. sold: unknown; o/p: unknown.

Notes: 1) Jacket text printed in black with brown titles and highlights. 2) The drawings in the text are by Mr. Arthur Smith, Miss Alison Birch and Dr. Angus Bellairs. 3) NN adverts to the last four pages for individual titles: *Botanical Illustration*, *British Plant Life*, *The Sea Shore*, *Mountains and Moorlands*, *Snowdonia*, *N. H. Highlands and Islands*, *Wild Flowers of Chalk*, *Birds and Men* and *The New Naturalist* listing 16 main series titles and 3 monographs; mailing list request.

NN2OB-DJ1 Revised [Second] Edition, First Jacket Variant, 1954. 'First published 1951 | Revised edition 1954'; no date to the title page; pp. xiv, 322; the plates and their position within text remain unaltered. The most significant revision is the addition of a tenth chapter: 'The Influence of Climate on the Distribution and Habits of the British Amphibians & Reptiles' as explained in the postscript inserted below the Editors' preface. Consequently the four pages of adverts have been omitted, otherwise revisions to the text are insubstantial with the setting unaltered. Jacket as first edition NN2OA but price clipped and over-printed 25s. net. Note: Presumably the jackets were left over from the first edition, but in quantity as this variant is not rare.

NN2OB-DJ2 Second Jacket Variant All text printed only in black; the NN library lists NN 1–30 inclusively (in a unique layout – see page 106); the rear flap is titled 'Some Press Comments on The British Amphibians and Reptiles' with four reviews cited; front flap unaltered. Price: 25s. net printed in a large font; o/p: 1961.

NN2OC Third Edition, 1964. 'First published 1951 | Second edition 1954 | Third edition 1964'. Essentially as NN2OB with the layout and pagination unaltered; the Editors' preface omitted and foreword by the two 'revisers' A. d'A Bellairs and J. F. D. Frazer inserted. Several new records have been added and Addenda to the bibliography extended. The NN library to the jacket lists NN1–45 (Type 42, variant 4); four press endorsements printed to rear flap, but different to those used for the second edition; the front flap reset; textually unaltered, but for omission of book title at head and addition of a reference to press opinions on back flap. Price: 35s. net. Print run: 3,000[?].

NN2OD Fourth Edition, 1969. 'First published 1951 | Second edition 1954 | Third edition 1964 | Fourth edition 1969'. But, in fact, a reprint; text, layout and pagination as NN2OC. Editors: JF, JG, JH, MD and EH. The jacket similar too, but all text heavier; the NN library lists NN1–50 (Type 42, variant 8); both flaps unchanged. Price: 36s. net. Print run: 3,000[?] inc. jacket variant below. Note: I have also seen this edition with the NN2OC jacket; presumably some were left over.

NN2OD-AP1 1st Repriced DJ (sold 1971–73), p. clipped and overprinted £1.80 net; no. sold: unknown, but not rare; o/p: 1973.

NN2OE Fifth Edition, 1973. ISBN 0002130297. 'First published 1951 | Second edition 1954 | Third edition 1964 | Fourth edition 1969 | Fifrth edition 1973'. Several revisions, mostly minor, including changes to the foreword and a resetting of the bibliography, but ostensibly a reprint of NN2OB. Editors: MD, JH, JG, KM and EH. The *Durasealed* jacket has reverted to a lighter type; the NN library lists NN1–56 (Type 42, variant 13); both flaps identical, but for inclusion of the ISBN to the rear. Price: £2.80 net. Print run: 2,500; no. sold: c. 1,000 plus variants below. Note: Sales reports indicate c. 1,000 quires were bound up later, but these later bindings appear indistinguishable.

NN2OE-AP1 1st Repriced DJ (1974–75?), £3.50 sticker, no. sold: unknown.
NN2OE-AP2 2nd Repriced DJ (1975–76), £4.00 sticker, c. 550 sold.
NN2OE-AP3 3rd Repriced DJ (1976–77), £4.50 sticker, c. 530 sold.
NN2OE-AP4 4th Repriced DJ (1978), £5.50 sticker, c. 280 sold.

POD2OA Print-on-demand digital copy of the first edition NN2OA.

21 British Mammals

'The Editors of the New Naturalist believe that this is the most important book on British mammals that has ever been published', so commences the jacket blurb. It was well reviewed by others too, but a year later sales were described as 'disappointing'. However, this was not a reflection on *Mammals* but merely indicative of a wider pattern of reduced sales within the series. Besides, it remained in print for 26 years. It was commissioned in February 1944, before a book in the series had been published and at a time when few colour photographs of mammals were available. Colour plate 13 of a badger taken by Ernest Neal first appeared as the frontispiece to his monograph in 1948 (M1) and plate 10 of a red squirrel by M.S. Wood was a touched-up colour version of the b/w original.

Mammals was reprinted four times but without any significant revision, but Collins used the terms 'impression' and 'reprint' interchangeably throughout these various printings. The first reprint of 1960 was stated as being the second edition, the second reprint of 1963 as the third impression, the third reprint of 1968 as the second edition (again!) and the fourth reprint of 1972 as the fifth impression. Matthews was aware of this confusion and insisted none of the reprints were editions, though his pleas, evidently, were not heeded. However, in the late 1960s Matthews was approached to revise the text for a new edition, but explained that this would necessitate extensive rewriting and therefore resetting. He was given no indication that this was would not be acceptable and so spent six months doing the work. He submitted the manuscript to Collins in 1971 and there it languished, never to be the subject of a compositor's attention – it was too long and too expensive and was unceremoniously passed over. Matthews was not unnaturally aggrieved but, when 'laid-up with a broken leg and feeling low', he acquiesced to the straight reprint of 1972. Collins approached him again in 1974 requesting yet another reprint and this time his reaction was more bellicose – 'It would be morally dishonest to sell a book so out of date and with so much misinformation, to innocent buyers.' And when in 1977 he was customarily offered the last few copies he dryly replied, 'I have three and it is so out of date that I can think of no use for additional ones'. But this was not the end of Matthews's literary partnership with Collins as he went on to write a completely new book published in 1982 as NN68 in the series: *Mammals in the British Isles*.

Mammals was also published by the Readers Union in 1960 but with a dedicated RU jacket and title page, never to be confused with the real thing. The 1972 fourth reprint was bound up in two tranches separated by several years, which has given rise to two binding variants.

British Mammals is not a difficult title to find in fine condition though jackets of the earlier impressions are prone to browning. Total no. of books printed: *c.* 25,000 (Collins h/b).

NN21A   **First Edition**, 1952 (17 March 1952).
Title: 'The New Naturalist | British Mammals'.

Author:	'L. Harrison Matthews	Sc.D. (Cantab.)'.
Illust:	'With 16 colour plates	48 black and white plates	and 92 figures in the text'.
Editors:	JF, JG, JH, LDS and EH (Photographic Editor).
Printer:	Mardon, Son & Hall, Ltd., Bristol.
Collation:	pp. xii, 410, [2 NN adverts]; 16 leaves of colour plates printed to one side only; 24 leaves of b/w plates printed to both sides (26½ × 16-page gatherings).
Jacket:	[Rear panel] The New Naturalist library, listing NN 1–23 inclusively. Rear flap: Advert for 'A New Naturalist Special Volume *The Badger*' with two reviews; seven 'Other Special Volumes' listed of which four in preparation including *The Fox* by Frances Pitt (never published).
Price:	25s. net.
Print run:	12,500; no. sold: *c.* 12,000[?]; o/p: 1960.
Notes:	1) Photographers: Predominantly John Markham with contributions from Fraser Darling, Eric Hosking, Ernest Neal, A. R. Thompson et al. See intro. regarding photographs. 2) Adverts to pages [411/412] for: 'The New Naturalist' listing 18 titles 'Already published in the Main Series' and 4 'Special Volumes'; overleaf: *Mountains and Moorlands*, *Snowdonia* and *Highlands and Islands* are featured, each supported with press reviews.

NN21B Second Impression (Second Edition), 1960 (Oct.). 'First Edition: 1952 | Second Edition: 1960'; no date to title page. Notwithstanding the reference to 'Edition' this is a reprint with minimal corrections and the adverts have been removed leaving the last two pages blank. Printer: Collins Clear-Type Press. The New Naturalist library to the jacket lists NN1–42 inclusively identifying NN6, 9 and 13 out of print (Type 41A), the rear flap features adverts for *Amphibians and Reptiles* and *British Game*, with press endorsements; the front flap is unchanged but title printed in black. Price: 30s. net. Print run: 2,500[?]. Note: The layout of NN library to jacket is a precursor to the familiar 'Type 42', but differs from that in that the authors' names are not italicised; also used for the 1960 reprint edition of *Mountains & Moorlands*.

TABLE NN21 Diagnostic features of the two binding variants of the 1972 fifth impression NN21E.

Mammals 1972 fifth impression	'Collins' to the spine of the book	Thickness of book	Hinges (internal)	Jacket
1st binding variant 'B1'	Smaller typeface – 17 mm long	34–35 mm	Mull evident under endpaper at hinges, not extending to top/tail of endpaper. Hinge with vertical lip of *c.* 4mm.	Jacket with original printed price of £2.75 net ; possibly a few repriced at £3.50.
2nd binding variant 'B2'	Larger typeface – 19–20 mm long	33–34 mm	Binding tape evident under endpaper at hinges which extends to top/tail of EP. Hinge flattish with *c.* 2mm vertical lip.	Jacket invariabley repriced at £3.50, £4.00, £4.95 & £5.50.

NN21C Third Impression, 1963 (Dec.). 'First Impression March 1952 | Second Impression: October 1960 | Third Impression December 1963'. Contents as NN21B. Jacket slightly revised: New Naturalist library lists NN1–45 (Type 42, variant 4); adverts to rear flap unchanged, but reset with *Amphibians and Reptiles* advertised '(Revised edition: 1964)'. Replacing the blurb to front flap are four long press reviews; the jacket design credit is omitted. Price: 35s. net. Print run: 3,000; no. sold: *c.* 2,850; o/p: 1967/8.

NN21D Fourth Impression (Second Edition), 1968. 'First Edition 1952 | Reprinted 1960 | Reprinted 1963 | Second Edition 1968'. But despite 'Edition' another straight reprint – contents as NN21B. Only revisions are to titles and post-nominals of author/ editors, but quality of printing poorer. The NN library to the jacket lists NN1–50 (Type 42, variant 8); both flaps identical. Price: 36s. net. Print run: 4,000. Note: The price has increased by just 1 shilling.

NN21E-B1 Fifth Impression, First Binding Variant, 1972. ISBN: 0002130211. 'First impression 1952 | Second impression 1960 | Third impression 1963 | Fourth impression 1968 | Fifth impression 1972'. As NN21D. Editors: JG, JH, KM, MD and EH. Quality of printing even poorer. New Naturalist library to the *Durasealed* jacket lists NN 1–54 (Type 42, variant 11); both flaps identical. Price: £2.75 net. Print run: 3,000 inc. 'B2'; no. bound thus *c.* 2,000. Note: This 1972 printing exists in two subtly but consistently different binding variants.

NN21E-B2 Fifth Impression, Second Binding Variant, 1972 [bound up *c.* 1975]. The New Naturalist Statement dated 18/10/74 states that the stock for *Mammals* was 816 +1030Q; i.e. *c.* 1,000 copies were held as unbound quires – and it is these which became this second binding variant. (These variations are similar to the binding variants of NN59 *Ants* – see photos on page 346). This second binding variant is likely to wear repriced jackets as below (all *Durasealed*). Print run: inc. above; no. bound thus: *c.* 1,000.

NN21E-B2-AP1 1st Repriced DJ (1975?), £3.50 sticker, no. sold: unknown.
NN21E-B2-AP2 2nd Repriced DJ (1975–76), £4.00 sticker, *c.* 500 sold[?].
NN21E-B2-AP3 3rd Repriced DJ (1976–77), £4.95 sticker, *c.* 550 sold[?].
NN21E-B2-AP4 4th Repriced DJ (1977), £5.50 sticker, *c.* 100 sold[?].

BC21A Readers Union Edition, 1960. As NN21B but specially printed for the RU; therefore with an integral title page displaying the RU imprint and tree logo, otherwise textually identical with the same composition of plates; the green buckram binding, stamped Readers Union to the spine. Fitted with the RU jacket Type 2; priced at 15/- net. Print run: unknown.

POD21A Print-on-demand digital copy of the 1972 fourth reprint NN21E.

BL21A Bloomsbury Edition, 31 December 1989. ISBN: 1870630688; pp. xii, 410, [2]; 40 leaves of integrated b/w illustrations (29 × 16-page gatherings). A b/w facsimile of the 1968 reprint NN21D. Price £12.95. Print run: unknown, but a significant proportion remaindered.

22 Climate and the British Scene

The memo of agreement between Gordon Manley and Collins was dated 12 October 1944 for 'Climate and Life', the working title, but Manley's preferred title was *Climate and the British Scene*. The book was originally advertised as NN14 in the series, but the delays were not of Manley's making: collecting together illustrations and the drawing of diagrams, and wrangling over the costs associated with these elements, were the culprits. *Climate and the British Scene* has a particularly nostalgic collection of photographs principally by Cyril Newberry, but assembled from wide and disparate sources. Three Editors contributed photographs: James Fisher, Julian Huxley and Eric Hosking and plate 32 is, I believe, the first colour photograph to appear in a New Naturalist taken by a Women – Anne Jackson. The photographs are nostalgic because the subject, technique and reproduction combine to epitomise the New Naturalist in the effervescent days of its infancy, where it was cradled at the confluence of the old and the new: succoured on a diet of enthusiasm and wonder from the former and science and learning from the latter. Plate 24 has a beautiful ethereal quality; evocative in a way that the crisp sharp, clear photographs of the modern series can never be.

Manley had suggested a Brolly for the jacket, but instead he got one of the Ellises' most impressionistic jackets: the brewing of the storm, full of menace and foreboding with a fist-shaped cloud descending from the heavens to smite the desolate church, or is it the still small 'hand' of calm reaching down through the earthquake, wind and fire to protect his church? Perhaps not, but intentionally or otherwise there is an allusion to childhood games of finding shapes in clouds (apologies to Peter Marren – it was not until later that I read his piece in *Art of the New Naturalists*, but as the analogy occurred independently, and therefore must be obvious enough, I have left it in.)

Early jackets printed on acidic paper are prone to tan, which, given the preponderance of pale areas on the spine, is more disfiguring than other, stronger coloured jackets. As always, brighter copies do exist, if you are prepared to wait, otherwise consider sending your browned copy to a paper conservator. Total no. of Collins h/b books printed: *c.* 25,000; o/p: 1979, but out of stock: end 1968/beginning 1969 to beginning of 1972.

NN22A **First Edition**, 1952 (13 October 1952).
Title: 'The New Naturalist | Climate and | the British Scene'.
Author: 'by | Gordon Manley | M.A. (CANTAB.), M.Sc. (MANC.) | Professor of Geography in the University of | London at Bedford College for Women'.
Illust: 'With 41 colour photographs | by Cyril Newberry and others | 40 photographs in black and white | and 75 maps and diagrams'.
Editors: JF, JG, JH, LDS and EH (Photographic Editor).
Printer: Mardon, Son & Hall, Ltd., Bristol.
Collation: pp. xviii, 314, [4 – NN adverts]; 16 leaves of colour plates printed to both sides; 24 leaves of b/w plates printed to both sides (21 × 16-page gatherings).
Jacket: [Rear panel] 'Published in The New Naturalist Library', advertising *Mountains and Moorlands* and *A Natural History of Man in Britain*. [Rear flap] 'A selection of volumes in the New Naturalist Library': *British Mammals*, *An Angler's Entomology*, and *A Country Parish* with 'in preparation' *Flowers of the Coast*, *The Weald* and *The Sea Coast*; send postcard for information.
Price: 25s. net.
Print run: 6,500.
Notes: Adverts to pp. [315–318] for: 'The New Naturalist' with endorsing clip from the TLS; 21 titles listed 'Already published in the Main Series' in a single column, and 5 'Special Volumes'; with specific adverts for *Fleas, Flukes & Cuckoos*, *Britain's Structure and Scenery*, *A Natural History of Man in Britain*, *A Country Parish*, *Mountains and Moorlands*, *Snowdonia* and *Natural History in the Highlands and Islands*.

NN22B **Second Impression**, 1953 (April). 'First impression October, 1952 | Second impression April, 1953'; no date to title page. As the first edition, seemingly without any revisions; now printed by Collins Clear-Type Press. NN adverts to rear unchanged. Jacket identical too but dark sage-green lettering to the rear panel a lighter grey green. Price: still 25s. net. Print run: 3,000.

NN22C **Third Impression**, 1955 (Dec.). 'First Impression October, 1952 | Second Impression April, 1953 | Third Impression December, 1955'. As NN21B but for minor additions and corrections as explained in the 'note to the third impression' on p. xviii. Bedford College to TP now without reference to women. Adverts to rear revised: 'The New Naturalist' lists 30 titles in single column (NN1–30 inclusive but unnumbered), TLS clip omitted; 'Special Volumes' lists 10 titles; specific adverts for *Butterflies*, *Britain's Structure and Scenery*, *A Natural History of Man in Britain*, *A Country Parish*, *Art of Botanical Illustration*, *British Plant Life* and *The Sea Shore*. Jacket exactly as NN22B and price remains at: 25s. net. Print run: 4,000; o/p: 1962.

NN22D **Fourth Impression**, 1962 (Aug.). 'First impression 1952 | Second impression 1953 | Third impression 1955 | Fourth impression 1962'. As NN22C but for minor additions and corrections as explained in the 'note to the fourth impression' on p. [xviii]. Editors: JH now Sir JH and JG awarded V. M. H. Adverts to rear revised: 'The New Naturalist' library reset, listing NN1–45 titles in two columns, omitting NN9 and 13. 'Special volumes' lists 15 titles; specific adverts for *Butterflies*, *Britain's Structure and Scenery*, *Birds and Men* and *Trees, Woods and Man*; last page blank. New Naturalist library to jacket lists NN1–45 (Type 42, variant 4); rear flaps with four press endorsements; blurb to front flap unchanged but 'for press opinions of this book see back flap' inserted below. Price: 30s. net. Print run: 3,000; o/p: end 1968/ beginning 1969.

NN22E **Fifth Impression**, 1971 (1972). ISBN: 0002130440 (to jacket only). 'First impression 1952 | Second impression 1953 | Third impression 1955 | Fourth impression 1962 | Fifth impression 1971'. As NN21d. Paper smoother, book very slightly thinner. Editors: JG, JH, MD, KM and EH. New Naturalist library to *Durasealed* jacket lists NN1–52 (Type 42, variant 9); new set of five press endorsements to rear flap and ISBN; blurb to front flap abridged and two press commendations inserted below, jacket design credit omitted. Price: £2.50 net. Print run: 4,000; no. sold: *c.* 2,000 + repriced variants below + probably *c.* 600 sold off, from stock, to a bookclub; o/p: 1979 (AP4). Note: No books were sold during 1971, which indicates was not published until 1972.
NN22E-AP1 **1st Repriced DJ** (1975–76), £3.95 sticker, *c.* 270 sold.
NN22E-AP2 **2nd Repriced DJ** (1976–77), £4.50 sticker, *c.* 330 sold.
NN22E-AP3 **3rd Repriced DJ** (1978–79), £5.50 sticker, *c.* 220 sold.
NN22E-AP4 **4th Repriced DJ** (1979), £6.00 sticker, *c.* 50 sold.

POD22A **Print-on-demand** digital copy of the 1971 fifth impression NN22E.

F22A **Fontana Paperback, First Edition**, 1962. ISBN: 000632326X (appears only in 1975 edition); pp. 382, [2]; 8 leaves of b/w plates bound in single central section printed on semi-glossy paper, to both sides (12 × 32-page gatherings). A reset copy of the Collins 1962 fourth impression, no colour and a reduced no. of b/w plates. The subtitle to the front cover and TP reads 'The Fontana Library'. Adverts for Fontana library at rear inc. 3 NN titles. Much better quality paper than later editions, creamy and not liable to tanning. Cover artwork by [Kenneth] Farnhill; rear cover carries 2 press endorsements. No printed price but 9/6 sticker to front cover. Total print run inc. reprints below: 36,000.
The following reprints exactly as preceding edition unless stated otherwise, changes to internal adverts ignored.
F22B **Second Impression**, October 1968. Half title and Fontana credo replaced with blurb; adverts at rear revised, paper poorer quality, liable to tanning, book thicker. Covers unchanged. Price: 12/6 to front cover.
F22C **Third Impression**, April 1970. 'The Fontana New Naturalist' to front cover and TP; adverts revised. Covers changed to traditional green livery; photographic front cover uncredited; rear cover reset but same press endorsements: Price: 12/-(60p).

F22D **Fourth Impression**, March 1971. (not seen)
F22E **Fifth Impression**, May 1972. Price: 60p. Thicker book.
F22F **Sixth Impression**, June 1975. Price: £1.00.

23 An Angler's Entomology

'The matter of importance is not so much how many fish are caught but rather how they are caught' so wrote Harris in the introduction to *An Angler's Entomology* and no doubt the book appealed to the purist angler in pursuit of this sentiment. The jacket blurb put it rather more prosaically 'Anglers, of all human groups devoted to a hobby or sport, are perhaps the most strongly obsessed with their occupation and with all that belongs to it.' This might explain why a book concerning an angler's entomology of the British Isles was published four times in the US. Harris was also somewhat of a fishing celebrity and when not lecturing (and fishing), managed Garnett & Keegan of Dublin, Ireland's leading tackle shop, where he oversaw the work of 10 full time fly-tiers. He was undoubtedly a celebrity in the then angling world, as reflected in the number of books he signed: to date I've come across eight signed copies. If the dedicatee was a friend or acquaintance he signed his name Dick Harris otherwise it was J.R. Harris.

In the early 1930s when Harris first had the idea for a book about angling entomology, he realised that the species described would need to be illustrated with colour pictures but at the time that necessitated paintings, which was beyond the scope of such a book. Later, in 1946, when Harris proposed the book to the Editorial Board, colour photography was suitably advanced to solve the problem and the photographer T. O. Ruttledge was commissioned. By today's standards the quality of the photographs is not good, particularly in the later reprints, but at the time they were well received; the *Daily Telegraph* reviewer wrote 'Full of superb coloured photographs…' – and note the use of 'coloured' rather than 'colour'. The reproduction in b/w of the photographs in the Bloomsbury reprint is so poor that it would be impossible to use any of them for identification purposes.

There is something singularly odd about the 1956 revised edition and all subsequent reprints. Odd, because some pages have a smaller, lighter type, though the setting is unchanged (to compensate for the smaller type, the rows are slightly shorter with greater space between them). These 'new' pages are

jumbled up with the old pages, and when side by side on a two-page spread are visually unsettling e.g. pp. 126/127. The reason for the smaller, lighter type is not exactly clear: the 'new' pages were apparently produced using a different reprographic technique – probably off-set lithography, whereas the original pages were letterpress. This does not however explain the degree of difference in scale – which might be attributable to nothing more complicated than carelessness. The first edition was, uniquely for a New Naturalist, printed in Austria; thereafter *An Angler's Entomology* was printed in house by the Collins Clear-Type Press (though it is a moot point whether all books stated as printed by Collins actually were). Variation was not confined to the book: each dust jacket printing exhibited a different colour emphasis.

An Angler's Entomology stayed in print for 31 years but, other than for a few corrections to the 1956 edition, was never revised. A new book was proposed by the angling writer Malcolm Greenhalgh in 1988, which resulted in a contract the following year, but was apparently abandoned not long after, due to other commitments. Greenhalgh did however go on to write other books for Collins, *Freshwater Life: Britain and Northern Europe*, with Denys Ovenden in 2007, and *An Encyclopedia of Fishing Flies – A Guide to Flies from Around the World*' with Jason Smalley in 2009.

All printings of Harris's New Naturalist, remain popular: the 1973 reprint is the scarcest, of which only 1,000 copies were printed, though the 1977 reprint is also rare despite a print run of 2,000. The first edition is not uncommonly in very good condition, though the jacket is liable to tanning. Total number printed: *c.* 17,500 (Collins) and *c.* 3,500 (USA); o/p: 1983 (Collins).

NN23A **First Edition**, 1952 (18 August 1952).
Title: 'The New Naturalist | an | Angler's | Entomology'.
Author: 'by J.R. HARRIS | F.R.E.S. | Demonstrator in Limnology, Department of Zoology' | Trinity College, Dublin'.
Illust: 'With 103 colour photographs | by T. O. Ruttledge | 24 black and white photographs | and 27 maps and diagrams'.
Editors: JF, JG, JH, LDS and EH (Photographic Editor).
Printer: Carl Ueberreuter, Vienna, Austria.
Collation: pp. xv, [1], 268, [4 – NN adverts]; 16 leaves of colour plates printed to both sides; 8 leaves of b/w plates printed to both sides (18 × 16-page gatherings).
Jacket: [Rear panel] 'The New Naturalist Library Three successful volumes in the Main Series' advertising *Life in Lakes and Rivers*, *Insect Natural History* and *Butterflies*; and above the lower edge 'see inside back flap for other New Naturalist publications'. [Rear flap] 'Some recent publication in the New Naturalist Library' listing in the main series *British Mammals*, *British Amphibians & Reptiles*, *A Country Parish*, *Wild Orchids of Britain* and *Birds and Men* and 'Special

Volumes' *Fleas, Flukes and Cuckoos* and *The Greenshank*; mailing list request below.

Price: 25s. net.

Print run: 7,500 but a few sold to the US imprint Praeger; o/p: 1956.

Notes: 1) Adverts to last four pages for: 'The New Naturalist' with endorsing clip from the *Yorkshire Post*; 19 titles listed 'Already published in the Main Series' in a single column, and 5 'Special Volumes'; mailing list request below. Overleaf specific adverts for *Butterflies, Insect Natural History, British Game, Wild Flowers of Chalk and Limestone, Birds and Men, Life in Lakes and Rivers, The Badger, The Redstart* and *The Yellow Wagtail*. each supported with two or three press commendations. 2) Book *c.* 27 mm thick.

NN23B Revised [Second] Edition, 1956. 'First published 1952 | Revised Edition 1956'; no date to the title page. This edition incorporates a fair number of corrections and changes. The most obvious is the change in the reprographic method used for some but certainly not all pages (see intro.), which, though the setting is largely unchanged, are printed in a smaller, lighter type. The length of a row of text of these 'new' pages is about 110 mm whereas in the original pages it is around 113 mm; examples are: p. [63], [121], 127 and 164 but there are many others besides. The typography of the title page, including the NN monogram, is also noticeably smaller, with a couple of textual revisions: Harris now with a M.A. and a 'sometime demonstrator'. Regarding revisions to the text, these are generally confined to small corrections e.g. first line of p. 164 now states there are five species of Caenis, (the first ed. stated there were four) but parts of the Keys extensively reordered: pp. 191,192, 195 and 196. The four pages of adverts unchanged. Printer: Collins Clear-Type Press; the paper rough and of poor quality; book 25 mm thick. Rear panel of jacket unchanged but previous reference to other NN publications on inside back flap omitted; rear flap with title 'Some press comments on *An Angler's Entomology*' under which four press endorsements cited; front flap unchanged. Price: 30s. net. Print run: 3,000; o/p: early 1965. Notes: 1) A few of the 'new' pages do not appear to exhibit any textural revision or, at least, any changes there might be are trifling e.g. words originally hyphenated are no longer so. 2) It is not unusual to find this book with a 1st ed. jacket and vice versa.

NN23C Second Edition, First Reprint, 1966 [Nov. 1966]. 'First Edition 1952 | Second Edition 1956 | Reprinted 1966'. As NN23B without any obvious textual revisions. Editors: JH and LDS now Sir JH and Sir DS and various post nominals added. Adverts at rear omitted. Book 24 mm thick. The NN library to the jacket lists nos. 1–47 (Type 42, variant 6); rear flap advertises *Insect Natural History, Moths* and *The World of the Honeybee*; the blurb to the front abbreviated and four press comments inserted below. Price: 35s. net. Print run: 2,000; o/p: around end 1969.

NN23D Second Edition, Second Reprint, 1970. SBN 002130017 (to jacket only). 'First Edition 1952 | Second edition 1956 | Reprinted 1966 | Reprinted 1970'. As NN23C. Editors: JF, JG, JH, MD and EH. The NN library to the jacket lists NN1–50 (Type 42, variant 8); both flaps unchanged, but for addition of SBN to rear. Dual Price: £2.25 net | 45s. net. Print run: 2,000; o/p: end 1974.

NN23E Second Edition, Third Reprint, 1973 [bound up end of 1974]. ISBN: 0002130017 (to imprint page only). 'First Edition 1952 | Second edition 1956 | Reprinted 1966 | Reprinted 1970 | Reprinted 1973'. As NN23D. Book 23 mm thick. The *Durasealed* jacket is decidedly bluer; the NN library lists nos. 1–55 (type 42, variant 12); both flaps unaltered and the rear still carries the obsolete SBN. No printed price. Print run: 1,000; no. actually bound up and sold thus: unknown. Note: This reprint was a 'run-on' to the US edition of the same date US23D, but at that time Collins had sufficient 1970 reprints in stock, so did not bind up this edition until required in late 1974. However the NN library to the jacket dates to 1973 so presumably these were printed at the same time as the books – and someone had the foresight not to print a price. A rare printing and, taking account of the usual wastage, fewer than 1,000 copies, would have been bound up.

NN23E-AP1 1st Priced DJ (1975), £2.25 sticker, no. sold: unknown.

NN23E-AP2 2nd Priced DJ (1975–76), £4.50 sticker, no. sold: unknown.

NN23F Second Edition, Fourth Reprint, 1977 (Feb.) ISBN: 002193728 (to imprint page and jacket). 'First Edition 1952 | Second edition 1956 | Reprinted 1966 | Reprinted 1970 | Reprinted 1973 | Reprinted 1977'. Editors: JG, MD, KM and EH; last sentence of NN credo omitted. Book 24 mm thick. The NN library to the *Durasealed* jacket lists NN1–58 (Type 42, variant 14); both flaps unaltered, but for the revised ISBN to the rear. Price: £5.50. Print run: 2,000; no. sold thus: *c.* 780 + repriced variants below.

NN23F-AP1 1st Repriced DJ (1979–80), £6.00 sticker, *c.* 400 sold.

NN23F-AP2 2nd Repriced DJ (1980–81), £7.50 sticker, *c.* 350 sold.

NN23F-AP3 3rd Repriced DJ (1981–82), £8.50 sticker, *c.* 100 sold[?].

NN23F-AP4 4th Repriced DJ (1982–83), £9.50 sticker, *c.* 400 sold[?].

POD23A Print-on-demand digital copy of the first edition NN23A.

BL23A Bloomsbury Edition, 1990 [31 December 1990]. ISBN: 1870630599; pp. xv, [1], 268, [4], [48 – b/w illustrations] (21 × 16-page gatherings). A b/w facsimile of the 1966 reprint NN23C. The blurb to the front flap is a précised form of the original jacket blurb. Price: £12.95. Print run: unknown, but remaindered, though now rarer than many other Bloomsbury NN titles, despite poor b/w images – see intro.

US23A US First Edition, 1952. Frederick A. Praeger, New York. As the Collins first edition NN23A, but with a Frederick A. Praeger inc. label pasted over the Collins imprint on the title page; otherwise no distinguishing marks, in the same green buckram casing and with the Collins imprint to the spine. Dust jacket not seen. Price and print run unknown. Note: As the book, unmodified but for an imprint label, was marketed in the States by Praeger, it is likely that the jacket too was identical to the Collins edition.

US23B US Second Edition. (1956). The Countryman Press, Woodstock Vermont. Not dated, but as the Collins revised edition of 1956 NN23B, and from the same printing, using the same rough cheap paper and displaying the same reprographic features. The half-title and title leaves, are the only textual differences: both omit references to the New Naturalist (inc. the monogram), the NN credo is omitted from the former and the latter carries The Countryman Press imprint, but both are integral leaves (i.e. not cancels). Bound in the same green buckram casing, but blocked 'The Countryman Press' to the spine and without the NN monogram. Dust jacket ostensibly as the Collins edition with the Ellises' design slightly modified: 'Collins' and the fly's three tails omitted from beneath the NN oval, and overprinted 'The Countryman Press'; the series no. '23' also omitted from the top roundel. The rear panel advertises 'Family Circle's Guide To Trout Flies And How To Tie Them'; the rear flap advertises 'Flies' by J. Edson Leonard; both these works published by A. S. Barnes and Company; the blurb to the front flap as NN23B but reset with smaller lettering, and the author and imprint added. Price: ?. Print run: 1,100 but 1,144 delivered.

US23C US Second Edition, First Reprint, 1966. 'A. S. Barnes and Co. South Brunswick New York'. From the same printing as the Collins 1966 reprint NN23C, but half-title and title pages not cancels; all references to the NN, etc. omitted as US23B. Bound in the same green buckram casing, but blocked 'A. S. Barnes' to the spine and without the NN monogram. Dust jacket modified as US23B but over-printed 'A. S. Barnes' and with the series no. '23' still omitted; rear panel lists nine titles under the title 'Barnes Books For The Fisherman'; rear and front flaps exactly as the Collins 1956 revised edition NN23B i.e. with four press comments to rear and unrevised blurb to front. No printed price. Print run: 1,100 but 1,057 delivered.

US23D US Second Edition, Second Reprint, 1973. ISBN: 0498080269. 'A. S. Barnes and Co. South Brunswick New York' (to TP) and 'A. S. Barnes and Co., Inc., New Jersey' (to imprint page). From the same printing as the Collins 1973 reprint NN23E, but half-title and title pages not cancels; all references to the NN, etc. omitted. Bound in the same green buckram casing, but blocked 'A. S. Barnes' to the spine and without the NN monogram. Dust jacket not *Durasealed*, decidedly bluer as NN23E jacket; modified as US23B but over-printed 'A. S. Barnes' and with the series no. '23' now retained; rear panel blank but for imprint; both flaps revert to the 1956 US second edition US23B but ISBN added to rear and imprint omitted from front. Price $8.95 to corner front flap. Print run: 1,000. Note: A Collins memo from September 1972 complained that 'selling off 1,000 of our old stock to America is going to have us…reprint for ourselves'. However the fact that this US edition has an integral title leaf would indicate, that in the event this did not happen.

US23D-AP1 1st Repriced DJ With '9.95' sticker applied over original printed price.

24 Flowers of the Coast

Peter Marren in the *Art of the New Naturalists* explains the printer's inability to match the colours of the Ellises' design, but from the collector's perspective, this is only part of the problem, as the jacket is, perhaps more than any other, impossible to find in an unfaded state – at least as a first edition. I have never seen one and suspect they don't exist. It is the pink on the spine which is particularly susceptible and the series number often fades to the point of illegibility. To compound matters, the paper used (pH < 6.5) is prone to tanning.

First printed in 1952, and reprinted in 1962, 1966 and again in 1972. All reprints without revision, but for a few minor corrections and a few changes to the publisher's adverts at the rear of the book. The 1972 reprint was bound up in two tranches, separated by three years, and consequently two binding variants exist; the differences are subtle but consistent, and outlined in table NN24. *Flowers of the Coast* finally went out of print in 1978, but was out of stock from 1958–1962. Total print run: c. 12,500.

NN24A   **First Edition**, 1952 (27 October 1952).
Title: 'The New Naturalist | Flowers of the | Coast'.
Author: 'by | Ian Hepburn | with a chapter | on coastal physiography | By J. A. Steers'.
Illust: 'With 17 colour photographs | by John Markham and others' | 43 black and white photographs | and 14 line drawings and maps'.
Editors: JF, JG, JH, LDS and EH (Photographic Editor).
Printer: Collins Clear-Type Press: London and Glasgow.
Collation: pp. xiv, 236, [6 NN adverts]; 16 leaves of colour plates printed to one side only; 20 leaves of b/w plates printed to both sides (16 × 16-page gatherings).
Jacket: Rear panel: Advert for *Wild Flowers of Chalk and Limestone*. Rear flap: Adverts for *Wild Orchids of Britain, British Plant Life; Mountains and Moorlands;* under which 'A list of published titles in the New Naturalist Library is given at the end of this book…'.
Price: 25s. net.
Print run: 6,000; no. sold: c. 5,600; o/p: summer 1958.
Notes: 1) Adverts to pp. [237–242] for: 'The New Naturalist', which lists 21 titles starting with *London's Natural History* and ending with *An Angler's Entomology*, but

TABLE NN24 Summary of differences between first and second binding variants of the 1972 reprint NN24D.

Flowers of the Coast 1972 reprint NN24d	'Collins' to the spine of the book	Other features	Hinges (internal)	Jacket
1st binding variant 'B1'	Larger typeface – 19–20 mm long	Book 23 mm thick. Lettering to spine less golden, more silver.	Mull evident under endpaper at hinges, not extending to top/tail of endpaper. Hinge with vertical lip of *c.* 4 mm.	Jacket with original printed price of £2.50 net, or repriced at £3.50.
2nd binding variant variant 'B2'	Smaller typeface – 17 mm long	Book 21.5mm thick. Lettering to spine golden gilt	Binding tape evident under endpaper at hinges, which extends to top/tail of EP. Hinge flattish with *c.* 2 mm vertical lip.	Jacket invariably repriced at £3.50, £4.00, £4.95 and £5.50.

titles not numbered and not necessarily in series sequence; followed by five 'Special Volumes' and then individual adverts for 13 titles. (*Fleas; Wild Orchids; Amphibians & Reptiles; Mammals; Wild Flowers of Chalk; Birds and Men, Life in Lakes; Botanical Illustration; British Plant Life; Sea Shore; Mountains and Moorlands; Snowdonia; Highlands and Islands.*) 2) All dust jacket text printed in blue.

NN24B First Reprint, 1962 (20 February 1962). 'First published 1952 | Reprinted 1962'; no date to the title page. As NN24A. Minimal revisions: address to TP reset, without building no.; adverts at the rear revised: The New Naturalist library lists nos. 1–45 inclusively (titles now numbered) and Special Volumes lists nos. M1–M19, omitting M6, M8, M10 and M14. The remaining four and half pp. of adverts revised. Rear panel of jacket with NN library listings NN1–44; last paragraph of blurb omitted, but augmented with two press endorsements; rear flap with adverts for *Wild Orchids* and *Weeds & Aliens*; all text printed in blue. Price: 30s. net. Print run: 1,500; no. sold: *c.* 1,420; o/p: summer 1965.

NN24C Second Reprint, 1966. (Jan 1966). 'First published 1952 | Reprinted 1962 | Reprinted 1966'. As NN24B. Adverts to rear of the book unaltered but for addition of M20 *The Wood Pigeon*. The NN library to the jacket lists NN1–47, (Type 42, variant 6). Both flaps identical; all text is printed in blue. Price: 32s. net. Print run: 2,500; o/p: 1971.

NN24C-AP1 1st Repriced DJ (sold 1971), p. clipped, with Collins £1.60 sticker (unverified: but *c.* 300 books were sold in 1971 so, in accordance with decimalisation, would have been repriced).

NN24D-B1 Third Reprint, First Binding Variant, 1972. ISBN: 000213067x. 'First published 1952 | Reprinted 1962 | Reprinted 1966 | Reprinted 1972'. As NN24c, apparently several minor corrections, but none obvious. Editors: JG, JH, MD, KM and EH. Adverts at rear unchanged. The NN library to *Durasealed* jacket lists NN1–53, (Type 42, variant 10); both flaps unaltered; all text now printed in black, paper brighter white. Price: £2.50 net. For diagnostic binding features see table NN24. Print run: 2,500 inc. 'B2'; no. bound thus: *c.* 1,500:

NN24D-B1-AP1 1st Repriced DJ (1975–76), £3.50 sticker, *c.* 300 sold[?].

NN24D-B2 Third Reprint, Second Binding Variant, 1972 [bound up *c.* 1975]. The New Naturalist Statement dated 18/10/74 gives the stock for *Flowers of the Coast* as 477+ 930Q; i.e. 930 copies were held as unbound quires – and it is these copies that became this second binding variant. For diagnostic binding features see table NN24. (These variations are similar to the binding variants of NN59 *Ants* – see photos on page 346). The *Durasealed* jackets of this second binding will be, almost without exception, repriced as described below. Print run: included in 'B1'; no. bound thus: *c.* 900; no. sold: as below + 250 copies, in 1977, either remaindered or pulped, probably the former.

NN24D-B2-AP1 1st Repriced Jacket (1975). £3.00 sticker, no. sold: unknown.

NN24D-B2-AP2 2nd Repriced DJ (1975–76), £3.50 sticker, < 50 sold[?].

NN24D-B2-AP3 3rd Repriced DJ (1976–77), £4.50 sticker, *c.* 400 sold.

NN24D-B2-AP4 4th Repriced DJ (1978), £5.50 sticker, *c.* 180 sold.

POD24A Print-on-demand digital copy of the 1972 reprint NN24D.

25 The Sea Coast

First published in 1953, *The Sea Coast* was a successful title, reprinted within a year, with further editions in 1962, 1963, 1969 and finally 1972, spanning a 20-year period and amounting to around 19,000 copies. However, the number of books offered on the second-hand market does not appear to reflect this cornucopia: was it prescribed as a textbook? The 1962 third edition includes an additional 16-page appendix on the Great Flood, otherwise there are no significant revisions to any edition.

The jacket artwork, which paints a dramatic and bleak landscape; does not carry the C & RE monogram and additionally all editions fail to credit the Ellises as the jacket's designers.

The Sea Coast, with a first edition print run of only around 6,000 copies and a jacket that is colourfast but prone to chipping, is difficult to find in fine condition. Some of the reprints have fared better. There is a marked difference in the shade and intensity of the colour of jackets between editions; the 1972 edition is particularly different.

The Sea Coast finally went out of print in 1982, but was out of stock from 1959 to the beginning of 1962 and again from the end 1967 to the end of 1969.

NN25A   **First Edition**, 1953 (16 February 1953).
Title: 'The New Naturalist | The Sea Coast'.
Author: 'by | J. A. Steers | Professor of Geography | and President of St. Catherine's College | in the University of Cambridge'.
Illust: 'With 10 colour photographs | taken by the author | 24 photographs in black and white | 52 maps and diagrams'.
Editors: JF, JG, JH, LDS and EH.
Printer: Collins Clear-Type Press: London and Glasgow.
Collation: pp. xii, 276; 8 leaves of colour plates printed to one side only; 12 leaves of b/w plates printed to both sides (18 × 16-page gatherings).
Jacket: [Rear panel] The New Naturalist library listing nos. 1–27, the last two noted as being in preparation. [Rear flap] Special Volumes listing NN1–7; followed by adverts for *Sea Shore* and *Britain's Structure and Scenery*.
Price: 25s. net.
Print run: 6,000; o/p: 1954.

Notes: 1) Errata slip tipped on to page v – the map appearing on p. 98 was printed upside down and several captions transposed. 2) The Preface is dated May, 1952.

NN25B First Reprint, Second Edition, 1954. 'First published in 1953… | …Reprinted with corrections and minor additions 1954'; no date to title page. Essentially a reprint of the first edition. The map on p. 98 now correctly orientated and plates correctly captioned. A four line 'Preface to the Second Edition' dated January 1954, added below author's original preface; this identifies a few of the additions, including a reference to the great flood of 1953. All additions inserted without resetting text or changes to pagination; plates remain the same. The NN library to the jacket lists NN1–29 (in the same format); both flaps unaltered; price remains at 25s. net. Print run: 3,000; no. sold: c. 2,850; o/p: 1959. Note: Occasionally this edition is found with first edition jackets – presumably a few were left over from the earlier printing.

NN25C Third Edition, 1962 (Feb./March). 'First published in 1953… | … Second Edition 1954 | Third Edition 1962'. Collation: pp. xii, 292 (19 × 16-page gatherings); the number of plates as previous editions. A three line 'Preface to the Third Edition', dated July 1960, replaces the 'Preface to the 'Second Edition" and identifies that an [16 page] appendix entitled 'The Storm of 1953 and its Aftermath' has been added, otherwise as NN25B. Editors: JH now Sir JH. The paper brighter and smoother. The NN library to the jacket lists NN1–44 (Type 42, variant 3); rear flap advertises *The Sea Shore, Structure & Scenery* and *Oysters*; front flap unaltered. Price: 30s. net. Print run: 1,500; no. sold: c. 1,300[?]; o/p: 1963[?]. Note: There was a 20-month delay between the author writing the preface and the publication of this edition, despite the book being out of print during this period.

NN25D Third Edition Reprint, 1963. 'First published in 1953… | … Third Edition 1962 | Reprinted 1963'. As NN25C. The NN library to the jacket lists NN1–45 (Type 42, variant 4); both flaps unaltered; price remains at 30s. net. Print run: 2,500; no. sold: c. 2,300; o/p: end 1967. Note: There is no mention of the 1954 second edition in the printing history on the imprint page and this theme continues through subsequent editions.
NN25D-DJ1 Jacket Variant. Fitted with a 1962 NN25C jacket. (Presumably some jackets were left over from that earlier printing and used before the dedicated NN25D jacket.)

NN25E Fourth Edition, 1969 (Oct.). 'First published in 1953… | … Fourth Edition 1969'. Essentially as NN25D: a two line 'Preface to the Fourth Edition' has been inserted below the third edition preface, and states '…a note has been added to Chapter 9 in order to call attention to recent work on raised beds'; to accommodate this, the list of 'Botanical Names Used in the Text', has been deleted. Editors: JF, JG, JH, MD and EH. The NN library to the jacket lists NN1–50 (Type 42, variant 8); rear flap advertises *Mountain Flowers*, *Wild Orchids* and *Flowers of Chalk and Limestone*; front flap unaltered. Price: '(£1.80 net) | 36s. net', printed in brown ink to the corner – not clipped. Print run: 3,000; no. sold: c. 2,700.

Notes: 1) The DJ rear flap is replicated on the rear flap of *Pollination of Flowers*, 1st ed., 1972; 2) a repriced variant of the 1963 jacket also appears on this book as catalogued below.

NN25E-DJ1 Jacket Variant. With the 1963 jacket NN25D but price-clipped and over-printed '(£1.80 net) | 36s. net' in brown ink. (Presumably there were sufficient jackets left over from the 1963 reprint to warrant overprinting them, especially considering that the NN library displayed on the rear panel was by then significantly out of date.)

NN25F Fourth Edition Reprint, 1972. ISBN: 0002132044 (to jacket only). 'First published in 1953 | Fourth Edition 1969 | Reprinted 1972'. As NN25E. Editors: JG, JH, MD, KM and EH. Lettering to the spine casing is silver-gilt. The *Durasealed* jacket with stronger colours; the NN library lists NN1–54 (Type 42, variant 11); the rear flap unaltered but for ISBN; the blurb is new, shorter and supplemented with five press clips. Price: £2.25. Print run: 3,000; no. sold *c.* 350[?] + repriced jacket variants below + probably 1,000 copies sold off from stock to RU; o/p: 1981. Note: unclipped jackets are exceptional.

NN25F-AP1 1st Repriced DJ (1974–75). £2.50: *c.* 350.

NN25F-AP2 2nd Repriced DJ (1975). £3.00 sticker, no. sold: unknown.

NN25F-AP3 3rd Repriced DJ (1975–76), £3.50 sticker, *c.* 300 sold.

NN25F-AP4 4th Repriced DJ (1976–77), £4.50 sticker, *c.* 400 sold.

NN25F-AP5 5th Repriced DJ (1978–79), £5.50 sticker, *c.* 300 sold.

NN25F-AP6 6th Repriced DJ (1979–80), £6.00 sticker, *c.* 150 sold.

NN25F-AP7 7th Repriced DJ (1980–81), £7.50 sticker, *c.* 100 sold.

NN25F-AP8 8th Repriced DJ (1981), £8.50 sticker, < 50 sold.

POD25A Print-on-demand digital copy of the 1972 reprint NN25F.

26 The Weald

The casing, jacket and title page of *The Weald* proclaim Wooldrige and Goldring as the authors, but in fact the text was solely written by Wooldridge and the photographs taken almost exclusively by Goldring. Apparently, the double authorship was a hangover from the time when colour photographs were regarded as a, if not *the*, critical selling point of the New Naturalist and where the photographer, working with the idiosyncrasies of primitive equipment, had to be more skilful than his modern counterpart. That being said there are many examples of foregoing NN titles where prominent photographers have not been credited with authorship e.g. *Butterflies, Sea Shore* and *A Country Parish*.

It is tempting to look back at the early days of the New Naturalist series and believe that all was well and somehow better than today, but as King Solomon pointed out, several thousand years earlier, this notion is not one spawned of wisdom. In the case of *The Weald*, the Editors managed to lose the manuscript and Wooldridge had to use a carbon copy for corrections. Additionally, the important NN credo was accidentally omitted and it was not until the fifth impression of 1972 that it was reinstated. There were other omissions too: perhaps due to the very long blurb, which left no space, the jacket designers went uncredited in all editions. And there was a bungle over the price of the 1962 third impression – priced, then clipped, then over-printed, then repriced with a label – at the original price! Then a new jacket was printed and this too had the wrong price so again had to be overprinted at the original price.

The Weald was reprinted four times but never updated, all revisions restricted to minor corrections and a short additional appendix on Piltdown Man. Perhaps the greatest oversight of the book was the omission of a general map. The Editors recognizing this stated that it was essential to include a map in all future editions, but this did not happen. Instead, in all reprints the suite of colour plates was reduced from sixteen to eight. Clearly, a title where the first edition is superior to reprints.

The colours of the 1960 reprint jacket are distinctly different from that of earlier and later jackets, generally more sombre, greyer, the grass a sage green, and the sky with more red in the blue – see illustration. The jackets of all editions, barring the 1972 reprint, are somewhat prone to chipping and toning. Total print run: *c.* 15,000; o/p: 1981, though it was o/s between 1956 and 1960.

NN26A	**First Edition**, 1953 [16 March 1953].
Title:	'The New Naturalist	The Weald'.
Authors:	'S. W. Wooldridge	C.B.E. D.Sc	Professor of Geography in the	University of London at King's College	and	Frederick Goldring'.
Illust:	'With 16 colour photographs	25 black and white photographs	and 53 maps and diagrams'.
Editors:	JF, JG, JH, LDS and EH.
Printer:	Collins Clear-Type Press: London and Glasgow.
Collation:	pp. x, 276, [2 NN adverts]; 16 leaves of colour plates printed to one side only; 12 leaves of b/w plates printed to both sides (18 × 16-page gatherings).
Jacket:	Front panel: Bright sap-green grass and bright blue sky, hedgerows dark green. Rear panel: *Snowdonia*; *Dartmoor* and *The Broads* are listed under the title 'In preparation' (The latter was not published for another 20 years). Rear flap: Adverts for *Climate and the British Scene, Mountains and Moorlands* and *A Natural History of Man in Britain*.
Price:	25s. net.
Print run:	6,000; no. sold: *c.* 5,650; o/p: unknown but it was o/s in Oct. 1956.
Notes:	1) The NN credo has accidentally been omitted. 2) The

recto of the last leaf advertises 'The New Naturalist A Survey of British Natural History' listing 23 titles already published; the verso advertises Special Volumes listing 5 titles with specific advert for *The Fulmar*. 3) All photographs are by Goldring with the exception of the Dartford Warbler which is by Eric Hosking. 4) The blurb at 384 words is about the longest found on any NN jacket.

NN26B First Reprint, 1960. 'First Published 1953 | Reprinted 1962'. No date to the TP. The no. of colour plates has been reduced to eight as reflected in the illustrations subtitle and list of plates, but printed to both sides, reducing the leaves of colour plates to four. A new Appendix B has been added to p. 253 – 'Notes on Piltdown Man | Addendum to Chapter 12', and what was Appendix B has become Appendix C; the adverts at the rear of the book have been omitted, the last leaf now blank. All other revisions appear to be restricted to minor corrections. The dust jacket colours are distinctly more sombre, greyer, the grass a sage green, the sky a dull blue with more red and the hedgerows dark grey-green; the NN library lists NN1–42 (same format as NN library to the *Dragonflies* jacket); the rear flap partly revised, substituting *Dartmoor* for *Climate and the British Scene*, otherwise unaltered as is the front flap. Price: 30s. net. Print run: 2,000; no. sold: *c.* 1,600; o/p: 1962.

NN26C-DJ1 Third Impression, First Jacket Variant, 1962. 'First Published 1953 | Second Impression 1960 | Third Impression 1962'. A reprint of NN26B without revisions or corrections. The jacket identical to NN26B including colour, but for the pricing arrangement: it would appear that the printed price was 30s. net, but it was agreed to increase the price to 35s. net, so the original price was clipped off and the new price overprinted along the bottom edge; however it then seems that there was a change of mind and it was decided the book should remain at the original price, so a 30s. net label was pasted over the 35s. net overprint (this jacket was probably not a new printing but a residue from the 1960 printing). Print run: 1,500; no. sold: *c.* 1,000[?] inc. DJ2 below.

NN26C-DJ2 Third Impression, Second Jacket Variant, 1962 [Sold: from 1963]. New jacket printing for NN26C. The jacket colours are much nearer the first edition NN26A but the sky now a mauve-blue, the NN library lists NN1–44 (Type 42, variant 3a); both flaps identical but for price: original price clipped from corner and overprinted 30s. net. No. jackets printed: unknown; o/p: 1966.

NN26D Fourth Impression, 1966. 'First Published 1953 | Second Impression 1960 | Third Impression 1962 | Fourth impression 1966'. Identical to NN26C. The jacket colours very near first edition NN26A; the NN library lists NN1–46 (Type 42, variant 5); *The Peak District* replaces *Natural History of Man* on rear flap, otherwise unchanged. Price: 30s. net. Print run: 2,500; no. sold: *c.* 2,100[?]; o/p: 1970/71.

NN26E Fifth Impression, 1972. ISBN: 0002132508. 'First Published

1953 | Second Impression 1960 | Third Impression 1962 | Fourth impression 1966 | Fifth impression 1972'. Editors: MD, JH, JG, KM and EH; the NN credos reinstated in shortened form. The NN library to the *Durasealed* jacket lists NN1–53 (Type 42, variant 10); rear flap unaltered but for addition of the ISBN; the blurb to the front flap rewritten and much shorter; now with press review by the *Kentish Express*. Price: £2.25 net. Print run: 3,000; no. sold: *c.* 1,550[?] plus repriced jacket variants below.

NN26E-AP1 1st Repriced DJ (1975?), £3.00 sticker, no. sold: unknown.
NN26E-AP2 2nd Repriced DJ (1975–76), £3.50 sticker, *c.* 280 sold inc. AP1.
NN26E-AP3 3rd Repriced DJ (1976–77), £4.50 sticker, *c.* 380 sold.
NN26E-AP4 4th Repriced DJ (1978–79), £5.50 sticker, *c.* 250 sold.
NN26E-AP5 5th Repriced DJ (1979–80), £6.00 sticker, *c.* 150 sold.
NN26E-AP6 6th Repriced DJ (1980–81), £7.50 sticker, *c.* 100 sold.
NN26E-AP7 7th Repriced DJ (1981), £8.50 sticker, < 50 sold.

POD26A Print-on-demand digital copy of the 1972 fifth impression NN26E.

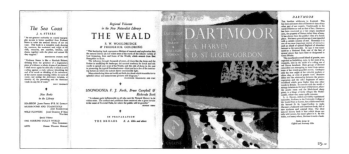

27 Dartmoor

While two authors are cited, *Dartmoor* is essentially Harvey's book; D. St. Leger-Gordon contributed only two chapters. It seems the two were aloof and it is perhaps telling that the Author's preface, written by Harvey, makes no mention of Leger-Gordon. Nor does Harvey's preface to the third edition, even though Leger-Gordon had died a few years earlier. Probably just an oversight, but it is not however rare for joint authors to become estranged.

The 1953 first edition did not sell particularly quickly and remained in print until 1960. It then went out of print for a couple of years until the second edition was published in 1962. Strangely it was reprinted within the year: presumably the uptake, following *Dartmoor's* two years absence from bookshop shelves, was much greater than Collins had envisaged, however the critical sales-sheets for the period 1962–1964 are missing, so quantities printed and sold remain ambiguous. *Dartmoor* went out of print for a second time from 1968–1970 and, then, for a third time from 1975–1978. While the third edition is dated 1977 it did not actually appear until spring 1978.

In the interim *Dartmoor* was published as a Fontana New Naturalist, which enabled extensive corrections and additions. There was an amount of debate at Collins regarding the profitability of this title in paperback format and the New

Naturalist Statement of April 1973 records 'Fontana edition unlikely (M.A.W. 28/2/72)'. Eventually, the decision was taken to publish, but it was probably the wrong one, as it was a poor seller. However it enabled the third hardback edition, which is, in fact, an enlarged photographic copy of the Fontana type setting and likewise omits the colour plates. This was a cost-saving expediency, as was the contract to supply a number of copies, of the third edition, to the Readers Union. These bookclub editions are almost identical but with the usual bookclub telltale features.

The first edition of *Dartmoor* is not a particularly difficult title to find in very good or fine condition, but the jacket, though not quick to fade, does, and is also prone to tanning.

Total print run: c. 14,000 (Collins) + 500 (RU); o/p: end of 1982.

NN27A   **First Edition**, 1953 (31 August 1953).
Title: 'The New Naturalist | Dartmoor'.
Authors: 'by | L. A. Harvey | and | D. St. Leger-Gordon'.
Illust: With 17 colour photographs | by E. H. Ware | 36 photographs in black and white | and 3 maps of the area'.
Editors: JF, JG, JH, LDS and EH (Photographic Editor).
Printer: Collins Clear-Type Press: London and Glasgow.
Collation: pp. xiv, 273, [1 – NN library]; 16 leaves of colour plates printed to one side only; 12 leaves of b/w plates printed to both sides (18 × 16-page gatherings).
Jacket: Rear panel: 'Regional Volumes in the New Naturalist Library', featuring *The Weald* and *Snowdonia*; *The Broads* appears under the heading 'In Preparation'. Rear flap: Advert for *The Sea Coast*; 'New Books in the Library' lists *Sea Birds*, *Mushrooms and Toadstools* and *Wild Flowers*, and as 'special volumes' *The Herring Gull's World* and *Ants*.
Price: 25s. net.
Print run: 6,500; total no. sold: c. 6,150; o/p: early 1961.
Notes: 1) Advert to p. [273] for: 'The New Naturalist A Survey of British Natural History' listing 18 titles 'Already published in the Main Series' followed by send postcard for information of each NN as published. 2) The DJ rear panel states that *The Broads* is in preparation but, in fact, it did not appear for a further 10 years. 3) The only New Naturalist to advertise Wragge Morley's *Ants* on the jacket. 4) Book 25 mm thick.

NN27B Second Edition, 1962 (02 July 1962). 'First published 1953 | Second edition 1962'; no date to the title page. Chapter 10 'Prehistoric Civilisations' completely rewritten and text reset, otherwise revisions confined to minor corrections and updates. JH now Sir JH and JG awarded V. M. H. Pagination and plates unaltered. The NN library to the last page omitted. The NN library to the jacket lists NN1–45 (Type 42, variant 4); rear flap carries an advertisement for *The Peak District* (an almost exact copy of the jacket blurb to the first edition of that title); blurb to front flap

omitted and five press endorsements inserted; the jacket design credit also omitted. Price: 30s.net. Print run: c. 1,500[?]

NN27C Second Edition, First Reprint, 1963. 'First published 1953 | Second edition 1962 | Reprinted 1963'. Book and jacket identical in every respect to NN27B. Price remains 30s.net. Print run: c. 2,500[?]; o/p: 1968.

NN27D Second Edition, Second Reprint, 1970. SBN 002130564 (to jacket only). 'First published 1953 | Second edition 1962 | Reprinted 1963 | Reprinted 1970'. As NN27C. Editors: JF, JG, JH, MD and EH. The NN library to the jacket lists NN1–50 (Type 42, variant 8), both flaps unaltered but for insertion of SBN to rear: Price: £2.25 net | 45s. net. Print run: 2,000; no. sold: c. 1,800; o/p: early 1975.

NN27D-AP1 1st Repriced DJ, £3.00 sticker, no. sold: unknown.

NN27E Third Edition, 1977 (1978). ISBN changed to 0002194236. 'First published 1953 | Second edition 1962 | Reprinted 1963 | Reprinted 1970 | Third edition 1977'; pp. 288; 8 leaves of b/w plates printed to both sides (18 × 16-page gatherings). The 'preface to the third edition' is dated December 1972: this edition copied from the 1974 Fontana edition FPB27A (blow-ups of the Fontana plates) and therefore text setting completely different to the previous Collins editions. The lengthy lists of plants and animals excised and in their place two additional chapters entitled 'Retrospective I' and 'Retrospective II', inserted. Colour plates omitted and number of b/w plates reduced, though some new photographs introduced. Editors: MD, JG, KM and EH. Last sentence of NN credo omitted. Book thinner, only 23 mm. The *Durasealed* jacket essentially unchanged from second edition jacket of 15 years earlier: the NN library lists NN 1–61 (Type 42, variant 16); ISBN to rear flap changed to suit; the Ellises design credit reinstated to front flap, one review omitted, otherwise unchanged. Price: £7.50 net printed diagonally with dotted line. Print run: 1,500; no. sold: c. 760 + repriced variants below + probably c. 400 copies remaindered to the RU.

NN27E-AP1 1st Repriced DJ (1981–82), £8.50 sticker, c. 100 sold[?].
NN27E-AP2 2nd Repriced DJ (1982), £9.50 sticker, c. 50 sold.

BC27A Readers Union Edition, 1977 (1978). Bound from the same sheets as the Collins third edition NN27E and almost indistinguishable but for following diagnostic features: casing of dark green imitation cloth; jacket identical but without a *Duraseal* protector and without a printed price. Print run: 500. A scarce edition.

POD27A Print-on-demand digital copy of the 1970 second edition, second reprint NN27D.

FPB27A Fontana Paperback Edition, 1974 (May). ISBN 0006334695; pp. 288; 8 leaves of b/w plates printed on glossy paper to both sides (18 × 16-page gatherings). Two new chapters entitled 'Retrospective I' and 'Retrospective II', replace the lists of plants and animals – as explained in the 'Preface to the Third Edition'. A reduced number of b/w plates only, but several new photographs have been

introduced. The subtitle to TP reads 'The Fontana New Naturalist'.
Advert for the New Naturalist series at front lists 17 titles available
in Fontana, inc. Lack's *The Life of the Robin*. Editors: JG, JH, MD, KM
and EH. The front cover photograph, by Barnaby's Picture Library,
features *Brent Tor, Dartmoor*. Price: 75p. Print run: 11,000; no. sold:
unknown, but it is likely that some copies were pulped. Notes: 1)
Dartmoor was not reprinted in Fontana p/b format; 2) the preface is
dated December 1972, *St Mary's, Isles of Scilly*, but the book was not
published until 1974 – Collins deliberated over the merits or
otherwise of publishing this edition.

28 Sea-Birds

Sea-Birds (note the hyphen) was commissioned in 1947, then with
the title 'Sea-Birds of the North Atlantic'. The reference to the
North Atlantic was retained as a subtitle, though this element is
rarely included in references. *Sea-Birds* remained in print for just
eight years, a particularly short period for a New Naturalist of that
era. Conflicting opinions, competing agendas and commercial
exigencies conspired to restrict *Sea-Birds* to just one impression.
Board minutes and sales-sheets record various proposals to
reprint in both hardback and Fontana softback formats, but
repeated delays brought the book to the point where it was so out
of date that only a completely new book would suffice. In the late
1960s and early 1970s the board looked at appointing various
authors to collaborate with Fisher on a fresh book and, at one
point or another, Dr W. R. P. (Bill) Bourne, Bryan Nelson, John C.
Coulson and George Dunnet were mentioned, but it was not to be.

Sea-Birds was published, more or less concurrently, in the US by
Houghton Mifflin, Boston who purchased 2,500 sets of printed
sheets from Collins. It was also subsequently reprinted in 1989 by
Bloomsbury.

An errata slip was printed for *Sea-Birds*, though it is unlikely that
one was issued with every book as few copies have them;
occasionally one is tipped onto the front free endpaper; conversely
an errata (of slightly different format) is found in all US books.

Sea-Birds was traditionally one of the rarest and most
sought-after titles in the series but it has become much more
readily available in the last twenty years or so. The jacket, one of
the most iconic of all, suffers a little from fading but more so
from browning. Fine, bright copies, their deep crimson unsullied,
are rich pleasures indeed: be patient and seek out the very best.

ERRATA

p. 5, line 22 should read: (See Fig. 54, page
  290.)
p. 132 line 4, for *Larns*, read *Larus*
Pl. XIV, opp. p. 133, transpose captions of
  a and *b*
p. 161. Caption fig. 29; last line should read:
  and *P.p. gavia* as far south as Cook Strait.
p. 206. Caption fig. 36; for Red-cormorant,
  read Reed-cormorant
Pl. XXXIV*b*, opp. p. 261, for Tern, read
  Terns

Errata slip for *Sea-Birds* that only appears in some copies.

NN28A **First Edition**, 1954 (01 March 1954).
Title: 'The New Naturalist | Sea-Birds | An Introduction to
         the | Natural History of the Sea-Birds of | the North
         Atlantic'.
Authors: 'by James Fisher | and | R. M. Lockley'.
Illust: 'With 9 colour photographs | 63 black and white
          photographs | and 66 maps and diagrams'.
Editors: JF, JG, JH, LDS and EH (Photographic Editor).
Printer: Willmer Brothers & Co. Ltd., Birkenhead.
Collation: pp. xvi, 320; colour frontispiece leaf printed to verso
           only; 6 leaves of colour plates printed to one side
           only; 20 leaves of b/w plates printed to both sides
           (21 × 16-page gatherings).
Jacket: [Rear panel] 'The New Naturalist, listing *The Sea Coast,
          Birds and Men* and *The Fulmar*'. [Rear flap] Some New
          Naturalist Publications, listing six titles.
Price: 25s. net.
Print run: 10,000; o/p: end 1961.
Notes: 1) Errata slipped occasionally loosely inserted or
          tipped-in on front free endpaper. 2) Printed above the
          rear jacket flap lower edge 'See list at end of this book
          for all New Naturalist volumes published to date',
          though this list does not exist in the book.

POD28A Print-on-demand digital copy.

BL28A Bloomsbury Edition, 31 December 1989. ISBN 1870630882;
pp. xvi, 320; 54 pages of integrated b/w illustrations. A b/w
facsimile (the errors identified on the errata slip have not been
corrected). Price: £12.95. Print run: unknown, but a significant
proportion remaindered.

US28A US Edition Houghton Mifflin Company, Boston. The
Riverside Press, Cambridge. 1954. Hardback with jacket; 155 × 223
mm, i.e. same format as Collins edition. Bound from the same

sheets as NN28A with same plates, but with integral title/imprint leaf carrying the HM imprint etc; original half-title leaf now blank; errata slip (different format to Collins slip) tipped onto p. v. Bound (probably in the US) in aquamarine cloth with gilt lettering. DJ designer uncredited; front panel carries strap line 'A lively exploration of the birds who share with us our ocean frontiers'; rear panel: 'Houghton Mifflin's library of bird books' listing seven titles; blurb to both flaps, unique to this edition. Price: $6.00. Print run: 2,500.

29 The World of the Honeybee

Not surprisingly this famous book was reprinted several times, and while other New Naturalist titles have sold many more copies, the *Honeybee*, in Collins hardback format, has more editions/ impressions than any other: eight in total. There are also two US editions and a Readers Union edition, but it is perhaps surprising that it was never published as a Fontana paperback as, undoubtedly, it would have sold well in that cheaper format.

The World of the Honeybee persisted in print for 34 years, its reviews were universerally positive; one bee-keeping periodical stated 'every serious beekeeper should have it' and the *British Bee Journal* commented 'One of the best books of this century on bees'. It remains popular with apiculturists today; some editions, particularly the American ones are virtually unobtainable.

During its long shelf-life it was revised three times, the 1974 revision being the most significant, but even that was not radically different from the first edition. Notwithstanding, in terms of content, this edition is the one to have, or its two subsequent reprints.

One strange and somewhat irksome feature of the *Honeybee* is its format: smaller than the main series and larger than the monographs. The story goes that because the *Honeybee* fell between two camps, Collins decided it should be in a 'standard biography page format', i.e. about 218/9 mm tall compared with 222/3 mm for the main series, but in a series of books where continuity was clearly so important, it was a curious decision. The 1977 reprint is a couple of mm shorter still.

There is considerable variation in the colours of the various jacket editions, the earlier ones tend to be softer and creamier, the later 1970s jackets are much brighter and more orangey. Unfortunately the first edition jacket is particularly susceptible to fading, not to mention chipping and toning. It is what is described, in the trade, as a 'difficult title'.

Total no. Collins books printed: *c.* 24,500 (it is likely that this figure includes *c.* 3,000 copies sold to US publisher and RU); o/p: 1985.

NN29A	**First Edition**, 1954 (24 May 1954).
Title:	'The New Naturalist | The World of the | Honeybee'.
Author:	'by | Colin G. Butler | M.A., Ph.D. | Head of the Bee Department | Rothamsted Experimental Station'.
Illust:	'With 2 colour photographs | and 87 black and white photographs | taken by the author'.
Editors:	JF, JG, JH, LDS and EH (Photographic Editor).
Printer:	Willmer Brothers & Co. Ltd., Birkenhead.
Collation:	pp. xiv, 226; 2 leaves of colour plates printed to one side only; 20 leaves of b/w plates printed to both sides (15 × 16-page gatherings).
Jacket:	Rear panel: 'Three successful volumes in the Main Series' – *Insect Natural History*, *An Angler's Entomology* and *Flowers of the Coast*. Rear flap: 'Some recent publications in the New Naturalist Library' listing special, and main series volumes with 'in preparation' volumes below.
Price:	21s. net.
Print run:	8,000; total no. sold: *c.* 7,620; o/p: early 1957 (These figures probably include *c.* 1,000 copies sold to Macmillan of USA, so figures for Collins ed. less *c.* 1,000.)
Notes:	Boards 218–9 mm tall.

NN29B First Edition, First Reprint, 1958. 'First Published 1954 \| Reprinted 1958.' Printed by Collins Clear-Type Press. No date to the TP. No apparent textual revisions. The NN library to the jacket lists NN1–35, omitting NN6 and 26; (Type 36) the rear flap with adverts for *Moths*, *Butterflies* and *Insect Natural History*; the blurb to the front flap, unaltered, but inserted below are three press commendations. The jacket has been price-clipped and a new price of 25s. net overprinted diagonally (presumably the jacket was printed originally with a price of 21s. net but most copies seem to have been clipped and over-printed). Print run: 4,000; no. sold: *c.* 4,100[?]; o/p: autumn 1961 (these figures may well include the 1959 Readers Union edition and if so require a downward adjustment of *c.* 2,100).

NN29C First Revised Edition, 1962. 'First edition 1954 \| Reprinted 1958 \| Revised edition 1962'. Only a few minor (though significant) revisions, e.g. footnote added to p. 58, info. on 'queen substance' added to pp. 107 and 109–110. The NN library to the jacket lists NN1–44 (Type 42, variant 3); the rear flap, unchanged but for the omission of *Insect Natural History*; front flap as NN29B. Price: 25s. net but now printed to the corner. Print run: 2,000[?]; o/p: spring 1966.

NN29D First Revised Edition, First Reprint, 1967 (early). 'First edition 1954 \| Reprinted 1958 \| Revised edition 1962 \| Reprinted 1967'. Editors' page reset otherwise appears exact reprint of NN29C, though the archive alludes to revisions having been made.

The NN library to the jacket lists NN1–47 (Type 42, variant 6); *Insect Migration* added to the rear flap which otherwise is unchanged; the front flap has an additional press review (*The Economist*). Price: 30s. net. Print run: 2,000; o/p: 1970.

NN29E First Revised Edition, Second Reprint, 1971. ISBN: 0002132540 'First edition 1954 | Reprinted 1958 | Revised edition 1962 | Reprinted 1967 | Reprinted 1971'. As NN29D. The jacket is *Durasealed*, the NN library lists NN1–52 (Type 42, variant 9); otherwise unchanged. Price: £2.10 net. Print run: 2,000; no. sold: c. 1,750[?]; o/p: summer 1974. Note: Often with silver-gilt lettering to the casing.

NN29F Second Revised Edition, 1974 [Jan 1975]. ISBN: 0002132540 (book); 0002195526 (Jacket). 'First edition 1954 | Reprinted 1958 | Revised edition 1962 | Reprinted 1967 | Reprinted 1971 | Revised edition 1974'; pp. [2], xii, 226. Plates unchanged. This ed. more substantially revised than any other, but still not greatly different from the first ed. The Editors' preface omitted and the author's preface with the title 'Preface to the Third Edition' (which of course it is), in which the author states there have been many changes to the text and many parts rewritten. While clearly the case, and therefore the best edition to have, the illustrations remain the same as does the majority of the type setting. Editors: MD, JH, JG, KM and EH; last sentence of credo omitted. The NN library, to the *Durasealed* jacket, lists NN1–58 (Type 42, variant 14); the rear flap, unaltered but for insertion of jacket design credit; the front flap blurb, unchanged but a new paragraph has been added that begins 'Fully revised and up-dated, this new edition....'; and one review omitted (*The Economist*). Price: £2.95 net. Print run: 1,500; no. sold: 1,160[?]; o/p: April 1975.
NN29F-AP1 1st Repriced DJ (1975), £2.95 sticker (why would Collins reprice at the same price?).

NN29G Second Revised Edition, First Reprint, 1976. ISBN now 0002195526 to book and jacket. 'First edition 1954 | Reprinted 1958 | Revised edition 1962 | Reprinted 1967 | Reprinted 1971 | Revised edition 1974 | Reprinted 1976'. Book and jacket textually identical to NN29F. Paper slightly textured. Price: £4.95 net, printed diagonally. Print run: 2,000; no. sold: c.1,950[?]; o/p: 1978[?] (AP1).
NN29G-AP1 1st Repriced DJ (1977–78?), £5.95 sticker, no. sold: unknown.

NN29H Second Revised Edition, Second Reprint, 1977. ISBN unchanged. 'First edition 1954 | Reprinted 1958 | Revised edition 1962 | Reprinted 1967 | Reprinted 1971 | Revised edition 1974 | Reprinted 1976 | Reprinted 1976'. Textually identical to NN29G. Editors: MD, JG, KM and EH. Boards only 216/217 mm tall. The NN table to the jacket lists NN1–60 (Type 42, variant 15), otherwise DJ as NN29F. Price: £5.95 net printed diagonally. Print run: 2,500; no. sold: c. 700[?] + repriced variants below, + tranche of 350 pulped or remaindered; o/p: 1985.
NN29H-AP1 1st Repriced DJ (1980–81), £7.50 sticker, c. 300 sold.
NN29H-AP2 2nd Repriced DJ (1981), £8.50 sticker, c. 150 sold.

NN29H-AP3 3rd Repriced DJ (1981–83), £9.50 sticker, c. 400 sold.
NN29H-AP4 4th Repriced DJ (1984–85), £7.50 sticker, c. 300 sold.

BC29A Readers Union First Edition, 1959. Exactly as the Collins 1958 reprint NN29B but with an integral title page displaying the RU imprint and tree logo, dated 1959. Casing of a unique green cloth, blocked in gilt with the RU logo to the spine. Green RU jacket 'Type 2'. Price: 15/- net. Print run: c. 2,100[?]

BC29B Readers Union Revised Edition, 1977. Bound from the same sheets as the Collins 1977 reprint NN29H and therefore textually identical. Casing of dark green imitation cloth. Jacket also identical but without a *Duraseal* protector and always price-clipped. Print run: 500.

POD29A Print-on-demand digital copy of the 1977 reprint NN29H.

US29A US First Edition, 1955. Macmillan. Not seen. Possibly with no other distinguishing mark than a Macmillan sticker or distribution stamp. Print run: c. 850 (possibly 975 supplied).

US29B US Second Revised Edition, 1975. ISBN: 0800839242. Taplinger, New York. Not seen. From the same printing as the Collins second revised edition NN29f. Print run: 500.

FOR29A German Edition, 1957. 'Die Honigbiene | Mit 47 Fotos des Verfassers'. Published by Eugen Diederichs Verlag Düsseldorf– Köln. Hardback with dust jacket; 145 × 208 mm, i.e. same format as Collins original; pp. 197, [3]; 12 leaves of b/w plates printed to both sides. All associations with the New Naturalist have been omitted including Editors' and Author's prefaces; reduced no. of b/w plates and without colour frontispiece. Bound in red-mahogany cloth, blocked with gilt lettering. The multicoloured jacket unpriced, designer uncredited. Print run: unknown, but not a scarce book.

30 Moths

Ford states in the introduction to Chapter 2 '...this is virtually the second volume of a work upon British Lepidoptera, of which *Butterflies*, already published in the New Naturalist series is the first'. *Moths* was planned to follow on the heels of *Butterflies*, but, in fact, did not appear for a further nine years.

Moths was sold over a 26-year period, but was out of stock for 12 months or so in 1966/67 and again in 1971 and in 1975/76. This protracted sales period required three reprints, but it did not get close to the success of Ford's first volume, with sales of *Moths* being only around one-quarter those of *Butterflies*.

A few hundred copies of the first edition were also sold in the US under the imprint Macmillan, and now a rare variant, particularly with the original jacket. A small batch of the 1976 reprint were bound up in imitation cloth and sold by the Readers Union, but in all other respects are identical to the Collins reprint. Otherwise *Moths* was not republished in any other format.

The dark tones of the *Moths* jacket mean that chips and tears are more conspicuous and it is a jacket that is prone to edge-wear but, on the plus side, it rarely fades. Total print run: 14,500 (Collins) + 460 (Macmillan – USA) + 500 (RU); o/p: late 1980.

NN30A	**First Edition**, 1955 (28 February 1955).
Title:	'The New Naturalist | Moths'.
Author:	'by | E. B. Ford | F.R.S. | Genetic Laboratories | Zoology Department, Oxford'.
Illust:	'With 77 photographs in colour | 71 photographs in black and white | taken by S. Beaufoy | 19 maps and diagrams'.
Editors:	JF, JG, JH, LDS and EH (Photographic Editor).
Printer:	Collins Clear-Type Press: London and Glasgow.
Collation:	pp. xix, [1], 266, [2-NN adverts]; 16 leaves of colour plates printed to both sides; 12 leaves of b/w plates printed to both sides (18 × 16-page gatherings).
Jacket:	[Rear panel] Advert for *The World of the Honeybee*. [Rear flap] Advert for *Butterflies* 'By the author of this Book'. 'Also in the Library main series' are listed *Insect Natural History* and *An Angler's Entomology* and as special volumes' *Fleas, Flukes & Cuckoos* and *Mumps, Measles & Mosaics*. Book details request.
Price:	35s. net.
Print run:	8,500; total no. sold: *c.* 8,140; o/p: early 1966.
Notes:	1) The two pages of adverts at the rear include 'The New Naturalist A Survey of British Natural History'; main series and special vols; and an advert for *Butterflies*. 2) Book 27½ mm thick.

NN30B Second Edition, 1967. 'First edition 1955 \| Second edition 1967'; no date to title page. The preface to the second edition states that the '…book has been extensively revised and also contains certain additional passages…', however these revisions and additions have been more or less incorporated into the existing typesetting, and pagination remains unaltered. Chapter 13 on melanism, significantly revised. The title and Editors' pages partly reset with Ford's post-nominals revised; Editors: JF, JG, JH, MD and EH. The NN adverts at rear unaltered. The plates are inferior, not as crisp, but textual printing and paper of an equal quality. Book 25 mm thick. The NN library to the jacket, lists NN1–50 (Type 42, variant 8); rear flap reset, carries same

advert for *Butterflies*, but titles listed under heading 'Also in the Library' are now: *Insect Natural History, The World of the Honeybee, Insect Migration, The World of Spiders, Bumblebees* and *Dragonflies*; Blurb to front flap précised with two press endorsements inserted below. Price: 45s.net. Print run: 2,000; o/p: 1970.

NN30C Third Edition, 1972. ISBN: 0002131412. 'First edition 1955 \| Second edition 1967 \| Third edition 1972'. As NN30B with minimal revisions. Editors: JG, JH, MD, KM and EH. Ford's post-nominals to the title page changed again. The two-page adverts at the rear substantially revised and now feature eight 'insect' titles, each with endorsing press snippet. The caption for image 2 of plate XI is incorrect and should read 'Waved Black', not 'Waved Umber' (much to the annoyance of Ford). B/w plates generally inferior, but colour plates are, if anything, an improvement. The NN library to the *Durasealed* jacket lists NN 1–54 (Type 42, variant 11); rear flap caries adverts for *Butterflies, The World of the Honeybee* and *Insect Natural History*, and ISBN added; the customary blurb to the front flap has been substituted by three press commendations. The colours of the jacket greener and brighter. Price: £2.50[?] Print run: 2,500; no. sold: *c.* 2,380 inc. repriced variant below; o/p: 1974 (AP1).
NN30C-AP1 1st Repriced DJ (1973–74), £3.00 sticker.

NN30D Third Edition, Reprint, 1976. ISBN changed to 0002194716. 'First edition 1955 \| Second edition 1967 \| Third edition 1972 \| Reprinted 1976'. Editors: JG, MD, KM and EH. Last sentence of NN credo omitted. Adverts at rear omitted leaving two blank pages. The image 2 caption of plate XI corrected. Reproduction of colour plates inferior to NN30C, but b/w plates similar quality. Book 24 mm thick. The NN library to the *Durasealed* jacket lists NN1–58 (Type 42, variant 14); flaps unchanged but for revised ISBN to the rear. Price: all copies price-clipped – see note below. Print run: 1,500; no. sold: see repriced variants below. Note: It appears that the jacket was printed with the incorrect price: a note in the March 1976 sales-sheet states '2,500 copies to be reprinted at £6.00', yet all books sold at this price have been clipped and repriced with a Collins £6.00 sticker. The reference to '2,500' was also incorrect: in the event 2,000 copies were printed of which 500 sold directly to the RU – see BC30A.
NN30D-AP1 1st Repriced DJ (1976–80), £6.00 sticker, *c.* 1,200 sold.
NN30D-AP2 2nd Repriced DJ (1980), £7.50 sticker, *c.* 150 sold.

BC30A Readers Union Edition, 1976. Bound up from the same sheets as NN30D, but in dark green imitation cloth. *Durasealed* jacket identical, always price clipped and without a Collins price sticker. Print run: 500.

POD30A Print-on-demand digital copy of the 1976 reprint NN30D.

US30A US Edition, 1955. The Macmillan Company, New York. Bound from the same sheets as Collins first edition NN30A, but with a cancel title leaf that states: 'The Macmillan Company \| New York'; and omits the date and NN monogram; the verso states

'First published in the U.S.A. in 1955', otherwise layout unaltered. Bound in same green buckram but 'Macmillan' blocked to the spine and NN monogram omitted. Jacket not seen, but probably the same Ellis design, with a similar layout to the 1957 Macmillan edition of *Butterflies* US1A. No. supplied to Macmillan: 465.

31 Man and the Land

The working title for this book was 'Land Use'; fine for a working title, but far too prosaic for a title that might kindle the fancy and encourage that all important journey from bookshop shelf to sitting-room table. Other potential titles were discussed by the board: 'Britain's Unnatural Landscape' or 'Britain's Unnatural Scenery', 'The Cultural Landscape', 'The Evolution of Land Use', 'Man and his Land', before settling upon the now familiar *Man and the Land*.

The author's preface is dated February 1954, but the book was not published until January 1955. This was put down to colour printing and block-making delays, but a good number of the colour plates were borrowed from previous New Naturalist titles: NN3 *London's Natural History*, NN6 *Highlands and Islands*, NN9 *Country Parish* NN13 *Snowdonia*; and NN21 *British Mammals* – presumably, at least in part, because the blocks had already been made?

Bibliographically, *Man and the Land* is complicated, principally due to a number of binding variants and repricings, but not because of multiple new editions. In fact, there is just one revised edition and two reprints: the book was not continually updated as the imprint pages of later printings infer, nor, as has been suggested, is it only the first edition with the full suite of colour plates – all impressions have them. Scattered, seemingly liberally,

through the text of the first edition were various mistakes, mostly typographical, but unfortunately Geoffrey Grigson writing in the *Observer* described a number of these as 'whoppers' and delighted in laying them before the public, as is the reviewer's way. And one reader sent in two pages' worth of incorrect plate references. These typos and howlers were corrected for the second edition, which also included a few updates but nothing substantial enough to require the resetting of the text.

The first edition is characterised by two binding variants: the first is identified by the irregular 'Type A' gilt-blocked monogram to the spine i.e. without a diamond in the middle of the conjoining vertical stroke (see page 60). Priority has been determined by examining copies with dated inscriptions; presumably the use of this 'obsolete' monogram was a mistake as all later printings revert to the standard monogram, for that period, with the diamond in the centre of the conjoining vertical stroke. There are also two binding variants for the 1973 imprint, but these are much less obvious and of little consequence to the majority of collectors who concentrate on first editions.

Notwithstanding these complications, *Man and the Land* was not published or sold by a bookclub, nor reprinted in Bloomsbury or Fontana formats.

The first edition jacket, printed on acidic paper, is often tanned and a little chipped, but fine copies are not uncommon. Total no. books printed: *c.* 18,500; total no. sold: 17,392 (326 quires without jackets were left in 1981 and these were pulped a few years later); o/p: 1982.

NN31A-B1	**First Edition, Primary Binding Variant**, (3 January 1955).
Title:	'The New Naturalist	Man And The Land'.
Author:	'by	L. Dudley Stamp'.
Illust:	'With 35 colour photographs	46 photographs in black and white	52 illustrations in the text'.
Editors:	JF, JG, JH, LDS and EH (Photographic Editor).
Printer:	Willmer Brothers & Co. Ltd., Birkenhead.
Collation:	pp. xvi, 272; 12 leaves of colour plates printed to both sides; 16 leaves of b/w plates printed to both sides (18 × 16-page gatherings).
Casing:	Blocked with the 'Type A' monogram, i.e. without a diamond in the middle of the conjoining vertical stroke.

TABLE NN31 Diagnostic features of the two binding variants of the 1973 reprint NN31D.

Man and the Land 1973 reprint NN31D	'Collins' to the spine of the book	Thickness of book	Hinges (internal)	Jacket
1st binding variant 'B1'	Larger typeface – 20 mm long	25½ mm thick (boards slightly thicker)	Mull evident under endpaper at hinges, not extending to top/tail of endpaper. Hinge with vertical lip of *c.* 4 mm.	Jacket priced at £1.60 or repriced at £3.00, £3.50 or £4.50
2nd binding variant 'B2'	Smaller typeface – 17 mm long	24 mm thick (boards slightly thinner)	Binding tape evident under endpaper at hinges, which extends to top/tail of EP. Hinge flattish with shallow vertical lip.	Jacket repriced at £4.50 but most between £5.50 & £9.50

Jacket: [Rear panel] 'The New Naturalist Library' under which advertised *A Natural History of Man in Britain*, *Climate and the British Scene* with *The Sea Coast*, *Dartmoor* and *The Weald* also listed. [Rear flap] 'Also by L. Dudley Stamp *Britain's Structure and Scenery* a best-selling volume in the New Naturalist Library', with two press reviews.

Price: 25s. net.

Print run: 9,961 (out-turn); no. sold: *c.* 9,620 (figures include 'B2') (subscription: 3,040).

NN31A-B2 First Edition, Second Binding Variant, 1955. (probably bound up later in 1955). Exactly as 'B1' but casing blocked with the 'Type C' monogram, i.e. with a diamond in the middle of the conjoining vertical stroke. This is the less common of the two variants; o/p: early 1964.

NN31B Second Edition, Revised, 1964 (September?). 'First published in 1955 | Second Edition, revised, 1964'. Printed by Collins Clear-Type Press. Title page (now) dated 1964. Smoother, better quality paper. 'Note to the Second Edition' dated October, 1963 inserted below the original author's preface. General corrections, e.g. Fig. 8 and Fig. 9 transposed to match captions, and a few up-dates to statistics, bibliography etc. but text not reset; same colour and b/w plates. 'Type B' monogram blocked to the spine. The jacket printed on bright white paper, colours colder, greener; NN library lists NN1–45 omitting NN6, 9 and 13 (Type 41), the rear flap virtually unchanged but now describes *Britain's Structure and Scenery* as 'New Naturalist volume No. 4'; blurb abbreviated and three press reviews inserted below. Price: 25s. net. Print run: 3,000; o/p: 1968.

NN31C Third Edition, 1969. 'First published in 1955 | Second Edition, revised, 1964 | Third Edition 1969'. No date to TP. Editors: JF, JG, JH, MD and EH. A straightforward reprint. The NN library to the jacket lists NN1–50 (Type 42, variant 8); rear and front flaps unchanged. Price: 32s. net. Print run: 3,000.

NN31C-AP1 First Repriced Jacket (1971–73). P. clipped, and boldly over-printed. £1.60 net, no. sold: *c.* 850 (repriced in accordance with decimalisation).

NN31D-B1 Third Edition, Reprint, First Binding Variant, 1973. ISBN: 0002131404. 'First published in 1955 | Second Edition, revised, 1964 | Third Edition 1969 | Reprinted 1973'. Editors: JG, JH, MD, KM and EH. Textually as NN31C. For diagnostic binding features see table NN31. The NN library to the *Durasealed* jacket lists NN1–54 (Type 42, variant 11); ISBN added to rear flap, otherwise unrevised. Price: £1.60 net. Print run: 3,000 inc. 'B2'. No. sold: *c.* 900 + repriced variants below + 326 quires without DJs pulped in 1980s. (The NN statement for April 1973 states: 'Price of £1.60 to be increased as soon as freeze is over', though does not mention why the freeze was imposed, but it explains why the price remained at 32s./£1.60 from 1969–1975 and then nearly doubled in price.)

NN31D-B1-AP1 1st Repriced DJ (1975), £3.00 sticker, no. sold: unknown.

NN31D-B1-AP2 2nd Repriced DJ (1976), £3.50 sticker, *c.* 150 sold.

NN31D-B1-AP3 3rd Repriced DJ (1976), £4.50 sticker, *c.* 250 sold.

NN1D-B2 Third Edition, Reprint, Second Binding Variant, 1973 [bound-up 1975/76]. As B1 but 'Collins' smaller on spine and different internal hinge arrangement – see table NN31. Would seem around 600 copies bound up thus. Always with repriced jackets as follows:

NN31D-B2-AP3 3rd Repriced DJ (1977), £4.50 sticker, *c.* 50 sold.

NN31D-B2-AP4 4th Repriced DJ (1978–79), £5.50 sticker, *c.* 200 sold.

NN31D-B2-AP5 5th Repriced DJ (1979–80), £6.00 sticker, *c.* 150 sold.

NN31D-B2-AP6 6th Repriced DJ (1980–81), £7.50 sticker, *c.* 100 sold.

NN31D-B2-AP7 7th Repriced DJ (1981), £8.50 sticker, *c.* 50 sold.

NN31D-B2-AP8 8th Repriced DJ (1981–82), £9.50 sticker, *c.* 50 sold.

POD31A Print-on-demand digital copy of the 1973 reprint NN31D.

32 Trees, Woods & Man

The idea of a tree volume was first mooted in 1951 and Sir William Taylor, late director of the Forestry Commission, offered to write a book about forests, but it was felt there were already similar books on the market and the Editors wanted a book on trees rather than forests. Edlin was approached in 1954 and by the spring of the next year he had submitted the manuscript; no wonder he was described as being a 'model author'.

Trees, Woods and Man was described as being 'the most readable of NN books' but initial sales were disappointing, and the Editors scratched their heads and pondered why: a lack of reviews especially in the 'Sundays' obviously did not help, but was it a natural antipathy towards forestry or possibly people already had Edlin books? Hosking recognised that the printing of some of the colour plates was poor, greens too blue, and this was picked up by reviewers, one of whom described them as atrocious and distorted with poor definition. By modern stands they are, of course, poor, but 'atrocious' is probably a bit harsh.

Trees, Woods and Man might not have sold, at first, in the numbers that the Editors would have wished for, but it was a dependable title and ran to five editions, finally going out of print 26 years later. The 1978 reprint, published posthumously, has half the number of colour plates; the reason for this is given on the jacket front flap: 'Except for the omission of some colour plates, which have unfortunately been damaged, this reprint is identical with its predecessor'.

The jacket, one of C & RE's best, is a universal favourite, especially the lithographed early editions, where the overlaid ink is so thick that you can feel its texture by running your fingers across it. The effect is so richly chromatic that it could easily be mistaken for original artwork, which, of course, it isn't – but each jacket is an original lithographic print. The jackets of the different editions vary considerably in both colour and printing quality; the last, the 1978 reprint, with its cold black shadows and flat colours is a travesty. Unfortunately the first edition jacket is often chipped and browned and consequently *Trees, Woods and Man* is one of the more 'difficult titles'. The endpapers of the first edition are unusual, like sugar paper, thick and often tanned too. Total print run: *c.* 17,650 (Collins) + 350 (RU); o/p: 1982 (Collins).

NN32A   First Edition, 1956 (27 February 1956).
Title: 'The New Naturalist | Trees, Woods | & Man'.
Author: 'by | H. L. Edlin | B.Sc., Dip. for. | Fellow of the Society of Foresters | of Great Britain'.
Illust: 'With 27 colour photographs | 30 photographs in black and white | and 2 line drawings'.
Editors: JF, JG, JH, LDS and EH (Photographic Editor).
Printer: Willmer Brothers & Co. Ltd., Birkenhead.
Collation: pp. xv, [1], 272; 12 leaves of colour plates printed to both sides; 12 leaves of b/w plates printed to both sides (18 × 16-page gatherings).
Jacket: [Rear panel] 'The New Naturalist Library Published in the Main Series' under which listed 30 preceding titles (not numbered), omitting *Highlands and Islands*; write for details. [Rear flap] Adverts for *Man and the Land* and *Squirrels*.
Price: 30s. net.
Print run: 7,989 (out-turn); no. sold *c.* 7,470; o/p: summer 1965.
Notes: 1) The title to the title page, i.e. the definitive title, is with an ampersand; whereas the title to the half-title, casing and jacket is with an 'and'. 2) Book 26 mm thick.

NN32B Second Edition, 1966 (between July and September). 'First Edition 1956 | Second Edition 1966'; no date to title page. Printed by Collins Clear-Type Press. Essentially a reprint of NN32A with minimal revisions. Editors: JH and LDS now Sir JH and Sir DS; JG awarded V. M. H. A sentence added to 'The Hoppus Foot' to appendix, but beyond this there do not appear to be any changes. Paper better quality, the print crisper. The green jacket design slightly less bright, warmer with an olive-green emphasis; NN library lists NN1–46 (Type 41, variant 5); rear flap unchanged; blurb to front flap abbreviated and three press endorsements inserted above. Price: 32s. net. Print run: 2,500; o/p: 1970[?].

NN32C Third Edition, 1970. SBN 002132303 to imprint page; ISBN 0002132303 to jacket. 'First Edition 1956 | Second Edition 1966 | Third (revised) Edition 1970'. Editors: JF, JG, JH, MD and EH.

Minor changes only, as identified in the 'Preface to 1970 revision' inserted on p. xv, which include: figures brought up to date; and 1947 and 1967 woodland stocktakings added to pp. 136 and [xvi] respectively (the former only amended). Paper smoother. The NN library to the jacket lists NN1–50 (Type 42, variant 8); rear flap advertises Edlin's book *Collins Guide to Tree Planting and Cultivation*, ISBN; front flap unchanged. Price: (dual) £2.25p. *net* and 45s. *net*. Print run: 2,500 inc. repriced variant below.
NN32C-AP1 1st Repriced DJ (1972), £2.50 sticker.

NN32D Third Edition, First Reprint, 1972. SBN 002132303 to imprint page; ISBN 0002132303 to jacket. 'First Edition 1956 | Second Edition 1966 | Third (revised) Edition 1970 | Reprinted 1972'. As NN32C. Book thinner – 24 mm. The jacket colours different still, trees now brown green; 2 mm two short for book; *Durasealed*; the NN library lists NN1–54 (Type 42, variant 11); both flaps unchanged. Price: £2.50 *net*. Print run: 3,000 inc. repriced variants below; o/p: beginning 1978 (AP4). Note: The SBN still used on the imprint page despite being 1972.
NN32D-AP1 1st Repriced DJ (1975), £3.00 sticker.
NN32D-AP2 2nd Repriced DJ (1975–76), £3.95 sticker, *c.* 500 sold.
NN32D-AP3 3rd Repriced DJ (1976), £4.50 sticker, *c.* 250 sold.
NN32D-AP4 4th Repriced DJ (1977–78), £6.95 sticker, *c.* 400 sold.

NN32E Third Edition, Second Reprint, 1978 (end of 1978/ beginning of 1979). ISBN changed to 0002195313. 'First Edition 1956 | Second Edition 1966 | Third (revised) Edition 1970 | Reprinted 1972 | Reprinted 1978'. As NN32D but only 12 colour plates (see intro.). Editors: JG, MD, KM and EH. Last sentence of NN credo omitted. Book 25 mm thick. Jacket less brown that NN32D, colours colder, shadows black, title band brighter green; *Durasealed*; the NN library lists NN1–61 (Type 42, variant 16); rear flap unchanged, but for ISBN; front flap has a new blurb which commences 'The late Herbert L. Edlin was one of the country's foremost authorities on trees'. Price: £8.50 net, printed diagonally with dotted line. Print run: 1,650; no. sold: *c.* 700 + repriced variant below + probably *c.* 700 copies, sold from stock to a bookclub; o/p: beginning of 1982 (AP1). Notes: 1) The total print-order was for 2,000 copies, of which 350 earmarked for the RU – see BC32A. 2) The 700 copies seemingly sold from stock to a bookclub would explain the preponderance of price-clipped jackets.
NN32E-AP1 1st Repriced DJ (1982), £9.50 sticker, *c.* 120 sold.

BC32A Readers Union Edition, 1978 [1979?]. Bound from the same sheets as the Collins third edition, second reprint NN32E and almost indistinguishable from it, but for following diagnostic features: casing of dark green imitation cloth; jacket identical but without *Duraseal* and without a printed price. Print run: 350. A scarce edition.

POD32A Print-on-demand digital copy of the 1978 reprint NN32E.

33 Mountain Flowers

The editor John Gilmour was quick to stress that this was the first comprehensive book on mountain flowers in the British Isles, and was keen that it should be marketed to the members of the Alpine Garden Society and Scottish Rock Garden Club. In fact it started off life with the title 'British Alpine Plants', but along the path to its final title, others were also considered: 'Flowers of the Hills'; 'Flowers of the Mountains', 'Flowers of Rocks and Mountains', 'British Mountain Flowers', before the board finally settled on *Mountain Flowers*.

It was reprinted in 1965 and 1971, the first time with a few minor changes; then again as an affordable paperback in 1984, but this last printing of just 1,500 copies was not particularly successful and was remaindered a few years later. An American edition of just a few hundred copies was published by Macmillan concurrently with the UK first edition.

Mountain Flowers, is not one of those 'difficult titles' and very good or fine first editions are regularly offered. It is not prone to fading and the paper often remains bright. Total print run: c. 12,000 (h/b); o/p: 1980/1981 (h/b).

NN33A	**First Edition**, 1956 (13 August 1956).
Title:	'The New Naturalist	Mountain Flowers'.
Author:	'by	John Raven	M.A.	Fellow of King's College, Cambridge, and	University Lecturer in Classics	and	Max Walters	M.A., Ph.D.	Curator of the University Herbarium,	Cambridge'.
Illust:	'With 16 colour photographs	28 photographs in black and white	and 20 distribution maps'.
Editors:	JF, JG, JH, LDS and EH (Photographic Editor).
Printer:	Willmer Brothers and Company Limited, Birkenhead.
Collation:	pp. xv, [1], 240; 8 leaves of colour plates printed to both sides; 12 leaves of b/w plates printed to both sides (16 × 16-page gatherings).
Jacket:	[Rear panel] Advert for *Wild Flowers* with supporting press reviews. [Rear flap] 'Other Plant Books in The New Naturalist Library,' under which are listed: *Flowers of the Coast, Wild Orchids of Britain, British Plant Life, Flowers of Chalk and Limestone, Art of Botanical Illustration* and *Tree, Woods and Man*. Information request.
Price:	25s. net.

Print run: 7,002 (out-turn); total no. sold: c. 6,470; o/p: end of 1964.

NN33B First Reprint, 1965 (Oct 1965). 'First published 1956 | Reprinted 1965'; no date to the title page. Essentially as the first edition. Additional titles and honours have been bestowed upon the Editors. A few very minor corrections and a nine-line addendum by Max Walters, regarding the 'Atlas of the British Flora' has been added to p. 209. Printed 'in house' by Collins Clear-Type Press, on smoother paper; the reproduction of the plates slightly improved. The NN library to the jacket lists NN1–46 (Type 42, variant 5); rear flap adds *Weeds and Aliens* and *Lords and Ladies* to the list of 'Other Plant Books'. The blurb abridged and three press endorsements added. Price: 30s.net. Print run: 2,500[?]; no. sold: c. 2,720; o/p: 1971[?]. Note: While the sales statements consistently indicate that the print-order was for 2,500 copies, the number of copies sold suggests that a figure of 3,000 is more likely.

NN33C Second Reprint, 1971. ISBN 0002131420. 'First published 1956 | Reprinted 1965 | Reprinted 1971'. As NN33B. Editors: JF, JG, JH, MD and EH; where JG has been (inexplicably) stripped of his V.M.H. (Victoria Medal of Honour). The NN library to the jacket lists NN1–52, (Type 42, variant 9a); rear flap omits *Lords and Ladies* and ISBN added, otherwise unchanged; blurb still abridged, but now supported with five press endorsements. Price: £2.50. Print run: 2,500; no. sold: c. 800[?] + repriced variants below.
NN33C-AP1 1st Repriced DJ (1975–76), £3.00 sticker, c. 300 sold[?].
NN33C-AP2 2nd Repriced DJ (1975–76), £3.50 sticker, c. 300 sold.
NN33C-AP3 3rd Repriced DJ (1976–77), £4.50 sticker, c. 400 sold.
NN33C-AP4 4th Repriced DJ (1978–79), £5.50 sticker, c. 300 sold.
NN33C-AP5 5th Repriced DJ (1979–80), £6.00 sticker, c. 100 sold.
NN33C-AP6 6th Repriced DJ (1980), £7.50 sticker, c. < 50 sold.

BPB33A Collins Paperback Reprint, 1984 (18 July 1984). ISBN: 0002190702; pp. [16], 240, [8 blanks], [40 – b/w illustrations] (19 × 16-page gatherings). A b/w copy of the 1965 reprint NN33B, with a new two-page preface by Max Walters (the original Editors' and Authors' prefaces retained); the last line of the NN credo omitted; reference to Collins Clear-Type Press removed; illustrations subtitle revised to reflect absence of colour plates in this edition. Front cover title band now grey-brown, title lettering reset, artwork colours distinctly different. Printed and bound by Biddles Ltd. Price: £6.50 net. Print run: 1,500; no. sold: c. 1,460 inc. 250 remaindered in 1988; o/p: 1988. (For generic features of the 'black paperbacks' see page 98.)

POD33A Print-on-demand digital copy of the 1971 reprint NN33C.

US33A US Edition, 1956. The Macmillan Company, New York. Bound up from the same sheets as the first UK edition NN33A. The integral title page (not a cancel) carries the US imprint 'The Macmillan Company, New York, 1956' and omits the NN monogram, otherwise setting unrevised. Imprint page omits reference to Collins. Bound in same green buckram, but with 'Macmillan' blocked to spine and NN monogram omitted.

The spine and front panel of the jacket identical to Collins edition and (strangely) even carry the Collins imprint, but rear panel and flap are blank; the front flap identical but sterling price omitted, with US price of $5.00 printed to the top corner. Print run: 400.

34 The Open Sea. Its Natural History: The World of Plankton

Of all New Naturalists, Alister Hardy's *Open Sea* duology possibly encompasses better than any other the ethos of the series; though Bristowe's *Spiders* must also be a contender for top spot. Suffice it to say that *Plankton* and the subsequent 'Part II' (NN37) have become classics of the natural history literature, and it is therefore not surprising that there are multiple editions and reprints of both. The American publisher Houghton Mifflin printed the two titles together as a single volume. 13,000 paperback copies were also published by Fontana, and for a book printed in such numbers it is now surprisingly scarce – perhaps reflecting the outstanding quality of the text and the ephemeral nature of these paperbacks.

The title to the first Collins edition neglects to state 'Part I' but perhaps in a sop to 'marketing', all subsequent editions state 'Part I' – clearly indicating more is to be had! From 1964 onwards the generic series title 'The New Naturalist' is omitted from the title page (and also from 1964, from the title page of *The Open Sea Part II*): it is present on every edition of every other New Naturalist.

The Ellises' monogram is always 'C & RE' and jacket credits reflect this, but inexplicably the order is swapped for all reprints of this book and instead reads 'Jacket design by Rosemary and Clifford Ellis'; unique in all NN jackets, and providing an instant way of telling a first edition from a later issue jacket.

A reprint was costed in 1977/78 with a new Ellis-designed jacket, but in the event did not materialise.

Though not rare in any edition, NN34 is difficult to find in fine condition, perhaps because it is so readable, and the white background colour on the spine is prone to browning. Total number of books (Collins) printed *c.* 26,500; total no. sold *c.* 25, 600; o/p: 1979 (Collins) but was o/s 1968–1969 before the printing of the second edition NN34E.

NN34A   **First Edition**, 1956 (22 October 1956).
Title: 'The New Naturalist | The Open Sea | Its Natural History: | The World of Plankton'.

Author: 'by Alister C. Hardy | M.A., D.Sc., F.R.S. | Fellow of Merton College and | Linacre Professor of Zoology and Comparative Anatomy | in the University of Oxford'.
Illust: 'With 142 watercolour drawings | by the author | 67 photographs in black and white | by Douglas Wilson and others | and 300 line drawings and maps'.
Editors: JF, JG, JH, LDS and EH (Photographic Editor).
Printer: Willmer Brothers & Co. Ltd., Birkenhead.
Collation: pp. xv, [1], 335, [1]; 12 leaves of colour plates printed to both sides; 12 leaves of b/w plates printed to both sides (22 × 16-page gatherings).
Jacket: [Rear panel] The New Naturalist Library listing in a single column NN1 *Butterflies* to NN33 *Mountain Flowers* but omitting *Highlands and Islands* and *Trees Woods and Man*. [Rear flap] Adverts for: *The Sea Shore*; *The Sea Coast* and *Sea-Birds*.
Price: 30s. net.
Print run: 9,883 (out-turn); no. sold: *c.* 9,460.

NN34B First Reprint (With Revisions), 1958. 'First published 1956 | Reprinted, with revisions, 1958'. Essentially as NN34A, The date omitted to the title page. Printer: Collins Clear-Type Press, London and Glasgow. Inconsequential revisions mostly confined to typographical errors, but 'Part I' has been added to the title (see intro.). The paper used is of slightly better quality than the first edition, smoother and silkier to the touch. The NN library to the jacket lists in double columns NN1 to 39 (Type 38), but omitting NN6, 26 and 37; rear flap unchanged; blurb to front flap slightly edited and review extract by C. M. Yonge, *Manchester Guardian*, added; followed by the usual design credit but order reversed (see intro.). Price: 30s. net. Print run: 6,000; no. sold: *c.* 6,300[?]

NN34C Second Reprint, 1962. 'First published 1956 | Reprinted, with revisions, 1958 | Reprinted, 1962'. As NN34B. The NN library to the jacket lists NN1–44 (Type 42, variant 3); the rear flap advertises *The Open Sea: II Fish and Fisheries*; front flap unchanged. Price 30s. net (but printed much larger). Print run: *c.* 3,000.
NN34C-AP1 1st Repriced DJ (1963–64?), overstamped 35s. net.

NN34D Third Reprint, 1964. 'First published 1956 | Reprinted, with revisions, 1958 | Reprinted, 1962 | Reprinted, 1964'. Title page reset; appreciably different in layout and type size, and omits the generic series title 'The New Naturalist'. Otherwise as NN34C. The NN library to the jacket lists NN1–45 (Type 42, variant 4); both flaps unchanged. Price 35s. Print run: *c.* 2,500; no. sold: *c.* 2,350.
NN34D-AP1 Earlier Repriced Jacket Some copies of this reprint were also issued in the repriced second reprint jacket NN34C (AP1) – presumably some were left over from that previous printing.

NN34E Second Edition, 1970. ISBN 0002131641. 'First published 1956 | Reprinted, with revisions, 1958 | Reprinted 1962 | Reprinted 1964 | Second edition, 1970'. But not a new edition; essentially as

NN34D, all revisions confined to minor details. Editors: JF, JG, JH, MD and EH. The NN library to the jacket lists NN1–50 (Type 42, variant 8); front and rear flaps unaltered. Dual price: 50s. net and £2.50p. net. Print run: *c.* 2,000.

NN34F Second Edition, Reprint, 1971. ISBN unchanged. 'First published 1956 | Reprinted, with revisions, 1958 | Reprinted 1962 | Reprinted 1964 | Second edition, 1970 | Reprinted 1971'. As NN34E including jacket but for price, which is now printed only in decimal currency – £2.50p.net. Print run: *c.* 3,000.

NN34F-AP1 1st Repriced DJ (1975?). £3.00 sticker.

NN34F-AP2 2nd Repriced DJ (1975–76), £4.00 sticker, *c.* 300 sold.

NN34F-AP3 3rd Repriced DJ (1976–77), £4.50 sticker, *c.* 550 sold.

NN34F-AP4 4th Repriced DJ (1978), £5.50 sticker, *c.* 50 sold.

NN34F-AP5 5th Repriced DJ (1979), £6.50 sticker, *c.* < 50 sold.

BC34A Readers Union Edition, 1959. As NN34B. Specially printed for the RU with an integral title page displaying the RU imprint and tree logo, otherwise textually identical with the same composition of plates. Bound in dark green imitation cloth with the title and RU logo gilt-blocked to the spine. RU jacket Type 2. Price: 17/- net. Print run: 2,000[?].

POD34A Print-on-demand facsimile of the 1956 first edition NN34A.

F34A Fontana Paperback First Edition, 1970 (8 May 1970). ISBN not known; pp. xviii, 393, [5]; 10 leaves of b/w plates, printed on glossy paper, to both sides, bound in three sections. A reset edition, but without colour plates and a reduced no. of b/w plates; the original colour drawings printed on the text paper. An 'Author's Preface to the Fontana Edition' added, 'signed' and dated A.C.H. 1968. The subtitle to the front cover and TP reads 'The Fontana Library'. Adverts for NN and Fontana Library titles at front and rear. Front cover photo of jelly-fish *Chrysaora hyoscella* by Dr. D. P. Wilson; blurb to rear cover. Price: 15/- (75p). Total print run inc. reprint below: 13,000. Note: The verso of the half-title page states 'Part II of *The Open Sea: Its Natural History* which is subtitled *Fish and Fisheries* will be published by Fontana in 1971'; but in the event this did not happen.

F34B Second Impression, May 1972 (as F34B). Advert for *Part II* omitted, other adverts slightly revised. Price: 90p.

US34A US First Edition, 1956. Houghton Mifflin Company, Boston, The Riverside Press, Cambridge. 'first published in the U.S.A in 1956'. Title unchanged. Hardback with dust jacket. From the same sheets as the first Collins edition NN34a and therefore textually identical to it, but for new integral half-title and title pages, the latter with the Houghton Mifflin imprint, both reset, with references to the New Naturalist removed. Casing of light green buckram with gilt lettering and dark green decoration, probably bound in the US. Dust jacket artwork by 'Bryant'; blurb to front

flap continues onto rear flap; rear panel with endorsement by Rachel Carson (author of *Silent Spring, Under the Sea-Wind; The Edge of the Sea* etc.). Price: $6.50. Print run: 2,000.

US34B US First Reprint. 1958. Houghton Mifflin. 'Reprinted, with revisions, 1958'[?]. From the same sheets as Collins first reprint (NN34B) and therefore presumed identical to it, but for cancel HTP and TP[?], latter with HM imprint. Casing of green cloth[?] with the same jacket[?] as US34A. Price: $6.50[?] Print run: *c.*1,600[?] (While the sales statements might indicate this print quantity, the scarcity of this edition would suggest less; not inspected).

US34/37A US First One-Volume Edition, January 1965. Houghton Mifflin Company, Boston, The Riverside Press, Cambridge. 'One-Volume Edition' and 'First Published January, 1965'; pp. xv, [1], 335, xiv, 322; plates. This edition combines Parts I (NN34 *Plankton*) and II (NN37, *Fish & Fisheries*). Part titles unchanged but jacket title reads 'The Open Sea | Its Natural History | Including: The World of the Plankton | and Fish and Fisheries'. Both parts from the same sheets as the 1964 Collins reprints NN34D and NN37B with the same suites of plates; both with separate, integral, half-title and title pages: all references on these pages to the New Naturalist omitted. The first TP follows the layout of the Collins 1964 ed., but with the HM imprint; the ruled lines and imprint have been omitted from the second part TP. Casing of dark green buckram with gilt lettering and light green decoration, probably bound in the US. The jacket is a hybrid – the upper part from US34A and the lower part US37A with a broad black title band in the middle; carries the same Rachel Carson endorsement as US34A to rear panel. Price: $15.00. Print run: unknown.

US34/37B US One-Volume Edition, First Reprint, March, 1965. Houghton Milfflin. 'One-Volume Edition' and 'First Published January, 1965 | Second Printing March, 1965'. Exactly as US34/37a, including jacket. Price: $15.00. Print run: unknown.

US34/37C US One-Volume Edition, Second Reprint. 1970. ISBN 039507777X. 'One- Volume Edition' and 'First Published January, 1965 | Second Printing March, 1965 | Third Printing 1970'. From the same sheets as the Collins 1970 printings NN34E and NN37C but with integral title pages. Format as US34/37A; same casing design but with dark blue cloth, gilt lettering to front board, black to spine, light green decoration; probably bound in the US. New dedicated jacket printed in blue and red on a white ground, artist unacknowledged, blurb and commendation unchanged but reset. Price: $20.00. No printed: unknown.

35 The World of the Soil

'A clod of earth seems at first sight to be the embodiment of the stillness of death'. So opened the blurb for the Fontana paperback edition of *The Soil*, of which 51,000 copies were sold. Conversely only 5,471 copies of the first edition hardback were printed: comparable with *Insect Migration* and just about 500 more than *Folklore of Birds* and *Dragonflies*.

The Soil is one of those titles, commonly perceived as being more abundant than is clearly the case. The first edition sold out in almost exactly a year.

This conservative print run reflected the commercial position of the New Naturalist at the time, as did the sanction of only four colour plates, all showing mineral deficiencies, even though the editor, Dudley Stamp, had considered a colour plate showing soil profiles was essential. This was noted in the minutes of the Board meeting of 27 November 1956 at which the following rather downbeat statement was also made: 'Mr Collins said that he was still interested in continuing the series, along the lines suggested. He agreed that it would be useful to make some announcement about the future of the series, giving an indication of the books to come, and the probable time of the termination of the New Naturalist, etc.'

Despite the sombre mood, *The Soil* ran to five editions, though most of these were in fact straightforward reprints. It was soon available as a cheaper Fontana paperback with the two formats on sale concurrently for over ten years; however there was no appreciable reduction in the sales of the hardback: the two formats appealing to two different markets that seemingly did not cross over.

The snout of the mole on the jacket spine, (thought it is not at all obvious that that is what it is) just below the title band, should be the same chestnut brown as the mole's paw on the front panel: it is extremely rare that it is; it is usually faded to a light grey. Total no. Collins books printed: *c.* 16,500; o/p: 1979.

NN35A   **First Edition**, 1957 (23 September 1957).
Title: 'The New Naturalist | The World of | the Soil'.
Author: 'by | Sir E. John Russell | D.Sc., F.R.S. | Late Director of | the Rothamsted Experimental Station'.
Illust: 'With 4 colour photographs | 44 photographs in black and white | and 11 text figures'.

Editors: JF, JG, JH, LDS and EH (Photographic Editor).
Printer: Willmer Brothers & Haram Ltd., Birkenhead.
Collation: pp. xiv, 237, [1], [4 – NN adverts]; 2 leaves of colour plates printed to one side only; 12 leaves of b/w plates printed to both sides (16 × 16-page gatherings).
Jacket: [Rear panel] The New Naturalist library listing NN1–34, omitting NN6. [Rear flap] Adverts for *Man and the Land*, and *Trees, Woods and Man*.
Price: 25s. net.
Print run: 5,471 (out-turn); o/p: early 1958.
Notes: 1) The four colour plates were electros all taken from the 1951 HMSO publication: Wallace, T.; 'The Diagnosis of Mineral Deficiencies in Plants by Visual Symptons. A Colour Atlas and Guide'. 2) The four pages of adverts at the end of the book include: *The New Naturalist* listing 32 titles; 'Special Volumes' listing 13 titles; adverts for specific titles *Birds of the London Area*, *The Rabbit*, *Man and the Land*, *Mountain Flowers*, *Mountains and Moorlands*, *Climate and the British Scene*, *Trees, Woods and Man* and *The Sea Coast*.

NN35B **Second Edition**, 1959. 'First published, 1954 | Second Edition 1959'. No date to TP. Printed by Collins Clear-Type Press. However not a new ed.; minimal revision only, e.g. footnote to p. 3 *Circium* and A. R. Chapham corrected to *Cirsium* and A. R. Clapham respectively. Adverts unchanged. Smoother, finer paper has resulted in a slightly thinner book. The NN library to the jacket lists NN1–39 omitting NN6, 26 and 37, (Type 37); both flaps unchanged. Price: 30s. net. Print run: 3,000; o/p: end 1962/ beginning 1963.

NN35C **Third Edition**, 1963. 'First published, 1957 | Second Edition, 1958 | Third Edition, 1963'. Minimal revisions to text (based on 1961 Fontana ed.), e.g. figures and footnote to p. 223 updated, bibliography slightly enlarged. Adverts to rear omitted. The NN library to jacket lists NN1–45 (Type 42, variant 4); rear flap unchanged, front flap reset with two press reviews inserted below abridged blurb. Price: 30s. Print run: 2,000[?]; o/p: summer 1967. Note: The printing history erroneously gives the date of the Second Edition as 1958 – an error repeated in all further editions.

NN35D **Fourth Edition**, 1967. 'First published, 1957 | Second Edition, 1958 | Third Edition, 1963 | Fourth Edition, 1967'. Notwithstanding, a reprint with minimal revisions; as NN35C. Editors: JF, JG, JH, MD and EH. No building no. to address on TP. The NN library to the jacket lists NN1–50 (Type 42, variant 8); both flaps unchanged. Price: 30s. net. Print run: 2,000.

NN35E **Fifth Edition**, 1971. ISBN 0002132559. 'First published, 1957 | Second Edition, 1958 | Third Edition, 1963 | Fourth Edition, 1967 | Fifth Edition, 1971'. As NN35D. The NN library to the jacket lists NN1–52 (Type 42, variant 9); ISBN added to rear flap, otherwise unchanged. Price: £2.25 NET. Print run: 2,000; o/p: 1975.

NN35F Fifth Edition, Reprint, 1975 [early 1975]. ISBN changed to 0002195550. 'First published, 1957 | Second Edition, 1958 | Third Edition, 1963 | Fourth Edition, 1967 | Fifth Edition, 1971 | Reprinted 1975'. As NN35E. Editors: JH, JG, MD, KM and EH. Last sentence of NN credo omitted. The jacket *Durasealed*; the NN library lists NN1–58 (Type 42, variant 14); revised ISBN to rear flap, otherwise unaltered. Price: £2.50 NET. Print run: 2,000; no. sold: few at original price + repriced variants below + probably *c.* 650 copies sold, from stock, to a bookclub; o/p: beginning 1979 but last few copies cleared to a remainder dealer in 1983.

NN35F-AP1 1st Repriced DJ (1975?), £3.00 sticker.

NN35F-AP2 2nd Repriced DJ (1975–76), £3.50 sticker, *c.* 300 sold.

NN35F-AP3 3rd Repriced DJ (1976–77), £4.50 sticker, *c.* 500 sold.

NN35F-AP4 4th Repriced DJ (1978–79), £5.50 sticker, *c.* 300 sold.

BC35A Readers Union Edition, 1959. As NN35B and from the same printing. With an integral title page displaying the RU imprint and tree logo. Bound in dark green imitation cloth with the title and RU logo gilt-blocked to the spine. RU jacket 'Type 2'. Price: 15/- net. Print run: 2,000[?].

POD35A Print-on-demand digital copy of the 1971 fifth reprint NN35E.

F35A Fontana Paperback, First Edition, 1961; pp. 285, [3]; 12 leaves of b/w plates, printed on glossy paper, to both sides, bound in single section in centre (18 × 16-page gatherings). A reset copy of the original Collins edition without colour plates, but same suite of b/w plates, of which some cropped. The subtitle to the front cover and TP reads 'The Fontana Library'. Internal adverts for Fontana Library titles and for *Britain's Structure and Scenery*. The cover artwork by [Kenneth] Farnhill; rear cover carries blurb (different to jacket) and author's biography. No printed price. Total print run including reprints below: 51,000.
The following reprints exactly as preceding edition unless stated otherwise, changes to internal adverts ignored.

F35B Second Impression, March 1966. (not seen)

F35C Third Impression, May. 1969. (not seen)

F35D Fourth Impression, April. 1970. Photographic front cover of soil laboratory, on which printed 'The Fontana New Naturalist'; rear cover has three press clips. TP reset with subtitle 'The Fontana New Naturalist'. Price: 10/- (50p).

F35E Fifth Impression, March 1971. (not seen)

36 Insect Migration

Migration, by definition, dictates that the subject must be explored beyond the shores of the British Isles and therefore it is not surprising that US, German and Japanese editions were also published. The second edition of 1965 [1966] is essentially very little more than a reprint, of which the 1971 reprint is virtually an exact copy. Only 5,860 copies of the Collins first edition were printed (on a par with *Folklore* printed in the same year, but never as expensive) and it would appear that a good proportion of these were sold overseas. The low print run coupled with a jacket that is prone to fading and tanning, renders *Insect Migration* somewhat of a collector's challenge. The butterflies on the spine should have distinct yellow-buff areas on a white ground, but when the paper is tanned, the buff areas are indistinguishable.

Both the later editions are comparatively scarce particularly the 1971 reprint. And as for the US edition – I have only been able to locate a single jacketed copy. Total no. of Collins books printed: *c.* 10,000; o/p: 1979.

NN36A	**First edition**, 1958 (05 May 1958).
Title:	'The New Naturalist	Insect	Migration'.
Author:	'by	C. B. Williams	F.R.S.'.
Illust:	'With 11 colour illustrations	22 photographs in black and white	49 maps and diagrams'.
Editors:	JF, JG, JH, LDS and EH (Photographic Editor).
Printer:	Willmer Brothers & Haram Limited, Birkenhead.
Collation:	pp. xiii, [1], 235, [1], [5 – NN catalogue], [1]; 4 leaves of colour plates printed to both sides; 8 leaves of b/w plates printed to both sides (16 × 16-page gatherings).
Jacket:	[Rear panel] 'The New Naturalist Library listing NN 1–35 inclusively'. [Rear flap] Adverts for *Insect Natural History*; *Moths*; and *The World of the Honeybee*.
Price:	30s. net.
Print run:	5,860 (out-turn); no. sold: *c.* 5,440; o/p: end of 1964.
Notes:	Adverts to pp. [237–241]: 'The New Naturalist Available in the Main Series', which lists NN1–35, omitting 6 and 26, followed by 'special volumes' listings NN M2–15, omitting M8, M10 and M14, followed by individual title adverts for: *Insect Natural History, Butterflies, Moths, Honeybee, Angler's Entomology, World of the Soil, Open Sea Part I, Mountain Flowers* and *British Amphibians and Reptiles*.

NN36B Second Edition, 1965 (Feb 1966). 'First edition 1958 | Second edition 1965'; date omitted from title page. Collation: xiii, [1], 237, [5]. Essentially a reprint of NN36A, not reset, with minimal revisions: a single leaf of additional migration tables covering years 1956–62, added at end of book (oddly, there is no reference to this additional material, nor has the appendix title been updated to reflect it – it still states '1850 to 1955'). The NN catalogue at the rear, one page less, revised with nos. 1–47 listed in the main series, but omitting NN9, 13 and 39, and special volumes M1–21, omitting M3, M6–8, M10, M11 and M14; individual adverts for *Insect Natural History*, *Butterflies*, *Moths*, *Honeybee*, *Angler's Entomology*, *World of Spiders*, *Dragonflies* and *Bumblebees*; 'A *New Naturalist Library* leaflet available'. Printed 'in house' by Collins Clear-Type Press, on smoother paper; the reproduction of colour plates slightly improved. Thicker, stiffer boards. The NN table to the jacket lists NN1–46 (Type 42, variant 5); rear flap identical; blurb to front flap abridged with three press clips inserted below. Price remains at 30s. net. Print run: 2,000; no. sold c. 1,770. Note: While dated 1965, this edition was not actually published until early 1966.

NN36C Second Edition, Reprint, 1971. ISBN 0002131010 3 – to jacket only. 'First edition 1958 | Reprinted 1971'. As NN36B. Editors: JG, JH, MD, KM and EH. The NN catalogue at the rear is textually unaltered but first page printed on verso rather than recto. The NN library to the jacket lists NN1–52 (Type 42, variant 9), rear flap identical but for the addition of ISBN; front flap unaltered. Price: £2.50 net. Print run: 2,000; no. sold: c. 800 + repriced variants below + possibly two hundred sold off to a bookclub. Note: The 1965 second edition is omitted from the printing history.

NN36C-AP1 1st Repriced DJ (1975–76), £3.50 sticker, c. 220 sold.
NN36C-AP2 2nd Repriced DJ (1976–77), £4.50 sticker, c. 230 sold.
NN36C-AP3 3rd Repriced DJ (1978–79), £5.50 sticker, c. 230 sold.

POD36A Print-on-demand digital copy of the 1971 reprint NN36C.

US36A US Edition, 1958. The Macmillan Company, New York. Bound up from the same sheets as the Collins first edition NN36A, but with a cancel title leaf that states: 'The Macmillan Company | New York'; and omits the date and NN monogram; the verso states 'First published in the U.S.A. in 1958' otherwise layout unaltered. Bound in same green buckram but 'Macmillan' blocked to the spine and NN monogram omitted. Likewise, dust jacket as NN36A, from the same print run, but overprinted *Macmillan* to the bottom of the spine and *Collins* obliterated with a thick black line; price-clipped with an adjacent overprinted price of $6.00. No. supplied to Macmillan: 518. (A rare edition, very difficult to find with a dust jacket.)

FOR36A German Edition, 1961 (In German). Title: 'Die Wanderflüge der Insekten'. 'Einführung in das Problem des Zugverhaltens der Insekten unter besonderer Berücksichtigung der Schmetterlinge. Übertragen und bearbeitet von Hubert Roer. Mit 79 Abbildungen im Text und auf Tafeln'. (An introduction to the problem of migratory behaviour of insects with special reference to butterflies. Edited and translated by Hubert Roer. With 79 illustrations in the text and plates.) Published by Paul Parey, Hamburg and Berlin; pp. 232; 8 leaves of b/w plates printed to both sides; errata slip at page 142, world-map end-papers. A reworking of the Collins edition, but with a number of changes: notably, the colour plates have been omitted and many of the original b/w illustrations replaced with new images. Bound in grey cloth with lettering and vignette of a swallowtail stamped in dark blue. Dust jacket: yellow, white and blue design on a blue-green ground; designer uncredited. No printed price. Print run: 3,000 (printed in Germany); no. sold: unknown, but only 1,117 sold by 1974.

FOR36B Japanese Edition, 1986. 昆虫の渡り ISBN 4806722936. Translated by Tsukiji Shokan. 'Japanese translation/reprint rights arranged with William Collins Sons & Co. Ltd. through Japan UNI Agency, Inc. Tokyo.' Hardback with dust jacket 158 × 229mm; pp. [2], 242, [3 – publisher's ads.]; 11 leaves of b/w plates printed on both sides; photographs as Collins edition but some reduced in size, all grouped together at the front. Title page printed in black and grey with attractive decorations of Monarch butterflies in flight, the design of which is repeated on the endpapers and dust jacket. Bound in ivory imitation cloth with an embossed marbling effect, a repeat of the Monarch patterns printed in blue and grey text to the spine. Bound-in ribbon bookmark. Silk laminated jacket with back text, blue and green Monarch butterflies on a white ground. Print run: unknown.

37 The Open Sea: Its Natural History Part II: Fish & Fisheries

The Open Sea II, for short, was reprinted four times and sold over a 22-year period, but the text remained unrevised: even the original addendum that starts, 'Just as the book is going to press', relating to a discovery published in 1958, appears unqualified and unrevised in the 1976 edition. But the emphasis of the book's title was significantly revised after the first edition: the Board minutes for 29 October 1963 record: 'To be called "Open Sea Part II" with Fish and Fisheries as subtitle only'. The reasons for the change are not recorded, but the 'busy' title page of the first edition is anachronistic: more like an 18th-century book than a progressive 20th-century New Naturalist. The title to reprint jackets was also revised, but the original wording to the casings and half-titles was retained. Like NN34 *Open Sea I*, later editions omitted the generic title 'New Naturalist' from the title page, for which they are unique in the series. Was this accidental or in preparation for a combined book outside the series?

The printing history of *Open Sea II* is straightforward, without bookclub editions and without any books remaindered, but the first edition was also published in the US by Houghton Mifflin, who in 1965 published the first combined *Open Sea I* and *II* edition. This 'one-volume' edition was a substantial tome of a nearly 700 pages and 50 leaves of plates: it was undoubtedly successful as it ran to three printings, each, seemingly, of *c.* 2,000 copies.

The acidic paper of the first and early reprint jackets is prone to tanning and bright copies are scarce: consider having them washed by a paper conservator. The 1970s jackets are greener with the 1976 edition *Durasealed*; this last edition now rare. Total no. of UK books printed: *c.* 16,200; o/p: 1981, but o/s 1967–1970.

NN37A   **First Edition**, 1959 (20 April 1959).
Title: 'The New Naturalist | the Open Sea: its Natural History | Part II | Fish and Fisheries | With chapters on Whales, Turtles | and Animals of the Sea Floor'.
Author: 'by Sir Alister Hardy | M.A., D.Sc., F.R.S. | Fellow of Merton College, | Hon. Fellow of Exeter College | and Linacre Professor of Zoology | and Comparative Anatomy | in the University | of Oxford'
Illust: 'With watercolour and line drawings | by the author | 68 photographs in black and white | by Douglas Wilson and others | and diagrams and maps'.
Editors: JF, JG, JH, DS and EH (Photographic Editor).
Printer: Willmer Brothers and Haram Limited, Birkenhead.
Collation: pp. xiv, 322; 8 leaves of colour plates printed to both sides; 16 leaves of b/w plates printed to both sides (21 × 16-page gatherings).
Jacket: [Rear panel] The New Naturalist library listing NN1–39 (omitting NN6, 26 and 37). [Rear flap] Adverts for *The Open Sea I, Life in Lakes and Rivers*, and *The Sea Shore*.
Price: 30s. net.
Print run: 7,715 (out-turn); o/p: 1963[?].
Notes: The first edition is characterised by particularly thick boards – about 3 mm as against the usual 1.5/2 mm, resulting in a noticeably thicker book.

NN37B-DJ1 First Reprint, (Second Impression). Title: 'The Open Sea: | Its Natural | History | Part II: Fish and Fisheries'. 'First published 1959 | Reprinted 1964'. A reprint of NN37A. Title page has been reset with changed emphasis of title as indicated (The gilt-blocked title to the casing spine has not changed.); no date and street no. added to Collins address and rules added to illustrations subtitle. Printer: Collins Clear-Type Press, London and Glasgow. Printing of letterpress and in-text diagrams not as fine as the first edition. The jacket is exactly as the first edition jacket NN37A, but price-clipped with the new price overprinted, diagonally, to the clipped corner. Price: 35s. net. Print run: 3,000 inc. new jacket variant below. (Presumably some jackets were left over from the first printing and these were put on the first books sold.)

NN37B-DJ2 New Jacket, 1964. A new dedicated jacket with title lettering reset (see intro.); the NN library lists NN1–45 (Type 42, variant 4); flaps unaltered. Price: 35s. net; o/p: 1967.

NN37C Third Impression, 1970. ISBN 000213165x. 'First published 1959 | Second Impression 1964 | Third Impression 1970'. As NN37B. Editors: JF, JG, JH, MD and EH. The blocked lettering to the spine of casing often appears silver-gilt. The NN library to the jacket lists NN1–50 (Type 42, variant 8); rear and front flaps unchanged. Price: £2.50 net and 50s. net (in accordance with decimalisation). Print run: 2,000.

NN37C-DJ Later Jacket. Some copies wear the 1971 jacket (NN37D), i.e. without the dual price. Presumably stock of the 1970 jacket ran out and so these later jackets were used; there was barely a year between the printing of the two impressions.

NN37D Fourth Impression, 1971. ISBN unchanged. 'First published 1959 | Second Impression 1964 | Third Impression 1970 | Fourth Impression 1971'. As NN37C. The jacket also identical but ISBN added to rear flap and without dual price. Price: £2.50 net. Print run: 2,000; o/p: end 1975.

NN37D-AP1 1st Repriced DJ (1975), £3.50 sticker, no. sold: unknown.

NN37D-AP2 2nd Repriced DJ (1975), £4.00 sticker, *c.* 200 sold.

NN37E Fifth Impression, 1976. ISBN 0002194953. 'First published 1959 | Second Impression 1964 | Third Impression 1970 | Fourth Impression 1971 | Reprinted 1976'. As NN37D. Editors: MD, JG, KM and EH. Last part of NN credo omitted. The combination of thinner paper and boards has resulted in a book about 4 mm thinner than the first edition. The NN library to the *Durasealed* jacket lists NN1–58 (Type 42, variant 14); both flaps are unchanged, but for the revised ISBN to the rear. Price: £6.50 net. Print run: 1,500; no. sold: *c.* 1,370 inc. repriced variants below; o/p: 1981 (AP2). Possibly handful also sold repriced at £9.50.

NN37E-AP1 1st Repriced DJ (1980–81), £7.50 sticker, *c.* 170 sold.

NN37E-AP2 2nd Repriced DJ (1981), £8.50 sticker, < 100 sold.

POD37A Print-on-demand digital copy of the 1964 reprint NN37B.

US37A First US Edition, 1959. Houghton Mifflin Company, Boston, The Riverside Press, Cambridge. Title page dated 1959; 'printed in Great Britain'. Title unchanged. Hardback with dust jacket. From the same sheets as the first Collins edition NN37A and therefore textually identical to it, but for new integral half-title and title pages, the latter with the Houghton Mifflin imprint; references to the New Naturalist removed. Casing of light green buckram with gilt lettering and dark green decoration, probably bound in the US. Dust jacket artwork by 'Bryant'; blurb to front flap continues onto rear flap; rear panel with endorsement by Rachel Carson (author of *Silent Spring, Under the Sea-Wind; The Edge of the Sea*, etc.). Price: $7.50. Print run: 2,500.

US34/37A US First/One-Volume Edition, January 1965. Houghton Mifflin. See NN34 on page 171.

US34/37B US One-Volume Edition, First Reprint, March, 1965. Houghton Milfflin. See NN34 on page 171.

US34/37C US One-Volume Edition, Second Reprint, 1970. ISBN 039507777X. See NN34 on page 171.

38 The World of Spiders

'It was sensational', is how Fisher described *Spiders* on first reading it in 1959. In all ways *Spiders* epitomises the New Naturalist ethos and is embellished throughout with Arthur Smith's fine drawings, for which Collins used particularly fine paper. Inexplicably, however, sales were disappointing and *Spiders* was not printed again until 1971, and then as a revised edition. But by now it was selling well and was quickly reprinted in 1971 and then in 1976. In fact, *Spiders* was revised a second time, in 1978, with a new introduction and a revised appendix by Bristowe, and despite numerous references to the imminent printing of this new edition, in NN reports (as late as 1980), it never actually materialised. It appears that it fell victim to rising costs, but the Collins archive does include a proof copy of this never-published edition. What is perhaps more perplexing is why *Spiders* was not chosen to be reprinted as a 'black paperback' (1984/5) or as Bloomsbury edition (1989/90): it would seem an obvious choice. The Readers Union did, however, buy into the 1976 reprint (1,000 copies), though there does not appear to be any distinctions between their books and the Collins edition. 350 copies of this same reprint were also sold to the US publisher Taplinger, but it is unknown how these differ, if at all, though they were allocated a dedicated ISBN.

The jacket features a garden spider: flip it 180 degrees and it mutates into a devilish warrior complete with war-paint and dreadlocks. Is this a deliberate reference to a commonly held perception of spiders? Probably not, but an appealing illusion nevertheless.

The rich russet of the jacket is unfortunately quick to fade on the spine, the first edition particularly so but all editions suffer in this way, and very few copies remain in their original bright state.

Total no. of books printed: c. 15,000 (Collins) +1,000 (RU); total no. sold: c. 12,450 + 1,000 RU; o/p: 1978.

NN38A   First Edition, 1958 (23 October 1958).
Title: 'The New Naturalist | the | World of | Spiders'.

Author: 'by W. S. Bristowe | M.A., Sc.D.'
Illust: 'With 14 plates of photographs | 4 in colour | and drawings by Arthur Smith | comprising 22 half tone plates | and 116 text figures'.
Editors: JF, JG, JH, LDS and EH (Photographic Editor).
Printer: Willmer Brothers and Haram Ltd., Birkenhead.
Collation: pp. xiii, [i], 304, [2 – NN catalogue]; 4 leaves of colour plates printed to one side only; 16 leaves of b/w plates printed to both sides (20 × 16-page gatherings).
Jacket: [Rear panel] The New Naturalist library listing NN 1–36 (omitting NN6). [Rear flap] Adverts for *Insect Migration; Insect Natural History* and *Moths*.
Price: 30s. net.
Print run: 7,500 (out-turn); no. sold: c. 7,340; o/p: 1968.
Notes: Two-page NN catalogue at rear listing NN1–22 (excluding NN6) in the main series and 'Special Volumes' M2–15 (excluding M8, M10 and M14).

NN38B Revised Edition, 1971 (February). SBN 002132567. 'First published 1958 | Revised Edition 1971'. Essentially a reprint of NN38A with three-page addendum, in which Bristowe writes, 'A need to reprint the book without revising the text, save for a few minor corrections, has caused the publishers to seek a brief addendum'. This is inserted after the author's preface and dated July 1968 (three years before publication). Preliminary blank page [xiv] and the two-page NN catalogue omitted; pagination now: xvi, 304; the insertion of the plates also very slightly revised. Editors: JF, JG, JH, MD and EH. Printer: Collins Clear-Type Press, London and Glasgow. The NN library to the dust jacket lists NN 1–50 (Type 42, variant 8); rear flap unaltered but for inclusion of the SBN; blurb to front flap précised, with four press endorsements inserted below. Price: £2.25 net and 45s. net. Print run: 2,500; o/p: 1972[?].

NN38C Revised Edition, First Reprint, 1971 (but probably 1972). 'First published 1958 | Revised Edition 1971 | Reprinted 1971'. Exactly as NN38B, with the same ISBN. The NN library to the *Durasealed* jacket lists NN1–53 (Type 42, variant 10); rear and front flaps unchanged. Price: £2.25 net. Print run: 2,000; o/p: 1974.
NN38C-AP1 1st Repriced DJ (1975?), £3.50 sticker, no. sold: unknown.
NN38C-AP2 2nd Repriced DJ (1975–76), £4.00 sticker, c. 250 sold.

NN38D Revised Edition, Second Reprint, 1976. ISBN 0002195585. 'First published 1958 | Revised Edition 1971 | Reprinted 1971 | Reprinted 1976'. As NN38C. The NN library to the jacket lists nos. 1–58 (type 42, variant 14); both flaps are unchanged, but for the ISBN to the rear. Price: £5.50 net. Print run: c. 2,500 (inc. RU and US copies); no. sold: c. 1,060; + repriced variant below. (1,000 copies were sold to the RU, which appear to be indistinguishable, but were probably all price-clipped.)
NN38D-AP1 1st Repriced DJ (1978), £8.00 sticker, < 50 sold.

POD38A Print-on-demand digital copy of the 1971 revised edition NN38C.

US38A US Edition, 1976. ISBN 0800885988. Published by Taplinger

Publishing Co., Inc. New York (or, at least, distributed in the US by them). Not inspected. But at only 350 copies, it is likely that the only distinguishing mark is a distribution or imprint sticker. No. sold: 350.

39 The Folklore of Birds

The first of the 39, 40 and 41 trio of scarce New Naturalist titles. Just one printing of the one Collins edition, though also published the following year in the US under the imprint Houghton Mifflin. It was subsequently enlarged and again published in the US, in 1970, this time by *Dover* – renowned for their reprints and facsimile editions. In 1975 the American imprint Crown, published in larger 4to format, a derivative of *Folklore*, entitled *The Life and Lore of the Bird in Nature, Art, Myth and Literature*, with a much simplified text but supported copiously with b/w and colour illustrations.

The print-order was small – 6,000 copies of which 1,000 had been ordered by the US publisher Houghton Mifflin and therefore just 5,000 books would have been available to Collins. *Folklore*, at just four years, had the shortest shelf-life of all the early titles. Nevertheless sales were comparatively slow, and the NN Board minutes for July 1962 record that 'sales do not justify a reprint but Collins will investigate [the] possibility of a paperback edition jointly with a USA publisher'. As we know this did not come to fruition and in 1965 the rights reverted to the author, who presumably negotiated directly with Dover for the 1970 enlarged edition.

The imprint page doubles as a dedication page and includes an advert for six other Armstrong titles – somewhat surprisingly, as only one of these was published by Collins and that, the NN monograph *The Wren*. Armstrong was evidently a canny negotiator.

Folklore sports one of the Ellises' most successful jackets, a favourite of many. The grey buckram binding of the Houghton Mifflin edition, with its simple black cave painting bird motifs, is graphically outstanding: a model of restraint; balanced, sophisticated and arresting. Regrettably the designer is uncredited.

Despite the rarity of the Collins edition, the jacket is often found in very good condition, perhaps because it is not an easy read; the series numeral '39' on the spine usually fades, sometimes to the point of illegibility – it should be the same bright yellow-orange as the highlights on the front panel. The jacket is also a couple of mm too short for the book.

NN39A   **First Edition**, 1958 (03 November 1958).
Title: 'The New Naturalist | The Folklore | of Birds | An Enquiry into the Origin & Distribution | of some Magico-Religious Traditions'.
Author: 'by | Edward A. Armstrong'.
Illust: 'With 55 photographs | 85 illustrations in the text'.
Editors: JF, JG, JH, LDS and EH (Photographic Editor).
Printer: Willmer Brothers and Haram Ltd., Birkenhead.
Collation: pp. xvi, 272; 1 colour plate leaf (frontispiece) printed to the verso only; 16 leaves of b/w plates printed to both sides (18 × 16-page gatherings).
Jacket: [Rear panel] The New Naturalist library listing NN1–38 inclusively (Type 38). [Rear flap] Advert for *The Wren*.
Price: 30s. net.
Print run: 5,969 (out-turn); no. sold: *c*. 5,420; o/p: August 1962. (Figures include 990 copies supplied to the Houghton Mifflin in US – see US39A.)

POD39A Print-on-demand digital copy.

US39A US First Edition, 1959. Houghton Mifflin Company, Boston. Bound up from the same sheets as the Collins edition with the same plates, but the title page bears the *Houghton Mifflin* imprint and omits the NN monogram; it is an integral part of first gathering, i.e. not a cancel leaf. 'Printed in Great Britain by Willmer Brothers & Haram Ltd., Birkenhead' Bound in grey buckram with black lettering and black decoration (see intro.) 157 × 226 mm, thick stiff boards. Jacket printed in black and white and orange, designer not credited. The blurb, which continues onto the rear flap is a revision of that on the Collins jacket, rear panel lists the contents of the book. Price ?. No. supplied to Houghton Mifflin: 990. (While the printing was done in the UK, it would seem that the binding, utilizing thick boards and a different stitching pattern, was undertaken in the US.)

US39B US Second Edition (Revised and Enlarged), 1970. Dover Publications Inc, New York. ISBN [0]486221458. 'Second edition, revised and enlarged with 71 photographs and 88 illustrations in the text'; manufactured in the United States of America. Paperback; pp. xviii, 284; [8]; 42 pages of illustrations (22 × 16-page gatherings); format slightly smaller at 136 × 203 mm; thin paper. All images b/w and integral to the text, i.e. imposed on the same sheets and printed on the same paper. Printed green card covers featuring a totem pole to front cover. *Armstrong* states in the 'Preface to the Dover Edition': '…this work has enabled me to make a number of corrections and additions, including an appendix containing much new material and a supplementary bibliography.' However, majority of text is a facsimile of the Collins edition, the pages photographically copied. Price: $3.50.

40 Bumblebees

'A work that is likely to remain the most informative summary of all that is known about the habits of these conspicuous and beautiful insects for a long time to come' so waxed the review in the *Times Literary Supplement* and, in 1984, Butler still regarded *Bumblebees* as the best, most up-to-date book on the subject. This might sound conceited but, in fact, it was really Free's book, with Butler contributing the photographs and helping with editing. It was, however, Butler who promoted the idea to Collins in 1954 and if it were not for his influence, it is unlikely that the book would have come to fruition.

Bumblebees did not have the same universal appeal as Butler's earlier book in the series NN28 *World of the Honeybee* and comparatively few copies were printed. It is, consequently, scarce and holds a fabled position within the series. Outside the G14 it is about number three in the rarity stakes but the first edition jacket suffers horribly from fading, making fine copies rarer still. It was originally to have been a special volume, i.e. a monograph and, perhaps because of this, as many collectors will know, it is slightly smaller than the conventional main series format.

Bumblebees was reprinted just once, but the first edition was also published in the States by Macmillan with a cancel title page and the same Ellis jacket but for the imprint. Collins had planned to reprint it again in paperback format in 1984 (the 'black paperbacks'), but Free refused to grant permission as he objected to the misely royalties offered.

As mentioned elsewhere in this book, few New Naturalist titles have conventional frontispiece plates, though *Bumblebees* is one of them that does, which is in fact a copy of Plate 40 from *Insect Natural History* published two years earlier. It features set specimens, however these were not keyed, at least not on the plate, and many previous owners took it upon themselves to annotate the frontispiece in manuscript – in varying degrees of neatness.

The richly coloured jacket is, to me, redolent of the setting sun on an early summer's evening when *Bombus* is still foraging long after her diurnal insect cousins have retired. But the warm mauve of the first edition jacket gives up its colour about as quickly as that dying sun, turning to a cold grey-blue on the spine. However the reprint is much more colourfast and unfaded copies are not rare: if you can put up with a reprint in your collection, the shelf will look the better for it.

NN40A	**First Edition**, 1959 (25 May 1959).
Title:	'The New Naturalist | Bumblebees'.
Authors:	'by | John B. Free | M.A., Ph.D. | and | Colin G. Butler | M.A., Ph.D., F.R.P.S. | Bee Department | Rothamsted Experimental Station | With two appendices by | Ian H. H. Yarrow | M.A., Ph.D. | Entomology Department | British Museum (Natural History)'.
Illust:	'Illustrated with 46 photographs | by Colin G. Butler'.
Editors:	JF, JG, JH, LDS and EH (Photographic Editor).
Printer:	Willmer Brothers & Haram Ltd., Birkenhead.
Collation:	pp. xiv, 208, [2]; 1 colour plate leaf (frontispiece) printed to verso only; 12 leaves of b/w plates printed to both sides (14 × 16-page gatherings).
Jacket:	[Rear panel] The New Naturalist library listing NN1–39, omitting NN6 and 26. [Rear flap] Advert for *The World of the Honeybee*.
Price:	25s. net.
Print run:	4,981 (out-turn) but including 371 for US (Taplinger); no. sold: *c.* 4,470; o/p: May 1967.
Notes:	1) *The World of the Honeybee* is advertised at the rear of the book. This, in addition to the advert to the jacket rear flap, which between them cite seven different press commendations for *Honeybee*. 2) The jacket is particularly quick to fade on the spine.

NN40B First Reprint, 1968. 'First published 1959 \| Reprinted 1968'. Appears a straight reprint. No date to TP. Editors: JF, JG, JH, MD and EH. Printer: Collins Clear-Type Press, London and Glasgow. Book very slightly thinner. The NN library to the dust jacket lists NN1–50 (Type 42, variant 8); rear flap unaltered; last paragraph of blurb omitted with 3 press commendations inserted below. Price: 30s. net. Print run: 2,000 including repriced variant below; o/p: summer 1973. Note: The jacket does not fade to the same degree as the first ed. jacket.

NN40B-AP1 1st Repriced DJ (1971–73), £1.50 net; p. clipped, overstamped £1.50 in accordance with decimalisation.

POD40A Print-on-demand digital copy of the first edition NN40A.

US40A US Edition, 1959. The Macmillan Company, New York. Bound up from the same sheets as NN40A, but with a cancel title page printed with the US imprint and without the NN monogram. 'First published in the United States of America 1959'. Bound in same green buckram over thicker boards, but with Macmillan blocked above the tail of the spine and the NN monogram omitted. The jacket, including the adverts and blurb, is unrevised but for Collins blacked-out to the spine, 'Macmillan' overprinted above the lower edge and the price of $5.00 printed to the top corner of the front flap. Print run: 371.

41 Dragonflies

A hallowed title, revered by the naturalist and bibliophile alike: well written, elegantly produced and ahead of its time; scarce and valuable, with a particularly becoming dust jacket. Just one small printing in hardback format, but reprinted 15 years later as an 'affordable' paperback in 1975, which purportedly sold out within a month of publication!

At 42/- *Dragonflies* was a comparatively expensive book when first published, for instance NN40 *Bumblebees* (1959) cost 25/- and NN42 *Fossils* (1960), 30/-. In the first year *c.* 2,400 copies were sold but by the second year sales were less than 400 copies. The Editorial Board meeting in November 1961 attributed this to the book being too expensive and too specialised. Thereafter it trickled out at around 200 copies a year, until going out of print in the spring of 1972.

There is a variant of the jacket with an errant blue blotch, which varies in size and intensity; looks very much like a printer's fingerprint, but the fault is subtle and mentioned only for curiosity's sake: no significance should be attached to it, though it does tend to be associated with books sold later.

The paper used for the dust jacket was obviously of good quality, strong and durable, as was that used in the book, so paradoxically, whilst a 'four-star title', it is comparatively easy to find in fine condition; the series numeral, on the spine, is prone to fading, but is otherwise colourfast.

NN41A	First Edition, 1960 (15 February 1960).
Title:	'The New Naturalist	Dragonflies'.
Authors:	'by	Philip S. Corbet	Cynthia Longfield	N. W. Moore'.
Illust:	'With 53 colour plates by S. Beaufoy	16 photographs in black and white	200 maps and diagrams	with key to larvae by A. E. Gardner'.
Editors:	JF, JG, JH, LDS and EH (Photographic Editor).
Printer:	Willmer Brothers and Haram Ltd., Birkenhead.
Collation:	pp. xii, 260; 12 leaves of colour plates printed to both sides; 4 leaves of b/w plates printed to both sides. (17 × 16-page gatherings).
Jacket:	[Rear panel] The New Naturalist library listing NN1–40, omitting NN6. [Rear flap] Adverts for *Insect Natural History, Insect Migration,* and *Moths.*

Price:	42s. net.
Print run:	5,000; no. sold: *c.* 4,750, inc. repriced jackets below.

NN41A-AP1 1st Repriced DJ (1971–72), Collins dual price sticker of £2.10 and 42/- stuck over the original printed price in accordance with decimalisation. No. sold: *c.* 300[?]; o/p: April 1972.

BPB41A Collins Paperback, Reprint, 1985 (21 January 1985). ISBN: 0002190648; pp. [14], 1–178, 181–260' [32 – b/w illus.]; (19 × 16-page gatherings). A new three-page Authors' preface has been added (the original Editors' and Authors' prefaces are retained) and text on p. 178 rearranged to enable omission of pp. 179/180: to ensure an overall total of 304 pages, but pagination remains unaltered. Price: £6.50. Print run: 1,600; no. sold: *c.* 1,530; o/p: 1985. Purportedly this paperback edition sold out inside a month – probably an exaggeration, but undoubtedly *Dragonflies* was very successful and by mid-February total sales were already around 1,000 copies.

POD41A Print-on-demand digital copy.

42 Fossils

Fossils, first printed in 1960, sold well and was out of print by the end of the following year. This was partly due to a first edition print run of only *c.* 5,000 copies and consequently it is now scarce. It was reprinted in 1962, again in 1970 and finally in 1973, without any significant revisions, though there is some variation in the thicknesses of the different reprints, depending on the weight of the paper used; the colours of the jackets vary considerably too. The 1973 reprint sports two binding variants and two different jackets, and in response to inflationary pressure nearly every one of these jackets has been price-clipped and repriced: seemingly very few were sold in their, original, entire state. *Fossils* was finally reissued as a Bloomsbury reprint in 1989, by which time much of the content was well out of date.

The first edition jacket, often chipped and foxed, is prone to fading on the spine where the ochre of the echinoids ages to a yellow, so a fine copy certainly now falls within the circumscription of what bibliophiles refer to as a *difficult* title. Total no. of *Collins* books printed: *c.* 15,000; total no. sold: *c.* 13,950; o/p: 1978.

NN42A   **First Edition**, 1960 (14 March 1960).
Title: 'The New Naturalist | Fossils'.
Author: 'by H. H. Swinnerton | C.B.E., D.Sc. | Professor
               Emeritus | The University of | Nottingham'
Illust: 'With one colour plate | by Maurice Wilson | 133 black
               and white photographs | and 21 text figures'.
Editors: JF, JG, JH, LDS and EH (Photographic Editor).
Printer: Willmer Brothers and Haram Ltd.; Birkenhead.
Collation: pp. xiv, 274; a single colour plate printed to verso only
               (frontispiece); 12 leaves of b/w plates printed to both
               sides (18 × 16-page gatherings).
Jacket: [Rear panel] The New Naturalist library listing NN1–41
               (Type 42, variant 1). [Rear flap] Adverts for *The Open
               Sea II Fish & Fisheries*; *Bumblebees* and *The Salmon* each
               supported with press comments.
Price: 30s. net.
Print run: 5,000; no. sold: *c.* 4,620; o/p: end of 1961.
Notes: 1) The first time that the 'Type 42' NN library
               appeared on the rear panel of a jacket – the format to
               be used unchanged for the next 23 years. 2) The
               captions for the b/w plates are not on the plate itself
               but on the adjacent page of letterpress – a unique
               arrangement in the NN library. 3) Book 24mm thick.

NN42B First Reprint, 1962 (May). 'First Edition, 1960 | Reprinted,
1962'. As NN42A with minimal textual changes: the title page has
been reset and the date omitted. However, changes to the
physical properties of the book are more significant: this is an
inferior production though still printed by Willmer Brothers and
Haram Ltd. The paper is rougher, lighter and more translucent,
resulting in a noticeably thinner book, 22 mm, the printing is
imprecise and fuzzy, not at all like the crisp letterpress of the first
edition. The jacket colours are stronger, the central spiral of the
ammonite now dark grey; the NN library lists nos. 1–45 (type 42,
variant 4); the rear flap advertises *Weeds and Aliens*, *The World of the
Soil* and *Dartmoor*; front flap unchanged. Price: 30s.net. Print run:
5,000; o/p: 1970.

NN42C Second Reprint, 1970. ISBN 0002130661 (to jacket only).
'First Edition, 1960 | Reprinted, 1962 | Reprinted, 1970'. As NN42B.
Editors: JF, JG, JH, MD & EH. Now printed by Collins Clear-Type
Press, but, ironically, the printing is even more fuzzy than the 1962
reprint; book 24mm thick. The jacket is lighter, colours closer to
the first edition; the NN library lists NN1–50 (Type 42, variant 8);
the rear flap unchanged, but for the ISBN; blurb to front flap
truncated and supplemented with 3 press commendations.
Dual-price: £1.80 & 36s. net. Print run: 3,000; no. sold: *c.* 2,500[?];
o/p: 1973. Note: This is, chronologically, the first New Naturalist to
have an ISBN; it does not appear on the book, only on the jacket.

**Note on the first and second states of the 1973 reprint (NN42D
and NN42E):** According to the NN statement for April 1974, around
half the 1973 reprint, that is, 942 copies, were not initially bound
up, but retained as quires – and, presumably, bound up later,
probably in 1975. These two bindings are very similar, but with a
few minor differences: the shoulders of the second state are more
pronounced, the joints more deeply impressed, but the two states
are principally separated by the length of 'Collins' on the spine of
the casing. However, two different jackets exist and it would
appear that the later binding was supplied only with the revised
jacket. That being the case, the two distinct bindings with their
respective dust jackets have been classified as first and second
states. But it is not unlikely that, a few 'hybrids' occurred, at the
point of transition from first to second state.

NN42D Third Reprint, First State 1973 [15/10/1973]. The ISBN
(0002130661) is now printed to the imprint page, as well as the rear
jacket flap. 'First Edition, 1960 | Reprinted, 1962 | Reprinted, 1970
| Reprinted, 1973'. As NN42C, but the paper is finer and the
printing is crisper, but still printed by Collins; book 22 mm thick.
'Collins' to the green buckram binding *c.* 20 mm long. The colours
of the *Durasealed* jacket are redder and the central ammonite
spiral now black; the NN library lists NN1–56 (Type 42, variant 13);
both flaps unaltered. Price: £2.75 net. Print run: 2,000 of which *c.*
1,050 bound up in the first instance. Note: The sales reports do not
list the two repriced variants below so the number of each sold is
impossible to determine.
NN42D-AP1 1st Repriced DJ (1974–75), £3.50 sticker.
NN42D-AP2 2nd Repriced DJ (1975–76), £3.95 sticker.

NN42E Third Reprint, Second State 1973 (bound-up 1975?). ISBN
to imprint page unchanged, but that to the jacket has changed to
0002194325, though this number appears to be invalid. Bound up
from the same sheets as NN42D. Book 21mm thick. 'Collins' to the
green buckram binding *c.* 18mm long. The *Durasealed* jacket is
2–3mm too short for the book, colours as NN42D first state; the NN
library lists NN1–58 (Type 42, variant 14); both flaps unaltered, but
for the revised ISBN. It would seem that all jackets have been
price-clipped and repriced. No. bound thus: *c.* 900[?]; no. sold:
unknown but probably a few copies pulped or remaindered to a
bookclub; o/p: 1975.
NN42E-AP1 First Repriced Jacket (1975–76). £4.00: *c.* 350[?]
NN42E-AP2 Second Repriced Jacket (1976–77). £4.50: *c.* 400.
NN42E-AP3 Third Repriced Jacket (1977–78). £5.50: *c.* 200[?]

POD42A Print-on-demand digital copy of 1970 reprint NN42C.

BL42A Bloomsbury Edition, 1989 [31/12/1989]. ISBN 1870630939;
pp. xiv, 274; [2] [26 – b/w illustrations]. A b/w facsimile of the 1973
reprint: NN43D. The blurb to the jacket is a combination of that to
the Collins jacket and extracts from the Editor's blurb. Price:
£12.95. Print run: unknown, but a significant proportion
remaindered.

43 Weeds & Aliens

Lawns are productive habitats for daisies as are bibliographies for pedants – and therefore please note that the correct title is 'Weeds & Aliens' with an ampersand. This form of title appears on the title page, the dust jacket and the spine of the book, though perhaps in a move to live by his own maxim 'consistency…is the foible of a feeble mind' (the author's preface) the half-title states 'Weeds and Aliens'! This latter title is almost invariably how it is given in Collins' lists, literature and elsewhere, though we will stick with bibliographic convention and the ampersand.

Just two editions though the second edition is really little more than a reprint. Despite remaining in print for over 11 years the price was not increased: at the end of this period the book cost, in real terms, about half that at the beginning.

It was also one of just a handful of main series books with a frontispiece plate, but in this case a befuddled photograph of the Monkey Flower – perhaps Salisbury felt obliged to use it as it was provided by the New Naturalist Editor and commissioner of the book, Sir Julian Huxley? In contrast to the title page is the fabulous jacket, but the poppies on the spine are quick to bleach in the sun, and as this design is more compromised than most when faded, it's worth seeking out ,and paying for, a bright copy.

Total print run: *c.* 8,000; total no. sold *c.* 7,900; o/p: end of 1972.

NN43A	**First Edition**, 1961 (24 April 1961).
Title:	'The New Naturalist	Weeds & Aliens'.
Author:	'by	Sir Edward Salisbury	C.B.B., D.Sc., LLD. (Hon.), V.H.M., F.R.S., F.L.S.	Late Director of The	Royal Botanic Gardens, Kew.'
Illust:	'With a colour frontispiece	29 photographs in black and white	and 34 line drawings, diagrams	and maps by the author'.
Editors:	JF, JG, JH, LDS and EH (Photographic Editor).
Printer:	Collins Clear-Type Press: London and Glasgow.
Collation:	pp. [8], 9–384; colour frontispiece plate printed to verso only; 8 leaves of b/w plates printed to both sides (24 × 16-page gatherings).
Dust Jacket:	Rear panel: The New Naturalist library listing NN1–43 (Type 42, variant 2). Rear flap: Advert for 'An Outstanding New Volume in the New Naturalist Series': *Lords & Ladies*.

Price: 30s. net.
Print run: 5,000; no. sold: *c.* 4,800[?]; o/p: 1963.
Notes: The production of the first edition was drawn out: the author's preface is dated 1959 but the book was not published until 1961.

NN43B Second edition, 1964. 'First edition 1961 | second edition 1964'. Essentially a reprint with minor revisions, all accommodated within the existing typesetting: a few misprints corrected, omissions inserted and the odd addition made; a 7-line 'Preface to the Second Edition', dated June 1963, added and a 'Postscript to Chapter 1. Nutrients in Weeds' squeezed onto bottom of last page. Casing and paper as NN43A. The NN library to the jacket lists NN1–45 (Type 42, variant 4); rear flap unchanged; press endorsement by the TES inserted to front flap, below same blurb. Price: 30s. net. Print run: 3,000; o/p: 1972 (AP1).

NN43B-AP1 Repriced DJ (*c.* 1971–72), over-printed £1.50 in accordance with decimalisation.

POD43A Print-on-demand digital copy of the 1964 second edition NN43B.

US43A US Edition 1961. The Macmillan Company, New York. The book and jacket identical to the Collins first edition NN43A but for a small printed sticker applied to the spine of the jacket 'Distributed by Macmillan'; the jacket price-clipped, with a $6.00 sticker applied.

44 The Peak District

K. C. Edwards first proposed *The Peak District* in 1953; it was to be written by him and a supporting team of appropriate specialists. The editor, James Fisher, was wary of the team approach and commented that from 'bitter experience' he preferred a single author. In 1956 a contract for a book of 100,000 words was awarded to Edwards as principal author, and while it is only his name that appears on the jacket and casing, *The Peak District* remained very much a collaboration of multiple authors, one of whom was Swinnerton, the author of NN42 *Fossils*.

The manuscript was submitted in 1958/9 but at around 75,000 words was slight. The Editors requested that the information on birds in the appendix should be expanded and, along with new information on mammals (this area of the park's fauna had been omitted), be put into a new chapter covering the animal life of the district. But a cursory inspection of the book will show that ornithology is still in the appendix and mammals omitted altogether. To pad the book out to 256 pages, i.e. 16 sets of 16-page gatherings, the number of lines per page was reduced to just 37 (the norm was around 40 lines/page).

The Peak District was scheduled for publication on 10 July 1961 but, due to a delay in the return of the proofs by the author, did not appear until spring 1962; it was reprinted three times with a new edition published in 1974. Unusually, this new edition has been completely reset with a new typeface (but not from the plates of the 1973 Fontana edition) and the textual revisions are fairly extensive. It was due to be reprinted again and corrections were made by the authors and submitted in early 1980, but costings from the Collins factory were 'horrific' and the project abandoned.

It was hoped that *The Peak District* would appeal to the tourist market, but it was students who were the principal purchasers and no doubt this influenced the decision to republish the title in 1973 as a Fontana paperback, though it was not reprinted in this format. It was also subsequently published in 1989 by Bloomsbury.

Due to missing sales statements it is not possible to state with certainty the number of first editions printed, but it was c. 5,000, which is in line with other titles published around this period. The same uncertainty applies to the reprints, though total figures are given below. However the first two reprints of *The Peak District* are, along with a handful of other titles reprinted in the early 1960s unique in the NN library for citing, on the imprint page, the month of publication with the year – *à la* Fontana titles.

Finding a fine or very good first edition copy of *The Peak District* does not usually present a challenge, though the soft grey-blue often fades to grey on the spine, but the abstract nature of the Ellis's design does a good job of camouflaging this defect; the jacket colours of the 1974 second edition are quite different. While it would appear that the same number of first editions was printed as its series neighbour, *Common Lands*, a like copy will cost significantly less than the latter.

Total print run (Collins editions): c. 14,500; total no. sold: c. 13,550; o/p: 1979.

NN44A	**First Edition**, 1962 (12 March 1962).
Title:	'The New Naturalist | The Peak District'.
Authors:	'by | K. C. Edwards | M.A., Ph.D. | assisted by | H. H. Swinnerton | C.B.E., D.Sc. | and | R. H. Hall | F.L.S.'.
Illust:	'With 7 colour photographs | 49 photographs in black and white | and 15 maps and diagrams'.
Editors:	JF, JG, JH, LDS and EH (Photographic Editor).
Printer:	Collins Clear-Type Press: London and Glasgow.
Collation:	pp. xvi, 240; 4 leaves of colour plates printed to one side only; 12 leaves of b/w plates printed to both sides (16 × 16-page gatherings).
Jacket:	[Rear panel] the New Naturalist library listing NN1–44 (Type 42, variant 3). [Rear flap] Adverts for *Mountains and Moorlands*, *Mountain Flowers* and *Britain's Structure*

and Scenery, each title supported with a press clip.

Price: 30s. net. Print run: 5,000[?].

NN44B Second Impression, May 1962. 'First Impression March, 1962 \| Second Impression May, 1962' (see note on inclusion of the month of publication in intro.). Date omitted from the title page, otherwise identical to NN44A. Jacket also identical. Price: 30s. net. Print run: 2,000[?]; o/p: end of 1964.

NN44C Third Impression, November 1964. 'First Impression March, 1962 \| Second Impression May, 1962 \| Third Impression November, 1964'. As NN44B. The NN library to the jacket lists NN1–45 (Type 42, variant 4a) otherwise unaltered. Price: 30s. net. Print run: 2,000[?]; o/p: autumn 1969.

NN44D Fourth Impression, 1970. ISBN: 0002131765 (to jacket only). 'First Impression 1962 \| Reprinted 1962 \| Reprinted 1964 \| Reprinted 1970'. (Note: The month of publication now omitted.) As NN44C. Editors: JF, JG, JH, MD and EH. The NN library lists NN1–50 (Type 42, variant 8); ISBN added to rear flap. Price: '£2.10p. net \| 42s. net'. Print run: 2,500; o/p: autumn 1973.

NN44E Second Edition, 1974. ISBN: 0002131765 (to imprint page and jacket). 'First Impression 1962 \| Reprinted 1962 \| Reprinted 1964 \| Reprinted 1970 \| Second Edition 1974'; pp. xvi, 223, [1] with same arrangement of plates as NN44A (15 × 16-page gatherings). Editors: JH, JG, MD, KM and EH. A fairly comprehensive revision based on the Fontana ed. of previous year: a preface to the second edition has been appended to the Author's Preface, which acknowledges Mr. J. M. Smith's assistance; Appendix III has been rewritten, and Appendix IV omitted. But the text completely reset in a new typeface with 39 lines to the page; the book, consequently a little shorter. The NN library to the *Durasealed* jacket lists NN1–56 (Type 42, variant 13); front and rear flaps unchanged. Price: £2.80. Print run: 3,000; no. sold: c. 1,110 + repriced variants below, + c. 600 either remaindered to a bookclub or pulped.

NN44E-AP1 1st Repriced DJ (1975–76), £3.50 sticker, c. 250 sold.
NN44E-AP2 2nd Repriced DJ (1976–77), £3.95 sticker, c. 380 sold.
NN44E-AP3 3rd Repriced DJ (1978), £4.95 sticker, c. 230 sold.
NN44E-AP4 4th Repriced DJ (1979), £6.50 sticker, < 50 sold.

POD44A Print-on-demand digital copy of the 1962 second impression NN44B.

F44A Fontana Paperback First Edition, 1973 (May). ISBN: 0006331939; pp. 251, [5]; 8 leaves of b/w plates, printed on glossy paper, to both sides; typical paper prone to tanning. A revised edition first published by Fontana. Editors omitted. Single p. of ads. for Fontana NNs at front and three pp. of ads for Fontana books at rear with headings: 'Fontana Social Science'; 'Fontana Politics' and 'Fontana Introduction to Modern Economics'. Integral order form (not loose). The front cover photograph of Monsal Dale by John McCrindle; rear cover carries 2 press reviews for *The Peak District*; price 60p. Total print run: 11,000 with total sales: c. 11,000.

BL44A Bloomsbury Edition, 1990 (31/12/1990). ISBN: 1870630343; pp. xvi, 223, [1], [32 b/w illustrations] (16 × 16-page gatherings). A b/w facsimile of the 1974 second edition NN44E. Price £12.95. Print run: unknown; a significant proportion remaindered.

45 The Common Lands of England and Wales

Common Lands, on the face of it, is quite straightforward with just one edition and a single reprint, but in fact is complicated by a number of anomalies, errors and binding variants. The first edition jacket erroneously puts Stamp before Hoskins, as does the casing. The title page was however correct, so 1 out 3. The order was corrected on the reprint jacket to Hoskins and Stamp, but the casing got overlooked, so 2 out of 3. However not all copies of the reprint were bound up in the first instance and later casings were corrected so finally, a good few years later, 3 out of 3! So, why all the fuss? Presumably, because Hoskins and Stamp were equal joint authors their names should be arranged alphabetically; additionally it would be both impolite and immodest for Stamp, as a series editor, to have his name before the invited author. Of course, all of this is inconsequential regarding the content of the book, but it helps to identify a binding history – and with the 1964 reprint there are three distinct binding variants. This is, perhaps, not surprising considering the reprint remained in print for 15 years, and it is for this reason too, that there are a number of repriced jackets, and during this period the Pound was decimalised too. Furthermore, jackets for the reprint were evidently printed in batches as required, some with and some without *Duraseal*, and the last printing was incorrectly trimmed, ending up a full 5mm taller than the book – by far the tallest New Naturalist jacket (as these jackets overlap the binding they are usually creased at the edges). All of this has rendered the *Common Lands* 1964 reprint one of the most challenging titles in the series to catalogue and I suspect that the full story is still not told.

One reviewer had remarked that there were 'too many *Morrismen*' and at Stamp's insistence plate IIIb (of May Day Dancing) in the first edition was changed, in the reprint, for a photograph of a New Forest road sign!

Common Lands is often in very good condition and while the first edition is a relatively scarce book, finding a copy in fine condition does not usually present a problem; it does not suffer from fading.

Total print run: 9,000; total no. sold: 8,250; o/p: summer 1979.

NN45A   **First Edition**, 1963 (08 April 1963).

Title: 'The New Naturalist | the Common Lands of | England & Wales'.

Authors: 'by | W. G. Hoskins | and | L. Dudley Stamp | Members of the Royal Commission | on Common Land, 1955–1958'

Illust: 'With 6 colour photographs | and 31 photographs in black and white'.

Editors: JF, JG, JH, LDS and EH (Photographic Editor).

Collation: pp. xvii, [1], 366; 4 leaves of colour plates printed to one side only; 12 leaves of b/w plates printed to both sides (24 × 16-page gatherings).

TABLE NN45B Diagnostic features of the three 1964 reprint NN45B binding variants.

Common Lands reprint 45B	Binding	Authors' names on casing spine	Casing Fabric	Joints (external)	Shoulder of Joint (external)	Jacket
Primary binding variant	Well produced – as associated with the series	STAMP above HOSKINS	Typical 'group 2' green buckram	Not impressed	Slightly proud of board	Not repriced. Series no. roundel usually truncated at head of spine *c.* 220–222 mm tall
Second binding variant	An inferior production, not well executed; fore-edge of book-block irregular	HOSKINS above STAMP	Smooth, bright green fine buckram; atypical for the series.	Not impressed	Rounded, ill-defined, in line with board	Not repriced. Series no. roundel usually in line with or a little below top edge; *c.* 222 mm tall.
Third binding variant	Well produced – as associated with the series	HOSKINS above STAMP	Typical 'group 2' green buckram	Deeply impressed	In line with or slightly above board	Jacket invariably repriced. Series no. roundel usually a few mm below top edge. 222 mm tall or 226–227 mm (DJ2). Often *Duraseal*ed.

Casing: L. Dudley Stamp above W. G. Hoskins on the spine.

Jacket: Size: 510 × 222 mm. [Rear panel] The New Naturalist library listing NN1–44 (Type 42, variant 4). [Rear flap] *Britain's Structure and Scenery* and *Man and the Land* are listed under the heading 'Also by L. Dudley Stamp'.

Price: 42s. net.

Print run: 5,000 (out-turn); no. sold: *c.* 4,540.

Notes: 1) On the jacket L. Dudley Stamp positioned above W. G. Hoskins; 2) For diagnostic features of the following three binding variants see table NN45B).

NN45B-B1 First Reprint, Primary Binding Variant, 1964 (November). 'First published March 1963 | | Reprinted November 1964'. A reprint of NN45A with minimal revisions, one plate substituted as explained in the intro. and a few minor corrections and additions e.g. new paragraphs on *The New Forest* added to page 175, insertion of item 32 on p. 291 and spelling corrections to Norfolk place names on pp. 300/301. 'Stamp' still appears above 'Hoskins' on the spine of the casing. More than one paper type has been used in this reprint variant, but neither with any discernible diminution of print quality. The jacket, 220–222mm high, essentially as NN45A, but 'Hoskins' now appears above 'Stamp' on the front panel and spine; rear panel and rear flap unaltered; blurb to front panel précised with three press commendations appended. Price: 42s. net. A feature of these jackets is that they are often a couple of mm. too short for the book and most appear to have been trimmed off-centre so that the roundel at the head of the spine is truncated to a greater or lesser degree. Print run: 4,000 (out-turn) including 'B1' and 'B2' & variants below.

NN45B-B2 First Reprint, Second Binding Variant, 1964 [probably bound up *c.* 1968]. 'Hoskins' now correctly positioned above 'Stamp' on the spine of the casing, which uses an atypical, smooth bright green buckram; the binding is poorly executed, the hinges often stiff so the boards do not lie flat. The jacket unchanged but generally trimmed centrally with the roundel entire at the head of the spine; the printed price remains at 42s. net. No. bound thus: unknown. Note: This unusual buckram was also used for some copies of the 1968 2nd, ed. of *Life in Lakes & Rivers* and *The Sea Shore* revised edition of 1966.

NN45B-B2 First Reprint, Third Binding Variant, 1964 [probably bound up early 1970s, with a further binding in 1974). 'Hoskins' now correctly positioned above 'Stamp' on the spine of the casing, which reverts to the typical NN buckram; the binding is well executed. The jacket unchanged but generally trimmed centrally with the roundel entire at the head of the spine; the printed price remains at 42s. net. However a number of other jackets were used as catalogued below. No. bound thus: unknown. Note: The April 1974 New Naturalist statement indicates that *c.* 950 copies were to be bound up for delivery in August of that year, but these are impossible to distinguish from this binding variant; most will wear repriced jackets.

NN45B-B3-DJ1 First Reprint, Third Binding Variant, First Jacket Variant (sold 1971–1974?). Jacket unchanged but now *Durasealed*; p. clipped, and over-printed £2.10 net (in accordance with decimalisation in 1971). No. sold: unknown.

NN45B-B3-DJ2 First Reprint, Third Binding Variant, Second Jacket Variant. Exactly as the first jacket variant i.e. *Durasealed* and overprinted £2.10 net, but a full 5 mm taller at 226–227 mm high. All copies seen price-clipped, and over-printed £2.10 net as DJ1, but the over-print manually cancelled in black pen, with a Collins price-sticker placed over the top, as follows:- .

NN45B-B3-DJ2-AP1 1st Repriced DJ (1975–76), £4.00 sticker, *c.* 200 sold.

NN45B-B3-DJ2-AP2 2nd Repriced DJ (1976), £4.95 sticker, *c.* 120 sold.

NN45B-B3-DJ2-AP3 3rd Repriced DJ (1977–79), £6.50 sticker, *c.* 300 sold. Note: The over-sized jacket is interesting in that it shows the full extent of the design.

POD45A Print-on-demand digital copy of the 1964 reprint NN45B.

46 The Broads

Just one printing of *The Broads*, but it remained in print for nine years. Collins was however keen to retain a Broads volume in print and was intending to replace the original book with a new edition by Ellis. However by 1975, Collins had given up hope of Ellis ever completing the new book (it took him nearly 15 years to complete the first, *The New Naturalists*, 2005) so approached Martin George to write it, but this again fell by the wayside. Finally 38 years after the appearance of the original *The Broads*, Moss's book was published: no. 89 in the series.

'E. A. Ellis' is the only name to appear on the title page, casing and jacket, but *The Broads* was very much a collaborative affair and while he oversaw the work, he only, in fact, wrote a little over half the text. The other contributors are listed below.

In the mistaken belief that a photographic dust jacket was more contemporary and therefore would increase sales, the Ellises' artwork was usurped for a laminated jacket featuring a photograph of a Norfolk Wherry on a Broadland water. This image, which also doubled as the colour frontispiece was uncredited, but was in fact by John Markham. Gone too was the wide title band running across the top of the front panel design, but was, at least, retained on the spine. The following title *Snowdonia National Park* suffered the same fate but fortunately this experiment, which did not increase sales, was quickly abandoned and the Ellises' artwork reinstated for NN48 *Grass and Grassland*.

Not only was the jacket a sore thumb aesthetically but it was also poorly made. It does not wear well; the clear laminate is often prone to craquelure, like the oil paint on an old master, or chipped with small creases showing as white lines. In 1973 a very small number of jackets, less than 300, were reprinted to replace 'faulty stock'. There is no reference, on file, as to the nature of the fault, but presumably they had already started to crackle. These replacement jackets were reset with the NN library brought up to date; they are particularly scarce and I have only seen a couple but perhaps not surprisingly, they were both in fine condition.

NN46A	**First Edition**, 1963 (13 May 1963?).
Title:	'The New Naturalist | The Broads'.
Author:	'by | E. A. Ellis'.
Illust:	'With 47 colour photographs | and 68 maps and diagrams'.
Editors:	JF, JG, JH, LDS and EH (Photographic Editor).
Printer:	Collins Clear-Type Press, London and Glasgow.
Contributors:	J. E. Sainty, J. N. Jennings, Charles Green, J. M. Lambert, C. T. Smith, & R. Gurney.
Collation:	pp. xi, [1], 401, [3]; colour frontispiece plt. printed to recto only; 14 leaves of black and white plates printed to both sides (26 × 16-page gatherings).
Jacket:	[Paper] glossy, laminated, surface prone to crackling, poor wearing. [Rear panel] The New Naturalist library listing NN1–46 (Type 42, variant 5). [Rear flap] Adverts for *Highlands and Islands*, *Dartmoor* and *The Weald*.
Price:	36s. net.
Print run:	8,500; total no. sold c. 7,810 inc. repriced and variant jackets below; o/p: spring 1974 (DJ1).
Notes:	1) Plates XIV & XV are printed upside down. 2) It would appear that not all sheets were bound up at the same time, or at least were bound in batches and subtle binding variations occur but these are so minor that no attempt has been made to separate them out.

NN46A-AP1 1st Repriced DJ (1971–73), overprinted £1.80 net in accordance with decimalisation.

NN46A-DJ1 First Jacket Variant (printed 1973; sold 1973–1974). The New Naturalist library now lists NN1–55 (Type 42 variant 12); front and rear flaps identical but with an integral printed price of £1.80 to the corner. Laminated with a glossy surface but slightly different to above. No. sold: < 300.

POD46A Print-on-demand digital copy.

47 The Snowdonia National Park

The comments for the preceding title regarding the photographic dust jacket apply equally to *Snowdonia*, though the jacket for this title is less prone to craquelure, but it is however particularly light-sensitive. Fine copies with bright spines where the number roundel is still dark red and the bracken at the base the same rust colour as the front panel are hard to find. But they do exist. Incidentally this is one of just a few titles where the series roundel is coloured.

Reprinted twice with revised jackets to suit, but with minimal revisions to the text. The total number printed was c. 15,500 but a tranche of c. 1,600 quires was lost in the vast Glasgow warehouse, with a further 950 or so bound copies probably sold to Readers Union. We do know that in the final analysis Collins sold c. 12,350 copies. *Snowdonia* finally went out of print in late 1980, but was out of stock for 17 months in 1975/1976, following the

TABLE NN48 Summary of differences between first and second binding variants of NN48 *Grass and Grasslands*.

Grass & Grasslands	Weight excl. Jacket	Binding	Joints (external)	Lettering to Spine	Hinges (internal)	Stitching	Jacket
1st Binding Variant B1	464–474 g	Medium green slightly shiny buckram; noticeably thicker: dimension across the spine approx. 24 mm.	Not impressed	'Collins' to base of spine approx. 20 mm long.	Mull evident under endpaper at hinges, the front edge of which is sharp.	Sewn with four stitches, each 25 mm long.	Printed price of 28s. net; if clipped, over-stamped £1.40 or Collins £3.00 sticker.
2nd Binding Variant B2	444–452 g	Dark green shiny buckram; dimension across spine approx. 21 mm.	Distinctly impressed	'Collins' to base of spine approx. 18 mm long.	Mull not used and therefore not evident at hinges, which are smooth.	Sewn with four stitches, each 30 mm long.	Always clipped, with Collins price sticker – £3.00 or more.

disappearance of the unbound quires and before the 1976 reprint was published.

NN47A   **First Edition**, 1966 (10 June 1966?).
Title: 'The New Naturalist | The Snowdonia | National | Park'.
Author: 'by | W. M. Condry'.
Illust: 'With 11 colour photographs | 52 photographs in black-and-white | and 9 maps and diagrams'.
Editors: JF, JG, JH, LDS and EH (Photographic Editor).
Printer: Collins Clear-Type Press, London and Glasgow.
Collation: pp. xvii, [1], 238; 4 leaves of colour plates printed to one side only; 12 leaves of black and white plates printed to both sides (16 × 16-page gatherings).
Jacket: [Paper] glossy, laminated. [Rear panel] The New Naturalist library listing NN1–46 (Type 42, variant 5). [Rear flap] 'Other New Naturalist Regional Volumes include' *Dartmoor, The Highlands and Islands* and *The Peak District.*
Price: 30s. net.
Print run: 7,500; no. sold: c. 7,200.
Notes: 1) The photograph on the front panel remains uncredited in all editions, but was by Kenneth Scowen. 2) The blurb states the Park was declared in 1956, when in fact it was 1951 – an error that remained uncorrected in all editions. 3) Plate III was badly trimmed and positioned, truncating Snowdon, so too the upper photograph on plate XIX decapitates the uppermost cormorant; both faults corrected in later editions.

NN47B Second Edition, 1967. 'First Edition 1966 | Second Edition 1967'. No date to the title page. Revisions are minor, e.g. on p. 125: [the siskin] '… probably now breeds in Coed-y-brenin and in the Dovey Forest…' and on p. 190: 'I should add that as a result of my mentioning these facts in the first impression of this book, an enterprising reader has traced Lhuyd's locality and found the spignel still growing there…' Additionally, a few minor corrections to the plates: Plate III now positioned to include all of Snowdon, but at the expense of the caption; also the upper photo. on plate XIX slightly repositioned. The NN library to the jacket lists NN1–50 (Type 42, variant 8), otherwise DJ unaltered. Price: 30s. net. Print run: 6,000 (but c. 3,000 delivered in 1967 with a further 1,500 in 1968, however c. 1,600 unbound copies disappeared – see intro.); no. sold: c. 2,200 + repriced variants below.
NN47B-AP1 1st Repriced DJ (1971–1975), £1.50 net sticker, c. 1,900 sold.
NN47B-AP2 2nd Repriced DJ (1975), £3.50 sticker, < 50 sold (unverified).

NN47C Second Edition, First Reprint, 1976. ISBN: 0002195259. 'First Edition 1966 | Second Edition 1967 | Reprinted 1976'. As NN47B. Editors: MD, JG, KM and EH. The paper is brighter and smoother though the plates are matter and the photographs more grainy. The NN library to the jacket lists NN 1–58 (Type 42, variant

14); rear flap now omits *Dartmoor* but *Highlands and Islands* and *Peak District* retained; ISBN added; front flap unaltered; price: £4.95. Print run: 2,000; no. sold: c. 550. Note: scarce with unclipped DJ – some copies repriced as catalogued below and would seem c. 950 copies were sold to RU.
NN47C-AP1 1st Repriced DJ (1978–1979), £5.50 sticker, c. 300 sold.
NN47C-AP2 2nd Repriced DJ (1979–1980), £6.00 sticker, c. 100 sold.
NN47C-AP3 3rd Repriced DJ (1980–1981), £7.50 sticker, c. 50 sold.

POD47A Print-on-demand digital copy of the 1967 second edition NN47B.

F47A Fontana Paperback First Edition, 1969. ISBN: 000631953X (appears on rear covers of 1973 and 1976 imp. only); printed by Collins Clear-Type Press; pp. 320; 12 leaves of b/w plates, printed on glossy paper, to both sides. A copy of the 1967 second edition NN47B but reset. Editors: JG, JH, MD, KM and EH. Adverts for Fontana NNs at front. The front cover photograph of Snowdon from Traeth Mawr by Kenneth Scowen; rear cover carries five press reviews for *Snowdonia*. Price: 10/6. Total print run including reprints: 12,000; o/p: 1978.
The following reprints exactly as preceding impression unless stated otherwise, changes to internal adverts ignored.
F47B Second Impression, July 1969.
F47C Third Impression, June 1970. Editors omitted. Smooth bright white paper. Price: 10/- (50p).
F47D Fourth Impression, April 1971.
F47E Fifth Impression, April 1973. Editors reinstated: JG, JH, MD, KM and EH. Usual tanned paper. Price: UK 75p.
F47F Sixth Impression, March 1976.

48 Grass and Grasslands

Moore kept his *Grass and Grasslands* short; in fact at 192 pages, just twelve 16-page gatherings, the shortest of all books in the main series.

Just one edition and one printing of c. 6,500 copies, but it wasn't popular and remained in print for 16 years (1966–1981). Seemingly just one printing too of the dust jacket. There are however two distinct binding variants. The New Naturalist statement of October 1974, under the heading 'Work in Progress', gives a figure '1,465Q' for *Grass and Grasslands* with a delivery date of December

1974, i.e. these were unbound quires in the process of being bound. From other sales reports we can deduce that all books sold during and after 1975 were these second bindings. The first binding variant has a noticeably thicker spine than the second, though there are several ways of telling them apart, as identified in table NN48 on page 186. In the second binding variant, the dust jackets are always clipped and repriced with a price sticker, though subsequent switching of dust jackets by collectors and dealers can make this an unreliable diagnostic feature. However, if your copy has a jacket with the original printed price of 28s. net intact, then almost certainly it will be on a first binding.

The fact that *Grass and Grasslands*, remained in print for such a protracted time, coupled with two binding operations, resulted in a comparatively high level of 'natural wastage'; additionally the sales figures for 1978/1979 show a sudden reduction of available stock of 400, which suggests pulping or remaindering, probably the latter to a bookclub.

Grass and Grasslands is not a difficult title to find in fine condition; it never looks well-read. The paper of the jacket does brown, but the design looks so much better on bright paper. Total number of copies sold by Collins was *c.* 5, 600 of which *c.* 4,600 were first binding variants; o/p: 1981.

NN48A-B1   **First Edition, First Binding Variant**, 1966 (31/10/1966).
Title: 'The New Naturalist | Grass And | Grasslands'.
Author: 'by | Ian Moore | C.B.E., M.Sc., Ph.D. (Leeds), N.D.A., | Dip. Ag. Sci (Cantab) | Principal, Seale Hayne Agricultural College, | Devon | Formerly Professor of Agriculture, | University College of the South-West, | Exeter'.
Illust: 'With 28 photographs in | black-and-white'.
Editors: JF, JG, JH, LDS and EH (Photographic Editor).
Printer: Collins Clear-Type Press, London and Glasgow.
Collation: pp. xiv, 175, [3]; colour frontispiece plate; 8 leaves of b/w photographic plates, printed to both sides (12 × 16-page gatherings).
Jacket: [Rear panel] The New Naturalist library listing NN 1–47 (Type 42, variant 6). [Rear flap] Adverts for *British Plant Life*, *Weeds and Aliens* and *The World of the Soil*.
Price: 28s. net.
Print run: 6,500; no. sold: *c.* 3,700 + repriced variant below.
Notes: The colour frontispiece was borrowed from NN14 *The Art of Botanical Illustration*.

NN48A-B1-AP1 1st Repriced DJ (sold 1971–74); p. clipped and over-stamped £1.40; *c.* 900 sold. Notes: In accordance with decimalisation in 1971. I have also seen this jacket on the second binding variant – difficult to explain unless a later marriage.
NN48A-B1-AP2 2nd Repriced DJ (1974), £3.00 sticker.

NN48A-B2 First Edition, Second Binding Variant. Bound up from the same sheets as NN48A, in late 1974, with a number of distinguishing features as identified in table NN48. The jacket

identical to NN48A, but price-clipped, with Collins sticker variously priced as described below. No. bound thus: *c.* 1,450; no. sold: as below + *c.* 400 remaindered to a bookclub[?].
NN48A-B2-AP2 2nd Repriced DJ (1975), £3.00 sticker, *c.* 120 sold[?].
NN48A-B2-AP3 3rd Repriced DJ (1975–76), £3.50 sticker, *c.* 250 sold.
NN48A-B2-AP4 4th Repriced DJ (1976–77), £4.50 sticker, *c.* 250 sold.
NN48A-B2-AP5 5th Repriced DJ (1978–80), £5.50 sticker, *c.* 350 sold.
NN48A-B2-AP6 6th Repriced DJ (1980–81), £7.50 sticker, < 50 sold.

POD48A Print-on-demand digital copy.

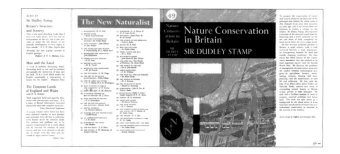

49   Nature Conservation in Britain

The period from August 1967 to October 1971 saw the publication of just one New Naturalist title and that was NN49 *Nature Conservation*, but oddly, it was NN50 *Pesticides & Pollution* that proceeded it. There are two reasons for this: firstly, the series was losing momentum and sales were down, hence lack of colour illustrations in *Nature Conservation* and secondly, the author, Sir Dudley Stamp, died two years before publication. But Stamp completed his preface before he died and the series is richer for it. It is a reflective, sometimes poignant, piece of writing that brilliantly evokes the pioneering spirit of the New Naturalist. But, unforgivably, it was omitted from the 1974 second edition.

James Fisher compiled the list of 'Conservation Areas in England, Wales and Scotland' which appears in Appendix IV, but much of this material was borrowed from his earlier book, *Shell Nature Lovers' Atlas of England, Scotland & Wales* published by Ebury Press and Michael Joseph in 1966 (31 annotated colour maps each with a page of letterpress).

From a bibliographic perspective, *Nature Conservation* is straightforward without any veiled pitfalls to trip up the unsuspecting collector, but there is one little quirk, which is unique in the series: the 1974 second edition is the only title to publicise, on the jacket, something other than a book; it fittingly carries a special appeal by Sir Peter Scott for readers to join the Fauna Preservation Society.

Nature Conservation sold well, the April 1973 NN statement described it as a best seller. A reprint was required within a year of the publication of the first edition; this, in turn, sold out quickly and the book was out of stock for the whole of 1973. By the time the new edition was published Collins had around 1,400 back orders.

Not a scarce book but difficult to find with the red of the jacket spine conserved in its natural brightness; but it looks so much better when it is. Total print run: *c.* 13,500; total no. sold: *c.* 12,460; o/p: summer 1982.

NN49A   **First Edition**, 1969 (16 June 1969).
Title: 'The New Naturalist | Nature Conservation | in Britain'.
Author: 'Sir Dudley Stamp | Late Member of the Nature | Conservancy and Chairman | of the English Committee'.
Subtitle: 'With a list of Conservation Areas in England, | Wales and Scotland compiled by James Fisher, | Deputy Chairman, the Countryside Commission'.
Editors: JF, JG, JH, MD and EH (Photographic Editor).
Printer: Collins Clear-Type Press, London and Glasgow.
Collation: pp. xiv, 273, [1]; 12 leaves of b/w plates printed to both sides (18 × 16-page gatherings).
Jacket: [Rear panel] The New Naturalist library listing NN1–50 (Type 42, variant 8). [Rear flap] 'Also by Sir Dudley Stamp', advertising *Structure and Scenery, Man and the Land* and *Common Lands*.
Price: 36s. net.
Print run: 8,000[?]; no. sold: unknown; o/p: 1970.
Notes: 1) Last sentence of NN credo omitted. 2) Book only 22 mm thick. 3) Jacket text is very dark green, almost appearing black.

NN49B Second Impression, 1970. SBN: 002131528. 'First Impression 1969 | Second Impression 1970'. Book and jacket essentially as NN49A. Date omitted from TP. SBN added to imprint page. Printed on thick smoother paper, resulting in book 29 mm thick, i.e. over 30 per cent thicker than the first ed. The jacket identical but text more obviously dark green; still priced at 36s. net. Print run: 1,500[?].
NN49B-AP1 1st Repriced DJ (1971–72), £1.80 sticker.

NN49C Second Edition, 1974 (March/April 1974). SBN: 002131528 (to imprint page); ISBN 0002131528 (to jacket). 'First Edition 1969 | Reprint 1970 | Second Edition' Printed on thick smoother paper, book now 23 mm thick. Text essentially as the first ed., with slight revisions only, e.g. addition of population figures for year 1969 on p. 2. The most important changes are found in the prelims, appendices and maps. Author's preface has been replaced (see intro.) by the Editors' 'short note on second edition'. Editors; JH, JG, MD, KM and EH. Appendixes 1, 2, and 3 brought up to date (to 1972), though Fisher's appendix remains unaltered. Maps 1–4 have been redrawn (but a combination of small typeface and poor printing render them difficult to read). Jacket now *Durasealed*; the NN library lists NN1–56 (Type 42, variant 13); rear flap carries a promotion for the Fauna Preservation Society, below which the full-length ISBN 0002131528; blurb to front flap edited and Mr M. J. Woodman credited for revising the lists and maps in the

second edition; two press reviews inserted below. Jacket colours are stronger. Price: £3.50 net. Print run: 4,000; no. sold: *c.* 2,300 plus repriced variants below.

NN49C-AP1 1st Repriced DJ (1975–76), £4.00 sticker, *c.* 300 sold.
NN49C-AP2 2nd Repriced DJ (1976–77), £4.50 sticker, *c.* 400 sold.
NN49C-AP3 3rd Repriced DJ (1978–79), £5.50 sticker, *c.* 300 sold.
NN49C-AP4 4th Repriced DJ (1979–80), £6.00 sticker, *c.* 250 sold.
NN49C-AP5 5th Repriced DJ (1980–81), £7.50 sticker, *c.* 100 sold.
NN49C-AP6 6th Repriced DJ (1981–82), £8.50 sticker, *c.* 100 sold.
NN49C-AP7 7th Repriced DJ (1982), £9.50 sticker, < 50 sold.

POD49A Print-on-demand digital copy of the 1974 second edition NN49C.

50 Pesticides and Pollution

The provisional title for Mellanby's books was 'Ecology of Toxic Chemicals', but *Pesticides and Pollution* was suggested at the Editorial Board meeting of 3 March 1964. In 1992 Collins published a new book by Mellanby entitled *Waste and Pollution: The Problem for Britain* and, when trawling the internet, you will occasionally see this book advertised with the New Naturalist subheading. Of course, it is not part of the series, but there is a good reason for this confusion – it was originally commissioned as a New Naturalist title and presumably at some stage was publicised as such. Mellanby was contracted to write a new book in 1988 with the title 'Waste, Wildlife and the Countryside', and this was intended to replace *Pesticides* and his later book, *Farming and Wildlife*. The manuscript was delivered for consideration by the board in April 1989 but it was thought unsuitable and this, coupled with the poor latter-day sales of *Farming and Wildlife*, buried it as a NN title. However, it was adapted and published outside the series as *Waste and Pollution*.

Pesticides is comparatively slight with only 224 pages and then with just 37 lines to the page, but even so, the book designers padded out the text with blank leaves at the front and rear and employed separate section-title pages for the bibliography and index, to fill the space dictated by the modular 14 × 16-page gatherings. With so much spare space it is perplexing, therefore, why the mandatory list of Editors and the NN credo were omitted from all editions? Presumably this was an oversight, but the omission of both is unique in the NN library.

Pesticides was a successful title with, in addition to the Collins hardback, 46,000 copies printed in Fontana paperback format. It was published at a time when there was heightened public concern over the use of chemicals and was quickly added to university reading lists. This popularity might explain why the Collins first edition, of which 6,500 copies were published, is disproportionately difficult to find in fine condition; it is often a little chipped/browned to the spine area.

Total no. Collins hardbacks. printed: *c.* 15,500; total no. sold: *c.* 14,320; o/p: summer 1980.

NN50A   **First Edition**, 1967 (21/08/1967).
Title: 'The New Naturalist | Pesticides and | Pollution'.
Author: 'Kenneth Mellanby'.
Editors: (omitted).
Printer: Collins Clear-Type Press, London and Glasgow.
Collation: pp. 221, [3]; 7 leaves of b/w plates printed to both sides (14 × 16-page gatherings).
Jacket: [Rear panel] The New Naturalist library listing NN 1–49 (Type 42, variant 7). [Rear flap] Other new books in this series listing: *Nature Conservation in Britain* and *The Trout*, both supported with synopses (despite this advert for *Nature Conservation* it was not to appear for another two years).
Price: 30s. net.
Print run: 6,500; no. sold: *c.* 5,800; o/p: end 1969.
Notes: The only NN that omits both the list of Editors and the NN credo.

NN50B Second Edition, 1970. SBN: 002131773. 'First Edition 1967 | Second (Revised) Edition 1970'. (Despite this statement, little more than a corrected reprint.) The only significant addition is a two-page appendix 'Composition of some chemicals described in the text', otherwise changes confined to preliminaries, e.g. date omitted from title page, street no. added to the address and the SBN added to the imprint page. The NN library to the jacket lists NN1–50 (Type 42, variant 8); the rear flap unchanged but for the insertion of the jacket design credit; the blurb has been précised with five press reviews inserted below. Dual price: 36s. net and £1.80 (the former nearer the corner to allow it to be excised post decimalisation). Print run: 3,000[?].

NN50C-B1 Second Edition, Reprint, Primary Binding Variant, 1971. (The second edition reprint exists in two subtly but consistently different binding variants – for diagnostic details see B2 below.) SBN unchanged. 'First Edition 1967 | Second (Revised) Edition 1970 | Reprinted 1971', otherwise identical to NN50B. The jacket too identical but for the insertion of the correct 10 figure ISBN: 0002131773 to the rear flap. Price: £1.80p. net and 36s. net. Print run inc. (B2) below: 3,000.

NN50C-B2 Second Edition, Reprint, Second Binding Variant, 1971, but bound up late 1974/early 1975. The New Naturalist statement dated 18 October 1974 states of *Pesticides* that 'work in progress' was

1,927[Q] with a completion date of Jan [1975], i.e. *c.* 1,900 quires were in the process of being bound up. These later bindings exhibit what can only be described as trifling differences, but are easily enough told apart by the arrangement of the internal hinges: there is no central strip of mull evident under the paste-down, but instead an impression of binding tape that runs the whole length of the hinge; the vertical step between the front board and text block is not pronounced, only *c.* 2 mm as against 4 mm in the primary binding. These variations are virtually identical to the binding variants of NN59 *Ants* – see photos on page 346. Barring perhaps a handful of copies, these second binding variants will wear repriced jackets. Print run: inc. above; no. bound thus: *c.* 1,900.

NN50C-B2-AP1 1st Repriced DJ (75?), £3.00 sticker, *c.* 100 sold[?].
NN50C-B2-AP2 2nd Repriced DJ (1975–76), £3.50 sticker, *c.* 350 sold[?].
NN50C-B2-AP3 3rd Repriced DJ (1976–77), £4.50 sticker, *c.* 550 sold.
NN50C-B2-AP4 4th Repriced DJ (1978–79), £5.50 sticker, *c.* 500 sold.
NN50C-B2-AP5 5th Repriced DJ (1979–80), £6.00 sticker, *c.* 300 sold.
NN50C-B2-AP6 6th Repriced DJ (1980), £7.50 sticker, *c.* 50 sold.

POD50A Print-on-demand digital copy of the 1971 second edition reprint NN50C.

BC50A Scientific Book Club Edition, 1967. The Scientific Book Club, London WC2. Hardback binding with dust jacket, 130 × 202 mm, i.e. smaller than the Collins edition; pp. 221, [3]; glued binding, not sown. Even though the format is smaller, it is printed from the same plates as NN50A, on cheaper paper with very narrow margins and without the photographic plates. Bound in blue imitation cloth, black lettering to the spine. Jacket designer uncredited; rear panel and rear flap advertise other titles and authors published by the Scientific Book Club; blurb to front flap as NN50A. Price: not given but states 'Originally published by William Collins at 30s. 0d.'. A utilitarian edition.

F50A Fontana Paperback First Edition, 1969 (April). ISBN: 0006319440 (ISBN appears only in the 1975 seventh imp.); pp. 219, [5]; 2 leaves of b/w plates, printed on glossy paper, to both sides. A copy of NN50A but reset, and with just four b/w plates and list of illus. omitted. Editors omitted. Adverts for NNs at front and rear. The front cover photograph, uncredited; rear cover carries five press reviews for *Pesticides*. Price: 8/6. Total print run including reprints: 46,000.

The following reprints exactly as preceding impression, unless stated otherwise, changes to internal adverts ignored.

F50B Second Impression, April 1970. Dark green border to lower edge of rear cover and spine. Price 8/- (40p).

F50C Third Impression, June 1970. Price 8/- (40p).

F50D Fourth Impression, Jan 1971.

F50E Fifth Impression, March 1972. Book thinner, brighter smoother paper. Price: 40p.

F50F Sixth Impression, Aug. 1972. Editors reinstated; JG, JH, MD, KM and EH; book thicker, tanned paper. Price: 45p.

F50G Seventh Impression, Aug 1975 (states sixth imp. in book). Price: 85p. ISBN to rear cover.

51 Man and Birds

The relationship between *Man and Birds* is complicated and multi-faceted, and so is the bibliography of *Man and Birds*. Firstly, there are two states of the first edition; secondly, both states have had a new (cancel) 'Plates' leaf pasted in, presumably replacing a significant error in the original text, which precipitates the question: are there any extant copies with the original uncorrected plates leaf? If so, that would mean three 'states' of the first edition. And to make the bibliography of *Man and Birds* a little more difficult, there are two distinct binding variants of the reprint.

Man and Birds is the first book in the series to be fitted with a *Duraseal* dust jacket protector though only second state first editions and reprints have them. *Duraseal*, a proprietary clear plastic protector, was to become a standard feature of New Naturalist jackets for the next 15 years. *Man and Birds* is also one of a handful of NN titles to sport a variant with silver-gilt lettering to the casing – often a diagnostic feature of the first edition, second state. It is likely that this has occurred as the result of a fault in the blocking process, as harlequin copies occur with both gilt and silver-gilt lettering. The stamping foil used to create the gilt lettering is made up of a coloured lacquer and condensed aluminium; if the lacquer is missing, rubs off, or fades the underlying colour will be silver. Silver-gilt lettering is a feature peculiar to 1971/72 bindings of various NN titles.

Man and Birds was reprinted just once, in 1973, but due a paucity of data in the Collins archive, the situation regarding dates and quantities is far from clear - and exacerbated by at least one, subsequent, variant binding. However, we do know that the reprint was undertaken almost exclusively for Taplinger (1,500 copies) and the Readers Union (750 copies). And with the presses already set up it made good economic sense for Collins to run off, for themselves, an additional 1,000 or so copies. But at this stage, Collins still had significant stocks of the first edition and therefore, seemingly, retained most of these reprints as unbound quires, to be bound up at a later date as required. It is likely that one of these later bindings was undertaken in 1977, which might explain why Marren mentions a 1977 reprint in *The New Naturalists*, which does not exist per se. To confuse matters yet further the RU books are indistinguishable from the Collins reprint – and are therefore not catalogued separately.

In line with bibliographic convention, the NN series drops the publication date from the title page for subsequent editions, but this was (almost uniquely) overlooked in *Man and Birds* and so the 1973 reprint confusingly retains the 1971 date on the title page.

As far as I am aware all reprint jackets have been price-clipped, which is probably attributable to two factors: firstly, significant delays between printing and binding and, secondly books sold by the RU would have been clipped in line with their own pricing policy.

Man and Birds is not difficult to find in fine condition but, as always with red, check the colour on the spine for fading. A significant number of copies have also been trimmed off-centre with the consequent cropping of the series no. roundel.

Total print run: *c.* 8,000? (Collins) + 750 (RU) + 1,500 (USA); o/p: 1981 (Collins).

TABLE NN51 Summary of differences between first and second state first edition *Man and Birds* and speculative pre-publication state without the corrected cancel plates leaf. Occasionally copies crop up that do not conform exactly with all criteria e.g. I have seen a 2nd state book with cloth more akin to that used for the 1st state, but the overriding diagnostic features (height and *Duraseal*) remain constant.

First Edition *Man and Birds*	Lettering to Buckram	Height	Buckram	Plates Leaf pp. [vii/viii]	Binding	Jacket
pre-publication state (speculative)	–	–	–	with original leaf i.e. with uncorrected errors and not the subsequent pasted-in (corrected) cancel leaf.	–	–
1st state	gold-gilt	bk. *c.* 221–222 mm. dj. *c.* 220 mm.	medium green, weave apparent, apt to fade	cancel leaf glued to top of the stub; pp. [viii/ix] glued together at gutter	spines and fore-edge of text-block distinctly rounded	without *Duraseal*
2nd state	often silver-gilt (slightly heavier than first state)	bk. *c.* 224 mm. dj. *c.* 220 mm. (too short for bk)	medium green with a waxy, finish; weave less pronounced, not apt to fade	cancel leaf glued to underside of stub; pp. [vii/viii] glued together at gutter	spine and fore-edge of text-block flattish	with *Duraseal*

NN51A-DJ1 First Edition, First State, 1971 (May? 1971).

Title:	'The New Naturalist	Man and Birds'.
Author:	'R.K. Murton	Ph.D.'
ISBN:	0002131323.
Editors:	JF, JH, MD & EH (Photographic Editor).
Printer:	Collins Clear-Type Press, London and Glasgow.
Collation:	pp. xx, 364; 16 leaves of b/w plates printed to both sides (24 × 16-page gatherings).
Jacket:	Without a *Duraseal* protector. [Rear panel] The New Naturalist library listing NN 1–50 (Type 42, variant 8). [Rear flap] Advert for *Woodland Birds*, ISBN above the bottom edge.
Price:	£2.50 net.
Print run:	6,000[?]; no. sold: *c.* 5,270 + repriced variants; o/p: probably 1976.
Notes:	1) For other distinguishing features see table NN51 above; but occasionally copies exist with intermediate features i.e. first state with a *Durasealed* jacket, but these might be later marriages. 2) The only jacket where the vertical joining stroke of the NN monogram bisects the central diamond. 3) The title to the HTP and TP is with an 'and' whereas the title to the casing and jacket is with an ampersand.

NN51B First Edition, Second State. (1971) [but sold later.] Bound up from the same sheets as NN51A and essentially identical but for a few differences identified in table NN51 above; the most significant being that the jacket is *Durasealed*, the book is several millimetres taller (rendering the jacket too short) and the lettering to the casing is often silver-gilt. Print run and no. sold: included in NN51A above. Note: Occasionally this second state book is found with a first state jacket i.e. without *Duraseal*, presumably some were left over from the first printing.

NN51B-AP1 1st Repriced DJ (1975–76), £4.00 sticker, *c.* 330 sold.

NN51B-AP2 2nd Repriced DJ (1976), £4.95 sticker, *c.* 160 sold.

NN51C-B1 First Reprint, First Binding Variant, 1973 (May?). ISBN unchanged. 'Reprinted 1973', but the 1971 date remains on the title page (presumably an error). Identical to NN51A. This first binding variant principally distinguished by 'Collins' to the casing which is 19/20 mm long, but see B2 below. The NN library to the *Durasealed* jacket now lists NN1–55 (Type 42, variant 12); rear flap unaltered; the blurb to the front flap likewise unaltered, but three press reviews inserted below. All jackets appear to be price-clipped. Notes: 1) For an overview see the intro., but this reprint principally produced for Readers Union and Taplinger. 2) It would seem that it was not actually sold by Collins until around 1976, once their first edition stock was exhausted. 3) Collins was commercially circumspect with the reprint, binding-up in batches in response to demand. The layout and gilt stamping to the spine of this B1 binding variant is as, or very similar to, the first edition NN51A, but there is some variation and this designation almost certainly represents more than one binding. 4) The number bound up thus is unknown, but an initial

batch of 750 copies were sold to the RU and it is likely another batch of *c.* 350 copies was remaindered to them in 1976. 5) Jackets without Collins replacement price stickers are probably RU copies.

NN51C-B1-AP1 1st Repriced DJ (1976–77), £4.95 sticker, *c.* 180 sold.

NN51C-B1-AP2 2nd Repriced DJ (1978–79), £5.50 sticker, *c.* 280 sold.

NN51C-B2 First Reprint, Second Binding Variant, 1973 (bound-up 1978?). In this variant the binding is clearly different with a number of distinctive elements, but the most straightforward diagnostic feature is 'Collins' on the spine, which is only 16 mm long and positioned further away from the NN monogram than in B1. All jackets are clipped and repriced with Collins price stickers as listed below.

NN51C-B2-AP2 2nd Repriced DJ (1978–79). £5.50: *c.* 280 sold.

NN51C-B2-AP3 3rd Repriced DJ (1979–80), £6.00 sticker, *c.* 280 sold.

NN51C-B2-AP4 4th Repriced DJ (1980–81), £7.50 sticker, *c.* 130 sold.

NN51C-B2-AP5 5th Repriced DJ (1981), £8.50 sticker, *c.* 80 sold.

POD51A Print-on-demand digital copy of the 1973 reprint NN51B.

US51A US First Edition, 1972 (but published 1973). ISBN 0800850831. Taplinger Publishing Co., Inc. New York. Identical to NN51B, but for title page, which is integral and carries the Taplinger imprint and omits New Naturalist from the title. Printed in Britain. Bound in same green buckram but with Taplinger blocked on the spine. The jacket, unlike Collins/RU editions, without a *Duraseal* protector; same Ellis design, but with Taplinger and the book specific part of the ISBN printed to the spine. The rear panel advertises five, non-NN, ornithological titles and the rear flap *The Pollination of Flowers*. The blurb to front flap entirely different to Collins edition. Price: $8.95 - printed to upper corner. No. supplied to Taplinger: 1,500. (A file note records that Collins sold *Man and Birds* to Taplinger for 72.5p per bound copy.)

52 Woodland Birds

An immediately successful title with 3,800 copies sold in the first two months, the figure growing to 4,500 by May of the following year. Despite a print-order for 8,000 copies of the first edition, only *c.* 6,900 copies were recorded as sold: a much greater disparity than normal, even if making generous allowances for review and complimentary copies, damaged copies, binding errors and returns. Whatever the reason, it has gone unrecorded.

The first edition was bound up in batches, or at least a few spare quires were bound up subsequently, leading to a variety of different casing fabrics. The majority of books are cased in the traditional green buckram, with the weave apparent and irregular and all early copies appear to use this cloth. Later bindings, identified by repriced jackets and dated inscriptions, display variant casing materials – fabric types which do not appear elsewhere within the NN library. It was as if the Collins bindery, bound up the remaining stock, with whatever bookcloth was to hand, provided it approximated to the usual NN buckram.

Woodland Birds was reprinted in 1976 with a contingent of this printing sold to Readers Union. Costings and tenders were undertaken for a proposed, later (1980) reprint, but did not progress beyond this point.

The bright red on the jacket spine is susceptible to sunning. Some titles when faded don't necessarily appear so when seen on the shelf, in isolation of the front panel, or at least the fading is not aesthetically too detrimental, but *Woodland Birds* is *not* one of these. Unfaded or at least tolerably faded copies are about. Total number of books printed: 10,000 (Collins) + 1000[?] (RU); o/p: 1981.

NN52A	**First Edition**, 1971 (4 October 1971).
Title:	'The New Naturalist	Woodland Birds'.
Author:	'Eric Simms, D.F.C., M.A.'
Editors:	MD, JH, JG, KM and EH (Photographic Editor).
Printer:	Collins Clear-Type Press, London and Glasgow.
ISBN:	0002132591.
Collation:	pp. xxii, 391, [3]; 4 leaves of colour plates printed to one side only; 12 leaves of b/w plates printed to both sides (16 × 16-page gatherings).
Casing:	Standard green buckram, weave apparent and irregular.
Jacket:	Without a *Duraseal* protector. [Front flap] 28 lines of blurb. [Rear panel] The New Naturalist library listing NN1–52 (Type 42, variant 9) [Rear flap] Advert for *Man and Birds*; ISBN.
Price:	£3.00 net.
Print run:	8,000; no. sold: *c.* 6,200 sold + repriced variants.
Notes:	The 'Illustrations' Leaf – pp. [xi/xii] is a cancel, so presumably the original integral printed leaf included errors, but the new cancel leaf has been tipped in so carefully that it is not at all obvious.

NN52A-BS Bookcloth Variants. Later bindings in non-standard buckrams/cloths. At least two types: 1) Very smooth green cloth with a semi-shinny finish, unique in the NN Library; endpapers pimpled (made from the minute impression of the dried glue to paste-down). 2) Acrylic[?] coated bluish-green buckram, shiny; similar to some of the later cloths used, but distinct.

NN52A-AP1 1st Repriced DJ (1975–76), £3.50 sticker, *c.* 450 sold.
NN52A-AP2 2nd Repriced DJ (1976), £5.95 sticker, < 250 sold.

NN52B Reprint, 1976 (Dec). ISBN changed to 000219564X. 'First published 1971 | Reprinted 1976.' As first edition, seemingly without any textural revisions; same plates. Editors: MD, JG, KM and EH. The 'Illustrations' leaf pp. [xi/xii] now integral. Printed on similar paper; bound in 'Group 2' buckram. The NN library to the *Durasealed* jacket lists NN1–60 (Type 42, variant 15); rear flap still advertises *Man and Birds* but reset, with three press reviews, revised ISBN; blurb to front flap omitted and four press endorsements introduced. Price: £5.95 net printed diagonally with dashed line. Print run: 2,000; no. sold: *c.* 1,200 + repriced variant below, + probably 650 copies sold off, from stock, in batches to RU in 1978/79.

NN52B-AP1 Repriced DJ (1980–81), £7.50 sticker, < 100 sold.

BC52A Readers Union Edition, 1976. Bound from the same sheets as NN52B, but with the 'usual' bookclub distinctions: jacket not priced and without a *Duraseal* protector; bound in imitation cloth. Print run: 1,000[?]. A rare edition.

BL52A Bloomsbury Edition, 1990. ISBN: 187063019X; pp. xxii, 391, [3], [32 b/w illustrations] (28 × 16-page gatherings). A b/w facsimile of the 1971 first ed. NN52A. The jacket blurb virtually as original DJ blurb. Price: £12.95. Remaindered.

POD52A Print-on-demand digital copy of the 1976 reprint NN52B.

53 The Lake District

I wandered lonely as a cloud
That floats on high o'er vales and hills,
When all at once I saw a crowd,
A host, of golden daffodils;
Beside the lake, beneath the trees,
Fluttering and dancing in the breeze.

William Wordsworth's famous poem *Daffodils*, which the Ellises' jacket so beautifully evokes – and explains the initials 'WW' incorporated into the design.

Just one Collins edition with a single reprint and few repriced jackets, though the reprint has a new ISBN and its jacket is significantly more yellow with the blue of the lake and sky turned to an Atlantic green. This reprint is inexplicably scarce, considering a couple of thousand were printed. Also rare is the Readers Union edition, but rarer still is the first edition marketed in the US by Taplinger with their label crudely applied to the spine of the jacket. In contrast the Bloomsbury edition, subsequently published in 1989, is readily obtainable.

The Lake District is often in fine condition and the colours of the jacket are comparatively colourfast, but look out for the series numeral on the spine, which should be the same bright yellow as the daffodils on the front panel.

NN53A **First Edition**, 1973 (July 1973?).
Title: 'The New Naturalist | The Lake District | A Landscape History'.
Authors: 'W. H. Pearsall D.Sc. F.R.S. | and | Winifred Pennington | (Mrs T. G. Tutin) Ph.D.'
Editors: MD, JH, JG, KM and EH (Photographic Editor).
Printer: Collins Clear-Type Press, London and Glasgow.
ISBN: 0002131331.
Collation: pp. 320; 16 leaves of b/w plates printed to both sides (20 × 16-page gatherings).
Jacket: [Rear panel] The New Naturalist library listing NN 1–56 (Type 42, variant 13). [Rear flap] Adverts for *Mountains and Moorlands* and *The Peak District*, jacket design credit and the ISBN.
Price: £3.15 net (printed parallel to the jacket edge).
Print run: 7,650; no. sold: *c.* 6,950 inc. repriced variants.
Notes: 1) Dust jacket with a *Duraseal* protector. 2) The ISBN to the jacket is incorrect – it has an additional digit and the penultimate 'o' should be omitted. 3) The print-order was for 8,000 books but 350 sold to USA. 4) The NN library to the jacket includes nos. 54–56.

NN53A-AP1 1st Repriced DJ (1975–76). £3.50 sticker, *c.* 1,000 sold[?].
NN53A-AP2 2nd Repriced DJ (1977), £5.95 sticker, *c.* 450 sold[?].

NN53B Reprint, 1977. The ISBN has changed to 0002194651. 'First published 1973 | Reprinted 1977'; date omitted from TP. As NN53A. Editors: MD, JG, KM & EH. The colours of the *Durasealed* jacket are significantly more yellow and 'Collins' bolder; the NN library lists NN1 –60 (Type 42, variant 15); rear flap identical but for revised ISBN; last paragraph of blurb omitted to front flap with clip from the *Northern Echo* inserted. Price: £5.95 net printed diagonally. No printed: *c.* 2,000; no. sold: *c.* 1,070 + repriced variants below + probably 250 copies sold off to RU (in addition to BC53A); o/p: 1982 (AP3).
NN53B-AP1 1st Repriced DJ (1980–81), £7.50 sticker, *c.* 230 sold.
NN53B-AP2 2nd Repriced DJ (1981), £8.50 sticker, *c.* 120 sold.
NN53B-AP3 3rd Repriced DJ (1982), £9.50 sticker, *c.* 130 sold.

BC53A Readers Union Edition, 1977. Bound up from the same sheets as NN53B, but with the usual BC distinctions: jacket not priced and without a *Duraseal* protector; bound in inferior imitation cloth (Type 1). A scarce edition.

BL53A Bloomsbury Edition, 1989 (31/12/89?). ISBN 187063058o; pp. 320, [32 – b/w illustrations] (22 × 16-page gatherings). A b/w facsimile copy of the 1977 reprint NN53B. Price: £12.95. Print run: unknown; a significant proportion remaindered.

POD53A Print-on-demand facsimile of the 1977 reprint NN53B.

US53A US Edition, 1973. Identical to first UK edition NN53A but binding tape used under hinges and not mull (unlike all UK copies) so probably a different batch; a Taplinger label has been pasted over the top of Collins on the jacket spine, which also *Durasealed*. Price clipped. Presumably a $US sticker was added. Print run: 350. A rare variant.

54 The Pollination of Flowers

One UK edition, first published in 1973, but reprinted twice, and a US edition that is dated 1972 so, theoretically, predates the UK first edition. However, in reality this is not the case but merely reflects a delay between printing and eventual publication.

The Pollination of Flowers was also sold off to the Readers Union from Collins stock, and accordingly there are no distinguishing features save for (presumably) price-clipped jackets and therefore have not been separately catalogued.

There are subtle differences in the bindings of the first edition and reprints, but these are insignificant and do not serve any diagnostic purpose, so are not described.

The brightest, sunniest Ellis jacket, though the scarlet colour tends to fade on the spine, which does detract significantly from the design, so it's worth seeking out an unfaded copy. Unlike *Fishes,* of a similar red, they are not too difficult to find, especially if you are happy with a reprint. As usual with books sold in the 1970s, they were repriced regularly in response to inflation. Total no. of Collins books printed: *c.* 8,000 (inc. copies sold to RU); o/p: 1985 but o/s for the first quarter of 1975.

NN54A **First Edition**, 1973 (02 April 1973).
Title: 'The New Naturalist | the | Pollination | of Flowers'.
Authors: 'Michael Proctor | M.A., Ph.D., F.R.P.S. | Senior Lecturer | Department of Biological Sciences | University of Exeter | and | Peter Yeo | M.A., Ph.D. | Taxonomist, University Botanic Garden, | Cambridge'.

Editors: JH, JG, MD, KM and EH (Photographic Editor).
Printer: William Collins Sons & Co Ltd Glasgow.
ISBN: 0002131781.
Collation: pp. [1–11], 14–418; 2 leaves of colour plates printed to
              both sides; 28 leaves of b/w plates, printed to both
              sides (26 × 16-page gatherings). (Note: The pagination
              is incorrect – the first numbered page should be
              numbered 12 not 14, so last page should be p. 416.)
Jacket: With *Duraseal* protector. [Rear panel] The New
              Naturalist library listing NN1–55 (Type 42, variant 12).
              (Note: The list includes NN55 *Finches*, which was
              actually published before NN54 *Pollination*.) [Front
              flap] The usual jacket designer's credit has been
              omitted (it was reinstated in later reprints to the rear
              flap). [Rear flap] Adverts for *Mountain Flowers*; *Wild
              Orchids of Britain*; and *Wild Flowers of Chalk and
              Limestone*; ISBN.
Price: £4.00 net.
Print run: 4,000 (out-turn); no. sold: *c.* 3,630; o/p: end 1974 (a note
              in the Collins archive states subscription was 1,888).

NN54B First Reprint, 1975 (April?). ISBN now 0002195046. 'First
published 1973 | reprinted 1975'. Identical to NN54A. The paper
used is of slightly inferior quality, resulting in a marginally
thinner book-block. The NN library to the *Durasealed* jacket lists
NN1–58 (Type 42, variant 14). Rear flap: jacket design credit
inserted, ISBN changed to suit, otherwise unrevised. Front flap:
three review extracts inserted below unrevised blurb. Price: £5.00
net. Print run: 2,000; no. sold: *c.* 1,050 + repriced variant + *c.* 370[?]
copies to the RU; o/p: 1979 (AP1).
NN54B-AP1 1st Repriced DJ (1978–79), £5.50 sticker, *c.* 350 sold.

NN54C Second Reprint, 1979. ISBN unchanged. Imprint page
states 'first published 1973 | reprinted 1975 | reprinted 1979'. As
NN54B. The NN library to the *Durasealed* jacket lists NN1–63
(Type 42, variant 18); both flaps identical. Price: £8.50 net. Print
run: *c.* 2,000[?]; no. sold: *c.* 770 + repriced variants below + *c.* 410[?]
copies to the RU; o/p: 1985 (AP2).
NN54C-AP1 1st Repriced DJ (1982–83), £9.50 sticker, *c.* 390 sold.
NN54C-AP2 2nd Repriced DJ (1984–85), £10.00 sticker, *c.* 130 sold.

POD54A Print-on-demand digital copy of the 1979 reprint NN54C.

US54A US Edition, 1972 (1973). ISBN: 0800864085. Taplinger
Publishing Co., Inc. New York. Bound up from the same sheets
and plates as the Collins first edition, but with an integral title/
copyright leaf that carries the Taplinger imprint and omits 'New
Naturalist' from the title; the copyright page states 'First
published in the United States in 1972', but was actually 1973.
Bound in the same green buckram but 'Taplinger' gilt-blocked to
the spine. The jacket ostensibly as Collins ed., but not *Durasealed*,
and with the Taplinger imprint and title-specific part of the ISBN
to the spine; the rear panel advertises *Irises* by Harry Randall; the
rear flap advertises: *Man and Birds*; the front flap carries a revised

blurb. Price: $14.95. Print run: 1,500. (A form on file, dated 05
December 1972, entitled 'Foreign Print Sale' quotes a price of
£1,420.65 for 1,500 copies i.e. 94.71p. per copy.)

55 Finches

Finches, generally perceived as being an exceptionally good
ornithological title, was not surprisingly one of the 7 NN titles
chosen to be reprinted in paperback format (the black paperbacks)
and predictably sold well. It is much rarer now than the hardback
edition – but few seem to want it.

Not only a fine book, but Billy Collins raved about the Ellises'
jacket artwork (*Art of the New Naturalists*) though the Editors forgot to
credit them; an oversight that remained uncorrected in later editions.
Given the very poor reproduction of the 1978 reprint jacket (and
worse was to come), the Ellises probably came to be thankful for the
omission. The yellow element is far too strong, but the 1985 limpback
reprint is even more intensely yellow, the once green teasels are now
yellow-ochre and the blue between, virtually non existent.

The 1975 reprint had a jacket price of £3.50, but this was a time
of rampant inflation and there seems to be hardly a copy that has
not been clipped and repriced with various Collins price stickers.
Likewise, all copies of the 1978 reprint have been price-clipped
and over-printed £8.00 net – did someone forget to revise the
price before printing or was it due to a time delay?

Finches was also sold by the Readers Union, but not as a special
bookclub edition. We know that Collins at the time used the RU as
a quasi-remaindering service and in addition to a large tranche of
over 2,500 reprints (1978) sold to the RU, it is probable that Collins
had already sold, in small batches over the preceding years, a total
of over 1,000 copies. It is likely that many of these copies sold to
the RU would have been price-clipped and the large number of
such copies in circulation supports this conjecture. As these RU
copies are indistinguishable from Collins editions, they have not
been separately catalogued.

1,500 copies were sold to the US and published under the
imprint Taplinger – the absence of 'British' in the title helped
facilitate the deal, and the American copies sold well.

Predictably, it is the red of the jacket which is prone to fading,
so check the goldfinch's mask and the series numeral on the spine
and compare them with the front panel.

Total UK hardbacks printed: *c.* 11,500[?]; o/p: 1982.

NN55A   **First Edition**, 1972 (25 September 1972).
Title: 'The New Naturalist | Finches'.
Author: 'I. Newton'.
Editors: JH, JG, MD, KM and EH (Photographic Editor).
Printer: William Collins Sons & Co Ltd Glasgow.
ISBN: 0002130653.
Collation: pp. 288; 2 leaves of colour plates printed to both sides; 12 leaves of b/w plates printed to both sides (18 × 16-page gatherings).
Jacket: With *Duraseal* protector. [Rear panel] New Naturalist library listing NN1–55 (Type 42, variant 12). [Rear flap] Advert for *Woodland Birds* and *Man and Birds*, each with three supporting press endorsements. The ISBN is positioned above the bottom edge.
Price: £3.00 net.
Print run: 4,750 (out-turn); no. sold c. 4,570; o/p: spring 1975.
Notes: 1) Illustrators: Hermann Heinzel (colour plates); Robert Gillmor (b/w in-text illustrations). The blurb to the jacket states, curiously, that Herman Heinzel's illustrations are depicted in semi-colour when in fact they are reproduced in full colour. 2) Heinzel also illustrated the classic Collins field guide *The Birds of Britain and Europe*; (with Richard Fitter and John Parslow) also first published in 1972. 3) Book 23 mm thick. 4) While no. 55 in the series, *Finches* was published after NN52 and before NN53 & 54.

NN55B First Reprint, 1975 (summer). ISBN has changed to 0002194295 – both to book and jacket. 'First published 1972 | Reprinted 1975'. Identical to NN55A. Book slightly thicker 25 mm. The NN library to the *Durasealed* jacket lists NN1–58 (Type 42, variant 14); rear flap unchanged; blurb to front flap unrevised, but four endorsing review extracts inserted. Price: £3.50 net. Print run c. 3,000; no. sold: c. 100[?] + repriced variants, plus probably an additional c. 900 copies to the RU. Notes: 1) It appears that very few copies were sold that were not price-clipped. 2) Bound up in two separate batches, but there does not appear to be any binding variation.

NN55B-AP1 1st Revised Price (1975–76), £4.00 sticker, c. 500 sold.

NN55B-AP2 2nd Revised Price (1976–77), £4.50 sticker, c. 600 sold.

NN55B-AP3 3rd Revised Price (1977–78), £5.50 sticker, c. 400 sold.

NN55C Second Reprint, 1978 (but published beginning 1979). ISBN unchanged. 'First published 1972 | Reprinted 1975 | Reprinted 1978'. As NN55B, book thinner – 23 mm. The jacket printed using new technique and colours noticeably different, more yellow, muddy; the NN library lists NN1–63 (Type 42, variant 18); both flaps unaltered. All copies price-clipped and over-stamped £8.00 net (the corner was clipped before *Duraseal* applied). Print run: c. 3,500[?]; no. sold: c. 800 copies + repriced variant below. Additionally, a tranche of c. 2,650 copies sold on to the RU, possibly more.

NN55C-AP1 1st Revised Price (1982), £9.50 sticker, very few sold.

CPB55A Collins Paperback Reprint, 1985 (21/01/1985). ISBN 0002190893; pp. [xix], 20–288, [4 blanks], [28- b/w illustrations], (20 × 16-page gatherings). A facsimile of NN55C, with a two-page 'Preface to the Limpback Edition' by Ian Newton. Price £6.50. No printed: c. 1,600; no. sold: c. 1,450; o/p: 1986. Note: An over-dominance of yellow in the reproduction of the cover design; the title band has been superimposed in a different colour and the title lettering reset.

POD55A Print-on-demand Facsimile copy of the first reprint, NN55B.

US55A US Edition, 1972. ISBN 0800827201. Published by Taplinger Publishing Co., Inc. New York. Bound up from the same sheets as the Collins first edition NN55A with same suite of plates; accordingly printed in Great Britain. The title and Editors' pages are cancels; in fact conjugate leaves, pasted over the stubs of the originals. New Naturalist references are dropped from the half-title and title pages as is the NN monogram from the latter, though the list of Editors and NN credo retained. Bound in the same green buckram, but thicker, stouter boards (book 25 mm thick) with 'Taplinger' blocked on the spine; the NN monogram is omitted. The jacket does not have a *Duraseal* protector, but is the same Ellis design, though more yellow; 'Taplinger 2720–1' printed to the spine; rear panel advertises *At The Turn of the Tide* by Richard Perry; rear flap advertises 'The New Naturalist Series', with a general blurb and three NN titles published by Taplinger in the US: *Man and Birds*, *The Mole* and *The Pollination of Flowers*; blurb to the front flap rewritten and adapted to US market. Price: $12.50. Print run: 1,541 (out-turn).

56 Pedigree: Essays on the Etymology of Words From Nature

Is it more than coincidence that a book on etymology should use four subtly different titles for the spine, jacket, half-title and title pages, which are respectively: 'PEDIGREE Words from Nature', 'Pedigree: Words from Nature', 'Pedigree Words from Nature' and (The New Naturalist) 'PEDIGREE Essays on the Etymology of WORDS FROM NATURE'? I suspect not, just poor editing and not all titles convey the same meaning. Michael Walter, then editor at Collins, recognised this confusion and in a letter to

Crispin Fisher wrote: 'the style of the lettering on the spine is silly giving the impression that it is a book about Pedigree Words' – but was also quick to point out that the error was not his. As previously discussed, bibliographic convention dictates that the title is taken from the title page, but I suspect this book will continue to be known simply and incorrectly as 'Pedigree Words from Nature'.

As this is a book on words, rather than specifically British wildlife, it is perhaps not surprising that there is an American edition too, published by Taplinger, but, 'predictably', with a modified title: 'Pedigree THE ORIGINS OF WORDS FROM NATURE', spelling out, in no-nonsense terms, exactly what the book is about!

If etymology is of interest to you seek out the review by Geoffrey Grigson that appeared in *Country Life* (24 January 1974) – well written and erudite, though one senses Grigson felt he could have written it better himself. But that is the wont of most reviewers. A peculiar title too in that it does not really conform to the stated aims of the series '…to interest the general reader in the wild life of Britain', and unique in that it is the only New Naturalist not to have an illustration of any sort. Just one impression of one edition, but a 1974 NN statement indicates that 1,250 copies were bound up later. In fact there are slight binding variations, but these are so subtle and inconsistent that no attempt has been made to differentiate them.

The jacket is susceptible to fading, the red geranium the most susceptible, but bright, unfaded copies are not that uncommon.

NN56A	**First Edition**, 1973 (01 September 1973).
Title:	'The New Naturalist	Pedigree Essays on the Etymology of	Words From Nature'.
Authors:	'Stephen Potter and	Laurens Sargent'.
Editors:	MD, JH, JG, KM and EH (Photographic Editor).
Printer:	William Collins Sons & Co Ltd Glasgow.
ISBN:	000213179X.
Collation:	pp. [15], 18–322 (20 × 16-page gatherings). (Note: The page-numerals are incorrect – the first 15 pages are unnumbered with the pagination starting on p. 16, which is incorrectly numbered 18 and so on throughout till the last page which is numbered 322, but is, in fact, p. 320.)
Jacket:	Paper: with *Duraseal* protector. [Rear panel] the New Naturalist library listing NN1–56 (Type 42, variant 13). [Rear flap] adverts for *A Natural History of Man in Britain* and *Man & the Land*; ISBN.
Price:	£3.15 net.
Print run:	4,650[?]; no. sold: *c.* 3,400 + repriced variants below; o/p: 1980 (AP4).

NN56A-AP1 **1st Repriced DJ** (1975–76), £3.50 sticker, *c.* 250 sold.
NN56A-AP2 **2nd Repriced DJ** (1976–77), £4.50 sticker, *c.* 250 sold.
NN56A-AP3 **3rd Repriced DJ** (1978–79), £5.50 sticker, *c.* 200 sold.
NN56A-AP4 **4th Repriced DJ** (1979–80), £6.00 sticker, *c.* 100 sold.

POD56A **Print-on-demand** digital copy.

US56A **US Edition**, 1974. 'Pedigree | The Origins of Words From Nature'. ISBN: 0800862481. Published by Taplinger Publishing Company, New York; pp. 320; large 8vo, slightly taller that the Collins edition (233 mm). Orange cloth-backed, dark orange-red boards; black lettering to the spine. Tan-orange jacket with design by Rus Anderson continuing on to rear panel; the blurb new, and the rear flap advertises *Naturalist in the Sudan* by Charles Sweeney. The preliminary sections reset and partly rewritten, but text identical to the Collins edition, printed from the same blocks, though titles and chapter headings reset. Price: $9.95. (An attractive production in a good-quality binding.)

57 British Seals

A single Collins edition, but the sales data is ambiguous: the total number printed jumps from 3,500 in 1975 to 4,500 in 1976, and then drops down to 4,000 from September 1977, where it remains. It might be that stock was released in two separate tranches from the binders and then a batch subsequently sold, from stock, to a bookclub. Notwithstanding, there is no ambiguity surrounding the number of copies sold – and that, from the collector's perspective is the more important figure. The total number sold was *c.* 3,550 over a 5-year period, which is, in fact, commensurate with a print-order of around 4,000 copies.

British Seals was published concurrently in the US by Taplinger with a new title page, but bound up from the same sheets printed in Britain. The jacket has the same Ellis design with a few revisions to reflect the US imprint.

The North Atlantic green of the jacket is particularly prone to fading: the flipper on the spine should be the same colour as the seal on the front panel. It seldom is.

NN57A	**First Edition**, 1974 (25 November 1974).
Title:	'The New Naturalist	British Seals'.
Author:	'H. R. Hewer	C.B.E., M.Sc., D.I.C.	Emeritus Professor in the	University of London'.
Illust:	'With 59 photographs in black and white	and 52 text figures'.
Editors:	MD, JH, JG, KM and EH (Photographic Editor).
Printer:	William Collins Sons & Co Ltd Glasgow.

ISBN: 0002130327.
Collation: pp. 256; 12 leaves of b/w plates printed to both sides
           (16 × 16-page gatherings).
Jacket: [Paper] with *Duraseal* protector. [Rear panel] New
           Naturalist library listing NN1–58 (Type 42, variant 14).
           (Note: NN58 *Hedges* inc. as published on the same
           day.) [Rear flap] Adverts for *The Pollination of Flowers*
           and *Finches*; jacket designer credit and ISBN.
Price: £3.50 net.
Print run: c. 4,000[?]; no. sold: c. 3,550 including repriced variants
           below; o/p: June 1980 (AP3).

NN57A-AP1 1st Repriced DJ (1976–77), £3.95 sticker, c. 280 sold.
NN57A-AP2 2nd Repriced DJ (1977–78), £4.95 sticker, c. 170 sold.
NN57A-AP3 3rd Repriced DJ (1978–79), £5.50 sticker, c. 100 sold.
NN57A-AP4 4th Repriced DJ (1979–1980), £6.00 sticker, c. 100 sold.

POD57A Print-on-demand digital copy.

US57A US Edition, 1974. ISBN: 0800810562. Published by Taplinger
Publishing Co., Inc. New York. Ostensibly book, contents and
jacket as Collins edition and from the same printing. The title
page is an integral leaf; it carries the Taplinger imprint and omits
New Naturalist from the title. The details to the imprint page have
changed to suit, otherwise the contents and paper identical – and
accordingly printed in Great Britain. Casing unchanged but
blocked with the Taplinger imprint and the boards significantly
thicker. The Ellis jacket now with the Taplinger imprint and
title-specific part of the ISBN to the spine, but not *Durasealed*; the
rear panel advertises *Sea Turtles* by Robert Bustard; the blurb to the
front flap is revised; the rear flap advertises seven NN titles: *Man
and Birds*, *The Mole*, *Pollination of Flowers*, *Finches*, *Lake District*,
British Seals and *Hedges* with prices in US dollars. Price: $14.95.
Print run: 1,500. Note: The rear flap NN titles are US editions
published or distributed by Taplinger.

58 Hedges

'Why is the bindery taking so long to get the quires bound up?
It is a pity to be out of stock with such a new book. If the authors
were less placid, they would be grumbling' wrote Michael Walters,
to S. Reid Foster in a memo dated 2 May 1975. *Hedges* was first
published on the 25 November 1974 and was out of print just a few

months later, but it appeared that 1,000 or so copies were not
initially bound up and it is likely that it is to these that Michael
Walters was referring. Jackets were reprinted for these unbound
copies, but with a couple of subtle differences: no printed price
and some with a different ISBN to the rear flap. It is not
uncommon to find first edition books wearing these unpriced
jackets with a Collins £3.50 sticker applied. This same jacket was
also used on the 1975 reprint. The reason for the price being
omitted was probably that this doubled as a bookclub edition –
and copies without price stickers lend weight to this hypothesis,
but it might have also been an expedient in those times of high
inflation (24.2 per cent in 1975).

This mix-and-match approach to jackets set the trend for
future impressions with seemingly endless permutations of
priced, un-priced and repriced jackets as catalogued below – and
this is probably not exhaustive.

An American edition was published a few months after the first
UK edition but was bound up from the same sheets, with the same
Ellis design to the dust jacket but without *Duraseal*.

The existence of bookclub variants and the fact that it would
seem existing warehouse stock was regularly siphoned off to the
RU, makes it very difficult to determine quantities actually printed
by Collins, but the sales figures have been interpolated as best
they can, hopefully without reading into them, more than there is
to be read – though I cannot guarantee my interpretations are
without error!

The dust jacket is often faded on the spine, the green becomes
blue-green and the orange of the number '58' becomes yellow – it
should be the same colour as the orange tip butterfly on the front
panel.

In total, c. 8,600 Collins copies were sold, plus 3,850 copies sold
to the Readers Union and c. 540 copies to Taplinger in the US.
Hedges remained in print for 10 years going out of print in 1984.

NN58A   First Edition, 1974 (25 November 1974).
Title: 'The New Naturalist | Hedges'.
Authors: 'E. Pollard, M. D. Hooper & | N.W. Moore'.
Editors: MD, JH, JG, KM and EH (Photographic editor).
Printer: William Collins Sons & Co Ltd Glasgow.
ISBN: 0002113406.
Collation: pp. 256; 10 leaves of b/w plates printed to both sides
            (16 × 16-page gatherings).
Jacket: With *Duraseal* protector. [Rear panel] The New
            Naturalist library listing NN1–58, (Type 42, variant 14).
            [Rear flap] Adverts for *Pollination of Flowers* and for
            Finches.
Price: £3.50 net.
Print run: 4,000; no. sold: c. 3,000. It would appear around 1,000
            were bound up a little later and supplied with
            unpriced jackets (NN58B and NN58C).
Notes: 1) 'Hooper' misspelt 'Hopper' on the spine of the
            book, but corrected in later impressions. 2) All jacket
            text printed in olive green.

NN58A-DJ1 First Jacket Variant. The *Durasealed* jacket, while identical to NN58A, does *not* have a printed price but with Collins £3.50 sticker. This jacket probably doubles as bookclub jacket (see intro.). No. sold: *c.* 1,000? (inc. NN58A-DJ2 below).

NN58A-DJ2 Second Jacket Variant. *Durasealed* jacket exactly as DJ1 but ISBN to rear flap is 0002190818.

NN58B First Reprint, 1975 (August?). ISBN unchanged (0002113406), but that to jacket now 0002190818. 'First published 1974 | Reprinted 1975'. As NN58A but 'Hooper' now correctly spelt on spine. The *Durasealed* jacket exactly as NN58A-DJ2, i.e. no printed price, revised ISBN and with a Collins price sticker in a variety of values as indicated below. It would appear that this first reprint was never issued in a jacket with a printed price. No. printed: 2,000.

NN58B-AP1 1st Repriced DJ (1975–76), £3.50 sticker, *c.* 1,100 sold.
NN58B-AP2 2nd Repriced DJ (1976), £3.95 sticker, *c.* 650 sold.
NN58B-AP3 3rd Repriced DJ (1976–77), £4.50 sticker, no. sold: unknown.

NN58C Second Reprint, 1977 (January). ISBN now 0002190818 to both imprint page and jacket. 'First published 1974 | Reprinted 1975 | Reprinted 1977'. As NN58B. Editors: MD, JG, KM and EH. Printing has converted from letterpress to litho; paper brighter and of better quality. The NN library to the *Durasealed* jacket lists NN1–60 (Type 42, variant 15); both flaps unchanged. Price: £4.50 net, printed diagonally. The print-order was for 3,500 copies but it seems around 1,800 of these were siphoned off for the bookclub over the following two years. No. sold: *c.* 600 inc. repriced variants.

NN58C-AP1 1st Repriced DJ (1978–79), £5.50 sticker, *c.* 750 sold.
NN58C-AP2 2nd Repriced DJ (1979), £6.00 sticker, *c.* 250 sold.

NN58D Third Reprint, 1979. ISBN unchanged. 'First published 1974 | Reprinted 1975 | Reprinted 1977 | Reprinted 1979'. As NN58D. The NN library to the *Durasealed* jacket lists NN1–63 (Type 42, variant 18a); both flaps unchanged. Price: £8.00 net. Print run: 2,000; no. sold *c.* 500 + repriced variants.

NN58D-AP1 1st Repriced DJ (1981), £8.50 sticker, *c.* 150 sold.
NN58D-AP2 2nd Repriced DJ (1982–83), £9.50 sticker, *c.* 500 sold.
NN58D-AP3 3rd Repriced DJ (1984–85), £10.00 sticker, *c.* 100 sold.

BC58B Readers Union First Reprint, 1975. Identical to NN58B but the *Durasealed* jacket *without* a price sticker. Note: As stated in the intro., the number of permutations of books and jackets makes this title difficult to catalogue and it is not unlikely that a bookclub variant of the first edition was also issued, and therefore catalogue this 1975 RU reprint with epithet 'B'.

BC58C Readers Union Second Reprint, 1977. Identical to NN58C but *Durasealed* jacket *without* a printed price.

BC58D Readers Union Third Reprint, 1979. Identical to NN58F but bound in cheaper dark green imitation cloth and with the dust jacket unpriced and without *Duraseal*. This would appear to be the only bookclub edition which is obviously so – with the telltale cheaper binding and unprotected jacket.

USA58A US Edition, 1975. ISBN: 0800838289. Taplinger Publishing Co., Inc. New York, Bound up from the same sheets as the first UK edition NN58A with the same suite of plates, accordingly 'Printed in Great Britain' to the imprint page. The title page is a cancel, but retains the series title 'The New Naturalist'; the half-title is unrevised. Casing of same green buckram but stamped 'Taplinger' to the bottom of the spine. The jacket is not *Durasealed*; has the same Ellis design but carries the Taplinger imprint and the title-specific part of the ISBN to the spine; the rear panel advertises the Taplinger edition of *Pollination of Flowers* and the rear flap advertises six other NN titles also published by Taplinger. The blurb to the front flap has been revised to reflect the North American market. Price: $14.95 printed to front flap top corner. Print run: 536 (out-turn).

POD58A Print-on-demand digital copy of the third reprint, 1979, NN58D.

59 Ants

Just one impression of one edition, however there are two subtly, but consistently different bindings. There are a number of factors that have informed the adopted priority. The primary binding, i.e. the earlier binding, is by far the commoner of the two and with such a small print run it is probable that the majority of books were bound up in the first instance, but more importantly the styles of binding fit an established pattern within NN books, which confirm the priority beyond doubt.

The two binding variants are essentially determined by the nature of the internal hinge and the manner in which the book-block is joined to the casing (see images on page 346). That said, the differences are really so slight that the desire to separate them is, in truth, academic, especially when it is remembered that all are bound from the same sheets, but that is the nature of bibliography – make of it what you will!

To complicate matters a little further it appears that around 1,000 copies were sold by the Readers Union, but without the usual bookclub signatures, and are therefore indistinguishable from the Collins edition. The sales statements suggest that books were sold off to the RU in more than one tranche and the preponderance of clipped jackets in both binding variants, supports this notion.

The yellow element of the green of the jacket is apt to fade, resulting in a bluer green on the spine, the series number on the spine should be the same brown as the ant on the front panel, but rarely is.

The ambiguity surrounding this title finds its way into the sales data, which is somewhat inconsistent, however it would seem that 4,500 copies were printed; o/p: 1981.

NN59A-B1   First Edition, Primary Binding Variant, 1977
(17 October 1977).

Title: 'The New Naturalist | Ants'.
Author: 'M.V. Brian'.
Editors: JG, MD, KM and EH (Photographic Editor).
Printer: William Collins Sons & Co Ltd Glasgow.
ISBN: 0002193787.
Collation: pp. 223, [1]; 2 leaves of colour plates printed to one side only; 8 leaves of b/w plates printed to both sides (14 × 16-page gatherings).
Binding: In this primary binding, the hinge (internal) is pronounced creating a step of approximately 4 mm between the front board and book-block, but more important diagnostically, is a strip of mull approximately 15 cm long, running part way along the length of the hinge, (used to join the text-block to the casing), which is apparent under the paste-downs. Buckram is slightly lighter green than B2.
Jacket: With *Duraseal* protector. [Rear panel] The New Naturalist library listing NN1–61 (Type 42, variant 17). [Rear flap] advert for *Inheritance and Natural History*; ISBN.
Price: £5.95 net.
Print run: 4,500[?]; no. sold: *c.* 3,350 (Collins) inc. B2 + *c.* 1,000 (RU).
Notes: 1) Colour plates by Gordon Riley. 2) *Ants*, while NN59 in the series, was published after NN60 *Birds of Prey* and a few weeks earlier than NN61 *Inheritance*, which explains why the NN library to the jacket includes NN60 and 61.

NN59A-B2 Second Binding Variant. Darker green buckram; the hinges/joints are tighter and the hinge (internal) is less pronounced creating a step of approximately 2 mm between the front board and text block, but more importantly, there is no central strip of mull; instead is an impression under the paste-downs of binding tape which runs the whole length of the hinge. There are a few other differences such as positioning of text on the spine, but the above are the most reliable diagnostically. (See intro. regarding priority.)

NN48A-B2-AP1 1st Repriced DJ (1980–81), £7.50 sticker, *c.* 150 sold.
NN48A-B2-AP2 2nd Repriced DJ (1981), £7.95 sticker, *c.* 50 sold.
NN48A-B2-AP3 3rd Repriced DJ (1981), £8.50 sticker, *c.* 50 sold.

POD59A Print-on-demand digital copy.

60   British Birds Of Prey

The best-selling title since the 1950s, and therefore not surprisingly it was reprinted four times; additionally there are three Readers Union editions and a Bloomsbury edition. 500 copies were also sold to the US and marketed by Taplinger, but, other than, probably, being price-clipped, are believed to be identical to the Collins first edition.

The reprints are in essence textually identical to the first edition, but with variations to the author's note and arrangement of plates; there are also variations in the paper and casing fabrics.

None of the RU editions is identified as such, but can be simply distinguished as the jackets are not priced, in contrast to the Collins jackets, which are. If your copy is price-clipped it's a little more tricky, but by looking at a combination of the casing material and the presence or otherwise of *Duraseal* on the jacket, it is always possible to tell – as described below.

The genuine Collins first edition is quite a rare book with less than 4,000 copies sold (there are many RU copies masquerading as firsts), but as with all issues of this title, the red-brown colour of the jacket is particularly prone to fading on the spine. If you have an unfaded copy, treasure it, show it to nobody and never let it see the light of day again.

Birds of Prey is about the rarest of the Bloomsbury New Naturalists, and in fact is considerably scarcer than the Collins first edition. But this doesn't mean you will have to pay much for it; you won't – that is, if you want one. It is worth noting that an entirely different book by Leslie Brown, but with virtually the same title, was published in the same year by Hamlyn (UK) and A & W Publishers (USA) – *Birds of Prey: Their Biology and Ecology*. Brown completed the manuscript for the New Naturalist title four years or so before Collins published it, which explains this apparent duplicity. In the event it did not seem to matter – the NN title sold out within a few months of publication.

Regarding the total number of Collins books printed, a figure is almost impossible to determine with any certainty as the sales statements tell only part of the story and almost certainly some of the print-figures cited include books printed for Readers Union, but an approximation would be around 11,000 copies with an additional *c.* 6,150 copies sold to the RU. The total no. of Collins books sold was *c.* 9,500. *Birds of Prey* finally went out of print towards the end of 1985.

NN60A   **First Edition**, 1976 (01 or 29 April 1976).

Title:	'The New Naturalist	British Birds of Prey	A study of Britain's 24 diurnal raptors'.
Author:	'Leslie Brown'.
Editors:	MD, JG, KM and EH (Photographic editor).
Printer:	William Collins Sons & Co Ltd Glasgow.
ISBN:	0002194058.
Collation:	pp. xiii, [1], 400, [2]; 8 leaves of b/w plates printed to both sides (26 × 16-page gatherings).
Casing:	Buckram.
Jacket:	With *Duraseal* protector. [Rear panel] New Naturalist library listing NN1–58 (Type 42, variant 14). [Rear flap] adverts for *Woodland Birds* and *Man and Birds*; ISBN.
Price:	£6 net, printed diagonally.
Print run:	4,250; no. sold c. 3,700.
Notes:	1) NN59 *Ants* is missing from the NN library to the jacket as it was not in fact published until October 1977. 2) Book 30 mm thick. 3) No colour illustrations, but 40 b/w photographs plus maps and diagrams.

NN60A-DJ1, Jacket Variant. The Collins first edition fitted with the RU jacket BC60A (i.e. without a printed price), but with a Collins £6.00 sticker attached. Presumably an expedient.

NN60B First Reprint, 1976. ISBN unchanged. 'First published April 1976 | Reprinted October 1976' (But in fact it did not appear until December). Pages x–xiii + [xiv] of the first edition have been reconfigured to allow space for the 'Author's Note on the Reprint' to which is tagged a 'Publisher's Note to the Reprint'. Otherwise, as NN60A and printed on the same quality paper and bound in buckram. The NN library to the *Durasealed* jacket lists NN1–60 (Type 42, variant 15) but NN59 *Ants* is still omitted; the designers' credit has been moved to the rear flap, which is otherwise unchanged; blurb to the front flap abbreviated, with two review extracts inserted below. Price: £6 net, printed diagonally. Print run: c. 2,000; no. sold: c. 2,000.

NN60C Second Reprint, 1978. ISBN unchanged. 'First published April 1976 | Reprinted October 1976 | Reprinted 1978'. As NN60B, but the 'Author's Note to the Reprint' has been rewritten and is now entitled 'Author's Note to the Second Reprint'. The paper is the same and bound in buckram. The NN library to the *Durasealed* jacket lists NN1–61 (Type 42, variant 16); both flaps unchanged. Price: £6.50 net, printed diagonally. Print run: c. 2,500 (inc. RU copies); no. sold: c. 1,650.

NN60D Third Reprint, 1979. ISBN unchanged. 'First published April 1976 | Reprinted October 1976 | Reprinted 1979'. Note: The 1978 second reprint NN60C omitted from the printing history. Textually as the 1976 first reprint NN60B. This edition was litho printed (text and illustrations), converted from letterpress, which might explain the reversion to the NN60B text. But it has been set up with 32-page gatherings with a new arrangement of the same plates, as reflected in the list of plates on p. vii. The paper is whiter, and of lighter weight, resulting in a noticeably thinner book – 27 mm thick, but still bound in buckram. The NN library to the *Durasealed* jacket lists NN1–63, (Type 42, variant 18a); both flaps unchanged. Price: £8.50 net, printed diagonally. Print run: c. 2,900 (inc. RU copies); no. sold: c. 1,400 including repriced variant below.

NN60D-AP1 First Repriced Jacket (1981–82?). £9.50: unknown.

NN60E Fourth Reprint, 1982. ISBN unchanged. 'First published April 1976 | Reprinted October 1976 | Reprinted 1979 | Reprinted 1982'. (Note: There is still no reference to the 1978 reprint.) This reprint retains 32-page gatherings as NN60D, but reverts back to the original plate arrangement and the unrevised 'Author's Note on the Reprint'; it is otherwise textually and graphically identical to NN60D. The paper is of better quality than NN60D, smooth and creamy, but the book, 30 mm thick, is bound in utilitarian light-green imitation cloth. The jacket without a *Duraseal* protector is otherwise identical to NN60D, but for the price of £10.50 net, printed diagonally. Print run: c. 1,000; no. sold: c. 700; o/p: 1985. Note: While this edition is bound in imitation cloth and has a jacket without *Duraseal*, there is not to my knowledge a dedicated RU edition, but perhaps price-clipped, it doubles as such.

BC60A Readers Union First Edition, 1976. Identical to NN60A and bound up from the same sheets, but in dark-green imitation cloth. The jacket identical too and *Durasealed*, but without a printed price. Print run and no. sold: unknown, but plentiful.

BC60B Readers Union First Reprint, 1978. Identical to NN60B and bound up from the same sheets, but in dark-green imitation cloth. The jacket identical too and *Durasealed*, but without a printed price.

BC60C Readers Union Third Reprint, 1979. Identical to NN60D and bound up from the same sheets, but in dark-green imitation cloth. The jacket identical too, but not *Durasealed* and without a printed price. Note: As this is a copy of the Collins 1979 third reprint it is referred to here as the RU *third reprint*.

BL60A Bloomsbury Edition, 1989 (31/12/1989). ISBN: 1870630637. pp. xiv, 400, [2], [16 – b/w illustrations] (27 × 16-page gatherings). A b/w facsimile of the 1982 reprint NN60E. The blurb to the jacket also as NN60E. Price £12.95.

POD60A Print-on-demand digital copy of the 1976 reprint NN60B.

US60A US Edition, 1976 (28/04/1976). ISBN 0800809955. Believed to be identical to the Collins first edition NN60A but marketed by Taplinger Publishing Company NY and possibly with their imprint label added; probably price-clipped. Price: $17.50. Print run: 500. Not inspected.

61 Inheritance and Natural History

Just one Collins edition of *Inheritance*, Berry's first book for the series, but an almost identical Readers Union edition was also published. The two editions were bound up from the same printed sheets and easily confused, but there are the usual RU trademarks: imitation cloth rather than buckram, no printed price to the dust jacket, and that jacket without a *Duraseal* protector. The Readers Union edition is comparatively scarce, so it is unlikely to trip up too many unsuspecting collectors. Additionally, 350 copies were sold in the US by Taplinger, and in 1989 *Inheritance* was reissued as a Bloomsbury reprint.

Unfortunately, the jacket is true to type for this period and suffers from fading: the blue is fugitive, but not to the same degree as the orange-brown colour – most telling is the roundel on the spine; it should be the same strong colour as the mouse on the front panel. It rarely is.

NN61A   **First Edition**, 1977 (28 November 1977).
Title: 'The New Naturalist | Inheritance and | Natural History'.
Author: 'R. J. Berry | Professor of Genetics in the University of London'.
Illust: 'With 12 colour photographs | 19 photographs in black and white | and 110 line drawings'.
Editors: MD, JG, KM and EH (Photographic Editor).
Printer: William Collins Sons & Co Ltd Glasgow.
ISBN: 0002190842.
Collation: pp. 350, [2 blanks]; 2 leaves of colour plates printed to both sides; 4 leaves of b/w plates printed to both sides (22 × 16-page gatherings).
Jacket: With *Duraseal* protector. [Rear panel] New Naturalist library listing NN1–61 (Type 42, variant 17). [Rear flap] adverts for *Butterflies* and Ford's *Moths*; ISBN.
Price: £6.50 net printed diagonally with dotted line.
Print run: 5,150; no. sold: *c.* 3,270 + repriced variants; o/p: 1985 (AP4).

NN61A-AP1 1st Repriced DJ (1980?), £7.50 sticker, no. sold: unknown.
NN61A-AP2 2nd Repriced DJ (1981–82), £8.50 sticker, *c.* 250 sold.
NN61A-AP3 3rd Repriced DJ (1982–84), £9.50 sticker, *c.* 300 sold.
NN61A-AP4 4th Repriced DJ (1984–85), £10.00 sticker, *c.* 100 sold.

BC61A Readers Union Edition, 1977. Identical to NN61A; bound up from the same sheets, but with dark green imitation cloth casing; jacket identical too, but without a printed price and without *Duraseal*. Print run: *c.* 500[?] (the sales reports also indicate 1,700 copies were sold to RU, but the scarcity of this edition would suggest, that if that many were sold off, many of them were from the ordinary Collins edition).

POD61A Print-on-demand digital copy.

BL61A Bloomsbury Edition, 1990 (31/12/1990). ISBN 1870630645; pp. 350, [2]; 12 pages of integrated b/w illustrations. A b/w facsimile. The blurb to the dust jacket front flap is identical to the Collins edition, but omits the last line. Price £12.95. Remaindered.

US61A US Edition (01/02/1978[?]). ISBN 0800841956. Taplinger Publishing Company, NY. Not seen. Presumed identical to the Collins edition, but marketed in the US by Taplinger, possibly with their applied imprint label, probably price-clipped with a Taplinger $17.50[?] sticker. Print run: 350. Note: Has a dedicated ISBN and appears to have been published in 1978.

62 British Tits

A successful title with total sales of around 15,000 copies, but, odd as it might seem, the majority (*c.* 9,300) were sold not by Collins but by the bookclub Readers Union. Christopher Perrins writing of this says, 'This came about because the book appeared too late for the Christmas sales and the bookclub asked Collins for a book which had missed the sales – nothing about the book's quality!' Though I have no doubt that the RU were aware that it was in fact a very good book and were aware, too, that it would appeal to that not inconsiderable peanut-buying section of the British public, some of whom might also be RU members – as proved to be the case.

British Tits was printed twice, but both impressions had variant bookclub bindings and dust jackets, so there are four distinct editions. However, it would appear that bookclub editions were borrowed by Collins when their stock ran low and vice versa. So strange 'anomalies' exist such as a 1979 bookclub edition with an added Collins £6.50 price sticker, and it is not unusual to find other 'incorrect' combinations of book and jacket. To confuse matters further, it is likely that some of these combinations are later marriages, arranged by collectors or dealers. Variants have only been catalogued if there is good evidence that they were actually issued by Collins or the RU.

What can be said with greater certainty is that the genuine Collins first edition is a much rarer book than commonly thought. Only *c.* 3,250 were printed and clearly there must be many RU editions masquerading as the real thing in collections. Notwithstanding the 'pick-and-mix' variants, all Collins impressions have *Durasealed* dust jackets with printed prices and are bound in buckram, whereas RU editions are bound in cheaper imitation cloth and their jackets are without *Duraseal* protectors and without printed prices.

There are no foreign editions of *British Tits* but Professor Perrins writes: 'there was also a strong rumour that there was a largish order from Israel that was cancelled when the purchaser discovered that the book did not cover the subject that they had hoped for....'

Despite the popularity of *British Tits*, in 1983 around 500 copies were remaindered, and interpolation of the sales statements suggests a further 500 or so copies were either remaindered or pulped at the end of 1985; the title finally going out of print in 1986. Total number of Collins copies sold was *c.* 5,400 (inc. remaindered books) and *c.* 9,300 RU copies sold.

NN62A   **First Edition**, 1979 (18 January 1979).
Title: 'The New Naturalist | British Tits'.
Author: 'C. M. Perrins'.
Editors: MD, JG, KM and EH (Photographic editor).
Printer: William Collins Sons & Co Ltd Glasgow.
ISBN: 0002195372.
Collation: pp. 304; 8 leaves of b/w plates printed to both sides (19 × 16-page-gatherings).
Casing: With NN Monogram 'Type D' (with large central diamond) to the spine.
Jacket: With *Duraseal* protector. [Rear panel] New Naturalist library listing NN1–63 (Type 42, variant 18a). [Rear flap] Adverts for *British Birds of Prey* and *Finches* both supported with press endorsements; ISBN.
Price: £6.50 net printed diagonally.
Print run: 3,250; no. sold: *c.* 3,500 (actually *c.* 3,100 – see notes below).
Notes: 1) *British Tits* employs two unusual NN monogram types: unembellished 'Type A' (i.e. without a central diamond) to the title page and 'Type D' (i.e. with large central diamond) to the spine casing; why these none standard monograms were used is unknown. 2) The number sold is greater than the number printed – on the face of it a discrepancy of impossible proportions! These figures, from the sales-sheets are for books sold before the 1980 reprint. The existence of NN62B, explains this discrepancy. Probably only *c.* 3,100 genuine first editions were sold.

NN62B Bookclub First Edition Sold by Collins. Seemingly, Collins 'requisitioned' stock of the 1979 RU ed. BC62A (presumably their own had run out) and either applied their own jacket to the book or a Collins price sticker to the RU jacket. Interpolation of the sales figures suggests around 400 such copies were sold, but this is ultimately conjectural. No. sold thus: 400[?].

NN62B-DJ1 RU book – BC62A, with a Collins first edition jacket NN62A i.e. priced and *Durasealed*.

NN62B-DJ2 RU book – BC62A, with Collins £6.50 price-sticker to the unpriced RU jacket.

NN62C Reprint, 1980. ISBN unchanged. 'First published 1979 | Reprinted 1980'. As NN62A, however the book-block is made up from nine 32-page gatherings and one 16-page gathering (same 304 pages), necessitating a revised placing of the plates, as reflected in the 'List of Photographs'. The binding is virtually identical but the NN monogram on the spine has changed to the 'Type A' variant and so now matches that on the title page. The blue to the *Durasealed* jacket noticeably darker and the NN library lists NN1–64 (Type 42, variant 19); both flaps unchanged. Price: £8 net, printed diagonally. Print run: 4,500; no. sold thus: *c.* 450. But it is likely that around 1,500 copies (quires?) were subsequently sold to the RU, and 496 copies were remaindered (at £1.50/unit to Booksmith) in 1983.

NN62C-AP1 1st Repriced DJ (1981–82), £8.50 sticker, *c.* 200 sold.
NN62C-AP2 2nd Repriced DJ (1982–83), £9.50 sticker, *c.* 400 sold.
NN62C-AP3 3rd Repriced DJ (1984–86), £10.00 sticker, *c.* 350 sold.

BC62A Readers Union First Edition, 1979. Bound up from the same sheets as NN62A, but cased in imitation cloth. The jacket too is identical to NN62A, but not *Durasealed* and without a printed price. No. sold: *c.* 9,300 inc. BC62B below.

BC62B Readers Union Reprint, 1980. Bound up from the same sheets as NN62C, but cased in imitation cloth. The jacket too is identical to NN62C, but not *Durasealed* and without a printed price. No. sold: inc. in BC62A above.

POD62A Print-on-demand digital copy of the first edition NN62A.

63 British Thrushes

Thrushes are ubiquitous garden birds and therefore it might seem surprising to learn that Collins managed to sell only *c.* 4,200 copies over an eight-year period; surprising, that is, until we learn that Readers Union (RU) had just under 8,000 copies, a further 1,400 copies were remaindered in 1983 and probably a further 350 copies in 1985.

Consequently there are far more RU copies around than genuine Collins editions, but they are at least easy to tell apart: the bookclub edition is an inferior product, bound in imitation cloth rather than buckram, the jacket is not *Durasealed* and is always price clipped. Usually with bookclub editions there is no printed price, but presumably someone forgot to remove the price before printing – who was the unlucky soul who had to clip 8,000 jackets?

Due to the high inflation rates of the early 1980s, only *c.* 3,100 copies of *British Thrushes* were sold at their original price, with the remainder price-clipped and repriced. Considering the jacket's propensity to fade, there cannot be many extant Collins editions that have unfaded entire jackets. In this condition, a much rarer book than commonly believed.

NN63A   **First Edition**, 1978 (07 September 1978).
Title: 'The New Naturalist | British Thrushes'.
Author: 'Eric Simms, D.F.C., M.A.'
Editors: MD, JG, KM & EH (Photographic Editor).
Printer: William Collins Sons & Co Ltd Glasgow.
ISBN: 0002196700.
Collation: pp. 304; 12 leaves of b/w plates printed to both sides (19 × 16-page gatherings).
Casing: Green buckram.
Jacket: With *Duraseal* protector. [Rear panel] The New Naturalist library, listing NN1–63, (Type 42, variant 18). [Rear flap] Adverts for *Finches* and *Woodland Birds*; ISBN.
Price: £6.50 net printed diagonally.
Print run: 6,500; no. sold: *c.* 3,100 + repriced variants listed below + 1,400 copies remaindered in 1983 and probably a further *c.* 350 copies in 1985; o/p: 1986[?]
Notes: It is a moot point as to whether the remaindered books were price-clipped, but the preponderance of clipped jackets and the fact that by 1983 Collins had increased the cover to £9.50 suggests that they probably were.

NN63A-AP1 1st Repriced DJ (1980–81), £7.50 sticker, *c.* 350 sold.
NN63A-AP2 2nd Repriced DJ (1981–82), £8.50 sticker, *c.* 200 sold[?].
NN63A-AP3 3rd Repriced DJ (1982–83), £9.50 sticker, *c.* 300 sold[?].
NN63A-AP4 4th Repriced DJ (1984–86), £10.00 sticker, *c.* 250 sold.

BC63A Readers Union Edition, 1978. Purchased by the Readers Union group and sold through their *Country & Garden Book Society*. As NN63A, bound up from the same sheets, casing in cheaper imitation cloth. Jacket also identical to NN63A but without *Duraseal* and all appear to have been price-clipped.
Print run: 7,880.

POD63A Print-on-demand digital copy.

64 The Natural History of Shetland

The printing history of *Shetland* is noteworthy for going out of print for a couple of years before being reprinted. It sold well at first but annual sales were down to 250 a few years later, so understandably Collins were reticent about a reprint. However, the promise of significant local sales by a Shetland Bookshop eventually prompted a reprint. In the event these sales did not materialise and the reprint sold particularly slowly: 353 copies in 1986, 152 copies in 1987 and 204 copies in 1988. *Shetland* was eventually remaindered. This was not, however, the end of the road for *Shetland*, as it was extensively revised by Johnston and published by T & A D Poyser under the title *A Naturalist's Shetland* in 1999 – 19 years after the Collins first edition.

The ISBN printed to the imprint page of the Collins first edition, is incorrect as it is the same as that assigned to the earlier title NN61 *Inheritance* (also by *Berry*), however, the correct ISBN is printed to the jacket and the error is corrected in the reprint. The first edition jacket is *Durasealed*, but the laminated reprint jacket is particularly flimsy, not unlike a laser facsimile and is the only jacket in the series printed on such paper. The colours are also markedly different; brighter with more yellow in the green. The reprint is bound, uniquely for the series, in cheaper dark blue-green imitation 'Type 7' cloth.

Shetland's jacket does suffer from fading, particularly the blue. However, when the spine is viewed on the shelf in isolation of the front panel, unless the fading is severe, it does not detract unduly from the aesthetics of the design.

NN64A   **First Edition**, 1980 (08 April 1980).
Title: 'The New Naturalist | The Natural History of | Shetland'.
Authors: 'R. J. Berry, D.Sc. | and | J. L. Johnston, B.Sc.'
Illust: 'With 29 colour photographs | 44 photographs in black and white | and 47 line drawings'.
Editors: MD, JG, KM and EH (Photographic Editor).
Printer: William Collins Sons & Co Ltd, Glasgow.
ISBN: 0002190419 to the dust jacket (correct). 0002190842 to the imprint page (incorrect).

204 · COLLECTING THE NEW NATURALISTS

Collation: pp. 1–264, [2], 265–380, [2]; 4 leaves of colour plates printed to both sides; 8 leaves of b/w plates printed to both sides (12 × 32-page gatherings). (Note: The Appendices title leaf has been omitted from the pagination, so total pp. = 382 + 2 = 384).

Jacket: With *Duraseal* protector. [Rear panel] The New Naturalist library listing NN1–63, (Type 42, variant 18a). [Rear flap] Advert for *Inheritance and Natural History;* ISBN.

Price: £8.50 net printed diagonally with dashed line.

Print run: 4,000; no. sold: *c.* 3,000 + repriced variant below; o/p: end of 1983.

Notes: *Shetland* was sponsored by Shell (who had significant commercial interests in Shetland) and it seems that part of the deal was a stock of gratis copies, which might explain the larger than normal discrepancy (15 per cent) between the print-order and books actually sold.

NN64A-AP1 1st Repriced DJ (1982–83), £9.50 sticker, *c.* 400 sold.

NN64B Reprint, 1986. ISBN 0002190419. 'First published 1980 | Reprinted 1986'. Textually identical to NN65A. ISBN corrected and matches that on the jacket. Bound in dark blue-green imitation cloth 'Type 7'. Jacket laminated, not *Durasealed,* (see intro.): the NN library lists NN1–71 inclusively (same format as *Orkney* jacket); both flaps unchanged. Price: £12.95, printed diagonally with dashed lined. Print run: 2,000; o/p: 1990[?] (it is probable that 500 or so copies remaindered around this time).

POD64A Print-on-demand digital copy of the 1886 reprint NN64B.

MIS64A T&AD Poyser Edition, 1999. ISBN: 0856611050. 'A Naturalist's | Shetland | by J. Laughton Johnston | Illustrations by John Busby'. Published by T&AD Poyser Ltd, London; pp. xii, 506, [2]. Text completely revised with colour illustrations integrated throughout, new diagrams and tables, map endpapers. Quarto format, 200 mm × 260 mm, larger than Collins original ed. Casing of light blue imitation cloth, gilt-blocked to spine, jacket laminated. An attractive edition, not scarce.

65 Waders

The genuine first edition *Waders* is a much rarer book than popularly thought: the print-order was for just 3,550 copies but the abundance of the very similar bookclub edition of the same date has muddied the waters. Marren, in his excellent book *The New Naturalists,* suggests that the first edition has edged into the 2-star category, but I would suggest it is firmly within it and knocking at the door of the 3-star establishment – especially when buoyed by an unfaded jacket.

The 1981 reprint would appear to have been solely produced for the bookclub Readers Union; unfortunately the sales statement, which would have recorded this issue, is missing, but I have not seen a copy in a jacket with a printed price, or with a Collins price sticker. Collins did, however, publish a reprint in 1982. All bookclub editions and reprints are inferior products in cheaper imitation cloth bindings of two different colours and with two different monograms.

There is noticeable colour variation of jackets between the different editions, but, regardless of edition, the pink band is particularly prone to fading on the spine.

NN65A **First Edition**, 1980 (10 November 1980).

Title: 'The New Naturalist | Waders'.

Author: W. G. Hale.

Editors: MD, JG, KM and EH (Photographic Editor).

Printer: William Collins Sons & Co Ltd, Glasgow.

ISBN: 0002197278.

Casing: Green, slightly shiny close-weave buckram.

Collation: pp. 320; 12 leaves of b/w plates printed to both sides (10 × 32-page gatherings).

Jacket: With *Duraseal* protector. (Note: The jacket is a couple of mm too short for the book.) [Rear panel] The New Naturalist library listing NN1–64 (Type 42, variant 20). [Rear flap] Adverts for *Finches, British Birds of Prey, British Tits* and *British Thrushes;* ISBN.

Price: £9.50 net diagonally printed.

Print run: 3,550; no. sold: unknown, but probably *c.* 3,000; o/p: 1981.

Notes: 1) b/w in-text illustrations throughout by Diane Breeze. 2) 'Type D' monogram to the casing spine. 3) Book 25 mm thick. 4) It is not unusual to find this first edition with a BC65A bookclub jacket; that is, not priced and without a *Duraseal* protector. It is likely that this union occurred as a warehouse expedient, but it is also not impossible that further harlequin copies have been unwittingly (or wittingly) created as second marriages arranged by dealers and collectors. Be warned, and make sure your first edition has a priced *Durasealed* jacket as originally intended.

NN65B Reprint, 1982. ISBN unchanged. 'First published 1980 | Reprinted 1982'. Textually as NN65A, but an inferior production. Cased in light green imitation cloth with 'Type C' monogram to the spine; the paper courser, resulting in a noticeably thicker book – 31 mm. The jacket as NN65A, but priced at £10.50 net and without a *Duraseal* protector. Print run: c. 2,650[?]; no. sold: unknown, but c. 1,300. Additionally 500 books were remaindered to Booksmith in 1983 (at £1.50 each) and it would appear that a further 500 books were remaindered or pulped in 1986; o/p: summer 1986.

BC65A Readers Union, First Edition, 1980. Identical with NN65A but bound in cheaper dark green imitation cloth. The jacket is also identical to NN65A, but without a price and without a *Duraseal* protector. Print run: unknown but seemingly a total of 5,300 copies, including BC65B below, were supplied to the Readers Union.

BC65B Readers Union, First Reprint, 1981. The ISBN as above. 'First published 1980 | Reprinted 1981'. As NN65A. Bound in dark sea-green imitation cloth (same as BC65A); the paper courser, resulting in a thicker book – 30 mm. The jacket identical to previous jackets but printed on much thinner, whiter paper; un-priced and without a *Duraseal* protector. Print run: unknown, but see BC65A. Note: It would seem that this 1981 edition was produced solely for the RU.

BC65C Readers Union, Second Reprint, 1982. Exactly as NN65B but without a printed price to the jacket. Print run: unknown but probably included in the Collins print number.

POD65A Print-on-demand digital copy of the 1982 reprint NN65B.

66 The Natural History of Wales

A beautifully written book, so much so that it is (to my knowledge) the only New Naturalist that has been recorded as a 'talking book' (11h. 48m.), read by Robin Holmes. But when compared with earlier New Naturalists and the standards we have grown accustomed to in recent titles, it is in terms of its physical attributes unprepossessing: slight and without colour plates; the reprint even more so, bound in inferior imitation cloth and printed on cheaper paper. However, from the bibliographic perspective, the first edition does possess two noteworthy physical features; firstly, it is one of only two New Naturalists stamped with its series number to the spine of the book (The other is NN95 *Northumberland)* and secondly the buckram cloth is a unique blue-green colour. The reasons for this are explained in a letter, dated 14 April 1981, from Robert MacDonald of Collins to Lord Mar: '...I have to admit that your question about the binding of *The Natural History of Wales* is slightly embarrassing. We knew that the binding material itself was slightly different because the factory ran out of stock of the usual buckram, and could not get the correct replacement in time. We were obliged to choose an alternative cloth finish as near as possible in texture and shade but, at such short notice, the choice was quite limited. The binding material is, incidentally, buckram as you suggest. The alteration of the design on the spine, however, was not intentional at all and, until the arrival of your letter, I confess, unnoticed. Clearly what has happened is that the jacket typography artwork has been used for preparation of the spine brass rather than a correct design in the usual style.'

The reprint reverts to the normal format of lettering on the spine without the series number. It doubled as a bookclub edition and consequently is bound in cheaper imitation cloth, and the dust jacket does not have a *Duraseal* protector. *Wales* was subsequently published in the Bloomsbury reprint series in 1989.

The *Wales* jacket is subject to fading on the spine, particularly so with the reprint, but unfaded first editions are not particularly rare and with a little perseverance can be found. The available sales data for *Wales* is both inconsistent and ambiguous and even makes mention of three printings, though to my knowledge there were only ever two. It is therefore impossible to state quantities with certainty but a cautious interpretation of the available figures does, at least, enable an overview.

NN66A	**First Edition**, 1981 (30 March 1981).
Title:	'The New Naturalist	The Natural History of	Wales'.
Author:	'William Condry, M.A., M.Sc.'.
ISBN:	0002195682.
Collation:	pp. 287, [1]; 12 leaves of b/w plates printed to both sides (9 × 32-page gatherings).
Casing:	Dark blue-green buckram with the number 66 stamped to the spine (see intro.).
Jacket:	With *Duraseal* protector, printed on bright white paper. [Rear panel] The NN library listing NN1–65, (Type 42, variant 21). [Rear flap] Advert for *The Natural History of Shetland* with 3 review extracts followed by 'Other books by William Condry' under which listed

six titles (Note: four of these titles were not published by Collins). The ISBN is positioned above the bottom edge. Note: The jacket is a couple of mm too short for the book.

Price: £9.50 printed diagonally with dotted line.
Print run: 3,970 (out-turn); o/p: 1982.

NN66B Reprint, 1982. ISBN unchanged. 'First published 1981 | Reprinted 1982'. Textually as NN66A. The spine of the casing has reverted to the normal layout without the series number. Cased in light straw-green imitation cloth (Type 4) and the paper used is poorer quality. Jacket identical, but not *Durasealed*, printed on cream-coloured paper. Price: £10.50 printed diagonally with dotted line. Print run: *c.* 2,500[?]; no. sold: *c.* 400[?] + 1,930 to the RU; o/p: 1986. Notes: 1) This reprint doubled as a RU bookclub ed., which might explain the preponderance of price-clipped jackets. 2) The jacket is very light sensitive, much more so than the first ed. – presumably cheaper inks were used.

BL66A Bloomsbury Reprint, 1990 (31/12/1990). ISBN 1870630440; pp. 287, [1]; 12 leaves of b/w illustrations. A facsimile of NN66A. Price £12.95. Remaindered.

POD66A Print-on-demand facsimile of the first edition.

67 Farming and Wildlife

Farming and Wildlife was first published in 1981 and reprinted in 1983, but the extant NN statements for this period are inconsistent regarding the number of books printed. A bookclub (RU) 'edition' was published concurrently with the Collins first edition and is virtually inseparable from it, but for the fact that the jacket is not priced; additionally it is probable that the RU was subsequently 'topped-up' from Collins stock. No doubt it is this RU connection that confuses the print quantities, but with a little interpolation and a few, not unlikely, assumptions it is possible to arrive at a figure that is probably fairly accurate – say ± 10 per cent. Notwithstanding, the sales figures cited in the NN statements are consistent, and it is these figures which are more important to the collector.

The jackets of all editions are a little prone to fading on the spine, but unfaded copies are available to those who seek them out.

NN67A   **First Edition**, 1981 (May[?]; not after June 1981).
Title: 'The New Naturalist | Farming and | Wildlife'.
Author: 'Kenneth Mellanby, C.B.E., Sc.D.'.
Illust: 'With 67 photographs in black and white'.
Editors: MD, KM, SMW and EH (Photographic Editor).
Printer: William Collins Sons & Co Ltd, Glasgow.
ISBN: 000219239x.
Collation: pp. [4], 7–178; 16 leaves of b/w plates printed to both sides (11 × 16-page gatherings). (Note: The pagination is incorrect – the page that is numbered '7' is actually p. 5, so last page should be p. 176.)
Jacket: [Rear panel] New Naturalist library listing NN1–66 (Type 42, variant 22). [Rear flap] Adverts for *Waders*, *Natural History of Shetland* and *British Tits*; ISBN.
Price: £9.50 net printed diagonally with dashed line.
Print run: *c.* 2,750[?]; no. sold *c.* 2,460.
Notes: 1) Bound in green buckram. 2) Collins address to TP: St James's Place, London. 3) Jacket with *Duraseal* protector. 4) Text to jacket printed in clay-brown.

NN67B Reprint, 1983. ISBN unaltered. 'First published 1981 | Reprinted 1983'. As NN67A; a few minor revisions to the prelims. Collins' address to TP now 'Grafton Street'. Editors: KM, SW and EH. Printed and bound by Biddles of Guildford and now with 32-page gatherings (5½ × 32-page). The casing of imitation cloth (Type 5). Paper and printing of better quality. The jacket, without a *Duraseal* protector, is distinctive: printed in green and dark brown to the rear panel is a general blurb for NN series, supported by three press reviews (the same format as the rear panel of NN69 *Reptiles & Amphibians*); front/rear flaps unaltered; colour emphasis slightly different to 1st ed. Price: £9.50. Print run: 1,000[?]; no. sold: *c.* 120 plus repriced variant below, plus in 1986, *c.* 220 copies either remaindered or pulped; o/p: 1987. Notes: 1) The imitation cloth used is unique to the series. 2) It is rare to find a jacket with the original printed price in tact – most copies have the £10 substitute price sticker.
NN67B-RP1 1st Repriced DJ (1984–1987), £10.00 sticker, *c.* 620 sold.

BC67A Readers Union Edition, 1981. As NN67A, binding and text indistinguishable and the *Durasealed* jacket identical too, but without a printed price. NN sales statements give a figure of 1,590 RU copies, but this, almost certainly, includes additional copies subsequently sold to the RU from Collins stock, as this unpriced variant is much scarcer than that figure would suggest.

POD67A Print-on-demand digital copy of the 1983 reprint NN67B.

Print run: c. 4,000[?] + 750 for the RU; no. sold: c. 2,200 (Collins) +
               750 (RU) + 700 (RU?) + 600 (remaindered/RU) = total of
               4,250; o/p: 1988 but still sold by RU and other outlets
               into the 1990s.
Notes: All lettering to the jacket is unusually printed in a
               russet colour to match the cover design.

POD68A Print-on-demand digital copy.

68 Mammals in the British Isles

Mammals is an unsatisfactory book from the bibliophile's
perspective: much key information is missing, or at best that
which is available is ambiguous. Firstly, there is some confusion
surrounding its publication date, purportedly June 1982, but
reviews did not appear until the end of the year. Secondly the
print-run is not recorded on file and thirdly there is uncertainty
surrounding the number, and nature of the books sold to the
Readers Union and/or remaindered. We do know that an initial
batch of 750 books were sold to the RU on publication; thereafter
it gets a bit more confusing: it is probable, but not certain, that
another batch of c. 700 were sold off to the RU in 1986 and a
further 600 or so remaindered in 1988. It has been suggested that
the (initial) RU edition was bound in an inferior imitation cloth,
but I am not aware of any such copies and presume that the RU
books are indistinguishable from the standard Collins edition,
though probably price-clipped.

The changing fortunes of the series and publishing generally
meant that it was no longer commercially viable to retain a large
range of historic titles in print, and *Mammals* is the last book in
the series to use the Type 42 library on the dust jacket rear panel,
which identifies all other titles contemporaneously in print. All
following books list either the full library or advertise specific
books.

With its *Duraseal* cover, *Mammals* is often found in fine
condition, but the russet colour of the dust jacket is prone to
fading and the weasel's head on the spine is often much paler
than it should be.

NN68A   **First Edition**, 1982 (30 June 1982?).
Title: 'The New Naturalist | Mammals | in the British Isles'.
Author: 'L. Harrison Matthews M.A., ScD., F.R.S.'
Editors: MD, KM, SMW and EH (Photographic Editor).
Printer: William Collins Sons & Co. Ltd, Glasgow.
ISBN: 0002197383.
Collation: pp. 207, [1]; 8 leaves of b/w plates printed to both sides
              (6½ × 32-page gatherings).
Jacket: With *Duraseal* protector. [Rear panel] New Naturalist
              library listing NN1–67 (Type 42, variant 23). [Rear flap]
              Adverts for *Waders*; *The Natural History of Shetland*; *The
              Natural History of Wales* and *Farming and Wildlife*; ISBN.
Price: £10.95 net printed diagonally with dashed line.

69 Reptiles and Amphibians in Britain

Bibliographically uncomplicated with a small print run of a single
Collins edition, which was also sold by the Readers Union and
later republished as a Bloomsbury facsimile edition. Extant file
notes in the Collins archive suggest that the bookclub edition was
to be bound in cheaper imitation cloth, but in the event this did
not happen and all books are identical. The preponderance of
price-clipped jackets does not seem to be any greater than usual,
which is odd, considering that around one-third of books were
sold by Readers Union, at a reduced price. The format of the jacket
rear panel is quite different and only shared with the reprint of
Farming and Wildlife (also published 1983); the customary NN
library is omitted and instead the complete library, uniquely, with
first edition publication dates is bound in at the end of the text.
The semi-shiny jacket is likewise unique in the series and the first
since NN50, *Pesticides* not to be protected with *Duraseal*;
additionally the first title to display Collins's new address –
Grafton Street.

Reptiles and Amphibians is not difficult to find in fine condition,
but the green of the jacket is prone to fade to a blue-green on the
spine.

NN69A   **First Edition**, 1983 (20 June 1983).
Title: 'The New Naturalist | Reptiles | and | Amphibians |
              in Britain'.
Author: 'Deryk Frazer'.
Illust: 'With 33 photographs | and 49 line drawing and |
              diagrams in the text'.
Editors: KM, SMW and EH (Photographic Editor).
Printer: William Collins Sons & Co. Ltd, Glasgow.
ISBN: 0002197065.
Collation: pp. 256; 8 leaves of b/w plates printed to both sides

Jacket: (16 × 16-page gatherings).
Upper side semi-glossy, underside matt. [Rear panel] General advert for The New Naturalist inc. three press reviews of the series. [Rear flap] Adverts for *Mammals in the British Isles, Farming and Wildlife, The Natural History of Wales* and *Waders*; ISBN.

Price: £11.00 net printed diagonally with dashed line.

Print run: 3,500; no. sold by Collins: *c.* 2,100; no. sold by RU: *c.* 1,050; o/p: 1986 (It is probable that a few additional copies were pulped/remaindered in 1986, but the extant sales-sheets are inconclusive).

Notes: 1) Copies sold by Readers Union are identical. 2) The first title to use the Grafton Street address on the title page. 3) Only NN jacket printed on this paper.

BL69A Bloomsbury Edition, 1989. ISBN 1870630041; pp. 256, [16 b/w illustrations] (17 × 16-page gatherings). Facsimile edition; hardback with jacket. Price: £12.95. Remaindered.

POD69A Print-on-demand digital copy.

70 The Natural History of Orkney

The bibliographic importance of *The Natural History of Orkney* and its neighbouring volume, NN71 *British Warblers*, within the New Naturalist library cannot be overemphasised. They were published on the same day and share a common design. This being the case, the notes for the two books should be read together. They were the heralds of a new style and represent a watershed in the New Naturalist series: they were the first titles to be printed concomitantly in hardback and paperback formats and the first to

have photographs integrated into the text. *Orkney* was the last title to sport an Ellis jacket, and *Warblers* the first to wear a Gillmor jacket.

However, more important than this and to the collector is the debacle surrounding the publication of *Orkney* and *Warblers* – see Peter Marren's comprehensive overview in *The New Naturalists*. These two titles were victims of a decision by Collins to switch emphasis to paperback production (a decision that underlined quite how out of touch Collins was with the collectors' market). The print run of the hardback edition was so absurdly small it could not nearly meet demand, but the Glasgow warehouse was awash with paperback copies. So Collins contracted Hunter & Follis Ltd: Publishers' Bookbinders (Edinburgh) in March 1986 to strip the covers off 500 paperbacks of each title and rebind them as hardbacks. In the process the text-blocks were significantly trimmed and then cased in correspondingly shorter bindings of lighter green utilitarian imitation cloth (the decision to use imitation cloth was a financial expedient – 24 pence per copy was saved reducing the rebinding cost to almost exactly £1/copy + 30 pence per jacket). The fact that the text-blocks were already stitched and glued meant that the books could not be rounded and backed in the normal way, so the spines and fore-edges are square. New jackets were printed and trimmed to suit, but laminated and without *Duraseal* protectors.

The original hardback edition has become known, in New Naturalist circles, as the first state and the rebound variant as the second state, and to avoid confusion, this terminology is retained here, though strictly speaking they should probably be distinguished as binding variants as both are bound up from the same sheets. Irrespective of terminology, the second state is a somewhat inferior product and being shorter, sits awkwardly in a collection of otherwise uniform books – an immediate giveaway to any visiting NN-*ophile*. Having said that, it is a genuine Collins first edition and represents an important episode in the history of the series: the diehard collector will want both. Table NN70 below summarises the differences between the two states.

Even though the hardback print run of *Orkney* coincides with that of the following title *Warblers*, it is generally regarded as being the scarcest of all New Naturalist titles and this is certainly my experience. The retail value of a fine first state copy of *Orkney* has increased by around 13,000 per cent! There are few other books published during the 1980s, in all genera, let alone natural history,

TABLE NN70 Summary of differences between first and second state variants of *Orkney*.

VARIANT	CASING FABRIC	CASE HEIGHT	CASE SPINE	LEAF SIZE	DUST JACKET
First state NN70A	Very smooth, shiny, almost waxy, dark green, buckram cloth	223 mm	Rounded	148 × 216 mm	Matt to both sides; with a clear plastic *Duraseal* protector to the upper side (223 mm tall).
Second State NN70B	Lighter pea-green imitation cloth (*Arlin*)	218 mm	Flat	144 × 210 mm	Laminated paper, glossy to the upper surface, without a *Duraseal* protector. Trimmed to the top and bottom edges with the series numeral very close to the top edge (217 mm tall).

that can match or better this, though a few children's books of the following decade come to mind – Philip Pullman's *Northern Lights* and of course J. K. Rowling's *Harry Potter and the Philosopher's Stone*. Inevitably, this price-tag puts *Orkney* beyond the reach of many collectors, and accordingly some dealers have commissioned full-height facsimile copies bound up from paperbacks, but these are generally easy enough to tell apart from the real thing. Presumably the introduction of affordable POD copies will prevent the manufacture of further 'fakes', though I don't believe the intention was ever underhand.

Around 4,500 copies of the paperback were printed, of which 500 copies were sold to the Readers Union (indistinguishable from the Collins edition) and 100 copies given free of charge to the book's sponsor: *Occidental North Sea Oil Consortium*. But general sales of the paperback were slow and Crispin Fisher (Collins), in a letter dated 17 June 1986 to Berry, stated 'the original paperback is a little disappointing. We printed approximately 3,700 and 500 of these are now hardbacks, and 1,100 sold. That leaves approximately 2,100 in the warehouse, and we expect to carry on selling steadily, but probably not dramatically.' By the end of August 1987, total sales had increased to only *c.* 1,360 copies, and by November of the same year Collins had agreed to reduce the list price to £5.95 and offer a 50 per cent promotional discount.

Berry in his preface points out that *Orkney* was in fact the collaboration of several authors, 'My name appears on the title page, but this book is truly a joint effort. There was a core which planned it from the start…'. This group of contributors is listed below. *Orkney* was subsequently revised and updated, and published in 2000, in hardback format, by Poyser with the title *Orkney Nature*: a lavish quarto production, with fine colour photographs throughout.

The colours of the second state dust jacket are lighter and brighter than the first state, but both are comparatively colourfast; copies with unfaded spines are not uncommon.

NN70A	**First Edition, First State**, 1985 (11 November 1985).
Title:	'The New Naturalist	The Natural History of	Orkney'.
Author:	'R. J. Berry, D.Sc., F.R.S.E.'.
Illust:	'With 20 colour photographs, and	over 100 photographs and diagrams	in black and white'.
Contributors:	[Miss Elaine R. Bullard; Dr. Paul Heppleston, Mr. David Lea and Mr Peter Reynolds et al].
Editors:	KM, SMW, RW and EH (Photographic Editor).
Printer:	Wm Collins Sons & Co. Ltd, Glasgow.
ISBN:	0002190621.
Collation:	pp. 304; 4 leaves of colour plates printed to both sides (9 ½ × 32-page gatherings).
Casing:	very smooth, shiny, almost waxy green buckram, 223 mm tall.
Jacket:	Matt to both sides, with *Duraseal* protector. [Rear panel] The New Naturalist library listing NN1–71 inclusively; ISBN and barcode. Front flap: In addition

to usual blurb, '*This title is also available in a limpback edition at £9.95'. [Rear flap] Author's biography and adverts for Berry's two previous NN titles: *Inheritance* and *Shetland*, both with press reviews.

Price:	£20.00 net printed diagonally across corner with dashed line.
Print run:	725; no. sold: *c.* 640; o/p: 1985.
Notes:	1) *Orkney* is the last book to be cased in the old-style buckram and the last NN to be printed by Collins. 2) The type size used is very small (for further details regarding these points see intro. to *Warblers*).

NN70B First Edition, Second State, 1985. Bound up from the same sheets and therefore textually identical to NN70A, including ISBN. These books were bound up from stripped-down paperbacks and it is therefore the bindings that are different, as explained in intro. above. Casing of a lighter pea-green imitation cloth, flatter across the spine and a full 5 mm shorter, being only 218 mm tall. Dust jacket is a new printing with noticeably brighter colours; laminated paper, glossy to the upper surface, without a *Duraseal* protector, and trimmed to suit. The jacket carried the same price of £20.00 net. Print run: 500; no. sold: *c.* 490; o/p: summer 1987.

CPB70A Collins Paperback First Edition, 1985. ISBN 0002194066. Concomitant with the hardback edition NN70A and bound-up from the same sheets. Paperback design Type 1. To the rear cover, a general blurb for The NN library and replica of the DJ blurb cover design credit (referred to as the 'jacket design'). Price: £9.95 net. Print run: *c.* 4,500[?]; no. sold: *c.* 2,800[?] + 600 to RU + 500 rebound as hardbacks; 100 copies given to *Occidental North Sea Oil Consortium*; o/p: 1990/91.

POD70A Print-on-demand digital copy.

MIS70A T & A D Poyser Revised Edition, 2000 (27/04/2000). ISBN: 0856611042. Title: 'Orkney Nature | R. J. Berry | Illustrations by John Holloway'. Published by T & A D Poyser in association with Academic Press, London. Hardback with dust jacket. Quarto format, 147 × 260 mm i.e. much larger than the original Collins ed.; pp. x, 308, [2]; (20 × 16-page gatherings). Completely revised with colour illustrations integrated throughout the revised text, some new diagrams and tables; map end-papers. Casing of dark green imitation cloth, gilt blocked lettering to spine. The laminated jacket features a photograph of The Old Man of Hoy to the front panel and a watercolour by Morton Boyd to the rear panel. Berry in his 'Apologia' writes '*Orkney Nature* is a much revised version of a book called *The Natural History of Orkney*, published in 1985 by Collins in their New Naturalist series…Much has happened since the first edition, and hence this new book rather than a simple reprint.' (No printed price.) Not scarce.

71 British Warblers

British Warblers suffered the same fate as the preceding title, *Orkney*, and as the notes for that title apply equally to this, they have not been duplicated here. Equally most of these notes apply to *Orkney*.

In order to give the series a contemporary look the design was restyled but it was ill-conceived. The traditional Baskerville typeface was replaced with Erhart but the type size used was mean, rendering reading onerous (9 pt for the main text and considerably smaller for *Orkney's* index). However, the blank fore-edge margins at over 40 mm were unnecessary wide. The new integrated format with half-tone photographs and diagrams dispersed throughout the text might have been a good idea if it was well executed, but, as a cost saving expedient, cheaper paper was used rendering the images blotchy with loss of detail.

While *Warblers* and *Orkney* were published on the same day and both were heralds of a new style, they were in fact printed and bound by different printers: *Warblers* by Butler & Tanner Ltd., Frome, Somerset, and *Orkney* in house by Collins' Glasgow Printers. This did not lead to any discernible variation in printing quality, but the casing fabrics and gilt lettering to the spine are quite different. *Orkney* is the last book to be cased in the old-style shiny, smooth, waxy buckram with the pleasing deeply indented gilt lettering to the spine – and in fact the last New Naturalist printed in-house. *Warblers* is cased in dark green non-shiny acrylic-coated *Arbelave* library buckram, variations of which have been used for every new naturalist since published. The gilt lettering is less deeply impressed and not so crisp.

Bearing in mind a generally higher level of demand for ornithological titles and given the identical print runs, it is somewhat perplexing that *Warblers* is, in both states, less scarce

than *Orkney*, particularly considering that it would seem only *c.* 380 copies of the second state were sold. Notwithstanding, Collins was optimistic when they ordered *c.* 8,000 paperback copies of *Warblers*, of which 2,100 copies were immediately sold to the Readers Union (indistinguishable from the Collins edition) and 1,200 copies were sold in the first couple of months. Thereafter sales slowed considerably. In 1988 the retail price was reduced to £4.95 with a bold red sticker applied to the front cover; even so, come April 1989, over 2,000 books still languished in the warehouse. A few months later all outstanding stock was remaindered.

During the eighties, Mr. Ronald Norman of Cleveland (presumably a bookseller) arranged with Collins to have 75–100 copies of each title signed by the author. In the case of *Warblers* and *Orkney* this represented over 10 per cent of first state books sold; additionally Collins had further copies signed, and therefore signed books are not uncommon. The *Warbler's* jacket spine is susceptible to fading, the brown elements particularly so, and most copies are lighter here than on the front panel, though the first state appears less fugitive than the second state. This might be because the colours generally of the second state have more yellow pigment, giving the impression of an overall brighter jacket.

NN71A	**First Edition, First State**, 1985 (11 November 1985).
Title:	'The New Naturalist | British Warblers'.
Author:	'Eric Simms D.F.C., M.A.'.
Editors:	KM, SMW, RW and EH (Photographic Editor).
Printer:	Butler & Tanner Ltd, Frome, Somerset, UK.
ISBN:	000219810X.
Collation:	pp. 432; 4 leaves of plates printed to both side, 6 sides of which in colour and 2 of which b/w text (13½ × 32-page gatherings + 1 × 16-page gathering).
Casing:	dark green non-shiny acrylic-coated *Arbelave* library buckram, 223 mm tall.
Jacket:	Matt to both sides, with *Duraseal* protector. [Rear panel] The New Naturalist library listing NN1–70 inclusively; ISBN and barcode. Front flap: In addition to the usual blurb, 'Jacket design by Robert Gillmor'. [Rear flap] adverts for three previous NN ornithological titles: *Waders, British Birds of Prey* and *British Thrushes* (unusually these are not supported

TABLE NN71 Summary of differences between first and second state variants of *Warblers*.

VARIANT	CASING FABRIC	CASE HEIGHT	CASE SPINE	LEAF SIZE	DUST JACKET
First State NN71A	Dark green non-shiny buckram (*Arbelave*).	223 mm tall	Rounded	148 × 216 mm	Matt to both sides; with a clear plastic *Duraseal* protector to the upper side (223 mm tall).
Second State NN71B	Lighter pea-green imitation cloth (*Arlin*).	218 mm tall	Flat	144 × 210 mm	Laminated paper, glossy to the upper surface, without a *Duraseal* protector. Trimmed to the top and bottom edges with the series numeral very close to the top edge (217 mm tall).

with press commendations but by extracts taken from the original jacket blurb for each title.)

Price: £20.00 net printed diagonally across corner with dashed line.
Print run: 725; no. sold: *c.* 660; o/p: 1985.
Notes: 1) Unlike *Orkney*, there is no illustrations blurb to the title page. 2) Artist: Ian Wallace.

NN71B First Edition, Second State, 1985. Textually identical to NN71A inc. the ISBN. Bound up from stripped-down paperbacks and it is therefore the bindings that are different – see entry for *Orkney*. The casing is of a lighter pea-green imitation cloth, flatter across the spine and a full 5 mm shorter, being only 218 mm tall. The jacket is a new printing with noticeably brighter colours; laminated paper, glossy to the upper surface, without a *Duraseal* protector, trimmed to suit. Price: £20.00 net. Print run: 500; no. sold: *c.* 380[?]; o/p: 1986.

CPB71A Collins Paperback First Edition, 1985. ISBN: 000219404X. Concomitant with the hardback edition NN71A and bound-up from the same sheets. Paperback design Type 1. To the rear cover an appraisal of the NN library and slightly abbreviated form of the jacket blurb; advert for three ornithological NN titles – NN60, 63 and 65 (as DJ rear flap); cover design credit (which erroneously refers to the 'jacket'). Price: £9.95 net. Print run: *c.* 8,000; no. sold: *c.* 3,000; 2,100 to RU (indistinguishable) + 500 rebound as hardbacks + *c.* 2,000 remaindered[?]; o/p: 1989/90.

POD71A Print-on-demand digital copy.

72 Heathlands

The existence of the much more common, but near-identical bookclub edition has caused much confusion. However the bookclub ed. is simply distinguished by the absence of 'Collins' on the dust jacket spine and the absence of a printed price – it is otherwise identical. It remains unrecorded why it was felt that the removal of the imprint from the jacket spine was sufficient to distinguish this book as a bookclub edition. But it does seem odd considering 'Collins' still appears on the casing and, internally, on both the title and imprint pages. Also, both the barcode and ISBN are unchanged. The same practice was employed with the following title *The New Forest*.

However, the confusion surrounding *Heathlands* is compounded by the presence of a Collins reprint of the same year. While the book is identified as a reprint to the imprint page, the jacket is identical to the first edition jacket with Collins on the spine – and if someone was inclined to put a reprint jacket on a bookclub book, the result would be indistinguishable from a genuine first edition – and no doubt some have been so inclined! The bookclub jacket is then put on the reprint book and this is the rub as, theoretically, this combination was never issued – at least not legitimately. But we know that, from other titles, the Collins warehouse was prepared to adopt a pragmatic approach when it came to fulfilling orders. It is also recorded that Collins attempted to buy back some of the bookclub editions but the RU refused. Additionally, I have been told by one collector that he purchased new, in a high street shop, a copy of the bookclub edition.

Whether any of this is important is ultimately for the collector to decide, but what can be said with certainty is that the genuine first edition as intended, with Collins printed to the spine, is a rare thing: the print-order was for just one thousand copies, but in the event only 880 copies were delivered, making the first edition of *Heathlands* the third rarest New Naturalist, at least in numerical terms. Not surprisingly the first edition went out of print almost immediately and before all subscription orders were fulfilled. However, the presence of the much more common bookclub edition has served to keep prices down, of which *c.* 2,000 copies were printed.

The paperback *Heathlands* was the first New Naturalist to be issued with a photographic cover – in the belief that it would appeal to the 'hoi polloi' who, apparently, visited heathlands by the million each year. But the hoi polloi were not persuaded and only *c.* 1,700 paperback copies were sold. Matters were not helped by the pitiable cover aesthetic. Looking back it demonstrates a miscomprehension of the New Naturalist readership.

Heathlands was the first NN to be fitted with a laminated jacket (notwithstanding reprints), highly glossy to the upper surface, and this remained the standard jacket finish until the publication of *Fungi* in 2005. Unfortunately this new finish did nothing to prevent the jacket from fading, and *Heathlands* is one of the worst culprits in this regard; unfaded copies are now the exception. Robert Gillmor writes in *Art of the New Naturalists*: 'For various reasons it is impractical to use light-fast inks for this kind of work, so the spines of many volumes have faded badly.'

Total print run: *c.* 1,650 (Collins h/b); *c.* 2,000 (Bookclub h/b); 2,000 (Collins p/b); o/p: 1993 (h/b), 1989 (p/b).

NN72A **First Edition**, 1986 (21 July 1986).
Title: 'The New Naturalist | Heathlands'.
Author: 'Nigel Webb. | B.Sc., Ph.D.'
Editors: KM, SMW, RW and EH (Photographic Editor).
Printer: Mackays of Chatham Ltd.
ISBN: 0002190206.
Collation: pp. 223, [1]; 4 leaves of colour plates printed to both sides (7 × 32-page gatherings).

Jacket: Laminated/highly glossy to upper surface. [Rear panel] The New Naturalist library listing NN1–72 inclusively; ISBN and barcode. [Rear flap] Biography of Nigel Webb with b/w portrait photograph.
Price: £20.00 net printed diagonally.
Print run: 1,000 (print order); 880 (out-turn); no. sold: *c.* 780; o/p: August[?] 1986.
Notes: 'Collins' printed to the base of the jacket spine.

NN72B First Reprint, 1986 (October). 'First published 1986 | Reprinted 1986'. The incorrect caption 'Bell Heather' to p. 96 corrected to 'Cross-leaved Heath' otherwise identical to NN72A; Jacket indistinguishable with same price and also with 'Collins' printed to base of spine. Print run: 750; no. sold: *c.* 730; o/p: 1993.

CP72A Collins Paperback First Edition, 1996. ISBN: 0002194198. Concomitant with the hardback ed. NN73A and bound-up from the same sheets. Paperback design Type 2. Front cover displays two photographs – heathland landscape (uncredited) and inset of an emperor moth (replica of plt. 13 by H. Clark); rear cover carries a summary of the *raison d'être* of 'The New Naturalist Series' and a copy of the jacket blurb. Price: £9.95. Print run: 2,000; no. sold: *c.* 1,680; o/p: 1989. (The spine is prone to fading.)

BC72A Bookclub Edition, 1986. Identical to NN72A, including ISBN etc. but 'Collins' is omitted from the dust jacket spine and there is no printed price. Print run: 2,000; 1,800 copies ordered by the Readers Union and 200 copies by Book Club Associates.

POD72A Print-on-demand digital copy of the 1986 reprint NN72B.

73 The New Forest

Like the previous title, *Heathlands,* the dust jacket exists in two different states: with a printed price and with 'Collins' to the spine, and without a printed price and without 'Collins' to the spine. Of course, that without is the bookclub variant, but unlike *Heathlands,* it is comparatively scarce as only 650 copies were produced. *The New Forest* and *Heathlands* jackets share one other unique feature: they both include a photographic portrait of the author on the back flap; an engaging addition, but why was it so quickly abandoned?

The New Forest was reprinted, but in paperback format only and as such is unique in the series. However, Colin Tubbs did completely rewrite and enlarge the book, and this revised edition was published posthumously in 2001 by his wife under the auspices of *New Forest Ninth Centenary Trust* and represents 'the most authoritative, up-to-date and in-depth survey available'. It is well worth seeking out but is now scarce.

Collins's archive on *The New Forest* is particularly comprehensive and includes the original invoices from Mackays of Chatham Ltd, who printed and bound the book. They offer an interesting insight into the costs associated with producing a high-quality product. The use of real bookcloth (buckram) and thick 32 oz boards increased the total binding cost by around 50 per cent. At a time when the series was in the doldrums, the temptation to use more utilitarian materials must have been strong, but mercifully was resisted.

The jacket is particularly light sensitive and copies with faded spines are the norm rather than the exception; it is not only the copper colour that fades but also the green, presumably there is a lot of yellow in it. The bracken at the foot of the spine should be the same colour as that on the front spine – exceptionally it is.

NN73A   **First Edition**, 1986 (03 November 1986).
Title: 'The New Naturalist | The New Forest'.
Author: 'Colin R. Tubbs'.
Illust: 'With 20 colour photographs and over | 100 photographs and diagrams in black and white'.
Editors: KM, SMW, RW and EH (Photographic Editor).
Printer: Mackays of Chatham Ltd.
ISBN: 0002191075.
Collation: pp. 300, [4]; 4 leaves of colour plates printed to both sides (9½ × 32-page gatherings).
Jacket: [Rear panel] The New Naturalist library listing NN1–73 inclusively; ISBN and barcode. [Rear flap] Biography of Colin Tubbs with b/w portrait photograph; advert for *Heathlands*.
Price: £22.50 net printed diagonally, with dashed line.
Notes: 'Collins' printed to the base of the jacket spine.
Print run: 1,850; no. sold: *c.* 1,620; o/p: early 1993.

CPB73A Collins Paperback First Edition, 1986. ISBN: 0002193701. Concomitant with the hardback edition NN73A and bound-up from the same sheets. Paperback design Type 2. Front cover features an uncredited photograph of a forest ride and an inset photograph of wild gladiolus, also uncredited. Rear cover carries a general account of the NN library and a copy of the jacket blurb. Price: £9.95 net. Print run: 2,000; no. sold: *c.* 1,800; o/p: 1988.

CPB73B Collins Paperback First Reprint, 1988. The imprint page, which has been partially reset, states: 'First Published 1986 | Reprinted 1988'. Otherwise identical to CPB73A in every respect, inc. ISBN, cover graphics and price. Print run: 1,000; no. sold: *c.* 830; o/p: 1991.

BC73A Bookclub Edition, 1986. Identical to NN73A, inc. ISBN, etc. but 'Collins' omitted from the jacket spine and without a printed price to the front flap (see intro. for further details). Print run: 650; 350 copies ordered by the Readers Union and 300 copies by Book Club Associates.

POD73A Print-on-demand digital copy of the single edition.

MIS73A Second (Revised) Hardback Edition, 2001 (09/11/2001). 'The New Forest | History, Ecology & | Conservation'. ISBN: 0952612062. Published by New Forest Ninth Centenary Trust, Lyndhurst. Printers: BAS Printers Ltd, Stockbridge, Hampshire. © Jennifer M. Tubbs 2001. A comprehensively revised, enlarged and updated edition, completely reset; one-third longer than the original. Hardback with dust jacket; 154 × 216 mm. Collation: pp. 400; 4 leaves of colour plates printed to both sides (12½ × 32-page gatherings). New forewords by D. A. (Derek) Ratcliffe and Verderers of the New Forest; Introduction & Acknowledgments and a Postscript by Jenni Tubbs replace the original prefaces. Most of the chapter titles remain the same and in the same order but a new chapter on the forest streams has been introduced. The suite of colour photographs is mostly unrevised, though a few have been substituted; there are very few changes to the b/w photographs that appear throughout, and reproduction is crisper; a b/w portrait frontispiece of Colin Tubbs has been inserted. A list of subscribers consisting of some 440 names is printed at the rear. Bound in dark green imitation cloth with gilt lettering to the spine. Dust jacket painting by Alison Bolton, lettering to the rear panel and flaps printed in black on a yellow ground. Price: ? Print run: 1,000. (Published posthumously – Collin Tubbs died on 17 October 1997 but completed the introduction in September of the same year in which he writes: 'This is a revised and updated version of *The New Forest*, published in 1986 in the Collins New Naturalist series, and long out of print'. Jenni Tubbs, Colin's wife, saw the book through to publication and in her postscript writes: 'Colin…was diagnosed with cancer in April 1995 and thus most of this book was revised during a period when he underwent three major operations and a number of other investigations and treatments. That he was able to research and write was both a diversion and often an enormous effort, but he was determined to complete it.')

MIS73B Second (Revised) Paperback Edition, 2001. ISBN: 0952612070. As MISM76A but in paperback format. Same cover illustration as dust jacket. No printed: 1,000.

74 Ferns

Ferns was the first purely botanical New Naturalist for 27 years, since the publication of *Weeds and Aliens* in 1961, but its history goes back much further than that. It started off life in 1948 or, at least, that is the date of the first reference to it in the Collins archive, but at that point the book was also to include mosses and was to be written by Francis Ballard. This first attempt at a fern book was abandoned in 1951 by mutual agreement, but Collins persisted with the idea; after all, a credible *Survey of British Natural History*, as the NN library was then subtitled, could not be conceived without a pteridological volume. By the mid-1960s Collins was suggesting a collaboration between Ballard and Clive Jermy but again this did not materialise. During the 1970s there are periodic references to a fern book, but it was in 1981 that the NN Board minutes record that Jermy thinks that Page is the 'obvious choice of author'. Christopher Page was duly contracted in November 1982 and the typescript delivered almost exactly two years later. It then took a further four years to take all the photographs, to finalise the text, and 'set the type'. Thus *Ferns* was finally published in 1988, 40 years after it was first conceived (for further details of *Ferns*' protracted gestation, see Page's interesting account in his author's preface).

Ferns has always been and will always be rare, but in recent years it has, puzzlingly, become more readily available and is now just outside the top ten, but it still is of course a revered member of the G14. P. Marren in *The New Naturalists* warns readers of an inferior bookclub edition with a dark green binding, but as far as I am aware this variant does not exist. However, 550 copies of the paperback were sold to the Readers Union, but as there appears to be no distinction, these bookclub copies have not been separately catalogued. The paperback binding is a muddle of a design and best ignored, but worth noting is the variant title to the front cover: 'A Natural History of Britain's Ferns'.

Ferns wears one of Gillmor's finest jackets but sadly it is particularly prone to fading – the red and yellow tones as always. Unfaded copies are the exception.

NN74A   **First Edition**, 1988 (07 November 1988).
Title: 'The New Naturalist | Ferns | Their Habitats in the British and Irish Landscape'.
Author: 'Christopher N. Page'.

Illust:	'With 21 colour photographs, and over | 160 photographs and diagrams in black and white'.
Editors:	MW, RW, DS and EH (Photographic Editor).
Printer:	Mackays of Chatham PLC, Chatham, Kent.
ISBN:	0002193833.
Collation:	pp. 430, [2]; 4 leaves of colour plates, printed to both sides (13½ × 32-page gatherings).
Jacket:	[Rear panel] The NN library listing NN1–74 inclusively; ISBN and barcode. [Rear flap] Biography of Dr Page.
Price:	£30.00.
Notes:	1) 'Collins' printed to the base of the jacket spine, but not immediately obvious as it is small and camouflaged by the cover design. 2) Unusually the jacket does not carry specific adverts for other books in the series.
Print run:	1,500; no. sold: c. 1,390; o/p: beginning 1995.

CPB74A Collins Paperback First Edition, 1988. ISBN: 0002193825. Concomitant with the hardback edition NN74A and bound-up from the same sheets. Paperback design Type 2. The front cover features two uncredited photographs of ferns. The rear cover carries a *raison d'être* of the New Naturalist, and a copy of the jacket blurb that omits the last paragraph. Price: £10.95. Print run: 2,000 + c. 550[?] for RU; no. sold: c. 1,850; o/p: summer 1994.

POD74A Print-on-demand digital copy.

75 Freshwater Fishes of the British Isles

The correct title for this volume is *Freshwater Fishes of The British Isles* as printed on the title page, though the jacket, casing and paperback simply state *Freshwater Fishes*. However, in the New Naturalist library and elsewhere it is invariably and incorrectly referred to as *British Freshwater Fish* or *Freshwater Fish*.

Freshwater Fishes is NN75 in the series but was longer in the making than originally planned and in fact was published two years after NN76 (*Hebrides*) and five months later than NN77 (*Soil*) and 78 (*British Larks*) and explains why these titles (and NN79 *Caves*) are included in the New Naturalist library on the dust jacket. For the same reason the paperback adopts the later design Type 3 format and if put in series order looks particularly incongruous sandwiched between *Ferns* and *Hebrides*. This delay might also explain the incorrect ISBN to the imprint page, which is in fact that for *Ferns*, though the ISBN to the jacket is correct.

The jacket, with its rich scarlet band, is eye-catching, but so light sensitive that it is more suited to the darkroom than the bookshelf; consequently most copies are badly faded. Unfortunately it is one of those designs which is unable to accommodate any colour loss without it being both noticeable and aesthetically detrimental. There are probably no more than a handful of extant unfaded copies. So what's the answer? There isn't one: except perhaps to put a bright facsimile jacket over the original?

The sales data for the paperback edition is inconsistent and ambiguous, probably as result of unrecorded sales to a bookclub and/or remaindering. What can be said with certainty is that the paperback, like the hardback, is a rare book and so the number printed could not have been great.

NN75A	**First Edition**, 1992 (23 July 1992).
Title:	'The New Naturalist | Freshwater Fishes | of The British Isles'.
Authors:	'Peter S. Maitland and | R. Niall Campbell'.
Illust:	'With 21 colour photographs, and over | 200 black and white | photographs and diagrams'.
Editors:	MW, RW, DS and SAC (Photographic Editor).
Printer:	Butler & Tanner, Frome, Somerset, UK.
ISBN:	0002193795 – as correctly stated on the jacket (the ISBN printed in the book: 0002193833 is incorrect and is, in fact, the ISBN for NN74 *Ferns*).
Collation:	pp. 368; 4 leaves of colour plates printed to both side (23 × 16-page gatherings).
Jacket:	[Rear panel] NN library listing NN 1–79 inclusively; ISBN and barcode. [Rear flap] Authors' biographies followed by 'Other Titles in the New Naturalist Series' under which *British Larks, Pipits & Wagtails, The Hebrides, The New Forest* and *Heathlands*, each supported with a short press endorsement. Listed under 'Forthcoming Titles' is *Caves*.
Price:	£30.
Print run:	1,470 (out-turn); no. sold c. 1,300 sold; o/p: summer 1995.
Notes:	'Collins' does not appear on the jacket spine but is blocked to the spine of the casing.

CPB75A Collins Paperback, First Edition, 1992. ISBN 0002193809. Concomitant with the hardback ed. NN75A and bound-up from the same sheets. Paperback design Type 3. Front cover photograph of salmon leaping in the River Lledr, Wales, by Frank Lane. Rear cover blurb is as the jacket and 'Other Titles in the New Naturalist Series' and 'Forthcoming Titles' are also textually as the jacket, but in revised layout; *The New Forest* and *Heathlands* omitted. Price: £14.99. Print run: variously given as 3,000 or 1,460 (out-turn); no. sold: c. 1,600[?]; o/p: summer 1994.

POD75A Print-on-demand digital copy.

76 The Hebrides

The Hebrides: A Natural History is the last title to acknowledge Eric Hosking as photographic editor; his name has graced every preceding NN title including all the monographs: just a couple shy of 100 volumes. At this stage Hosking's involvement was token, as reflected by the poor reproduction of the b/w images. But there are a number of firsts too: the first (and only) NN to be written by a father and son team, and to have a Royal foreword.

As far as value is concerned, *Hebrides* sits firmly in bronze medal position. Why this is so is not entirely clear; certainly the print run was small but the Collins sales-sheets record that more copies were sold than *Caves & Cave Life*, *The Soil*, *Wild and Garden Plants* and *Ladybirds*. Neither, at the time of publication, was the demand for *Hebrides* overwhelming, as the hardback remained in print for three years. Perhaps more copies were purchased by libraries, or perhaps *Hebrides* was confused with *Orkney*. Whatever the reason, *Hebrides* now has an established reputation underwritten by substantial investment by collectors and dealers alike, and this is likely to maintain it in third spot.

The paperback is now, if anything, even rarer; 3,000 copies were printed but most of these were sold to libraries and individuals who wanted reference copies. Consequently few find their way back onto the market in anything near collectable condition.

The Hebrides was not republished by Collins but it was revised and published as a three-volume paperback set (essentially conforming to the original three parts of the Collins edition) by the Edinburgh publisher Birlinn, in 1996, each book with a different subtitle: *A Habitable Land?*, *The Mosaic of Islands* and *The Natural Tapestry*. A scarce trilogy, but not expensive.

The Hebrides dust jacket suffers from fading: look at the Gannets' heads on the spine – they should be the same butterscotch colour as those on the front panel design; they rarely are. The paperback is particularly difficult to find in fine condition, the spine is usually creased and faded.

NN76A   **First Edition**, 1990 (04 June 1990).
Title: 'The New Naturalist | The Hebrides | A Natural History'.
Authors: 'J. Morton Boyd | and | Ian L. Boyd'.
Foreword: 'Foreword by HRH Prince Philip, | Duke of Edinburgh'.

Illust: 'With 21 colour photographs, and over | 150 photographs in black and white'.
Editors: SAC, MW, RW, DS and EH (Photographic Editor).
Printer: Mackays of Chatham PLC, Chatham, Kent.
ISBN: 0002198843.
Collation: pp. 416; 4 leaves of colour plates printed to both side (13 × 32-page gatherings).
Jacket: [Rear panel] NN library listing NN1–76 inclusively; ISBN and barcode. [Rear flap] Authors' biographies.
Price: £30.00.
Print run: 1,500; no. sold: *c.* 1,290; o/p: spring 1993.
Notes: 1) It appears that the book designer struggled to keep the text within the confines of the prescribed module of 13 × 32-page gatherings. To accommodate the b/w frontispiece map (an integral leaf of the first gathering and included within the pagination), the Editors' list and NN credo were moved to the imprint page, and the bibliography and index are in smaller fonts with minimal margins; in some copies the running title of the index is almost flush with the top edge. 2) 'Collins' does appear on the jacket spine.

CPB76A Collins Paperback First Edition, 1990. ISBN: 0002198851. Concomitant with the hardback edition NN76A and bound-up from the same sheets. Paperback design Type 2. Front cover features a photograph of the St Kilda gannetry (not credited but a copy of the photograph by J. M. Boyd that features on the sixth page of colour plates), with an uncredited inset photograph of a seal pup. Rear cover carries a general blurb for the NN library and a copy of the jacket blurb. Price: £12.95. Print run: 3,000 (out-turn); no. sold: *c.* 2,800; o/p: spring 1993.

POD76A Print-on-demand digital copy.

MIS76 (A, B and C) Birlinn Revised Edition, 1996. Titles: as below – three-volume set, each with separate subtitle. J. Morton Boyd and Ian L. Boyd. Published by Birlinn Limited, Edinburgh. Paperbacks 138 × 216 mm, i.e. slightly smaller than Collins paperback. Colour printed laminated card covers. Most of the text has not been reset (excluding page numbers and chapter headings) with the b/w illustrations and diagrams positioned as Collins ed. But this trilogy without colour plates, instead some are reproduced in b/w within the new chapters. Preface to *A Habitable Land?* states '…substantially Part III "Islands and People" of the HarperCollins New Naturalist volume *The Hebrides – A Natural History*. Chapters 1 and 6 [in fact, Chapter 2] are new, but the core of the book is Chapters 17–20 of that previous work. This book has two companions: *The Hebrides – A Natural Tapestry* and *The Hebrides – A Mosaic of Islands*, which are respectively parts I and II of that previous work'. (Chapter 1 of *A Mosaic of Islands* is also new.) These books published with a grant from the Scottish Arts Council, seemingly in small numbers as they are now scarce.

MIS76A Title: 'The Hebrides | A Habitable Land? (Book I)'.
ISBN: 1874744556; pp. xii, 124. Price £8.99.
MIS76B Title: 'The Hebrides | A Natural Tapestry (Book II)'.
ISBN: 1874744564; pp. xii, 208. Price: £9.99.
MIS76C Title 'The Hebrides | A Mosaic of Islands (Book III)'.
ISBN: 1874744564; pp. xii, 136. Price: £8.99.

77 The Soil

The Soil started off life in 1975 when Davis was commissioned to revise Russell's *The World of The Soil* (NN35) but it was soon realised that a new book was needed. Four years later, in 1979, the new book was contracted but without a specified delivery date. By 1988 Davis had co-opted three further authors to write specific chapters and while the editorial panel were not initially enamoured of this proposal, they came, in time, to accept and endorse it.

It is interesting that the authorship is attributed to four people; firstly, because the Editors wished to see only two names and, secondly, because it suggests equal authorship – albeit Davis's name does come first. Looking at the text of *The Soil* we see that 46 per cent was written solely by Davis, 12 per cent by Walker, 9 per cent by Ball and 7 per cent by Fitter with collaborations between Davis/Ball and Davis/Walker contributing a further 17 per cent and 9 per cent respectively. Bearing in mind the bulk of the work was written by Davis, it was noble of him to share the honours with his collaborators (compare with NN46 *The Broads* where around one-third was written by others but only Ellis was credited as author on the book – probably on the insistence of the board.)

The book was eventually published in 1992. It is perhaps ironic that a book that was so many years in the making and that employed more authors than any other New Naturalist, excepting *The Broads* (NN46) and *Birds of the London Area* should end up sharing with *Grass and Grassland* the dubious distinction of being the shortest main series title (both were only 192 pages long).

The dedicated band of New Naturalist collectors ensures that all new hardback titles are met with a warm reception and in this respect *The Soil* was no different, but beyond the devotees it proved less popular and, despite a print run of fewer than 1,500

hardback copies, it remained in stock for over four years. It was undoubtedly expensive for what it was, but the lower-priced paperback met with the same indifference and was eventually remaindered. Even now *The Soil* does not appear particularly popular and is seemingly one of the last titles to be purchased when assembling a collection. This, of course, does not mean that it is not a good book, but merely suggests that many collectors perceive it as being less appealing than other titles. Notwithstanding, very few were printed and it remains expensive.

An albino mole cricket is a rare aberrant of a rare thing, but yet you will find one on almost every copy of *The Soil* as regrettably the light brown-ochre of Gillmor's jacket design is quick to bleach on the spine. Unfaded copies are now virtually unobtainable.

NN77A   **First Edition**, 1992 (13 February 1992).
Title: 'The New Naturalist | The Soil'.
Authors: 'B. N. K. Davis, N. Walker, | D. F. Ball and A. H. Fitter'.
Illust: 'With 14 colour photographs, and 100 | black and white photographs and | drawings'.
Editors: SAC, SMW, RW and DS.
Printer: Butler & Tanner Ltd., Frome, Somerset, UK.
ISBN: 0002199033.
Collation: pp. 192; 2 leaves of colour plates printed to both sides (6 × 32-page gatherings).
Jacket: [Rear panel] NN library listing nos. 1–79 inclusively; ISBN and barcode. [Rear flap] Authors' biographies followed by 'Other Titles in the New Naturalist Series' under which are advertised *The Hebrides*, *The New Forest* and *Heathlands*. *Larks, Pipits & Wagtails* and *Caves* are listed under 'Forthcoming Titles'.
Price: £27.50.
Print run: 1,481 (out-turn); no. sold: *c.* 1,250; o/p: beginning 1996.
Notes: 'Collins' not printed to dust jacket spine.

CPB77A Collins Paperback First Edition, 1992. ISBN: 0002199041. Concomitant with the hardback edition NN77A and bound-up from the same sheets. Paperback design Type 3. Front cover features a photograph by David Woodfall of a potato prairie in Lincolnshire. Rear cover carries blurb and adverts for 'Other Titles in the New Naturalist Series' and 'Forthcoming Titles' exactly as jacket text. Price: £12.99. Print run: 2,078 (out-turn); no. sold: *c.* 1,310 + unknown qty remaindered (copies were available from *Summerfields* reduced to £3.99); o/p: 1995.

POD77A Print-on-demand digital copy.

78 British Larks, Pipits and Wagtails

Eric Simm's fourth and last book for the series. From a bibliographic perspective, simple and unencumbered, just one edition with one printing and available in the usual hardback and paperback formats. And no bookclub editions, either. *Larks* was published on the same day as NN77 *The Soil*; these two titles predating NN75 *British Freshwater Fishes* by five months, and are the first books in the series to exhibit the HarperCollins imprint.

Almost exactly 1,600 hardback copies of *Larks* were printed, that is around 200 more than *Caves*, *Ladybirds* and *Wild and Garden Plants* and around 100 more than *Fishes* and *Ferns*. In percentage terms this is significant and perhaps explains why *Larks* is a little less expensive than those titles. Nevertheless, it is still a scarce title – look out for rebound paperbacks masquerading as the hardback with facsimile jackets, though generally easy enough to tell apart.

Amusingly, the blurb to the rear cover of the paperback is a 'dumbed-down' version of that to the dust jacket and 'difficult' phrases such as 'a degree of elegance and ethereal magic' and 'cryptically coloured' have been commuted to 'something especially attractive' and 'drab-looking' respectively! Presumably HC was hoping to appeal to a different market with the paperbacks. However, in the event, that different market proved to be far from profligate and of the 3,000 or so paperbacks printed, a little more than one third were sold. The remainder either pulped or remaindered; probably the former as the paperback is undoubtedly a scarce book.

The dust jacket, particularly the yellow pigment, is prone to fading and the yellow wagtail on the spine frequently suffers from progressive albinism, though unfaded specimens are not particularly rare.

NN78A	First Edition, 1992 (13 February 1992).
Title:	'The New Naturalist	British Larks,	Pipits and Wagtails'.
Author:	'Eric Simms, D.F.C., M.A.'.
Illust:	'With four colour plates and over 200	black and white photographs and	drawings'.
Editors:	SAC, SMW, RW and DS.
Printer:	Butler & Tanner Ltd., Frome, Somerset, UK.
ISBN:	0002198711.

Collation:	pp. 320; 2 (tipped-in) leaves of colour plates printed to both sides (10 × 32-page gatherings).
Jacket:	[Rear panel] NN library listing NN1–79 inclusively; ISBN and barcode. [Rear flap] Biography of Simms; 'Other Titles in the New Naturalist Series' under which advertised *The Hebrides*, *The New Forest* and *Heathlands*. Listed under 'Forthcoming Titles' are *The Soil* and *Caves*.
Price:	£30.00.
Print run:	1,601 (out-turn); no. sold: c. 1,380.
Notes:	1) Many of the b/w bird portraits are by Eric Hosking – his last significant contribution to a New Naturalist. 2) Colour plates by Norman Arlott. 3) 'Collins' not on jacket spine.

CPB78A Collins Paperback, First Edition, 1992. ISBN 0002198703. Concomitant with the hardback edition NN78A and bound-up from the same sheets. Paperback design Type 3. The front cover photograph of a Pied Wagtail by John Buckingham. The rear cover carries a simplified version of the blurb (see intro.) and 'Other Titles in the New Naturalist Series' and 'Forthcoming Titles' as found on the jacket. Price: £14.99, Print run: 2,846 (out-turn); no. sold: c. 1,080. Notes: 1) The sales statements record that 1,763 copies 'unaccounted for': their fate is not recorded. 2) The blue spine is prone to fading. 3) A scarce edition.

POD78A Print-on-demand digital copy.

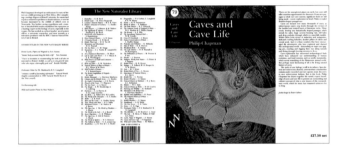

79 Caves and Cave Life

'The Natural History of Caves' was first suggested by Huxley as a subject for the New Naturalist in 1952, but it would be another 41 years before the book was published. Given its history of repeated setbacks and stoppages, it bears testimony to the obduracy of Collins and their Editors that it ever came to fruition. In 1963 Dr G. T. Warwick of Birmingham University was invited to write the book, but at that time was busy, though commented that the book should only take him a year to write. That year never came along and in 1972, by mutual consent, Collins, Caves and Warwick parted company. In due course Dr G. T. Jefferson was contracted but it was the same old story, or rather lack of it. This partnership came to an end in 1988 when Jefferson died. Other authors were considered and synopsises submitted, before Philip Chapman was finally commissioned in 1989; unlike his predecessors he quickly completed the manuscript and *Caves and Cave Life* was published in the summer of 1993.

The preceding nine G14 titles all have a complement of colour plates but *Caves* reverts to an earlier black and white period and, in fact, is without plates altogether but, admittedly, is enriched with Brian Edwards' excellent in-text pencil drawings.

According to the NN sales-sheets only 1,401 hardback copies were delivered to the warehouse, whereas 2,064 paperbacks were delivered, but evidently many p/bs went missing and only 1,239 were recorded as being sold. Not surprisingly *Caves* in both formats is scare, but the paperback particularly so. It features on its front cover a photograph of long-fingered bats, which is somewhat anomalous considering this is a Mediterranean species when the book is predominantly about British and Irish caves. Perhaps HC were hoping for a wider readership with the p/b.

Like all G14 books, the jacket spine is susceptible to fading, but unlike many, *Caves* can tolerate a degree of sunning without it adversely affecting the design, especially when the spine is seen on the shelf in isolation of the front panel.

NN79A   **First Edition**, 1993 (15 July 1993).
Title: 'The New Naturalist | Caves and Cave Life'.
Author: 'Philip Chapman'.
Illust: 'With 97 black and white | photographs, line drawings and maps'.
Editors: MW, RW, DS, SAC and DR.
Printer: Butler & Tanner Ltd., Frome, Somerset, UK.
ISBN: 0002199076.
Collation: pp. 219, [5, index]; (7 × 32-page gatherings).
Jacket: NN library listing NN1–80 inclusively; ISBN and barcode. [Rear flap] Author biography; 'Other Titles in the New Naturalist Series' under which advertised *British Larks, Pipits and Wagtails* and *Freshwater Fishes*; *Wild and Garden Plants* listed under 'Forthcoming Title'.
Price: £27.50.
Print run: 1,401 (out-turn); no. sold: c. 1,190; o/p: early 1996.
Notes: 1) b/w pencil illustrations by Brin Edwards. 2) One of just a handful of main series New Naturalists with a frontispiece included within the general pagination with the Editors' list and NN credo relegated to the half-title. 3) 'Collins' not printed to jacket spine.

CPB79A Collins Paperback, First Edition, 1993. ISBN: 0002199084. Concomitant with the hardback edition NN78A and bound-up from the same sheets. Paperback design Type 4. Front cover photograph of long-fingered bats by Chris Howes. Rear cover carries the blurb and 'Other Titles in the New Naturalist Series' and 'Forthcoming Title' as found on the jacket. Price: £12.99 net. Print run: 2,064 (out-turn); no. sold: c. 1,240; o/p: beginning 1998. Note: Contemporary sales reports state 825 copies 'unaccounted

for' i.e. the difference between the number printed and the number sold; what exactly happened to these books is unknown, but the paucity of available copies would suggest that they were (eventually) pulped.

POD79A Print-on-demand digital copy.

80 Wild & Garden Plants

Wild & Garden Plants is one of the most difficult titles to obtain – scarcer than *Ferns, Fishes, Caves* and *Ladybirds*, all with equally small print runs. In fact it is on a par with, or just below *Hebrides*, at about fourth in the rarity table, but for some inexplicable reason, when available it is always less expensive than the above-mentioned titles. Perhaps drawing attention to this anomaly will put the kibosh on it; if so, apologies to all prospective purchasers. While the print-order was for 1,500 hardback copies, in the event only 1,404 copies were delivered, but surprisingly *Wild & Garden Plants* remained in print for two years. It was a familiar story with the paperback; few wanted them and with sales reduced to a little more than 100 copies per annum, Collins remaindered 1,000 copies during the winter of 1995/96.

The bright mustard-yellow colour band and orange honeysuckle of the jacket is particularly susceptible to fading and quickly the contrast between the white lettering and yellow is lost, rendering the title virtually illegible. Completely unfaded copies are an absolute rarity if indeed they exist at all, but there are still a few copies around with just a minimal level of fading. Notwithstanding fading the strength of the yellow colour varies appreciably.

NN80A   **First Edition**, 1993 (11 November 1993).
Title: 'The New Naturalist | Wild & Garden Plants'.
Author: 'Max Walters | Sc.D., V.M.H.'.
Illust: 'With sixteen colour plates and | over 60 black and white photographs and | drawings'.
Editors: MW, RW, DS, SAC and DR.
Printer: Butler & Tanner Ltd., Frome, Somerset, UK.
ISBN: 0002193760.
Collation: pp. 200; 8 (tipped-in) leaves of colour plates printed to both sides (6½ × 32-page gatherings).
Jacket: [Rear panel] NN library listing NN 1–81 inclusively;

ISBN and barcode. [Rear flap] Author's biography followed by 'Other Titles in the New Naturalist Series' under which advertised *British Larks, Pipits and Wagtails* and *Freshwater Fishes. Ladybirds* listed under 'Forthcoming Titles'.

Price: £27.50.

Print run: 1,404 (out-turn); no. sold: *c.* 1,180; o/p: autumn 1995.

Notes: 1) The title to the title-page, half-title and jacket uses an ampersand, whereas that to the casing uses an 'and'. 2) Many of the photographs are by the author's son Martin Walters. 3) 'Collins' not on jacket spine.

CPB80A Collins Paperback, First Edition, 1994. ISBN: 0002198894. Concomitant with the hardback edition NN80A and bound-up from the same sheets. Paperback design Type 4. Front cover features a photograph by Martin Walters of wild honeysuckle and the rambling rose 'Paul's Scarlet'. Rear cover blurb and 'Other Titles in the New Naturalist Series' and 'Forthcoming Titles' textually as that on the jacket. Price: £12.99 net; print run: 3,040 (out-turn); no. sold: *c.* 1,350 + 1,000 remaindered; o/p: autumn 1999, but remainders available beyond that date. Note: The cover photograph is a copy of Plate 1, but more subtly alludes, albeit perhaps serendipitously, to Gillmor's jacket design which also featured roses and honeysuckle.

POD80A Print-on-demand digital copy.

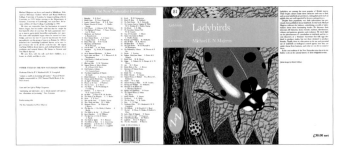

81 Ladybirds

Another highly desirable title – about fourth in the valuation stakes. The print-order was for 1,500 hardback copies, but in the event only 1,400 copies were delivered to the warehouse. Not surprisingly, therefore, the hardback was out of print a year or so later. The paperback had been printed in greater numbers, but at the beginning of 1997 Collins remaindered the last 896 copies. That being the case, why is the paperback today such a rare book?

The string of ladybirds on the jacket spine is quick to fade to a soft pink, but, irrespective of fading the strength of the red is by no means consistent and some jackets are brighter than others – presumably jackets printed at the beginning of the run were more intense than those at the end. And this is not unique to

Ladybirds – many jackets, particularly the later laminated ones, vary considerably in colour intensity.

NN81A   **First Edition**, 1994 (06 October 1994).

Title: 'The New Naturalist | Ladybirds'.

Author: 'Michael E. N. Majerus'.

Illust: 'With sixteen colour plates and over 150 black | and white photographs and drawings'.

Editors: SAC, SMW, RW, DS and DAR.

Printer: Butler & Tanner Ltd., Frome, Somerset, UK.

ISBN: 0002199343.

Collation: pp. 367, [1]; 8 leaves of colour plates printed to both sides (11½ × 32-page gatherings).

Jacket: [Rear panel] NN library listing NN1–82 inclusively; ISBN and barcode. [Rear flap] Author's biography followed by 'Other Titles in the New Naturalist Series' under which adverts for *Freshwater Fishes* and *Caves and Cave Life; The New Naturalists* listed under 'Forthcoming Titles'.

Price: £30.00 net.

Print run: 1,400 (out-turn); no. sold: *c.* 1,190; o/p: 1995.

Notes: 1) 'Collins' not printed to jacket spine. 2) The New Naturalist table to the rear panel of the dust jacket includes NN82.

CPB81A Collins Paperback First Edition, 1994. ISBN: 0002199351. Concomitant with the hardback edition NN81A and bound-up from the same sheets. Paperback design Type 4. Front cover features a photograph of hibernating 11-spot ladybirds by M. Tweedie. Rear cover features blurb and 'Other Titles in the New Naturalist Series' and 'Forthcoming Titles', all as found on the jacket. Price: £14.99 net. Print run: 2,478 (out-turn); no. sold: *c.* 1,190 + *c.* 900 remaindered copies; o/p: beginning of 1996 but remaindered copies were available beyond this date.

POD81A Print-on-demand digital copy.

82A The New Naturalists

A superb exposition of the series and the men and women behind it, and for this reason appropriately titled *The New Naturalists*.

The book was published to coincide with the 50th anniversary of the series and was universally well reviewed. A party to celebrate this milestone was held at HarperCollins in London on 24 April 1995 with around 300 guests in attendance. A round, white sticker printed in gold stating '50 Years, 1945–1995, Celebrating Collins Natural History' was fitted to the front cover/jacket of all first edition hardbacks and all paperbacks. This wording is somewhat odd as it is the New Naturalist that is 50 years old, not Collins natural history publishing *per se*, which is a little older.

The New Naturalists was officially published on the 6 April 1995 (though had been available from early March) and was out of print by the end of November 1995, prompting a hardback reprint in February 1996 of just 497 copies. The paperback didn't fair quite as well, but sales figures suggest that over 650 copies were unaccounted for: some of these would have been the usual gratis copies, but presumably the greater part were either lost or pulped? Additionally a tranche of 250 paperback copies were sold off to Book Club Associates in May 1995 and, as these were sold from stock, are inseparable from the Collins edition. Whatever the true fate of those missing copies, the paperback is a rare book, particularly so in fine, unfaded condition without creases to the spine.

The New Naturalists was republished as an updated and significantly enlarged edition in 2005 with a new jacket design, but retained the same series number, hence the use of the additional 'A' or 'B' epithet to distinguish editions. It is only the 2005 edition that is available in Print-on-demand format.

Most jackets are faded to a greater or lesser degree; the orange books depicted on the spine should be the same strength of colour as the books on the front panel.

NN82AA   **First Edition**, 1995 (06 April 1995).
Title: 'The New Naturalist | The New Naturalists'.
Author: 'Peter Marren'.
Illust: 'With sixteen colour plates and over 100 black | and white photographs and drawings'.
Editors: SAC, SMW, RW, DS and DAR.

ISBN: 000219998x.
Printer: Butler & Tanner Ltd., Frome, Somerset, UK.
Collation: pp. 304; 8 leaves of colour plates printed to both sides (9½ × 32-page gatherings).
Jacket: [Rear panel] NN library listing NN1–82 inclusively; ISBN and barcode. [Rear flap] Author's biography followed by 'Other Titles in the New Naturalist Series' under which advertised *Caves and Cave Life* and *Wild and Garden Plants*.
Price: £30.00 net.
Print run: 1,489 (out-turn); no. sold: c. 1,280; o/p: end of November 1995.
Notes: 1) The half-title reads 'The New Naturalists | Half A Century of British Natural History'. 2) Due to the frontispiece, the Editors' list and the NN credo have been moved to the HTP. 3) Chapter 1 begins (in unconventional fashion) on the verso. 4) The NN monogram on the jacket has been embellished with a pen device, but it is only the standard 'Type E' that appears on the casing. 5) A round sticker celebrating 50 years of Collins natural history is fixed to the front panel of all first edition jackets. 6) 'Collins' not printed to jacket spine. 7) The price includes 'net'.

NN82AB Reprint, 1996. ISBN unchanged. 'First published 1995 | Reprinted 1996' otherwise identical in every respect, but for a slightly revised stitching pattern. The jacket also identical but omits 'net' from the price and does not have the 'Celebrating 50 years' sticker. Price: £30. Print run: 497 (out-turn); no. sold: c. 380[?]; o/p: 1997.

CPB82AA Collins Paperback First Edition, 1995. ISBN: 0002199971. Concomitant with the hardback edition NN82AA and bound-up from the same sheets. Paperback design Type 4. Front cover features an uncredited photograph of NN1 *Butterflies* amongst various natural history specimens to which is fixed the 'Celebrating 50 years sticker'. Rear cover carries a replica of the blurb and adverts that appeared on the dust jacket. Price: £14.99 net. Print run: 1,751 (out-turn); no. sold: c. 1,110 + c. 250 bookclub copies; o/p: 1996. A scarce book.

82B The New Naturalists

A revised and enlarged edition of 82A with a new jacket design and over 60 additional pages, including an appendix on *The Australian Naturalist Library*, supplementary notes for the original chapters, a new suite of colour plates depicting Robert Gillmor's jacket designs, bibliographic details on NN books published in the interim and a postscript by John Sykes. The two editions of *The New Naturalists* are different enough to merit ownership of both.

This edition includes a new preface by Stefan Buczacki, in which he describes *The New Naturalists* as 'Peter Marren's …utterly excellent and beautifully-written series tribute.' Of course he's right. Any further bibliographies are likely to live in its shadow! But Collins requires praise, too, for allowing a candid account that does not always reflect positively on them; many publishers would not, but the book is richer for it, and Collins the nobler. This book does, however contain one annoying trait: the recompiled index contains a huge number of incorrect references, particularly for page numbers higher than 250.

The first edition was published to celebrate the 50th anniversary of the series and this updated edition to mark the 60th anniversary and, like the first edition, a party was held to celebrate the event, but in this case was scheduled to coincide with the official publication date. The partygoers were given a commemorative mug featuring six Gillmor jacket designs (see pages 53–4) and a miscellany of other items including bags, books, bookmarks and a chocolate bar.

This revised edition was not reprinted, but the hardback exists in two distinct binding states, one the standard NN format but the other distinctly shorter. The reason for this still remains somewhat of a mystery, though a number of theories have been propounded to explain it, and these are explored in the introduction to the chronologically following title NN96 *Fungi*. But with 82B *The New Naturalists* there is another possibility. The then Collins editor, Helen Brocklehurst, reported that the printer put the colour plate section at the back instead of the middle and all such copies had to be returned for rebinding. Did this rebinding operation involve the trimming of the text-block? In the truncated variant the running titles virtually coincide with the top edge, but more than this they look out of place on the shelf, where conformity is all important.

The jacket design does not suffer unduly from fading though there is considerable variation in the strength of the colours; including an early 'variant' where the bookcase, depicted in the design, is decidedly green.

NN82BA   **Second Edition, First State**, 2005 (04 April 2005).
Title: 'The New Naturalist | The New Naturalists'.
Author: 'Peter Marren'.
Illust: 'With sixteen colour plates and over 100 black | and white photographs and drawings'.
Editors: SAC, SMW, RW, DS and DAR.
ISBN: 0007197160.
Printer: Printed and bound in Thailand by Imago.
Collation: pp. 363; [5]; 8 leaves of colour plates printed to both sides (23 × 16-page gatherings).
Casing: Full height 223 × 157 mm wide; without a decorative headband, rounded and backed; NN monogram embellished with a pen device.
Jacket: [Rear panel] NN library listing NN1–95 inclusively; ISBN and barcode. [Rear flap] Author's biography followed by advert for *Nature Conservation* with 6 press endorsements; ISBN, Collins logo and website address.
Price: £40.00.
Print run: 2,677 (out-turn) inc. B2 below; o/p: see B2 below.
Notes: 1) While the layout has been rejigged, the majority of pages are not reset. 'The Author's Foreword to the Second Edition' appears on p. [14] and Chapter 1 now begins (conventionally) on the verso. 2) As NN82A, half-title reads 'The New Naturalists | Half A Century of British Natural History'. 3) Also as NN82A due to use of a frontispiece, Editors' list and the NN credo are on the HTP. 4) Again as NN82A, the NN monogram on the jacket has been embellished with a pen device. 5) Unlike 82A, 'Collins' printed to the jacket spine.

NN82BB Second Edition, Second State (Shorter Binding Variant), 2005 (bound-up 2006?). Bound up from the same sheets, but only 216 mm high by 150 mm wide. Spine is flat and the fore-edge of the book-block square; one or both rear blank leaves excised; now with shiny green/white-striped decorative head and tail-bands. This variant was sold towards the end of the in-print period. Print run: inc. above[?]; o/p: end 2006[?]

CPB82BA Collins Paperback, Second Edition, 2005. ISBN: 0007197152. Concomitant with the hardback edition NN95A and bound-up from the same sheets. Paperback design Type 6. Front cover features a photograph by David Hosking, of a hand withdrawing *The Pollination of Flowers* from a bookcase of New Naturalists. Rear cover carries a replica of the blurb that appeared on the dust jacket. 'Other Titles in the New Naturalist Series' features thumbnails of p/b titles: *Seashore, Moths,*

Northumberland and *Lakeland*; Price: £25.00. Print run: 900 (out-turn). A scarce book.

POD82BA Print-on-demand digital copy. Note: It is only this edition 82B that is available in POD format; 82A was not scanned.

83 The Natural History of Pollination

There is a general perception that New Naturalists are of a uniform size, notwithstanding a couple of well-known exceptions, namely *The Honeybee* and *Bumblebees*, but in point of fact there is much greater variation than commonly believed and at 226 mm high *The Natural History of Pollination* is the tallest of all New Naturalists, a good 3 mm taller than the average; the leaf size is correspondingly larger too.

Pollination is the last member of the G14 and one of the few books of this period to be reprinted, and though the reprint does not declare itself as such, it is easy enough to detect. The recto/verso of the reprint half-title page is strangely bereft of the usual NN Editors' list, NN credo and, for that matter, any reference to the NN series. These NN-specific features were removed for the US edition – and seemingly this US set-up was at hand and erroneously used when the reprint was undertaken. For a summary of the differences between the two books see table NN83. However, perhaps the most striking distinction of all rests in the dust jacket: the colours of the first are soft and muted, those of the second stronger and brighter and more faithful to the artist's

original: it is interesting to note that it is this second impression jacket that is reproduced in *Art of the New Naturalists*. Regrettably the soft colours of the first edition jacket are particularly prone to fading and it is virtually impossibly to find a copy that is unfaded: the orange of the title band fades to a light lemon yellow on the spine, such that there is minimal contrast between this and the reversed-out lettering rendering it, in the worst cases, illegible. The second impression is much more colourfast (which demonstrates that the fading of dust jackets need not be inevitable), and unless you must have a first edition, it is undoubtedly superior. Also, at only *c.* 500 copies printed, in numerical terms, the reprint is about the rarest of any single NN impression.

The US edition was published in hardback and paperback formats by Timber Press a month after the UK edition. This was the last time a New Naturalist was to be published in the US by an American imprint; the end of a 45-year tradition.

NN83A	**First Edition**, 1996 (27 March 1996).
Title:	'The New Naturalist	The Natural History	of Pollination'.
Authors:	'Michael Proctor, Peter Yeo and Andrew Lack'.
Illust:	'With eight colour plates and over 250 black	and white photographs and drawings'.
Editors:	SAC, SMW, RW, DS and DR.
Printer:	Bath Press.
ISBN:	000219905X
Collation:	pp. 479; [1]; 4 leaves of colour plates printed to both sides (15 × 32-page gatherings).
Jacket:	[Size] 225.5 × 530 mm. [Rear panel] NN library listing NN1–83 inclusively; ISBN and barcode. [Rear flap] Authors' biographies; 'Reviews of the Previous Edition' with two press comments. 'Other Titles in the New Naturalist Series', advertises *Wild and Garden Plants* and *Ladybirds*.
Price:	£30.00.
Print run:	1,472 (out-turn); no. sold: *c.* 1,370; o/p: end of 1996.

TABLE NN83 Summary of differences between the first edition and reprint – *The Natural History of Pollination*.

NN83	HALF TITLE	HALF TITLE VERSO (diagnostic features only)	IMPRINT PAGE	DUST JACKET
first ed.	The New Naturalist Library	A SURVEY OF BRITISH NATURAL HISTORY	THE NATURAL HISTORY OF POLLINATION	Editors' list and NN credo	HarperCollinsPublishers London Glasgow Sydney Auckland Toronto Johannesburg/First published 1996 ISBN 000219905X (hardback) ISBN 0002199068 (paperback)	Printed price: £30.00 Colours soft and muted. Very prone to fading.
reprint	THE NATURAL HISTORY OF POLLINATION	blank	HarperCollinsPublishers 77–85 Fulham Palace Road London W6 8JB First published 1996 98 00 01 99 97	2 4 6 8 10 9 7 5 3 ISBN 000219905X	Printed price: £35.00. Colours stronger and brighter. Less prone to fading.

Notes: 1) The 'previous edition' referred to on the rear flap is NN54 *The Pollination of Flowers*. 2) 'Collins' not on jacket spine.

NN83B Reprint, 1996 (1997). ISBN unchanged. While dated 1996 it was, in fact, not published until late 1997. Not identified as a reprint, but a number-line has been introduced to the imprint page running from 2–10, omitting '1', which declares it as a second impression. For other diagnostic features see table NN83, but essentially a straightforward reprint of NN83A. Jacket printed in stronger colours. Price: £35.00. Print run: 513 (out-turn); no. sold: *c.* 450; o/p: 2000.

CPB83A Collins Paperback, First Edition, 1996. ISBN: 0002199068. Concomitant with the hardback edition NN83A and bound-up from the same sheets. Paperback design Type 4. As expected, the leaf size identical to NN92A and therefore *Pollination* is slightly taller than its p/b counterparts. The front cover features a photograph of a solitary bee on a wallflower (copy of photograph (a) on Plate 7 by Michael Proctor). Rear cover carries blurb and 'Reviews of the Previous Edition' as on the jacket. Price: £16.99. Print run: 1,956 (out-turn); no. sold: *c.* 1,550; o/p: end 1999. (Widely purchased as a 'textbook' and now very scarce in fine condition. The reprint was not published in p/b format.)

US83A US Hardback Edition, 1996 (15/4/1996). ISBN: 0881923524. Published by Timber Press of Portland Oregon. Hardback with jacket; 155 × 226mm, i.e. same format as Collins edition. Essentially as Collins reprint NN83B (but published earlier); title page with Timber Press imprint; and all references to the New Naturalist omitted. Jacket replicates the same layout, colour scheme and photograph as the Collins paperback, spine and rear panel have a solid orange ground, text of the front and rear flaps virtually identical but order modified and references to other Collins publications removed. Price $42.95. Print run: 500. (With such a short print run; now a scarce edition; Timber Press is a specialist publisher of gardening, horticulture and natural history titles.)

USPB83A US Paperback Edition, 1996. ISBN: 0881923532. Timber Press. As US hardback edition. Wrappers also based on the Collins softback ed. Price $24.95. Print run: *c.* 2,000.

POD83A Print-on-demand digital copy of the first edition NN83A.

84 Ireland

Ireland was first mooted at the Editorial Board meeting of 9 November 1966: 'JG read out a letter about Cabot…[he] is young with considerable energy and ability, and it was agreed we should ask him for a specimen chapter…' And 23 years later the book was published.

Often referred to as 'A' or 'The Natural History of Ireland' or 'Ireland: A Natural History', when in fact the title page simply states *The New Naturalist Ireland* and the dust jacket and binding even more simply *Ireland*. It is only the half-title page which reads *Ireland: A Natural History* and it is this title which appears in all Collins literature, including the ubiquitous New Naturalist library.

The appearance of *Ireland* followed a three-year publishing hiatus and was the first of the modern New Naturalists to have a sensible print run of *c.* 3,100 hardback copies; about twice that of the preceding G14 titles. Consequently, it is now much more affordable. It was the first of a run of titles to be priced at £34.99.

Despite the larger print run, *Ireland* sold prodigiously well: within two weeks of the official release 2,000 copies had gone and within eight months it had sold out completely. Undoubtedly this was fuelled by speculative buying – Bob Burrow writing in *The New Naturalist Book Club* newsletter suggested that it would be a £50.00 book by Christmas and encouraged readers generally to salt away investments for future years.

Collins did consider a reprint but, for reasons unknown, this did not materialise, though many collectors believe, to the contrary, that *Ireland* was reprinted. However, not all copies of the single hardback edition were bound up in the first instance and it is probably this that has led to the confusion. The existence of this later binding has always been a frustration to collectors as it

TABLE NN84 Summary of differences between the first state and second state *Ireland*.

NN84 IRELAND	QTY	STITCHING PATTERN	DUST JACKET
First state	*c.* 2,730	6 stitches of 15.5 mm each with 16 mm gaps between = total sequence of 173 mm (evident at centre of gatherings: i.e. pp. 16/17, 48/49, 80/81 etc).	222 mm tall (some second state books wear this jacket).
Second State	*c.* 400	5 stitches of 20 mm each with 18 mm gaps between = total sequence of 172 mm (evident at centre of gatherings i.e. pp. 16/17, 48/49, 80/81 etc).	1) 219 mm tall. 2) Barcode number flush with bottom edge. 3) Printing error evident as v. small white dots to the top part of the spine.

appeared to be impossible to tell from the first. But in researching this book, reliable diagnostic features have finally become apparent, the clearest of which is the stitching: in the first state six stitches; in the second only five. The presence of dated inscriptions, the fact that the five-stitch variant is much the scarcer of the two, and also the pattern of stitching in titles after *Ireland* confirm this chronology. New jackets were also printed for the second binding variant and these are very subtly different too, though some second binding variants wear first jackets. The differences are summarised in table NN84. Note that in both bindings the spine is relatively flat, which has led some collectors to question the authenticity of their copy – but you need not worry; that is how it should be.

The rich greens of the jacket are synonymous with Ireland, a land from which the sun is often withheld, as it must always be from the jacket, otherwise the emerald green on the spine will quickly become a cold viridian-green.

NN84A   **First Edition, First State**, 1999 (01 March 1999).
Title: 'The New Naturalist | Ireland'.
Author: 'David Cabot'.
Illust: 'With 8 colour plates and over 230 black and white photographs and line | drawings'.
Editors: SAC, SMW, RW, DS and DAR.
Printer: Bath Press.
ISBN: 0002200791.
Collation: pp. 512; 4 leaves of colour plates printed to both sides (16 × 32-page gatherings).
Binding: 6 stitches of 15.5 mm each (see table NN84).
Jacket: [Rear panel] NN library – listing NN1–84 inclusively; ISBN above bottom edge. [Rear flap] Author's biography. *The New Naturalists* and *The Natural History of Pollination* are advertised under 'Other Titles in the New Naturalist Series'.
Price: £34.99.
Print run: 3,120 (out-turn); no. sold: *c.* 2,920 (figures inc. second state binding); o/p: 1999.
Notes: 1) A map of Ireland improvises as a frontispiece, relegating the usual Editors' credits and the NN credo to the half-title page. 2) 'Collins' not printed to jacket spine.

NN84B First Edition, Second State, 1999. From the same sheets as NN84A but bound up slightly later. Binding almost identical but with 5 stitches of *c.* 20 mm each. Jacket is a new printing, only 219 mm tall, barcode number flush with bottom edge and printing error evident as v. small white dots to the top part of the spine. No. bound up thus: *c.* 400; no. sold: inc. in NN84A; o/p: 1999. Note: Some second state books wear first state jackets.

CPB84A Collins Paperback First Edition, 1999. ISBN: 0002200805. Concomitant with the hardback edition NN84A and bound up from the same sheets. Paperback design Type 4. Front cover

photograph of Glen Inchiquin, Co. Kerry is by the author. Rear cover carries an abbreviated, version of the jacket blurb. *The Natural History of Pollination*, advertised under 'Other Titles in the New Naturalist Series'. *Lichens* and *Plant Disease* are listed under 'Forthcoming Titles'. Price: £17.99. Print run: 3,053 (out-turn); no. sold: *c.* 2,520; o/p: spring 2000. Notes: 1) Such a large discrepancy between no. printed and no. sold (*c.* 530) might suggest that some copies were either remaindered or pulped, though there is nothing in the sales reports to suggest either; 2) Paperback copies of this title can vary in height by a couple of mm or so – a not uncommon phenomenon of NN paperback editions.

POD84A Print-on-demand digital copy.

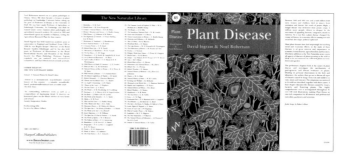

85 Plant Disease

Any publishing venture that has spanned as many years as the New Naturalist series will have been subject to many changes and developments and inevitably will reflect influential events of the time: it seems almost inconceivable in a world where the internet is inextricably woven into the fabric of our lives, that *Plant Disease*, published only 14 years ago, was the first New Naturalist to embrace cyberspace by including adverts for Collins' website. Which, of course, has been a standard feature of all titles since this date.

'*Plant Disease* [is] an essential companion for all amateur and professional naturalists, gardeners and scientists', so states the blurb to the dust jacket. However, less than 2,000 hardback copies were printed, suggesting that the sales team did not share quite the same level of faith in the title as its marketing counterpart. In the event, 1,500 hardback copies were sold within the first few months and it was out of print within a year – the last copy being sold to the founder of the New Naturalist Collectors' Club, Bob Burrow. Collins did seriously consider reprinting *Plant Disease* but as we know, this did not materialise. The fortunes of the softback edition were less auspicious: it sold slowly and 500 copies were remaindered at the beginning of 2001 and an additional 343 at the beginning of 2004. The Book Depository Ltd. was still advertising these remaindered copies, for a little more than £7.00, at the end of 2012.

With such a small print run the hardback is undeniably a scarce book, but inexplicably this paucity is not reflected in either the number or price of books offered on the second-hand market. I suspect the subject matter and relatively dull (but graphically sophisticated) jacket, combine to demote *Plant Disease* towards the bottom of most collectors' desirability lists.

The brown ochre of the jacket is susceptible to fading, but it doesn't take too much searching to find an unfaded copy.

NN85A   **First Edition**, 1999 (04 October 1999).
Title: 'The New Naturalist | Plant Disease | A Natural History'.
Authors: 'David Ingram and Noel Robertson'.
Illust: 'With 8 colour plates and over 100 black | and white photographs and line drawings'.
Editors: SAC, SMW, RW, DS and DAR.
Printer: Bath Press.
ISBN: 0002200740.
Collation: pp. 287, [1]; 4 leaves of colour plates printed to both sides (9 × 32-page gatherings).
Jacket: [Rear panel] NN library listing NN1–84 inclusively; ISBN and barcode. [Rear flap] Authors' biographies. *Ireland: A Natural History* advertised under 'Other Titles in the New Naturalist Series'. *Lichens* listed as a 'Forthcoming Title'. ISBN, 'HarperCollinsPublishers' and www.fireandwater.com website advert.
Price: £34.99.
Print run: 1,964 (out-turn); no. sold: c. 1,820; o/p: July 2000.
Note: 'Collins' not printed to jacket spine.

CPB85A Collins Paperback First Edition, 1999. ISBN: 0002200759. Concomitant with the hardback edition NN85A and bound-up from the same sheets. Paperback design Type 4. Front cover photograph of rust on Juniper is by Debbie White (this is a copy of photograph (a) on Plate 7). Rear cover replicates the blurb and adverts that appeared on the jacket with *Ireland: A Natural History* and *Lichens* featured. Price: £19.99. Print run: 1,960 (out-turn); no. sold: c. 1,050 + c. 840 remaindered; o/p: beginning 2004 (but remaindered copies were still available at the end of 2012).

POD85A Print-on-demand digital copy.

86 Lichens

Lichens, not only 'the still explosions on the rocks' but the first New Naturalist of the new millennium, appropriate, perhaps, for these ancient organisms. A successful title that sold quickly with many paperbacks seemingly purchased by libraries and lichenologists rather than collectors; at any rate few have found their way onto the second-hand market. In June 2010, not one paperback copy was being offered on the internet – it took a year to find a single copy. Conversely the hardback is readily available, and paradoxically more expensive.

The jacket is prone to fading, though faded copies are not immediately obvious: the abbey's masonry on the spine is often straw yellow, but it should be the caramel colour of the masonry on the front panel; having said that, *Lichens* is a jacket that looks well on the shelf, even when a little faded.

NN86A   **First Edition**, 2000 (06 March 2000).
Title: 'The New Naturalist | Lichens'.
Author: 'Oliver Gilbert'.
Sub-Title; ''The still explosions on the rocks' | Elizabeth Bishop'
Illust: 'With 16 colour plates and over 120 black | and white photographs and line drawings'.
Editors: SAC, SMW, RW, DS and DAR.
Printer: Bath Press.
ISBN: 0002200813.
Collation: pp. 288; 8 leaves of colour plates printed to both sides (8 × 32-page gatherings).
Jacket: [Rear panel] NN library listing NN1–85 inclusively; ISBN and barcode. [Rear flap] Author's biography. *Ireland: A Natural History* advertised under 'Other Titles in the New Naturalist Series'. *Reptiles and Amphibians* listed as a 'Forthcoming Title'. ISBN, 'HarperCollinsPublishers' and www.fireandwater.com website advert.
Price: £34.99.
Print run: 2,502 (out-turn); no. sold: c. 2,330; o/p: summer 2001.
Notes: 1) The rear flap advertises *Reptiles and Amphibians* (NN87) which should be *Amphibians and Reptiles*. 2) 'Collins' not printed to jacket spine.

CP86A Collins Paperback First Edition, 2000. ISBN: 0002200821
Concomitant with the hardback edition NN86A and bound-up from the same sheets. Paperback design Type 4. The front cover photograph, of a lichen-covered gravestone in Wensley Churchyard, by Tom Chester. The rear cover replicates the blurb and adverts that appeared on the jacket with *Ireland: A Natural History* and *Reptiles and Amphibians* featured. Price £19.99. Print run: 1,978 (out-turn); no. sold: *c.* 1,780; o/p: early 2003.

POD86A Print-on-demand digital copy.

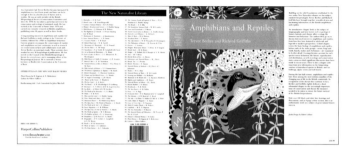

87 Amphibians and Reptiles

Herpetology is the only area of British natural history which has been examined in the series on three separate occasions: 1951, 1983 and now in 2000. The title of NN87 *Amphibians and Reptiles* is presumably so ordered to distinguish it from NN69 *Reptiles and Amphibians in Britain,* and additionally omits *British* from the actual title, to distinguish it from NN20 *The British Amphibians and Reptiles,* but puts it back in to the subtitle.

Amphibians is illustrated with the usual (for this period) suite of colour plates, plus 84 numbered b/w figures, but the title page blurb states over 80 b/w figures, the jacket over 100 and the paperback blurb over 70!

The paperback edition is much scarcer than the hardback, probably because most copies were bought to be studied – and then subsequently discarded. The jacket's golden ochre band is apt to fade on the spine.

NN87A   **First Edition**, 2000 (05 October 2000).
Title: 'The New Naturalist | Amphibians and Reptiles | A Natural History of the British | Herpetofauna'.
Author: 'Trevor J. C. Beebee and Richard A. Griffiths'.
Illust: 'With 8 colour plates and over 80 black | and white photographs and line drawings'.
Editors: SAC, SMW, RW, DS and DAR.
Printer: Bath Press.
ISBN: 000220083x.
Collation: pp. 270, [2]; 4 leaves of colour plates printed to both sides (8½ × 32-page gatherings).
Jacket: [Rear panel] NN library listing NN1–86 inclusively; ISBN and barcode. [Rear flap] Authors' biographies.

Plant Disease and *Lichens* listed under 'Other Titles in the New Naturalist Series'. *Loch Lomondside* listed as a 'Forthcoming Title'. ISBN, 'HarperCollinsPublishers' and www.fireandwater.com website advert.
Price: £34.99.
Print run: 3,023 (out-turn); no. sold *c.* 2,620; o/p: 2004.
Notes: 'Collins' not printed to jacket spine.

CPB87A Collins Paperback First Edition, 2000. ISBN: 0002200848.
Concomitant with the hardback edition NN87A and bound up from the same sheets. Paperback design Type 4. Front cover photograph of a sand lizard is by P. Edgar. Rear cover carries an almost identical copy of the jacket blurb, but revises the no. of b/w illustrations and adds 'reader-friendly text' as an appeal to the perceived paperback market. *Lichens* and *Loch Lomondside* featured. Price: £19.99. Print run: 2,050 (out-turn); no. sold: *c.* 1,690; o/p: 2003.

POD 87A Print-on-demand digital copy.

88 Loch Lomondside

Loch Lomondside is by New Naturalist standards a slight book of just 232 pages and just four leaves of colour plates. The author had to take out several sections he had hoped to include to comply with the initial commission of 80,000 words. However at the eleventh hour this was increased to 92,000 words by which time 'the text was virtually complete and anything but minor additions would have significantly affected the book's carefully considered balance'. The omitted sections were subsequently serialised in six parts in *The Glasgow Naturalist,* the journal of the Glasgow Natural History Society. For wider circulation just a dozen sets of the six parts were put together under the title *Loch Lomondside Depicted and Described* and deposited in various libraries (for a fuller account see John Mitchell's article in the The New Naturalist Collectors' Club Newsletter No. 43. Winter 2008).

The designers of *Loch Lomondside* (and the four following titles NN89–92) followed suit, adopting a less-is-more philosophy, with the gilt lettering on the buckram spine so small that the author's name is almost illegible.

The hardback was characteristically successful and sold 2,000 copies within just 5 months of publication. The fortunes of the paperback were considerably less auspicious with *c.* 1,110 copies remaindered in 2004 – and at the end of 2012 new (remaindered) copies were still available on the internet at around £10.00. The jacket does not appear to suffer unduly from fading.

NN88A   **First Edition**, 2001 (05 March 2001).
Title: 'The New Naturalist | Loch Lomondside | Gateway to the Western Highlands | of Scotland'.
Author: 'John Mitchell'.
Illust: 'With 8 colour plates and over 120 black | and white photographs and line drawings'.
Editors: SAC, SMW, RW, DS and DAR.
Printer: Bath Press.
ISBN: 0002201453.
Collation: pp. 232; 4 leaves of colour plates printed to both sides (7½ × 32-page gatherings).
Jacket: [Rear panel] NN library listing NN1–87 inclusively; ISBN and barcode. [Rear flap] Author's biography. *Plant Disease*, *Lichens* and *Amphibians and Reptiles* listed under 'Other Titles in the New Naturalist Series'. *Ponds, Pools and Puddles* and *Moths* listed under 'Forthcoming Titles'. ISBN, 'HarperCollinsPublishers' and www.fireandwater. com website advert.
Price: £34.99.
Print run: 2,510 (out-turn); no. sold *c.* 2,200; o/p: summer 2002.
Notes: 1) A sketch map of Loch Lomond improvises as a frontispiece, relegating the usual Editors' credits and the NN credo to the half-title page. 2) Despite being listed on the jacket *Ponds, Pools and Puddles* has not yet been published. 3) 'Collins' not printed to jacket spine.

CPB88A Collins Paperback First Edition, 2001. ISBN: 0002201461. Concomitant with the hardback edition NN87A and bound up from the same sheets. Paperback design Type 4. Front cover photograph of *Loch Lomondside* by the author. Rear cover carries the blurb, and advertises *Plant Disease*; *Lichens*; *Amphibians and Reptiles*; *Ponds, Pools and Puddles* and *Moths*, all as, and in the same format as the dust jacket. Price: £19.99. Print run: 1,960 (out-turn); no. sold: *c.* 630 with *c.* 1,110 copies remaindered in 2004; o/p: 2004 but remaindered copies still available in 2012.

POD88A Print-on-demand digital copy.

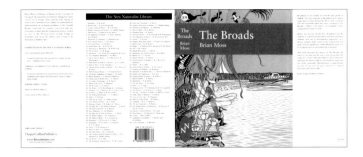

89 The Broads

The original *Broads* by C. E. Ellis went out of print in spring 1974. Despite Collins' desire to retain a *Broads* volume on their list a gap of 25 years ensued before Moss's book was published. Clearly a lot had changed in the interim to both the *Broads* and the New Naturalist series.

By mid-January 2002, just a couple of months after publication, Collins had less than 200 hardback copies of *The Broads* in stock. Perhaps not surprising, considering only *c.* 2,500 of this format were printed. However, the paperback was not so popular, with 600 copies being remaindered in 2003.

The title band of the dust jacket is bright red, generally a fatal colour for New Naturalists and this one is no exception – the ink used is more fade-fast than colourfast and books with pink spines are not uncommon.

NN89A   **First Edition**, 2001 (05 November 2001).
Title: 'The New Naturalist | The Broads | The People's Wetland First Edition. 2002'.
Author: 'Brian Moss'.
Illust: 'With 29 colour plates and over 14 black | and white photographs and line drawings'.
Editors: SAC, SMW, RW, DS and DAR.
Printer: Bath Press.
ISBN: 0002201631.
Collation: pp. 392; 8 leaves of colour plates printed to both sides (12½ × 32-page gatherings).
Jacket: [Rear panel] NN library listing NN1–88 inclusively; ISBN and barcode. [Rear flap] Author's biography. *Loch Lomondside* and *Amphibians and Reptiles* advertised under 'Other Titles in the New Naturalist Series'. *Moths* and *Conservation* listed under 'Forthcoming Titles'. ISBN, 'HarperCollinsPublishers' and www. fireandwater.com website advert (*Conservation* was published as *Nature Conservation*).
Price: £34.99.
Print run: 2,540 (out-turn); no. sold: *c.* 2,270; o/p: end of 2002.
Notes: 'Collins' not printed to jacket spine.

CPB89A Collins Paperback First Edition, 2001. ISBN: 0007124104. Concomitant with the hardback edition NN87A and bound up from the same sheets. Paperback design Type 4. Front cover photograph of a yacht on the Broads, is by the author. Rear cover carries a copy of the jacket blurb below which listed *Loch Lomondside* and *Amphibians and Reptiles*, *Moths* and *Conservation*. Price: £19.99. Print run: 1,981 (out-turn); no. sold: *c.* 1,180 + 600 copies remaindered; o/p: beginning 2005.

POD89A Print-on-demand digital copy.

90 Moths

Majerus's second New Naturalist and the second New Naturalist with the title *Moths*; a successor to NN30, Ford's work of 47 years earlier. The hardback edition was particularly successful and remained in print for little more than a year, but conversely the paperback was still available 3 years later. *Moths* wears one of Gillmor's boldest and most effective jackets, but watch the red colour on the spine, otherwise the Garden Tiger will soon be mistaken for an aberrant pink form.

NN90A	**First Edition**, 2002 (04 February 2002).
Title:	'The New Naturalist | Moths'.
Author:	'Michael E. N. Majerus'.
Illust:	'With 16 colour plates and over 180 black | and white photographs and line drawings'.
Editors:	SAC, SMW, RW, DS and DAR.
Printer:	Bath Press.
ISBN:	0002201410.
Collation:	pp. 310, [2]; 8 leaves of colour plates printed to both sides (9 × 32-page gatherings + 1 × 8-page gathering + 1 × 16-page gathering).
Jacket:	[Rear panel] NN library listing NN1–89 inclusively; ISBN and barcode. [Rear flap] Author's biography. *The Broads* and *Loch Lomondside* advertised under 'Other Titles in the New Naturalist Series'. *Nature Conservation* and *Lakeland* listed under 'Forthcoming Titles'. ISBN, 'HarperCollinsPublishers' and www.collins.co.uk website advert.
Price:	£34.99.
Print run:	2,984 (out-turn); no. sold: *c.* 2,740; o/p: May 2003.
Notes:	'Collins' not printed to jacket spine.

CPB90A Collins Paperback First Edition, 2002. ISBN: 0002201429. Concomitant with the hardback edition NN90A and bound-up from the same sheets. Paperback design Type 4. Front cover featuring a photograph of a 5-spot burnet moth by the author. Rear cover carries the blurb and advertises *The Broads, Loch Lomondside, Nature Conservation* and *Lakeland*, all as, and in the same format as the dust jacket. Price £19.99. Print run: 1,944 (out-turn); o/p: April 2007.

POD90A Print-on-demand digital copy.

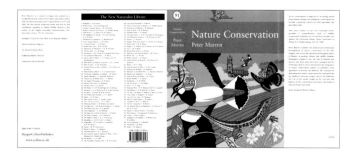

91 Nature Conservation

Nature Conservation is bibliographically unremarkable: just one impression of one edition. Less than 3,000 hardback copies were printed and as such it is a rare book. Given this, and considering it is such a good read, it is surprising that it is not worth more: there is always a good number offered on the second-hand market, but it was certainly popular at the time, with over 2,000 copies sold in the first five months.

The red colour is a little prone to fading on the jacket spine, but it is not difficult to find bright unfaded copies.

NN91A	**First Edition**, 2002 (07 May 2002).
Title:	'The New Naturalist | Nature Conservation | A Review of the Conservation of Wildlife in Britain 1950–2001 First Edition. 2002'.
Author:	'Peter Marren'.
Illust:	'With 16 colour plates and over 130 black | and white photographs and line drawings'.
Editors:	SAC, SMW, RW, DS and DAR.
Printer:	Bath Press.
ISBN:	0007113056.
Collation:	pp. 344; 8 leaves of colour plates printed to both sides (12 × 32-page gatherings).
Jacket:	[Rear panel] NN library listing NN1–90 inclusively; ISBN and barcode. [Rear flap] Author's biography. *Moths* and *The Broads* advertised under 'Other Titles in the New Naturalist Series'. *Lakeland* listed under 'Forthcoming Title'. ISBN, 'HarperCollinsPublishers' and www.collins.co.uk website advert.
Price:	£34.99.

Print run: 2,862 (out-turn); no. sold: *c.* 2,550; o/p: early summer 2004.
Notes: 1) The dedication and two quotes have been inserted onto the Editors' and NN credo page (page opposite the title page) resulting in a layout both cramped and alien to the series. 2) 'Collins' not printed to jacket spine.

CPB91A Collins Paperback First Edition, 2002. ISBN 0007113064. Concomitant with the hardback first edition NN90A and bound-up from the same sheets. Paperback design Type 4. The front cover photograph of a wildflower meadow is by Bob Gibbons. The rear cover carries a précis of the dust jacket blurb; author's biography (different to jacket) and features *Moths*; *The Broads* and *Lakeland,* as the jacket. Price: £19.99. Print run: 1,980; no. sold: *c.* 1,760; o/p: autumn 2003.

POD91A Print-on-demand digital copy.

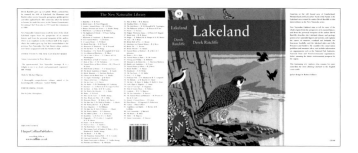

92 Lakeland

The initial sales of hardback *Lakeland* were characteristically high as collectors snapped up their copies. Six months following publication nearly 2,300 copies had been sold with only a few hundred left in stock. Sales of the paperback were far less propitious: in the same period only 860 copies were sold. Odd, as *Lakeland* is generally recognised as being an excellent book and, as it covers a popular area, one would assume its appeal would go beyond the collectors' fold – especially at the more affordable softback price. In 2004, 600 paperback copies were remaindered.

The jacket does not appear to be susceptible to fading and fine copies are readily available.

NN92A   **First Edition**, 2002 (07 October 2002).
Title: 'The New Naturalist | Lakeland | The Wildlife of Cumbria'.
Author: 'Derek Ratcliffe'.
Illust: 'With 43 colour plates and over 130 black | and white photographs and line drawings'.
Editors: SAC, SMW, RW, DS and DAR.
Printer: Printed and bound in Great Britain by the Bath Press.
ISBN: 000711303x.
Collation: pp. 384; 10 leaves of colour plates printed to both sides (12 × 32-page gatherings).

Jacket: [Rear panel] NN library listing NN 1–91 inclusively; barcode and ISBN. [Rear flap] Author's biography. *Nature Conservation* and *Moths* advertised under 'Other Titles in the New Naturalist Series'. *Bats* is listed under 'Forthcoming Titles'. ISBN, 'HarperCollins*Publishers*' and 'everything clicks at www.collins.co.uk'.
Price: £35.00.
Print run: 2,938 (out-turn); no. sold: *c.* 2,560; o/p: March 2004.
Notes: 'Collins' not printed to jacket spine.

CPB92A Collins Paperback First Edition, 2002. ISBN: 0007113048. Concomitant with the hardback edition NN92A and bound up from the same sheets. Paperback design Type 4. Front cover photograph of Eagle Crag is by Derek Ratcliffe. Rear cover carries a précis of the jacket blurb, author's biography and titles *Nature Conservation, Moths, Bats,* as the jacket. Price: £19.99. Print run: 1,974 (out-turn); no. sold: *c.* 1,110 + 600 remaindered in 2004; o/p: 2005[?].

POD92A Print-on-demand digital copy.

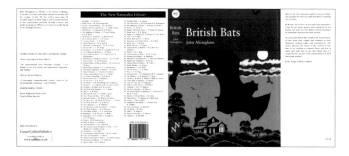

93 British Bats

The publication of *Bats* coincided with an upsurge of general interest in these mammals, and this coupled with a comparatively small print run of *c.* 3,000 hardbacks and *c.* 2,000 paperbacks resulted in this title quickly going out of print. The 'non-collector' tended to buy the cheaper softback and the collector the jacketed hardback, but sales of the latter were no doubt fuelled by speculative buying: in the event a thoroughly good investment as it quickly quadrupled in value, though has come down a little since. The paperback was the first display on the rear cover the colourful band of thumbnail illustrations of 'Other Titles in the New Naturalist Series'; an attractive feature that has persisted to date. *Bats* was not reprinted. The jacket appears colourfast.

NN93A   **First Edition**, 2003 (03 March 2003).
Title: 'The New Naturalist | British Bats'.
Author: 'John D. Altringham'.
Illust: 'With 8 colour plates and over 120 black | and white photographs and line drawings'.
Editors: SAC, SMW, RW, DS and DAR.
Printer: Printed and bound in Great Britain by the Bath Press.

ISBN: 0002201402.
Collation: pp. 218, [6]; 4 leaves of coloured plates, printed to both sides (7 × 32-page gatherings).
Jacket: [Rear panel] NN library listing NN1–92 inclusively; ISBN and barcode. [Rear flap] Author's biography. *Nature Conservation* and *Moths* advertised under 'Other Titles in the New Naturalist Series'. *British Wildfowl* and *Fungi* listed under 'Forthcoming Titles'. ISBN, 'HarperCollinsPublishers' and www.collins.co.uk website advert.
Price: £35.00.
Print run: 3,036 (out-turn); no. sold: c. 2,720; o/p: 2004.
Notes: 1) b/w line illustrations throughout by Tom McOwat. 2) 'Collins' not printed to jacket spine. 3) *British Wildfowl* listed on the jacket was not to be published for another six years and then simply with the title *Wildfowl*.

CPB93A Collins Paperback First Edition, 2003. ISBN: 000220147X. Concomitant with the hardback first edition NN93A and bound-up from the same sheets. Paperback design Type 5. Photographic front cover features a Natterer's Bat by Frank Greenaway. Rear cover carries a general advertisement for the NN series, followed by the blurb (different from and more extensive than that on the jacket). 'Other Titles in the New Naturalist Series' features thumbnail illustrations of p/b titles: *Lakeland, Nature Conservation, Moths, The Broads, Loch Lomondside*, and *Amphibians and Reptiles*. Price: £20.00. Print run: 1,951 (out-turn); no. sold: c. 1,680; o/p: 2003.

POD93A Print-on-demand digital copy.

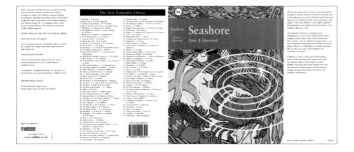

94 A Natural History of the Seashore

A Natural History of the Seashore, to give it its full title, replaces or accurately supplements Russell's *The Sea Shore* (NN12) of 55 years earlier. Russell's book was enriched with colour photographic plates, and while this book has a good array of marine photographs, it is perhaps the fine line drawings throughout the text that stand out. These are unacknowledged, but are, in fact, by the author.

From a bibliographic perspective *Seashore* is straightforward with just one impression of one edition. The hardback with

a print-run of only c. 3,200 copies went out of print within about a year. The fortunes of paperback were less propitious and after four years of slow sales, the outstanding stock was remaindered: in 2012 The Book Depository was still advertising the paperback at little more than a fiver. This is surprising considering a print-run of only c. 2,250 copies. It is now the norm, on internet sites such as Amazon, for new books to be offered at prices significantly lower than the publisher's recommended price, and therefore, the jacket price has become somewhat academic, but when *The Seashore* was first published this was not the case. *The Seashore* was the first hardback to be priced at £40 and therefore it was, comparatively speaking, one of the most expensive New Naturalists; notwithstanding, its second-hand value is now significantly higher.

Early Collins marketing images of the paperback showed a more muted design with a soft blue ground, but presumably Collins felt this design would not stand out well and substituted the adopted photographic design on a vibrant pink ground.

The dust jacket is a little prone to fading on the spine – look at the red of the anemones by the NN monogram, it should be the same colour as that on the front panel.

NN94A First Edition, 2004 (05 April 2004).
Title: 'The New Naturalist | A Natural History of the | Seashore'.
Author: 'Peter J. Hayward'.
Illust: 'With 16 colour plates and over 60 black | and white line drawings'.
Editors: SAC, SMW, RW and DS .
Printer: Printed and bound in Great Britain by the Bath Press. Colour reproduction by Colourscan, Singapore.
ISBN: 0002200309.
Collation: pp. 288; + 8 leaves of colour plates printed to both sides (9 × 32-page gatherings).
Jacket: [Rear panel] NN library listing NN1–93 inclusively; barcode and ISBN. [Rear flap] Author's biography. 'Other Titles in the New Naturalist Series' under which advertised *British Bats* and *Lakeland*. Listed under 'Forthcoming Titles' are *Northumberland* and *Fungi*. ISBN, Collins 'ripple-logo' and website advert.
Price: £40.00.
Print run: 3,224 (out-turn); no. sold: c. 2,950[?]; o/p: May 2006.
Notes: 1) The inclusion of a frontispiece illustration to the verso of the half-title, has usurped the usual Editors' list and NN credo to the imprint page, onto which the dedication and now defunct HarperCollins website 'www.fireandwater.com', have also been shoe-horned, creating a thoroughly busy page of eclectic content. 2) The last of the tranche of NN77–94 without 'Collins' printed to the spine of the jacket.

CPB94A Collins Paperback First Edition, 2004. ISBN: 0002200317. Concomitant with the hardback first edition NN94A and bound-up from the same sheets. Paperback design Type 5. Front cover photograph of a sea anemone by D. N. Huxtable. Rear cover carries a copy of the blurb (reordered) and author's biography as that on the jacket. 'Other Titles in the New Naturalist Series' features thumbnail illustrations of p/b titles: *Lakeland, Nature Conservation, Moths, Amphibians and Reptiles, The Broads,* and *British Bats.* Price: £25.00. Print run: 2,250 (out-turn); o/p: July 2006 (964 copies remaindered – these copies still available in 2012).

POD94A Print-on-demand digital copy.

95 Northumberland

There is little to write about the printing history of *Northumberland,* no reprints, no second states, no variant jackets; all simple and straightforward. There are, however, a few points worth mentioning. Firstly, *Northumberland* is the last title in the series to have separate plates printed on different paper: the end of a 49-year tradition. Secondly, and of particular note, is the scarcity of the paperback version. Just 1,016 copies were printed, the majority of which were sold to libraries, institutions and individuals who purchased the book principally for the purposes of study; consequently fine copies of the paperback are now virtually unobtainable. Thirdly, the hardback edition of *Northumberland* is one of only two titles that has the series number blocked to the casing of the book, the other being NN66 *Wales* (how much better it would have been if all books had their series no. stamped to the spine of the book, as arranging greenbacks into their correct order is a singularly frustrating exercise; it might also have established a greater interest in non-jacketed books). Lastly *Northumberland* reintroduces the imprint Collins to the spine of the jacket following an interlude of 14 years; it last appeared on NN76, *Hebrides.*

    Northumberland jacket does not appear prone to fading, but it does tan; also it is a couple of mm too tall for the book, so is liable to rubbing at the edges – a protective sleeve is a good countermeasure.

NN95A	**First Edition,** 2004 (04 October 2004).
Title:	'The New Naturalist	Northumberland	With Alston Moor'.
Author:	'Angus Lunn'.
Illust:	'With 16 colour plates and over 160 black	and white photographs and line drawings'.

Editors:	SAC, SMW, RW, DS and DAR.
ISBN:	0007184840.
Printer:	Printed and bound in Thailand by Imago. Colour reproduction by Colourscan, Singapore.
Collation:	pp. 304; 8 leaves of colour plates printed to both sides (19 × 16-page gatherings).
Jacket:	[Rear panel] NN library listing NN1–94 inclusively; barcode and ISBN. [Rear flap] Author's biography. 'Other Titles in the New Naturalist Series' under which advertised *British Bats* and *Lakeland. Fungi* is listed under 'Forthcoming Titles'; ISBN, Collins 'ring logo' and Collins website advert.
Price:	£40.00.
Print run:	3,295: (out-turn); o/p: 2006.
Notes:	*Northumberland* is one of only three NN titles [*Natural History of Pollination* reprint and *Lichens*] that uses a number-line device (imprint page), but in the absence of reprints, it is an superfluous feature.

CPB95A Collins Paperback First Edition, 2004. ISBN: 0007184832. Concomitant with the hardback first edition NN95A and bound-up from the same sheets. Paperback design Type 5. Front cover photograph by Graeme Peacock features *Hadrian's Wall.* The Collins 'ring logo' has been introduced to both covers and spine (this logo has been used ever since). Rear cover carries the blurb and author's biography as appears on the dust jacket. 'Other Titles in the New Naturalist Series' features thumbnail illustrations of p/b titles: *Lakeland, Seashore, Moths, Plant Disease, the Broads,* and *British Bats'.* Price: £25.00. Print run: 1,016 (out-turn); o/p: November 2005.

POD95A Print-on-demand digital copy.

96 Fungi

Fungi is a landmark New Naturalist; it is, if you like, the first of the new model and introduces a number of now familiar features. It has undergone a comprehensive redesign (managed by Collins Art Director Mark Thomson) and uses the FF Nexus typeface designed by Martin Majoor, though the old style ('Type E') NN monogram is still retained. The text is now justified only to the left – much to the chagrin of the classical bibliophile. The title to the title page is printed in colour as is the large initial letter of each new chapter, a contemporary take on the traditional historiated letter, and 'Library' has been added to the series title. Importantly, *Fungi* is the first NN to be printed throughout in colour, with the illustrations integrated into the text (see also intro. to NN97 *Mosses and Liverworts*). While *Fungi* introduces these innovations, it paradoxically reverts back to the conventional form of pagination where the preliminary pages are numbered using Roman numerals, with the main text numbered separately using Arabic figures. This traditional form of pagination was last used, for NN52 *Woodland Birds*, 34 years earlier, but has been adopted ever since its reappearance in *Fungi* (excepting NN108 *Southern England*).

Fungi was also the first title with the thick 'reversed' laminated jacket, that is, glossy on the underside but matt on the upper. At the time this jacket created quite a stir in NN collecting circles, some liked it and some didn't, while others declared it a mistake! This latter view was not perhaps unreasonable as a number of jackets were replaced as the originals were inclined to smudge; see below for details. The binding style remains pretty much unaltered but decorative headbands have been added to the head/tail of the spine, a now familiar feature.

Fungi is the second of three titles to be published in 2005, the other two being *The New Naturalists*, second edition and *Mosses and Liverworts*, all three of which are distinguished by undersized hardback variants or reprints. These runtish bindings are immediately obvious as they are about 6 mm shorter than they should be. Collins has explained that that they ran on sheets of the first printing, i.e. printed more copies than they intended to bind, to allow them to respond to demand by binding up these spare sheets as required, in the future, in either paperback or hardback formats. In the event they were bound as hardback copies and seemingly this was done in the UK, rather than the Far East, but the shorter variant of *Fungi* is apparently a reprint. However, for reasons unknown, the binder bound them up as hybrid 'perfect-bindings', that is, they were prepared, stitched and glued as if to be paperbacks, but then cased. As rounding and backing (R&B) is not part of the perfect binding process, these shorter variants have flat spines and correspondingly, the fore-edges of the text-blocks do not have the usual and pleasing concave profile. This has led to speculation that they are rebound paperbacks. Quite why they were so overly-trimmed is likewise not known, but inevitably they are generally perceived as being an inferior product.

The paperback version of *Fungi* is also annoyingly shorter than the standard height – and inconsistently so. It should be around 216 mm, but is only 210–213 mm. It is, however, another comparatively scarce paperback with only 1,850 copies printed: clean copies are now rarely offered.

The dust jacket is a little prone to fading on the spine.

NN96A   **First Edition**, 2005 (03 May 2005).
Title: 'The New Naturalist Library | Fungi'.
Authors: 'Brian Spooner & | Peter Roberts'.
Editors: SAC, SMW, RW and DS.
Printer: Printed in Thailand by Imago.
ISBN: 0002201526.
Casing: 157 × 223 mm.
Collation: pp. xi, [1], 594, [2] (19 × 32-page gatherings).

Jacket: Laminated, upper surface matt, underside glossy (see notes). [Rear panel] NN library listing NN1–95 inclusively; barcode and ISBN. [Rear flap] Authors' biographies; 'Other Titles in the New Naturalist Series' under which advertised *Seashore* and *Northumberland*. Listed under 'Forthcoming Titles' are *Mosses and Liverworts* and *History of Ornithology*. ISBN, Collins ring logo and Collins' website.
Price: £40.00.
Print run: 3,524 (out-turn); o/p: see NN96B.
Notes: 1) Title and initial letter of each chapter printed in carmine. 2) At 608 pages *Fungi* is a substantial tome, but this is, in part, due to the unusually generous spacing of text lines that appear almost double spaced: just 35 lines to the page. Compare this with the following volume, *Mosses*, which has 39 – almost the same number of words are in fifty fewer pages (for further comment on recent NN book design, read Roger Long's short but excellent article in the New Naturalist Book Club [NNBC] newsletter no. 32, No. 4, 2005). 3) A jacket glossy to the upper surface and another glossy to both surfaces were developed as prototypes but were never actually issued: a few examples have found their way into specialist collections. Some of the original issued jackets did have a tendency to smudge and John Burrow, in the NNBC newsletter no. 30, no. 2. 2005, wrote 'those of you who bought *Fungi* through the NNBC will find a new dust wrapper enclosed with this newsletter. The originals are inclined to smudge, so the wrapper was reprinted'. Additionally there is noticeable colour variation between batches of dust jackets.

NN96B Reprint (Shorter Binding Variant), 2005. Textually, appears identical to NN96A but casing is only 217 mm high by 150 mm wide. Spine flat and the fore-edge of the book-block square, rear blank leaf excised, the decorative head and tail-bands are different too, bright green stripes and shiny, (those of NN96A have dark blue-green stripes and are matt). This variant sold later, in 2006. The colours of the jacket are slightly more muted, but the paper is appreciably thinner. Print run: 695 copies; o/p: November 2006.

CPB96A Collins Paperback First Edition, 2005. ISBN: 0002201534. Concomitant with the hardback edition NN96A and bound-up from the same sheets. Paperback design Type 6. The text-blocks of all copies have been variously over-trimmed resulting in a smaller leaf size of only 210–213 mm. Cover photograph (copyright of the authors) of an orange toadstool. Rear cover includes blurb (part of) and authors' biographies as found on the jacket. 'Other Titles in the New Naturalist Series' features thumbnail illustrations of p/b titles: *Lakeland, Moths, Seashore, The Broads, British Bats* and *Northumberland*'. Price: £25.00. Print run: 1,850 (out-turn); o/p: May 2007.

POD96A Print-on-demand digital copy.

97 Mosses and Liverworts

Mosses and Liverworts, like the preceding title, *Fungi*, adopts the new full-colour internal layout and also has a secondary binding variant which is significantly shorter. For details of these features see the intro. to *Fungi*. When *Mosses* was first commissioned it was to be in black and white with the usual small complement of colour plates, but Ron Porley, supported by his editor Derek Ratcliffe, persistently argued the case for full colour. It was, of course, only a matter of time before Collins would have to embrace full colour, but undoubtedly the persuasive arguments of Porley and Ratcliffe precipitated the decision: in a letter to Porley of March 2004, Ratcliffe wrote that he understood the first full colour NN was to be NN100. He also advocated the use of large-format photographs 'instead of trying to cram in as many as possible at three or four per page (as...in *Lichens*)', and astutely observed 'The NNs are not large-format books and the size of the photographs always presents problems...'. Thus *Mosses* includes a number of fine full-page colour photos e.g. Fig. 145 on page 364.

Mosses paperback reintroduces the Ellis's artwork to the front cover in a design layout that has been used consistently to date (Paperback design type 7 – see page 100), but originally it featured a photograph by Ron Porley of a moss (*Tortella tortuosa*) creeping over a rock, and it was this version that was advertised, in the first instance, on Amazon, though no copies were actually produced.

NN97A	**First Edition, First State**, 2005 (05 September 2005).
Title:	'The New Naturalist Library	Mosses and	Liverworts'.
Authors:	'Ron Porley & Nick Hodgetts'.
Editors:	SAC, SMW, RW, DS and DAR.
Printer:	Printed in Thailand by Imago.
ISBN:	0002202123.
Collation:	pp. xiii, [1], 495, [3] (16 × 32-page gatherings).
Casing:	158 mm (including curve of spine) × 223 mm.
Jacket:	[Rear panel] NN listing NN1–96 inclusively; barcode and ISBN. [Rear flap] Authors' biographies; 'Praise for the New Naturalist Series' under which advertised *Northumberland*. *Bumblebees* listed under 'Forthcoming Titles'. ISBN, www.collins.co.uk and Collins ring logo.
Price:	£40.00.
Print run:	3,561 (out-turn); o/p: September 2008.
Notes:	1) Title and initial letter of each chapter printed in crimson. 2) Derek Ratcliffe wrote the Editors' Preface.

NN97B First Edition Second State (Shorter Binding Variant). Seemingly bound up from the same sheets as NN97A, but noticeably shorter by about 7 mm (casing 151 × 216 mm), bound without the rear blank leaf. The spine is flat, with the fore-edge of the text-block correspondingly square. The head/tail-bands are subtly different too. This variant was sold towards the end of the in-print period. For a more detailed explanation of this shorter binding see preceding entry for NN96 *Fungi*. No. printed (bound thus): *c.* 680[?]; o/p: 2008[?]. Note: Sales statements from Collins mention a reprint of 684 copies, but it is assumed that this refers to this subsequent second state binding.

CPB97A Collins Paperback First Edition, 2005. ISBN: 0007174004. Concomitant with the hardback first edition NN97A and bound-up from the same sheets. Paperback design Type 7 with Gillmor's artwork reinstated. Rear cover carries abridgements of the jacket blurb and authors' biographies. 'Other Titles in the New Naturalist Series' features thumbnail illustrations of p/b titles: *Lakeland, Moths, Seashore, The Broads, Fungi* and *Northumberland*. Price: £25.00. Print run: 1,557 (out-turn); o/p: March 2008.

POD97A Print-on-demand digital copy.

98 Bumblebees

Bumblebees was well reviewed, sold well and was out of print within a couple of years, and this has led to a comparatively high second-hand value. But it is impossible to discuss *Bumblebees* without mentioning the superlative jacket, which no doubt played a significant role in its success. Of the 50 New Naturalist dust jackets designed by Robert Gillmor to date, *Bumblebees* is perhaps his finest and one that has achieved iconographic status. The design was also used as the cover illustration for the catalogue accompanying Gillmor's New Naturalist Art Exhibition of 2009, held at the Pinkfoot Gallery in Cley, Norfolk, at which an edition of 65 original linocut prints of this jacket quickly sold out, amounting to a total catalogue value in excess of £24,000. It's a design that, due to its fine colour combinations and strong sense of rhythm, could equally be applied to a fabric or wallpaper.

The dust jacket follows the trend of recent titles in that the underside is glossy, however the upper surface, rather than being the usual matt, has a satin finish: in this respect it is unique in the series. To date it appears colourfast.

NN98A   **First Edition**, 2006 (06 March 2006)
Title: 'The New Naturalist Library | Bumblebees | The
              Natural History & | Identification of the | Species
              Found in Britain'.
Author: 'Ted Benton'.
Editors: SAC, SMW, RW and DS.
Printer: Printed in Singapore by Imago.
ISBN: 0007174500.
Collation: pp. xi, [1], 580 (37 × 16-page gatherings).
Jacket: Laminated, upper surface with a satin finish,
              underside glossy. [Rear panel] NN library listing
              NN1–97; ISBN and barcode. [Rear flap] Author's
              biography; 'Praise for the New Naturalist Series';
              'Praise for *Fungi*'; *Gower* appears under 'Forthcoming
              Titles'; ISBN and website address.
Price: £45.00.
Print run: 4,622 (out-turn); o/p: May 2007.

CPB98A Collins Paperback First Edition, 2006. ISBN: 0007174519.
Concomitant with the hardback first edition NN98A and bound-up
from the same sheets. Paperback design Type 7. Rear cover carries a
facsimile of the blurb and an abridgement of the author's
biography, as on the jacket. 'Other Titles in the New Naturalist
Series' features thumbnail illustrations of p/b titles: *Moths, British
Bats, Seashore, Northumberland, Fungi* and *Mosses and Liverworts*.
Price: £25.00. Print run: 1,516 (out-turn); o/p: January 2007.

POD98A Print-on-demand digital copy.

99 Gower

Gower was well received, with the first edition selling out within a
year. It was reprinted twice, a feat not achieved since NN65 *Waders*,
25 years earlier. The reprints extended to both h/b and p/b formats
and, helpfully, are acknowledged on the imprint page, so with
Gower there is no need for dreary tables of diagnostic details.
Barely 1,000 copies of the first edition paperback were printed,
but both reprints, in both formats, were printed in even smaller
numbers, so numerically, at least, these are scarce editions.

Note the correct title – simply *Gower* without the definite article
and this, as the author explains in Chapter 1, because the original
name was *Gwyr* and not *Y Gwyr* – and not because of any

whimsical notion that, currently, it might be *de rigueur* to ditch the
definite article.

The paper used for later impressions was slightly different
resulting in marginally thicker books. The jackets of the different
impressions vary noticeably in shade and intensity of colour; less so
within the same printing, but the colours of the paperbacks are
more distinctive still. Total no. of books printed: *c.* 6,750 (h/b and
p/b).

NN99A   **First Edition**, 2006 (02 May 2006).
Title: 'The New Naturalist Library | Gower'.
Author: 'Jonathan Mullard'.
Editors: SAC, RW and DS.
Printer: Printed in China by Imago.
ISBN-10:   0007160674, ISBN-13: 9780007160674.
Collation: pp. xviii, 445, [1] (29 × 16-page gatherings).
Jacket: [Rear panel] NN library listing NN1–98; 10 digit ISBN
              and barcode. [Rear flap] Author's biography; 'Praise
              for the New Naturalist Series'; under which
              advertised *Northumberland*. *Woodlands* appears under
              'Forthcoming Titles'. 10-digit ISBN; Collins 'ring
              logo'; www.collins.co.uk.
Price: £45.00.
Print run: 3,064 (out-turn); o/p: 2006.
Notes: 1) *Gower* is the first NN to have a 13-digit ISBN, but
              printed to the imprint page only. 2) Text-block: 28.5
              mm thick. 3) 'Silk' headband: green/white banded
              with *c.* 17 green 'teeth' along length. 4) Spine well
              rounded and fore-edge concave.

NN99B First Reprint, 2006. ISBN unchanged. 'First published
2006 | Reprinted 2006'. Book and jacket as NN99A. Book-block
29.5 mm thick. 'Silk' headband chequered, *c.* 18 green 'teeth' along
length. Price: £45.00. Print run: 550 (out-turn); o/p: 2007[?] (With
just 550 copies printed, a rare edition.)

NN99C Second Reprint, 2007. ISBN unchanged. 'First published
2006 | Reprinted 2006 | Reprinted 2007'. As NN99A. Book-block
29.5 mm thick. 'Silk' headband: green/white banded with *c.* 17
green 'teeth' along length; Spine flatter and fore-edge only
shallowly concave. Jacket unchanged, but ISBN to the rear panel
now the 13-digit number, and barcode enlarged accordingly
(10-digit number remains to rear flap). Print run: 751 (out-turn);
o/p: 2013.

NN99C-DJ1 Second Reprint, Earlier Jacket. The second reprint
was also supplied with the earlier jacket showing the 10-digit ISBN
to the rear panel.

CPB99A Collins Paperback First Edition, 2006. ISBN-10:
0007160666, ISBN-13: 9780007160662. 'First published 2006'.
Concomitant with the hardback edition NN99A and bound-up
from the same sheets. Paperback design Type 7. Book 29.5 mm
thick, inc. covers. Rear cover carries a copy of the jacket blurb, but

in revised order. 'Other Titles in the New Naturalist Series' features thumbnail illustrations of p/b titles: *Moths*, *Seashore*, *Northumberland*, *Fungi*, *Mosses and Liverworts* and *Bumblebees*. 10-digit ISBN to rear cover. Price: £25.00. Print run: 1,050 (out-turn); o/p: 2006.

CPB99B Collins Paperback First Reprint, 2006. 'First published 2006 | Reprinted 2006'. As CPB99A but 30.5 mm thick inc. covers. 10-digit ISBN to rear cover. Print run: 550 (out-turn); o/p: 2007.

CPB99C Collins Paperback Second Reprint, 2007. 'First published 2006 | Reprinted 2006 | Reprinted 2007'. As CPB99B. 30.5 mm thick inc. covers. Now, with 13-digit ISBN to rear cover. Print run: 780 (out-turn); o/p: April 2011. (Some copies were available from remainder outlets for around £10.00 in spring 2011).

POD99A Print-on-demand digital copy of the first edition NN99A.

100 Woodlands

A prophetic advert for The New Naturalist appeared on the jacket of *Both Sides of the Road*, illustrated by Tunnicliffe, and published by Collins in 1949, which stated 'A library that will exceed 100 volumes' – and that 100th volume was *Woodlands*, published 57 years later.

The combination of this milestone and a book thoroughly good in its own right (and, unusually, recognised as such in its own time) resulted in far greater publicity than usual; it was reviewed in the broadsheets with accompanying order forms, and not surprisingly *Woodlands* sold prodigiously well. Moreover, many copies were seemingly ordered by readers outside the usual NN fold and consequently the first edition is now scarce. It was reprinted five times in both hardback and paperback formats; the first time six printings has been achieved since NN35 *The World of the Soil* (1957–75). A total of *c.* 17,000 NN copies of *Woodlands* were printed: such a figure had not been attained since NN60 *British Birds of Prey* (1976), but many of those were bookclub copies; for NN books sold by Collins alone, NN34 *The Open Sea I*, (1956) was the last title to exceed this number.

Following the NN reprints, in 2010 *Woodlands* was republished in a cheaper hardback format, without a jacket, but a particularly well designed and coordinated production (by Myfanwy Vernon-Hunt) with a crisp, fresh and restrained cover design printed in black and red on a cream ground, the row of trees,

growing from the bottom edge, continuing onto the cream endpapers and cropping up again on chapter headings. In 2012, a utilitarian paperback edition was published, essentially the same design as the 2010 edition but the colour way reversed for the covers. With the publication of these two later editions, the total number of copies printed rises to an unprecedented, (in modern times), 24,300.

Perhaps fittingly for the 100th volume, *Woodlands* at 624 pages is the longest New Naturalist to date. It is also the first book to sport the now familiar patterned endpapers, an excellent innovation, and the first to display the new Martin Majoor NN monogram to the title page, but unlike the four preceding titles the first letter of each new section is printed in black rather than in colour. A batch of first edition books were bound with plain endpapers: apparently the binder ran out of pattern endpapers and as an expedient used plain stock.

To celebrate the 100th volume, one hundred copies were bound in leather and these sold via a ballot. This venture, fuelled by no small amount of speculation, was outstandingly successful and, within a few days of the books being distributed, they were changing hands on eBay for around £2,000. While it was entirely proper to commemorate this notable landmark with a limited edition, the introduction of a pastiche leather binding (with raised bands) to a series celebrated for its outstanding and conforming jacket art was seen as an inappropriate incongruity by some collectors: akin to replacing the bluebells in a famed bluebell wood with a finely manicured lawn – *Scilla non-scripta* or silly and nondescript? They felt that the aesthetic core of the New Naturalists runs through its dust jackets (it is perhaps telling that since NN112 *Books and Naturalists*, limited edition leather bindings are covered up with jackets).

NN100A-VAR1

First Edition, Patterned Endpapers, 2006 (14 September 2006).

Title: 'The New Naturalist Library | Woodlands'.
Author: 'Oliver Rackham'.
Editors: SAC, RW, DS and JF.
Printer: Butler & Tanner Ltd., Frome, Somerset, UK.
ISBN-10: 0007202431. ISBN-13: 9780007202430 (see notes).
Collation: pp. xiv, 609, [1] (19½ × 32-page gatherings).
Jacket: [Rear panel] NN library listing NN1–99; 10-digit ISBN and barcode. [Rear flap] Author's biography; 'Praise for the New Naturalist Series'; under which advertised *Gower* and *Bumblebees*. *Galloway and the Borders* listed under 'Forthcoming Titles'. Collins 'ring logo'.
Price: £45.00.
Print run: 4,160 (out-turn); o/p: 2006.
Notes: 1) Endpapers: patterned – dark green NN motifs on a yellow-green ground. 2) The 13-digit ISBN is erroneously given on the imprint page as 9780007202431, but the check digit (last digit) should

be 'o'. 3) The series number '100' is printed in gold to the jacket.

NN100A-VAR2 First Edition, Plain Endpapers, 2006. Exactly as 'VAR1' but with plain white endpapers. This plain endpaper variant is much rarer than the intended patterned variant; no. bound up thus: unknown.

Note: *Woodlands* was reprinted five times in NN livery, but unfortunately, only three have been acknowledged in the printing histories on the imprint pages. It has not been possible to determine which printings these actually represent and therefore the number printed cannot be correctly ascribed. The numbers (out-turns) printed were as follows:

	HB	PB	TOTAL
1st reprint	996	983	1,979
2nd reprint	772	1,008	1,780
3rd reprint	1,047	792	1,839
4th reprint	367	1,848	2,215
5th reprint	1,200	1,575	2,775
Totals	4,382	6,206	10,588

NN100B First Reprint, 2006. ISBN unchanged (13-digit ISBN still incorrect to imprint page). 'First published 2006 | Reprinted 2006'. Book and jacket as NN100A. Price: £45.00; o/p: 2007[?].

NN100C Second Reprint, 2007. ISBN unchanged (13-digit ISBN still incorrect to imprint page). 'First published 2006 | Reprinted 2006 | Reprinted 2007'. Book as NN100B; jacket unchanged, but ISBN to the rear panel is now the 13-digit number (correct), and barcode enlarged accordingly; o/p: 2007[?].

NN100D Third Reprint, 2007. ISBN unchanged but 13-digit ISBN corrected to imprint page with 'o' being the last digit. 'First published 2006 | Reprinted 2007'. Book and jacket as NN100C; o/p: 2008[?].

CPB100A Collins Paperback First Edition, 2006. ISBN-10: 000720244X, ISBN-13: 9780007202447 (The 13-digit ISBN is erroneously given to the imprint page as 978000720244X). 'First published 2006'. Concomitant with the hardback first edition NN100A and bound-up from the same sheets. Paperback design Type 7. Rear cover carries an abridgement of the jacket blurb; 'Other Titles in the New Naturalist Series' features thumbnail illustrations of p/b titles: *Seashore, Northumberland, Fungi, Mosses and Liverworts, Bumblebees* and *Gower*. 10-digit ISBN to rear cover and the slogan 'Collins. Do More'. Price: £25.00. Print run: 2,524 (out-turn); o/p: 2006.

CPB100B Collins Paperback First Reprint, 2006. ISBN unchanged (13-digit ISBN still incorrect to imprint page). 'First published 2006 | Reprinted 2006'. Concomitant with the hardback edition NN100B and bound-up from the same sheets; otherwise as CPB100A inc. covers. Price: £25.00; o/p: 2007[?].

CPB100C Collins Paperback Second Reprint, 2007. ISBN unchanged (13-digit ISBN still incorrect to imprint page). 'First published 2006 | Reprinted 2006 | Reprinted 2007'. Concomitant with hardback ed. NN100C and bound up from same sheets; otherwise as CPB100B inc. covers, but ISBN to rear cover now the 13-digit number (correct), and barcode enlarged accordingly. Price: £25.00; o/p: 2007.

CPB100D Collins Paperback Third Reprint, 2007. ISBN unchanged but 13-digit ISBN corrected to imprint page with '7' the last digit. 'First published 2006 | Reprinted 2007'. Concomitant with hardback ed. NN100D and bound up from same sheets. Rear cover displays a number of revisions: 'Other Titles in the New Naturalist Series' features thumbnail illustrations of p/b titles: *Mosses and Liverworts, Gower, Galloway and the Borders, Garden Natural History, The Isles of Scilly*, and *A History of Ornithology*; the border to the ISBN and price now dotted; slogan 'Collins. Do More' omitted. Price: £25.00; o/p: 2007[?].

COE100A Collins Hardback Cheaper Edition, 2010 (01/05/2010). ISBN 9780007315147; 160 × 240 mm (little taller than NN original); pp. 508, [4]; 36 leaves of colour plates printed to both sides on glossy paper; 12 leaves of b/w plates printed to both sides on glossy paper (16 × 32-page gatherings). Text printed on matt paper. A reprint of NN100A but text completely reset and all colour photographs and b/w diagrams that were previously reproduced within the text now gathered together in separate plate sections; many of the colour illustrations are printed at a larger size than the original NN edition. Casing of printed paper-covered boards; red head and tail-bands; three press reviews to rear board. Despite the cheaper production a very well designed book; for instance chapter headings are deliberately positioned on the verso but balance well with the text that begins on the recto. Price: £20.00. Print run: 3,964 (out-turn); o/p: December 2012.

COE100B Collins Paperback Cheaper Edition, 2012 (16/08/2012). ISBN 9780007481040. Paperback; perfect bound. As COE100A without any apparent textual revisions, but all plates printed in b/w on the same cheaper, cream paper as the text. Front cover with same design as COE100A but colourway reversed, though white not cream; rear cover reset and includes blurb and two press reviews. Price: £14.99. Print run: 3,054 (out-turn). Still in print 2014.

POD100A Print-on-demand digital copy of first ed. NN100A.

NNL100A Collins Leatherbound Limited Edition, 2006. Limited to 100 copies. Bound in dark brown 'Ross Napa' leather, all edges gilt, raised bands on the spine; with a brown cloth-covered slipcase.

101 Galloway and the Borders

Derek Ratcliffe died just days after completing the manuscript of *Galloway and the Borders* and therefore his name appears as author but does not appear in the list of Editors.

A unique graphic emblem woven into the NN monogram, symbolizing the subject matter of the title was a delightful and subtle device used for all the early NN titles and then resurrected for a few later books; regrettably *Galloway* is the last title in the series to be thus embellished, and in this case with a golden eagle. *Galloway* is also the last title to display the New Naturalist library on the rear panel of the dust jacket; thereafter there just wasn't the room to add further titles and so from NN102 onwards the New Naturalist library was bound in at the rear of the book.

Galloway was reprinted once in 2007, but as a pre-publication order made in 2006; unhelpfully, reprints are not marked as such, but there are differences, albeit negligible, which allow the books to be distinguished as categorised in table NN101. Variation is restricted to the jacket and binding; textually they appear identical. The first edition jacket is brighter, the colours warmer, with the yellow pigment in greater emphasis; having said that there is often variation in jackets anyway and so it is probably wise not to apply this diagnostically. But the first edition jacket is considerably thicker. Both are categorised by thick boards but the reprint has about the thickest of any book in the series.

NN101A **First Edition**, 2007 (03 January 2007).
Title: 'The New Naturalist Library | Galloway | and the | Borders'.
Author: 'Derek Ratcliffe'.
Editors: SAC, RW, DS and JF.
Printer: Printed in China by Imago.
ISBN-10:   0007174012. ISBN-13: 9780007174010.
Collation: pp. xxx, 385, [1]; (26 × 16-page gatherings).
Jacket: [Rear panel] NN library listing NN1–100 inclusively. [Rear flap] Author's biography. 'Praise for the New Naturalist Series' under which advertised *Gower* and *Bumblebees*. Listed under 'Forthcoming Titles' is *Garden Natural History*.
Price: £45.00.
Print run: 3,150 (out-turn).

Notes: Patterned EPS: dark charcoal NN motifs on enamel blue ground. Title printed in black; initial chapter letters printed in black.

NN101B Reprint, dated 2007. Virtually indistinguishable from NN101A, but with several diagnostic features as identified in table NN101. Perhaps the easiest way to tell the two apart is to look at the headbands. Print run: 736 (out-turn); o/p: January 2008.

CPB101A Collins Paperback First Edition, 2007. ISBN-10: 0007174020, ISBN-13: 9780007174027. Concomitant with the hardback first edition NN110A and bound-up from the same sheets. Paperback design Type 7. Rear cover carries précised versions of blurb and author's biography as on the dust jacket. 'Other Titles in the New Naturalist Series' features thumbnail illustrations of p/b titles: *Northumberland, Fungi, Mosses and Liverworts, Bumblebees, Gower* and *Woodlands* . Price: £25.00. Print run: 1,312 (out-turn); o/p: February 2011.

[CPB101B Collins Paperback Reprint], 2007. Indistinguishable from CPB101A. Print run: 240 (out-turn); o/p: February 2011.

102 Garden Natural History

Garden Natural History was reprinted once in 2007 and like its predecessor *Galloway*, was ordered pre-publication and is not acknowledged as a reprint in the book itself: it is textually and graphically identical to the first edition. However, there are a few subtle differences in the binding and dust jacket which enable them to be told apart. When the two are compared side by side these differences are obvious enough, the problem is when you only have just one copy, but by looking at table NN102 it should be possible to determine, with a fair degree of certainty, which edition you have. The reprints are also much rarer and are generally an inferior production. However with the paperback, it has not yet been possible to distinguish one from the other and therefore the reprint remains within the circumscription of the first edition, but has been provisionally catalogued.

Garden Natural History is the first title to have the New Naturalist library bound in at the back of the book, with the jacket rear panel once again used to advertise specific and forthcoming titles, as was the case with the earliest titles in the series.

TABLE NN101 *Galloway and the Borders*: Summary of differences between the first edition and reprint.

NN 101	CASING	BOARDS	INTERNAL HINGE	HEADBAND	DUST JACKET
First Edition	Well executed with crisp lines. Spine: well rounded. Joints: deeply impressed.	Heavy boards. Overall thickness of book *c.* 32mm.	Hinge at endpaper with rounded step, convex at fold.	Matt, finely chequered, c.16 green 'teeth' along its length.	Laminated, glossy to the underside, thick, stiff, ground colour slightly off-white, (approx. 20g).
Reprint	Not so well executed, less crisp. Spine: flattish, not well rounded. Joints: flatter, only slightly impressed.	Very heavy boards. Overall thickness of book *c.* 33mm.	Hinge at endpaper sharp well-defined, with rounded step, concave at fold.	Shiny, silky finish, not finely chequered, banded green and white, with only c.14 'teeth' along its length.	Dust jacket laminated, glossy to the underside, comparatively thin and flimsy, ground colour bright white, (approx. 16 g).

TABLE NN102 *Garden Natural History*: Summary of differences between the first edition and reprint.

NN102	Casing	Gilt Lettering	Headband	Dust Jacket
First Edition	Spine well rounded.	Golden yellow, neatly stamped.	Matt, finely chequered, 13–15 green 'teeth' along it's length.	Laminated, glossy to the underside, thick, stiff, ground colour slightly off-white, (approx. 20g).
Reprint	Spine flattish, not well rounded.	Duller less golden-yellow, not sharply stamped.	Shiny, silky finish, not finely chequered, alternately banded green and white, with only 10–11 green 'teeth' along its length.	Laminated, glossy to the underside, comparatively thin and filmsy, ground colour bright white, (approx. 16 g).

NN102A **First Edition**, 2007 (01 May 2007).

Title:	'The New Naturalist Library	Garden	Natural	History'.
Author:	'Stefan Buczacki'.
Editors:	SAC, RW, DS and JF.
Printer:	Printed in China by Imago.
ISBN-10:	0007139934. ISBN-13: 9780007139934.
Collation:	pp. x, 324, [2 NN library] (21 × 16-page gatherings).
Jacket:	[Rear panel] 'Format 102' with three press endorsements for *Woodlands*; listed under 'Forthcoming Titles' are *Isles of Scilly* and *A History of Ornithology*. [Rear flap] Author's biography.
Price:	£45.00.
Print run:	3,150 (out-turn).
Notes:	1) Patterned EPS: magenta NN motifs on a mars-orange ground. Title printed in dark sage green. 2) New Naturalist library at rear.

NN102B First Reprint, 2007. Not identified as a reprint; textural and graphically identical to NN102A, including jacket, but has several diagnostic distinguishing features as identified in table NN102 above. Print run: 736 (out-turn); o/p: October 2010.

CPB102A Collins Paperback First Edition, 2007. ISBN-10: 0007139942, ISBN-13: 9780007139941. Concomitant with the hardback first edition NN102A and bound-up from the same sheets. Paperback design Type 7. Rear cover carries the blurb and an abridgement of the author's biography as featured on the dust jacket. 'Other Titles in the New Naturalist Series' features thumbnail illustrations of p/b titles: *Fungi, Mosses and Liverworts, Bumblebees, Gower, Woodlands* and *Galloway*. Price £25.00; Print run: 2,086 (out-turn).

[CPB102B Collins Paperback Reprint]. 2007 but reprinted 2008[?]. To date, indistinguishable from CPB102A. Print run: 227 (out-turn); o/p: July 2011. (See notes above regarding the h/b reprint which equally apply to the p/b.)

103 The Isles of Scilly

Scilly follows the theme of the previous two titles: that is, reprinted, but without any acknowledgement in the reprint to that effect. Both printings are textually and graphically identical and therefore all books appear to be first editions. Fortunately there are a few subtle and consistent differences in the binding and dust jacket which enable us to tell them apart as identified in table NN103 overleaf. The reprints are not quite as well made as the first editions, though the printing quality, paper and casing fabric are identical. None of the reprinted sheets was bound up as paperbacks and therefore all p/b copies are straightforward first editions.

TABLE NN103 *The Isles of Scilly*: summary of differences between the first edition and reprint.

EDITION	CASING	FORE-EDGE OF TEXT-BLOCK	POSITION OF COLLINS ON SPINE	HEADBAND	DUST JACKET
First Edition	Spine well-rounded	Distinctly concave	4 mm or less from lower edge	Matt, (usually) chequered, c. 18 green 'teeth' along it's length	Laminated, glossy to the underside, thick, stiff (approx. 20 g.)
Reprint	Spine flat, not well-rounded	Flattish, at best slightly concave	c. 7 mm from the lower edge	Shiny, silky finish, banded green and white, with c. 14 green 'teeth' along its length	Dust jacket laminated, glossy to the underside, comparatively thin (approx. 16 g.)

A few hardback copies (all reprints) of *Scilly* were remaindered in late 2008 and sold by Postscript Books for £10.00 each – strange as this was two years before the book went out of print.

NN103A   **First Edition**, 2007 (06 August 2007).
Title: 'The New Naturalist Library | The Isles | of Scilly'.
Author: 'Rosemary Parslow'.
Editors: SAC, RW, DS, JF and JS.
Printer: Printed in China by Imago.
ISBN-10:   000220150X. ISBN-13: 9780002201506.
Collation: pp. xii, 450, [2 – NN library] (29 × 16-page gatherings).
Jacket: [Rear panel] Type 102. *Galloway and the Borders*, *Woodlands* and *Gower* advertised under 'Praise for the New Naturalist Series'; *A History of Ornithology* & *Wye Valley* listed under 'Forthcoming Titles'; price, ISBN, barcode and Collins' Website. [Rear flap] Author's biography.
Price: £45.00.
Print run: 4,100 (out-turn).
Notes: 1) Patterned EPS: light brown-green NN motifs on Indian blue ground. Title in light sage green. 2) b/w line drawings of various artists throughout. 3) NN library at rear. 4) First title which includes the editor Jonathan Silvertown.

NN103B Reprint, 2007. Not identified as a reprint, textural and graphically identical to NN103A, including dust jacket, but has several diagnostic distinguishing features as identified in table NN103. Print run: 920 (out-turn); o/p: October 2010. Note: Copies of the reprint were supplied in boxes of eight with the printer Butler & Tanner's labels, and dated November 2007.

CPB103A Collins Paperback First Edition, 2007. ISBN-10: 0002201518, ISBN-13: 9780002201513. Concomitant with the hardback first edition NN103A and bound-up from the same sheets. Paperback design Type 7. Rear cover replicates the blurb and author's biography of the dust jacket. 'Other Titles in the New Naturalist Series' features thumbnail illustrations of p/b titles: *Mosses and Liverworts, Bumblebees, Gower, Woodlands, Galloway* and *Garden Natural History*. Price: £25.00. Print run: 2,580 (out-turn); o/p: October 2010.

104   A History of Ornithology

'*Ornithology*' is one of just a few titles in the series that is not directly concerned with the study of natural history, but instead examines the study itself. The c. 4,100 hardback copies of the first edition were insufficient and a reprint of c. 1,000 books was ordered in 2007, but frustratingly the reprint is not identified as such and, to date, I have been unable to tell it apart. However, it would seem not unlikely that it would share the same distinguishing features as the reprints of the forgoing three titles, all reprinted around 2007 and also without reference. The paperback was not reprinted.

NN104A   **First Edition**, 2007 (01 October 2007).
Title: 'The New Naturalist Library | A History of | Ornithology'.
Author: 'Peter Bircham'.
Editors: SAC, RW, DS, JF and JS.
Printer: Printed in China by Imago.
ISBN-10:   0007199694. ISBN-13: 9780007199693.
Collation: pp. xii, 482, [2 – NN library] (31 × 16-page gatherings).
Jacket: [Rear panel] Type 102. Adverts for *Galloway* and *Woodlands*. *Wye Valley* and *Dragonflies* are listed under 'Forthcoming Titles'. [Rear flap] Author's biography.
Price: £45.00.
Print run: 4,104 (out-turn).
Notes: 1) Patterned EPS: burnt-orange NN motifs on a porcelain blue ground. Title in yellow ochre. 2) Jacket is printed on particularly thick paper, which has a tendency to crease along the fold lines.

NN104B Reprint, 2007. Not identified as a reprint; textural and graphically identical to NN104A, inc. jacket. Print run: 984 (out-turn); o/p: November 2010.

CPB104A Collins Paperback First Edition, 2007. ISBN-10: 0007199708, ISBN-13: 9780007199709. Concomitant with the hardback first edition NN104A and bound up from the same sheets. Paperback design Type 7. Rear cover carries abridgements of blurb and author's biography as that of the jacket. 'Other Titles in the New Naturalist Series' features thumbnail illustrations of p/b titles: *Bumblebees, Gower, Woodlands, Galloway and the Borders, Garden Natural History,* and *The Isles of Scilly.* Price: £25.00. Print run: 2,085 (out-turn); o/p: February 2009.

105 Wye Valley

Wye Valley is the fourth volume in the series to cover an Area of Outstanding Natural Beauty (AONB), the first being *Gower,* and like that book the definite article is omitted from the title. But unlike *Gower,* it was not omitted in the interests of nomenclatural correctness but, instead, to follow a modern trend – much to the chagrin of traditional New Naturalist readers. Despite their consternation, it seems that they will have to get used to life without definite articles as *Art of the New Naturalists* and *Badger* quickly followed suit.

Notwithstanding 'inconsequential' issues of grammar, *Wye Valley* is an excellent and successful book. The 4,000 or so copies of the first edition hardback sold out quickly, requiring a reprint in July 2008, though unfortunately these books are not identified as such: they appear identical to the first edition. They have therefore not been catalogued separately. The paperback was not reprinted.

NN105A	**First Edition**, 2008 (04 February 2008). Title 'The New Naturalist Library | Wye Valley'.
Author:	George Peterken.
Editors:	SAC, RW, DS, JF and JS.
Printer:	Printed in China by Imago.
ISBN:	9780007160686.
Collation:	pp. xii, 466, [2-NN library] (30 × 16-page gatherings).
Jacket:	[Rear panel] Type 102 but the New Naturalist website information has been added immediately above the

barcode; an addition that has remained in subsequent titles to date. Adverts for *Garden Natural History* and *Galloway and the Borders. Dragonflies* and *The Grouse Species of Britain and Ireland* (published as *Grouse*) are listed under 'Forthcoming Titles'. [Rear flap] Author's biography.

Price:	£45.00.
Print run:	4,032 + 792 reprints (out-turns); o/p: October 2010.
Notes:	Patterned EPS: sage-green NN motifs on bright uranium green. Title in lettuce-green.

CPB105A Collins Paperback First Edition, 2008. ISBN 9780007160693. Concomitant with the hardback first ed. NN105A and bound-up from the same sheets. Paperback design Type 7. Rear cover carries a copy of the blurb and an abridgement of the author's biography as found on the jacket. 'Other Titles in the New Naturalist Series' features thumbnail illustrations of p/b titles: *Gower, Woodlands, Galloway and the Borders, Garden Natural History, The Isles of Scilly* and *A History of Ornithology.* Price: £25.00. Print run: 2,100 (out-turn); o/p: October 2010.

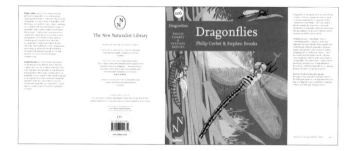

106 Dragonflies

'We find dragonflies to be limitless sources of wonder and delight', so the authors wrote in their preface. *Dragonflies* augments NN41 of the same title, but was published nearly 50 years later. Philip Corbet was a joint author of both and clearly, in the interim, had not lost his enthusiasm for these insects, but sadly he died a few months before the publication of this volume. A short obituary by Michael Parr was inserted.

Dragonflies, at over 5,500 hardback copies, had the largest first edition print run since *British Thrushes,* published 30 years earlier, and furthermore has not been exceeded since. Neither was it remaindered.

Robert Thompson took most of the fine colour photographs that illustrate *Dragonflies,* but the b/w photograph of the Fish Pond, Wokefield Common (Fig. 44) first appeared in the 1960 edition and appropriately was taken by Sam Beaufoy, pioneer of natural history photography and responsible for the colour photographs of dragonflies that lit up the 1960 edition; a fitting allusion to a previous era of the New Naturalist.

NN106A   **First Edition**, 2008 (02 June 2008).
Title: 'The New Naturalist Library | Dragonflies'.
Authors: 'Philip S. Corbet & | Stephen J. Brooks'.
Illust.   'With many colour photographs by | Robert Thompson'.
Editors: SAC, RW, DS, JF and JS.
Printer: Printed in Hong Kong by Printing Express.
ISBN: 9780007151684.
Collation: pp. xvi, [2], 454, [2 – NN library], [6] (15 × 32-page gatherings).
Jacket: [Rear panel] Type 102. Adverts for *A History of Ornithology*, *Garden Natural History* and *The Isles of Scilly*. *The Grouse Species of Britain and Ireland* and *Southern England and Islands* are listed under 'Forthcoming Titles'. [Rear flap] Authors' biographies.
Price: £45.00.
Print run: 5,544 (out-turn); still in print (2014).
Notes: Patterned EPS: dark parsley-green NN motifs on bright pea-green ground. Title in sage-green.

CPB106A Collins Paperback First Edition, 2008. ISBN: 9780007151691. Concomitant with the hardback first ed. NN106A and bound up from the same sheets. Paperback design Type 7. Rear cover carries précised versions of the blurb and authors' biographies that feature on the jacket. 'Other Titles in the New Naturalist Series' features thumbnail illustrations of p/b titles: *Woodlands, Galloway and the Borders, Garden Natural History, The Isles of Scilly, A History of Ornithology*, and *Wye Valley*. Price: £25.00. Print run: 2,376 (out-turn); o/p: May 2014.

NNL106A Collins Leatherbound Limited Edition, 2008. Limited to 250 copies. *Dragonflies* was the first title to be issued concurrently in limited edition format as part of the standard suite of editions, i.e. hardback, paperback and leatherbound limited edition (limited-edition *Woodlands* was a one-off issued to celebrate the 100th New Naturalist titles and available only by ballot). Collins, unsure of demand but aware that there was considerable interest in the limited-edition *Woodlands*, commissioned 400 leatherbound copies as stated on the limitation plate tipped onto the front free endpaper. However, subscriptions were significantly less than anticipated and the limitation subsequently revised to 250 copies, as explained on the loosely inserted errata slip. There was some debate, at the time, amongst collectors as to the fate of the surplus 150 copies, but they have not, to my knowledge, entered the second-hand market. Many of the cloth slipcases were sub-standard and Collins offered to replace these free of charge.

107 Grouse

Grouse was the first bird book to appear since the publication, in 1992, of Simms's *Larks, Pipits and Wagtails*, but at 544 pages it is nearly twice as large, and with *c.* 5,000 hardback copies, enjoyed a print run three times greater. With such a long-running and comprehensive series there are always comparisons and connections to be made. Admittedly, they are often trivial, but they sew a uniting thread through the NN library. A colour photograph, by Adam Watson (Fig. 116 on p. 214), shows tracks in the snow made by two displaying red grouse, but the same photograph reproduced in b/w first appeared 40 years earlier in Stamp's *Nature Conservation*, though then attributed to John Edelstein (plate 22). Comparing the two images and pages side by side, powerfully demonstrates the extent to which NN book production has changed over those years.

Grouse was well-reviewed and presumably appealed beyond the shores of the British Isles; it sold well but the comparatively large initial print-run ensured that no reprints were required.

NN107A   **First Edition**, 2008 (01 September 2008).
Title: 'The New Naturalist Library | Grouse | The Natural History | of British and Irish Species'.
Authors: 'Adam Watson | and | Robert Moss'.
Editors: SAC, RW, DS, JF and JS.
Printer: Printed in Hong Kong by Printing Express.
ISBN: 9780007150977.
Collation: pp. xii, 529, [2 – NN library], [1] (17 × 32-page gatherings).
Jacket: [Rear panel] Type 102. Adverts for *Wye Valley, A History of Ornithology*, and *The Isles of Scilly*. *Southern England* and *Islands* are advertised under 'Forthcoming Titles'. [Rear flap] Authors' biographies.
Price: £50.00.
Print run: 5,025 (out-turn); o/p: October 2012.
Notes: Patterned EPS: dark charcoal NN motifs on light cerulean blue ground. Title in black.

CPB107A Collins Paperback First Edition, 2008. ISBN 9780007150984. Concomitant with the hardback first edition NN107A and bound-up from the same sheets. Paperback design Type 7. Rear cover carries blurb and abridgments of the authors' biographies as featured on the jacket. 'Other Titles in the New

Naturalist Series' features thumbnail illustrations of p/b titles: *Galloway and the Borders, Garden Natural History, The Isles of Scilly, A History of Ornithology, Wye Valley,* and *Dragonflies.* Price: £30.00. Print run: 2,100 (out-turn); o/p: July 2011.

NNL107A Collins Leatherbound Limited Edition, 2008. Limited to 250 copies.

108 Southern England

Southern England was the fourth New Naturalist title to be published in 2008, bringing the total number of NN books printed in the year to over 30,000 (including reprints). A figure not exceeded since 1971 and a testament to the recent resurgence of the series.

The photograph (Fig. 297) on p. 370 of the sea cliffs at Hunstanton clearly shows the inspiration for Gillmor's fine jacket. A small point, but notice how 'Collins' on the spine is now printed in the same green as the title band; an innovation that Gillmor has used a number of times since *Southern England* but in his previous designs 'Collins', if present, was always either printed in black or reversed out in white.

NN108A   **First Edition**, 2008 (03 November 2008).
Title: 'The New Naturalist Library | Southern | England'. Subtitle: 'Looking at the Natural Landscapes'.
Author: 'Peter Friend'.
Editors: SAC, RW, DS, JF and JS.
Printer: Printed in Hong Kong by Printing Express.
ISBN: 9780007247424.
Collation: pp. 414, [2 – NN library] (13 × 32-page gatherings).
Jacket: [Rear panel] Type 102. 'The New Naturalist Library'. *Dragonflies, Wye Valley* and *A History of Ornithology* advertised under 'Praise for the New Naturalist Series'. I*slands* and *Wildfowl* listed under 'Forthcoming Titles'. NN website, price, ISBN and barcode. [Rear flap] Author's biography.
Price: £50.00.
Print run: 5,124 (out-turn); o/p: October 2010.
Notes: 1) Patterned EPS: sap-green NN motifs on light porcelain blue ground. Title in dark sage green. 2) Roman numerals for the pagination of the preliminary pages are discarded for this title.

CPB108A Collins Paperback First Edition, 2008. ISBN: 9780007247431. Concomitant with the hardback first ed. NN108A and bound-up from the same sheets. Paperback design Type 7. Rear cover carries blurb (abridged) and author's biography as found on the dust jacket. 'Other Titles in the New Naturalist Series' features thumbnail illustrations of p/b titles: *Garden Natural History, The Isles of Scilly, A History of Ornithology, Wye Valley, Dragonflies,* and *Grouse.* Price: £30.00. Print run: 2,055 (out-turn); o/p: July 2011.

NNL108A Collins Leatherbound Limited Edition, 2008. Limited to 150 copies.

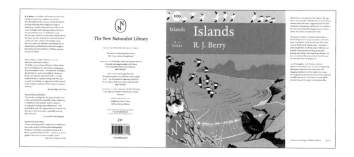

109 Islands

The Natural History of Islands, to give it its full title, took 20 years from commission to publication; not in itself a record (that accolade goes to Cabot's *Ireland*) but it is Professor Berry's fourth New Naturalist title – which is a record (shared with Dudley Stamp). Perhaps this is why the publisher's chose to list his three other books on the rear jacket flap, each with a supporting press review – even though these titles were out of print and only available as 'print on demands'. Professor Berry is a geneticist by trade, though it as a nissologist that he makes his greatest contribution to the series. This, his third book on islands.

NN109A   **First Edition**, 2009 (05 February 2009).
Title: 'The New Naturalist Library | The Natural History of | Islands'.
Author: 'R. J. Berry'.
Editors: SAC, RW, DS, JF and JS.
Printer: Printed in Hong Kong by Printing Express.
ISBN: 9780007267378.
Collation: pp. xiii, [1], 384, [2 – NN library] (12½ × 32-page gatherings).
Jacket: [Rear panel] Type 102. Adverts for *Dragonflies, Wye Valley* and *A History of Ornithology. Wildfowl* and *Dartmoor* are advertised under 'Forthcoming Titles'. [Rear flap] Author's biography with adverts for his previous titles *Inheritance and Natural History, Natural History of Shetland* and *Natural History of Orkney.*
Price: £50.00.
Print run: 5,112 (out-turn); o/p: November 2010.

Notes: Patterned EPS: light grey-brown NN motifs on light Indian blue ground. Title in light grey-brown.

CPB109A Collins Paperback First Edition, 2009. ISBN: 9780007267385. Concomitant with the hardback edition NN109A and bound-up from the same sheets. Paperback design 'Type 7'. Rear cover carries the blurb as found on the jacket and a four line author's biography. 'Other Titles in the New Naturalist Series' features thumbnail illustrations of p/b titles: *The Isles of Scilly, A History of Ornithology, Wye Valley, Dragonflies, Grouse* and *Southern England*. Price: £30.00. Print run: 2,176 (out-turn); o/p: July 2011.

NNL109A Collins Leatherbound Limited Edition, 2009. Limited to 150 copies.

110 Wildfowl

Wildfowl, as a potential subject for the New Naturalist library, was first mooted over half a century before the book was finally published. The Editorial Board minutes of 4 March 1957 record the title *Wildfowl Resources*, with Severn Wildfowl Trust cited as potential authors. Six years later, *Water Birds* was put forward as a possible new title at the board meeting of 16 May 1963. Later in the same year Julian Huxley suggested that Peter Scott might do it, but the minutes record the board's terse response: 'never get him to do it.' By 1966 Hugh Boyd was to write it with George Wills and the title, on James Fisher's suggestion, had changed to *Wildfowl*. It then drifted for many years until David Cabot was commissioned to do it, but *Wildfowl* continued to be dogged by unavoidable delays: *British Bats,* published in 2003, carried an advert for it under the heading 'Forthcoming Titles,' but it was to be a further six years before it was published.

Wildfowl, when it finally arrived, sold quickly: the long delays, it would seem, did not dent its appeal. The paperback sold out within a year and in the same period around 3,000 hardback copies were sold. From and including the publication of *Wildfowl*, Gillmor's artwork is generally reproduced at a smaller scale on the paperbacks than that on the jackets.

NN110A **First Edition**, 2009 (29 May 2009).
Title: 'The New Naturalist Library | Wildfowl'.
Author: 'David Cabot'.
Editors: SAC, RW, DS, JF and JS.

Printer: Printed in Hong Kong by Printing Express.
ISBN: 9780007146581.
Collation: pp. xiii, [1], 460, [2 – NN library], [4 – blanks] (15 × 32-page gatherings).
Jacket: [Rear panel] 'Type 102'. Adverts for *Dragonflies* and *A History of Ornithology*. *Dartmoor* and *Nature Publishing in Britain* are listed under 'Forthcoming Titles' (pub. as *Books and Naturalists*). [Rear flap] Author's biography followed by 'Praise for David Cabot's previous title *Ireland*'.
Price: £50.00.
Print run: 5,112 (out-turn); still in print (May 2014).
Notes: Patterned EPS: burnt orange NN motifs on light porcelain blue ground. Title in dark sage green.

CPB110A Collins Paperback First Edition, 2009. ISBN: 9780007146598. Concomitant with the hardback first edition NN110A and bound-up from the same sheets. Paperback design 'Type 7'. Rear cover carries abridgements of the blurb and author's biography as found on the jacket. 'Other Titles in the New Naturalist Series' features thumbnail illustrations of p/b titles: *A History of Ornithology, Wye Valley, Dragonflies, Grouse, Southern England*, and I*slands*. Price: £30. Print run: 1,700 (out-turn); o/p: 2010.

NNL110A Collins Leatherbound Limited Edition, 2009. Limited to 150 copies.

111 Dartmoor

Ian Mercer's account is the second New Naturalist title to examine Dartmoor, following Harvey's and Leger's book of 56 years earlier (NN27). The two books are of course very different, both in their content and in their production, and their jackets contrast well the styles of C&RE and Gillmor. In terms of the New Naturalist they are equally fine statements of their times (to borrow Mercer's subheading), embodying the ethos of the series. They are both thoroughly good and the thorough bibliophile will want both. The paperback cover artwork is reproduced at a distinctly smaller scale than that of the jacket, about 88 per cent in fact, allowing more of the peripheral design to be included – the jacket version has been trimmed.

NN111A   **First Edition**, 2009 (17 September 2009).
Title: 'The New Naturalist Library | Dartmoor |
           A Statement of its Time'.
Author: 'Ian Mercer'.
Editors: SAC, RW, DS, JF and JS.
Printer: Printed in Hong Kong by Printing Express.
ISBN: 9780007184996.
Collation: pp. xiv, 402 (13 × 32-page gatherings).
Jacket: [Rear panel] Type 102; advert for I*slands. Nature*
           Publishing in Britain [pub. as *Books and Naturalists*]
           and *Badger* are listed under 'Forthcoming Titles'.
           [Rear flap] Author's biography.
Price: £50.00.
Print run: 5,100 (out-turn); still in print (May 2014).
Notes: Patterned EPS: dark green NN motifs on light oriental
           blue ground. Title printed in dark sage green.

CPB111A Collins Paperback First Edition, 2009. ISBN: 9780007146598. Concomitant with the hardback first edition NN111A and bound-up from the same sheets. Paperback design Type 7. Rear cover carries abridgements of the blurb and author's biography as found on the jacket. 'Other Titles in the New Naturalist Series' features thumbnail illustrations of p/b titles: *Wye Valley, Dragonflies, Grouse, Southern England,* I*slands,* and *Wildfowl*. Price: £30.00. Print run: 2,048 (out-turn); o/p: July 2011.

NNL110A Collins Leatherbound Limited Edition, 2009. Limited to 100 copies.

112   Books and Naturalists

In September 1968 David Elliston Allen submitted the manuscript to Collins of his book *The Naturalist in Britain,* which he had been gestating for sixteen years and had, all along, envisaged as a New Naturalist (with some encouragement from James Fisher). However, this was rejected by the then editor Michael Walter. Understandably Allen was disappointed, but the book was eventually published by Allen Lane in 1976 under the same title.

    With the approaching 60th anniversary, in 2005, of the New Naturalist, it was suggested that a book exploring the outstandingly rich legacy of British natural history books would be a fitting way of marketing that milestone, and *Books and Naturalists* was the eventual result. Chapter 20 is devoted to *New*

Naturalists – in the plural and without the definite article, as is the modern wont.

    Books and Naturalists started life with the title *Nature Publishing in Britain,* as advertised on the rear jacket of the preceding two titles NN110 *Wildfowl* and NN111 *Dartmoor.* It completes a trio of books in the series principally concerned with 'works on paper', the other two being *Botanical Illustration* and *The New Naturalists.* If one includes the adjuncts *Art of The New Naturalists* and this volume, then it is a quintet.

NN112A   **First Edition**, 2010 (04 February 2010).
Title: 'The New Naturalist Library | Books and | Naturalists'.
Author: 'David Elliston Allen'.
Editors: SAC, RW, DS, JF and JS.
Printer: Printed in Hong Kong by Printing Express.
ISBN: 9780007240845.
Collation: pp. xiv, 495, [1], [2 – NN library] (16 × 32-page gatherings).
Jacket: [Rear panel] Type 102. Advert for I*slands, Bird Migration*
           and *Badger* are listed under 'Forthcoming Titles'. [Rear
           flap] Author's biography.
Price: £50.00.
Print run: 4,080 (out-turn); still in print (May 2014).
Notes: Patterned EPS: brick red NN motifs on dark brown
           ground. Title in pillar-box red.

CPB112A Collins Paperback First Edition, 2010. ISBN: 9780007300174. Concomitant with the hardback first ed. NN112A and bound up from same sheets. Paperback design 'Type 7'. Rear cover carries abridgements of blurb and author's biography as found on the jacket. 'Other Titles in the New Naturalist Series' features thumbnail illustrations of p/b titles: *Dragonflies, Grouse, Southern England,* I*slands, Wildfowl* and *Dartmoor.* Price: £30. Print run: 1,518 (out-turn); o/p: July 2011.

NNL112A Collins Leatherbound Limited Edition, 2010. Limited to 75 copies. This was the first leatherbound edition to be issued with a dust jacket, which was also signed by Robert Gillmor.

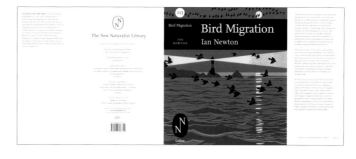

113   Bird Migration

Bird Migration, in terms of rate of sales, was the most successful of the recent New Naturalists and quickly went out of stock in both formats. The Editors describe it as a 'seminal new book',

which no doubt it is, but is also accessible to the layman in the best tradition of the New Naturalist. Furthermore, it is clearly a book that, by its nature, appeals to readers beyond the shores of the British Isles, and now, a year or so later, the hardback has a retail price approaching twice that of the jacket price. Unusually, c. 3,000 copies of the paperback were printed, perhaps to cater for the international demand; in any case they quickly sold out.

No doubt some of this success is due to Gillmor's outstanding jacket, perhaps inspired by a striking illustration in Eagle Clarke's *Studies in Bird Migration* (1912) that depicts a mass attraction of birds to a lighthouse beam, and reproduced in the preceding New Naturalist *Books and Naturalists* (Fig. 162).

NN113A   **First Edition**, 2010 (01 April 2010).
Title: 'The New Naturalist Library | Bird | Migration'.
Author: 'Ian Newton'.
Editors: SAC, RW, DS, JF and JS.
Printer: Printed in Hong Kong by Printing Express.
ISBN: 9780007307319.
Collation: pp. x, 596, [2 – NN library] (19 × 32-page gatherings).
Jacket: [Rear panel] Type 102. 'The New Naturalist Library'. NN series commendations, I*slands* and *Dartmoor* advertised under 'Praise for the New Naturalist Series'; *Badger* and *British Climate and Weather* listed under 'Forthcoming Titles'; NN website, price, ISBN and barcode. [Rear flap] Author's biography.
Price: £50.00.
Print run: 4,032 (out-turn); o/p: August 2011.
Notes: Patterned EPS: canary yellow NN motifs on light cerulean blue ground. Title in dark sage green.

CPB113A Collins Paperback First Edition, 2010. ISBN: 9780007307326. Concomitant with the hardback first edition NN113A and bound-up from the same sheets. Paperback design 'Type 7'. Rear cover carries an abridgement and modification of blurb, and a replica of the author's biography, as found on the jacket. 'Other Titles in the New Naturalist Series' features thumbnail illustrations of p/b titles: *Grouse, Southern England, Islands, Wildfowl, Dartmoor,* and *Books and Naturalists*. Price: £30.00. Print run: 3,012 (out-turn); o/p: April 2011.

NNL113A Collins Leatherbound Limited Edition, 2010. Limited to 75 copies. Issued with a jacket, signed by Robert Gillmor.

114 Badger

The New Naturalist library has a history of replacing earlier titles with new books by new authors, bringing the latest research and knowledge to bear, but until *Badger* this has not happened with the monographs. Of course the monograph series has long since been discontinued, so this has only been possible by including this volume within the main series. This is recognised in the Editors' preface, which begins: '*Badger* is a new departure for the New Naturalist library: a volume on a single species in the main series.' However, this is not strictly true as *The World of the Honeybee* was also published in the main series and more or less devoted to *Apis mellifera* as is the current volume to *Meles meles*. And in the preface to the *Honeybee*, the Editors begin 'A monograph…would normally be published by the New Naturalist in its series of Special Volumes.' Déjà vu.

At exactly 400 pages *Badger* is rather short in comparison to recent NN titles, but that is perhaps fitting for what is after all a monograph. The brown of the paperback is distinctly different from that of the jacket and the cover artwork reproduced at a reduced scale.

NN114A   **First Edition**, 2010 (27 May 2010).
Title: 'The New Naturalist Library | Badger'.
Author: 'Timothy J. Roper'.
Editors: SAC, RW, DS, JF and JS.
Printer: Printed in Hong Kong by Printing Express.
ISBN: 9780007320417.
Collation: pp. xi, [1], 386, [2 – NN library] (12½ × 32-page gatherings).
Jacket: [Rear panel] Type 102. 'The New Naturalist Library'. NN series commendations, I*slands* and *Dartmoor* advertised under 'Praise for the New Naturalist Series'; *Climate and Weather* and *Crop Pests* listed under 'Forthcoming Titles'; NN website, price, ISBN and barcode. [Rear flap] Author's biography.
Price: £50.00.
Print run: 4,056 (out-turn); still in print (May 2014).
Notes: 1) Patterned EPS: nut brown NN motifs on light porcelain blue ground. Title in nut brown. 2) *Crop Pests* advertised on jacket published as *Plant Pests*.

CPB114A Collins Paperback First Edition, 2010. ISBN

9780007339778. Concomitant with the hardback first edition NN114A and bound-up from the same sheets. Paperback design 'Type 7'. Rear cover carries abridgements of the blurb and author's biography, as found on the jacket. 'Other Titles in the New Naturalist Series' features thumbnail illustrations of p/b titles: *Southern England*, I*slands, Wildfowl, Dartmoor, Books and Naturalists* and *Bird Migration*. Price: £30.00. Print run: 2,048 (out-turn); o/p: January 2014.

NNL114A Collins Leatherbound Limited Edition, 2010. Limited to 75 copies. Issued with a jacket, signed by Robert Gillmor.

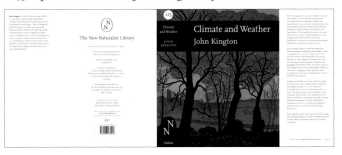

115 Climate and Weather

Climate and Weather is not so much a replacement of Manley's *Climate and the British Scene* (NN22, 1952) but a supplement to it, as over half the text (Part II) is devoted to a 'Chronology of Climatic History'. This represents more of a reference element than we are perhaps used to seeing in the New Naturalist and, as such, is a little unusual. But it proved to be another successful title.

As with a number of recent books, the colours of Gillmor's design are much brighter and stronger on the paperback than they are on the jacket.

NN115A   First Edition, 2010 (02 September 2010).
Title: 'The New Naturalist Library | Climate and | Weather'.
Author: 'John A. Kington'.
Editors: SAC, RW, DS, JF and JS.
Printer: Printed in Hong Kong by Printing Express.
ISBN: 9780007185016.
Collation: pp. x, 484, [2 – NN library] (15½ × 32-page gatherings).
Jacket: [Rear panel] Type 102. 'The New Naturalist Library'. NN series commendations, *Dartmoor* and *Bird Migration* advertised under 'Praise for the New Naturalist Series'; *Plant Pests & Plant Galls* listed under 'Forthcoming Titles'; NN website, price, ISBN and barcode. [Rear flap] Author's biography.
Price: £50.00.
Print run: 3,540 (out-turn); still in print (May 2014).
Notes: Patterned EPS: slate grey NN motifs on oriental blue ground. Title in dark sage green.

CPB115A Collins Paperback First Edition, 2010. ISBN 9780007185023. Concomitant with the hardback first edition

NN115A and bound-up from the same sheets. Paperback design 'Type 7'. Rear cover carries abridgements of blurb and author's biography, as found on the jacket. 'Other Titles in the New Naturalist Series' features thumbnail illustrations of p/b titles: I*slands, Wildfowl, Dartmoor, Books and Naturalists, Bird Migration* and *Badger*. Price: £30.00. Print run: 1,534 (out-turn); still in print (May 2014).

NNL115A Collins Leatherbound Limited Edition, 2010. Limited to 75 copies. Issued with a jacket, signed by Robert Gillmor.

116 Plant Pests

'Until now books on plant pests have generally been more concerned with controlling pests than with exploring their lives.' so states the Editors' preface. And to a few observers the topical and complicated issue of chemical control is insufficiently dealt with, but it remains a thoroughly readable account. The print run of the hardback at *c.* 3,000 copies is 25 per cent less than immediately preceding titles, and in spring 2013 was still in print, indicating perhaps that demand for New Naturalist titles is somewhat down, though this must be tempered by the sales of electronic formats.

Gillmor's design on the paperback is slightly reduced, i.e. printed at a smaller scale (approximately 95 per cent) and is much greener, due to a greater proportion of yellow in the ink and the cabbage white butterfly and its caterpillars are more strongly coloured.

NN116A   **First Edition**, 2011 (06 January 2011).
Title: 'The New Naturalist Library | Plant Pests | A Natural History of Pests of Farms and Gardens'.
Author: 'David V. Alford'.
Editors: SAC, RW, DS, JF and JS.
Printer: Printed in Hong Kong by Printing Express.
ISBN: 9780007338498.
Collation: pp. x, 500, [2 – NN library] (16 × 32-page gatherings).
Jacket: [Rear panel] Type 102. 'The New Naturalist Library'. NN series commendations, *Bird Migration* and *Badger* advertised under 'Praise for the New Naturalist Series'; *Plant Galls* and *Marches* listed under 'Forthcoming Titles'; NN website, price, ISBN and barcode. [Rear flap] Author's biography.

Price: £50.00.
Print run: 3,108 (out-turn); still in print (May 2014).
Notes: 1) Patterned EPS: blue-green NN motifs on bright yellow ground; title in chocolate brown. 2) A 'frontispiece plate' is included on p. [vi] rather than in conventional fashion opposite the title page.

CPB116A Collins Paperback First Edition, 2011. ISBN: 9780007338481. Concomitant with the hardback first ed. NN116A and bound up from the same sheets. Paperback design 'Type 7'. Rear cover carries abridgements of the blurb and author's biography, as found on the jacket. 'Other Titles in the New Naturalist Series' features thumbnail illustrations of p/b titles: *Wildfowl, Dartmoor, Books and Naturalists, Bird Migration, Badger* and *Climate and Weather*. Price: £30.00. Print run: 1,296 (out-turn); still in print (May 2014).

NNL116A Collins Leatherbound Limited Edition, 2011. Limited to 50 copies. Issued with a jacket, signed by Robert Gillmor.

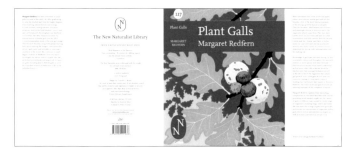

117 Plant Galls

Few New Naturalist collectors would consider themselves cecidologists, nevertheless *Plant Galls* has been a welcome addition to the library – and possibly the most specialised title in the main series to date. Not all reviews were positive, but regarding Gillmor's outstanding jacket, it would be difficult to be anything other than positive. *Plant Galls* follows the format of the preceding titles and bibliographically there is little to be said about it, but there is one small quirk – the jacket is not priced to the front flap, but nothing should be read into this: it was simply an oversight.

NN117A   **First Edition**, 2011 (28 April 2011).
Title: 'The New Naturalist Library | Plant Galls'.
Author: 'Margaret Redfern'.
Editors: SAC, RW, DS, JF and JS.
Printer: Printed in Hong Kong by Printing Express.
ISBN: 9780002201438.
Collation: pp. xi, [1], 562, [2 – NN library] (18 × 32-page gatherings).
Jacket: [Rear panel] Type 102. 'The New Naturalist Library'. NN series commendations, *Bird Migration* and *Badger*

advertised under 'Praise for the New Naturalist Series'; *Marches* and *Scotland* listed under 'Forthcoming Titles'; NN website, price, ISBN and barcode. [Rear flap] Author's biography.
Price: £50.00 (printed only to the jacket rear panel.)
Print run: 3,032 (out-turn); o/p: April 2014.
Notes: 1) Patterned EPS: Mahogany red NN motifs on a lurid lime-green ground; title in chocolate brown.

CPB117A Collins Paperback First Edition, 2011. ISBN: 9780002201445. Concomitant with the hardback first ed. NN117A and bound-up from the same sheets. Paperback design 'Type 7'. Rear cover carries abridgements of the blurb and author's biography, as found on the jacket. 'Other Titles in the New Naturalist Series' features thumbnail illustrations of p/b titles: *Plant Pests, Climate and Weather, Badger, Bird Migration, Books and Naturalists* and *Dartmoor*. Price: £30.00. Print run: 1,001 (out-turn); still in print (May 2014). Notes: 1) For some inexplicable reason, the thumbnail adverts of other p/b titles are in reverse chronological order; for all other paperbacks they are in chronological order. 2) Unlike preceding and succeeding titles the cover artwork is reproduced at 100 per cent of that on the jacket and the colours are very similar but the title band is a different colour – reddish brown rather than mahogany red.

NNL117A Collins Leatherbound Limited Edition, 2011. Limited to 50 copies. Issued with a jacket, signed by Robert Gillmor.

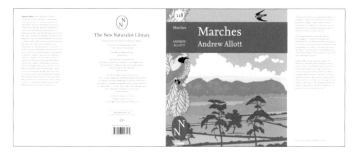

118 The Marches

The first chapter commences, 'The Welsh Marches are the parts of England that border on to Wales ... though almost always abbreviated to the Marches'. And while the jacket, the casing, the NN library, adverts and even Amazon refers to this book simply as 'Marches', the title page, which is the custodian of the definitive title, states 'The Marches' with the definite article alive and well.

It has already been identified that Gillmor's artwork on paperback covers is, from NN110 *Wildfowl* onwards, usually reproduced at a smaller scale than that of the dust jackets, but not at a consistent ratio: in the case of *The Marches* it is reproduced at a significantly smaller scale (c. 92 per cent), which importantly allows the inclusion of the dark hedgerow along the bottom edge, as presumably intended, lending a balance to the composition, missing from the jacket version. The paperback artwork is reproduced in bluer and stronger colours and the title band a different green.

NN118A	**First Edition**, 2011 (01 September 2011).
Title:	'The New Naturalist Library	The Marches'.
Author:	'Andrew Allott'.
Editors:	SAC, RW, DS, JF and JS.
Printer:	Printed in Hong Kong by Printing Express.
ISBN:	9780007248162.
Collation:	pp. x, 452, [2 – NN library] (14½ × 32-page gatherings).
Jacket:	[Rear panel] Type 102. 'The New Naturalist Library'. NN series commendations, *Wye Valley* and *The Isles of Scilly* advertised under 'Praise for the New Naturalist Series'; *Scotland* and *Grasshoppers and Crickets* listed under 'Forthcoming Titles'; NN website, price, ISBN and barcode. [Rear flap] Author's biography.
Price:	£50.00 (printed only to the rear jacket panel, accidentally omitted from front flap.)
Print run:	3,060 (out-turn); still in print (May 2014).
Notes:	Patterned EPS: Sage green NN motifs on a duck-egg green ground; title in dark green.

CPB118A Collins Paperback First Edition, 2011. ISBN: 9780007248179. Concomitant with the hardback first edition NN118A and bound-up from the same sheets. Paperback design 'Type 7'. The rear cover carries abridgements of the blurb and author's biography, as found on the dust jacket. 'Other Titles in the New Naturalist Series' features thumbnail illustrations of p/b titles: *Books and Naturalists*, *Bird Migration*, *Badger*, *Climate and Weather*, *Plant Pests* and *Plant Galls*. Price: £30.00. Print run: 1,004 (out-turn); still in print (May 2014).

NNL118A Collins Leatherbound Limited Edition, 2011. Limited to 50 copies. Issued with a jacket, signed by Robert Gillmor.

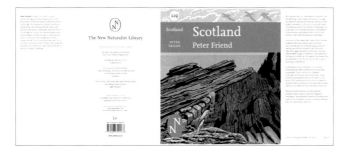

119 Scotland

Scotland is Peter Friend's second book in the series, his first being NN108 *Southern England* with just 25 months separating them; a feat indeed. However, *Scotland* is the result of a three-author collaboration with the other two authors, Leah Jackson-Blake and James Sample appearing on the title page, though it is only Peter Friend whose name appears on the casing and the jacket and only his name that features in all electronic data and general blurb; the division of labour is not noted in the book. The full title is *Scotland, Looking at the Natural Landscapes*, though the book is geology-focussed, as alluded to in Gillmor's jacket artwork of Siccar Point, 'an unusually good example of an uncomformity', a photograph of the same appearing on page 163. The jacket is Gillmor's 50th for the series; the Ellises managed 86, but 19 of those were monograph jackets.

NN119A	**First Edition**, 2012 (05 January 2012).
Title:	'The New Naturalist Library	Scotland	Looking at the Natural Landscapes'.
Author:	'Peter Friend	with	Leah Jackson – Blake	and	James Sample'.
Editors:	SAC, RW, DS, JF and JS.
Printer:	Printed in Hong Kong by Printing Express.
ISBN:	9780007309566.
Collation:	pp. xii, 466, [2 – NN library] (15 × 32-page gatherings).
Jacket:	[Rear panel] Type 102. 'The New Naturalist Library'. NN series commendations and *Bird Migration* advertised under 'Praise for the New Naturalist Series'; *Grasshoppers and Crickets* and *Vegetation* listed under 'Forthcoming Titles'; NN website, price, ISBN and barcode. [Rear flap] Author's biography.
Price:	£50.00.
Print run:	3,067 (out-turn); still in print (May 2014).
Notes:	Patterned EPS: Brown-green NN motifs on an electric-blue ground; title in black.

CPB119A Collins Paperback First Edition, 2012. ISBN: 9780007359066. Concomitant with the hardback first ed. NN119A and bound-up from the same sheets. Paperback design 'Type 7'. Rear cover carries abridgements of the blurb and author's biography, as found on the jacket. 'Other Titles in the New Naturalist Series' features thumbnail illustrations of p/b titles: *Books and Naturalists*, *Bird Migration*, *Badger*, *Climate and Weather*, *Plant Pests* and *Plant Galls*. Price: £30.00. Print run: 1,004 (out-turn); still in print (May 2014).

NNL119A Collins Leatherbound Limited Edition, 2012. Limited to 50 copies. Issued with a jacket, signed by Robert Gillmor.

120 Grasshoppers and Crickets

Grasshoppers and Crickets is the first multimedia New Naturalist and includes a DVD featuring an hour of exclusive video and audio material. Introduced by Ted Benton, it enables readers to put a face and voice to the author: a welcome bonus. *Grasshoppers* offers another first – the first main series title since NN33 *Mountain Flowers*, published in 1956, not to include, either on the jacket or in the book, the New Naturalist library – due simply to a lack of space. It will be noticed that the jacket is additionally priced in Canadian Dollars (CAN $115); this is line with other HarperCollins books and underlines a future desire to market New Naturalist titles in that territory. There is also a first for Gilmour: the NN monogram and lettering on the title band of the jacket is black; on his previous 50 jackets these features have been reversed-out white; the last NN artwork jacket to have black lettering was NN36 *Insect Migration*, published in 1958.

Previously, it has been pointed out that the jacket art is not infrequently reduced when applied to the slightly smaller format of the paperback covers. However, in the case of *Grasshoppers* the reduction is negligible (96 per cent), but the title band is significantly thinner, allowing greater space for the design. Only 731 copies of the paperback were printed, making it numerically the scarcest of all the concomitant paperbacks: it went out of print within a few weeks of publication.

NN120A   **First Edition**, 2012 (5 July 2012).
Title: 'The New Naturalist Library | Grasshoppers | & Crickets'.
Author: 'Ted Benton'.
Editors: SAC, RW, DS, JF and JS.
Printer: Printed in Hong Kong by Printing Express.
ISBN: 9780007277230.
Collation: pp. xii, 532 (17 × 32-page gatherings).
Jacket: [Rear panel] Type 102. 'The New Naturalist Library'. NN series commendations and *Bird Migration* advertised under 'Praise for the New Naturalist Series'; *Partridges* and *Vegetation* listed under 'Forthcoming Titles'; NN website, price, ISBN and barcode. [Rear flap] Author's biography.
Price: £50.00 | CAN $115.
Print run: 3,120 (out-turn); still in print (May 2014).
Notes: 1) Patterned EPS: Orange NN motifs on a dark green ground; title printed in orange. 2) The DVD is housed in a clear plastic wallet pasted to the rear cover.

CPB120A Collins Paperback First Edition, 2012. ISBN: 9780007277247. Concomitant with the hardback first ed. NN120A and bound up from the same sheets. Paperback design 'Type 7'. Rear cover carries abridgements of the blurb and author's biography, as found on the jacket. 'Other Titles in the New Naturalist Series' features thumbnail illustrations of p/b titles: *Books and Naturalists, Badger, Climate and Weather, Plant Pests, Plant Galls* and *Scotland*. Price: £30.00; CAN $66.99. Print run: 731 (out-turn); o/p: August 2012. The DVD is housed in a clear plastic wallet pasted to the rear cover. Note: Being out of print, *Bird Migration* is omitted from the list of thumbnail titles on the rear cover and *Birds and Naturalists* reinstated.

NNL120A Collins Leatherbound Limited Edition, 2012. Limited to 50 copies. Issued with a jacket, signed by Robert Gillmor.

M1 The Badger

'Mr Ernest Neal with his indefatigable labour, has removed a vast amount of the debris concealing the Badger's life…He has made himself a patient watchman, a cunning photographer, an ingenious detective and a careful judge. The number of hours he has spent in the field is one of which every professional ecologist will be jealous. He has done, in fact, an honest job of natural history observation and deduction in the best English tradition.' This statement, part of the blurb, epitomises the defining spirit of the New Naturalist – an amateur naturalist investigating the ecology of an animal and presenting his findings in an honest and readily assimilable manner, supported with pioneering photography (the frontispiece was the first colour photograph of a wild badger). Reviewers at the time also noted and commended Neal's enthusiasm and warmth. Brian Vesey-Fitzgerald, author of NN2 *British Game*, wrote in *The Field* : 'His book is warm and full of life. He has not made the mistake common to modern scientists of believing that truth to be truth must be frigid. "Cold facts" is a favourite catch-phrase of the scientist. How pleasant to have the facts with some warmth for a change! How much more Human!' (Perhaps modern NN authors and their Editors should take note?)

The Badger soon assumed classic status and was likened to David Lack's celebrated monograph, *The Robin* (an honorary New Naturalist monograph in the Fontana series), and therefore it is not surprising that it was such a commercial success. Writing in his autobiography '*The Badger Man*' Neal says, 'I have a feeling that the success of this book gave some financial incentive for Collins to publish others'. He is probably correct, though with perhaps the exception of M9 *The Herring Gull's World*, none of the succeeding monographs reaped the same rewards for Collins as *The Badger*. But the 'war effect' must not be overlooked – see the intro. to NN1 *Butterflies*.

It is Harrison Matthews (author of NN21 *British Mammals* and NN68 *Mammals in the British Isles*) we have to thank for *The Badger*, as it was when he was lunching with Billy Collins in 1945 that he informed the publisher of Neal's work on badgers and his pioneering photography. While the first edition is dated 1948 to the imprint page, due to a 'great rush of autumn books' the publication was delayed until February 1949. Five further

printings followed, including a Readers Union edition, a Penguin (Pelican) paperback edition, German and Japanese editions. The 1958 Penguin edition is interesting in that it was given preference over reprinting the Collins edition and so between 1957 and 1962 the Collins book was out of print. It is not clear why Collins made way for Penguin, but c. 24,000 copies of the latter paperback edition were printed.

Despite the fact that four of the five reprints were called editions, none of them, textually, is in fact much more than a straightforward reprint. The January 1961 board meeting minutes record that (for the 1962 second edition) only 'minimum alteration to be asked for' as the author would eventually write a completely new book with a different title. The suggested title for this new book was 'World of Badgers', although the book of course never materialised, but almost half a century later a new book by Timothy Roper was published as NN114 in the main series, simply with the title *Badger*.

The 1969 third edition has a revised suite of b/w plates, three are new, all are enlarged and a number differently orientated. The reason for this is unknown, and no attention is drawn to the new plates in the prelims, but the most likely explanation is that the original blocks were lost: that is usually the reason! The jacket too is distinctly different, a product of a new reprographic technique and apparently re-originated as it includes sections of the design to the horizontal edges that were cropped from the preceding jackets, however it is cruder and the colours more yellow.

The 1976 reprint was not actually published until January 1977, by which time the printed price was obsolete, so all Collins jackets were price clipped. It was seemingly bound up in more than one batch, the first in buckram and the second in imitation cloth, the latter doubling as the Readers Union edition. The jacket was also reprinted, but without a printed price. The Collins jackets are *Durasealed*, whereas the RU ones are not. A complicated business, but one compounded by an open-minded warehouse staff who had no qualms when it came to mixing and matching – and to find Readers Union jackets with Collins price stickers is by no means unusual; most Collins books, in their various permutations, have been repriced at £4.50 net.

Despite the superfluity of first edition copies, few are offered with fine or even very good jackets: the paper readily tans and is apt to chip, the pink of the title oval on the spine gives up its colour without struggle, fading to a nondescript taupe; in fact all editions are prone to fading.

The sales reports include a number of inconsistencies and errors regarding *The Badger*, but it would seem c. 20,000 hardback copies were printed and an additional 2,000 copies for the Readers Union; Neal's notes record that he received royalties on approximately 20,500 hardback copies (inc. RU), which, given 'natural wastage', lends credence to these figures. *The Badger* finally went out of print in 1980.

M1A   **First Edition**, 1948 (07 February 1949).

Title: 'New Naturalist Monograph | The Badger'.

Author: 'by Ernest Neal | M.Sc. (Lond.)'.

Illust: 'With one colour photograph taken by the author | 29 black-and-white photographs | & 12 maps and diagrams'.

Editors: JF, JG, JH, LDS and EH (Photographic Editor).

Printer: Collins Clear-Type Press, London and Glasgow (in conjunction with Adprint).

Collation: pp. xv, [1], 158, [2]; 1 colour plate leaf (frontispiece) printed to verso only; 12 leaves of b/w plates, printed to both sides (11 × 16-page gatherings).

Jacket: [Rear panel] The New Naturalist listing 'The first fourteen titles in the main series'; publication information and request, Collins address. [Rear flap] 'Announcing the New Naturalist Monographs' under which an explanation is given and the first four monographs listed. List of Editors.

Price: 12s. 6d. net.

Print run: 11,000; no. sold: c. 10, 630; o/p: 1957.

Notes: 1) b/w plates printed on matt paper – most by Neal but also by Harold Platt, Arthur Brook and T. Ormsby Ruttledge. 2) Colour frontispiece photograph positioned towards the top of the plate. 3) Book 15–16 mm thick. 4) Flaps of the jacket are particularly wide, covering most of the pastedown.

M1B Second Edition, 1962. 'First published 1948 | Second edition 1962'. Date omitted from TP. As M1A with a few minor corrections and revisions e.g. pp. 144–145 revised and reset. 'Ph.D.' added to Neal's name on TP; imprint page reset and now only Collins Clear-Type Press mentioned. Editors: JH now Sir JH and V.M.H. added to JG. The b/w plates printed on smoother semi-glazed paper; text paper rougher and book slightly thicker – 17/18 mm. Jacket rear panel advertises *British Mammals* and *The Rabbit*; rear flap lists (and numbers) monographs M1–19 but omitting M6, M8, M10, and M14; blurb to the front flap omits first sentence reset with press endorsements from the *Sunday Times* and *Manchester Guardian* inserted. Price: 18s. net. Print run: 1,500; no. sold: c. 1250[?]; o/p: spring 1967.

M1C Third Edition, 1969. 'First published 1948 | Second edition 1962 | Third edition 1969'. As M1B and despite 'edition' appears a straight reprint, though, significantly, b/w plates have been 'reworked' and all now bleed to the edges of the plate leaf, i.e. enlarged; most also cropped, thereby making them appear as 'close-ups', or differently orientated (plates III and XIX); plates IIb, XIV, XX and XXIV are new images replacing the originals; all captions reset and now printed on glossy paper. No reference to the revised plates in the prelims and list of illustrations not revised to suit. Editors: JF, JG, JH, MD and EH. Atypical brighter blue-green buckram. Jacket printed on bright white paper, using a different technique, producing a distinctly different effect (see

intro.); rear panel unchanged as is the rear flap, but now lists monographs M1–21, omitting M3, M5–8, M10, M11 and M14; blurb to front flap omitted and in its place four press endorsements (*Observer*, *The Field*, *Sunday Times* and *Guardian*). Price: 25s. net. Print run: 1,500.

M1D Third Edition, Reprint, 1971. ISBN: 0002130289. 'First published 1948 | Second edition 1962 | Third edition 1969 | Reprinted 1971'. As M1C without any revision. Book 17 mm thick. Editors: JG, JH, MD, KM and EH. Rear panel of the *Durasealed* jacket unchanged, rear flap still lists the Monographs but adds M22 *The Mole* and additionally omits M12, M13, M15 and M17; ISBN added; front flap unaltered. Price: £1.80 net. Print run: 2,000; o/p: end 1974.

M1E Fourth Edition, 1975 (April). ISBN unchanged. 'First published 1948 | Second edition 1962 | Third edition 1969 | Reprinted 1971 | Fourth edition 1975'. Despite 'edition' a straightforward reprint without any obvious revision. Last sentence of the NN credo omitted. Colour frontispiece printed using a new reprographic technique producing colder colours, printed on bright white glossy paper, the image now centred on the plate. Text paper slighter textured, whiter. Book 16–17 mm thick. *Durasealed* jacket identical to M1D. Price: all jackets appear to be clipped and repriced as below. Print run: 2,000. Note: A combination of delays in printing and inflation probably resulted in the printed jacket price being obsolete, which would explain why all copies seen have been price-clipped.

M1E-AP1 1st Repriced DJ (1975[?]), £2.75 sticker, no. sold: unknown.

M1E-AP2 2nd Repriced DJ (1975–76), £3.00 sticker.

M1E-AP3 3rd Repriced DJ (1976), £3.95 sticker (unverified).

M1F Fifth Edition, 1976 (January 1977). ISBN: now 000219399X. 'First published 1948 | Second edition 1962 | Third edition 1969 | Reprinted 1971 | Fourth edition 1975 | Fifth edition 1976'. Despite 'edition' appears as another straightforward reprint. Book 18 mm thick. Jacket rear panel lists five 'New Naturalist Monographs' with information request below; the rear flap advertises *The Mole* and *British Seals*, front flap unaltered; always price-clipped or without a printed price. Print run: 2,000; o/p: 1980. This is the 'basic' book of which all copies are variants as described below. The genuine Collins edition in primary binding and jacket is M1F-B1-DJ1.

M1F-B1-DJ1 Fifth Edition, First Binding Variant, First Jacket Variant, 1976 (January 1977). Bound in green buckram cloth. Jacket is *Durasealed* and always price clipped and repriced with a Collins sticker as follows.

M1F-B1-DJ1-AP1 1st Repriced DJ (1977), £3.95 sticker (unverified).

M1F-B1-DJ1-AP2 2nd Repriced DJ (1978–1980), £4.50 sticker.

M1F-B2-DJ2-AP2 Fifth Edition, Second Binding Variant, Second Jacket Variant, Repriced 1976 (sold from 1978–1980). Cased in dark green imitation cloth (Type 1). Jacket *Durasealed* but without a printed price (therefore not price-clipped), and repriced with a Collins £4.50 sticker.

M1F-B2-DJ3-AP2 Third Jacket Variant 1976 (sold from 1979?). Jacket identical, i.e. no printed price but not *Durasealed*. This jacket produced for the Readers Union but as an expediency used by Collins with their £4.50 sticker applied; o/p: 1980.

BCM1A Readers Union Edition, 1976 [1977]. Bound up from the same sheets as the 1976 Collins fifth ed. M1F, but cased in dark green imitation cloth (Type 1). Jacket without *Duraseal* and without a printed price, otherwise identical. Print run: 2,000 (this ed. also sold by Collins with their price sticker, as described above).

MISM1A Penguin Paperback Edition
Title: 'The Badger'. 1961 (Pelican Books, no. A410) Published by Penguin Books Ltd, Harmondsworth, Middlesex. Made and printed in Great Britain by Spottiswoode, Ballantyne & Co Ltd, London and Colchester. 'A-format' paperback (111 × 180 mm), stitched and glued; pp. 176; 8 leaves of b/w plates printed to both sides bound in a single central section (11 × 16-page gatherings). Typical cheap but elegant Penguin production; cover illustration by Paxton Chadwick; same suite of plates, but no colour and arranged differently. No printed: *c.* 24,000; Neal records that 23,147 copies were sold.

FORM1A German Edition, 1975. ISBN: 3405115086. Title: 'Der Dachs | Mit einer Ergänzung | »Der Dachs in Deutschland« | von Dr. Friedrich Goethe'. Translated from the English by Elisabeth Goethe. Published by BLV Verlagsgesellschaft München; printed in Germany. In the series 'BLV Wildbiologie'. Hardback without dust jacket; square 8vo, 150 × 200 mm; pp. 152, [1], [1]; 8 leaves of b/w plates, evenly distributed through the book. Adapted for the German market; all associations with the New Naturalist omitted as have Editors' and author's prefaces, instead a foreword to the German Translation by Friedrich Goethe. A new chapter 'Der Dachs in Deutschland | Eine Ergänzung,' (*The Badger in Germany | A Supplement*), also by Goethe, appended. Many of the b/w photographs new to this edition. Bound in laminated bright green boards printed in black and red; rear board carries the blurb. Print run: unknown, but a reasonably scarce book.

FORM1B Japanese Edition, 1974. アナグマの森 Translated by Syunji Shibanai (No. 6 in the Chronicles of the Animal World series). 'Rights arranged through Orion Press, Tokyo © Syunji Shibanai 1974, by Shisakusha Publishing Co.' Hardback with jacket, 137 × 197 mm; pp. (2), 241, (2); 2 leaves of b/w plates printed to both sides; photographs as Collins ed. but only using 6 out of the 30 original plates. All plates grouped together at the front. Title page printed in dark maroon. Bound in shiny orange imitation cloth with silver gilt lettering to the spine. Glossy, laminated jacket printed in orange, green and black on a white ground, supplied with a black and white printed wrap-around or Obi. Print run: unknown.

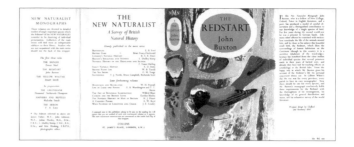

M2 The Redstart

Conceived in a German WWII POW camp and published in 1950, *The Redstart* was the first of the 11 ornithological titles in the monograph series, but it persisted for 23 years, finally going out of print in the autumn of 1973. Buxton was due to write another bird monograph for the series – *The Oystercatcher* – but in 1967 wrote in a letter to Collins '…Anyhow there is not much attraction in writing another book that might take 15 years to earn £200.'

Bibliographically, *The Redstart* is not particularly remarkable: just one Collins edition, but a Swedish edition (*Rödstjärten*), in both hardback and paperback formats, was published in 1953.

The Redstart is a thin book and looking at the Ellises' jacket, it is evident that they designed it for a somewhat thicker tome: the title lettering to the spine spills onto the boards as do the eyes of the redstart, peering from its hole, and the design extends well onto the front flap. To get an impression of this jacket, as intended by the artists, wrap it around a thicker monograph, and what is already recognized as a superb design, gets better still. *The Redstart* is not a particularly difficult book to find in fine or very good condition, though the jacket spine is apt to brown and fade.

M2A	**First Edition**, 1950 (10 March 1950).
Title:	'New Naturalist Monograph	The Redstart'.
Author:	'by John Buxton'.
Illust:	'With one Colour Photograph by Eric Hosking	19 Black-and-White Photographs	20 Maps and Diagrams	& 2 Text Figures'.
Editors:	JF, JG, JH, LDS and EH (Photographic Editor).
Printer:	In conjunction with Adprint; printed in Great Britain by Collins Clear-Type Press, London and Glasgow.
Collation:	pp. xii, 180; 1 colour plate leaf (frontispiece) printed to verso only; 8 leaves of b/w plates, printed to both sides (12 × 16-page gatherings).
Jacket:	[Rear panel] The New Naturalist with 9 titles listed under title 'Already published in the main series' followed by 7 titles listed under the heading 'some forthcoming volumes'. [Rear flap] New Naturalist Monographs announcing 'The first three titles' with three further titles listed under the heading 'in preparation' (see notes below).

Price: 12s.6d. net.
Print run: 6,000; no. sold: *c.* 4,700 + repriced variants below; o/p:
              autumn 1973 (AP2).
Notes: 1) 'Amphibia and Reptiles' is advertised on the DJ rear
              flap as a monograph in preparation, but was, of
              course, published in the main series in 1951 with the
              title *The British Amphibians and Reptiles* 2) The b/w
              plates are matt and feature photographs by Eric
              Hosking and John Markham with a single
              photograph by Robert M. Adam. The 3 plates of b/w
              drawings are by 'Fish Hawk' [David K. Wolfe Murray]
              and the in-text drawing (p. 135) of close species by
              D. M. Henry.

M2A-AP1 1st Repriced DJ (1967–70), 18/- sticker, *c.* 500 sold[?].
M2A-AP2 2nd Repriced DJ (1971–73), 90p sticker, *c.* 400 sold[?].

FORM2A Swedish Edition Hardback, 1953. Title: 'Rödstjärten | Nr
ett 1 Svensk Naturs Serie | Populära Djurmonographier' (*No. 1 in
the Swedish Nature popular monograph series*). Published by
Bökforlaget Svensk Natur; Stockholm, 1953. Printed in Sweden.
Hardback with jacket, 140 × 206 mm, i.e. almost identical to the
original Collins ed; pp. 157, [3]; 1 colour plate leaf (frontispiece)
printed to recto only; 8 leaves of b/w plates printed to both sides.
The colour frontispiece of a redstart (which is printed on thick
card and tipped-in) is by Harald Wiberg. The 3 plates of b/w
drawings by 'Fish Hawk' are retained, however only a few of Eric
Hosking's photographs have been used, all others substituted
with new photographs by E. K. Barth and G. Håkansson (redstarts)
and K. Curry-Lindahl (Swedish habitats & landscapes). Casing of
light green buckram with gilt-blocked redstart to the front board
and lettering to the spine. The colour printed jacket replicates the
frontispiece illustration on the front panel; the rear panel carries
the blurb, price and publisher's adverts; front and rear flaps are
blank. Not scarce.

FORM2B Swedish Edition Paperback, 1953. As FORM2A but in
paperback format, 144 × 214 mm. Note: The page edges are
untrimmed and therefore this paperback format is, unusually,
larger than the hardback. Without colour frontispiece plate. The
colour printed card covers replicate the front/rear panels and
spine of the jacket. Not scarce.

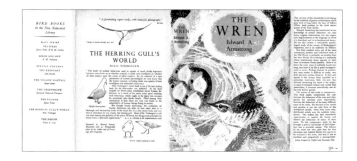

M3 The Wren

The Wren: rare and fabled, wrapped in a superb and quintessentially
Ellis jacket. And if you don't collect the monographs make this the
exception, because it is the same full height format as the main
series and will complement your collection. This book never fails to
excite me; it stirs up strong sentiments and reminds me of my
early, often unfulfilled, days of collecting, when I coveted my
neighbour's *Wren*. But now it emboldens me, and with a fine
jacketed copy in hand, I no longer fear the Kindle, the POD, and any
other, yet undefined, pretender that the future may throw up.

 The Wren was essentially subsidised by Collins: it made a loss,
and that after much wrangling to reduce costs (even the Editors
forfeited their fees). Billy Collins was unimpressed but this affair
is excellently explained by Peter Marren in *The New Naturalists*.
Most copies of *The Wren* were sold within the first two years of
release, thereafter they trickled out, on average, at 80 copies a year.
It was a comparatively expensive book, for a monograph, and
presumably at the time there was a very limited audience for such
a detailed ornithological study. Not surprisingly, therefore, it was
not reprinted and just one edition exists, but 250 copies were sold
to Macmillan and distributed in the US.

 It might appear a little odd that the rear dust jacket panel of M3
advertises M9, *The Herring Gull's World*, but this is because *The Wren*
was, in fact, published two years after *The Herring Gull* and
chronologically should be M13 (is this why the '3' is so diminutive
on the spine?). Perhaps a more noteworthy feature of *The Herring
Gull* advert is that it is enlivened with Tinbergen's idiosyncratic
line drawings of gulls. New Naturalist jackets are characterised by
restricting the graphic element to the front panel and spine, with
the rear panel given to text only, and in this respect *The Wren* is
almost exceptional – almost exceptional because, as it so happens,

TABLE M4 Diagnostic features of the two states of M4 *The Yellow Wagtail.*

Yellow Wagtail	'Collins' to the spine of the book	Buckram	Jacket (usually)
first state	smaller font 16 mm long	early type green buckram, often unevenly aded, weave open and irregular	'The New Naturalist' to the rear panel; priced at 12s.6d. net or repriced with 18p/- sticker
second state	larger font 18.5/19 mm long	later darker green buckram cloth, close weave, slightly shiny	advert for *The Badger* to the rear panel; priced at 90p. net or repriced with Collins sticker at £2.50

the rear panel of *The Herring Gull* carries an advert for *The Fulmar* also supported with a line drawing.

As already identified, *The Wren* is a rare book, particularly so in a fine jacket, which seems more prone to chipping than usual and is often toned, dust soiled and foxed. Expect to pay handsomely for a fine copy and do so willingly – in the knowledge that Billy Collins did so 55 years earlier.

M3A	**First Edition**, 1955 (28 March 1955).
Title:	'The New Naturalist	The Wren'.
Author:	'by Edward A. Armstrong'.
Illust:	'With 20 black and white photographs	41 drawings and diagrams'.
Editors:	JF, JG, JH, LDS and EH (Photographic Editor).
Printer:	Collins Clear-Type Press: London and Glasgow.
Collation:	pp. viii, 312; 8 leaves of b/w plates, printed to one side only (20 × 16-page gatherings).
Jacket:	[Rear panel] Advert for *The Herring Gull's World* supported by Tinbergen's line drawings. [Rear flap] 'Bird Books in the New Naturalist Library' listing *Sea Birds, Birds and Men, The Redstart, The Yellow Wagtail, The Greenshank, The Fulmar, The Herring Gull's World* and *The Heron*.
Price:	30s. net.
Print run:	2,975 (out-turn) inc. 250 copies to the States (USM3A); no. sold: *c*. 2,450; o/p: spring 1964.

USM3A US Edition, 1955. Exactly as M3A but with a 'Distributed by Macmillan' label to the jacket. (The only copy I have seen was not price clipped, still showing the UK price of 30s.net, with no evidence of there having been a US $ price label or sticker.) Print run: 250 (order).

M4 The Yellow Wagtail

The final draft of *The Yellow Wagtail* was ready by June 1947, but it was a further three years before it was published. The reason for the delay is unrecorded but it was probably because Fisher, the book's editor, was unhappy with aspects of the text. Clearly, as revealed by its chronological inaccuracies, the jacket was also completed well before the book was published: the blurb to the front flap states 'this book, the first New Naturalist Monograph

on a species of bird...' and the rear flap advertises *The Yellow Wagtail* as 'Already Published', yet *The Redstart* and *The Wren* are 'In Preparation'. In the event, the latter two titles were published ahead of *The Yellow Wagtail*. *Parasites of Birds* is also advertised which, of course, was published in 1952 as *Fleas, Flukes and Cuckoos*.

The Yellow Wagtail, despite being a monograph dedicated to one of Britain's most colourful birds and supported with fine colour illustrations by Edward Bradbury, albeit in a somewhat anachronistic style, did not sell well. Once the initial burst of subscription sales was over, the book trickled out at a few hundred copies a year. Ten years on, the total number of copies sold was a little over 4,000 and, the Collins archive records that, in late October 1962 the decision was taken to pulp 1,000 quires. At that stage there were 800 bound copies and 2,300 quires left.

Later, probably around or a little after decimalisation, the remaining quires were bound up giving rise to a 'second binding variant', most copies of which, wear a revised jacket with a printed decimal price of '90p. net'. Referred to collectively as the second state, these later bindings are easy enough to tell apart as identified in table M3; the surest way is to look at 'Collins' at the base of the spine: the font of the second variant is significantly larger.

The Yellow Wagtail remained in print for over quarter of a century, uninterrupted, with essentially just one price increase. There are no reprints, paperback or foreign editions.

The Yellow Wagtail is not a rare book, in fact one of the most readily available and cheapest of the monographs, but it is not easy to find in fine condition, particularly with the first edition jacket. While the yellow pigment is comparatively colour fast, the paper is apt to tone, with subsequent loss of definition to the yellow areas. Being a particularly thin book, the jackets are often off centre on the spine. Predictably, second binding variants and their jackets are easier to find in fine condition.

M4A	**First Edition, First State**, 1950 (20 February 1950).
Title:	'New Naturalist Monograph	The Yellow Wagtail'.
Author:	'by	Stuart Smith	BSc., Ph.D.'.
Illust:	'With 26 paintings by Edward Bradbury	11 black and white photographs	taken by the author	4 line drawings and 4 maps'.
Editors:	JF, JG, JH, LDS and EH (Photographic Editor).
Printer:	Collins Clear-Type Press: London and Glasgow (produced in conjunction with Adprint).
Collation:	pp. xiv, 178; 4 leaves of colour plates printed to both sides; 2 leaves of b/w plates, printed to both sides (12 × 16-page gatherings).
Binding:	Early type green buckram, often unevenly faded, weave open and irregular; 'Collins' on spine 16 mm long.
Jacket:	[Rear panel] The NN library listing the first 14 titles in the main series; publication info, and mailing list. [Rear flap] 'New Naturalist Monographs' with *The Badger* and *The Yellow Wagtail* listed under heading 'Already Published'; with *The Redstart, The Wren, The*

Greenshank and *Parasites of Birds* listed under heading 'In Preparation'; Editors named below.

Price: 12s. 6d. net.
Print run: 8,000 but 1,000 quires pulped in 1962; no. sold: *c.* 5,000[?].
Notes: 1) Photographs by the author. 2) I have seen one example of the smaller font 'Collins' on a later closer weave buckram, but this appears atypical.

M4A-AP1 1st Repriced DJ (1968–70[?]), 18/- sticker, *c.* 280 sold[?].

M4B First Edition, Second State Dated 1950 (sold 1971?– 75). Bound up, probably around 1971, from the same sheets as M4A therefore identical, however the casing is subtly different as identified in table M4: Rear panel of the jacket advertises *The Badger*; rear flap advertises *Oysters* and *The Open Sea* (both parts); front flap unaltered. Price: 90p.net (the flaps are not as wide as the first ed. jacket). Print run: inc. in M4A; no. sold: *c.* 900[?] + repriced variant below; o/p: summer 1975 (AP1). Note: Occasionally this second binding variant is found in a first state jacket, but these might be later marriages.

M4B-AP1 1st Repriced DJ (1975), £2.50 sticker, *c.* 50 sold[?].

M5 The Greenshank

'It is anticipated that the publication of *The Greenshank* will cause a considerable stir in ornithological circles', so concluded the blurb to the dust jacket. It was certainly well reviewed (see adverts bound in to the rear of *The Hawfinch*) and probably sold well at first but for the last ten years of its shelf-life it averaged sales of only 90 copies a year. Such emaciated sales are difficult to perceive in today's world, as is the fact that *The Greenshank* remained in print for 15 years without a price increase – the real cost of the book at the end of this period was about half that at the beginning! It is a very readable, very 'personable' book, so it is perhaps surprising that it did not sell better. There is just one edition; all books apparently of the same binding and all in the same jacket. Nethersole-Thompson did write an updated version, published by A. D. Poyser in 1979 simply titled *Greenshanks* with 275 pages, four colour plates and numerous b/w illustrations.

The Greenshank is often found in very good condition though the white areas on the jacket spine are prone to tanning, but clean copies are still reasonably plentiful.

M5A **First Edition**, 1951 (15 November 1951).
Title: 'The New Naturalist | The Greenshank'.
Author: 'by | Desmond | Nethersole-Thompson'.
Illust: 'With 4 colour photographs | by John Markham and F. C. Pickering |42 black and white photographs |and 12 maps and diagrams'.
Editors: JF, JG, JH, LDS and EH (Photographic Editor).
Printer: Collins Clear-Type Press: London and Glasgow.
Collation: pp. xii, 244; 4 leaves of colour plates printed to one side only; 12 leaves of b/w plates, printed to both sides (16 × 16-page gatherings).
Jacket: [Rear panel] The New Naturalist library listing 18 main series and three monograph titles. [Rear flap] Adverts for *The Redstart*, *The Yellow Wagtail* and *Birds and Men*.
Price: 15s. net.
Print run: 4,000; no. sold: *c.* 3,690; o/p: summer 1966.

M6 The Fulmar

A classic of the ornithological literature and a monumental achievement: as the jacket blurb states '…probably the most complete study of an important species of wild bird yet undertaken.' So much so that it required over 500 pages and was published in the larger format of the main series – even then Fisher was required to omit its 2,378 supporting references! In fact it remained the longest New Naturalist until the publication of *Bumblebees* in 2006. But from a commercial perspective it was a flop: a note in the Collins file states that it needed to sell 5,000–6,000 copies to be profitable and in the event less than 2,600 copies were sold (at the original published price of 35/-, soon to rise to 42/-, it was an expensive book and was unlikely to sell in large numbers). It is interesting to note that Collins paid an author's fee of £700, i.e. the equivalent of £17,500 in today's money.

The Fulmar's reputation as an outstanding work probably helped to exaggerate its purported scarcity to the extent that copies were being sold for hundreds of pounds in the early 1980s. The internet has now shown that it is not quite as rare as legend suggested, but it will always remain in the upper tiers of most bookseller's offerings. Collins, in response to this rarity and

Frontispiece for *The Fulmar* by Sir Peter Scott.

so, but very occasionally books turn up that are still bright. Have you considered having your copy washed by a paper conservator?

M6A   **First Edition**, 1952 (15 September 1952).
Title: 'The New Naturalist | The Fulmar'.
Author: 'by | James Fisher'.
Illust: 'With a painting by Peter Scott | 4 colour photographs | 78 black and white photographs |and 70 maps, diagrams and line drawings'.
Editors: JF, JG, JH, LDS and EH (Photographic Editor).
Printer: Love and Malcomson, London and Redhill.
Collation: pp. xv, [1], 496; 4 leaves of colour plates printed to one side only; 24 leaves of b/w plates, printed to both sides (32 × 16-page gatherings).
Dust jacket: [Rear panel] advertisement for *The Greenshank*; under the heading 'Other New Naturalist Special Volumes' are listed *Fleas, Flukes and Cuckoos*, *The Redstart*, *The Yellow Wagtail* and *The Badger*. [Rear flap] advertisements for *Birds and Men* and *A Country Parish*. Followed by 'Some forthcoming books' under which are listed *Sea Birds* in the 'Main Series' and *The Herring Gull's World* and *The Wren* under 'Special Volumes'.
Price: 35s. net.
Print run: 3,000; no. sold: *c.* 2,570 including repriced variant below.

M6A-AP1 First Revised Price (1956–58). 42s. net label pasted over the original printed price – presumably this was towards the end of the in-print period.

CPBM6A Collins Paperback Reprint, 1984 (18/06/1984). ISBN: 0002190656; pp. [xvi], 496, [10-blanks] [54-b/w illustrations] (36 × 16-page gatherings). A b/w facsimile, but with a new preface and list of corrections to the text; last sentence of NNM credo omitted. Price: £7.50. Print run: *c.* 1,600[?]; no. sold: *c.* 1,200; o/p: 1989. Notes: 1) The contents pages are a muddle referring to preliminaries that no longer exist and the list of plates stops at plt. VII, missing off the last 3 pages of plates – yet there are 10 blank pages at the rear. 2) The Ellises' cover design has distinctly different tones and textures to the original dust jacket; it is a little stained and appears to have been copied from the (soiled) original artwork, the title crudely reset so that it no longer fits within the oval.

USM6A US First Edition, 1958. Identical with M6A but with a stamp to the title page 'Distributed in the U.S.A. by | John de Graff, Inc. | 31 East 10th Street | New York 3, N.Y.'. Just 200 copies were supplied to John de Graff.

demand, printed a 'limpback form' in 1984, which enjoyed a new preface by Dr William Bourne (who was paid £50 worth in books for his troubles) and a useful list of corrections by James Fisher. This limpback edition is otherwise greatly inferior without any colour plates; moreover the photographs are in many cases so dark and muddy that they are 'illegible'. While Collins deliberately used an inferior process of manufacture to achieve an economic price, it does rankle somewhat to see Fisher's painstaking work treated so shoddily. But it remains the only monograph to have been also published by Collins in paperback format and is the most affordable text of *The Fulmar*, albeit an elusive one.

The hardback edition has a fine colour 'frontispiece' plate by Peter Scott, but strangely it has been sandwiched between the author's preface and the beginning of the text; how much better it would have been to have had it in the customary place opposite the title page. The white areas on the dust jacket spine are particularly prone to tanning and the vast majority of copies are

M7 Fleas, Flukes and Cuckoos

'The story behind the publication of *Fleas, Flukes and Cuckoos* was disgraceful! I wrote it to order of the committee selected by Collins but on completion Collins refused to publish it! Julian Huxley, chairman of the committee, said they would resign if he [Billy Collins] did not do so but I had to pay for the illustrations and finally had to the pay for printing too. Collins said it would not sell – but it went into 5 editions! (The Collins concerned has long since died).' So wrote Miriam Rothschild in a letter to Dave Hutchinson over 50 years later. This debacle is further chronicled in *The New Naturalists* (pp. 187–188).

Fleas, Flukes and Cuckoos is the first of the three 'special volumes' and is the larger main series format; regrettably it is clothed in a plain non-Ellis jacket – we can only imagine what the Ellises might of made of such rich subject matter: a cuckoo was discussed. But what it lacks in a jacket, *Fleas* more than compensates for in content: it is erudite and witty, not at all dry or overly academic. Another classic, and following rave reviews it sold well; in fact the first edition purportedly sold out within two weeks; vindication indeed for Miriam Rothschild! Two Collins reprints, a Readers Union edition, two US hardback editions and a paperback by Arrow Books followed. (*The New Naturalists* also refers to a paperback edition published by Pelican, but the British Library does not hold a copy nor does any other Copac library and therefore one must conclude that it probably does not exist. Presumably Collins were in negotiation with Pelican or Penguin at some stage, which led to the supposition that it was actually published, but the minutes of the Editorial Board meeting of 5 June 1956 state 'the author…was not interested in a Penguin Edition'.)

The first edition is a scarce book; only 2,000 copies were printed: the smallest first edition print-run of any monograph. Presumably, many of these are now either lost or no longer in 'collectable condition' so clearly there cannot be nearly enough copies to satiate all collectors. But such are the vagaries of collecting the New Naturalist series that a very good copy of *Fleas* will cost only half that of a similar copy of say *Mumps*, *The Wren* or *The Hawfinch*.

The first edition jacket is particularly prone to foxing or browning and the crimson of the title roundel fades to pink – much more so than the reprint of the same year and fresh copies are scarce. The jacket of the first reprint is identical to that of the first edition but for one subtle difference: the lettering to the rear panel and flaps is printed in the same grey-green colour as the front panel and spine, whereas that of the first edition is printed in black: be warned – it is not unknown for them to be find their way onto the wrong book!

The available sales data for this period is sketchy and not always consistent, but from 1957 to 1960 the total number printed is repeatedly given as '2k + 2k + 2k + 2k', and as there were only three Collins printings one assumes the other set of 2k refers to the RU printing.

M7A	**First Edition**, 1952 (05 May 1952).
Title:	'The New Naturalist | Fleas, Flukes & | Cuckoos | A Study of Bird Parasites'.
Authors:	'by | Miriam Rothschild | and | Theresa Clay'.
Illust:	'With 99 Black and White Photographs | 4 Maps & 22 Drawings'.
Editors:	JF, JG, JH, LDS and EH (Photographic Editor).
Printer:	Willmer Brother & Co. Ltd. Birkenhead (produced in conjunction with Adprint).
Collation:	pp. xiv, 304, [2]; 20 leaves of b/w plates printed to both sides (20 × 16-page gatherings).
Jacket:	[Rear panel] NN library listing NN1–23 inclusively; *Manchester Guardian* quote. [Rear flap] 'The New Naturalist Special Volumes' listing *The Badger, The Redstart, The Wren, The Yellow Wagtail, The Greenshank* and *The Fulmar;* Further information request; below which advertised: *The Redstart, The Yellow Wagtail* and *Insect Natural History*.
Price:	21s net.
Print run:	2,000; o/p: 1952 (allegedly 2 weeks after publication).
Notes:	1) Text to the jacket printed in black. 2) Fine b/w line illustrations by Arthur Smith, whose work also appeared in NN38 *World of Spiders*. 3) The photograph on plate XL of birds crowding the sea-shore quickly became a classic – especially taken for this book by Eric Hosking. 4) Adverts to pages [305–306] for: 'The New Naturalist' listing 19 titles 'Already published in the Main Series' and 4 'Special Volumes'; then: request for information on further titles; overleaf: advert for *The Greenshank* supported with 5 press commendations.

M7B First Reprint, 1952. 'First published in 1952 by… \| Reprinted 1952'; no date to TP. As M7A. Jacket graphically and textually identical too, but text now printed in the same grey-green as the front panel and spine; price remains at 21s. net. Print run: 2,000. Note: A few copies have first ed. jackets, suggesting a few jackets were left over from the first printing.

M7C Second Reprint (Third Edition), 1957. 'First published in 1952 by… \| Reprinted 1957'; pp. xiv, 305, [1 blank]. A slightly updated edition as described in 'Additions to The Third Edition' on pp. xiii/xiv. These additions incorporated without any significant resetting of text: last paragraph of Editors' preface omitted; adverts also omitted; pagination slightly revised: Text to jacket reverts to black type for rear panel and flaps; rear panel features: 'Some Press Comments on *Fleas, Flukes and Cuckoos*' with 8 separate review endorsements; rear flap unrevised and a press clip from *Lilliput* inserted on front flap. Price: 25s. net. Print run: *c.* 2,000; o/p: 1964. Notes: 1) Despite the title to p. xiii, this is strictly speaking the second edition. 2) *Fleas* was out of stock for a year, or so, prior to publication of this edition.

BCM7A Readers Union Edition, 1953. The title page, dated 1953, carries the RU imprint and tree logo, otherwise textually as the Collins ed. M7B, with the same suite of plates. The paper is slightly different and not quite as smooth, which suggests that this RU edition was a separate printing and not a run-on of the M7B printing. The casing is of the same green buckram with gilt titling, but blocked with the RU tree monogram. RU jacket Type 1. Price: 10s. 6d net. Print run: 2,000[?]. Note: This RU edition is half the price of the Collins first edition – and without any appreciable diminution of quality, barring the jacket, which due to the poor, very thin paper, is usually missing or, at best, in poor condition.

MISM7A Paperback Edition, 1961. Published by Arrow Books Ltd., London; pp. 304; b/w plates and illustrations. In the 'Grey Arrow Series'. No printed: unknown. Note: The authors were not consulted over this edition and their permission not sought. Neither were they given an opportunity to correct proofs and the book is allegedly full of misprints. Rothschild writing of this later described it as an atrocious paperback and added, 'I would have sued the publisher if I had had the time'. Fortunately, perhaps, it is a scarce book.

USM7A US First Edition, 1952. Philosophical Library, Inc. New York. Published concurrently with the first UK ed. and bound up from the same sheets; but with cancel title and half-title leaves. The setting of these pages ostensibly the same but all references to the New Naturalist, including NN credo, omitted; Philosophical Library imprint and logo appear on the title page; the last two pages of adverts excised. Casing of same green buckram with gilt titling, but blocked with the imprint 'Philosophical Library'. Likewise, jacket from the same printing as M7A (lettering printed in black) but over-stamped 'Philosophical Library' above, and not obliterating, 'Collins' to the spine. Print run: 250[?]. Note: Being for the North American market, the jacket would have been price-clipped, with a replacement US $ label adjacent. The Philosophical Library also distributed this book in the UK, price-clipped with a 21S. net label adjacent. A scarce edition, particularly in the original jacket.

USM7B US Second Edition, 1957. The Macmillan Company, New York. Bound up from the same sheets as the 1957 UK edition M7C, but with integral title and half-title leaves (i.e. not cancels), the former displaying the Macmillan imprint and dated 1957. The NN credo omitted but other references to the New Naturalist retained;

typesetting ostensibly as M7C. Imprint page exactly as the Collins 1952 first edition and presumably printed from the same block. Casing of identical green buckram and gilt titling, but blocked with the imprint 'Macmillan' to the spine. Jacket design as Collins ed. but significantly modified: 'Macmillan' overstamped to spine and 'Collins' obliterated in maroon ink to match jacket design; rear panel and flap blank; blurb to front flap unchanged, but without the Lilliput commendation, no printed sterling price, but $5.00 printed to top corner; print run: 250[?]. (A scarce edition, particularly in the original jacket.)

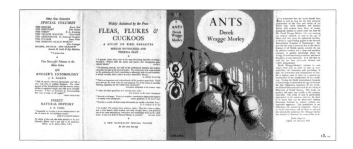

M8 Ants

Ants is an infamous book, mainly on account of a few poor reviews, and it has even been suggested that it was withdrawn and pulped. But it is not a particularly rare book, and therefore that seems unlikely, at least, in any meaningful quantity. Moreover, the review in the *Entomologist's Monthly Magazine*, that did all the damage, did not appear until a good six months after publication – and it is unlikely that many of the buying public read that esoteric publication anyway. The truth is much more prosaic: *Ants* was under-printed and sold well, so well in fact that it was out of print by the end of 1953. But by this time the Editors and Collins had lost faith in it and in Wragge Morley and chose not to reprint. Wragge Morley was somewhat of a maverick and, no doubt, ruffled a few professional feathers: a spat broke out between him and the *British Medical Journal* in 1950, over an alleged secret remedy for cancer, which itself became the subject of a BBC Radio 4 play called 'Taming the Wart' and was broadcast in February 2000. Fascinating, black and white British Pathe footage of Mr. Morley (with his ubiquitous pipe) and a maze of ants has survived and can be viewed online (British Pathe historical archive 24/04. 1950 Film ID. 1277.11).

Returning to the book, *Ants* was the first monograph to be written, starting in 1945 as an independent publication, that is, independent of the New Naturalist Series. D. W. M.'s preface is dated 14 July 1952 and the official publication date was 22 May 1953, but copies do exist with dated inscriptions that predate May 1953.

Ants is often found in reasonably good condition, though the jacket is prone to chipping and tanning.

M8A   **First Edition**, 1953 (22 May 1953).
Title: 'The New Naturalist | Ants'.
Author: 'by Derek | Wragge Morley | M.A., F.L.S.'.
Illust: 'With 27 Photographs by | Raymond Kleboe, Ronald
             Startup | and others, 50 Drawings and Maps, and | a
             Key for the Identification of | British Ants drawn by |
             Alison Birch'.
Editors: JF, JG, JH, LDS and EH (Photographic Editor).
Printer: Collins Clear-Type Press: London and Glasgow.
Collation: pp. xii, 179, [1]; b/w frontispiece plate printed to the
             verso only; 7 leaves of b/w plates printed to both sides
             (12 × 16-page gatherings).
Jacket: [Rear panel] Advert for *Fleas, Flukes & Cuckoos* with 7
             press endorsements. [Rear flap] 'Other New Naturalist
             Special Volumes' listing 8 titles; adverts for *An Angler's
             Entomology* and *Insect Natural History*.
Price: 18s. net.
Print run: 3,900 (out-turn); no. sold: *c.* 3,660; o/p: 1953.

M9 The Herring Gull's World

'One of the most brilliant volumes in the whole *New Naturalist*
series' so opened the jacket blurb on the 1971 reprint. Forty years
later it is possible to make claims for *The Herring Gull's World* even
bolder and say that it is the most internationally influential of all
New Naturalist texts: it has been translated into French, German,
Japanese, Lithuanian, Russian, Swedish, and probably other
languages, too (Marren mentions an Italian translation but this
remains unverified). It has been published in the US under
a variety of American imprints, but surprisingly it was not
published in paperback format by Collins and neither by any of
the bookclubs. *The Herring Gull* set a new standard in bird
behavioural books and was 'ahead of its time' (see Marren's
account in *The New Naturalists*) and remains prescribed reading
on various university courses.

Unsurprisingly, with so many editions the bibliography of *The
Herring Gull* is complicated – and not entirely resolved! But this
plethora of editions has led to a number of interesting aberrations,
for instance the designers of the Swedish book were clearly not
ornithologists as they inserted Talbot Kelly's line drawing of a
Fulmar onto the title page and rear cover! (This drawing appeared
as an advert for *The Fulmar* on the jacket of the Collins 1st ed.). And
the Ellises' artwork was carefully, but inexpertly, redesigned for the
1967 US p/b edition, resulting in a single, somewhat stubby-billed
herring gull, and with the design continuing onto the rear cover;
even the Ellises' monogram has been forged!

There are some rarities amongst these books – it would appear
that only *c.* 500 copies of the Collins 1963 reprint were published
and this printing is virtually unobtainable, perhaps the rarest of
all Collins editions. The non-English editions in all their guises,
are likewise almost impossible to find – assuming, of course, you
want them.

The blurb to the 1961 US edition (M9US2) commenced,
prophetically: 'If a Nobel prize were awarded for work in the
science of behavior, Niko Tinbergen would certainly be one of
the leading candidates'. As it was, the Nobel price for Physiology
was awarded in 1973 to Tinbergen and his fellow ethologists, Karl
von Frisch and Konrad Lorenz, and it was the last who fittingly
wrote the foreword to the *The Herring Gull*. Undoubtedly the
status of *The Herring Gull* soared on the making of the award, and
a band advertising the Nobel prize was wrapped around the
jacket of the 1971 reprint, but Lorenz's foreword, to the great
annoyance of some commentators, was omitted from the 1976
fifth reprint, M9F.

The 1971 and 1976 reprints accidentally omitted the 1965 reprint
from the 'printing history' given on the imprint page; consequently
when the new foreword was written for the 1976 reprint (usurping
Lorenz's foreword) it was erroneously titled 'Foreword to the Fifth
Impression' when it was, the sixth impression.

Like a number of other NN authors, Tinbergen wrote a few
children's books, including a delightful tale of a herring gull
called 'Kleew' written in Tinbergen's inimitable style: 'When the
beast left at last it left a very curious thing behind. It was a tent
– Mr. Tinbergen's tent, for that was the monster's name.' It was
first published by Oxford University Press, New York, in 1947, and
while a children's book, it is a precursor to *The Herring Gull* and is
embellished with dozens of Tinbergen's idiosyncratic but
charming line drawings, some of which were borrowed for *The
Herring Gull*, e.g. Fig. 1 on p. 29 and Fig. 3 on p. 46. If you have
children or grandchildren, it is well worth seeking out a copy;
in fact, seek out a copy even if you don't! *Kleew* was subsequently
published, in 1991 in the US, by Lyons & Burford, and then
published in Spanish by Plural in 1992 with the title *Kleew,
Historia de una Gaviota*.

Fine copies of *The Herring Gull's World* are not particularly
difficult to find, but the jackets of early editions are often tanned
on the spine. Total print run: *c.* 11,750; total no. sold: *c.* 10,900; o/p:
end 1980 (Collins editions only).

M9A   **First Edition**, 1953 (28 September 1953).
Title: 'The New Naturalist | The Herring Gull's World |
             A Study of the | Social Behaviour of Birds'.
Author: 'by Niko Tinbergen'.
Illust: 'Illustrated with | 51 Photographs taken by the Author
             | 58 Drawings and Diagrams'.

Editors: JF, JG, JH, LDS and EH (Photographic Editor).
Printer: Collins Clear-Type Press: London and Glasgow.
Collation: pp. xvi, 255, [1]; b/w frontispiece leaf printed to the verso only; 15 leaves of b/w plates, printed to both sides (17 × 16-page gatherings).
Jacket: [Rear panel] Advert for *The Fulmar;* b/w line drawing of a Fulmar by Talbot-Kelly. [Rear flap] Advert for 'Special Volumes in the New Naturalist Library', with 11 titles listed including *The Wren.* A footnote for this latter title states 'For 1953 Publication' (though in fact it did not appear until 1955).
Price: 18s.net.
Print run: 5,000; no. sold: *c.* 4,900 (inc. 400 copies supplied to the US); o/p: by summer 1959.
Notes: 1) 'Collins' to the base of the jacket spine is printed in a serrifed font. 2) All line drawings uncredited, but by the author. 3) The 'List of Plates' is unusually positioned at the rear and not at the front as part of the contents. 4) The last page [256] advertises 'Bird Books in the New Naturalist Library' listing 9 titles.

M9B First Reprint, 1960 (early 1961). 'First published 1953 | Reprinted 1960'. Date omitted from title page. As M9A. Adverts omitted from p. [256] (presumably to be compatible with the parallel 1961 US edition M9US2). Jacket rear panel advertises *The Herring Gull's World* with four press clips from *Birmingham Post; Star, Manchester Guardian* and *The Field;* rear flap lists New Naturalist Special Volumes M2 to M18 omitting M6, M8, M10 and M14; front flap unaltered. Price: 21s. net. Font for 'Collins' to the base of the jacket spine as M9A. Print run: 1,250[?]; a scarce edition.

M9C Second Reprint, 1963. 'First published 1953 | Reprinted 1960 | Reprinted 1963' Identical to M9B. Jacket not inspected but, presumably, either identical to M9B or intermediate between M9B and M9D. Price probably 21s. net. Print run: 500. A very scarce printing; perhaps the scarcest of all Collins NN printings; seemingly printed as a 'run-on' to a US order, but no evidence for a 1963 US ed. has come to light.

M9D Third Reprint, 1965. 'First published 1953 | Reprinted 1960 | Reprinted 1963 | Reprinted 1965'. As M9B, barring changes to Editors' titles and post nominals. 'Collins' to the base of jacket spine, now printed in a plain, large, bold typeface; rear panel as M9B; rear flap lists 'Special Volumes' M2 to M21 omitting M6, M8, M10 and M14; front flap unaltered. Price: 25s. net. Print run: 1,250.

M9E Fourth Reprint, 1971. ISBN: 0002130912 (to jacket only). 'First published 1953 | Reprinted 1960 | Reprinted 1963 | Reprinted 1971' (Note: the 1965 reprint is missing). As M9D. Editors: JG, JH, MD, KM and EH. Jacket rear panel advertises 'New Naturalist Monographs' under which are listed 9 titles; rear flap cites six press reviews for *The Herring Gull*, with the jacket design credit and ISBN below; blurb to the front flap has been rewritten and précised with 3 press reviews inserted – *Birmingham Post, Shooting*

Times and *The Listener.* Price: £1.80 net. Print run: 2,000[?]; o/p: end 1974. (A red band or obi advertising the Nobel Prize was wrapped around the jacket of copies sold after the award was made in 1973.)

M9F Fifth Reprint, 1976. ISBN changed to: 0002194449 (now to both imprint p. and jacket). 'First published 1953 | Reprinted 1960 | Reprinted 1963 | Reprinted 1971 | Reprinted 1976' (the 1965 reprint is still omitted). As M9E with a few revisions, the most significant of which is the new 'Foreword to the Fifth Impression', which replaces the Editors' preface and the foreword by Konrad Lorenz. Editors: MD, JG, KM and EH. Printed on whiter, slightly textured paper. Rear panel of the *Durasealed* jacket lists only five titles under the heading 'New Naturalist Monographs'; rear flap unchanged, but for new ISBN; front flap unaltered. Price: £4.50 NET, printed diagonally. Print run: 1,500; no. sold: *c.* 1.350; o/p: end 1980.

USM9A US First Edition, 1953. Frederick A. Praeger, Inc. New York. Not seen. Collins sales statements record that 400 copies of the first edition of 1953 were sold to the US under this imprint and were marketed at $4.00, but how this differs, if at all, from the Collins first edition is unknown. Internet searches reveal a number of reviews of this title published by the Praeger imprint.

USM9B US Second Edition, 1961. Basic Books, Inc. Publishers, New York. From the same printing as the Collins 1960 reprint M9B but copyright, to the imprint page, as the '1960 Revised Edition'. Textually identical to M9B, but the integral (i.e. not a cancel) title/imprint leaf reset to reflect the American publisher, the NMN monogram is dropped from the TP and 'The New Naturalist' omitted from the half-title as are the Editors and NN credo from the verso of the same. Paper as Collins ed. and book and jacket both state printed in Great Britain, though the binding of quarter white cloth with blue paper-covered boards, blocked in black, looks distinctly American and probably manufactured there. The jacket displays the same Ellis artwork and title lettering as the Collins ed., including the NMN monogram and series no., but 'Basic | Books' has been overprinted to the base of the spine; rear panel advertises *Curious Naturalists*, rear flap carries the author's biography; blurb to the front flap rewritten and prophetic. Price: $5.00 printed to top corner. Not a scarce book.

USM9C US Third Edition, 1967. Anchor Books, Doubleday & Company, Inc. Garden City, New York. Paperback, perfect binding, 'A-format' 106 × 182 mm; pp. xxi, [1], 297; 16 leaves of b/w plates printed to both sides. A reset and reduced edition (inc. in-text illustrations) of the 1960 ed. M9B; plates also reset from the original photographs, which remain the same but many have been cropped differently e.g. plt. 15a; the frontispiece has been added to the first group of plates and plt.17a has been reversed. Colour printed card covers after the Ellises' design but completely redrawn including the rear panel to style. Price $1.75 and Anchor book no. A567 are printed to the front cover. A common book.

USM9D US Fourth Edition, 1971. ISBN: 06131594x. Harper Torchbooks, Harper & Row, Publishers New York. Paperback, perfect binding 135 × 203 mm, i.e. same format as original. A photo-lithographic[?] copy of the 1961 Basic Books ed. (USM9B). 'This book was originally published by Basic Books, Inc. and is here reprinted by arrangement…Printed in the United States of America'. The plates are reproduced on the same paper as the 'letterpress' and part of that printing; consequently of poor quality. Card covers, printed in blue and black, designed by Catherine Hopkins. (the English spelling of behaviour has been retained on the TP but spelt 'behavior' on the front cover). A common book.

USM9D-B1 Exactly as above but with the price $2.95 added to the front cover after the book number.

USM9E US Fifth Edition, 1989. ISBN: 1558210490. Lyons & Burford, New York. Paperback, perfect binding 136 × 198 mm i.e. same format as original. A copy of the 1961 Basic Books ed. (USM9B); pp. 255, [1]. The plates are reproduced on the same paper as the 'letterpress' and integral to that printing – and of poor quality. Card covers carry the same Ellises' design though spine area overprinted to dissociate it from the NN brand, a red strapline has been added to the lower edge of the front cover 'The classic field study by a Nobel-prizewinning naturalist' (sic).

FORM9A Swedish Edition, 1956. Title: 'Gråtruten | En Studie Över Fåglarnas Sociala Beteende'. Published by Svensk Natur; Stockholm 1956. Printed in Sweden. Paperback, perfect binding 140 × 210 mm, i.e. slightly larger format than original Collins ed., but plates and in-text illustrations reproduced at the same size; pp. 323, [1]; arrangement of plates as Collins ed. Colour-printed card covers replicate the Ellises' artwork, but lettering ovals redrawn to accommodate the Swedish titles. The rear cover carries an advert for *Gråtruten* erroneously supported by Talbot Kelly's line drawing of a Fulmar also reproduced on the title page. A scarce edition.

FORM9B German Edition, 1958. Title: 'Die Welt der Silbermöwe | Eine Untersuchung | des Sozialverhaltens von Vögeln'. Published by Musterschmidt-Verlag; Gottingen, Berlin and Frankfurt. Printed in Germany. Hardback with dust jacket; 140 × 205 mm, i.e. same format as Collins original; pp. 279; frontispiece and 15 leaves of b/w plates, arranged exactly as Collins ed. All associations with the New Naturalist omitted including Editors' preface; in its place is a new and much longer foreword by Konrad Lorenz 'signed' 'Seewiesen, Dezember 1956'. Bound in pale blue buckram, blocked in black with gilt lettering to the spine. Jacket printed in blue and black on cream paper, the designer uncredited but effective and not unlike some of the Ellises' work; rear panel is blank. both the very narrow flaps are used for the book's blurb. A rare book.

FORM9C Russian Edition, 1974. ISBN: XXX. Title: '   '. Translated from the English by I. G. Gurov from the 1971 Harper Torchbooks ed. (M9US4); edited and foreword by K. N. Blagosklonova. Published by Mir, Moscow 1974. Paperback size mm; pp. 272; frontispiece and 15 leaves of b/w plates, arranged exactly as Collins ed. Card covers printed in black and white. Scarce.

FORM9D French Edition, 1975. ISBN: 2800300922. Title: 'L'univers du | goéland | argenté'. Published by Elsevier Séquoia, Paris, Bruxelles. 'Imprimé en France'. Based on the 1971 Collins edition. Perfect bound paperback, 147 × 210 mm, i.e. slightly larger than the Collins original; pp. 223, [1]; 15 leaves of b/w plates printed to both sides. Frontispiece and plate 30b omitted, plate 17a reversed, otherwise very close to Collins ed., all association with the NN series omitted. Bound, appropriately, in silver card covers with white and black lettering, the rear cover carries a photograph of Tinbergen (the same photo appeared in *The New Naturalists*, 20 years later). Not scarce.

FORM9E Japanese Edition, 1975. Title: 'セグロカモメの世界'. Translated by Naoya Abe and Takashi Saito (no. 11 in the Chronicles of the Animal World series edited by Kinji Imanishi). 'Rights arranged through Orion Press, Tokyo © Naoya Abe & Takashi Saito, 1975 by Shisakusha Publishing Co.' Hardback with dust jacket 140 × 197 mm; pp. [2], 391, [5]; 12 leaves of b/w plates printed to both sides; photographs as Collins ed. but some omitted and others reduced in size, all grouped together at the front. Title page printed in red; book, of course, reads right to left. Bound in shinny orange imitation cloth with silver gilt letter to the spine. Glossy, laminated jacket printed in orange, blue and black on a white ground, supplied with a brown printed wrap-around band or Obi.

FORM9F Lithuanian Edition, 1978. Title: 'Sidabrinio | Kiro | Pasaulis'. Tinbergen spelt 'Tinbergenas' Published by Mokslas, Vilnius. Translated from the Russian edition. Hardback; paper-covered boards, printed in blue and black, no dust jacket, 135 × 173 mm, i.e. significantly smaller than the Collins original; pp. 210, [2]; 19 b/w illustrations on 8 leaves; photographs as Collins ed. but some omitted and others cropped, all grouped together at the rear. A utilitarian production with the plates poorly reproduced.

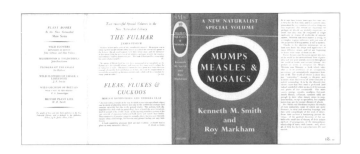

M10 Mumps, Measles & Mosaics

This, the second of the special volumes (see entry under *Fleas*), began life with the working title 'Viruses', but this was usurped by the more seductive *Mumps, Measles and Mosaics*. Despite the title, Collins did not have sufficient faith to commission a suitably enticing jacket from the Ellises' but followed the design format of the *Fleas* jacket, the ground colour being of a rather drab grey, with the ovals in green. It is, however, graphically well designed and has a restrained sophistication.

Just one edition and without any binding variants, but 250 copies were distributed in the US under the American imprint Frederick Praeger of New York. Peter Marren in *The New Naturalists* suggests that this is the rarest of the monographs and this is certainly my experience, but in terms of print run it is equal to or greater than several other titles. The nature of *Mumps* meant that it probably sold well to institutions and libraries and therefore there are fewer copies available today. While a scarce book, when available it is often in very good condition, though the paper used is acidic and prone to tanning and foxing.

M10A	**First Edition**, 1954 (01 February 1954).
Title:	'The New Naturalist | Mumps, Measles & | Mosaics | A Study of Animal and | Plant Viruses'.
Authors:	'by | Kenneth M. Smith | D.Sc., F.R.S. | Honorary Fellow | Downing College, Cambridge | and Roy Markham | M.A., Ph.D.'.
Illust:	'Illustrated with 25 Photographs | and 10 Diagrams'.
Editors:	JF, JG, JH, LDS and EH (Photographic Editor).
Printer:	Collins Clear-Type Press: London and Glasgow.
Collation:	pp. xii, 160; [4]; colour frontispiece plate printed to verso only; 8 leaves of b/w plates printed to both sides (11 × 16-page gatherings).
Jacket:	[Rear panel] Adverts for *The Fulmar* and *Fleas, Flukes & Cuckoos*. [Rear flap] 'Plant Books in the New Naturalist Series' under which listed *Wild Flowers, Mushrooms & Toadstools, Flowers of the Coast, Wild Orchids of Chalk & Limestone, Wild Orchids of Britain* and *British Plant Life*. Postcard request for details of other books.
Price:	18s. net.
Print run:	2,750; no. sold: *c.* 2,500; o/p: spring 1956.
Notes:	1) 4 pages of adverts at rear: NN library listing NN1–28 but omitting NN5. 'Special Volumes' listing 8 titles. Specific adverts for *Fleas, Flukes & Cuckoos, The Herring Gull's World, The Fulmar, The Badger, Flowers of the Coast, British Plant Life* and *Wild Orchids of Britain*. 2) Jacket text printed in green.

USM10A US Edition, 1954. Published by Frederick Praeger of New York. Bound up from the same sheets as Collins ed. M10A and therefore identical but for following distinguishing features: cancelled title page with Praeger imprint; cased in the same buckram with Praeger stamped to the bottom of the spine. Jacket not seen but believed to be a copy of the Collins jacket, but price-clipped and overstamped with a US dollar price, and likewise the Collins imprint to the spine is overstamped Praegar. *Mumps* was retailed at $4.00. Print run: 250. A very rare variant – only a handful of copies were sold to the US and it seems that many of these ended up in institutional libraries never to see the light of day again.

M11 The Heron

The Heron: a masterclass in jacket design. It should be bought for that alone (the reproduction in *Art of the New Naturalists* does not do it justice as there is insufficient contrast between the blue-grey ground colour and the black elements). But it is a scarce book, especially so with a fine jacket, as many are chipped and browned. It is consequently expensive.

The Heron is refreshingly simply bibliographically: just one binding of a single edition, and not reprinted.

M11A	**First edition**, 1954 (12 July 1954).
Title:	'The New Naturalist | The Heron'.
Author:	'by | Frank A. Lowe'.
Illust:	'With a Colour Frontispiece | 15 Black and White Photographs | 13 Drawings & Maps'.
Editors:	JF, JG, JH, LDS & EH (Photographic Editor).
Printer:	Willmer Brothers & Co. Ltd., Birkenhead.
Collation:	pp. xiii, [1], 177; [1]; colour frontispiece plate printed to the verso only; four leaves of b/w plates printed to both sides (12 × 16-page gatherings).
Jacket:	[Rear panel] NN library listing NN1–30 inclusively. [Rear flap] 'Special Volumes' listing 10 titles, with additional adverts for *Life in Lakes and Rivers* and *An Angler's Entomology*.
Price:	18s. net.
Print run:	3,000; no. sold: *c.* 2,790; o/p: 1962.
Notes:	1) Main Photographs by Eric Hosking and the author. 2) Adverts at rear: eight monograph titles under heading 'Special Volumes' on p. 177 and 'The New Naturalist Library' on p. [178] listing NN1–28 inclusively.

M12 Squirrels

James Fisher wrote to Monica Shorten in early 1949 inviting her to write *Squirrels*. This was a book that Billy Collins was keen to publish as he believed it was potentially very saleable (there was a lot of public feeling and misinformation surrounding the grey squirrel). The book was published six years later, but was not perhaps the runaway success that Collins had hoped for: it trickled out at around 200 copies a year for the last 15 years of its shelf-life. Despite offering the book to six US publishing houses, the desire to publish in the US remained unfulfilled. It was not reprinted and is unencumbered by binding variants.

Reading *Squirrels* one gets the impression that Monica Shorten was particularly personable, her book is dedicated to her husband (who took some of the photographs that appear in it) and she appends her home address to the author's preface. She often writes in the first person and tells us how her conservative friends unwittingly requested second helpings of squirrel pie. Her film, entitled 'Miss Monica Shorten on grey squirrels', survives in the Natural History Museum Archive (ref. no. DF ZOO/234/42).

The bold jacket employs unusual colour combinations, which on a design level work. It is graphically excellent and no doubt was, as intended, visually arresting on the bookshop shelf. But the animal depicted looks more like a Louis Wain cat than a squirrel! Inexplicably, the series number on the spine is absurdly small. The jacket is hard wearing and does not fade; fine and very good copies are not uncommon.

M12A	**First edition**, 1954 (01 November 1954).
Title:	'The New Naturalist	Squirrels'.
Author:	'by	Monica Shorten'.
Illust:	'Illustrated with	32 Photographs in Black and White	22 Maps & Drawings'.
Editors:	JF, JG, JH, LDS and EH (Photographic Editor).
Printer:	Willmer Brothers & Co. Ltd., Birkenhead.
Collation:	pp. xii, 212; b/w frontispiece plate printed to verso only; 7 leaves of b/w plates printed to both sides (14 × 16-page gatherings).
Jacket:	[Rear panel] 'In the New Naturalist Library' under which advertised *The Badger* and *British Mammals*. [Rear flap] Adverts for *The British Amphibians & Reptiles* and *Sea-Birds*.
Price:	15s. net.
Print run:	6,000; no. sold: *c.* 4,900 + repriced variant below; o/p: 1971.

Notes: Plate 4a of a wild cat was wrongly credited to Douglas English; it was in fact by Frances Pitt.

M12A-AP1 First Repriced Jacket (sold 1967?–70). P. clipped, with small 18/- sticker; no. sold thus: *c.* 700[?]. Note: A few copies were probably sold in 1971 with a replacement price sticker of £0.90 net, but, to date, not verified.

M13 The Rabbit

The Rabbit is a sombre book about a verminous mammal and its associated virus; it has no colour plates and only four leaves of b/w plates; neither is the mood lightened by the Ellises' masterful but sinister jacket. Even though press reviews for *The Rabbit* were positive and it was published during the midst of a revolution in the natural history of the rabbit in Britain, with widespread concern surrounding the catalyst of that revolution – myxomatosis, sales were disappointing. Over the last eight years of its shelf-life, an average of only 200 copies were sold per annum.

The Rabbit remained in print, at the same price, for 12 years. Published at 16 shillings, or the equivalent of £14 at 2011 prices, it was not an expensive book, but with the effects of inflation it was 30 per cent cheaper when last on sale in 1968, i.e. £10 at 2011 prices.

Not a difficult book to find in fine condition, though the jacket does tend to brown. The aesthetic effect of the skull on the spine is somewhat diluted when displayed on tanned paper, so it is worth seeking out a bright copy.

M13A	**First Edition**, 1956 (24 October 1956).
Title:	'The New Naturalist	The Rabbit'.
Authors:	'by Harry V. Thompson	and	Alastair N. Worden	With an Appendix on Legal Aspects	by Valerie Worrall'.
Illust:	'Illustrated with	16 photographs in black and white	31 maps and diagrams'.
Editors:	JF, JG, JH, LDS and EH (Photographic Editor).
Printer:	Willmer Brother & Co. Ltd., Birkenhead.
Collation:	pp. xii, 240, [4]; 4 leaves of b/w plates printed to both sides (16 × 16-page gatherings).
Jacket:	[Rear panel] 'Two Special Volumes in the New Naturalist Library' with adverts for *Squirrels* and *The Heron*. [Rear flap] 'New Naturalist Special Volumes'

listing 9 monograph titles and 'In the Main Series'
advert for *British Mammals*.

Price: 16s net.
Print run: 4,920 (out-turn); no. sold: *c.* 4,660; o/p: June 1968.
Notes: Plates v and vi are transposed – errata slips were
meant to be inserted to this effect.

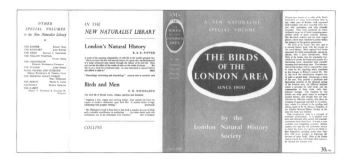

M14 The Birds of the London Area

The Birds of the London Area is the only truly collaborative New
Naturalist, written by a committee of the London Natural History
Society (LNHS) chaired by R. C. Homes. It is the last of the three
'special volumes' and is the larger main series format with a
non-Ellis jacket.

In 1945 Fitter had proposed it as a complement to his *London's
Natural History*. Collins was reluctant, rejecting it in the first
instance on the basis that it was contrary to the concept of the New
Naturalist, but was eventually persuaded to publish the book on the
strength of a guarantee from the LNHS that they would purchase
400 copies for sale to their members. Tradition has it that *Birds of the
London Area* was commercially unsuccessful: it only made a profit of
£85. But the book went out of print within 8 months of publication,
so even with large subscription sales, it could not have been that
unpopular. We know that there was an amount of acrimony
between R. Trevelyan of Collins and Homes, and it is probably this
that ultimately put paid to a Collins reprint. The minutes of the
Editorial Board for March 1959 record: 'Question of reprint raised
again by Mr Fisher and discussed. Mr Fisher's final suggestion was
that if Collins printed a minimum economic reprint of 2,000 the
London Natural History Society would then agree to take up 1,000
over a period of four years. Mr Smith to examine costs on this basis'.
Clearly the NN Editorial Board was keen to find a mechanism that
would enable a reprint, but this was seemingly resisted by Collins.
The minutes of the next meeting, held three months later in June
1959, state: 'Type distributed. Mr Smith to ask R. Trevelyan if he told
the Natural History Society before type was dispersed' – i.e. the type
that the book was printed from had been disassembled, thereby
sabotaging, either deliberately or accidentally, the possibility of a
conventional reprint.

However, in 1963 Rupert Hart-Davis purchased the plant (line
and half-tone blocks) for £8 and paid a fee of £40 to offset
photographically the Collins edition, then republished it the
following year with virtually the same title. It is a revised edition

with a few pages reset but most are identical to the Collins
edition; a supplementary chapter has been added at the end,
bringing the text up to date. A new suite of photographs has been
used including a colour frontispiece photograph of a kingfisher,
appropriately, by Eric Hosking and this is repeated on the front
panel of the dust jacket. The Collins jacket is particularly prone to
tanning and to a lesser degree chipping, consequently with just
1,800 books sold, it can be a challenge to find a fine jacketed copy.

M14A   **First Edition**, 1957 (04 March 1957).
Title: 'The New Naturalist | The Birds of | The London Area
| Since 1900'.
Authors: 'By a Committee of | The London Natural History
Society | R. C. Homes (Chairman) | Miss C. M. Acland
C. B. Ashby | C. L. Collenette R. S. R. Fitter | E. R.
Parrinder B. A. Richards'. Not all the authors were on
the committee and additionally they were S. Cramp,
W. G. Teagle, R. B. Warren, Dr. Geoffrey Bevan, H. F.
Greenfield and W. D. Melluish.
Illust: 'Illustrated with 40 photographs | and 6 maps and
diagrams'.
Editors: JF, JG, JH, LDS and EH (Photographic Editor).
Printer: Willmer Brother & Co. Ltd., Birkenhead.
Collation: pp. x, 305, [5]; 12 leaves of b/w plates printed to both
sides (20 × 16-page gatherings).
Jacket: [Rear panel] 'In the New Naturalist Library'
advertising *London's Natural History* and *Birds and
Men*. [Rear flap] 'Other Special Volumes in the New
Naturalist Library' listing 11 monograph titles.
Price: 30s net.
Print run: 2,247 (out-turn); no. sold: *c.* 2,030; o/p: 1957.
Notes: Four pages of adverts at the end of the book for:
'The New Naturalist' listing 32 titles; 'Special Volumes'
listing 12 titles; and specific adverts for *The Heron*,
The Rabbit, *The Redstart* and *London's Natural History*.

M1SM14A Revised Edition, 1964. 'The Birds of The London Area.
By a Committee of the London Natural History Society A New
Revised Edition'. Published by Rupert Hart-Davis, 1964. 'This new,
revised edition has been prepared by Mr. R. C. Homes, with the
assistance of Messrs. S. Cramp and D. I. M. Wallace', with the
addition of a new chapter (Part 3) covering the years 1955 to 1961.
Hardback (same format as Collins ed.) with jacket. Collation: pp. x,
332, [2]; colour frontispiece plate printed to verso only; 12 leaves of
b/w plates printed to both sides (21½ × 16-page gatherings).
Original photographs almost entirely replaced with a new set, inc.
colour frontispiece of a kingfisher by Eric Hosking. Bound in blue
imitation cloth with gilt lettering blocked to the spine. Jacket
front panel repeats Hosking's kingfisher photograph; rear panel
carries the blurb, printed in black on a blue ground; rear flap
blank, and four press reviews to the front flap. Price: 42s. net.
Common and inexpensive.

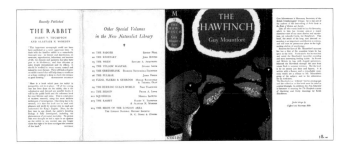

M15 The Hawfinch

To many collectors *The Hawfinch* is the holy grail of the monographs, dressed in one of the Ellises' finest jackets, elegantly written and, of course, scarce and valuable. At first inspection the bibliography of this legendary title appears straightforward, with just a single impression of a single edition, but on closer examination, it's much more complicated. Peter Marren was observant when in *The New Naturalists* he wrote 'Many of the dustwrappers are slightly smaller than the book', but in point of fact he should have written 'many of the books are slightly too large for the dustwrappers', because it is the books that vary in size, and the Ellises' jackets that remain constant (and presumably all of the same printing).

Three distinct states exist; bound up at different times, but all from the same original sheets. The first, and most common, bears the dubious distinction of being the smallest of all New Naturalist books, the binding being unmistakably smaller in height and width than the standard monograph format and the pages trimmed to suit. The second is larger and in fact the standard monograph size. The third is also the correct monograph size but wears a completely different plain green jacket.

The same Ellis jacket was fitted to the first two states, but because of the varying book sizes, they look quite different when folded on the books: the first state will show just one bird's-eye to the front panel, whereas on the second, two. Because the width (horizontal dimension) of the first state book is too small for the jacket design, the eye of the second (right-hand) finch ends up under the cover on the inside flap; clearly unintentional and upsetting the balance of the image. What did the Ellises' make of it? With the second state, the jacket design fits the front cover of the book perfectly, as intended, however the jacket appears to be part of the original printing and apparently trimmed to fit the undersized first state format. Therefore it is approximately 4 mm too short for the corrected second state, resulting in an annoying thin band of green buckram showing at the head or tail.

The third state has a slightly different binding, but is easy to tell as it has a completely different, plain-green, non-Ellis jacket. This last state appeared much later; one copy inspected was dated '9.10.70' alongside a Foyles sticker, which indicates it was on sale just before the book went out of print. It would seem a few cartons of unbound quires, without jackets, were lying about the warehouse and, as stocks were running low, these were bound up. The reason for the plain green jackets is unknown but it is not unlikely that the original plant for the Ellis jacket was lost and rather than go to the significant expense of commissioning new blocks, a cheaper alternative was sought. The front flap includes four press reviews, not found on the Ellis jacket, which indicates that someone went to some trouble over this jacket. It seems that around 300 copies were printed; it is certainly now particularly scarce, and in its own muted way, not unattractive.

The priority described, has been determined by a variety of factors: firstly, all review copies have been the smaller format; secondly, dated inscriptions agree with this chronology; thirdly, the smaller format is by far the most common, and given just one printing, it is likely that the majority of sheets were bound

TABLE M15 Diagnostic features of the three different states of M15 *The Hawfinch*.

Hawfinch M15	Width (horizontal dim.)	Board height (vertical dim.)	Leaf Size (width × height)	Joints (external)	Book thickness (inc. boards)	Buckram	Jacket (total width/ length × height)
1st State	136 mm (from apex spine curve to fore-edge).	202 mm	129 × 196 mm	Rounded, shallow.	17 mm	Dark green, weave apparent.	Ellis design. 500 × 202.5 mm. Jacket trimmed to correct height for book but design too large for book's format: only left-hand hawfinch's eye evident on front panel – other on front flap.
2nd State	141 mm (from apex spine curve to fore-edge).	206 mm	135 × 199 mm	Well-defined shoulder.	16 mm	Slightly lighter than 1st state; weave apparent.	Ellis design. 500 × 202.5 mm. Jacket trimmed too short for book but design fits format: Both hawfinches' eyes evident on front panel.
3rd State	142 mm (from apex spine curve to fore-edge).	206 mm	135 × 200 mm	Deeply impressed.	18 mm	Lighter green, waxy, smoother; weave less apparent.	Plain green design. Thick paper. 478 × 204.5 mm.

up in the first instance; fourthly, the Ellis jackets would have been trimmed to fit the book and assuming they were all printed at the same time, a stock of shorter jackets would be available for later bindings; and fifthly, the printed price on the plain green jacket is 21s. rather than 18s. as on the Ellis jackets. The russet colour on the spine of the (Ellis) jacket is particularly prone to fading and unfaded copies are very much in the minority.

M15A   **First Edition, First State**, 1957 (15 April 1957).
Title: 'The New Naturalist | The Hawfinch'.
Author: 'by | Guy Mountfort'.
Illust: '18 black and White Photographs | by the Author, Eric Hosking & others | 32 Drawings & Maps'.
Editors: JF, JG, JH, LDS and EH (Photographic Editor).
Printer: Collins Clear-Type Press, London and Glasgow.
Collation: pp. xii, 176, [4]; 4 leaves of b/w plates printed to both sides (12 × 16-page gatherings).
Casing: Undersized format c. 136 × 202 mm; jacket design too large for front panel.
Jacket: [Rear panel] 'Other Special Volumes in the New Naturalist Library' listing M1–14 inclusively. [Rear flap] 'Recently Published The Rabbit', with reviews.
Price: 18s. net.
Print run: 2,751 (out-turn); no. sold: c. 2,620[?] – figures include 2nd and 3rd states; subscription sales: 970.
Notes: 1) For diagnostic features of the first state see table M15 and intro. 2) Black and white scraperboard drawings by Keith Shakleton, as advertised to the jacket front flap, but reproduced poorly due to inferior paper, which was used as cost-saving expedient.

M15B First Edition, Second State, 1957. Bound up from the same sheets as M15A, probably during the first half of 1962. Format larger, conforming to the standard monograph size (141 × 206 mm), but jacket probably from the original printing and trimmed to fit undersized first state format and therefore now approximately 4 mm shorter than the binding, but artwork now displayed as intended, with both birds' eyes showing on the front cover. Print run: included in M15A. Considerably scarcer than the first state.

M15C First Edition, Third State, 1957. Bound up from the same sheets as M15A. Book same format and very similar to M16B, but probably bound up in 1969. Fitted with a plain green jacket, printed in black on thick green paper; four press reviews to front flap (Maxwell Knight, *School Nature Study*; R. S. R. Fitter, *New Scientist*; E. A. Ellis, *Eastern Daily Press* and *The Field*); rear panel and flap blank. Price: 21s. net. No. bound thus c. 300; no. sold: c. 260[?]; o/p: 1971.

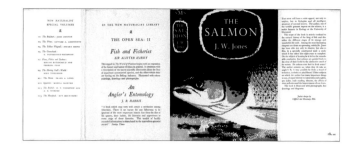

M16 The Salmon

The minutes of the New Naturalist board reveal that the Editors, not infrequently, lacked confidence in the ability of their authors to write well. Their remarks were often scathing and unequivocal. Regarding *The Salmon's* author, Huxley stated: 'Jones would never write good English'. But belying such censure was a spirit of pragmatic support, and in the case of *The Salmon* James Fisher rewrote the early chapters – such direct intervention by the Editors seems now to be a thing of the past.

Despite the supposed shortcomings of Jones's prose, *The Salmon* was a good book and though just one edition, it was reprinted three times, with a tranche of c. 1,000 copies published in the US by Harper & Brothers, New York.

Only half of the 1972 fourth impression was bound up in the first instance; the remainder bound up around 1975 and consequently there are two binding variants. *The Salmon* is often found in fine condition.

M16A   **First Edition**, 1959 (04 May 1959).
Title: 'The New Naturalist | The Salmon'.
Author: 'by J. W. Jones | D.Sc., Ph.D., | Senior Lecturer in Zoology | University of Liverpool'.
Illust: '27 Black-and-White Photographs | 24 Diagrams'.
Editors: JF, JG, JH, LDS and EH (Photographic Editor).
Printer: Willmer Brothers & Haram Limited, Birkenhead | for Collins Clear-Type Press, London and Glasgow.
Collation: pp. xvi, 192; 6 leaves of b/w plates printed to both sides (13 × 16-page gatherings).
Jacket: [Rear panel] adverts for *The Open Sea: II Fish and Fisheries* and *An Angler's Entomology*. [Rear flap] 'New Naturalist Special Volumes': M2, M3, M4, M5, M7, M9, M11, M12, M13 and M15.
Price: 18s net.
Print run: 4,000; no. sold c. 3,400[?]; o/p: 1961.
Notes: 1) The type size used for prefaces and appendices noticeably smaller than that used for main text. 2) The flaps of the jacket are particularly wide and cover ¾ of the paste-downs. 3) Book 20 mm thick.

M16B Second Impression, 1961. 'First published 1959 | Reprinted 1961'; date omitted from the title page. As M16A, seemingly without any alterations to the text. Printer: Collins Clear-Type

Press. Jacket also identical; price remains at 18s. net. Print run: 2,000[?]; o/p: summer 1967. Note: While the imprint page refers to this edition as a reprint, all later editions refer to it and themselves as impressions.

M16C Third Impression, 1968. 'First published 1959 | Second Impression, 1961 | Third Impression, 1968'. As M16B. Editors: JF, JG, JH, MD and EH. Book appreciably thinner: *c.* 18 mm. Jacket rear panel as previous impressions, but slightly reset; blurb to front flap unaltered, but reset, with a quote from the *New Statesman* inserted and 'continued on back flap' with other press commendations and advert for *The Trout*. Price: 25/- net. Print run: 1,500. Note: '1968' print history to imprint p. poorly printed and partially illegible; the scarcest of all editions.

M16C-AP1 1st Repriced DJ (sold 1971–72?), £1.25 sticker; o/p: 1972[?].

M16D-B1 Fourth Impression, First Binding Variant, 1972. ISBN: 000213201x. 'First published 1959 | Second Impression, 1961 | Third Impression, 1968 | Fourth Impression, 1972' As M16C. ISBN added to imprint page. Editors: JG, JH, MD KM and EH. Binding subtly but consistently different from B2 – for diagnostic features see B2 below. *Durasealed* jacket textually as M16C but printed, using a different process, on bright white paper with noticeably different colours. Price: £2.00 net. Print run: 2,000 inc. variants below; no. bound thus: *c.* 1,000. (It is likely that a few copies of this binding were also sold with jackets repriced at £3.00, but have not been recorded.)

M16D-B1-AP1 1st Repriced DJ (sold 1974?), £2.50 sticker.

M16D-B2 Fourth Impression, Second Binding Variant, 1972 (Bound up 1975?). The New Naturalist Statement dated 18/10/74 states that the stock for *The Salmon* was 201 +1024Q, i.e. the majority of stock was held as unbound quires and as the sales figures for the following few years do not reveal a break in sales, we can surmise that this unbound stock was bound up around 1975. These later bindings exhibit what can only be described as trifling differences, but are easily enough told apart by the arrangement of the internal hinges. In this second binding variant there is no central strip of mull evident under the endpaper paste-down, but instead an impression of binding tape that runs the whole length of the EP. The vertical step between the front board and text block is not pronounced, only *c.* 2 mm as against 4 mm in the primary binding (these variations are similar to the binding variants of NN59 *Ants* – see photos on page 346. Most, if not all, of these second binding variants will wear repriced jackets). Print run: inc. in M16D-B1 above; no. bound thus: *c.* 1,000; no. sold: *c.* 600[?] including repriced variants and tranche of *c.* 350 either pulped or remaindered.

M16D-B2-AP1 1st Repriced DJ (sold 1975–76), £3.00 sticker, *c.* 150 sold[?].

M16D-B2-AP2 2nd Repriced DJ (sold 1976–77), £3.95 sticker, *c.* 300 sold.

M16D-B2-AP3 3rd Repriced DJ (sold 1977–78), £4.50 sticker, *c.* 150 sold.

USM16A US Edition, 1959 (1961). Harper & Brothers. Printed from the same plates as the English edition and therefore format, text and illustrations exactly as the first UK ed. M16A, but with a new integral title/imprint leaf (not a cancel); the layout of the title page unaltered but NMN monogram and date omitted; imprint added 'Harper & Brothers | New York'. The imprint page gives the copyright date of 1959, but in point of fact this US edition was published in late 1961 and seemingly of the same printing as the UK second impression M16B. Casing is blue buckram blocked in black. Jacket same Ellis design with Harper overprinted to spine and Collins blacked out; rear flap advertises 'Other Outstanding Harper Books on Nature and Outdoor Life' and rear flap advertises 'Complete Field Guide to American Wildlife'; blurb to front flap remains unaltered and a price of $4.50 is printed to top corner (some copies have this printed price excised and instead are rubber stamped $4.50 – why?). Print run: 1,000; not scarce.

FORM16A Japanese Edition, 1974. Translated by Hiroaki Matsui (No. 4 in the *Chronicles of the Animal World* series). 'Rights arranged through Orion Press, Tokyo © Hiroaki Matsui, 1974, by Shisakusha Publishing Co.' Hardback with dust jacket 137 × 197 mm; pp. [2], 235, [2]; 1 leaf of b/w plates printed to both sides. Other photographs and diagrams printed within text, images as Collins ed. but some omitted and others reduced in size. Title page printed in dark maroon. Bound in shiny orange imitation cloth with silver gilt lettering to the spine. Glossy, laminated jacket printed in orange, pale green and black on a white ground. Supplied with a black and white printed wrap-around or Obi.

M17 Lords & Ladies

Just as there are two species of Arum native to the UK, so there are just two editions of *Lords & Ladies;* the first published by Collins in 1960 and the second, a facsimile reprint printed by the Pendragon Press and published posthumously by the author's widow Frances Prime, 21 years later. The Collins edition is rare and sought after, whereas the reprint is generally spurned – even at a tenth the cost. It is, however, a well-produced book printed on *Conqueror* watermarked paper and bound in a pale yellow buckram. It fittingly includes an additional b/w portrait plate of Cecil Prime and Frances's additional preface, concludes with a fine and poignant poem by Thomas Moult. But it is let down by the murky photographic jacket of muddy yellow and brown tones – in contrast to the Ellis jacket.

It is fitting that a book about one of our most striking hedgerow plants, and in fact the only botanical monograph to grace the series, is clothed in one of the Ellis's finest designs, though the Editorial Board at the time didn't agree (see *Art of the New Naturalists* p. 295). The Ellis jacket, printed on heavy paper, does not readily tan and consequently is often found in very good condition.

M17A	**First Edition**, 1960 (04 July 1960).
Title:	'The New Naturalist	Lords & Ladies'.
Author:	'by	Cecil T. Prime	M.A., Ph.D., F.L.S.'.
Illust:	'With a Colour Frontispiece	6 Photographs in Black and White	and Line Drawings and Diagrams	by Robert J. Jones	MA., PH.D., F.G.S.'.
Editors:	JF, JG, JH, LDS and EH (Photographic Editor).
Printer:	Willmer Brothers & Haram Limited, Birkenhead.
Collation:	pp. xiv, 241, [1]; 1 colour plate (frontispiece) printed to verso only; 4 leaves of b/w plates printed to one side only (16 × 16-page gatherings).
Jacket:	[Rear panel] Adverts for three other botanical New Naturalists: *Wild Flowers; Wild Flowers of Chalk and Limestone, Wild Orchids of Britain*. [Rear flap] Advert for 'The New Naturalist Library' with endorsing review by the *Guardian*.
Price:	21s. net.
Print run:	2,501 (out-turn); no. sold: *c.* 2,200; o/p: 1969.
Notes:	1) The title to the TP and jacket is with an ampersand, whereas that to the spine casing and half-title page is

with an 'and'; in the text Prime always uses 'lords-and-ladies'. 2) Frontispiece photo by John Markham.

M1SM17A Pendragon Press Reprint, 1981. No ISBN. Published by Frances Prime. Hardback binding with dust jacket, 140 × 207 mm, i.e. same size as Collins ed; pp. xv, [1], 241, [3]; 1 colour plate (frontispiece) printed to verso only; 5 leaves of b/w plates printed to one side only (7 × 32-page + 1 × 16-page + 1 × 20-page gatherings). Printed from the same plates, or electros of those plates, on Conqueror watermarked paper; new photographic colour frontispiece plate (by Dr. Robert Jones) and new portrait plate of Cecil Prime (uncredited), otherwise same suite of monochrome photographic plates; additional preface by Frances Prime. Bound in pale-yellow buckram, gilt blocked to the spine. Photographic jacket which replicates the frontispiece plate, rear panel and flap blank; unrevised blurb to front flap. Price: £9.50. Print run: unknown, probably remaindered, not scarce. Note: Essentially a facsimile of original edition; instigated by Frances Prime and probably paid for by her, too – there is no reference to a publisher, just printer and without an ISBN.

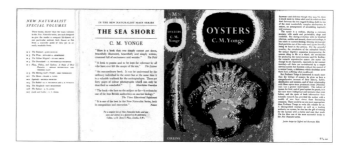

M18 Oysters

Oysters enjoys a relatively simple publishing history; just two printings in 1960 and 1966 and an American imprint, though the latter consists of no more than a Macmillan label applied to the jacket. While the 1966 printing is referred to in the book as a second edition, it is ostensibly a reprint as there is little material difference in the two texts. Perhaps the most notable difference is the quality of the paper: in the first edition it is thick, smooth and creamy, a pleasure to touch, whereas in the second, thin, rough and annoyingly transparent, and much more prone to foxing. The print quality of the second edition is also inferior, though this might be more to do with the poor paper than the printing. The first edition was printed 'out of house', but the second edition was printed by Collins. The first edition jacket was initially used on the reprint with the original price of 21/- intact; it then appeared price-clipped and overstamped 25/-. When these first edition jackets finally ran out a bespoke second edition jacket was introduced.

The dust jacket holds its colour well and is often found in fine bright condition.

M18A   **First Edition**, 1960 (3 September 1960 also given as 29 August 1960).

Title: 'The New Naturalist | Oysters'.

Author: 'by | C. M. Yonge | C.B.E., D.Sc., F.R.S.'.

Collation: pp. xiv, 209, [1]; b/w frontispiece plate printed to verso only; 8 leaves of b/w plates, printed to both sides (14 × 16-page gatherings).

Printer: Willmer Brothers & Haram Ltd., Birkenhead for Collins Clear-Type Press.

Jacket: [Rear panel] advert for *The Seashore* with four press commendations. [Rear flap] 'New Naturalist Special Volumes' listing nos. M2–5, 7, 9, 11–13, 15, 16 and 17.

Price: 21s. net.

Print run: 4,000; no. sold: *c.* 3,720 (both figures inc. 250 US copies); o/p: 1965.

M18B Second Edition, 1966 (November). 'First Edition 1960 | Second Edition 1966'. Date omitted from title page; pp. xiii, [i], 209, [1]. Printer: Collins Clear-Type Press. The two-page Editors' Preface of first ed. substituted for a half-page 'Preface to Second Edition', which identifies a handful of corrections to the text. The paper significantly inferior (see intro.). Print run: 1,500; no. sold: *c.* 1,480 including variants below.

M18B-DJ1 First Edition Jacket. With first ed. M18A, jacket, not clipped.

M18B-DJ1-AP1 1st repriced DJ. With first ed. M18A, jacket, but now price-clipped by Collins and overprinted with '25s. net'.

M18B-DJ2 Second Edition Jacket. With new jacket: rear panel unchanged; monographs M18 and M19 added to list on rear flap; blurb precised and three press commendations added. Price: 25s. net.

M18B-DJ2-AP1 1st Repriced, 2nd Ed. DJ. £1.25 sticker, o/p: 1972.

USM18A US Edition, 1960 (sold 1962 onwards). The Macmillan Company, New York. Book and jacket identical to M18A but for a small printed sticker applied to front panel of the jacket 'Distributed by Macmillan'; jacket price-clipped. 250 copies were sold to Macmillan during the winter 1961/62.

M19 The House Sparrow

'Do I love the house sparrow? That I find difficult to answer, though I do know that I should find life extremely dull without them as my constant neighbours'. So wrote Dennis Summers-Smith in the introductory chapter of *The House Sparrow*, a classic of the ornithological literature, not least because of the author's evident affection for the bird; his observations, at times, refreshingly light-hearted, 'The house sparrow has a remarkably short working day….Perhaps this liking for his bed is picked up by the sparrow from his close association with man!' Of course there is great scholarship here too, but always delivered in a readable manner: a lesson perhaps for NN authorship wannabes?

Despite the endearing quality of this book and the ubiquitous nature of the subject, it only achieved modest sales of around 5,600 copies spanning a ten-year period. It was reprinted just once, in 1967, though correspondence in the Collins archive alludes to plans for a 1976 reprint. Peter Marren, presumably picking up on this, mentions a 1976 reprint in *The New Naturalists*, and writes '[it] represented the last printing of any New Naturalist monograph'. In the event this second reprint never materialised (the accolade of the last monograph printing going to the 1976 [1977] reprint of *The Badger*). *The House Sparrow* was offered to 6 US publishers, all of whom turned it down; odd considering the impact of the 'English Sparrow' on the US agricultural scene. Later, Foyles Scientific Book Club toyed with republishing a cheaper edition without photographs, but this too fell from the nest.

With such a limited print run *The House Sparrow* is now a scarce book, especially the reprint, though of course worth significantly less than the first edition. On the plus side it is often found in good condition, the jackets wearing well.

The first edition was out of stock by the spring of 1965 and Collins, in a deliberate move to build demand, delayed the reprint until the autumn of 1967.

M19A   **First Edition**, 1963.

Title: 'The New Naturalist | The | House Sparrow'.

Author: 'by | D. Summers-Smith'.

Illust: 'With a colour frontispiece | 32 photographs in black and white | and 36 text figures'.

Editors: JF, JG, JH, LDS and EH (Photographic Editor).

270 · COLLECTING THE NEW NATURALISTS

Printer: Willmer Brothers & Haram Limited., Birkenhead.
Collation: pp. xvi, 269, [3]; 1 colour frontispiece leaf printed to
             verso only; 12 leaves of b/w plates printed to both
             sides (18 × 16-page gatherings).
Jacket: [Rear panel] 'New Naturalist Monographs' listing
             M1–5, M7, M9, M11–13 and M15–18. [Rear flap]
             'New Naturalist Monographs' Advertising
             The Hawfinch and *The Wren*.
Price: 25/- net.
Print run: 4,000; no. sold: *c.* 3,500; o/p: spring 1965.
Notes: 1) The author's name appears as J. D. Summers-Smith
             on the jacket and casing, but simply D. Summers-
             Smith on the title page. 2) The quality of the text
             printing to the jacket is poor, the ink has bled into
             the paper – particularly noticeable on the rear panel.

M19B Reprint, 1967 (September). 'First published, 1963 |
Reprinted, 1967'; date omitted from TP. As M19A. Printer: Collins
Clear-Type Press, London and Glasgow. Editors: 'LDS' now 'Sir DS'
and his post nominals multiplied. The jacket text now crisp; rear
panel unchanged but for addition of M20 *Wood Pigeon* (M19 still
missing from list); both flaps unrevised and still priced at 25s. net.
Print run: 2,000; no. sold: *c.* 2,100[?] inc. repriced variant below.
Notes: 1) There does not appear to be any textual revisions, though
board minutes refer to a small no. of corrections, however these
might not have materialized. 2) Impossibly, more copies were sold
than printed: either the out-turn was significantly larger than the
print-order or a mistake made in the sales figures.
M19B-AP1 1st Repriced DJ (sold 1971), Collins £1.25/25/- sticker
applied (in accordance with decimalisation), *c.* 600 sold[?].
M19B-AP2 2nd Repriced DJ (sold 1972–73), p. clipped, and boldly
overprinted £1.25; no. sold: inc. in AP1; o/p: autumn 1973.

M20 The Wood Pigeon

The Wood Pigeon was printed just once in 1965, but not all copies
were bound up initially and a Collins 'New Naturalist Statement'
of April 1974 noted a stock of '1936Q' [Q = quires], i.e. nine years
later, one-third of the original print run of 6,000 still remained as
unbound quires. A similar statement of a few months later alludes
to these quires being bound up for delivery at the end of the year.
Consequently two binding states exist and are easy enough to tell
apart, principally by the arrangement of the internal hinges, but
other diagnostic features are also given in table M20. Though, in
truth, the differences are really rather trifling. Whether such
subtleties are important is not for me to decide; but if your copy
wears an original unclipped jacket, then it will almost certainly be
a first state binding.

The Wood Pigeon remained in print for 14 years, without any
revisions or further printings of the jacket. In 1971, when sterling
was decimalised, the printed price of 25s net was clipped off the
remaining stock of jackets and these, then, over-stamped,
accordingly £1.25. This was a period of high inflation and it was
not long before the jacket price needed increasing, which
required the additional excision of the overprinted price. As a
result many jackets have a significant proportion of their lower
corner missing. It would seem that only around half of all copies
sold were not price-clipped.

TABLE M20 Diagnostic features of the two binding variants of *The Wood-Pigeon*.

Wood-Pigeon	Weight (excl. jacket)	Spine	Width of boards (horizontal dimension)	Joints (external)	Hinges (internal)	Jacket
1st binding variant	496–520g.	Distinctly rounded; max. dimension across spine *c.* 27 mm.	Approx. 145 mm from fore-edge to outermost point of spine.	Joints slightly impressed	Mull evident under endpaper at hinges, *not* extending to top/tail of endpaper.	Printed price of 25s. net; if clipped, over-stamped £1.25.
2nd binding variant	488–496g.	Flatter, less rounded; max. dimension across spine *c.* 24 mm.	Approx. 143 mm from fore-edge to outermost point of spine.	Joints distinctly impressed	Binding tape used which extends to top/tail of the endpaper.	*Always* clipped, over-stamped £1.25 or Collins price sticker of £3.00 or more.

M20A-B1   **First Edition, Primary Binding Variant**, 1965[?].

Title: 'The New Naturalist | The Wood-Pigeon'.

Author: 'by | R. K. Murton'.

Illust: 'With 39 Black and White Photographs | & 22 Text Figures'.

Editors: JF, JG, JH, DS and EH (Photographic Editor).

Printer: Collins Clear-Type Press, London and Glasgow.

Collation: pp. 256; one colour plate leaf (frontispiece); 8 leaves of b/w plates printed to both sides (16 × 16-page gatherings).

Jacket: [Rear panel] List of 12 monographs starting with *The Badger* and ending with *The House Sparrow*. [Rear flap] Adverts for *The House Sparrow* and for *The Herring Gull's World*.

Price: 25s net.

Notes: 1) See table M20 for diagnostic feature of this primary binding variant. 2) Two different stitching patterns exist in this variant: one with 25 mm stitches (4 × 25 mm stitches with 18 mm gaps between) and the other with 30 mm (4 × 30 mm stitches with 10 mm gaps between). These probably reflect different binding batches, but as it has not been possible to identify a chronology no priority has been given. The bindings are otherwise identical.

Print run: 6,000; no. sold: *c.* 2,700[?] + repriced decimal variant below.

M20A-B1-AP1 1st Repriced DJ (1971–?). The pre-decimal price has been clipped and the jacket overprinted £1.25 adjacent to the excised corner, *c.* 1,000[?] sold. Note: There appear to be two variants of this repriced jacket – one over-stamped and one overprinted; presumably there will also be a dual priced variant.

M20A-B2 First Edition, Second Binding Variant (bound up 1974/74). Bound up from the same sheets as M20A, but in a distinct binding: the joints are clearly impressed and mull is *not* evident under the end-paper at the internal hinges – see table M20 for further diagnostic features. The buckram is all but indistinguishable from B1. Seemingly all books of this second binding wear clipped jackets, inc. the repriced variants below. Additionally it would seem that 500 books were remaindered to a bookclub and the large number of clipped, but not repriced jackets would support this conjecture.

M20A-B2-AP1 1st Repriced DJ (1975), £1.25 sticker, *c.* 150 sold?

M20A-B2-AP2 2nd Repriced DJ (1975–76), £3.00 sticker, *c.* 450 sold.

M20A-B2-AP3 3rd Repriced DJ (1976–77), £3.95 sticker, *c.* 250 sold.

M20A-B2-AP4 4th Repriced DJ (1978–79), £4.50 sticker, *c.* 400 sold.

M21 The Trout

In April 1946 Winifred Frost of the Freshwater Biological Association (FBA) asked the New Naturalist Board if they were interested in a book in which she would collaborate with Miss M. E. Brown. They were. But 21 years went by before the book was finally published in 1967. It was reprinted once in 1972 and it is this latter printing, which, bibliographically, is more interesting. It was bound up in two batches, the first at publication and the second around 1975, resulting in two binding variants, both of which, due to the use of a lighter-weight paper, are significantly thinner books than the first edition. Additionally, the reprint accidentally omits '21' from the spine of the jacket – the only New Naturalist jacket, in both series, not to have a series number.

Originally to have had the title 'The Brown Trout', but later changed to the more encompassing *The Trout*. It was also published as a Fontana paperback in 1970 and again in 1973, but with a new subheading *The Natural History of the Brown Trout in the British Isles*. It was translated into Spanish and published in 1971, with the title *La Trucha*, but of particular interest, the translator was the celebrated Spanish polymath Luis Saenz de la Calzada: medical doctor, artist, poet and actor, and accordingly, he painted the jacket artwork too! A bold, striking, piece of work, but the fish appears to be floating amongst clouds, rather than swimming in water.

TABLE M21 Diagnostic features of the two 1972 reprint binding variants of *The Trout*.

The Trout Reprint M21B	'Collins' to spine of casing	Joints (external)	Shoulder of Joint (external)	Weight (without Jacket)
Primary binding variant (B1)	*c.* 20 mm long, impressed into cloth.	Not deeply impressed.	Stands proud of board.	430–436g
Second binding variant (B2)	*c.* 19 mm long, blocked onto surface of cloth without an impression.	Deeply impressed.	In line with or below board.	420–424g

The Editorial Board minutes record that *The Trout* was to have a colour frontispiece, and indeed it does have a single colour plate, but oddly, it was tipped in opposite page 32, where it is easily missed.

The Collins edition is generally not difficult to find in fine condition.

M21A   **First Edition**, 1967 (01 May 1967?).
Title: 'The New Naturalist | The Trout'.
Authors: 'by W. E. Frost | and M. E. Brown'.
Illust: 'With 4 photographs in colour | and 42 in black and white | and 26 text figures'.
Editors: JF, JG, JH, DS and EH (Photographic Editor).
Printer: Collins Clear-Type Press, London and Glasgow.
Collation: pp. 286, [2]; 1 colour plate leaf (tipped in) printed to recto only; 8 leaves of b/w plates printed to both sides (18 × 16-page gatherings).
Jacket: [Rear panel] adverts for *The Salmon* and *Oysters*, both supported with press reviews. [Rear flap] advert for 'An Angler's Entomology' with five endorsing press reviews.
Price: 25s. net.
Print run: 6,000; no. sold: *c.* 5,700[?].
Notes: Book 26 mm thick.

M21B-B1 Reprint, Primary Binding Variant, 1972. ISBN: 0002132311. 'First Edition 1967 | Reprinted 1972'. No date to title page. As M21A without any apparent textual revisions; Editors: JG, JH, MD, KM and EH. Due to a lighter weight of paper, the book is noticeably thinner – 22 mm. For the diagnostic features of this primary binding variant see table M21. The *Durasealed* jacket omits the series number, (21), from the spine; rear panel unaltered; rear flap unchanged but for addition of the ISBN; same blurb to front flap, but now supported with two press reviews – *The Sunday Times* and *The Salmon and Trout Magazine*. Price: £2.00 net. Print run: 2,500 including B2, of which *c.* 1,000 books bound up thus.
M21B-B1-AP1 1st Repriced DJ (sold 1975), p. clipped, with Collins £3.00 sticker, no. sold: unknown.
M21B-B2 Reprint, Second Binding Variant, 1972. Bound up 1975[?]. Differences restricted to casing only, as explained in table M21. Additionally, all jackets likely to be price-clipped, with Collins replacement price stickers adjacent. A maximum of 1,480 books bound up thus. The number sold impossible to determine with any certainty but 500 copies probably sold off to a bookclub in 1978/79, otherwise pulped.
M21B-B2-AP1 1st Repriced DJ (sold 1976?), p. clipped, with Collins £3.00 sticker, no. sold: unknown.
M21B-B2-AP2 2nd Repriced DJ (sold 1976–77), p. clipped, with Collins £3.95 sticker, *c.* 350 sold.
M21B-B2-AP3 3rd Repriced DJ (sold 1978–79), p. clipped, with Collins £4.50 sticker, *c.* 400 sold.

FM21A Fontana Paperback First Edition, 1970 (18/05/1970). ISBN: 0006322859 (appears only on second impression). Title: 'The Trout | The Natural History of the Brown Trout in the British Isles'; pp. 316, [4]; 8 leaves of b/w plates, printed on glossy paper, to both sides, bound in two sections. Ads. for Fontana books at front/rear inc. Fontana NN titles; Editors omitted. A reset edition, but without colour plate. Front cover features an unacknowledged photograph of three trout; two press commendations to rear cover. Price: 10/- (50p). Total print run inc. reprint. *c.* 5,500[?].
FM21B Second Impression, April 1973. As FM21A. Editors added: JG, JH, MD, KM and EH; ads. now solely for Fontana NN titles. ISBN (0006322859) added to rear cover. Price: 60p; o/p: 1976[?].

FORM21A Spanish Edition, 1971. Title: 'La Trucha'. Translated into Spanish by Luis Saenz de la Calzada. Published by Editorial Academia, S. L. Leon (España). Printed in Spain. Paperback, stitched and glued, with stiff printed card covers and separate dust jacket; 136 × 196 mm. i.e. same format as Collins original; pp. 319, [1]; 1 colour plate leaf printed to recto only; 8 leaves of b/w plates printed to both sides (20 × 16-page gatherings). All references to the New Naturalist omitted, but Editors' and authors' prefaces retained: appears a faithful translation of the Collins original including plates, text figures and maps. The textured card covers printed in black and purple on a white ground; jacket features artwork also by Calzada to the front panel; rear panel and rear flap advertise other titles published by Editorial Academia; front flap with usual blurb. Not rare.

M22 The Mole

Like the first of the monographs, this, the last, is about a mammal, but unlike *The Badger* published 23 years earlier it is without a colour frontispiece and has half the number of black and white plates. Essentially the monographs had become commercially non-viable – they had always been marginal.

The bibliography of *The Mole* is, on the surface, quite straightforward, but a little digging reveals a more interesting picture. The first edition exists, or at least appears to exist, in two binding variants: the primary is common and displays the non-characteristic 'Type A' NN monogram gilt-blocked to the casing, whereas the second, if that is what it is, is particularly scarce but displays the more familiar 'Type C' NN monogram (incidentally, *The Mole* is the only monograph not to use the NMN monogram). Telling them apart physically is easy enough, but the status of the second variant is unclear; it was supplied with a jacket repriced with a £2.50 Collins sticker so it was later. There would appear to be three possibilities:

1) A few spare sheets of the first edition were bound up subsequently, once the principal stock had been sold and before the appearance of the delayed reprint, or
2) It represents an undeclared reprint of the first edition. Marren in *The New Naturalists* refers to a 1971 reprint, but there is no reference to this in the printing/sales statements, or
3) It was bound up from sheets left over from the 1973 US printing. The text and paper of the Collins 1971 and US 1973 editions appear identical but for the title pages, however the US title leaf is a cancel and therefore almost certainly was printed with the Collins 1971 title page. The stitching pattern for the 'second variant' is the same as the US edition which might suggest the two were bound up at roughly the same time.

But in the absence of conclusive information and as this 'second variant' is dated 1971, I have for the purpose of this bibliography treated it as a variant binding of the first edition.

The 1974 reprint is equally interesting, though not as mysterious. While this is the date printed in the book, it was not, in fact, published until May 1975. The reasons for the delay are unknown, but this was a period of high inflation, and by the time the book left the printers, the printed price (of £2.50) was obsolete, so all jackets are price-clipped with a replacement £3.00 price sticker (or more, later). The reprint is additionally complicated by two distinct binding variants, though these are easy enough to tell apart, principally from the style of the NN monogram on the spine casing.

The Mole was also published by the Readers Union bookclub and in the US by Taplinger, both in 1973, but these are clearly distinct and not likely to confuse. Also unlikely to confuse is Mellanby's chaming children's book *Talpa: The story of a Mole* published in 1976, again by Collins. A number of NN authors have ventured into this genera and the minutes of the New

Naturalist Editorial Board for April 1965 record '… and all agreed, that eventually we do a Child's Natural History – not necessarily in the NN series itself, but intended to stimulate interest in NN books'.

Finding a fine copy of *The Mole* doesn't usually present a problem; the jackets are not susceptible to fading, chipping or any other notable ills. Total no. Collins books printed: *c.* 6,500; total no. sold: *c.* 5,500; o/p: spring 1980.

M22A-B1 **First Edition, Primary Binding Variant**, 1971 (1 November 1971).

Title: 'The New Naturalist | The Mole'.
Author: 'Kenneth Mellanby'.
Illust: 'With 18 photographs and | 35 text figures'.
Editors: JG, JH, MD, KM and EH (Photographic Editor).
Printer: William Collins Sons & Co Ltd Glasgow.
ISBN: 0002131455.
Collation: pp. 159, [1]; 6 leaves of b/w plates printed to both sides (10 × 16-page gatherings).
Casing: Gilt blocked monogram 'Type A' (see page 60), i.e. no diamond in the middle of the conjoining vertical stroke.
Jacket: [Rear panel] Single advert for *The Badger* supported by four press reviews. [Rear flap] Adverts for *The Salmon* and *The Trout*; ISBN.
Price: £2.00 net.
Print run: 4,500; no. sold: *c.* 3,730 including 'B2' below.
Notes: 1) *c.* 24 mm thick across spine. (Stitching: 4 × 25 mm stitches with 18 mm gap between = 154 mm.) 2) Jacket without *Duraseal*. 3) Ad. to p. [160] for *Pesticides and Pollution* with 5 press endorsements.

M22A-B2 First Edition, Second Binding Variant, 1971. Sold 1974[?] As B1 but monogram 'Type C' to spine casing i.e. with diamond motif in the centre of the conjoining vertical stroke. (Stitching: 3 × 38 mm stitches with 26 mm gap between = 166 mm.) Jacket

TABLE M22 Diagnostic features of the two reprint binding variants of *The Mole*.

The Mole reprint M22B	Monogram to casing	External dimensions	Leaf size
Primary binding variant (B1)	No central diamond – Monogram 'Type A'	142 x 206 mm	136 x 200 mm
Second binding variant (B2)	With central diamond – Monogram 'Type C'	138 x 207 mm	134 x 200 mm

unchanged but price-clipped with a Collins £2.50 sticker; o/p: beginning 1975.

M22B-B1 Reprint, Primary Binding Variant, 1974 (published May 1975 – see intro.). ISBN unchanged. 'First published 1971 | Reprinted 1974'. Contents unrevised but book appreciably thinner than M22A (*c.* 20 mm across spine). This primary variant a larger format than the second variant and with monogram 'Type A' to the casing, i.e. no diamond in the middle of the conjoining vertical stroke (see table M22 for details). Jacket *Durasealed*; rear panel unaltered as is rear flap but for the introduction of jacket design credit, moved from the front flap, which has allowed two press reviews (*Birmingham Post* and *Scotsman*) to be inserted below the unrevised blurb. All jackets price-clipped and repriced with Collins £3.00 price sticker. No printed: *c.* 2,000 inc. variants below.

M22B-B2 Reprint, Second Binding Variant. Bound from the same sheets as M22B-B1 but smaller format and with monogram 'Type C' to the casing, i.e. with diamond motif in the centre of the conjoining vertical stroke (see table M22 for details). This variant probably always wears jackets repriced in excess of £3.00 as follows.

M22B-B2-AP2 2nd Repriced DJ (sold 1976–77), p. clipped, with Collins £3.95 sticker, *c.* 300 sold.

M22B-B2-AP3 3rd Repriced DJ (sold 1978–80), p. clipped, with Collins £4.50 sticker, *c.* 350 sold.

BCM22A Readers Union edition, 1973. Text and plates as M22A but title page imprint reads 'The Country Book Club | Newton Abbot 1973' and imprint page states 'This edition was produced in 1973 for sale to its members | only by the proprietors, Readers Union Limited...' Accordingly no ISBN. Title page is an integral leaf, not a cancel. Casing of grey imitation cloth, gilt-blocked to the spine. Jacket with the same Ellis design (uncredited) not *Durasealed* and carries the RU monogram to the base of the spine; rear panel advertises non-related RU titles; rear flap is a membership enrolment form for Readers Union; blurb abbreviated. No printed price.

USM22A US edition, 1973. ISBN: 0800853164. Taplinger Publishing Company, New York. As M22A with same suite of plates, but the title and Editors' pages are cancels; in fact conjugate leaves, pasted over the stubs of the originals. (Stitching: 3 x 38 mm stitches with 26 mm gap between = 166 mm.) New Naturalist references are dropped from the half-title and title pages as is the NN monogram from the latter, though list of Editors retained. Printed in Great Britain. Binding same green buckram with Taplinger blocked to spine, but boards significantly thicker. The jacket: Ellis's artwork, title lettering, NMN monogram and series no. all as Collins editions, but 'Tapliinger 085316' printed to spine; rear panel advertises *Man and Birds* (Taplinger ed.); rear flap promotes *The Behaviour of Animals* by J. Kikkawa and M. J. Thorne; v. short blurb to front flap. Price: $7.50 to top corner. Print run: *c.* 1,500.

The Artists and Their Designs

BESIDES SEARCHING FOR THE VARIOUS BOOKS and related ephemera, another absorbing addition to a good New Naturalist collection is original artwork. The most striking and obvious examples are the dust jacket designs. The artwork created by Clifford and Rosemary Ellis has never really been available to acquire by collectors, as most of this material is held in the Collins archive. For many years only the published jackets had been seen in public until the publication of *Art of the New Naturalists* and the associated exhibition of original artwork held at Nature in Art, Twigworth in March 2010. The only known example of original Ellis New Naturalist artwork in private hands is for *Waders*. This was originally acquired by the author Bill Hale from Clifford Ellis in 1981 and is now part of his private collection. Clifford Ellis painted a number of watercolours, often depicting landscapes, and these very occasionally turn up at auction. The paintings display the familiar characteristics as seen on the jackets of the New Naturalists, particularly in the treatment of the sky. From time to time original posters by Clifford and Rosemary Ellis also come up for auction, such as the Shell Landmark series of lithographically printed posters. These are rare and sought after and always command high prices at auction. There are also limited-edition lithographs by Clifford Ellis made during the 1950s. These are signed and dated and usually fetch high prices at auction. Auction houses such as Christies, Lyon & Turnbull and Onslows (who specialise in vintage posters and ephemera) are good potential sources and it is worth joining their databases to receive notifications of forthcoming auctions. Many of these auction houses produce lavish catalogues which illustrate in colour the various posters for sale. In cases where the original posters are beyond the reach of many collectors, the catalogues themselves provide a good record of the image together with the price realised and are also likely to become quite collectible.

Considerably easier to find is the artwork of Robert Gillmor, particularly through his numerous exhibitions. He began designing the dust jackets after Clifford Ellis died in 1985 and has continued to create them ever since.

Robert's linocuts have become very popular and the limited edition print runs always sell out very quickly. A number of the more recent New Naturalist jacket designs have also been available to buy, but only in very small editions, sometimes of only one or two prints. Art galleries such as the Pinkfoot Gallery and Birdscapes, both based in Norfolk, are a good source of Robert Gillmor original prints and it is worth joining their mailing lists to receive information of forthcoming exhibitions.

Illustrations used within the various New Naturalist volumes, although perhaps more numerous, hardly ever appear on the market. Diagrams, along with manuscript material, will usually be stored by the author or publisher and may even be destroyed. Occasionally when a library is broken up, after the owner's death, drawings may come to light, such as with the library of Eric Simms, where drawings by Robert Gillmor, Ian Wallace and Eric Simms himself were discovered which had featured in his four New Naturalist books. Dedicated collectors have a great skill in discovering such items when they appear on the market and it is a case of continually keeping a lookout amongst art and book dealers, with the potential of discovering a New Naturalist piece of artwork from a most unexpected source.

In this section we will take a look at the three major artists who have so far contributed so much to the covers of the New Naturalist library, and also at a selection of other artists and their artwork which have appeared within the pages of the series.

To many New Naturalist collectors, Clifford and Rosemary Ellis are well known for their striking dust jacket designs, the importance of which cannot be overestimated with the success of the series. Clifford Ellis was born in 1907 at Bognor, West Sussex, and at the age of nine he went to live for several formative and memorable months with his grandparents in Arundel. W. B. Ellis, his grandfather, was a countryman, a painter, naturalist and taxidermist. He introduced Clifford to the natural world on vividly recalled walks in Arundel Park, along the riverbank and at his home, where amongst other animals he kept butterflies and a tame otter. Clifford Ellis attended Owen's Boys' School, Islington, between 1918 and 1923, where he was encouraged in his wide interests. His skill in drawing developed, thanks in particular to his habit of sketching animals at London Zoo. He spent a year at St Martin's School of Art before studying pictoral design and art history at the Regent Street Polytechnic (1924–7), followed by post-graduate courses in art history at University College London (1927–9). In 1928 he was awarded the Board of Education's Art Teacher's Diploma, and while at the London University Institute of Education he was especially inspired by the teaching of Marion Richardson (painter and teacher). She encouraged her students to look at original contemporary art from Paris and Germany, one day even bringing a work into the studio '…there it was, a small sheet of paper…shapes variously tinted in clear transparent water colour. It was by somebody called [Paul] Klee'.

From 1928–36 Clifford Ellis was a full-time member of staff of the Regent Street Polytechnic, teaching perspective and in charge of first year students. In 1931 he married Rosemary Collinson, born in 1910 in Totteridge, North London. Her childhood, during the war years, was spent at her grandparents' house in the New Forest where she developed an everlasting interest and love for the countryside. Rosemary was also at the Polytechnic (1927–1931), where, after a broad preliminary period, she studied sculpture and art history. From the early days of their marriage Clifford and Rosemary worked as a team and signed their design work jointly to indicate the nature of their partnership. Their distinctive sense of fresh bright colour and bold design is seen to great effect in the numerous posters they created in the 1930s. These posters were for some of the leading patrons of poster design at that time, including London Passenger Transport Board, Shell-Mex and BP Ltd. One of these early works, commissioned by Frank Pick, inspirational Chief Executive at London Transport, was 'Down', in 1932, one of a set of four images featuring birds and their habitats. These are in many ways evocative of the New Naturalist covers to come a decade later. Shell-Mex and BP Ltd, with Jack Beddington as Publicity Director, also produced a large number of superb posters designed by such artists as Paul Nash, McKnight Kauffer as well as the Ellises. Other commissions in the 1930s included artwork for the Empire Marketing Board, The Post Office, book jackets for Jonathan Cape, decorative tiles for Messrs Carter & Co, Poole and a mosaic floor for the British Pavilion at the Paris Exhibition in 1937.

Clifford and Rosemary Ellis left London in 1936 to take up posts in Bath; Clifford as Assistant at Bath School of Art, becoming Headmaster in 1938, and Rosemary as art teacher at the Royal School for Daughters of Officers of the British Army, which moved to Longleat during the war years. In 1943 Clifford and Rosemary made a series of watercolours for the 'Recording Britain' scheme and other paintings from the war years were acquired by the War Artists Advisory Committee (three of Clifford Ellis's watercolours are illustrated in volume IV of *Recording Britain*, Oxford University Press, 1946). During a few years of optimism at the end of the war there were new opportunities and amongst the possibilities at Bath was that of moving out into the country and starting the first English residential art academy. This 'a School of Visual Arts (in direct descent from Bath School of Art) and a Training College for Art Teachers' opened in 1946 as Bath Academy of Art at Corsham Court, the home of Lord Methuen, who was himself a distinguished painter. Corsham was 10 miles north east of Bath. There was a broad range of teaching not only in art and design but also in music, drama and science. Clifford was Principal and Rosemary an active and later senior member of staff.

Clifford continued to run the Academy with enthusiasm and vigour until his retirement in 1972. Almost concurrent to the founding of BAA was Clifford and Rosemary's introduction to a new, important series of books on natural history and in 1944 they began their first designs for Collins and the New Naturalist Library, an association which was to last until Clifford's death in 1985. Clifford and Rosemary Ellis worked as a creative team from the time they were married. In the early days, if Rosemary initiated and did most of the work her name was signed first, and if it was Clifford, his name went first. All of the New Naturalist jackets were designed in this partnership and the authorship was always, and now alphabetically, C & RE. Clifford Ellis himself

Rosemary and Clifford Ellis (left and centre) at BAA, Beechfield, Corsham, in 1966. In cannot be underestimated how important their dust jacket designs were towards the success of the New Naturalist library. They created over 80 of these until Clifford Ellis died in 1985, *The Natural History of Orkney* being their final design. (Mary Evans Picture Library)

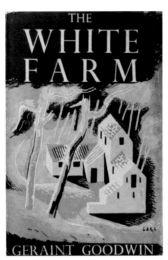

A selection of striking dust jacket designs by Clifford and Rosemary Ellis for non-New Naturalist books. Many of these are quite scarce but make beautiful and interesting additions to any New Naturalist collection .

TABLE 1: Books and book jackets by Clifford and Rosemary Ellis.

JONATHAN CAPE

1934	*The White Peony*	Evelyn Herbert
1935	*North-West by North*	Dora Birtles
1937	*The White Farm and Other Stories*	Geraint Goodwin

THE STUDIO

1939 (rev. 1945)	*Modelling for Amateurs*	Clifford and Rosemary Ellis

KING PENGUIN

1946	*Flowers of the Woods* (signed R & CE)	E. J. Salisbury
1947	*A Book of English Clocks*	R. W. Symonds

COLLINS

1945	*How to Study Birds*	Stuart Smith
1946	*The Wind Protect You*	Pat Murphy
1946	*The Swift Trout*	H. E. Towner Coston
1946	*Brensham Village* (frontispiece)	John Moore
1947	*The Rumour in the Forest*	Madeleine Couppey
1958	*Collins Guide to English Parish Churches*	John Betjeman (editor)

COLLINS COUNTRYSIDE SERIES

1974	1. *Life on the Seashore*	John Barrett
1974	2. *Birds*	Christopher Perrins
1974	3. *Woodlands*	William Condry

An unusual design by C & RE for a wallpapers exhibition at the Suffolk Galleries, London in 1945. (Mary Evans Picture Library)

Set of four posters (top and centre) was designed in 1932 for London Transport. They were used to encourage the public to explore and enjoy the countryside and are evocative of the New Naturalist dust jacket designs to come. (London Transport Museum). The Ocean Cable poster (left) was designed in 1935 for The Post Office and is one of a number of bold and powerful commercial graphic images designed by Clifford and Rosemary Ellis during the 1930s and 40s. (Mary Evans Picture Library)

regarded the book jackets as being 'a small poster: it is part of the machinery of book selling…the jacket should be immediately interesting; its forms and colours should make a very clear and distinctive image.' It cannot be overemphasised how much of an impact the Ellis jackets had on the book market in the 1940s and 50s which, in their way, contributed to the huge success of the New Naturalist library.

After retiring from the Bath Academy of Art, Clifford and Rosemary Ellis moved to a house below the Downs in Wiltshire where they continued to work. Clifford with part-time teaching on adult education courses and other art-related work, Rosemary with photographic exhibitions and, with others, books for children. Together they worked on the New Naturalist jackets until Clifford died, after a short illness in March 1985. Rosemary continued to live in the same house with its landscaped valley garden until her death in May 1998. They are buried in the same grave in the nearby village cemetery, marked with a Portland headstone carved simply with the letters C & RE.

Although finding original artwork by Clifford and Rosemary Ellis can be very difficult, it is possible to discover a few limited edition lithographic prints from the 1950s. The printed travel posters from the 1930s are particularly sought after by collectors. When they do become available to buy, usually at auction houses, they command very high prices. Perhaps just as much fun is to try to track down the other (non-New Naturalist) book jackets which were designed by Clifford and Rosemary Ellis. As well as these, C & RE also wrote a book, *Modelling for Amateurs*, which was published as part of the *How to do it* series (the Studio, 1939 and revised edition 1945).

Original watercolour paintings by Clifford and Rosemary Ellis from War Artists Advisory Committee and 'Recording Britain' are held at the Victoria Art Gallery, Bath, Bristol City Art Gallery, the Victoria and Albert Museum and the Imperial War Museum (who also hold a taped recording). LPTB and Shell posters are held, respectively, by London Transport Museum and Shell Art Collections, National Motor Museum, Beaulieu.

ROBERT GILLMOR

Robert was born in 1936 and educated in Reading. He studied Fine Art at Reading University and taught art at his old school, Leighton Park, from 1959 until 1965 when he became a full-time illustrator. He was greatly influenced by his grandfather, Allen Seaby, who had been Professor of Fine Art at Reading University. As a small boy Robert spent a great deal of time watching him in his studio, carefully printing his colour woodcuts. This was also Robert's first introduction to the New Naturalist books, as his grandfather had a painting of 'Blackcock Lekking' featured in the second volume of the series, *British Game*. With a strong interest in birds and drawing, Robert spent much time bird-watching and studying bird behaviour at the various flooded gravel pits around Reading. He was an active member of the Reading Ornithological Club, and in

1949, while still a young schoolboy, illustrated the first cover of their Annual Report and has continued to design these ever since, (although now it is the annual *Berkshire Bird Report*). Robert's first commercial use of linocuts was in 1958 for the cover of David Snow's book, *A Study of Blackbirds*, for which he had done the line drawings. Around this time he became involved with the annual RSPB film shows, brought to Reading by Frank Hamilton, a member of the Society's tiny staff. Frank saw and admired Robert's early artwork and this lead to occasional line drawings for society publications and covers for the film programmes, which in turn lead to covers for *Birds Magazine* and eventually Christmas cards. He also helped re-design the RSPB's Avocet logo.

Robert also got to know the writer and broadcaster Tony Soper, who had come to Reading to film with him for the BBC television series, *Out of Doors*. Drawings were soon commissioned from the BBC and also for Tony Soper's *Bird Table Book*, which was published in 1965. This book became hugely popular and has gone through many editions. The striking original jacket design, using a four-colour linocut, featured a great tit and great spotted woodpeckers.

In the late fifties, with the support of leading bird artists of the day, including Eric Ennion and Peter Scott, Robert organised the 'Exhibition by Contemporary Bird Painters', which led directly to the founding of the Society of Wildlife Artists in 1964. Having spent six years running the art and craft department at Leighton Park, Robert retired from teaching in 1965, when he found himself doing two full-time jobs. He was also becoming more involved with The Society of Wildlife Artists, of which he was the first secretary and went on to serve two terms as its president. In 1966 Robert became art editor of the prestigious publication *Birds of the Western Palearctic*. He continued to illustrate over 100 books as well as work for the RSPB, BTO and his local wildlife trust. Eventually he returned to his great love for printmaking when he and his wife, Susan Norman (herself an accomplished pastel and oil painter), moved to the north Norfolk coast in 1998, where they had enjoyed numerous family holidays. Although Robert is one of Britain's leading wildlife illustrators, he now spends nearly all his creative time printmaking and doing the occasional watercolour for a Poyser jacket and pen and ink drawings for the local bird reports.

Robert had long admired the work of Clifford and Rosemary Ellis, especially their jacket designs for the New Naturalist books. In April 1985 he was approached by Crispin Fisher, who was the Natural History Editor at Collins at that time, to design the dust jackets for the New Naturalist series. Clifford Ellis had died earlier that year, aged 78, and his widow Rosemary felt that she could no longer carry on with the series. The remarkable team of Clifford and Rosemary Ellis had designed more than 86 covers over a period of 40 years, giving the series its distinctive branding. Crispin Fisher was quite adamant that he wanted Robert to take over the mantle of the Ellises and although Robert was very cautious about following in the footsteps of such eminent artists, he eventually accepted the commission. Crispin and Robert both agreed that it was important to retain the basic layout and use of

The Tree Sparrow
J. Denis Summers-Smith

THE HANDBOOK OF
BRITISH
MAMMALS

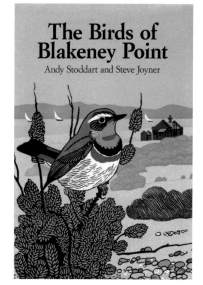

The Birds of
Blakeney Point
Andy Stoddart and Steve Joyner

A DREAM OF
JEWELLED FISHES
Reflections on Angling
'A special book' Chris Yates

JOHN ASTON

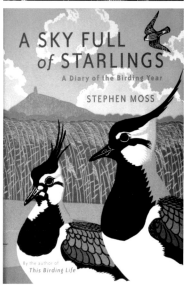

A SKY FULL
of STARLINGS
A Diary of the Birding Year
STEPHEN MOSS

By the author of
This Birding Life

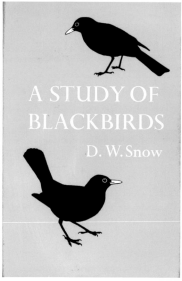

A STUDY OF
BLACKBIRDS
D. W. Snow

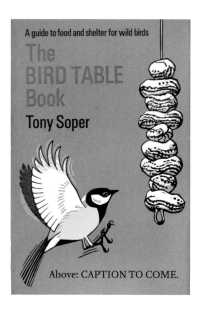

A guide to food and shelter for wild birds
The
BIRD TABLE
Book
Tony Soper

Above: CAPTION TO COME.

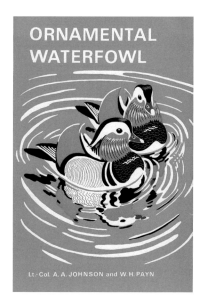

ORNAMENTAL
WATERFOWL

Lt.-Col. A. A. JOHNSON and W. H. PAYN

A small selection of more than 100 book
jackets designed by Robert Gillmor. His
versatile skill as an artist is used to great
effect, showing a range of delicate
watercolours and bold linocuts.

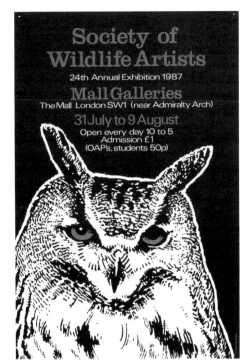

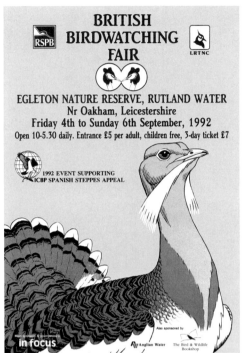

four flat colours and his first NN jacket design was for *British Warblers*.

After an initial brief from the publisher with a possible hint from the author or editor, a series of pencil doodles eventually becomes the basis for the final design, and a more finished full-size drawing is made in crayon or felt-tip pen. Occasionally an author might be quite specific about the cover design. Jonathan Mullard suggested the precise spot on the Gower peninsula for the view of Worm's Head which he hoped Robert would depict on the jacket of NN99. The colour visual is presented to Collins and that is usually followed by the go-ahead to produce the final artwork, although sometimes there may be changes required, or in one or two cases an entire re-think might be requested, such as the designs for *Freshwater Fishes* and *A History of Ornithology*. On a visit to Robert's Norfolk studio he described the process further: 'The "visual" is intended to give an idea of the overall design and how I suggest using the spaces on the jacket. Within the design I see three distinct areas. The spine, the narrow top register above the title band and the main area on the front.' He went on to explain, 'Now that my designs are also being used on the soft backs, which do not include the spine, I try to ensure that this area does not spread uncomfortably onto the front, and vice versa. At this early stage I often do not have the actual spine width, which can lead to slight changes once it is known.'

The final design is created by drawing four separate pieces of artwork in black Indian ink onto transparent acetate sheets, creating a series of overlays which eventually become the four plates from which the four colours (one of which is black) are printed. Overlapping colours are planned to create extra colours.

Robert produced his first seventeen jackets in this way.

Once Robert and Sue moved to the north Norfolk coast, he began to resume his passion for printmaking and the design for *The Broads*, published in 2001, used a linocut for the first time. Since NN95, *Northumberland*, all the jacket designs have been full linocuts often involving around a dozen blocks and up to twenty colours. The entire process is carried out by hand using his magnificent 1860 Albion Press. Once all the lino blocks are cut, they are ready for proofing. At this stage the colours are determined and also the important final order of printing, which is done using water-based inks. The colour of the title band is left until last so that a colour which goes well with the print can be chosen from the Pantone range.

Robert finds inspiration for his designs all around his Norfolk studio. Binham Priory was the basis for the jacket of *Lichens* with the tombstones blotched in orange, white and grey against the facade of the ruined priory. Look out for the beautifully camouflaged little moth resting on lichens on the tombstone in the foreground. *British Bats* featured Pipistrelle and Natterer's bats flying around Wiveton Church and ideas for the dust jacket designs of *Fungi* and *Bumblebees* were found in the Gillmor garden. In 2007 Robert heard from Peter Friend, who he had first met on an expedition to Spitsbergen in 1957. He had been commissioned to write volume 108 in the series *Southern England* and the manuscript persuaded Robert to visit the sea cliffs at Hunstanton where he made a series of sketches which would provide the basis for the jacket design.

Robert is tremendously unassuming and not the least bit pretentious, in spite of all the recognition his work has earned

him. In 2001, he was awarded the RSPB medal in recognition of outstanding contribution to bird conservation. He is one of Britain's leading ornithological illustrators and his work is up there with the best of our wildlife artists, such as Charles Tunnicliffe and Eric Ennion. He has brought his own distinctive style and craft of printmaking to the New Naturalist series and continues to keep them fresh and exciting.

Robert's work has been available to collect for many years at various exhibitions. Original drawings and paintings are very collectable. His distinctive style has been used to great effect in numerous greetings cards, postcards, posters and book jackets. Robert Gillmor prints are always printed in small editions, typically between 35 and 75, and as the demand for these is always very high, they tend not to be available for long. In 2010 he made 24 full-colour linocut designs for Royal Mail's *Post & Go* stamps, issued in four sets of six.

In October 2009, the Pinkfoot Gallery in Cley-next-the-Sea, on the north coast of Norfolk was host to a very special exhibition of Robert Gillmor's New Naturalist artwork. The exhibition was launched at midday on 24 October with a book signing by Peter Marren and Robert Gillmor of the recently published *Art of the New Naturalists*. From 10am three phone lines had been kept frantically busy while the vast majority of artwork was sold within a couple of hours. The gallery produced a fine catalogue illustrating much of the artwork and limited edition prints which were for sale, and this itself is now a sought-after collectors' item. Amongst the exhibits were original pencil sketches, final colour visuals, watercolour studies and 15 linocut prints of the recent New Naturalist jacket designs. Robert also

reprinted the artwork for *Bumblebees* as a limited edition of 65, which featured the main artwork without the title band. Also available were postcards of the artwork for *Bumblebees* and *Wildfowl*.

Some New Naturalist collectors also endeavour to have the dust jackets signed by Robert. This certainly adds interest and individuality to the book. One avid collector from Cambridge now has all of his Gillmor NN jackets signed. Occasionally it is possible to find something a little more elaborate with an original drawing or colour sketch by Robert Gillmor alongside his signature. These are very scarce and would undoubtedly increase the value not only of the dust jacket, but also of the book itself.

PHILIP SNOW

Philip was born in Cheshire in 1947 and educated at Lymm Grammar School, Northwich College of Art and Manchester Polytechnic. He has been a freelance painter and illustrator since 1977, specialising in wildlife and landscape work. Philip has illustrated a large range of items including prints, postcards, calendars and nature reserve signs. Among the books he has illustrated are *Collins Field Notebook of British Birds, Birds and Forestry, The Cottage Book* and *The Marsh Harrier,* as well as numerous illustration commissions for magazines including *BBC Wildlife*. Recent books include *Light and Flight – a Hebridean Wildlife & Landscape Sketchbook,* which includes 23 years of field sketches, and the *Collins Guide to Birds by Behaviour* in 2004.

Philip is also well known for his jacket artwork for the Bloomsbury New Naturalist books published in 1989 and 1990. He

Two delicately painted watercolours (left top & left) by Philip Snow for the Bloomsbury editions of the New Naturalist books from 1989 (*Wild Flowers* & *London's Natural History*). Commissioned by Crispin Fisher, these reprints were designed to be very different from the well-established main series. A preliminary pencil sketch for the cover of *British Birds of Prey* (above).

was contacted by Crispin Fisher in the summer of 1989 to paint the covers of a selection of New Naturalist reprints. They had already worked together on several other projects including *Collins European Bird Guides* and the *Birdwatchers' Quiz Book*. Peter comments 'Alas both Crispin and Collins were then at the "end of an era", a "golden age" when handshakes were all that was needed to ensure understanding and initial "contract", and before the gloriously casual Georgian Mayfair offices were replaced with that razor-wire and security-ringed cell block in Hammersmith.'

The idea of producing a series of New Naturalist reprints was instigated in the back of Crispin's brother Edmund's Rolls-Royce. Edmund Fisher was at that time associated with Godfrey Cave Associates Ltd, who operated the remainder company, Bloomsbury Books. These books were going to be printed as cheaply as possible and 24 titles were chosen to start with and a further 24 at a later stage if the reprints were successful. Crispin Fisher's part of the project was to commission a set of new jacket designs and to provide the camera-ready texts for the books. These were photographed from the most recent editions of the books, so were not technically new editions.

Philip was then given complete freedom to illustrate the covers with only vague indications as to what needed to be depicted. There was a requirement for a paler section where the title and author were to be placed, but the important thing was that they needed to be very different to the existing New Naturalist jackets designed by the Ellises and Robert Gillmor. For that very reason Philip Snow had been chosen to illustrate these new covers. Crispin had admired Philip's almost pastel wildlife and landscape watercolours and wanted full scenes on the wrap-around dust jackets, showing as much natural history, landscape and detail as possible. 'I produced A3 pencil "roughs" of all the covers first, usually two alternate versions and working on three different books at a time, photostatted them and sent them to Collins and Bloomsbury Books for criticism before painting the final ones. Naturally, I adapted as many covers as possible to my own preferred landscapes and subjects, and was delighted to find such personal favourites as *Birds of Prey*, *Highlands and Islands*, *Natural History of Wales*, *Mountains and Moorlands* and *The Lake District* amongst the 24 reprints. *The Sea Shore*, *Seabirds* and *Fossils* all used local Anglesey landscapes.

Mammals showed an urban red fox climbing over my old Bowden (Cheshire) garden wall, but several others were amalgams of various landscapes to show as much variety as possible – like the made-up aerial view of ancient and industrial man's architecture in *The Natural History of Man in Britain*.

'As always with Crispin, humour was never far away, and he allowed me several comic touches, as usual, if not that evident, like the escaped Golden Eagle chasing a terrier in Regent's Park, in the background of the *London's Natural History* cover!'

Halfway through the project, and mainly due to the problems of ensuring the safe passage of large flat parcels, the finished artworks were reduced from A2 to A3 size. All of the paintings were completed within 8 months and it wasn't long before the finished books were sent to Philip. It was then revealed that they were to be 'remaindered' at once, never going into the book shops at the jacket price – apparently remaindered stickers were printed at the same time! Philip was fairly pleased with the final results of his work but as he says 'just wished I could have had more time to do them …'.

Crispin Fisher had hoped that the Bloomsbury reprints would give the New Naturalist series a new lease of life. The new jackets were printed in four colours on laminated paper. The designs are actually rather beautiful paintings but they do not sit comfortably on the bookshelf with the Ellis and Gillmor jackets.

Philip Snow's delicately painted artwork is frequently offered for sale at his various exhibitions. His paintings that were used for the Bloomsbury New Naturalist jackets have long since been sold but it is worth keeping a look out in case any of them resurface on the wildlife art market.

OTHER ARTISTS

The New Naturalist library was from the beginning well regarded for its lavish colour photographs. Billy Collins had always intended that the books would be well illustrated with as many colour plates as possible and the Collins-Adprint partnership made this a reality. The books offered an exciting opportunity for a number of talented natural history photographers to work in some inspirational locations. In the early days of the New Naturalist series, professional wildlife photographers were extremely rare, with the major exception of Eric Hosking, the pioneer of nature photography. He had been invited by James Fisher and Julian Huxley to be the photographic editor of the series towards the end of 1942. It was to be Eric Hosking's task to find and commission photographers to take part in the various projects and also supply the precious colour Kodachrome film. One of the most prolific of these was John Markham, who must have climbed many a hillside and mountain to create his masterly shots for such titles as *The Natural History of the Highlands and Islands, Mountains and Moorlands* and *Snowdonia*. He also took many of the pioneering photographs for *British Mammals* in 1952. Another talented photographer, particularly of marine and microscopic subjects, was Douglas Wilson, a zoologist at Plymouth's Marine Biological Association, who produced the fine images for *The Sea Shore*. Other photographers from those early days included Robert Atkinson and Brian Perkins and they frequently accompanied the various authors on field trips to take the many photographs. Many of the earlier volumes included detailed diagrams and maps created by Adprint and in some cases by the authors. Occasionally, if the author was a particularly skilled artist, the books were full of exquisite illustrations. The first of these was probably the two volumes by Sir Alister Hardy. The first of these books *The Open Sea: The World of Plankton* covered a subject that almost defied the most skilled and determined of photographers. Douglas Wilson, almost the only photographer to have specialised in marine subjects, did contribute to the book, but many of the deep ocean planktonic life were beyond the technical capabilities of any camera at that time. Alister Hardy was a talented artist and he painted the 142 watercolour drawings for the book. He went on to paint a further 16 plates of colourful illustrations for *The Open Sea II: Fish and Fisheries*. These beautiful paintings, together with other paintings from the Discovery expeditions (*Great Waters*, Collins 1967) are now in various collections such as Department of Zoology, Oxford University, and the National Maritime Museum. Alister Hardy also painted a series of exquisite watercolour sketches of protozoa for Clifford Ellis to help him with the jacket design for the ill-fated *Ponds, Pools and Puddles*.

Another book for which photography was very difficult was William Bristowe's *The World of Spiders*. Sam Beaufoy, who had worked with E. B. Ford taking many of the delightful images for *Butterflies*, was invited to take part in the project, but even he had to admit defeat. Although the book did include some spectacular photos of spiders, most of the illustrations were magnificent line and wash paintings and drawings by Arthur Smith.

Although the earlier books were published with exotically coloured photographic plates, from the 1960s fewer and fewer colour plates were included. By the 1970s the books were illustrated entirely with black and white photographs. At this time, however, there were more line drawings included, particularly with the bird volumes. For *Finches* Robert Gillmor produced the line drawings of displays and postures and Hermann Heinzel provided several other line drawings and painted the four coloured plates. Heinzel also contributed a few line drawings to *British Birds of Prey*. Robert Gillmor provided a number of line drawings for *British Thrushes* and Diane Breeze contributed the sketches for *Waders*. The third New Naturalist title with drawings by Robert Gillmor was for *British Larks, Pipits and Wagtails*. Two drawings were included and taken from *A Natural History of British Birds*, also written by Eric Simms in 1983.

Colour plates began to reappear in the books from the 70th volume in the series, *The Natural History of Orkney*, which contained 20 coloured photographs. This was followed by *British Warblers* which, although it did not include any colour photographs, did benefit from six plates of colour paintings by Ian Wallace, together with a number of line drawings.

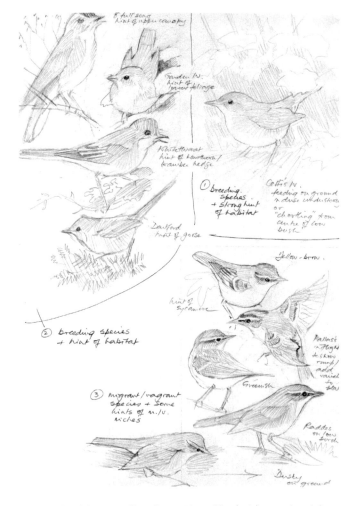

An early sketch by Ian Wallace for *British Warblers* (1985). Ian painted the exquisite colour plates for this scarce book but unfortunately it is not known what happened to the original watercolours.

BRIN EDWARDS

Perhaps the most recent New Naturalist title to include a large number of illustrations was *Caves and Cave Life*. The author, Phil Chapman, commissioned the natural history artist Brin Edwards to illustrate the text with a series of 50 fine and very beautiful pencil drawings. Born in 1957, Brin spent his early childhood in Singapore and was inspired by the colourful tropical species in his back garden. He went on to study Biology and Ecology at the University of Exeter, intending to follow a career in scientific research. He soon realised that he was much more interested in painting and illustration and gradually built up an impressive portfolio based on a variety of work commissioned by UK and European book and magazine publishers. His illustration work is precise and detailed with subjects as far ranging as fossils, marine life and amphibians, but especially birds. Brin's work has appeared in numerous books and magazines as well information and interpretation boards for such organisations as The Wildfowl

and Wetlands Trust. More recently he has been working in oils; concentrating on birds and the effects of light. Much of his inspiration comes from the Suffolk countryside, where he lives, and also the wide expanses of the Norfolk coast. He has held several successful exhibitions and continues to experiment and develop his skills as one of the country's leading bird artists.

'It was always about the jackets for me.' Brin recalls. 'Those wonderful Ellis designs just drew me in – indeed I recall taking out library copies just so I could colour photocopy the dust jackets. The first volume I owned was *Inheritance and Natural History*, which was on my undergraduate reading list, and I soon started looking out for the cheaper common titles in second-hand bookshops. A few years after leaving university I embarked upon an uncertain "career" as a wildlife illustrator, which mostly involved me hawking my portfolio around whichever London book publishers would look at it. Sometime in the late eighties I had an appointment with Myles Archibald at Collins and I sat mesmerised by the massed ranks of first editions on the bookcases behind him – I cannot remember a word of what he said, just those gorgeous books!

'A couple of years later I had a phone call out of the blue from Phil Chapman at the BBC Natural History Unit in Bristol. He had seen some of my work in BBC *Wildlife* magazine and wondered if I would be interested in illustrating a book he was writing on the wildlife of caves. When he mentioned in a rather offhand way that it would be published in the New Naturalist series my jaw hit the floor. Needless to say, I accepted the commission. I have often stated since that whatever else I might achieve in my working life at least I can say that I illustrated a New Naturalist; perhaps I should have this inscribed on my gravestone. My ambitions may have moved on a bit since then but I still feel hugely proud to have been associated in even a small way with the series. Phil was keen to have the drawings feature heavily in the book, which was music to my ears, with Bristowe's *The World of Spiders* as a sort of artistic template. It was a big challenge to emulate those exquisite drawings and I did get stuck for a while using pen and ink before switching to pencil. I soon found that graphite was a more sensitive medium which meant I could render subtle tones and shadows. I was delighted to find that some of my drawings were generously allocated a whole page in the final text. (See page 144 for a nightmare image of a Heleomyza fly sprouting the fruiting bodies of an insect-eating fungus.)

'Phil provided me with much of the reference material as photographs and specimens and left me to get on with it whilst he was overseas on filming trips. In many ways it was the perfect commission as I wasn't under too much time pressure and could work steadily. There was no budget for artwork and I was paid out of the author's fee, so let us say the money wasn't great but I'd probably have done the work for nothing anyway. With hindsight I wish I had arranged payment as a dozen copies of New Naturalist NN79 but how was I to know the ridiculous amount of money those 216 pages are now worth?'

The Broads (2001) included two full-colour watercolour paintings and three line drawings by Alan Batley. From the publication of *Fungi* in 2005 onwards, all books in the series have been illustrated in full colour throughout with a light scattering of drawings. The most recent New Naturalist volume to include line drawings was *Bird Migration* and Ian Newton commissioned the well-known and highly respected wildlife artist Keith Brockie to draw a set of four detailed and charismatic pencil illustrations.

Original artwork from any of the New Naturalist books is exceptionally difficult to find. Sometimes the originals are returned to the artists and at other times they become the property of the author or even the publisher. Work from the earlier books, such as that of Alister Hardy, has become part of the National Archive, whilst other pieces of artwork have found their way into private collections. Some artists, such as Robert Gillmor, produce rough working drawings as a guide to show the author what might be expected and these working drawings, although not actually used in the books themselves, are an interesting part of the illustrative process.

Collecting natural history illustration has become increasingly popular and to own an original drawing or painting as used within the pages of a New Naturalist book, and therefore part of the history of the series, is probably the most desirable collectible of all.

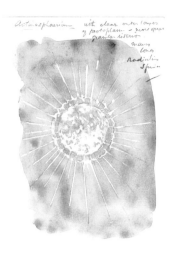

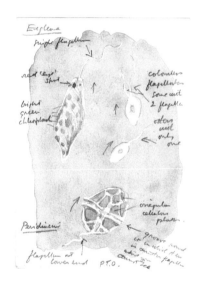

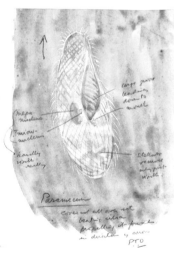

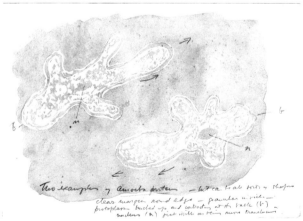

A beautiful set of watercolour sketches painted by Sir Alister Hardy in 1975 to assist Clifford Ellis with the dust jacket design for *Ponds, Pools and Puddles* which was never published.

A Cluster of Collectors and Their Reflections on a Bibliophilic Passion

We hope this book will work on several different levels. As a broad guide to the series from its beginnings in war-torn London, through the many authors and editors who shaped it over the last 65 years, and as a detailed collectors' guide to the many printed variations and associated books. Above all the book is a celebration of these esteemed books. With this in mind a selection of special guest writers were invited to contribute a series of short essays on what they love about the books and why they collect them. We have tried to select as wide a variety of New Naturalist collectors as possible, including a couple of NN authors, some very well-known television personalities and a few not so well-known but equally enthusiastic collectors. Here, then, we hand over to the collectors themselves to try to discover what lies behind their passion for the magnificent New Naturalist library.

Collecting the New Naturalists by Nick Baker

Nick Baker is a professional naturalist with a passion for wildlife since early childhood, especially invertebrates. After studying at the University of Exeter, he began to feature on local radio and local newspapers, leading to appearances in the national press and television. Since then Nick has become a full-time presenter of wildlife natural history programmes for BBC, Channel Five, National Geographic *and* Animal Planet. *He has also written a number of successful books including* Nick Baker's Bug Book *and* Nick Baker's British Wildlife. *He now lives on Dartmoor with his wife and daughter.*

Like most obsessions, this one slowly crept into my life, imperceptible at first, just a random chance purchase of a dusty old second-hand copy of *Seashore* picked up in a book store as a kid which led to a now dedicated dark corner of the house, a floor to ceiling regiment of the best of British wildlife knowledge condensed and compiled, a colourful colonnade of spines, a shelf of order and beauty. It's a place to ponder and pore over a double passion and not dwell on how much the collection has set me back financially.

The contrast between this bookcase and all the others in my house couldn't be more apparent; books on the whole for me are tools and as essential a part of the naturalist's arsenal as a microscope or magnifying lens. As a consequence of working on the frontline they usually become pretty battered and well thumbed over time. They are also stacked and piled in any way the shelf (or floor) will take them; those used more frequently inhabit the surface layers of this literary chaos while more obscure subjects have to be dived for, hunted out and in some cases divined for.

My NNs, on the other hand, are treated like royalty in comparison – for a start they get dedicated shelf space and are arranged in order and they all have, no matter how obscure the subject material within, equal status with each other. At a glance their spines can be read and whether they are read and referred to regularly (like Altringham's brilliant bat key) or whether they remain in their cellophane wrapper awaiting their turn – they exist in a world of bibliographical equality.

These books bring out in me strange behaviours and qualities that seem very atypical; the fact that I order them is just one of them, I have developed a habit of buying two copies of the ones I'm likely to use a lot – such as *Bats, Badgers* and *Dartmoor*. I also lovingly encase them in special cellophane jackets; preposterous madness for me as that constitutes double wrapping. I get twitchy if anyone else even touches them and nobody dare even suggest borrowing a copy to take out of the house.

In order to try and get to the bottom of this addiction and make sense of this I need to take a journey back to the early days; for many years I only possessed the one original copy, the battered *Seashore*, but later on in life when I began to expand my horizons and when books became the only justifiable expense on a student grant I found myself trawling the remaindered book stores. It was while doing this I discovered for a ridiculously low outlay of around about £1 an assortment of books with strange titles that will be familiar to all other NN collectors, but rather than being sumptuous and strokable these looked cheap. But I'm pretty sure that it wasn't just the low price that had me scurrying to the checkout with my treasure, after all, in those days £5 bought the best part of a Saturday night on the razzle –something of high importance in the life of a student.

I still have these copies; literally literal shadows of their former incarnations these pale green-sleeved look-a-likes were the Bloomsbury reprints. It seems these facsimiles are rarely mentioned in collecting circles but even in such a basic form with new generic sleeve art and with the contents all printed in monochrome they still had a certain something. Enough for me to get to know them sufficiently intimately that several years later I recognised a title on a book that looked so different to the copy I owned that I pulled it off the shelf. The rest, as they say, is history – I was hooked.

I think back to these copies and wonder if I could put my finger on and distil out of the situation what it was that caught my eye. If I could cure this hopeless case of bibliographical OCD I know my wife would be pleased, just think of the holiday we could have… But no, I continue to crave the copies I've missed, long to fill the gaps; I stroke them, hold them, behold them, pamper them in cellophane and give them the sort of privileged molly codling that none of my other books get.

So what happened? Why do I collect them? What's the big attraction? Especially since the chances of me reading, yet alone understanding or even referring to the information in some of the titles is as likely as me penning a New Naturalist myself.

For a start they have numbers on the spine, which makes collecting them simply irresistible, and in addition to this the exquisite dust jackets and the clever spine design created over the years by the Ellises and Robert Gillmor not only dazzle but infatuate the naturalist in the same way as the minutiae and beauty that they look for in all their subjects. It is in these details that I believe part of the appeal of this most original and celebrated series of books lies. By accident or as if setting a beguiling trap to capture the naturalist it seems Billy Collins and team tapped into what has become known to psychologists as the 8th Intelligence, or the 'Naturalist intelligence'. It has been described by some as a form of autistic thinking and, to quote Leslie Owen Wilson from *New Horizons*:

'Naturalist intelligence deals with sensing patterns in and making connections to elements in nature. Using this same intelligence, people possessing enhanced levels of this intelligence may also be very interested in other species, or in the environment and the earth. Children possessing this type of intelligence may have a strong affinity to the outside world or to animals, and this interest often begins at an early age. They may enjoy subjects, shows and stories that deal with animals or natural phenomena. Or they may show unusual interest in subjects like biology, zoology, botany, geology, meteorology, palaeontology or astronomy. People possessing nature smarts are keenly aware of their surroundings and changes in their environment, even if these changes are at minute or subtle levels. Often this is due to their highly-developed levels of sensory perception. Their heightened senses may help them notice similarities, differences and changes in their surroundings more rapidly than others. People with naturalistic intelligence may be able to categorise or catalogue things easily too. Frequently, they may notice things others might not be aware of.'

Sound familiar? I'm pretty confident that anyone living with a New Naturalist collector will recognise most of these traits. Autism or not, the affinity with nature and the sensitivity to order, natural patterns and detail are all qualities more than satisfied by this 'one of a kind' series and, let's face it, if one needs an excuse to collect these books then the above paragraph seems like a good enough reason to me!

The New Naturalist Collector: A Personal Odyssey by Stefan Buczacki

Professor Stefan Buczacki is probably Britain's most experienced media gardening celebrity. He was educated at the Universities of Southampton and Oxford and has received accolades, honorary degrees and awards for his research, writing, broadcasting and photography. He has published almost sixty books on gardening and natural history including a field guide to British Fungi for Collins. He is also the author of Garden Natural History, *volume 102 in the New Naturalist library. Stefan has travelled widely throughout the world and is always in demand as a speaker, consultant and garden designer.*

Leaders of nations, so they say, are born and not made. So are book collectors. And there was never any doubt from a very early age that in the absence of an opportunity to become Prime Minister or Pope, book collecting would be for me. The fact that I was born in the same year as the New Naturalists clearly meant I was destined eventually to end up collecting them. But the path to being a New Naturalist collector is paved with a multitude of other volumes.

The first natural history book I owned as a small child was inherited from elsewhere in the family. It was called *My Book of Insects, Seashore Animals and Fish*, a fairly eclectic subject mixture but they did in truth hang together rather well – lobsters and spiders, periwinkles and perch, the lappet moth and the John Dory. It was published by Macmillan during the War and written by the ubiquitous Kate Harvey M.Sc and E.J.S. Lay with illustrations taken from Frohawk and elsewhere. (Isn't it odd how the custom of putting your degrees and other qualifications on the title page has tended to pass away. I treasure one early twentieth-century volume in my library where the author lists, in addition to such worthy achievements as Fellow of the Linnean Society, the rather more prosaic Member of The National Trust.)

I loved my cloth-bound, well-worn Kate Harvey volume and it was this humble bit of print that set me on the road to proper book collecting, but I became even more excited a few years later when I discovered it was in fact one of a series! So it was followed onto the book shelf by *My Book of Animals and Trees* (pretty eclectic too come to think of it), *My Book of Wild Flowers* and *My Book of Birds*. It had become apparent I was not just destined to be a serious book collector but a serious series collector.

Once I was committed to series collecting, practically anything in a series was fair game and this meant that inevitably I came into contact with some pretty large, and pretty important, publishing ventures. For reasons I have never quite understood, two of the most obvious, the *Observer's Books* and *King Penguins*, rather passed me by and although, like everyone, I had a few, I never quite caught their bug.

But then my eye lighted on Collins' *Britain in Pictures*. This magnificent series of around 140 books was in some ways the forerunner of the New Naturalists. They were published during the Second World War, in large measure as propaganda to show the world what a splendid, clever and creative nation we are; something well worth fighting to preserve. The series had some hugely distinguished authors – John Betjeman, James Fisher, Vita Sackville-West, Cecil Beaton, George Orwell. But, above all, they were numbered. It is truly astonishing what a number on the spine can do for a book collector's pulse. I remember some years ago when beginning to write what was destined to be a fairly long-running series of gardening books and fighting tooth and nail with my publisher (not HarperCollins); or more specifically with my publisher's marketing department, to have the books numbered. Eventually I won the day (something that doesn't often happen in contests between author and publisher) and I am convinced it boosted sales no end.

Britain in Pictures thus became the first series I collected in its entirety. My next target was another Collins venture – the delightful numbered *About Britain* guides 'Published for the Festival of Britain Office'. They were soon swallowed whole and swiftly followed by John Betjeman's brilliantly conceived *Shell Guides* from Faber. Delving into county guides, and having a love of architecture, inevitably led to one of the greatest of single person (or at least single person driven) of all British publishing ventures in Nikolaus Pevsner's *Buildings of England*. I had to have them all, so hardbacks and paperbacks (the twenty-six paperbacks with numbers!) were gobbled up with alacrity. And I reckon I still refer to one or more at least once a week. A less obvious target and a highly dated and distinctly diverse series were the sporting volumes of the Lonsdale Library, with subject matter ranging from river management to steeple chasing.

And so the shelves continued to fill as series after series rolled in – David & Charles' *Islands*, the motley range of Warne's *Wayside and Woodlands* of course, all the Batsfords with Brian Cook jackets – which led inevitably to all the Batsfords without Brian Cook

jackets. And I would add in parenthesis how much more absorbing (and easy) it is to collect a series for which some well-meaning and devoted person (usually Peter Marren) has produced a bibliographic volume.

I do believe book collecting, especially series collecting, is governed by the same genes that turns some people into taxonomists. So it should surprise no one to know that I studied taxonomy as one of my university options. It is the pigeon-holing mentality, the mind that is most at ease when things are ranked, ordered, neat, tidy. In my experience, not many book collectors are untidy (unlike booksellers of course; but that is another story altogether); and series collectors never are. Yes, after owning and reading the books the next greatest satisfaction comes from seeing the serried rows, the blends of colours and those mounting sequences of numbers.

Now, the New Naturalists themselves, as we all know, are numbered. I obtained my first many years since – when I was in the Sixth Form in truth, which really is a long time ago – but the beguiling digits on the spine didn't work their magic until some years later; quite simply because a sixth former's income didn't allow of such things. Proper collecting of the New Naturalists couldn't begin until I had a proper income and they could compete with mortgage repayments and the week's grocery bill.

That first acquisition was NN43 Salisbury's *Weeds and Aliens* and it was given to me as a Sixth Form prize. I chose it because it was a subject that genuinely interested me, although with hindsight I rather suspect that I felt the title might raise an eyebrow on the part of the headmaster, who would probably have preferred me to choose something translated from the Greek.

I can't in truth remember the second volume I acquired, although I can recall the last time I found one of the early titles simply languishing on a bookseller's shelf awaiting an enlightened purchaser. It was a new copy of NN14 Blunt's *Art of Botanical Illustration* that I found in a long-gone bookshop in Oxford in 1970 – at a knock-down price because no one wanted it.

But from then on, it was downhill (or do I mean uphill?) all the way; and then being the 1970s and 80s, it was fairly easy to obtain first editions of everything relatively quickly. The Monographs were a bit harder, even then; and quite a bit more costly, but along they came. Then from around 1985 onwards, I automatically bought each title as it appeared. The books were as wonderful as ever but the thrill of the chase had gone. So what was left for a by-then-committed New Naturalist aficionado to do?

Association copies? Associated ephemera – letters from authors and the like? Other collectors have done this to remarkable effect but I embarked instead on related volumes – including what Peter Marren might call 'Honorary New Naturalists'. The first comprised a small series aimed at younger readers and that perhaps more than anything are the sons (or daughters) of New Naturalists; and indeed the nephews or nieces of Britain in Pictures: the Country Naturalists. Six volumes were published between 1952 and 1954, each using a few plates from the most relevant New Naturalist proper. They were (and are) fairly easily obtainable, although the card jackets are often rather the worse for wear. I have always had a special affection for these slim tomes which are too readily passed by as insignificant adjuncts.

It is a fairly short step from Collins Country Naturalists to Collins Countryside series: eight volumes (although rather more versions), and all a bit disappointing but leavened by three of them having Ellis jackets. Having then acquired the *New Naturalist Journal* and exhausted these possibilities, I returned to the main series. Buying all the reprints seemed a bit pointless and destined simply to take up more shelf space – always a consideration as we live in a timber-framed house where several of the walls are made of cow manure and not really up to book-bearing fortitude. I thought I should have the Bloomsbury reprints as a matter of course – and as much as anything because some of the jackets of this much-maligned venture really are rather attractive. Then came the Fontana and other paperbacks which didn't take up much room. Then came the oddments among the reprints – the privately printed *Lords and Ladies* and the three-way split of *The Hebrides*, for example. Then I was again running short of ideas. The American editions were helpful to keep the appetite going then, while in Australia, I chanced on the Australian Naturalists. Not real New Naturalists, of course, but Collins Australia's attempt to climb on the NN bandwagon. Only six ever appeared, all except one with rather striking artwork jackets that look handsome alongside the real thing. But that seemed to be that. Where could I go next?

Of course! The translations. Peter Marren listed a number of putative translations but he has confessed to me that some may not exist – and my experience suggests he is probably right. His list was based on intentions as revealed in the notes of New Naturalist editorial meetings rather than actual publishing contracts and, despite exhaustive trawling of the world, I have only managed to track down versions from Sweden, Spain and Germany. I don't think the Italian editions exist and fear the Japanese translations may be just a Far Eastern illusion. I have had a Japanese friend combing their second-hand book market in vain for years. The translated New Naturalists that do exist, however, are in some ways revelatory and I thank Verlag Paul Parey and their edition of C. B. Williams' *Insect Migration* for introducing me to the fabulous German word *Wanderflüge*. But is it astonishing or is it just depressing to see what can happen to New Naturalists when foreigners get their hands on them? Just as the triumph of the entire New Naturalist publishing venture has been NN102 *Garden Natural History* (but then I would say that), so the pits has been the German translated edition of Ernest Neal's monograph *The Badger*. The lurid, practically luminous green, cheap shiny plastic jacket of *Der Dachs* is quite frankly enough to make you sick.

Series collecting is indeed an obsession. It is an obsession that is ninety-nine per cent challenging and ninety-nine per cent richly rewarding but, like all obsessions, it occasionally has a downside. And when I look at *Der Dachs*, I know exactly what the downside is and feel that having to have that thing in my

bookcase just serves me right for taking my personal New Naturalist obsession to its ultimate conclusion.

Confessions of a New Naturalist Eater by David Cabot

David Cabot became absorbed with nature from an early age when his parents took the family on summer vacations to Vermont where colourful birds, snakes and intriguing butterflies fascinated him. He began collecting books in 1952, particularly when delving in second-hand bookshops in Devon and is now a serious collector specialising in eighteenth- and nineteenth-century Irish Natural History and Darwiniana. He worked in an Irish Government Research Institute for 20 years, integrating biodiversity into the physical planning system. He then was a documentary film producer and a radio/tv presenter for the BBC and RTE, followed by consultancy in Eastern Europe for 10 years. He now works as a writer and ecological consultant. His third New Naturalist volume, Terns, *written with Ian Nisbet, was published in June 2013.*

As a very young and green thing, more than half a century ago, I wandered one afternoon into a bookshop in the town of Totnes, South Devon, close to where I then lived. I used to make regular sorties there to sniff out new arrivals in the natural history section and to furtively sneak reads before being reprimanded by one of the assistants. There, that afternoon, I spotted a smallish book with a stunning dust wrapper design, sporting a fabulous looking Greenshank, its head turned over its back. Leafing through the book was a new experience – no, not another identification guide, nor a turgid tome with a boring text, nor a large format book with mostly close up shots of birds. I had come upon a new type of book. It was written by Desmond Nethersole-Thompson, who had devoted decades of painstaking and original field research to unravel the breeding biology and behaviour of this elegant bird. To me, *The Greenshank* was a 'New Naturalist' type of book – original, fresh, displaying an almost obsessive pursuit of the subject as well as being well written. He opened up the secret life of the greenshank, one of our most elusive breeding birds and known only to me as a graceful and almost aristocratic wintering bird to the Exe Estuary. Scratching together all my meagre pocket money, I bought the book for 15 shillings when it was published in 1951. My collection of NNs had commenced.

The publication of *The Greenshank* occurred at a time when there was a flourish of other New Naturalist books – monographs and mainstream titles – during the late 1940s and early 50s. Several of these joined my embryonic library: *Natural History in the Highlands and Islands* (1947); *The Yellow Wagtail* (1950); *The Redstart* (1950); *Dartmoor* (1953) and *Sea-Birds* (1954). Then a period of quiescence set in and no more NNs were purchased from the Totnes bookshop.

Looking back now at the time when I was at university I was such a stupid and naive student. I made no connection between my zoology tutor, Dr. E. B. Ford, and his two great NN volumes *Butterflies* (1943) and *Moths* (1955), often lauded as amongst the best NNs. If I had, I would have bought both volumes and asked him to sign them. Similarly, when we were being lectured by Sir Alaister Hardy on the detailed anatomical structure of some obscure copepod, I failed to make the association between this great man and his wonderful NNS – *The World of Plankton* (1956) and *Fish and Fisheries* (1959). Oh, the collector follies of youth! But, I would argue in my defence, that in those days it was not fashionable to pester authors for their signatures and dedications. How things have changed! Many collectors now go to great lengths to have their NNS signed. Ironically I know of some cases, in the field of poetry, where the unsigned book of a certain famous poet is rarer and more expensive than the signed one.

However, after these encounters with some of the eminent NN authors it was not until years later that I got back on track and started to collect more earnestly, filling gaps and seeking recently published titles. After my modest start, a critical mass soon developed and I was hooked; subject, book and dust wrapper! I became an obsessive collector, as bad as any alcoholic who hides their gin or whiskey in hot water bottles for fear of being detected by those nearby. In my case it was to conceal a disproportionate amount of family income being diverted into NNS.

My collection, mostly first editions with dust wrappers and a few signed by authors, is now as complete as it can ever be. Today I feel that should I suddenly die at least I would have achieved 'something' in my life. But to my shame I have not supported several booksellers as I should have done by purchasing my NNS through them. Today I buy the new titles through Amazon after the price has been discounted, often by as much as 50 per cent and before the print run has been exhausted – a sometimes rather tricky judgement, rather like trying to catch the last bus home on a Friday night, missing it and then spending a fortune on the taxi.

I am glad to say that my collection was put together not by lashing out hundreds, maybe thousands, of pounds for the scarcer itemsm such as *British Warblers* (1985) – only 725 hardback copies – and *The Natural History of Orkney*, again, only 725 copies. No, the real challenge and excitement of building a complete set of NNS was doing it on a minimal budget by swapping titles with friends, poking around the stalls at church bazaars and outwitting booksellers. I did buy several titles from a wonderful natural history bookseller in Amsterdam – Antiquariat Kok in Oude Hoogstraat – as Amsterdam was just up the road, so to speak, from EU meetings in Brussels which I used to regularly attend. But other than that, and together with my first purchases in Totnes, I have generally steered clear of booksellers who often think certain NNS are worth far more than they actually are. I also went through a joyful period when a generous benefactor, who has to remain anonymous in case you might try to tap him, used to supply me with freshly published titles.

There is a major problem confronting the obsessive collector – getting the books into the home. This was both a challenging and daunting operation. There was a mortgage to pay, three young mouths to feed and a house to run. How could I be spending scarce money on books? So the volumes were gathered at the office and then brought home in the briefcase, sometimes bulging like a boa constrictor after swallowing a wild pig. On enquiry by the wife as to the nature of the enlarged briefcase, my reply was

'Oh, yes dear, those are documents I have to work on for tomorrow'.

A serious collector always worries about the completeness of his or her collection. In a moment of wild and abject craziness I once thought: why not collect every single edition and reprint of each hard and softback, book wrapper variants, leatherback copies, limited edition author signed copies, titles published in other countries, any foreign translations and now all the PODS? To achieve such a collection I reckon it would take me another fifty years. But the gas will soon be running low, so time is limited. However, if I am not mistaken there is at least one NN collector in these islands who is suffering from this malady and is trying to assemble such a unique set.

I collect NNS not for their dust wrappers (the sheer brilliance of their designs is undisputed) nor for their potential monetary appreciation (although there is something reassuring when gazing at the scarcer titles while fretting about rising medical costs and the need to get to the sun and snow sometimes), but principally for their content. The body of knowledge carried in the NNS is simply amazing. Most of it is extraordinarily original and brilliant, some of it quirky, very little of it mundane. I know no other natural history book series, past or present, that comes within an ass's roar of the quality of material and its presentation as in NNS. All of us owe a great deal of gratitude to the persistence and patience of HarperCollins, its NN Editorial Board and the editors of natural history. The current editor, Myles Archibald, who I have described elsewhere as 'irrepressible', reinvigorated the series when it was endangered by potential demise several years ago. But, of course, without the eclectic band of enthusiastic authors who write, certainly not for monetary gain, but more for the honour of contributing to the NN series, these books would not exist.

Which brings me to the question how did I get involved as an NN author? Many years ago, in the early 1960s, the study of natural history in Ireland had reached a low ebb after a period dominated by the great Irish naturalist Robert Lloyd Praeger. His magnificent *The Way That I Went* (1937 and many later printings) was one of the best natural history books ever written about Ireland. Collins published his *Natural History of Ireland* in 1950 – it had been written in 1944 but the war delayed its publication. I believe the intention was that it would be part of the New Naturalist family but for some reason it never made it and was published 'out of series', so to speak. Perhaps, as an arrogant young pup, I thought I would like to have a go at a new *Natural History of Ireland*. It was certainly time for a new one. In the mid-1960s I proposed a structure and sent it, with support from Miriam Rothschild and David Webb, to Michael Walters, who was the NN editor at Collins at the time. The Editorial Board were interested but thought the task too great for one person and suggested I secure other collaborators. Anyway, a requested sample chapter on the geology of Ireland was sent off but wasn't met with great enthusiasm. I retired into my burrow but reemerged for another bite nearly 30 years later. By then I was a little more mature and experienced. It took me two years to write *Ireland: a Natural History* (1999), mostly during weekends and in the evenings while working in Slovenia.

A book on wildfowl had been planned for sometime by the NN Editorial Board but for a variety of reasons, not an unusual NN situation, it failed to fly. So, as a ducks, goose and swan man I was keen to have a go at it and *Wildfowl* was published at the end of May 2009. I recently published another NN, *Terns* with Ian Nesbit as co-author. I am extraordinarily lucky to have worked with Ian as he is one of the foremost tern researchers in the world.

If someone asked me which were my favourite NNs I would find it hard to say. But the top group would certainly include William Condry's *The Natural History of Wales* (1981) for its elegant prose and readability; Edward Armstrong's *The Folklore of Birds* (1958) for its scholarship and cultural articulations and also his *The Wren* (1955) for its amazingly detailed study, by a parson ornithologist in the tradition of Gilbert White. Peter Marren's *The New Naturalists* (second edition 2008) is a stunning account of all NN authors, their books and the stories that surround them: details of all print runs, variants, price guidelines and much more – an essential vade mecum for any NN collector. Other favourites are John Raven and Max Walter's *Mountain Flowers* (1956); Ian Hepburn's *Flowers of the Coast* (1952); Miriam Rothschild and Theresa Clay's *Fleas, Flukes and Cuckoos* (1952) and James Fisher's *The Fulmar* (1952). Amongst the more recent titles I would include Oliver Rackham's *Woodlands* (2006); Sam Berry's I*slands* (2009) and Ian Newton's *Bird Migration* (2010).

What about the future? Despite the electronic net closing in on us, and some NNs now being available on Kindle, I believe that the New Naturalist series will continue to flourish in traditional book form as there are too many of us who just love books and would die for them. So, to my thinking, there is no way that NNs, in their present format, will become obsolescent. However, I can envisage the possibility of video inserts in future NNs, and maybe some other strange innovations. But that would be a small price to pay for continuance of this remarkable series in its present form.

The New Naturalists and I by Ken Davies

Ken Davies took an honours degree in Classics in the 1960s at St David's University College in Wales, where he had ample opportunity to develop his twin passions for birds and books. At that time just a few pairs of red kites retained a tenuous hold in the nearby hills, while the surrounding woods and valleys held redstarts, pied flycatchers and wood warblers. His first teaching post in Huntingdonshire led him to discover the wildlife of the Fens, the Brecks and the Norfolk coast, as well as the delights of East Anglian second-hand bookshops! He retired as Assistant Head from the same school thirty-six years later, and has spent each summer season since then as a volunteer with the Rutland Water Osprey Project.

I bought my first New Naturalist in a little second-hand bookshop in Southport on 1 May 1969 for ten shillings. I know this because (unfortunately) I wrote my name and the date on the front free endpaper. It was John Buxton's exquisite monograph on *The Redstart* (M2), a favourite bird I had studied at length during undergraduate days in mid-Wales, and later in wooded parts of Lancashire. The book was already nearly twenty years old when I bought it, and the observations which led to its writing were first made several years earlier than that. I already 'knew' John Buxton as the recipient of his brother-in-law R. M. Lockley's *Letters from Skokholm*, and I was also aware that Buxton had carried out his studies during his years of confinement as a prisoner-of-war in Bavaria. For me this added glamour and excitement to the book. There had certainly been times when I regarded my three-year Classics degree at University in Central Wales as a 'confinement' – albeit a wholly different one – and I too had found solace in studying the redstarts. I took the book home and immediately covered the beautiful dust-wrapper with a see-through plastic sleeve – which probably helps to explain why it is as bright and crisp today as it was then, over forty years ago. I read and re-read the book during that summer of 69, until I knew every page, every paragraph even. I admired the very fine photographs by Eric Hosking and John Markham, and the drawings by 'Fish Hawk' and D. M. Henry. I loved the quotations at the head of each chapter and recited them in Greek (ϖ ....), Latin (*aeriae primum volucres te, diva, tuumque / significant initum perculsae corda tua vi*) and French (*Tout part: le plus jeune peut-être / Demande, en regardant les lieux qui l'ont vu naître...*), and I learned by heart the lines from John Clare....

'Around the rotten tree the firetail mourns
As the old hedger to his toil returns,
Chopping the grain to stop the gap close by
The hole where her blue eggs in safety lie.
Of everything that stirs she dreameth wrong
And pipes her 'tweet tut' fears the whole day long'

And Gilbert White...

'Amusive bird! say where your hid retreat
When the frost rages and the tempests beat;
Whence your return, by such nice instincts led,
When spring, soft season, lifts her bloomy head?'

Above all, though, I admired and revelled in the unique insight into an individual species' social and domestic life, in language and style I could relate to and fully understand. Buxton and his fellow prisoners were 'not scientists, not trained in school and university to the technicalities of biology, but mere naturalists who delighted in the birds and were content to note down what [they] saw or heard without any opinion about its significance'. Whilst such a statement might definitely not please the present generation of professional monograph writers, it had an immediate appeal then to a young man whose redstarts inhabited woodland edges around the Dinas in Cardiganshire, the Forest of Bowland in Lancashire, and, in later years, the spinneys of coastal Suffolk. For me, it was this book, more than any other, which set the trend for my involvement with birds and books over the next forty years, and ensured that my mantra would always be 'watch, note, and watch again'. And if that sounds like 'the enquiring spirit of the old naturalists', then so be it.

At first I could only afford to buy the books for special occasions – *Mountain Flowers* (33) for a trip to Scotland, *The Broads* (46) for a holiday in Norfolk, *The Yellow Wagtail* (M4) after finding a nest while spending a summer bean-picking near Ormskirk – but from the beginning I only bought second-hand copies with bright, sparkling wrappers which I immediately encased in plastic sleeves to protect them in a rucksack or in the panier of a motorcycle. These early purchases are mostly still on the bookshelf as part of the complete set, although one or two have been replaced with better copies over the years. The books I chose to buy never failed to thrill me whatever the topic – birds, flowers, insects, mammals, amphibians, fungi, even fossils! – and all the time my interests were widening.

I tended not to buy books at that stage which had a 'text book' feel about them and titles like *Britain's Structure and Scenery* (NN4) and *Man and the Land* (NN31) had to be added much later when I was 'filling in the gaps'. I did buy a copy of *The Weald* (NN26) which looked perfect at first sight, but when I got it home, proved to be rather imperfect as the pages were bound in the wrong order – some were repeated and some missing altogether! I kept it anyway as a curiosity but have to admit this is one of the very few in the series I have never attempted to read.

The first New Naturalist I bought brand new was *British Birds of Prey* (NN60) by Leslie Brown, in May 1976. By this time I had a 'proper' job and could just about afford the £6 it cost on publication. I ordered it from Heffers in Cambridge and had to wait months and months for it. The expected publication date came and went, was replaced with another which was also changed, and so on and so on, until finally I had a postcard to say it had arrived and I could go and collect it. It was a massive moment for me. Leslie Brown's passion and intensity inspired me to devote hours, days and weeks of each year since then to studying and helping to protect Britain's birds of prey. What a pity Leslie Brown is not here today to share with us the upturn in fortunes for so many of the species which, at that time, appeared to be still in decline. The marsh harrier, for example, which in the early 1970s was reduced, in Brown's words, to a 'beleaguered remnant' in East Anglia, thanks in part to 'noisy, pleasure-seeking human beings', can now be found widely in many regions, even on the outskirts of large, inland cities. Peregrines on Tate Modern, red kites in the Chilterns, ospreys in central England, buzzards everywhere, even goshawks, honey buzzards and sea eagles regaining a foothold – how thrilled Leslie Brown would be. His chapters on pesticides and other 'burning issues' as he called them, alerted his readers to the plight of birds of prey and for this reason I would put this New Naturalist very high on my personal list of 'influential' books. My original copy is still on the shelf, spine unfortunately faded, contents out of date, author sadly deceased – but never forgotten.

The late 1970s and 1980s were nervous years for the New Naturalists, although at the time I was unaware of the financial difficulties in the background. I continued to buy the titles I really wanted. William Condry's *Natural History of Wales* (NN66) was a 'must' after my three-year sojourn in Lampeter and a memorable day spent with him at the RSPB Ynys-hir reserve, where he was the warden. That book cost me £9.50 new, but just four years later I was shocked to hear from my local bookshop that *Orkney* (NN70) would be priced at a whopping £20! Little did I know that my copy was one of only 725 printed!

Despite the tiny print, I found the book an indispensable companion during a long stay on the islands that summer, with the hen harriers, whimbrel and Arctic skuas over my head (and even *on* my head in the case of the skuas!). The book is now worth approximately ten times more than the total cost of that holiday (including the rather decrepit car that took me there), so perhaps £20 was not too bad after all. Throughout the rest of that decade, titles continued to attract, prices continued to rise ('£30 for a book? Ridiculous!' – but I bought *Ferns* (NN74) anyway), until, in August 1995, I bought the book (*The New Naturalists*, NN82) which succeeded in 'putting new heart into a by then moribund series' (Peter Marren, pers comm.) and left me, and many others, feeling vindicated for sticking with the series for so long. 'Don't stop now', urged Peter Marren, and most of us haven't. I still feel the same anticipation for a new book as I did forty years ago.

I had gaps to fill, scarce monographs to find, updates of *Mammals* (NN21, 68), *Moths* (NN30, 90), *Amphibians and Reptiles* (NN20, 69, 87), *The Soil* (NN35, 77), and others as they appeared, to add. It took time, but with patience, and the help of a couple of excellent book dealers, the missing volumes were slotted in one by one, and each one has added to my experience and enjoyment of Britain's rich wildlife. Admittedly one or two were, and still are, beyond me – I still have trouble when confronted with ants or diseased plants!

The New Naturalists have been one of the few constant factors in my life for forty years now – that's well over two-thirds of my existence! I've bought, on average, three or four books a year. And it didn't break the bank … well, apart from that special NN100! Through all the ups and downs – births, deaths, job-changes, house moves – the books have always been my companions and the source of so much of my knowledge of the natural world in Britain. Added to which, it's true that their colourful wrappers, whether Ellis or Gillmor, do indeed 'light up a room like a Ming vase', as someone once said. Which reminds me, I just need to check in *Ladybirds* (NN81) to identify that little yellow and black creature I found in the garden today …

Collecting New Naturalist Books by Mildred Davis

Mildred Davis was born in Newcastle upon Tyne in 1946. She did a degree in pharmacy at Sunderland College of Advanced Technology (now University) followed by a preregistration year at Newcastle General Hospital. After qualifying as a pharmacist, she completed a PhD in pharmaceutical microbiology at Bradford University in 1973. Work in the editorial department of the Royal Pharmaceutical Society in London was followed by work in Sheffield as a hospital drug information pharmacist.

In the 1980s she completed an Open University BA degree in humanities. Since 1995 Mildred has worked as a freelance editor, mainly involved in the revision and updating of pharmacy reference books and as a proof reader. Her main interests outside of work include travel, walking, gardening, natural history, art history and reading.

The first New Naturalist book was published in 1945, about a year before I was born. However, throughout my childhood I had no idea that these books existed. Nevertheless, my interest in natural history started in childhood. At that time, primary school children were encouraged to create collections of pressed dried flowers or take items to school for the nature table. I loved to go on walks with my family and dog near my home at Ryton-on-Tyne (then in Co Durham, now part of Tyne and Wear). In the post-war years, Ryton was still relatively small, but although there were several housing developments in those years, it retained a village core and there were lots of good walks on nearby farm land, woodland or by the riverside, 'Ryton Willows', that provided the chance to find a good range of plants. My source of plant identification at this time was a copy of *The Observer's Book of Wild Flowers*. My interest in natural history was broadened when at the age of eleven, I was given a copy of Collins *Britain's Wonderland of Nature*. Although written for children, this book provided quite detailed information on most aspects of British natural history. I found it fascinating. Even so, I did not follow some of the more practical information, although given with some reservations, such as how to cage squirrels or snakes to keep as pets. In a similar way to my flower collecting, this reflected a more intrusive approach to natural history than is acceptable today.

The first time I became aware of the existence of the New Naturalist series of books was when I went to a party at a house shared by postgraduate students in the Moor Side area of Bradford in 1973. Obviously the party could not have been very exciting because what has stuck in my memory about the occasion was seeing a set of about a dozen books in pride of place on the living room mantelpiece that turned out to be the New Naturalist collection of one of the biology students. As someone with an interest in natural history who loved reading and collecting books, this set triggered such possibilities.

The first New Naturalist book I bought was a reprint of NN19 *Wild Orchids of Britain* in 1976. At the time I was working in London and it was bought from a bookshop in Bromley where I lived, as a birthday present for my then boyfriend, Barry. Happily, as we married in 1977, the book was the start of our collection of New Naturalist books and remains a treasured book.

The next New Naturalist was the paperback Fontana edition of NN6 *Highlands and Islands*. I bought this before visiting the Hebrides, reading it from cover to cover and also as it was fairly portable and inexpensive taking it with maps and other guides on the holiday. It was many years later that I found and bought a copy of the 1947 edition of NN6 *Natural History in the Highlands and Islands*.

The pattern of New Naturalist acquisition until the early 1980s was guided solely by our particular interests. They were books to read or dip into for information, rather than collect. Moving to Derbyshire in 1977, meant that NN44 *The Peak District* was a must. A growing interest in bird watching put volumes such as NN60 *British Birds of Prey*, NN63 *British Thrushes* and NN65 *Waders* on birthday and Christmas present lists, while one of Barry's research interests in the use of vegetable refuse material as a potential soil conditioner, prompted another present, NN35 *The World of the Soil*.

As well as finding the books a fantastic resource for information on British natural history, part of the obvious attraction was the acquisition of more books of a series. Added to this was the obvious attractiveness of the books themselves, not least in the wealth of illustrations within the books, but also in the artwork of the dust jackets. I really like the striking picture of the great spotted woodpecker on the jacket of NN52 *Woodland Birds* and the *flypast* of gannets and puffins over St Kilda witnessed by the wren on the dust jacket of NN109 I*slands*.

In 1983 I bought NN69 *Reptiles and Amphibians in Britain* for £11. However, by the time NN70 *The Natural History of Orkney* appeared in 1985 at £20, I had stopped working to look after two small sons so in no way could the household budget justify the expenditure for this book. Price increases to £30 or more for the volumes that appeared through to NN85 *Plant Disease* in 1999 also countered any ideas for buying them. However, we still loved to visit bookshops, but the focus shifted towards children's books for several years, although we always looked to see whether any new New Naturalist books had been published, particularly looking longingly at titles such as NN76 *The Hebrides*, as these wonderful islands have remained one of our favourite holiday destinations. I suppose it only dawned on us how collectable New Naturalist books were when we spotted NN82 *The New Naturalists* in 1995 and also began to notice how prices of the rarer titles had risen.

However, during the late 80s and 90s, looking for New Naturalist books provided a pleasant focus for browsing around second-hand bookshops, both those we knew of locally in Derbyshire, but also those found, often by chance, a bit further afield at holiday destinations throughout England and Scotland. As a result, our collection began to grow substantially. One piece of luck occurred when, in 1987, the university Barry worked at cleared some redundant books from its library. Fortunately before consigning them to a skip, the books were offered to staff. Barry rescued several New Naturalist volumes including NN34 and 37, the two volumes of *The Open Sea*, NN36 *Insect Migration* and NN38 *The World of Spiders*. Although not first editions, all were in good condition with dust jackets intact. For us, a great find. This luck was repeated in the 1990s, when at a second library cull, another batch of New Naturalist books rescued from the skip included the 2nd edition of NN6 *The Highlands and Islands*. However, we were not always so lucky. I remember, Barry and I discussing whether or not to buy a copy of NN14 *The Art of Botanical Illustration* at a bookshop in Northumberland. Just as we made our decision an assistant arrived with another customer and removed the book from the locked bookcase. We had been too slow.

Some gaps were also temporarily filled with the cheap

Bloomsbury editions of 1989 and 1990. They provided good reading editions which have now found their way to our sons' bookshelves.

As well as meeting the needs of an ever growing interest in natural history, I think the late 1980s and 1990s marked a transition from reader to reader/collector. In 2000, I bought the first new New Naturalist for almost two decades. It was NN86 *Lichens* and from then on I have bought each new volume as it is published.

Over the last decade the collection has grown steadily and a copy of each volume from NN1 *Butterflies* up to the most recently published, NN115 *Climate and Weather* as well as copies of the 22 New Naturalist monographs, are on the bookshelves. Some of the latter were found in second-hand bookshops, but much of this part of the collection was found via the internet, an option that has added a new dimension to collecting books. Although not all the New Naturalist volumes collected are first editions, they are all very special to me and my family. Interest in British natural history remains strong, the collecting bug is firmly in place and with new books to look forward to, just gets better.

A Passion for Nature by David Kings

David Kings has spent a career in the construction industry working on a wide range of projects for multi-national clients such as IBM and GlaxoSmithKline. Retirement has enabled him to spend more time on his four key interests: as a university researcher, carrying out conservation and habitat creation work on his nature reserve, bird ringing for the British Trust for Ornithology and maintaining and, where necessary, restoring his early 17th-century stone house in Warwickshire.

My lifelong obsession with natural history began during the latter part of the Second World War. Typical early memories include observing the unsettled behaviour of barn swallows *Hirundo rustica* on overhead power lines prior to migration (behaviour that I would later understand as migratory restlessness). Nature walks were an important part of my early schooling and often resulted in later nest-finding and egg-collecting 'expeditions' with other like-minded boys. My first two natural history books were E. A. R. Ennion's *The British Bird* (1943), reprinted 1945, and *Wild Animals of Britain* (1946) by W. Kenneth Richmond – both published by Oxford University Press – although I was largely self-taught about the British countryside at that time. Interestingly, Ennion's book has a comprehensive bibliography which I had little knowledge of how to use and was unaware that in future years many of those volumes would be in my library. Several of the authors listed such as E. A. Armstrong, James Fisher, Ronald Lockley, Max Nicholson and Brian Vesey-Fitzgerald would later write influential books in the New Naturalist series.

While studying ornithology at Birmingham University and conservation and ecology at Warwick University during the 1970s, several New Naturalist books were on the recommended and set reading lists. Borrowing those library books was often problematic due to their limited numbers. It was therefore more convenient to purchase relevant volumes such as Eric Simms' *Woodland Birds*, Ian Newton's *Finches*, Chris Perrrin's *British Tits*, Ian Moore's *Grass* and *Grasslands and Hedges* by Pollard et al. Initially, condition seemed unimportant and one or two early purchases were bookclub editions and fairly battered paperbacks. But the seeds of my obsession with the New Naturalist series had been sown and soon my collection had grown considerably. After so many decades those early books are still some of my personal favourites and are regularly consulted.

Although the scientific aims of the original Editorial Board remained important, an appeal of the early New Naturalist books was their unusually bright dust jackets, which became one of the key reasons for the longevity of the series. The beautiful hand-drawn artwork, designed by Clifford and Rosemary Ellis, intriguingly suggested the books' contents, thereby influencing potential readers to look inside. Having numbered and sometimes quirky dust-wrappers appealed greatly to collectors and to cite Marren (2009) on p. 21: 'They caught the eye, as intended, but the books also sat sweetly together on the shelf, more and more as the series expanded', resulting in collectors feeling the desire to fill any gaps in their collection. Before long my first set of hardback copies, including the monographs and special volumes, was complete. But, being an 'obsessive' bibliophile, I started looking for ways to enhance the collection and began writing to authors requesting that they dedicate and sign a copy of their book or, alternatively, an enclosed bookplate. Their reply letters being loosely inserted with the relevant volume. This method worked well and provided closer connections with the authors. Interest was widened by collecting review copies, signed association copies and emails and letters between authors. For example, the collection includes two signed letters from Desmond Nethersole-Thompson (author of *The Greenshank*) to his close friend Derek Ratcliffe (author of *Lakeland* and *Galloway and the Borders*) and another to the author of *Waders*, Prof. Bill Hale. The signatures of all five members of the original Editorial Board are also included on various books, papers and letters. One unusual book in my collection is Sir Julian Huxley's personal copy of *Pedigree: Words from Nature* by Stephen Potter and Laurens Sargent, with details of the dispersal of Julian's estate on the front endpaper. There are extensive minute notes and underlining in red ink throughout by Huxley – the book is evidently: 'the last book he read all the way through'.

The collection was further extended to include authors' own copies signed by them, such as E. B. Ford's personal copy of *Butterflies* inscribed by him on the front free endpaper and with minor corrections in the author's hand; and presentation copies from one author to another, such as James Fisher's *The Fulmar* signed by the author for Eric Simms. These books often included reviews and obituaries from newspapers and journals and, occasionally, photographs. A further example is Eric Simms' copy (signed by him on the free endpaper) of *British Mammals* by L. Harrison Matthews. The book is dedicated to Eric Simms and signed by Matthews on the title page and contains three letters from Leo to Eric dated 15.12.61, 16.8.68 and 23.8.68. Also loosely inserted is a newspaper article about Captain Scott's return to the Antarctic in 1925, annotated by Eric: 'Leo sailed with the Discovery on the 1925 voyage and had a tooth removed by the ship's carpenter with the aid of a bottle of rum and a hammer and chisel'. Evidently, under similar circumstances, it was not unusual to extract teeth using such excruciating methods.

My fascination with New Naturalist authors was extended to collecting their memoirs, such as Ernest Neal's *The Badger Man: Memoirs of a Biologist* (1994), signed and dated by Ernest on title page; Bruce Campbell's *Bird-Watcher at Large: Autobiography of an Ornithologist* (1979), dedicated to Eric Simms, dated and signed by the author and *The Song of The Sandpiper: Memoir of a Scottish Naturalist* (1999) by Morton Boyd. This posthumously published book is dedicated and signed on the title page by his wife Winifred. Sometimes, however, memoirs of New Naturalist authors are somewhat oblique; for example, *Wandering Albatross: Adventures among the Albatrosses and Petrels in the Southern Oceans* (1951) dedicated and signed by Leo Matthews: 'The book was about real albatrosses, but in another sense the wandering albatross was Matthews himself' (*see* Marren, 1995, p. 163).

Anecdotes about the authors' lives, their books and associated politics also interest me greatly. For example, my collection includes the author's personal copy of *Woodland Birds*, inscribed: 'To my brother Wilfrid with affection and esteem Eric, January 1972' – the book being subsequently returned to Eric Simms after his brother's death. Within this volume are letters which, when used in conjunction with Peter Marren's 1995 book, tell an intriguing and lengthy story: In November 1951 James Fisher approached Bruce Campbell to write *Woodland Birds* but, some weeks later, Bruce decided that he was not sufficiently keen or self-confident for the project. The contract was subsequently signed with W. B. Yapp who worked on the book until June 1956 when Fisher asked Yapp to withdraw from the contract as he thought the book was disappointing and uninteresting. Yapp's book – renamed *Birds and Woods* – was subsequently published in 1962 by Oxford University Press. Bruce Campbell was re-approached in June 1957 but he was too busy; however, in February 1962 he said that he was keen to write the book because he was leaving the BBC, but changed his mind yet again in April 1965. Collins were keen to publish the book as the main series had few volumes on ornithology at that time, and so the eminent ornithologist David Snow was asked to write the book early in June 1966, but he also declined the offer. Finally, Fisher wrote to Eric Simms on 23 June 1966 asking him to, 'write a scholarly and interesting work for the New Naturalist? – the subject: Woodland Birds'. The offer was accepted, the book eventually published in 1971 and Eric was destined to become the first New Naturalist author of four volumes in the series. Twenty years from approaching an author to final publication may seem an exceedingly lengthy time but is by no means the longest; for example, the synopsis of David Cabot's *Ireland* was submitted in 1966 but publication was not until 1999, some 33 years later. It can

also be interesting to try and solve dedication mysteries. For example, my copy of *A Country Parish* by A. W. Boyd (with the author's signature opposite the title page) is inscribed: 'M. K. B. from J. N. B. December 1951'. Investigation suggests that it is from Arnold Boyd's father James to his mother, Mary Boyd. My collection includes other unique items such as *Dragonflies* (2008), including the leatherbound deluxe edition, by Philip Corbet and Stephen Brooks, which have bookplates fortuitously signed by Philip the day before his untimely demise and a letter showing provenance.

The key volume stimulating collectors' interest in the authors is undoubtedly Peter Marren's *The New Naturalists* (1995) which has proved to be an invaluable reference work for avid collectors. My copy is inscribed: 'For Eric Simms with warm wishes and thanks for all your help and enthusiasm from Peter Marren 1st March 1995', with three signed handwritten letters from Peter to Eric. The dust-wrapper is signed by Robert Gillmor, as is every jacket designed by Robert in my collection. Fortunately I have been able to contact many of the authors at conferences, such as the British Trust for Ornithology annual ringing conference where a number of other ornithologist/bird ringers are also enthusiastic collectors of the New Naturalist library.

Although for many years I have been fascinated with the dust-wrapper artwork of the New Naturalist series, it is only recently that I started collecting such unique artwork; for example, Clifford and Rosemary Ellis's artwork for *Waders* (1980) by Bill Hale, and Robert Gillmor's preliminary design for *Garden Natural History* (2007) by Stefan Buczacki. Ian Wallace's pencil sketches for the layout of warblers for *British Warblers* (1985) by Eric Simms, and the original photographic plates (including those by Eric Hosking) for *Waders* (1980) by Bill Hale were also recently added to the collection. In October 2009, a representative selection of the above was displayed at the first symposium of The New Naturalist Collectors' Club at Nature in Art, Twigworth, Gloucestershire. It was at this event that Peter Marren and Robert Gillmor's latest book *Art of the New Naturalists* was launched, stimulating considerable interest in dust-wrapper art. Throughout March 2010, a special exhibition of largely publicly unseen artwork from the New Naturalists series, featuring the unique dust-wrapper artwork of Clifford and Rosemary Ellis, was also held at Twigworth. The *Mountains and Moorlands* poster advertising the exhibition was subsequently added to my collection. Key highlights of the event were thought-provoking talks by Peter Marren and Robert Gillmor on the 24 March, creating yet further interest in the series by a growing band of devoted collectors.

My current aim is to have the complete New Naturalist library in mint, or very good, condition with all copies signed by their author/s, or with at least one signed letter from the author/s. To achieve this, fifteen signatures are required to complete the main series and eight signatures for the monographs and special volumes.

New Naturalists by Nigel Marven

Nigel Marven showed promise as a budding naturalist from an early age. Family holidays in the Mediterranean became zoological expeditions with Nigel collecting snakes and lizards for study. He read Botany and Zoology at Bristol University and got his first break in television working on Galactic Garden, *he went on to become a researcher and later producer for the* BBC *Natural History Unit. Nigel stepped from behind the camera to in front of it to present Granada Television's* Giants. *He has also presented many other television programmes including* Walking with Dinosaurs *specials and recent adventures with polar bears, penguins, pandas and piranhas. He now runs his own wildlife film production company, Image Impact, based in Bristol.*

I've always relished top facts, surprising statistics or intriguing pieces of information, and the New Naturalists series is full of them. As a kid reading by torchlight under the covers when I was meant to be asleep, I discovered the largest British specimen of one creature was found in Surrey in 1968; it was 6' 3" (1,830 mm) long. An awe-inspiring thought – I wished I could find a record-breaker!

Another species I was desperate to see at any size was described: 'The adult male in spring has a high denticulated crest starting behind the eyes and terminating abruptly at the loins.' Or what about an animal which, as the male ages, sometimes develops bright blue spots, described beautifully by the author.

Of course I'm quoting from the first New Naturalist I ever owned, *The British Amphibians and Reptiles* by Malcolm Smith. I already had an interest in herptiles [ALT: cold-blooded creatures], but the book was the fertiliser for my interest to become a passion. I read the book from cover to cover, over and over again; I was determined to see the creatures Smith's words brought so vividly to life.

A few springs after reading the book, I was pond-dipping on Hadley Common, North London. Something moved in the weeds in the bottom of my net, a jet-black creature with a high denticulated crest. Reading Smith made the find even sweeter – a male crested newt with an eye-popping belly of orange and black from eyes to loins, a silver stripe along its tail. Smith had described it so perfectly.

I never did find a grass snake over a metre long in Britain, though (and as far as I know, the 1,830 mm record still stands). However, for the BBC dramatisation of Gerald Durrell's book *My Family and Other Animals*, I caught an individual that was 1.5 metres long on the Greek island of Corfu. Not that great a feat really – as a rule, grass snakes from the Mediterranean do grow larger than British ones. And in Russia, while filming desmans (an aquatic member of the mole family), I found a grass snake that seemed to have passed away, lying motionless on its back with its mouth open, forked tongue hanging out. I instantly knew from reading Smith that playing dead is a defensive strategy to put off predators. It's rarely seen in British grass snakes, but it was a fact he mentioned.

Some male slow worms develop a blue-spotted back as they mature; I've only ever found two, one under a piece of old carpet in St Albans when I was growing up, the other crossing a woodland path in Belarus this spring. Even then, some 35 years after reading Smith's book, his slow worm facts came back to me.

The New Naturalist series has had a great impact on my life, and in my job as a television naturalist, it's been invaluable. I have a complete set now and on entering my library, the colourful kaleidoscope of dust-wrappers is like an old and very knowledgeable friend. I'm not sure whether mine are first, second, or third editions – I'm interested in the information they contain.

Alister Hardy's *The Open Sea: The World of Plankton* helped me impress David Attenborough's production team enough for them to offer me my first job in television as a researcher on the Attenborough series *First Eden*, a natural history of the Mediterranean. Hardy had written eloquently about the glories of the Mediterranean plankton, a community of transparent creatures: salps, ctenophores and jellyfish. Those glories weren't, in the end, filmed for *First Eden*, but I stored Hardy's top facts away and eight years later, went to Villefranche, a small French marine laboratory on the Mediterranean coast which Hardy had visited, to document them. The stunning sequences of this jelly world featured in a programme about the mysterious lifecycle of freshwater eels in *Incredible Journeys*, a series about remarkable migrations.

My favourite New Naturalist book must be Bristowe's *The World of Spiders*. After reading his words on Scytodes, a spider that spits strands of sticky silk that glue down its prey, I always wrote a Scytodes sequence into any film proposal I could, but unfortunately I never had the chance to include it. I think the behaviour has been videoed successfully now, although I've never seen it on the box.

The World of Spiders also includes what, for me, is one of the most thrilling sentences in British natural history: 'Only one species is found in Britain and so gorgeous is the male *Eresus niger* that it is every collectors dream to find one'. The ladybird spider has black legs ringed with white and a body of vivid scarlet. When Bristowe was writing about them in 1958 they'd last been seen in Britain 52 years before, and were presumed extinct in this country. Rather wonderfully, they were rediscovered at a single heathland site in Devon in 1979. Now strictly protected, these arachnids are the subject of a captive-rearing project, using individuals brought in from Denmark to boost the British population. But I've still never seen one!

Then recently, while filming in Hohhot, the capital of Inner Mongolia province, China, I met a research student who had on her door a photo of a scarlet spider with black and white legs. Bristowe's wondrous words came back to me once more; *Eresus niger*, the ladybird spider, has a wide distribution, and Inner Mongolia is at the southern and eastern limit of its range. This was my chance to see one, even include it in our documentary, but we were thwarted. The research student agreed to try, but a severe drought in China had forced the spiders deep underground and none could be found. *Eresus niger* is still on my wish-list.

So, even though my job takes me far away from Britain for much of the time, the New Naturalist series is still very relevant for me. I owe it a great debt of gratitude for inspiring me as a boy and for generating top facts and ideas for my films.

New Naturalist Companion by Stephen Moss

Stephen Moss is a television producer, writer and broadcaster specialising in British wildlife, especially birds. He currently works at the BBC Natural History Unit in Bristol where he has been responsible for many successful series including The Nature of Britain, Springwatch *and* Birds Britannia, *a series on the cultural and social history of birds and the British people. His books include* This Birding Life, A Sky Full of Starlings *and* The Bumper Book of Nature. *He lives with his family on the Somerset Levels.*

More than 100 New Naturalists stand in the corner of my bedroom, in serried ranks, in a tall wooden bookcase. Take a closer look and you'll see that the numbers form a pleasing continuum – apart, of course from NN76 (see below). The 22 monographs sit modestly in the opposite corner of the room, in another, smaller bookcase. My wife Suzanne puts up with their presence, as she knows how much they mean to me.

Sometimes I wish they had a room of their own – my own, personal New Naturalist library, with specially designed shelves to show them front-on, so I could sit and savour the subtle beauty of the Ellis dust-jackets, and the more striking, graphic style of the Gillmor ones.

Of course, looking at the New Naturalists is never quite enough. You have to take one off the shelf – *A Country Parish*, perhaps, or *The Wren* – open up its pages, and inhale deeply. That familiar, slightly musty smell of these iconic volumes always transports me to a bygone, less complicated, age.

Unlike many New Naturalist collectors my obsession began quite late – I never won a volume as a school prize; nor did I study them as part of a university science degree (I read English, not Zoology). In fact the first volume I ever owned was bought for purely practical reasons.

During my three years at Cambridge University I had pursued many things, including women, a career in television and occasionally my degree; but I had sadly neglected my interest in birds. So when I graduated in the summer of 1982, with a couple of months free until I started work at the BBC, I decided to give it one more go. I would find out whether birding was purely a childhood hobby, such as collecting stamps, coins or football cards, or whether it would truly become my lifelong passion.

I headed off on the long train and boat journey to Shetland, the northernmost archipelago of the British Isles, in search of snowy owls, red-necked phalaropes, and thousands upon thousands of seabirds. I found them, and I also discovered, in a bookshop in Lerwick, *Natural History of Shetland* by R. J. (Sam) Berry. During my stay I read it from cover to cover, and discovered the fascinating story behind the ecology and history of the islands and their wildlife.

A couple of years later I found myself spending three months at the BBC Natural History Unit in Bristol; a place that would eventually become my permanent place of work. While there I managed to blag, from Crispin Fisher at Collins, paperback copies of *Natural History of Orkney* and *British Warblers*. Later on I would have these rebound into 'faux hardbacks' (I'm reluctant to pay more than £1,000 for a car, let alone a book!), but for the next decade or so they travelled with me in boxes from one home to another, largely forgotten.

Then, one summer in the mid-1990s, I went on holiday to France. I took a variety of reading matter, but the book that really grabbed my attention was not the latest airport novel or non-fiction bestseller, but Peter Marren's masterful *The New Naturalists*. Peter is, for me, the finest writer of all on books and natural history, and I read this fascinating volume from cover-to-cover – twice.

On my return I dashed off to Foyle's bookshop in the Charing Cross Road and snapped up pristine hardback copies of *British Freshwater Fish, The Soil, British Larks, Pipits and Wagtails, Wild and Garden Plants* and *Ladybirds*. I recall seeing that cursed NN76, *The Hebrides*, but I neglected to buy it – a decision I later regretted, for obvious reasons. Nevertheless, my quick thinking had saved me a small fortune, as I soon discovered when prices of these hardbacks went into the stratosphere.

Fired with enthusiasm, I decided to collect the set, and spent many a happy weekend visiting bookfairs, or browsing second-hand bookshops in market towns – this was in those prehistoric, pre-internet days we'll tell our grandchildren about one day. On a work trip to East Anglia I popped into a bookshop in Colchester and found *Ferns* at the bargain price (even then) of £25. Occasionally I picked up a copy closer to home – my local second-hand shop sold me a fifty-year-old, box-fresh copy of *Mountains and Moorlands*, for just £20.

I loved the thrill of the chase – like most men I retain the boyhood thrill of collecting – and in particular I would enjoy getting a copy of an old volume in the post, opening it and savouring the brilliance of the dust-jackets – *Weeds and Aliens* and the splendid Puffin on the cover of *Seabirds* being amongst my favourites.

As Peter Marren has pointed out, though, the main reason we collect NNs is a very basic one: the fact that they are numbered, enabling us to place them in order on our bookshelves, notice the gaps – and try to fill them!

Fill them I did – not just with the main series, but with the monographs – which in some ways I enjoyed finding even more. I loved both their exquisite beauty in miniature and their eccentric choice of subjects – whoever today would think of publishing a book on lords and ladies or oysters – or even the mole?

The dust-jackets of many of the monographs are, if anything, even more beautiful than those of the main series – when asked by Peter Marren to choose my favourite NN dust-jacket I knew immediately it had to be *The Redstart*. Talking of dust-jackets, whoever decided that some of the main series and monographs should appear in photographic or plain jackets should have been put up against a wall and shot!

So, bit by bit, I collected the set – not all first editions, and some 'cheats' (see *Orkney* and *Warblers* above). But all treasured and loved

– and even, occasionally, read. Some, of course, are better written than others: Miriam Rothschild's *Fleas, Flukes and Cuckoos* and *Lords and Ladies* are unexpected delights; while amongst more recent volumes, Oliver Gilbert's *Lichens* and Sam Berry's I*slands* are both rattling good reads. I won't mention the dullest ones – but if you are thinking of curling up for the evening with *The World of Soil* then make sure you drink plenty of coffee beforehand.

And now, apart from the blasted *Hebrides*, I have a complete set. It's tempting to log on to the Collins website and shell out fifty quid for a print-on-demand version – but then I would have come to the end of my quest – and whoever wants to come to the end of a quest as fascinating, frustrating and enjoyable as collecting the New Naturalists? And there's always a chance, I tell myself, of a pristine copy of Boyd and Boyd's magnum opus turning up for 50p at our school jumble sale.

Incidentally, I have also had the privilege – and the pleasure – of meeting several NN authors in person. I have signed copies of *London's Natural History* and *Birds and Men*, personally inscribed by the late Richard Fitter and Max Nicholson. I once enjoyed a splendid day with Eric Simms, but forgot to take my books for him to sign. I often bump into Phil Chapman, author of *Caves and Cave Life*, at work, as he is a colleague of mine. And I also have the pleasure of calling Peter Marren and Robert Gillmor, joint authors of *The Art of the New Naturalists*, friends of mine.

My favourite New Naturalist? For its cover – *The Redstart*. For content – *Fleas, Flukes and Cuckoos*. And for the story behind how I got hold of it – definitely *The Hawfinch*. Back in spring 2001 I was in a second-hand bookshop in Canterbury, where I discovered an immaculate copy of Guy Mountfort's delightful little book. The only drawback – the cost – more than £200. Suzanne and I were about to move house and get married, so after much debate I decided not to part with the money.

A week or so later I mentioned that I wished I had bought the book, as I was never likely to find such a pristine specimen again. Suzanne suggested I should telephone the bookshop, which I did, only to discover that I was too late – it had already been sold.

Six months later, on our wedding day, she gave me a present – a box whose size and shape suggested it contained a shirt. I opened it, and nestling amongst the crepe paper was a copy of – you've guessed it – *The Hawfinch*. And not just a copy, but the very copy I had turned down the opportunity to buy. Sometimes it's not just the thought that counts, but the deed!

New Naturalists: Natural Wonders by Michael McCarthy
Michael McCarthy was the long-standing Environment Editor of The Independent *and has won numerous awards for his writing about the natural world, including Specialist Writer of the Year in the British Press Awards. In 2007 he was awarded the medal of the* RSPB *for 'Outstanding Services to Conservation' – the only time in the medal's 100-year history that it has been given to a journalist – and in 2009 he published* Say Goodbye to The Cuckoo *(John Murray), a study of Britain's declining migrant birds.*

Struggling for a long time to put into words just why the attraction is so intense, I kept coming back to a phrase which maybe doesn't really do it, but which I couldn't really better: there is something perfect about them.

It is a series of books, a long-running sequence of volumes on British natural history (126, to date), and they have titles like *Wild Flowers of Chalk and Limestone, A Country Parish, The World of Spiders, Life in Lakes and Rivers* or *The Greenshank*. Written by men (it's usually men) expert in their own fields, they are solid tomes, typically of 300 pages or so – they feel weighty in the hand – and they proclaim a serious and idealistic purpose, which is to make deep knowledge of the natural world accessible to non-specialists, to interested amateurs.

But there's more. They are jacketed in the most exquisite modernist dust-wrappers, each one making a bold impressionistic visual statement about the contents, like a mini-poster, yet in a restricted palette of colours which only adds to the charm. And when they sit together in a bookcase as a set, the Collins New Naturalists, they present a peerless mingling of noble aim and physical beauty, a combination of idealism and restrained visual harmony, for which perfection does not seem too strong a word.

You think I exaggerate? Well, it's not only me that feels like that. Across the country about 2,000 people are thought to be seriously collecting New Nats, as we say, trying determinedly to build up complete sets of the series that was launched by Collins and Co. (as it then was) in 1945 and is still going, and such is their longing for the scarcer ones that they have bidden up prices to what may seem completely crazy levels.

You want a copy – we are talking first editions only, in fine or at least very good condition, both for the book and the dust-wrapper – of NN9, *A Country Parish*, A.W. Boyd's famous 1951 portrait of Great Budworth in Cheshire? That'll set you back about £200–£250. Or if you fancy NN41, *Dragonflies* (1960), that'll be more like £350–£400.

But, hey, that's nothing. Wait till we get to more recent titles. A copy of NN81, Michael Majerus's *Ladybirds* (1994) will currently cost you about £450. NN74 and 75, *Ferns* (1988) and *Freshwater Fish* (1992), will each lighten your wallet by about £650, while NN76, *The Hebrides* (1990), will set you back another £850. And we're still not finished.

The two rarest of all are NN70 and 71, R. J. Berry's *The Natural History of Orkney* and Eric Simms' *British Warblers* (both 1985). To buy Simms' book you will need to shell out about £1,200; this week *Orkney* was being advertised for sale on a well-known natural history books website for £1,750. That's right. For just one copy of a book published just 20 years ago, which you could have bought then for £20. Even house prices haven't done that.

You want to add it all up? There are to date 95 titles in the main series, and another 22 in the New Naturalist monographs, which are smaller volumes that tend to deal with individual species such as *The Mole* or *The Salmon*. To buy a full set of both at current prices, all 117 volumes, will cost you (depending on condition) about £16,000 to £18,000. Let's say £20,000 to be on the safe side

(I've been quoted more). Two thousand collectors at £20,000 a time means something like £40m worth of second-hand books potentially in play, in just one series.

This astonishing phenomenon is surely one of the most remarkable events in the British book trade in recent years. But it has had virtually no publicity in the world at large, so speculation is thought to have played little part so far in driving prices up so dizzily.

'It's simply the operation of the market,' says Bob Burrow, who founded and ran the New Naturalist Book Club, for collectors, from his bookshop in Jersey. He points out that there are now more serious collectors than the numbers actually printed of many of the volumes from the mid-1980s on, when Collins's faith in the series underwent a wobble. The two most valuable titles, *Orkney* and *Warblers*, for example, were both given minuscule print runs of only 725 hardbacks each. 'It's just supply and demand,' he says.

But what accounts for the demand in the first place? Why do people want to collect New Naturalists?

There is no doubt that the series has been seen as very special from the outset, both by those who conceived it and by those who have bought the books (and at the start they were numbered in tens of thousands). It was an idealistic, hugely ambitious publishing project, dreamed up during the Second World War as a contribution to the ensuing peace, to the better world that soldiers, it was hoped, would be returning to.

Its aim was to bring to the interested public the advances that had been made in the study of the natural world between the wars. Natural history throughout the Victorian era, and after, had been largely based on collecting – birds' eggs, stuffed birds, pressed wild flowers, mounted butterflies in trays – but in the inter-war years the science of ecology, or the study of organisms in the context of their natural environment, began to flourish. The New Naturalists library was to document this extensive new knowledge over the whole spectrum of British wildlife and the British landscape, in a way that was serious, yet accessible to the general reader.

In today's dumbed-down world to launch such a series would not even be contemplated, but at the end of the Second World War, before the short attention span was even visible on the horizon, the moment was propitious: there was an intelligent readership at hand, and also a pool of naturalist authors who were as skilled and elegant at writing English as they were scientifically knowledgeable.

The story of the launch, and indeed of the series as a whole, is told in detail by Peter Marren in his book *The New Naturalists*, which was republished by HarperCollins – as it now is, of course, part of the Murdoch Empire – to mark the 60th anniversary of the series in 2005. (Marren's book was first published in 1995 to mark the 50th birthday and is itself a New Naturalist, NN82. Price of the original now, 1st, fine, with fine dust-wrapper? Don't ask.)

Three men were the progenitors. The leader was the well-connected ornithologist James Fisher, who, after Sir Peter Scott,

was Britain's best-known naturalist in the post-war years, a familiar face in the early decades of television. The series was his idea, but he was enthusiastically partnered by the biologist Julian Huxley, grandson of T. H. Huxley, Darwin's celebrated defender, and most importantly, by the maker-possible: W. A. R. Collins, universally known as Billy, chairman of the family publishing firm. Billy Collins was looking for distinction for his imprint, but, hard-nosed as he was, he also sensed he could make money.

He was right. The first title, E. B. Ford's *Butterflies*, priced at 16s, a hefty enough sum in 1945, sold out its first edition of 20,000 and was reprinted several times. NN2 and 3, Brian Vesey-Fitzgerald's *British Game* (1946) and R. S. Fitter's *London's Natural History* (1945) – the first-ever detailed study of the wildlife of a city – flew off the shelves in similar fashion. Gradually sales settled down, but for the next 35 years, through 50 or so titles, they were steady and highly respectable.

It is not hard to see why. Not only was there an eager reading public, but many of the titles were and are marvellous books, now regarded as classics. The contribution of Ford, for example, an eccentric, misogynist Fellow of All Souls who liked to test the toxicity of moths by eating them, is widely regarded as the best book on butterflies ever written.

Colour photography was another great attraction. It was just coming in and widely used in the series. But the icing on the cake – perhaps a not inappropriate metaphor here – was the dust-wrapper on each volume. These were designed by a husband-and-wife team, Clifford and Rosemary Ellis, who had been poster designers in the 1930s, and for each title they produced a strongly stylised image instantly suggestive of the content. The Ellises did all the covers up to and including *Orkney* in 1985, when Clifford died and Rosemary retired, and they were then succeeded by Robert Gillmor, who has carried on their stylised tradition.

The New Naturalist dust-wrappers are hugely attractive and turn the volumes into objects of real beauty; it is what makes the books so collectible, so irresistible, almost, to a bibliophile with a love for the natural world.

I have been collecting them for five years. (My favourite is actually one of the few that has a plain wrapper, Miriam Rothschild's marvellously engaging 1952 study of bird parasites *Fleas, Flukes and Cuckoos*.) I have about half the series, although I possess none of the really expensive ones, and such are their prices now that, barring a substantial lottery win, I reckon I never shall.

But when I look at the ones I do have on the shelves, *The Highlands and Islands*, *The Art of Botanical Illustration*, *An Angler's Entomology*, I am reminded of the idea of perfection: this great intelligent enterprise, of such noble purpose, brought about with such harmonious grace and elegance. It's just a pity that with these wonderful books, as I suppose with everything else, perfection doesn't come cheap.

First published in the *Independent Magazine*, 26 March 2005.

New Naturalist Companion by Jonathan Mullard

Jonathan Mullard started his career in the environmental sector working on urban nature conservation in central London and nearly thirty years later is once again employed in the city. In between, he has been responsible for the management of Heritage Coasts, Areas of Outstanding Natural Beauty and National Parks. Jonathan spent over ten years on Gower, the first AONB, and is appropriately author of NN99 Gower. He has recently written another book in the series covering the Brecon Beacons, which was published in May 2014.

I first encountered the New Naturalist series when I was a student, studying biology at Portsmouth Polytechnic in the 1970s. Brought up in landlocked Shropshire I had become fascinated by the sea and was intent on becoming a marine biologist. The annual family day trip to Barmouth on the Welsh coast and regular doses of Jacques Cousteau on our black and white television only served to increase my enthusiasm for this seemingly hard-to-reach habitat. Several books in the series, in their guise as Fontana paperbacks, were required reading for my course, although at the time I did not appreciate the link. I think the first one I bought was *Britain's Structure and Scenery*, which was closely followed by *The Open Sea: The World of Plankton* and *Pesticides and Pollution*; the latter a key environmental concern in that period and one which has unfortunately not gone away. As I write this, thousands of tonnes of floating oil are beginning to reach the Gulf coast of the United States, following an explosion on an oil rig.

One of the paperbacks in particular, *The Sea Shore*, was responsible for strengthening my interest in marine biology and for ensuring that I spent much of my final year removing hermit crabs from their shells in order to study the associated organisms, including ragworms and anemones, and complete the thesis for my degree. The realisation that the paperbacks were related to a wider series came about in the first summer holiday after I started college, in 1975, when I was browsing in Blackwell's bookshop in Birmingham. Amongst a pile of rather boring looking biology textbooks I came across Pollard, Hooper and Moore's *Hedges*, published the previous year. This book, the first 'proper' New Naturalist volume that I encountered, subsequently became famous, or perhaps infamous, for introducing the 'Hooper Rule', which suggested that in every 300 ft of hedgerow each individual shrub species represented 100 years in the life of the hedge. The formula has subsequently proved a difficult one to apply, but it certainly helped to galvanise the historical study of hedges.

All the same *Hedges* really stood out on the shelves, the dust jacket by Clifford and Rosemary Ellis, doing its job, as ever. It took me a while, though, through looking at the list of books in the series on the back cover, before I connected the well-thumbed paperbacks of my reading list with the solid and beautiful looking hardback I held in my hands. There seemed a gulf between the two. I particularly remember looking longingly at the book, turning it over in my hands and spending some time reading it, missing my train as I did so. I could not afford to buy it on my student grant. Instead I walked away, passed my degree in biological sciences and eventually forgot about the series. The copy of the book I have now is the third reprint of 1979. Neither did I buy *British Seals, Ants, British Birds of Prey*, or *Inheritance and Natural History*; all which came out during my college years. Only now am I beginning to fill these gaps on my bookshelves, but a good first edition of *Ants* is proving especially elusive.

A year after completing a post graduate course in applied ecology, in 1982, I met my first New Naturalist author through being asked to join the Ecological Parks Trust. This was a small urban wildlife charity, based in London, set up and ably guided by Max Nicolson, the pioneer conservationist and author of *Birds and Men*. How sexist that title seems now. Somehow *Man and the Land* by Dudley Stamp does not seem so bad and, of course, later there was *Man and Birds* by Ron Murton. Max's book was long out of print and I did not manage to find one second-hand, although there was a badly sunned copy in the Portacabin on the William Curtis Ecological Park, the Trust's main site near Tower Bridge. Situated next to an equally aged *London's Natural History* it occupied the shelf alongside pond-dipping nets and field guides used by the visiting school groups. One of my abiding memories of this time is being enthusiastically videoed by Japanese tourists standing on the bridge, while cutting the few square metres of grassland that served as our demonstration 'hay meadow' with a traditional scythe. It was also here at the Ecological Park that I first met David Goode, then Senior Ecologist for the Greater London Council and now author of the forthcoming New Naturalist *Nature in Towns and Cities*. Just by chance, clearing out my study a few weeks ago I came across a copy of BBC *Wildlife Magazine* from October 1984, which contained a photograph of David and me, together with two local boys, in the Ecological Park, intently staring into a pond net for the photographer. It seemed exciting work at the time, but existing in London in the 1980s, on just over £3,000 a year, meant I did not buy many books. I spent all my spare funds on Kodachrome slide film instead, intent on building up a portfolio of landscape and wildlife photographs.

It took a move to South Wales later that year, to take up a job with the local wildlife trust and a new girlfriend, who eventually became my wife, to reconnect me with the series. An enthusiastic archaeologist and, like me, a lover of quiet countryside and good books, it was Melanie's inspired choice to buy me NN66, *The Natural History of Wales*. Back in contact with the series and perhaps in a better position to appreciate it, I subsequently picked up a number of volumes, including hardback copies of *The Sea Shore* (my Fontana paperback having disintegrated long ago), *Wild Orchids of Britain, The Folklore of Birds* and a special favourite of mine, *Natural History in the Highlands and Islands*. Quite a few of my subsequent trips to the west coast of Scotland owe their origin to Fraser Darling's enthusiastic prose. Although, like the series as a whole, not really designed as a field guide, *The Sea Shore* must, at some time in its life, have been taken out onto the coast as occasionally when opening it a few grains of sand fall out onto my desk. Certainly the cover shows signs of being left in the sun.

Unfortunately a move north in 1986, to look after the Flamborough Headland Heritage Coast, disrupted my purchases and I missed a number of key volumes; including *The New Forest* and *Ferns* (although I later got the paperback of *Ferns*). I did, however, buy a number of the remaindered Bloomsbury reprints of otherwise hard to find items in the series, including *The Peak District*, in Sheffield when Melanie was based there for a while and we were exploring the area at weekends. It was only on my return to Wales in 1990, to manage the Gower Area of Outstanding Natural Beauty, that I started purchasing New Naturalists regularly; again, though, with a lamentable gap due to the disruption of the move. In this way I missed *The Hebrides,* which was published that year. I could have bought the revised book which was published as three separate paperbacks in 1996, as I saw them in the Portacabin that served as the local bookshop in Mallaig in 1997, while waiting for the ferry to Rum. A friend of mine was the Assistant Warden there at the time. For some reason, which I will never be able to explain, I also missed *Ladybirds,* though I do have the paperback, which was a lucky find for a few pounds in a second-hand bookshop that did not realise its value.

From 2000, when I moved to Northumberland to work for the National Park Authority (and in doing so met Angus Lunn, author of *Northumberland*) I have been a consistent purchaser of the series and have not missed a volume, though four books a year has sometimes proved too much; as I understand it has for other enthusiasts [NB: Collins now publish three volumes a year]. There is not time to read them all in detail. I have not been tempted yet by the reprints and am still looking for first editions I can afford. Indeed I have probably been too enthusiastic at times and have ended up with three first editions of *Ireland* and duplicates of a number of others such as *Fungi* and *Mosses and Liverworts*. The books have gradually taken over most of the bookshelves in my attic study and displaced other books from lesser publishers to sites elsewhere in the house. After my experience in Swansea, where I stored my New Naturalists on shelves in a north-facing room and still experienced 'spine fade', I now have a blackout blind on the roof light in the room, which is firmly closed when the room is not in use. *Heathlands,* which I bought as revision prior to setting up a major conservation project on the Gower commons, was the worst affected and I am still looking for a good copy to replace it.

Thanks to the publishers I do, of course, have numerous copies of my first book in the series, *Gower,* which brings together my twelve years of landscape and wildlife management in the area. The opportunity to produce my own contribution to the series was a wonderful experience, (especially the chance to liaise with Robert Gillmor on the cover design) and I have finished work on a second publication, covering the Brecon Beacons National Park. As part of my research I purchased the missing volumes in my collection covering other National Parks, including *The Snowdonia National Park* and *The Lake District,* so as to compare the approaches to structure and content. I am also looking for *Lords and Ladies* in the monographs.

I do not, yet, own many of the monographs. I bought *Badger* very early on as a result of an excellent weekend course on badgers run by the Field Studies Council, at Preston Montford in Shropshire, which set me up for a lifetime of badger watching. As regards the rest of the series, like most people interested in New Naturalists, when I should have been buying monographs I wasn't! A former role as Company Secretary for the Tweed Forum did result though in the acquisition of *The Salmon* and I am still on the lookout for *The Trout*.

So my collection has grown rather unevenly, and rather slowly, over the years but, unlike perhaps the libraries of dedicated book collectors, each volume that I have purchased has some link or relationship to my career in the environmental sector. Indeed, if I were to lose all other records of my activities over the last 30 years I feel I could summon them up again by merely looking at a collection of New Naturalists. I also find that volumes come back into focus again after being 'neglected' for some time. Recently I joined the Civil Service and I am now once again spending part of my week in central London. Walking regularly through St James's Park, past the pelicans on the lake, has prompted me to reach again for my well-used copy of *London's Natural History* and compare what I am seeing now to what Richard Fitter recorded in the 1940s – and add additional memories to the book.

Cop Lane By John Sykes

John Sykes was born in London in 1949 and brought up in Lancashire. He became a language teacher and then a gardener. John bought his first New Naturalist in the 1970s and started collecting them in 1998. He heard of Bob Burrow in Jersey and joined the New Naturalist Book Club for which he wrote several reviews and articles for the newsletter, one of which, 'The Big Bang Theory', was published in Peter Marren's second edition of The New Naturalists *in 2005.*

Immediately beyond the overbridge at Cop Lane railway station there existed in my boyhood a large flat area of land, excavated long before by the Lancashire and Yorkshire Railway Company, presumably as a site for sidings, an engine shed, or simply for material with which to build the embankment further down the line towards Preston. After excavation the land certainly seemed to have been left to its own devices. I passed this sunken triangular area on my way to school every morning, and, where the bushes permitted, would look down at it, while I waited to see the 8.30 Preston to Southport train, which was often pulled, unusually, by an express engine, a Jub, a Scot or a Brit filling in its turn of duty.

The five or six acres were overgrown, wild, mysterious, foreign, a strange area beyond the mind as much as a physical presence. A vague sort of track led, twisting between hawthorns and elders, no more than a sheep track, down the steep slope and then through it; but come summer come winter, I never saw man or beast there. In fact, nobody else appeared even to mention the place, so that years later I wondered if it had ever existed.

I was not obsessed. Far from it. I hardly gave the place a second thought when I didn't have it in front of me. As now-forgotten months passed, and years, the urge to explore it became too strong to resist. The place had to be known, had to be made conscious, to be conquered and accommodated within the perimeter of my mind.

These were the times when adults had far fewer worries about theft or children being outside and simply wandering off!

I cannot number the occasions I descended into that small flat wilderness – no more than half dozen, to be honest. Always alone though, or the magic would be broken. It was thirty feet or so below the general level of the land, but it seemed like a lost world, as lost from the ordinary world as any inaccessible crater of some Venezuelan mountain. The wind seemed to pass overhead, in summer heat the air seemed stifling; the noise of traffic, the distant hum of the town, receded into oblivion.

Look around and listen! The insects are louder. And nearer. The birds, if they sing, sing more clearly. The blackberries are earlier and juicier and sweeter than anywhere else. The flowers are more pungent and deeper in colour. In everything there is cradled a deep still reverence. I am an intruder, and yet, in some indefinable way, I know I belong.

I am no longer aware of all that was there. Knapweeds I remember in the August heat, with butterflies, a linnet singing, burnet moths and frogspawn in masses in two small ponds. Ordinary things, but all more than ordinary. Then I recall the excitement of finding a common twayblade; and on my hands and knees, amid the steaming scent of earth, an adder's-tongue fern, almost unseen from a standing position. More visible the wild pear-tree, with fruits as hard as conkers. But never another soul did I see there, nor wanted to see. My own personal kingdom.

The railway line was closed in September 1964. The area remained inviolate for several years after. I moved away. I have been back once or twice, have driven along the new road that has been built along the old track-bed. I doubt if my area still exists as it did. It doesn't matter – it is now a place you can never find again, a young dream that dies with adult knowledge. Its mystery would be dead, its paradise compromised.

NN23 was my first, my very first. 'Ali!' I hear you thinking, *An Angler's Entomology*! Get real, man! (I do mean 'man'. Let's face it, not many of you are going to be women, are you?) No, I mean the *real* Number 23 – *The Observer's Book of Railway Locomotives*, by H. C. Casserley (a great man, surely – why was *he* never asked to write an NN?) Number 23 was the first book I ever bought, and it cost me five bob. That was a few weeks' pocket-money, I can tell you, and it cost me dear: a painful period of abstinence from gobstoppers, sherbet dips and Uncle Joe's Mint Balls.

More *Observer's Books* followed, bought or received as presents, not a great number, just relevant to my interests. That's how I recognised that adder's-tongue fern, thanks to number 12, learnt the name of tufted vetch, or told the lady at the jumble-sale that it was a guillemot's egg she had at her stall. Good books, the *Observer's*. And particularly pleasing because at the top of the spine was a number. Now isn't that a lovely perfect mathematical thing, a whole number. You can't argue with a number, it has

power and position, it creates tidiness out of chaos, and puts everything in its due order. And with books it defines a series, it includes but mainly excludes, it promotes the collection and by extension, the collector! It's perfect, unchallangable, it banishes grey areas to the outer darkness.

And oh! So many numbered things you could collect. Not just *Observer's Books*. Railway engines, buses, car registrations (ever tried spotting them in order from 1 to 999? When did you give up?), PG Tips cards (number 3, Wild White Cattle – wasn't that a rare one?), bubble-gum cards of well-known and not so well-known footballers. Yes, I did it all, at one time or another. The absurdity of it hit me one day. Two of us had gone to Morecambe. We were looking for the bus depot of Morecambe and Heysham Corporation. It was a Sunday morning in late October, cold, wet and miserable, and the wind was tearing in. Off one of the streets I noticed row upon row, a series even, of Fina petrol tankers. Instinctively going over to inspect them and seeing that each lorry sported a number, I decided then and there to start another collection. With my notebook and pen poised, my friend Ian, more nonchalant and far-seeing than I, put his hand on my arm and, giving me an apprehensive, pitying look, slowly shook his head. There was a moment of recognition. We turned away, into the face of the gale being hurled at us across Morecambe Bay. Madness, by a hair's breadth, had been averted.

Several years later, with a job and a bit of money in my pocket, I found myself in Birmingham, in a shop called, if I remember correctly, Midland Educational (the heart sinks at such a title). In my hand *The Highlands and Islands*. Mmm. Nice weight to this book, very nice wrappers. My sort of title. Wait, what's this at the top of the spine? Well, bless my soul, a number! There were other titles in the same series, all numbered. My sort of book, I thought. I bought four: NN6, together with *British Plant Life*, *Wild Flowers of Chalk and Limestone* and *A Natural History of Man in Britain* (please notice the underlying numerical order). All bright and spanking new. None of them were first editions. In spite of the numbers, I didn't buy them to collect at all, it was the subject matter and, for want of a better expression, that authoritative feel they had.

The books re-awakened my interest in wild plants ('botany' would be an altogether too grand a word). I read them all in the space of about two weeks. I am not a scientist, always formed the base-line of science results at school, dislike analysis, loathe walls of facts that seem to hide rather than reveal/any truth, and have no professional connection with nature conservation or study. These books tell you things which you would never find out yourself, they give insights, feed the imagination. They may become bogged down with statistics and tables at times, they may with grim determination seek to be comprehensive at the expense of interest, but if they get you outside, if they show you what there is and what to look for, if they fill in the background to what you have observed, they are of great value.

Of course, collecting them as a series is quite another walk in the park.

After my initial purchases, I added *Mountain Flowers* and *Wild*

Orchids and *Flowers of the Coast*. I had a family, and other interests too. Twenty years or so elapsed. I had no idea that New Naturalists had something of a cult following. I don't know how it happened, but I must have looked, as I had looked many times before, at the list of titles on the back of the wrappers. This time not so idly, perhaps. I had always known that there were gaps in the numbering. Where was NN9, for example, and, more fundamentally, what was it? Where NN13 and 28, 39 and 41? This was a series, wasn't it, not just numbers plucked from a lottery bag? The collecting instinct re-asserted itself. I began to look in second-hand bookshops in the area. They had New Naturalists. I bought. Soon I had forty or fifty of them, and, I was pleased to say, with no great outlay. But oh, how green I was! As green as the buckram of my new books. My collection consisted primarily of – greenbacks!

How naïve, how foolish! I didn't know no better, me lud! Oh how they must have laughed in Charing Cross Road, among the gloomy bookshelves of Hay-on-Wye. Oh no, I was no book-collector, just a pathetic resting-place for books at the end of their days. Well, they'd looked alright to me. And it was the contents that were important. Wasn't it?

How the scales soon fell from my eyes when I purchased the volume that brought enlightenment! In a book fair at Droitwich of all places. Fifty smackaroos it cost me. Exorbitant! NN82 *The New Naturalists* entered my life. It was the Word of God, and Peter Marren his Isaiah.

Divers Great Truths were herein revealed –

1. There is but *one* Natural History series
2. There is a large Church of Worshippers
3. Numbers are of mystical significance and inviolate
4. All things strive towards *Orkney*
5. Warblers attend the throne of the Most High
6. Reading the Good Books is not essential
7. First Editions require additional adulation
8. In Light lurks the evil one
9. Signed copies accelerate Immortality
10. The unpossessed title must have dominance over the one possessed.

Imagine the stomach-churning humiliation with which I now beheld my grubby, faded, naked also-rans with their sunned spines and illegible titles. Before such copies the daily ritual of full-length prostration was no longer possible. I entered Limbo. The King is dead! Long live the King!

A new determination arose. Yes! No more a limit of £5 per book. Cancel the holiday in the Cevennes, blow the box of Belgian chocolates every Friday night, and no Hereford United season ticket next year. I'd be a fancy collector from now on!

It was a New Dawn. Cool, bracing, uplifting. If you decide to collect with an idea of completion, then you must be prepared to fork out for the highest-priced items. So, at the time, I had to be prepared to spend five or six hundred on an *Orkney*, a *Warblers* or,

coming up in the fast lane, a *Hebrides*. I garnered catalogues, visited book-fairs, got to know the market. You couldn't hang around. Nice copies were being snapped up as soon as they were seen, the prices were rising tangibly. It was the classic situation for deluding oneself and others with the timeless phrase: it's an investment, you know.

Eventually, I got the lot, and, yes, there is always the copy which isn't as nice as the rest, and is occasionally replaced by a better one, or one which seemed better but turns out to have a different annoying little fault. The greenbacks were sold off or given away, possibly ending up as land-fill. I've sold some of the pricey hardbacks in the seventies, to raise some cash, and haven't replaced them, though I do have all the limpback versions. I rather think the limpbacks are more worthy, more genuine, in that they were produced to be read, not to be put in a bookcase and brought out on bended knee on high days and holidays, like a Royal Worcester vase.

A bookseller, John Capes, once told me that a man walked into his shop in Sheffield and told him that he wanted to collect books. Which ones would he recommend? It is, of course, should you be more than a mere investor, a ludicrous question. The books should choose themselves. It's an emotional thing, and sometimes I wonder whether I have been collecting NNs or collecting something more, the concept of them. After all, if all the books in the series were not NNs but separately published by different companies in a multitude of shapes, colours and sizes, would I have bought them? The answer is probably yes, but only a handful, as I did in the seventies.

So, why buy all the others? I find the question easy to answer, but the answers difficult to justify. There are many reasons for collecting, most probably spurious, fatuous and rationally unsound. The difficulty lies in rising above the inadequate must-get-them-all collecting mania, however appropriate that particular description may be. By possessing them, I think I want to make a statement (a phrase I dislike in this particular modern usage), if only to myself. Even if we ignore the commercial aspect of the series, the hype, the financial speculation, the salesmanship of recent years, there still remains that statement – a commitment, through the unified multiplicity of the series, to beyond it, to the multiplicity, wholeness and wonder of the natural world itself.

New Naturalist Books by Alan Titchmarsh

Alan Titchmarsh was born and brought up on the edge of Ilkley Moor. He became an apprentice gardener in the local nursery, followed by full-time training at horticultural college and the Royal Botanic Gardens, Kew. Alan is well known as the main presenter for television programmes such as Gardeners' World, Ground Force *and* The Nature of Britain *and has his own daytime show in ITV. He has written numerous books including seven novels, four memoirs and more than 50 gardening books. He lives with his wife and family in an old farmhouse in Hampshire.*

It all began rather innocently. And slowly. I think E. B. Ford's *Butterflies* was the first New Naturalist title to grace my shelves – rather fitting since it is number one in the series. But that was pure chance. I must have picked it up in a jumble sale – those were the days long before I discovered book fairs, or even 'proper' second-hand and antiquarian booksellers. It did not have a dust-wrapper. But back then – in my mid-teens – I would probably have discarded the dust-wrapper if it had been a bit tatty. It seemed so much nicer to have a green book on my shelf with a neatly gilded title. Don't gnash your teeth. I was very young…

The NN series was clearly a cut above my junior school reading – the *Observer* books. I still have all the ones I treasured at the age of nine or ten – *Wild Animals* (signed by George Cansdale when he came to talk to the Wharfedale Naturalists' Society, of which I was about the youngest member), *Horses and Ponies, Pond Life* (a particular favourite), *Geology* (a bit serious, that one), *Dogs, Cacti, Automobiles* and *Painting*. It was an eclectic mixture, but then my interests have always been pretty eclectic.

Over the years that followed I ceased to add to my library of *Observer* books – it remains at a round dozen – but the New Naturalists began to increase in number. It was a while before I had to devote one shelf entirely to them, but as individual animals – or subjects – interested me, I began to acquire the appropriate volumes.

Two of the monographs were among the first to be bought – Kenneth Mellaby's *The Mole*, and Ernest Neale's *The Badger* – the first because I spotted moles wreaking havoc on the local rugby pitch and wanted to know more about them, and *The Badger* when I noticed their activity in the local woods.

Over the years I suppose *The Badger* is the book I have referred to most. When we acquired a few acres of Hampshire woodland almost twenty years ago it came in handy to check the likelihood of their appearance at a certain time of day in a particular season of the year.

Other titles followed perhaps at the rate of two or three a year until, quite recently, I decided that I really should make an effort to possess the entire collection.

Now as any collector of anything knows, this can be dangerous. Rationality can fly out of the window in the thrill of the chase, and so I tried to be sensible. I decided that where possible I would collect first editions – if you are going to do something…. But I had not reckoned with *Orkney* and *British Warblers*. I suspect all NN collectors have tales to tell where the acquisition of those two titles is concerned. They invariably are the last to be bought, and I would suspect that few collectors have confessed to their other halves what they actually paid for these two jewels in the crown. Peter Marren may suggest in *The New Naturalists* that they can be had for X, but in my experience it is usually Y. This is the only NN title whose information I have ever had cause to doubt, but the blame cannot be laid at the door of the author, only at the doors of the collectors who read about them and then want to acquire the elusive volumes.

I did manage to find bound second state copies which satisfied me for a while, but there was this niggling feeling that they were not quite up to par. So I now have copies in both first and second states and a lurking feeling of guilt.

My collection was finally completed in 2009 and I have a standing order for new titles which are greeted with feverish anticipation and delight – not just for their collectability but also for the information, knowledge and industry that is sandwiched between their Ellis or Gillmor covers – and I can never decide which designs I like best.

I cannot claim to be a New Naturalist collector who has read every one of the books cover to cover, and I find myself experiencing a hybrid emotion of admiration and suspicion about those who insist they have devoured them all. But I do dip – almost on a daily basis – to discover how long newts live, or when the swallows are likely to arrive, or what wild flowers I am likely to encounter in my chalky meadow.

Favourites? Aside from those already mentioned, I have a soft spot for Wilfrid Blunt's *The Art of Botanical Illustration*, and not simply because of its content. I interviewed the author many years ago now – when he was curator of The Watts Gallery at Compton near Guildford – for a series on gardening writers I was penning for the Royal Horticultural Society's Journal. He was charming – good company, wise and witty – and kindly signed my copy for me. It remains the only New Naturalist in my collection that has been signed by the author. (Oh, but it was not a first edition, so an unsigned first sits alongside it now!)

I love Victor Summerhayes's *Wild Orchids of Britain* and regret that I never met him – I worked at Kew some years after he retired. Max Walters and John Gilmour's *Wild Flowers* has been with me almost since the beginning of my acquaintance with the books and is another stalwart.

I occasionally keep an eye open for a copy of earlier titles with better dust jackets than the ones I possess, but having bought one or two online and discovered on their arrival that they were in a worse state than the ones I already possessed I took it as a sign that such pedantry was not really for me. Neither is keeping new titles in their cellophane, or storing them in the dark under dust sheets. Or in the vault at the local bank. Well, there is no telling where it will end. I do take care of them, though. Mine are neatly shelved out of bright sunshine so that the dust-wrappers don't fade, and I have backed them with library cellophane, partly to preserve them but also because I find the repetitive operation therapeutic, rather like mowing the lawn. And I am quite neat and orderly by nature. But that's as far as it goes. I like them to be to hand, and used, since I'm sure that's what the authors intended.

It is tempting – having seen the soaring prices of titles published only a few years ago – to order a dozen copies of each title as it is published. But I have resisted, in the belief that such an arrangement would be both antisocial and slightly cynical. No, I treasure my one copy and take care of it and if, on my demise, my children can make a few bob – all well and good.

But that is not what New Naturalists are about for me. They are a source of pleasure and, sometimes, daunting scholarship; a chance to find out from specialists what it is about a particular subject – from the soil to the flora and fauna of a particular region – that makes it so special. And because their content is special, so too are the books. Every last one of them, from *Fleas, Flukes and Cuckoos* to *Lords and Ladies* – oh, and yes that is another particular favourite…

From Book Club To Collectors' Club With
The New Naturalists by Roger Long

Roger Long was born in the early thirties and spent some of the war years in the Chilterns, where his interest in the countryside and its wildlife flourished. This was followed by a number of years in London training in industrial chemistry. He moved to Jersey in 1957 after marrying Margaret, a Jersey native who he had met there whilst on holiday. Roger was a key influence behind the beginnings of the New Naturalist Book Club. He has written a number of articles on wide-ranging subjects from birds and insects to milestones and cricket.

Many members of the New Naturalist Collectors' Club, especially new ones, will not be familiar with its origins, and therefore I offer this account as a tribute to the founder of the club and his achievement in successfully seeing it through its early years.

Robert Burrow – 'Bob' to many members – was always fun to be with; full of initiative and ideas for projects, many of which were instant responses to events, having little chance of taking flight, although some became major features in a life lived to the full. Natural history was the underlying stimulus for most of Robert's activities and enterprises, but the terms 'natural environment' and 'wildlife' better characterise his practical rather than academic approach.

Robert was born in Jersey in 1950, his formal education ending with his leaving a small, private school as soon as was allowed for him to start bringing a wage home. He repeatedly told of his regret at not being rather more schooled, and at not having had an introduction to wider intellectual landscapes. His first employment was with the Jersey New Waterworks Company, in the footsteps of his father and grandfather, the latter having been its founder. He discovered that the potential for family nepotism would work against him rather than in his favour and he left, complaining that he was being treated as general dogsbody. He did, however, acquire a formidable ability to turn his hand to almost any practical task. He soon broke free of this and launched himself, with moderate success, in several directions in turn, as each failed to satisfy him. Commercial sea-fishing on a small scale and fishing trade supplier were examples, but his good nature and absence of business experience left him vulnerable to traders less easy-going and honest than he was and he had to move on.

My wife and I first met Robert as a young teenager, bursting with enthusiasm and vitality into the activities of the Ornithology Section of the Société Jersiaise, an untutored but keen and responsible birdwatcher. Some of us wondered how long it would be before other attractions captured his lively attentions, but quite soon we realised that he had a deep and genuine feeling for, initially, birds but, later, most of the living components of Jersey's wildlife. Later still, as he matured and we became colleagues in other disciplines, it was evident that Robert was one of those truly rare people having an innate empathy with all the creatures around them, to an extent that we have encountered in only one or two others. He qualified as a first-class bird-ringer, and immersed himself in the lives of Jersey's limited but interesting reptiles and amphibians which led to his pioneering efforts, eventually successful, in conserving the endangered, remaining population of Jersey's non-British Agile Frog. He later took up light-trapping for Lepidoptera and rapidly became a first-class recorder and a valuable contributor to the small group studying Lepidoptera.

While still a teenager Robert proudly showed us his bird books, acquired with no particular family encouragement and, later, we introduced him to the New Naturalists. He bought those relevant to his interests, which is how my wife and I had started, a good few years before. An early acquaintance with books on remote Scottish islands, particularly Fraser Darling's, was the stimulus for her buying *Natural History in the Highlands and Islands*, and she bought me my first title, *London's Natural History*, its being relevant to my home. Titles on botany were purchased, as funds permitted, for their subject, and particularly because of what was in those days a generous use of colour. Although there was never the slightest thought of the books being part of a set, possibly to be collected, we gradually widened our acquisitions as opportunities arose, but it was much later that completing the collection became an option, albeit a distant one, rather than an essential goal. It is difficult to remember exactly when the far-off possibility became a fervent hope and, in due course, an implacable ambition. Perhaps it was when we began ordering every title in advance regardless of subject or merit, and soon Robert was asking us to order a copy for him as well. In those far-off, pre-internet days I had overlooked ordering one issue and was apologising to him. With typical impatience with our slow postal method he offered to take over and, there and then, he telephoned Collins in Glasgow, saying, on that first call, 'Please send me three copies, and will you open a trade account for me'! To my surprise they immediately agreed, but I suspect that our revered publisher has tightened up its wholesale practices since then.

Robert was quick to keep up with modern ideas and practice and he casually began to buy books on the internet to add New Naturalists at modest prices to his burgeoning collection. It must have been about then that he told us he had had a bright idea. 'I'll start a bookclub for collectors of New Naturalists', he said, 'I can sell new issues to members at an attractive discount for them, make a little profit to cover expenses, and act as a clearing house for second-hand copies'. And that is how, in the autumn of 1998, the New Naturalist Collectors' Club was born.

Robert regularly frequented auctions here in Jersey, buying and selling all manner of things. For him this was a way of life as much as a business, and his attic was already bulging with tea chests of general books – and much else besides – which were bought quite cheaply, and from which he had removed the ones he wanted to keep or to sell on at a profit, sometimes a handsome one. With, to me, astonishing initiative he established links with specialist second-hand book-dealers all over the UK who seemed keen to take surprising numbers of the valuable items he would find lurking in ostensibly uninteresting lots at auctions.

This led to Robert's taking a lease on a small shop just out of St Helier and starting trading, part-time, in second-hand books. He sought occasional general bibliographic advice from myself and from his many contacts in the trade, for his easy and friendly manner soon led to first-name acquaintanceships with numerous dealers on the mainland.

The shop was invaluable as a store and distribution centre for each new issue of the New Naturalists. At one stage, before the present relatively large print-runs, Robert's wholesale order was probably one of the largest that the publisher received.

Robert's early circulars and advertisements seeking members for his new club claimed that they would receive six newsletters a year. He would not listen to my wet-blanket doubts that he could keep up such an ambitious schedule and I think he achieved it in only one year. His intention was genuine enough but he had too many irons in the fire. With some editing experience behind me I offered to help, if only to dot his 'i's and cross his 't's, but too often he left himself insufficient time, and I was unable to copy-edit several newsletters before he issued them.

The newsletters were a varied mixture, depending heavily for a while on reprinting relevant, published material, of which obituaries of New Naturalist authors provided sometimes interesting but frequently repetitive comparisons. He enjoyed selecting a single title and delving into variations or anomalies relating to its bibliography. His findings were popular with many members often as aids to identifying false descriptions of books for sale. As deadlines approached he would sometimes badger me for another contribution – a habit common to editors of serial publications.

In addition to his bird-ringing and moth-trapping, the wider aspect of conservation in Jersey was high on Robert's agenda. He represented the Société Jersiaise on the crucial St Ouen's Bay Preservation Committee, he served for fourteen years as a Trustee of the Jersey Ecology Fund, and for a while on the Lands Committee of the National Trust for Jersey. When local enthusiasts were building up the Jersey group of the RSPB so successfully, Robert became leader of the group for a while and was an industrious helper with the Young Ornithologists Club. Perhaps more important to him than all that honorary work

for the island, was his time as a senior member of Jersey's Honorary Police Service, spanning more than twenty years, a most responsible, unpaid and time-consuming occupation in a community where the honorary police work very closely with their professional colleagues. A worrying heart condition, which had been a cloud on his horizon for a few years, worsened rapidly in 2006 and, after treatment in London and a brief spell in hospital in Jersey he died, aged only 56. His huge, wide-ranging friendships and great popularity ensured a crowded gathering to pay their respects at his funeral.

Robert's widow, Sarah, was keen initially that the shop and the club should be kept going and I was happy to help. Between us we distributed three or four new titles, but soon unforeseen circumstances rendered her hopes for both the club and shop unrealistic. The shop lease was relinquished and Robert's lovingly-assembled stock of over a thousand New Naturalist volumes, including at least one of every title, was sold to a dealer in London.

It was our greatest good fortune, as well an enormous relief that, after keeping the club afloat for about eighteen months, we were able to hand it over as an ongoing concern to one of its keenest members, Tim Bernhard, who was both able and willing to take it on. It was as if he was an understudy waiting in the wings to assume the leading role and at the same time bring fresh ideas and great enthusiasm to ensuring the continued prosperity of the renamed New Naturalist Collectors' Club.

Club membership was just over two hundred when Tim took charge of it, and he has done wonders expanding membership, which at the time of writing is more than five hundred, and introducing new enterprises. Tim's initiative in dreaming up the idea of symposiums devoted to the NN Library, and his hard work in bringing it to such a successful fruition at the first gathering, held in October 2009, has drawn wide attention to the remarkable impact these books have had on the broad community of naturalists, amateur and professional, throughout the British Isles. I have no doubt that this will be further evident at the second meeting planned for June 2011.

My wife Margaret and I retain fond memories of Robert Burrow, an exceptional person in many ways, and we hope he will be remembered for his brilliant idea and for founding the club based on these very special books. He would have been astonished and delighted that it has proved such a lasting success.

New Naturalist Authors and Editors and Their Publications

This part of the book began as a simple list of well-known books written by New Naturalist authors. It became increasingly evident that there were a huge number of publications including many scientific papers and leaflets. Due to space limitations, these have had to be edited quite severely. Only the major books are listed, and only those associated with natural history or the landscape. Many NN authors were extremely prolific writing on a number of different subjects. E. B. Ford wrote on *Church Treasures in the Oxford District* (Alan Sutton, 1984), John Raven on *Pythagoreans and Eleatics, an Account of the Interaction Between the Two Opposed Schools During the Fifth and Early Fourth Centuries B.C.* (Cambridge University Press, 1948), Oliver Rackham published on the *Treasures of Silver at Corpus Christi College, Cambridge* (Cambridge University press, 2002), and Stephen Potter produced *A First Study of D. H. Lawrence* (Cape, 1930) as well as his well-known series on One-upmanship. Such books have not been listed. Other cases are books which border on biology but only marginally. Decisions about them are not straightforward. Brian Vesey-Fitzgerald wrote books on the *Beauty of Dogs* (Scribner, 1965) and *Keep Your Cage Bird Happy* (News of the World, 1968) and R. J. Berry on *Darwin, Creation and the Fall* (IVP, 2009). These books have not been included, but Alister Hardy on the *Biology of God* (Cape, 1975), Edward Armstrong on *Saint Francis: Nature Mystic* (University of California Press, 1973) and R. J. Berry on *God and the Biologist* (Apollos, 1996) are listed.

All books listed here are first editions with extensively revised editions also noted.

Once the lists of books had been assembled it was decided to elaborate the entries for each author and to include a copy of the author's signature. The idea was that anyone using this book would be able to refer to this appendix to read a basic summary of the author and in some cases check to see if a signed book they might have discovered is genuine.

The search for signatures was difficult and the completed bibliographical appendix is a tribute to these men and women without whom the New Naturalist library would not have been written.

The New Naturalist Editorial Board

Corbet, Sarah Alexandra (Sally) 1940–
Member of the Board since 1992

Sally Corbet was a lecturer in both the Department of Applied Biology and later in the Department of Zoology at the University of Cambridge until she retired in 1999. She has been a series editor of the Naturalists' handbooks, including the author of three of them. Brother of Philip Corbet, the co-author of both New Naturalist books on dragonflies.

Editor of the series of Naturalists' Handbooks (Richmond Publishing Company, London), including authorship of: 3. *Solitary Wasps* (with Peter Yeo), 1983; 6. *Bumblebees* (with Oliver Prys-Jones), 1991. Originally published by Cambridge University Press, 1987; 15. *Insects, Plants and Microclimate* (with D. M. Unwin), 1991.

Davies, Margaret (née Dunlop) 1914–1982
Member of the Board 1967–82

Margaret Davies studied at the University of Manchester writing her MA thesis on the distribution of Bronze Age objects in Britain and France, and her PhD was on the coastal megalithic monuments of the Irish Sea. She was concerned with nature conservancy and served on the National Parks Commission and the Countryside Commission. Her other interests included farming in Wales, Celtic field systems and the English and Welsh languages.

Fisher, James Maxwell McConnell 1912–1970
Member of the Board 1943–70
Author of *The Fulmar* (M6, 1952) and (with Ronald Lockley) *Sea Birds* (NN28, 1954).

James Fisher's father was the Headmaster of Oundle School and his maternal uncle was Arnold Boyd, author of NN9, *A Country Parish*. Educated at Eton and Magdalen College, Oxford, he became assistant curator at London Zoo, then ornithologist at the Ministry of Agriculture. James Fisher was a busy and multi-talented writer, broadcaster and traveller, an expert on rooks and seabirds and an influential voice in publishing. His energy, intelligence and panache lay at the heart of the New Naturalist library's success in the 1940s and 1950s. The Orkney island of Copinsay is dedicated to his memory.

BIOGRAPHY **Vever, H. G.** (revised **Clemency Fisher**) *Oxford Dictionary of National Biography.*

BOOKS *Animals as Friends and How to Keep Them* (with Margaret Shaw). Dent, London, 1939, 1952; *Birds as Animals.* Heinemann, London, 1939; revised and reissued in Hutchinson's University Library and by Houghton Mifflin, Boston, 1954; *The Living Thoughts of Darwin* (with Julian Huxley). Cassell, London, 1939; new edition 1958; *Watching Birds.* Pelican, 1941. Revised by Jim Flegg and re-published by Poyser, Berkhamsted, 1974; *The Birds of Britain* (Britain in Pictures series). Collins, London, 1942; *Birds of the Village.* Penguin (Puffin Picture library), 1944; *Bird Recognition.* Volume 1. *Sea-Birds and Waders.* Pelican, London, 1947; Revised edition 1954; *The Natural History of Selborne by Gilbert White* (Ed). The Cresset Press, London, 1947; *The New Naturalist Journal* (Ed). Six parts issued. Collins, London, 1948; *Natural History of the Kite.* Royal Society for the Protection of Birds, Sandy, 1949; *Bird Recognition.* Volume 2. Birds of Prey and Water-Fowl. Pelican, London, 1951; *Bird Preservation.* Royal Society for the Protection of Birds, 1951; *Birds of the Field (Country Naturalist Series).* Collins, London, 1952; *Nature Parliament* (with L. Hugh Newman and Peter Scott). Dent, London, 1952; *Watching Birds.* Collins, London, 1953; *A Thousand Geese* (with Peter Scott). Collins, London, 1953; *Fine Bird Books, 1700–1900* (with Sacheverell Sitwell & Handasyde Buchanan). Collins, London and Van Nostrand, New York, 1953; *A History of Birds.* Hutchinson's University Library, London and Houghton Mifflin, New York, 1954; *The Wonderful World: The Adventure of the Earth we Live on.* Hanover House, New York, 1954; *Bird Recognition 3. Rails, Game-Birds and Larger Perching and Singing Birds.* Pelican, London, 1955; *The Shell Nature Studies, Birds and Beasts* (Ed). Phoenix House, London, 1956; *Adventure of the Sea.* Rathbone, London, 1956 and (as the *Wonderful World of the Sea*) Garden City Books, New York, 1957; revised and published Macdonald, London, 1970; *Rockall.* Geoffrey Bles, London, 1956; *Wild America: The record of a 30,000 mile journey around the North American continent by an American naturalist and his British colleague* (with Roger Tory Peterson). Collins, London, 1956 and Houghton Mifflin, New York, 1955; *The Wonderful World of the Sea.* Garden City Books, New York, 1957 and Macdonald, London, 1970; *Adventure of the Air.* Rathbone Books, London, 1958; *Shackleton* (with Margery Turner Fisher). Barrie, London, 1958. Published in North America as *Shackleton and the Antarctic* by Houghton Mifflin, Boston, 1958; *The Wonderful World of the Air.* Doubleday & Garden City Books, New York, 1959; *The Macdonald Illustrated Library. Volume 2. Nature: Earth, Plants and* Animals (with Julian Huxley). Macdonald, London, 1960; *Field Guide to the Birds of Texas and Adjacent States* (with Roger Tory Peterson). Houghton Mifflin, Boston, 1963; *Shell Nature Book* (with Geoffrey

Grigson). Phoenix House, London, 1964; *The World of Birds* (with Roger Tory Peterson). Macdonald, London and Doubleday, New York, 1964. Reprinted by Aldus Books, 1971 and Crescent Books, 1988; *The Shell List of British and Irish Birds.* Ebury Press & Michael Joseph, London, 1966; *The Migration of Birds* (illustrated by Crispin Fisher). Bodley Head, London, 1966; *The Shell Bird Book.* Ebury Press, London, 1966; *Zoos of the World.* Aldus Books, London and Natural History Press, New York, 1966; *Shell Nature Lovers' Atlas of England, Scotland and Wales.* Ebury Press, London, 1966; *Thorburn's Birds* (edited and text) Ebury Press, London, 1967, reprinted Mermaid Books, London, 1976; *The Red Book. Wildlife in Danger* (with Noel Simon and Jack Vincent). Collins, London and International Union for the Conservation of Nature, 1969; *Wildlife Crisis* (with HRH the Duke of Edinburgh). Hamish Hamilton, London, 1970; *Birds: An Introduction to General Ornithology* (posthumously with Roger Tory Peterson). Aldus Books, London, 1971; *List of Mammals which Have Become Extinct or are Possibly Extinct since 1600* (posthumously with H.A. Goodwin and J.M. Goodwin). Morges: International Union for Conservation of nature and Natural Resources, 1973; *Watching Birds* (with Jim Flegg). Poyser, Berkhamsted, 1974.

Flegg, Jim OBE 1937–
Member of the Board since 2005

Jim Flegg specialised in plant parasitic nematodes and spent much of his career at the fruit Research Station in Kent. His is also an ornithologist and has written numerous books on birds. Jim was a former director of the BTO and president of the Kent Ornithological Society. He also became a household name due to his television programmes *Country Ways* and *Coastal Ways.*

BOOKS *Watching Birds* (with James Fisher). Poyser, Berkhamsted, 1974; *In Search of Birds.* Blandford, Poole, 1983; *Parasitic Worms.* Shire, Princes Risborough, 1985; *Birdlife.* Pelham, London, 1986; *Field Guide to the Birds of Britain and Europe.* New Holland, London, 1990; *Poles Apart.* Michael Joseph, London, 1990; *Deserts.* Cassell, London, 1993; *Eric Hosking's Classical Birds.* Collins, London, 1993; *Birds.* HarperCollins, London, 1994; *Time to Fly, Exploring Bird Migration.* BTO, Thetford, 2004.

Gillmour, John Scott Lennox 1906–1986
Member of the Board 1943–79
Author (with Max Walters) of *Wild Flowers* (NN5, 1954)

A Cambridge botanist to his fingertips, John Gilmour was urbane, equally interested in horticulture and wild plants, and consumed by

the complexities of scientific names. The early part of his career was spent in administration at Kew and Wiley, but it is as head of the University Botanic Gardens at Cambridge that he is remembered.

BIOGRAPHY **Max Walters** In *Oxford Dictionary of National Biography.*

BOOKS *British Botanists* (Britain in Pictures series). Collins, London, 1944; *Wild Flowers of the Chalk.* Penguin, London, 1947; *Gardening Books of the Eighteenth Century.* Hunt Botanical Library, Pittsburgh, 1961; *Thomas Johnson c. 1600–1944. Botanical Journeys in Kent & Hampstead: facsimile reprint with introduction and translation of his Iter Plantarum 1629, Descriptio Itineris Plantarum 1932.* Hunt Botanical Library Museum Facsimile Series no. 3, 1972; *Humphrey Gilbert-Carter, a Memorial Volume* (with S. Walters). Cambridge Botanic Garden, Cambridge, 1975).

Hosking, Eric John, OBE 1909–1991
Photographic Editor of the series 1943–91

The world famous bird photographer, Hosking's images of birds broke new ground and illustrated bird books over five decades. He lost an eye to a tawny owl in 19. Hosking's role in the series was to supply or commission photographs, especially colour photographs, for each title.

AUTOBIOGRAPHY *An Eye for a Bird.* Hutchinson, London (1970).

BOOKS (Eric Hosking's pictures have been widely used. This list is books by Hosking himself, and books based around his photographs): *Intimate Sketches from Bird Life.* Country Life, London, 1940; *Art of Bird Photography.* Country Life, London, 1944; *Masterpieces of Bird Photography* (with Harold Lowes). Collins, London, 1947; *Birds in Action.* Collins, London, 1949; *Birds Fighting* (with Stuart Smith). Faber, London, 1955; *Bird Photography as a Hobby* (with Cyril Newberry). Stanley Paul, London, 1961; *Antarctic Photography* (with Bryan Sage). Croom Helm, London, 1962; *Nesting Birds, Eggs and Fledglings* (with Winwood Reade). Blandford Press, Poole, 1967; *Minsmere, Portrait of a Bird Reserve* (with Herbert Axell). Hutchinson, London, 1977; *Wildlife Photography: a Field Guide* (with John Gooders). Hutchinson, London, 1973; *Nature Through the Seasons* (with Peter Gerrard). Midas, Tunbridge Wells, 1976; *Eric Hosking's Birds. Fifty Years of Photographing Wildlife.* Pelham Books, London, 1979; *Antarctic Wildlife* (photos by Eric Hosking, text by Bryan Sage). Croom Helm, Beckenham, 1983; *Eric Hosking's Waders* (with W. G. Hale). Pelham, London, 1983; *Eric Hosking's Seabirds* (text by Ronald M. Lockley). Croom Helm, Beckenham, 1983; *Eric Hosking's Classic Birds. Sixty Years of Bird* Photography (text with Jim Flegg). HarperCollins, London, 1993.

Huxley, Julian Sorrell, KT, FRS 1887–1975
Chairman of the Board 1943–75

A famous evolutionary biologist, humanist and internationalist, his wide-ranging contributions to science and human thought are difficult to summarise briefly. He was one of the main authors of the 'evolutionary synthesis' which reconciled genetics with behavioural and population biology – and made field-based natural history academically respectable again. Through his books and media appearances he was a major science populariser. He was an innovative director of London Zoo and was the first head of UNESCO. Among his other lifelong causes were eugenics, secular humanism and ornithology.

AUTOBIOGRAPHY *Memories* (2 volumes, 1970, 1973). George Allen & Unwin, London.

BIOGRAPHY **Baker, John R.** (1976). Julian Sorrell Huxley, *Biographical Memoirs of fellows of the Royal Society,* **22**: 207–38; **Baker, John R.** (1978). *Julian Huxley, scientist and world citizen, 1887–1975.* UNESCO, Paris; **Clark, Ronald W.** (1960). *Sir Julian Huxley.* Phoenix, London; **Clark, Ronald W.** (1968). *The Huxleys.* Heinemann, London; **Dronamraju, Krishna R.** (1993). *If I am to be remembered: the life & work of Julian Huxley, with selected correspondence.* World Scientific, Singapore; **Green, Jens-Peter** (1981). *Krise und Hoffnung, der Evolutionshumanismus Julian Huxleys.* Carl Winter Universitatsverlag; **Keynes, Milo & Harrison, G. Ainsworth** (editors) (1989). *Evolutionary studies: a centenary celebration of the life of Julian Huxley. Proceeding of the 24th annual symposium of the Eugenics Society, London (1987).* Macmillan, London; See also: **Bates, S.C. & Winkler, M.G.** (1984). *A Guide to the Papers of Julian Sorrell Huxley.* Fondren Library, Rice University, Houston TX.

BOOKS *The Individual in the Animal Kingdom.* Cambridge University Press, Cambridge, 1912; 'The courtship habits of the Great Crested Grebe (*Podiceps cristatus*); with an addition to the theory of natural selection'. *Proceedings of the Zoological Society of London,* **2**: 491–562, 1914 [a landmark in ethology: reprinted as a book: Cape, London 1968]; *Essays of a Biologist.* Chatto & Windus, London, 1923; *Essays in Popular Science.* Chatto & Windus, London, 1926; *The Stream of Life.* Watts, London, 1926; *Animal Biology* (with J. B. S. Haldane). Oxford University Press, Oxford, 1927; *Religion Without Revelation.* Benn, London, 1927, revised edition 1957; *The Tissue-culture King* [science fiction short story. First published in *The Yale Review* for April 1926; reprinted in many anthologies], 1926; *The Science of Life: a summary of contemporary knowledge about life and its possibilities* (with H. G. & G. P. Wells), 1929–30. London: Amalgamated Press – first issued in 31 fortnightly parts, bound up in three volumes

as publication proceeded. First issued in one volume in 1931, reprinted 1934, 1937; popular edition, fully revised 1938, Cassell, London. Published as separate volumes: *I The living body. II Patterns of life. III Evolution – fact and theory. IV Reproduction, heredity and the development of sex. V The history and adventure of life. VI The drama of life. VII How animals behave. VIII Man's mind and behaviour. IX Biology and the human race.* Cassell, London; Doubleday, Doran & Co., New York 1931, 1934, 1939; *Ants.* Benn, London, 1930; *Bird-watching and Bird Behaviour.* Chatto & Windus, London, 1930; *Africa View.* Chatto & Windus, London, 1931; *The Captive Shrew and Other Poems of a Biologist.* Basil Blackwell, Oxford, 1932; *Problems of Relative Growth.* Methuen, London, 1932 (reprinted John Hopkins Press, Baltimore, 1993; *Scientific Research and Social Needs.* Watts & Co., London, 1934; *Elements of Experimental Embryology* (with Gavin de Beer). Cambridge University Press, Cambridge, 1934; *Animal Language* (includes recordings of animal calls with Ludwig Koch). Country Life, London, 1938, reprinted 1964; *The Living Thoughts of Darwin, presented by Julian Huxley* (with James Fisher) Cassell, London, 1939; new edition 1958; *The New Systematics* (Ed) [this multi-author volume, is one of the foundation stones of the 'New Synthesis', with essays on taxonomy, evolution, natural selection, Mendelian genetics and population genetics]. Clarendon Press, Oxford, 1940; *The Uniqueness of Man.* Chatto & Windus, London, 1941; reprint 1943 (published in US as *Man Stands Alone.* Harper, New York; *Evolution: the Modern Synthesis.* Allen & Unwin, London, 1942, reprinted 1943, 1944, 1945, 1948, 1955; 2nd ed., with new introduction and bibliography by the author, 1963; 3rd ed., with new introduction and bibliography by nine contributors, 1974). US first edition by Harper, New York, 1943; *Evolutionary Ethics* (Romanes Lecture). Oxford University Press, Oxford, 1943; *Evolution and Ethics 1893–1943.* [includes text from both T. H. Huxley and Julian Huxley] Pilot, London; in US as *Touchstone for Ethics.* Harper, New York, 1947; *Soviet Genetics and World Science: Lysenko and the Meaning of Heredity.* Chatto & Windus, London; in US as *Heredity, East and West.* Schuman, New York, 1949; *Evolution in Action.* Chatto & Windus, London, 1953; *Evolution as a Process* (edited with Hardy A. C. and Ford E. B.) Allen & Unwin, London, 1954; *New Bottles for New Wine.* Chatto & Windus, London and Harper, New York, 1957; reprinted as *Knowledge, Morality, Destiny.* New York, 1960; *Biological Aspects of Cancer.* Allen & Unwin, London, 1958; *The Humanist Frame* (Ed). Allen & Unwin, London, 1961; *Essays of a Humanist.* Chatto & Windus, London, 1964; *The Human Crisis.* University of Washington Press, Seattle, 1963; *Darwin and his World* (with Bernard Kettlewell). Thames & Hudson, London, 1965.

Mellanby, Kenneth, CBE 1918–1993
Member of the Board 1971–87, Chairman from 1975
Author of *Pesticides and Pollution* (NN50, 1967), *The Mole* (M22, 1971), and *Farming and Wildlife* (NN67, 1981)

A senior scientific administrator, Kenneth Mellanby was in charge of Monks Wood Research Station in its greatest years, after serving as head of entomology at Rothamsted and in the colonies as Principal of University College at Ibadan, Nigeria. Original and outspoken in his opinions, Mellanby was regularly in the news in the 1970s and 1980s on farming and conservation topics.

BIOGRAPHY **Weindling, P.** *Oxford Dictionary of National Biography.*

BOOKS *Human Guinea Pigs.* Gollancz, London, 1945; *Scabies.* Oxford University Press, Oxford, 1943; *Can Britain Feed Itself?* Merlin Press, London, 1975; *Ecological Effects of Pesticides* (editor with Franklyn Perring).Linnean Society, London, 1977; *Biology of Pollution Studies.* Edward Arnold, London, 1980; *Waste and Pollution.* HarperCollins, London, 1981; *The DDT Story.* The British Crop Protection Council, Farnham, 1992.

Ratcliffe, Derek Almey 1929–2005
Member of the Board 1993–2005
Author of *Lakeland* (NN92, 2002) and *Galloway and the Borders* (NN101, 2007)

Derek Ratcliffe was the Nature Conservancy's (later the NCC's) Chief Scientist for sixteen years and one of the most versatile and influential (and most modest) British naturalists of the twentieth century. His skill as a nest-finder helped him to produce evidence of the catastrophic decline of the Peregrine in the 1960s and to elucidate its cause – persistent pesticides. He also instituted the first review of wild habitats in Britain, the Nature Conservation Review (1977). He was an authority on mountain vegetation and bryophytes, and on birds of moorland and Lapland, where he spent many summers after his retirement.

AUTOBIOGRAPHY *In Search of Nature.* Peregrine, Leeds (2000).

BOOKS *Plant Communities of the Scottish Highlands* (with Donald McVean). Nature Conservancy Council/HMSO, London, 1962; *Nature Conservation Review* (Ed). Cambridge University Press, Cambridge, 1977; *Highland Flora.* Highlands and Islands Development Board, Inverness, 1977; *The Peregrine Falcon.* Poyser, London, 1980; *Birds, Bogs and Forestry* (edited, with P. H. Oswald). Nature Conservancy Council, Peterborough, 1987; *Bird Life of Mountain and Upland.* Cambridge University Press, Cambridge, 1991; *The Raven.* Poyser, London , 1997; *Lapland: a Natural History.* Poyser, London (2005).

Silvertown, Jonathan 1954–
Member of the Board since 2006

Jonathan Silvertown is Professor of Evolutionary Ecology at the University of Edinburgh. His research broadly covers plant population biology, including population dynamics, life history evolution, evolutionary ecology and community ecology. He is especially interested in the connections between ecology and evolution of plants. He created iSpot and Evolution MegaLab.

BOOKS *Introduction to Plant Population Biology* (with Charlesworth, D.). Blackwell, Oxford (4th ed., 2004; *Demons in Eden: The paradox of plant diversity*. Chicago University Press, Chicago, 2008; *99% Ape* (editor, with others). Natural History Museum, London, 2008; *An Orchard Invisible. A natural history of seeds*. Chicago University Press, Chicago, 2009; *Fragile Web: What Next for Nature?* (Ed). Natural History Museum, London, 2010.

Stamp, Laurence Dudley KT, CBE 1898–1966
Member of the Board 1943–66
Author of *Britain's Structure and Scenery* (NN4, 1946), *Man and the Land* (NN31, 1955), *The Common Lands of England and Wales* (with W. G. Hoskins) (NN45, 1963), and *Nature Conservation in Britain* (NN49, 1969)

A prolific writer of geography textbooks, Sir Dudley Stamp was also professor at the London School of Economics, and found time to serve on a large number of important committees and commissions, including the one that set up the National Parks and the Nature Conservancy. One of the original Editorial Board, he managed to write four New Naturalists before his untimely death in 1966.

BIOGRAPHY **Wise, M.J.** *Oxford Dictionary of National Biography.*

BOOKS [Dudley Stamp was voracious writer of textbooks. Many of them went into many editions and were often reprinted in different formats or combinations].
An Introduction to Stratigraphy: British Isles. Thomas Murby, London, 1923, later reprints published by Methuen; *The Indian Empire. Part IV. India, Burma, Ceylon.* Longmans, Calcutta, 1926; *An Intermediate Geography.* Longmans, Green, London, 1927; *The World: a General Geography.* Longmans, Green, London, 1929; *A Practical Atlas of Modern Geography* (Ed). G. Gill, London, 1930; *The British Isles* (with Stanley Beaver). Longmans, Green, London, 1933; *A Commercial Geography.* Longmans, Green, London, 1936; *Chisholm's Handbook of Commercial Geography, entirely*

rewritten by L. Dudley Stamp. Longmans, Green, London, 1937; *Physical Geography and Geology.* Longmans, Green, London, 1938; *An Introduction to Commercial Geography.* Longmans, Green, London, 1940; *The British Isles: a Geographic and Economic Survey.* Longmans, Green, London, 1937; *The Land of Britain.* The Report of the Land Utilisation Survey of Britain (Ed), 1937 onwards) [A comprehensive survey of land utilisation in many volumes]; *The Face of Britain.* Longmans, Green, London, 1940, revised 1948, 1956; *Physical Geography and Geology.* Longmans, Green, London, 1938, 1946; *A New Geography of India, Burma and Ceylon.* Longmans, Green, London, 1942; *The Land of Britain: Its Use and Misuse.* Longmans, Green, London, 1948; *An Introduction to Economic Geography* (with G. H. T. Kimble). Longmans, Green and Co., Toronto, New York and London, 1949; *The British Commonwealth.* Longmans, Green, London, 1951; *The Earth's Crust. A New Approach to Physical Geography and Geology.* Harrap, London, 1951; *London Essays in Geography* (edited, with S. W. Wooldridge). Longmans, Green for London School of Economics, London, 1951; *Our Undeveloped World.* Faber & Faber, London, 1953; *Our Developing World.* Faber & Faber, London, 1960; *Applied Geography.* Penguin, London, 1960; *A Glossary of Geographical Terms.* Longmans, London, 1961; *An Introduction to Commercial Geography.* Longmans, London, 1962; *Our Developing World.* Faber & Faber, London, 1963; *Geography of Life and Death.* Fontana, London, 1964; *Some Aspects of Medical Geography. The 1962 Heath Clark Lectures.* Oxford University Press, Oxford, 1964; *Europe and the British Isles.* Longmans, London, 1969).

Streeter, David MBE 1937–
Member of the Board since 1986

David Streeter is Reader in Ecology at the University of Sussex. He has served on a number of committees including the Countryside Commission, Nature Conservancy, British Ecological Society and the Sussex Downs Conservation Board. He is also chairman of Conservation Committee of the BSBI and President of the Sussex Wildlife Trust.

BOOKS *Discovering Hedgerows* (with Rosamund Richardson). BBC Books, London (1982). *The Wild Flowers of the British Isles* (with Ian Gerrard). Midsummer Books, London (1983, 1998). *The Natural History of the Oak Tree* (with Richard Lewington). Dorling Kindersley, London (1993).*Collins Flower Guide.* HarperCollins, London, 2009).

Walters, Stuart Max VMH 1920–2005
Member of the Board 1980–2005.
Author (with John Gilmour) of *Wild Flowers* (NN5, 1954), *Mountain Flowers* (with John Raven) (NN33, 1956), and *Wild and Garden Plants* (NN80, 1993)

Max Walters followed his friend John Gilmour as director of Cambridge Botanic Garden and a member of the New Naturalist Editorial Board. He was a leading experimental taxonomist, and an authority on the British and European flora, helping to edit the standard work on the latter, *Flora Europaea*. Together with Franklyn Perring, he masterminded the BSBI mapping scheme.

BOOKS *Flora of Cambridgeshire* (with Franklyn Perring and F. D. Sell). Cambridge University Press, Cambridge, 1964; *Atlas of the British Flora* (edited with Franklyn Perring). Botanical Society of the British Isles Publications, Oundle, 1968; *Plant Variation and Evolution* (with David Briggs). Weidenfeld & Nicolson, London, 1969; *Darwin's Mentor: John Stevens Henslow (1796–1861)* (with E. A. Stow). Cambridge University Press, Cambridge, 2001; *Trees: a Field Guide to the Trees of Britain and Northern Europe* (with John White and Jill White). Oxford University Press, Oxford, 2005.

West, Richard Gilbert FRS 1926–
Member of the Board 1983–2013

Richard West is Fellow of Clare College, Cambridge, where he has been Professor of Palaeoecology and Professor of Botany. He has written a number of books on the Palaeoecology and geology of Britain and northern Europe.

BIOGRAPHY **Turner, C. & Gibbard, P.** (1996). Richard West – an Appreciation. *Quaternary Science Reviews*, **15**: 375–89.

BOOKS *Pleistocene Geology and Biology.* Longmans, Green, London, 1968; *Ice Age in Britain* (with Bruce Sparks). Methuen, London, 1972; *Pre-Glacial Pleistocene of the Norfolk and Suffolk Coasts.* Cambridge University Press, Cambridge, 1980; *Pleistocene Palaeoecology of Central Norfolk.* Cambridge University Press, Cambridge, 1991; *Plant Life in the Quaternary Cold Stages.* Cambridge University Press, Cambridge, 2000; *From Brandon to Bungay – an expedition of the landscape history and ecology of the Little Ouse and Waveney Rivers.* Suffolk Naturalists' Society, Ipswich, 2009).

Main Series Authors

Alford, David Victor 1938–
Author of *Plant Pests* (NN116, 2011)

David Alford was a government entomologist serving first at Rothamsted and then the Ministry of Agriculture based at Cambridge where he was Regional Entomologist. With a doctorate in bumblebee ecology he is an authority on the insects and mites that ravage crops and horticulture.

BOOKS *Bumblebees*. David-Poynter, London, 1975; *The Life of the Bumlebee*. David-Poynter, London, 1978; *Colour Atlas of Fruit Pests*. Wolfe, London, 1984; *Colour Atlas of Pests of Ornamental Trees, Shrubs and Flowers*. Wolfe, London, 1991). Second edition, Manson, London, 2012; *Textbook of Agricultural Entomology*. Blackwell Science, Oxford, 1999; *Biocontrol of Oilseed Rape* (ed.). Blackwell Science, Oxford, 2000; *Pest and Disease Management Handbook* (ed.). Wiley-Blackwell, Oxford, 2000; *Pests of Fruit Crops*, Manson, London, 2007.

Allen, David Elliston 1932–
Author of *Books and Naturalists* (NN112, 2010).

Bibliophile, botanist and historian, David Allen is best known as the author of *The Naturalist in Britain* (1976), a ground-breaking social history of British natural history. He is also a botanist of note, author of a flora of the Isle of Man and an authority on brambles. His day job was administering academic research grants.

BOOKS *The Victorian Fern Craze*. Hutchinson, London, 1969; *The Naturalist in Britain: a Social History*. Allen Lane, London, 1976, re-issued Princetown University Press, 1994; *Flora of the Isle of Man*. Manx Museum, Douglas, 1984; *The Botanists: a history of the Botanical Society of the British Isles through 150 years*. St Paul's Bibliographies, Winchester, 1986; *Naturalists and Society: the Culture of Natural History in Britain. 1700–1900*. Ashgate, Aldershot, 2001; *The Isle of Wight Flora*. (with Colin Pope and Lorna Snow), Dovecote, Wimborne, 2003; *Medicinal Plants in Folk Tradition: an Ethnobotany of Britain and Ireland*. (with Gabrielle Hatfield), Timber Press, Portland, 2004.

Allott, Andrew Jonathan 1956–
Author of *Marches* (NN118, 2011)

Andrew Allott is head of biology at Shrewsbury School and an authority of natural history in the Welsh Marches. He has also committed to the development of the International Baccalaureate, especially its biology courses.

Altringham, John Derek 1954–
Author of *British Bats* (NN93, 2003).

Professor of Biomechanics, Leeds University who specializes in animal locomotion and the ecology of bats. Recently he discovered a new British species, the Alcathoe Pipistrelle.

BOOKS *Bats. Biology and Behaviour*. Oxford University Press, Oxford, 1996.

Armstrong, Edward Allworthy 1900–78
Author of *The Folklore of Birds* (NN39, 1958) and *The Wren* (M3, 1955).

One of the twentieth-century's most distinguished 'parson-naturalists': Edward Armstrong was a parish priest who loved birds, their behaviour and their cultural associations. He combined meticulous studies of wrens with a searching interest in folklore, for example the 'psychology'
of legends associated with St Francis. Apparently his church superiors were unaware of any of it.

BIOGRAPHY Simmonds, K. E. L., *Oxford Dictionary of National Biography*.
BOOKS *Birds of the Grey Wind*. Oxford University Press, Oxford, 1940; *Bird Display: an introduction to the study of bird psychology*. Cambridge University Press, Cambridge, 1942, re-issued as *Bird Display and Behaviour*, Lindsay Drummond, London, 1947 and Dover Publications, New York, 1965; *The Way Birds Live*. Lindsay Drummond, London, 1943; *Bird Life*. Lindsay Drummond, London, 1949; *A Study of Bird Song*. Oxford University Press, London, 1963; *Saint Francis, Nature Mystic: The derivation and significance of the nature stories in the Franciscan legend*. University of California Press, Berkeley and London, 1973; *Life and Lore of the Bird in Nature, Art, Myth and Literature*. Crown

Publishers, New York, 1975; *Discovering Birdsong*. Shire, Princes Risborough, 1975.

Ball, David Francis 1927–
Author of *The Soil* (NN77, 1992) with Brian Davis, Norman Walker, and Alastair Fitter.

A soil scientist at the Agricultural Research Council who later became a member of the scientific team of the Nature Conservancy based at Bangor. There was involved with academic studies in soil science, clay mineralogy, glacial geology, and geomorphology, relating these to the ecological issues and management of conservation sites throughout Britain.

Beebee, Trevor John Clark 1947–
Author of *Amphibians and Reptiles* (NN87, 2000) with Richard Griffiths.

A herpetologist based at Sussex University, Trevor Beebee is well known for his work on the conservation of our rarest amphibians and reptiles, notably the natterjack toad and pool frog. Long-term involvement with the British Herpetological Society and Amphibian and Reptile Conservation Trust. His second love is for pond life.

BOOKS *Natterjack Toad*. Oxford University Press, Oxford, 1983; *Frogs and Toads*. Whittet Books, London, 1985; *Gene Structure and Transcription* (with Julian Burke). Oxford University Press, Oxford, 1988; *Pond Life*. Whittet Books, London, 1992; *Ecology and Conservation of Amphibians*. Chapman & Hall, London, 1996; *Introduction to Molecular Ecology* (with Graham Rowe). Oxford University Press, Oxford, 2004.

Benton, Edward (Ted) 1942–
Author of *Bumblebees* (NN98, 2006) and *Grasshoppers and Crickets* (NN120, 2012).

A field entomologist and one of our leading experts on bumblebees and grasshoppers, Ted Benton's day job was as Professor of Sociology at Essex University.

BOOKS *The Dragonflies of Essex*. Essex Field Club, 1988; *Natural Relations: Ecology, Animal Rights and Social Justice*. Verso, London, 1993. *The Bumblebees of Essex*. Lopinga Books, Saffron Walden, 2000; *The Butterflies of Colchester and North East Essex* (with J. Firmin). CNHS, Colchester, 2002; *Easy Guide to Butterflies* (with T. Bernhard). Aurum, London, 2006; *Dragonflies of Essex* (new edition) (with J. Dobson). Essex Field Club with Lopinga Books, Saffron Walden, 2007.

Berry, Robert James (Sam) FRSE 1934–
Author of *Inheritance and Natural History* (NN61, 1977), *The Natural History of Shetland* (NN64, 1980) with J. Laughton Johnston, *The Natural History of Orkney* (NN70, 1985) and I*slands* (NN109, 2009).

A distinguished geneticist, 'Sam' Berry took science into the field to study the effects of isolation on islands, especially on small mammals. As a Christian he also intercedes between science and religion, winning the Templeton Award for 'sustained advocacy of the Christian faith in the world of science'.
BOOKS *Teach Yourself Genetics*. English Universities Press, London, 1965; *Biology of the House Mouse* (Ed). Academic Press, London, 1981; *Neo-Darwinism*. Edward Arnold, London, 1982; *Evolution in the Galapagos* (Ed). Academic Press, London, 1984; *The Collins Encyclopaedia of Animal Evolution* (with A. Hallam). Collins, London, 1986; *Nature, Natural History and Ecology* (Editor with John Crothers). Academic, London, 1987; *God and Evolution*. Hodder & Stoughton, London, 1988; *Environmental Dilemmas* (Ed). Chapman & Hall, London, 1993; *God and the Biologist*. Apollos, Leicester, 1996; *Orkney Nature*. Poyser, London, 2000; *God's Book of Works*. T&T Clark , London, 2003; *Environmental Stewardship* (Ed). Continuum, London, 2006; *When Enough Is Enough* (Ed). Apollos, Nottingham, 2007; *Ecology and the Environment*. Templeton, Philadelphia, 2011.

Bircham, Peter Michael Miles 1947–
Author of *A History of Ornithology* (NN104, 2007).

An ornithologist with a background in 'Continuing Education' at Cambridge, Peter

Bircham is interested in the historical background to birding and its leading personalities. His full-time work is as a pharmacologist. Involved with research and recording at Wicken Fen.
BOOKS *Birds of Cambridgeshire*. Cambridge University Press, Cambridge, 1989; *The Cambridge Encyclopaedia of Ornithology* (advisory editor and contributor). Cambridge University Press, Cambridge, 1991; *Wicken Fen: the making of a wetland nature reserve* (contributor). Harley Books and The National Trust, 1997.

Blunt, Wilfrid Jasper Walter 1901–87
Author of *The Art of Botanical Illustration* (NN14, 1950).

A celebrated artist, author and polymath, Wilfred Blunt taught art at Haileybury and then at Eton. A bachelor, he found the leisure to dabble with Islamic art, biography and of course botanical art. He helped to revolutionise children's handwriting, using a fourteenth century Italian script as the basis.
AUTOBIOGRAPHIES *Married to a Single Life*. Michael Russell, Salisbury, 1983; *Slow on the Feather*. Michael Russell, Salisbury, 1986.
BOOKS *Tulipomania*. King Penguin, London, 1950; *Of Flowers and Village: an Entertainment for Flower Lovers*. Hamish Hamilton, London, 1963; *The Compleat Naturalist: A Life of Linnaeus*. Collins, London, 1971; *Flora Superba*. Tryon Gallery, London, 1971; *Captain Cook's Florilgeium* (with William Stearn). Lion & Unicorn Press, London, 1973; *The Golden Road to Samarkand*. Hamish Hamilton, London, 1973; *The Ark in the Park: The Zoo in the Nineteenth Century*. Hamish Hamilton, London, 1976; *Flora Magnifica*. Tryon Gallery, London, 1976; *In for a Penny. A Prospect of Kew Gardens*. Hamish Hamilton, London, 1978; *Illustrated Herbal* (with Sandra Raphael). Thames & Hudson, London, 1979; *Great Flower Books, 1700–1900* (with Sacheverell Sitwell and Patrick Synge). Witherby, London, 1990; *The Art of Botanical Illustration* (new edition, revised and enlarged) (with W. Stearn). Antique Collectors' Club, Woodbridge and Royal Botanic Gardens, Kew, 1994.

Boyd, Arnold Whitworth MC 1885–1959
Author of *A Country Parish* (NN9, 1951).

An old-style naturalist devoted to his home patch in Cheshire, Arnold Boyd was also a soldier (earning the MC at Gallipoli where he lost an eye), a leading ornithologist and agent for the family yarn business. He was James Fisher's uncle.
BOOKS *The Country Diary of a Cheshire Man*. Collins, London, 1946.

Boyd, Ian Lamont FRSE 1957–
Author of *The Hebrides* (NN76, 1990) with J. Morton Boyd.

Son of Morton Boyd, Ian Boyd is an authority on marine mammals, especially seals. He worked for the British Antarctic Survey for thirteen years before becoming Director of the Sea Mammals Research Unit and Scottish Oceans Institute at Edinburgh University. He is Chief Scientific Adviser to the Department of Environment, Food & Rural Affairs.
BOOKS *Conserving Nature*. Scotland and the Wider World (editor, with Roger Crofts). John Donald, Edinburgh, 2005; *Marine Mammals; Advances in behavioural and population biology*. Zoological Society of London Symposium, Clarendon, Oxford, 1992; *Seals, Fur Seals, Sea Lions and Walrus: Status Survey and Conservation Action Plan* (with P. Reijnders, S. Brasseur , J. van der Toorn, P. van der Wolf, J. Harwood, D. Lavigne and L. Lowry). IUCN, Gland, Switzerland, 2006; *Marine Mammal Ecology and Conservation: A Handbook of Techniques* (with Don Bowen and Sara Iverson). Oxford University Press, Oxford, 2010.

Boyd, John Morton CBE FRSE 1925–1998
Reviser of *The Natural History of the Highlands and Islands*, re-titled *The Highlands and Islands* (NN6b, 1964) and author of *The Hebrides* (with Ian Boyd) (NN76, 1990).

A zoologist, Morton Boyd directed the Nature Conservancy Council in Scotland in the 70s and 80s. Scotland's best-known conservationist, he was a passionate man who immersed himself in everything he did. He loved the islands (he had a second home on Tiree), dabbled in poetry and art, and was a Church Elder.

AUTOBIOGRAPHY *The Song of the Sandpiper.* Colin Baxter, Grantown-on-Spey, 1999.

FESTSCHRIFT *Conserving Nature: Scotland and the Wider World* (eds Roger Crofts and Ian Boyd). Edinburgh: John Donald.

BOOKS *St Kilda Summer* (with Kenneth Williamson). Hutchinson, London, 1960; *A Mosaic of Islands* (with Kenneth Williamson). Oliver & Boyd, Edinburgh and London, 1963; *Island Survivors. The Ecology of the Soay Sheep of St Kilda* (with Peter Jewell and Cedric Milner). Athlone Press, London, 1974; *The Natural Environment of the Outer Hebrides* (Ed). Royal Society of Edinburgh & Nature Conservancy Council, Edinburgh, 1979; *Natural Environment of the Inner Hebrides* (Ed): Proceedings of the Royal Society of Edinburgh, vol. 83., 1983; *Fraser Darling's Islands.* Edinburgh University Press, Edinburgh, 1986; *Fraser Darling in Africa: a rhino in the whistling thorn.* Edinburgh University Press, Edinburgh, 1992.

Brian, Michael Vaughan OBE 1919–1990
Author of *Ants* (NN59, 1977).

M.V. Brian was an entomologist who specialised in social insects, especially ants. First a lecturer at Glasgow University he spent most of his career in the Nature Conservancy (later ITE) at Furzebrook research station in Dorset studying local ants in his spare time.

BOOKS *Social Insect Populations.* Academic, New York and London, 1965; *Social Insects: Ecology and Behavioural Biology.* Chapman & Hall, London, 1983.

Bristowe, William Syer (Bill) 1919–90
Author of the *The World of Spiders* (NN38, 1958).

The doyen of spider study in Britain, Bill Bristowe observed the behaviour of spiders with enormous commitment and energy, earning a Cambridge doctorate on the strength of it. His New Naturalist is widely regarded as one of the immortal classics of the series. His day job was a senior administrator at ICI.

BOOKS *Comity of Spiders.* 2 vols. Ray Society, London, 1939, 1941; *Book of Spiders.* King Penguin, London, 1947; *A Book of Islands.* G. Bell & Sons, London, 1969.

Brooks, Stephen John FRES 1955–
Author of *Dragonflies* (NN106, 2008) with Philip Corbet.

A leading expert on dragonflies, Stephen Brooks is a member of the entomology department at the Natural History Museum. His research takes him around the world, as well as recording and studying dragonflies at home.

BOOKS *Dragonflies and Damselflies.* Natural History Museum, London, 2003; *Field Guide to the Dragonflies and Damselflies of Great Britain and Ireland* (with R. Lewington). British Wildlife Publishing, Hook, 1997, 4th ed. revised 2004; *The Identification and use of Palaearctic Chironomidae larvae in palaeoecology* (with P. Langdon and O. Heiri). Quaternary Research Association Technical Guide no. 10, 2007.

Brown, Leslie Hilton OBE 1917–80
Author of *British Birds of Prey* (NN60, 1976).

An African-based ornithologist specialising in birds of prey, especially eagles, Leslie Brown was one of the more colourful New Naturalists, fiercely independent, prickly, voluble and fearless. He had a busy career in agriculture in Kenya, briefly becoming Chief Agriculturist before retiring in 1963 to study and write about birds full time.

BOOKS *Outlaw of the Air.* Geoffrey Bles, London, 1939; *Birds and I.* Michael Joseph, London, 1947. *Eagles.* Michael Joseph, London, 1955; *The Mystery of the Flamingos.* Country Life, London, 1959; *The Continents We Live On: Africa a Natural History.* Hamish Hamilton, London, 1965; *Ethiopian Episode.* Country Life, London, 1965; *Eagles, Hawks and Falcons of the World* (with Dean Amadon). Hamlyn, London, 1968; *African Birds of Prey.* Collins, London, 1970; *Eagles.* Arthur Barker, London, 1970; *Birds of the African Bush* (with R. Fennessy). Collins, London, 1971; *The Life of the African Plains.* McGraw-Hill, New York, 1972; *Birds of Prey, their Biology and Ecology.* Hamlyn, London, 1976; *Eagles of the World.* David & Charles, Newton Abbott, 1976; *Encounters with Nature.* Oxford University Press, Oxford, 1979; *Birds of the African Waterside* (with R. Fennessy). Collins, London, 1979; *Birds of Prey of the World* (with Friedhelm Weick). Collins, London, 1980; *The African Fish Eagle.* Bailey, Folkestone, 1980; *The Birds of Africa* (with Emil Urban and Kenneth Newman) 2 volumes. Academic, London, 1982.

Buczacki, Stefan Tadeusz 1945–
Author of *Garden Natural History* (NN102, 2007).

A well-known broadcaster, the chair of *Gardener's Question Time* for many years, Stefan Buczacki is an expert on gardens and garden design with a specialist knowledge of fungi and plant diseases. He is also a prolific author and much in demand as a speaker on gardening matters. More quietly, he is a book collector.

BOOKS *Collins Guide to the Pests, Diseases and Disorders of Garden Plants* (with Keith Harris). Collins, 1981; *Gem Guide to Mushrooms and Toadstools.* Collins, London, 1982; *Collins Shorter Guide to the Pests, Diseases and Disorders of Garden Plants* (with Keith Harris). Collins, London, 1983. *Zoosporic Plant Pathogens* (Ed). Academic Press, London, 1983; *Beat Garden Pests and Diseases.* Penguin, London, 1985; *Gardeners' Questions Answered.* Collins, London, 1985; *Three Men in a Garden* (with Geoffrey Smith and Clay Jones). BBC, London, 1986; *Ground Rules for Gardeners: a Practical Guide to Garden Ecology.* Collins, London, 1986; *Creating a Victorian Flower Garden.* Collins, London, 1988; *The Conran Beginner's Guide to Gardening.* Conran Octopus, London, 1988; *Garden Warfare.* Souvenir, London, 1989; *New Generation Guide to the Fungi of Britain and Europe.* Collins, London, 1989; *A Garden for All Seasons.* Conran Octopus, London, 1990; *Understanding Your Garden.* Cambridge University Press, Cambridge, 1990; *The Essential Gardener.* Macmillan, London, 1991; *The Plant Care Manual.* Conran Octopus, London, 1992; *Mushrooms and Toadstools of Britain and Europe.* HarperCollins, London, 1992; *Dr Stefan Buczacki's Garden Hints.* Pan, London, 1992; *Stefan Buczacki's Gardening in Britain.* BBC, London, 1996. *Best Container Plants.* Hamlyn, London, 1986; *Stefan Buczacki's Garden Dictionary.* Hamlyn, London, 1998; *Stefan Buczacki's Plant Dictionary.* Hamlyn, London, 1998; *Plant Problems.* David & Charles, Newton Abbott, 2000; *Best Kitchen Herbs.* Hamlyn, London, 2000; *Hamlyn Encyclopaedia of Gardening.* Hamlyn, London, 2002; *The Commonsense Gardener.* Frances Lincoln, London, 2004; *Young Gardener* (with Beverley Buczacki and Anthea Sievking). Francis Lincoln, London, 2006; *Fauna Britannica.* Hamlyn, London, 2005; *Collins Wildlife Gardener.* HarperCollins, London, 2007; *Churchill and Chartwell.* Frances Lincoln, London, 2007; *Pests, Diseases and Disorders of Garden Plants* (with Keith Harris and Brian Hargreaves). Collins, London, 2010; *Collins Fungi Guide* (with Chris Shields and Denys Ovenden). Collins, London, 2012

Butler, Colin Gasking OBE FRS 1913–
Author of *The World of the Honeybee* (NN29, 1954) and *Bumblebees* (NN40, 1959) with John Free.

Colin Butler spent his professional career at Rothamsted as head of bee research and latterly head of entomology. A world authority on honey bees, he discovered the 'queen substance', secreted by queen bees, that makes sure there is only one queen in the hive.
BOOKS *The Honeybee: An Introduction to her Sense-Physiology and Behaviour.* Oxford University Press, London, 1949.; *Beekeeping Bulletin Number 9*, ninth edition. HMSO, London, 1957.

Cabot, David Boyd Redmond 1938–
Author of *Ireland* (NN84, 1999), *Wildfowl* (NN110, 2009) and *Terns* (NN123, 2013) with Ian Nisbet.

Irish naturalist and ornithologist, David Cabot worked as a government ecologist responsible for Ireland's conservation policy before becoming an independent consultant on ecology and conservation. He is an author, broadcaster and film maker, as well as a bibliophile.
BOOKS *Irish Sea Birds.* Folens, Dublin, 1976. *Irish Pond Life.* Folens, Dublin, 1977.; *Inventory of Outstanding Landscapes in Ireland* (Ed). An Foras Forbartha/Department of Environment, Dublin, 1977.; *Irish Birds of Prey.* Folens, Dublin, 1978.; *Inventory of Areas of Scientific Interest in Ireland* (Ed). An Foras Forbartha/ Department of Environment, Dublin, 1981.; *State of the Environment* (Ed). An Foras Forbartha/ Department of Environment, Dublin, 1982.; *Biological Expedition to Jameson Land, Greenland, 1984* (with Richard Nairn, Steve Newton and Michael Viney). Barnacle Books, Dublin, 1984.; *eec Environmental Legislation* (with Nigel Haigh). An Foras Forbatha/ Department of Environment, Dublin, 1987.; *Irish Expedition to North-East Greenland, 1987* (with Michael Viney and Roger Goodwillie). Barnacle Books, Dublin, 1988.; *Irish Birds.* HarperCollins, London, 1995. Revised 2004, reprinted 2006, Reprinted as *The Complete Irish Birds*, 2008, 2010.

Campbell, Bruce 1912–93
Author of *Snowdonia* (NN13, 1949) with F. J. North and Richenda Scott.

A well-known ornithologist, Bruce Campbell worked for many years as the first full-time secretary at the BTO putting his nest-finding skills to good use. He also served as producer of the BBC's Natural History Unit, before becoming freelance writer, broadcaster and journalist. Although his was the first doctorate for bird study in the field, he always regarded bird-watching as first and foremost 'a sport'.
AUTOBIOGRAPHY *Birdwatcher at Large.* Dent, London, 1979;
BOOKS *Bird Watching for Beginners.* Penguin, London, 1952; *Finding Nests.* Collins, London, 1953; *Birds in Colour.* Penguin, London, 1960; *Oxford Book of Birds.* Oxford University Press, London, 1964; *The Pictorial Encyclopedia of Birds* (with Jan Hanzák). Hamlyn, Feltham, 1967; *British & European Birds in Colour* (with Bertel Bruun and Arthur Singer). Hamlyn, Feltham, 1969; *The Hamlyn Guide to Birds of Britain and Europe* (with Bertel Bruun and Arthur Singer). Hamlyn, Feltham, 1970; *The Dictionary of Birds in Colour.* Michael Joseph, London, 1970; *Field Guide to Birds' Nests* (with James Ferguson-Lees). Constable, London, 1972; *Guide to the Birds of the Coast* (revised edition) (with Robert Campbell). Constable, London, 1976; *The Bird Paintings of Henry Jones.* Folio Fine Editions for the Zoological Society of London, London, 1976; *Birds of the Coast and Sea.* Oxford University Press, Oxford, 1977; *The Natural History of Britain and Northern Europe.* Five Volumes (edited with James Ferguson-Lees). Hodder & Stoughton, London, 1979; *A Dictionary of Birds* (with Elizabeth Lack). Poyser for the British Ornithologists' Union, Berkhamsted, 1985.

Campbell, Ronald Niall 1924–2005
Author of *Freshwater Fishes* (NN75, 1992) with Peter Maitland.

A fisheries biologist who specialised in wild brown trout, Niall Campbell spent most of his career in the Nature Conservancy (later the NCC) as regional officer in North-west Scotland.

Chapman, Philip 1950–
Author of *Caves and Cave Life* (NN79, 1993).

Philip Chapman is a much-travelled film-maker for the BBC Natural History Unit, producing, for example, *Dragons Alive* (on reptiles) and *Wild China.* He is an authority on caves and cave life and has led numerous caving expeditions.

Condry, William Moreton 1918–98
Author of *The Snowdonia National Park* (NN47, 1966) and *The Natural History of Wales* (NN66, 1981).

Wales' best-known nature writer was an in-comer from Birmingham. He helped to set up a bird observatory on Bardsey and was for many years warden of the Ynys-hir nature reserve. He is remembered as a diarist and essayist as well as for his books and personality. His legacy lives on in a Welsh festival of outdoor writing.
AUTOBIOGRAPHY *Wildlife, My Life.* Gomer, Llandysul, 1995;
BOOKS *Birds and Wild Africa.* Collins, London, 1967; *Thoreau* (Great Naturalists Series edited by R. M. Lockley). Witherby, London, 1954; *Exploring Wales.* Faber, London, 1972; *Woodlands* (Collins Countryside Series). Collins, London, 1974; *Pathway to the Wild.* Faber, London, 1975; *The World of a Mountain.* Faber, London, 1977; *A Welsh Country Diary.* Gomer, Llandysul, 1993; *Welsh Country Essays.* Gomer, Llandysul, 1996; *Wildflower Safari: the life of Mary Richards.* Gomer, Llandysul, 1998.

Corbet, Philip Steven FRSE 1929–2008
Author of *Dragonflies* (NN41, 1960) with Cynthia Longfield and Norman Moore and *Dragonflies* (NN106, 2008) with Stephen Brooks.

Our leading dragonfly biologist, Philip Corbet was a full-time entomologist on four continents, latterly as professor of biology at Dundee. Much of his research was directed at insect control in tropical diseases, crop protection and freshwater management, but his first love was always for dragonflies.
BOOKS *Biology of Dragonflies.* Witherby, London, 1962; *The Microclimate of Arctic Plants and Animals, on Land and in Fresh Water.* Munksgaard, Copenhagen, 1972; *Dragonflies: Behaviour and Ecology of Odonata.* Harley Books, Colchester, 1999.

Darling, Frank Moss Fraser FRSE KT 1903–79
Author of *Natural History in the Highlands and Islands* (NN6a, 1947) heavily revised in collaboration with Morton Boyd and republished as *The Highlands and Islands* (NN6b, in 1964).

Fraser Darling was one of the best-known conservationists of the 1960s and 1970s, well ahead of his time in arguing for sustainable development and scientific principles in planning. He spent his early years in remote parts of the Scottish Highlands and Islands studying deer, seals, gulls and the crofting life. He later extended the principles of his West Highland Survey (1955) to 'odysseys' in Africa and North America.

BIOGRAPHY **Boyd, J. Morton** *Fraser Darling's Islands.* Edinburgh University Press, Edinburgh, 1986; **Boyd, J. Morton** *Fraser Darling in Africa: a Rhino in the Whistling Thorn.* Edinburgh University Press, Edinburgh, 1992; **Mellanby, K.** (revised **V. M. Quirke**) *Oxford Dictionary of National Biography.*

BOOKS *Animal Breeding in the British Empire. A Survey of Research and Experiment.* Imperial Bureau of Animal Genetics, Edinburgh, 1934; *A Herd of Red Deer. A Study in Animal Behaviour.* Oxford University Press, London, 1937; *Bird Flocks and the Breeding Cycle: a Contribution to the Study of Avian Sociality.* Cambridge University Press, Cambridge, 1938; *Wild Country. A Highland Naturalist's Notes and Pictures.* Cambridge University Press, Cambridge, 1938; *The Seasons and the Farmer: A Book for Children.* Cambridge University Press, Cambridge, 1939; *A Naturalist on Rona: Essays of a Biologist in Isolation.* Clarendon Press, Oxford, 1939; *Island Years.* Bell and Sons, London, 1940; *The Seasons and the Fisherman.* Cambridge University Press, Cambridge, 1941; *The Story of Scotland* (Britain in Pictures series). Collins, London, 1942; *Wild Life of Britain* (Britain in Pictures series). Collins, London, 1943; *Island Farm.* Bell and Sons, London, 1943; *The Story of Scotland* (Britain in Pictures series). Collins, London, 1945; *Crofting Agriculture. Its Practice in the West Highlands and Islands.* Oliver and Boyd, Edinburgh, 1945; *West Highland Survey: An Essay in Human Ecology.* Oxford University Press, London, 1955; *Pelican in the Wilderness: A naturalist's odyssey in North America.* Allen & Unwin, London, 1956; *Wilderness and Plenty: the Reith Lectures,* 1970. BBC, London, 1969; *A Conversation on Population, Environment, and Human Well-Being.* Conservation Foundation, Washington, 1970.

Davis, Brian Noel Kittredge 1934–
Author of *The Soil* (NN77, 1992) with Norman Walker, David Ball and Alastair Fitter.

Brian Davis spent nearly all his professional career at Monks Wood, the famous research station near Huntingdon, latterly as its deputy head. He broke his scientific teeth on soil fauna, later moving into pesticide research, plant-eating insects and the environmental effects of modern farming.

BOOKS *Insects on Nettles.* Cambridge University Press, Cambridge, 1983; *A Field Guide to the Grasses of the East Midlands.* Huntingdonshire Fauna & Flora Society, 2009.

Edlin, Herbert Leeson MBE 1916–76
Author of *Trees, Woods and Man* (NN32, 1956).

The twentieth century's best-known writer on forestry matters, Bill Edlin produced a stream of publications for the Forestry Commission as well as books on trees, timber and woodmanship as a freelance author.

BOOKS *British Woodland Trees.* Batsford, London, 1944; *Forestry and Woodland Life.* Batsford, London, 1947; *Woodland Crafts in Britain.* Batsford, London, 1949; *The Changing Wildlife of Britain.* Batsford, London, 1952; *The Forester's Handbook.* Thames and Hudson, London, 1953; *The Living Forest.* Thames and Hudson, London, 1958; *England's Forests. A survey of the woodlands old and new in the English and Welsh Counties.* Faber, London, 1958; *Wildlife of Wood and Forest.* Hutchinson, London, 1960; *Wayside and Woodland – Trees.* Warne, London, 1964; *Man and Plants.* Aldus, London, 1967; *Trees and Timbers.* Routledge & Kegan Paul, London, 1973; *Collins Guide to Tree Planting and Cultivation.* Collins, London, 1970; *The Natural History of Trees.* Weidenfeld and Nicolson, London, 1976; *Trees.* Orbis, London, 1978; *Tree Key.* Scribner, New York, 1978; *Observer's Book of Trees and Shrubs.* Warne, London, 1975; *Illustrated Encyclopaedia of Trees* (with Maurice Nimmo). HMSO, London, 1978.

Edwards, Kenneth Charles CBE 1904–82
Author of *The Peak District* (NN44, 1962).

A geographer at Nottingham University, 'KC' Edwards was also a great proponent of field study, and a keen rambler. Much involved in local planning matters he was for many years professor and head of the geography department.

FESTSCHRIFT **Osborne, R.H., Barnes, F.A. & Doornkamp, J.C.** (Eds) *Geographical Essays in Honour of K. C. Edwards.* Nottingham University Press, Nottingham, 1970.

BOOKS *The ABC of Climate.* John Hamilton, London, 1930; *Luxembourg* (with Monkhouse, F. J. and Edwards, B. J.). Cambridge University Press, Cambridge, 1944.

Ellis, Edward Augustine (Ted) 1909–86
Author of *The Broads* (NN46, 1965).

Perhaps the best-known East Anglian naturalist, Ted Ellis was a self-taught all-rounder and an expert on the Broads, as well as on his chosen specialty, micro-fungi. He kept a daily diary in the local newspaper for forty years, which, together with his radio broadcasts, made him a much-loved local personality. Established Wheatfen Broad as a nature reserve in 1945, which is now run as field centre by the Ted Ellis Trust.

BIOGRAPHY **Stone, Eugene.** *Ted Ellis: The People's Naturalist.* Jarrold, Norwich, 1988.

BOOKS Several local wildlife guides: *The Countryside in Spring, Summer, Autumn and Winter* (four vols). Jarrold, Norwich, 1975.

Fisher, James Maxwell McConnell 1912–70
Author of *The Fulmar* (M6, 1952) and of *Sea Birds* (NN28, 1954) with Ronald Lockley. See under Editorial Board.

Fitter, Alastair CBE FRS 1948–
Author of *The Soil* (NN77, 1992) with Brian Davis, Norman Walker and David Ball.

Alastair Fitter is professor of ecology at York University and an influential voice in plant science. He also follows in his father, Richard Fitter's, footsteps as author of field guides and other illustrated books on British natural history.

BOOKS *The Wild Flowers of Britain and Northern Europe* (with Marjorie Blamey and Richard

Fitter). Collins, London, 1977; *An Atlas of the Wild Flowers of Britain and Northern Europe*. Collins, London, 1978; *A Wood in Ascam: a Study in Wetland Conservation. Askham Bog 1879–1979* (with C. J. Smith). Ebor Press, York, 1979; *Trees* (with David More). Collins, London, 1980; *Environmental Physiology of Plants* (with Robert Hay). Academic, London, 1981; *The Complete Guide to British Wildlife* (with Richard Fitter and Norman Arlott). Collins, London, 1981; *Collins Guide to the Countryside* (with Richard Fitter). Collins, London, 1984; *Collins Guide to the Grasses, Sedges, Rushes and Ferns of Britain and Northern Europe* (with Richard Fitter and Anne Farrar). Collins, London, 1984; *New Generation Guide to the Wild Flowers of Britain and Northern Europe*. Collins, London, 1987; *Collins Guide to the Countryside in Winter* (with Richard Fitter). Collins, London, 1988; *The Wild Flowers of the British Isles* (with Richard Fitter and Marjorie Blamey). A & C Black, London, 2003.

Fitter, Richard Sidney Richmond 1913–2005
Author of *London's Natural History* (NN3, 1945) and contributor to *The Birds of the London Area* (M14, 1957).

The name of Richard Fitter is synonymous with natural history field guides for which his polymathic knowledge, energy and literary talent made him the ideal author. Throughout his life he also worked for nature conservation, often in partnership with his wife, Maisie, as a leading light of the Fauna and Flora Preservation Society.

BIOGRAPHY **Greenwood, J. J. M.** *Oxford Dictionary of National Biography*.

BOOKS *London's Birds*. Collins, London, 1949; *The Pocket Guide to British Birds*. Collins, London, 1952; *Birds of Town and Village* (The Country Naturalist Series). Collins, London, 1953; *The Natural History of the City* (with J. E. Lousley). Corporation of the City, London, 1953; *The Pocket Guide to Nests and Eggs*. Collins, London, 1955; *Fontana Bird Guide*. Collins, London, 1956; *The Pocket Guide to Wild Flowers* (with David McClintock). Collins, London, 1956; *Fontana Wild Flower Guide*. Collins, London, 1957; *The Ark in Our Midst: The Story of the Introduced Animals of Britain; Birds, Beasts, Reptiles, Amphibians, Fishes*. Collins, London, 1959; *The 'Countryman' Nature Book: An Anthology from 'The Countryman'*. Brockhampton Press, Leicester, 1960; *Collins Guide to Bird Watching*. Collins, London, 1963; *Fitters Rural Rides: 'The Observer' Illustrated Map-Guide to the Countryside*. The Observer, London, 1963; *Wildlife in Britain*. Penguin, London, 1963; *Pocket Guide to British Birds* (with Richard Richardson). Collins, London, 1966; *Britain's Wildlife, Rarities and Introductions*. Kaye, London, 1966; *The Penguin Dictionary of British Natural History* (with Masie Fitter). Penguin, London, 1967; *Pocket Guide to Nests and Eggs*. Collins, London, 1968; *Vanishing Wild Animals of the World*. Kaye, London, 1968; *Guide to Bird Watching*. Collins, London, 1970; *Finding Wild Flowers*. Collins, London, 1971; *Birds of Britain and Europe with North Africa and the Middle East* (with illustrations by Hermann Heinzel and maps by John Parslow). Collins, London, 1972; *The Wild Flowers of Britain and Northern Europe* (Collins Pocket Guide) (with Alastair Fitter and Marjorie Blamey). Collins, London, 1974; *The Penitent Butchers: The Fauna Preservation Society 1903–1978* (with Peter Scott). Fauna Preservation Society, London, 1978; *Handguide to the Wild Flowers of Britain and Northern Europe*. Treasure Press, London, 1979; *The Complete Guide to British Wildlife* (with Alastair Fitter and Norman Arlott). Collins, London, 1981; *Grasses, Sedges, Rushes & Ferns of Britain and Northern Europe* (Collins Pocket Guide) (with Alastair Fitter and Ann Farrer) Collins, London, 1984; *Collins Guide to the Countryside* (with Alastair Fitter). Collins, London, 1984; *The Wildlife of the Thames Counties. Berkshire, Buckinghamshire & Oxfordshire* (Ed). BBONT, Oxford, 1985; *A Field Guide to Freshwater Life in Britain and North-West Europe* (Collins Field Guide) (with Richard Manuel). Collins, London, 1986; *Wildlife for Man. How and why we should conserve our species*. Collins, London, 1986; *Collins Guide to the Countryside in Winter* (Collins Handguide) (with Alastair Fitter) Collins, London, 1988; *Wild Flowers* (Collins Gem Series) (with Martin Walters). Collins, London, 1999; *The Wild Flowers of Britain and Ireland: The Complete Guide to the British and Irish Flora* (with Alastair Fitter and Marjorie Blamey) Collins, London, 2003.

Fleure, Herbert John FRS 1877–1969
Author of *A Natural History of Man in Britain* (NN18, 1951).

A distinguished anthropologist and geographer, H. J. Fleure pioneered the study of the social evolution of man through his papers, books and editorship of *The Corridors of Time*. He was the first geographer to be elected Fellow of the Royal Society.

BIOGRAPHY **Garnett, A.,** 1970). Herbert John Fleure. *Biographical Memoirs of Fellows of the Royal Society*, 16: 253–78; **Gruffudd, P.** In *Oxford Dictionary of National Biography*

BOOKS *Human Geography in Western Europe*. Williams and Norgate, London, 1918; *The Peoples of Europe*. Oxford University Press, London, 1922; *The Races of England and Wales*. Benn, London, 1923; *The Corridors of Time* (series of 10 vols) (with H. J. E. Peake). Clarendon Press, Oxford, 1927–56; *The Races of Mankind*. Benn, London, 1927; *An Introduction to Geography*. Benn, London, 1929; *The Geographical Background to Modern Problems*. Longmans Green, London, 1932; *Problems of Population in Europe*. Percy Bros., Manchester, 1942; *Some Aspects of British Civilization*. Clarendon, Oxford, 1948.

Ford, Edmund Brisco (Henry) FRS 1901–88
Author of *Butterflies* (NN1, 1945) and *Moths* (NN30, 1955).

As an undergraduate he was considerably influenced by Julian Huxley. 'Henry' Ford was the pioneer of ecological genetics, or, to borrow the title of one of his books, 'taking genetics into the countryside'. At the same time he turned his hobby of collecting butterflies and moths into a tool for studying the workings of inheritance. A lifelong Oxford man, he is now as famous for his eccentricities as for his science.

BIOGRAPHY **Clarke, B. C.,** 'Edmund Brisco Ford'. *Biographical Memoirs of Fellows of the Royal Society*. 41: 145–68, 1995; **Cooper, J.** *Of Moths and Men: a critical account of E. B. Ford and his associates*. Fourth Estate, London, 1995.

FESTSCHRIFT *Ecological Genetics and Evolution. Essays in Honour of E. B. Ford* (edited by Robert Creed). Blackwell Scientific Publications, Oxford, 1971.

BOOKS *Mendelism and Evolution*. Methuen, London, 1931; 8th edition 1965; *Mimicry* (with G. D. Hale Carpenter). Methuen, London, 1933; *The Study of Heredity*. Thornton Butterworth, London, 1938; *Genetics for Medical Students*. Methuen, London, 1942; *British Butterflies*. Penguin, London, 1951; *Ecological Genetics*. Methuen, London, 1964; *Genetic Polymorphism*. Faber & Faber, London, 1965; *Evolution Studied by Observation and Experiment*. Oxford University Press, London, 1973; *Ecological Genetics*. Chapman & Hall, London, 1975; *Genetics and Adaptation*. Edward Arnold, London, 1976; *Understanding Genetics*. Faber & Faber, London, 1979; *Taking Genetics into the Countryside*. Weidenfeld & Nicolson, London, 1981.

Frazer, John Francis Deryk 1916–2009
Author of *Reptiles and Amphibians* (NN69, 1983).

A physiologist and expert on amphibians, Deryk
Frazer turned to nature study and conservation
in the 1950s, ending in charge of international
matters at the Nature Conservancy. In retirement
he devoted himself to surveying and rescuing
beleaguered amphibians in Kent.
  BOOKS *The Sexual Cycle of Vertebrates.*
Hutchinson, London, 1959; *Amphibians.* Taylor &
Francis, London, 1972.

Free, John Brand 1927–2006
Author of *Bumblebees* (NN40, 1959) with
Colin Butler.

An expert on bumblebees and a lifelong
promoter of beekeeping, John Free worked with
Colin Butler at Rothamsted research station on
the social life and pollination ecology of bees.
  BOOKS *Insect Pollination of Crops.* Academic Press,
London, 1970, 2nd Ed 1993; *The Social Organization
of Honeybees.* Edward Arnold, London, 1977;
Honeybees. A&C Black, London, 1978; *Insects We
Need.* A&C Black, London, 1980; *Life Under Stones.*
A&C Black, London, 1981; *Bees and Mankind.* Allen
& Unwin, Hemel Hempstead, 1982; *Pheromones of
Social Bees*; Chapman & Hall, London, 1987.

Friend, Peter Furneaux 1934–
Author of *Southern England* (NN108, 2008) and
Scotland (NN119, 2012).

Brought up in Edinburgh and the Scottish Borders,
Peter Friend was based at the Department of
Earth Sciences at Cambridge University, where
he contributed to research programmes from
the Arctic to India and Pakistan, with a particular
interest in the role of rivers in shaping the landscape.
  FESTSCHRIFT *Sedimentary Processes, Environments
and Basins* (edited with Gary Nichols, Ed Williams
and Chris Paola). Blackwell, Oxford, 2007.
  BOOKS *Tertiary basins of Spain: the stratigraphic
record of crustal kinematics* (editor with Cristino
Dabrio). Cambridge University Press, Cambridge,
1996; *New Perspectives on the Old Red Sandstone*
(editor with Brian Williams). Geological Society
of London, 2000.

Gilbert, Oliver Lathe 1936–2005
Author of *Lichens* (NN86, 2000).

A lichenologist, he 'invented' the sport of lichen
hunting, investigating remote or unlikely sites
with unflagging enthusiasm. He was also an
authority on landscape restoration from his
base in the landscape department at Sheffield
University.
  BOOKS *The Ecology of Urban Habitats.* Chapman
& Hall, London, 1989; *Habitat Creation and Repair*
(with Penny Anderson). Oxford University Press,
Oxford, 1998; *The Lichen Hunters.* The Book Guild,
Lewes, 2004.

Gilmour, John Scott Lennox 1906–86
Author of *Wild Flowers* (NN5, 1954) with
Max Walters. See under Editorial Board.

Goldring, Frederick (Fred) 1897–1997
Author of *The Weald* (NN26, 1953) with
Sidney Wooldridge.

A talented amateur photographer with a special
interest in the churches and historic buildings
of the Weald, Fred Goldring ran Timberscombe
Guest House, Haslemere, where S.W. Wooldridge
and his students often stayed in the 1930s and 40s.

Griffiths, Richard 1957–
Author of *Amphibians and Reptiles* (NN87, 2000)
with Trevor Beebee.

A zoologist at the University of Kent, currently
Professor of Biological Conservation. He is also
a leading herpetologist, running conservation
projects both at home and around the world.
  BOOKS *How to Begin the study of Amphibians.*
Richmond Publishing Company, London, 1987;
Newts and Salamanders of Europe. Poyser,
London, 1995.

Hale, William Gregson (Bill) 1935–
Author of *Waders* (NN65, 1980).

Bill Hale was head of the biology department
at what was then Liverpool Polytechnic (now
Liverpool John Moores University), and later
emeritus professor of animal biology. He made a
long-term study of the redshank, and was inter-
ested in the ecology and variation among wading
birds. Founder member of the Lancashire
Ornithologists Club.
  BOOKS *Eric Hosking's Waders.* Pelham, London,
1983; *Basic Biology* (with J. P. Margham). Collins,
London, 1983; *Coastal Waders and Wildfowl in
Winter* (with P. R. Evans and J. D. Goss-Custard);
Cambridge University Press, Cambridge, 1984;
Martin Mere – its history and natural history;
Causeway Press, Ormskirk, 1985; *Collins Dictionary
of Biology* (with J. P. Margham and V.A. Saunders).
Collins, London, 1988, 3rd ed 2005; *The Redshank.*
Shire Publications, Princes Risborough, 1988;
Martin Mere: Lancashire's Lost Lake (with Audrey
Coney). Liverpool University Press, Liverpool,
2005; *The Meyer's Illustrations of British Birds.*
Maggs Bross and Peregrine Books, London, 2007.

Hardy, Alister Clavering KT FRS 1896–1985
Author of *The Open Sea: the World of Plankton*
(NN34, 1956) and *The Open Sea: Fish and Fisheries*
(NN37, 1959).

A world-famous marine biologist, Hardy started
his career as an expedition zoologist, inventing
ways of sampling ocean plankton, and finished
it as the revered Linacre Professor of Zoology at
Oxford. Today he is remembered as much for his
investigations into the occult and 'encounters
with the divine'. There is an Alister Hardy
Foundation and an Alister Hardy Trust, and a full
biography in preparation.
  BIOGRAPHY Marshall, N. B., 1985. *Alister
Clavering Hardy.* Biographical Memoirs of Fellows
of the Royal Society, 32: 223–73; Lucas, R. In *Oxford
Dictionary of National Biography.* Hay, D., 2011.
God's Biologist. Darton Longman Todd, London
  BOOKS *The Living Stream: a Restatement of
Evolutionary Theory and Its Relation to the Spirit of
Man.* Collins (Gifford Lectures), London, 1965;
*The Divine Flame: an Essay Towards a Natural
History of Religion.* Collins (Gifford Lectures),
London, 1966. *Great Waters.* Collins, London, 1967;
The Biology of God. Jonathan Cape, London, 1975;

Harris, J. Richard (Dick) 1910–1994
Author of *An Angler's Entomology* (NN23, 1952).

An Irish fishing consultant and tackle merchant, who lectured part-time on limnology at Trinity College, Dublin. He regularly contributed to the angling magazines *Trout and Salmon* and *Stream and Field* under the assumed names of Notata and A. J. Berine.

Harvey, Leslie Arthur 1903–86
Author of *Dartmoor* (NN27, 1953) with D. St Leger-Gordon.

A university teacher, latterly Professor of Zoology at Exeter University, whose courses often included field expeditions in and around Dartmoor. Involved with the Devonshire Association and the Dartmoor National Park Committee.
FESTSCHRIFT Clark, R. B. and Wootton, R. J. (Eds) (1972). *Essays in Hydrobiology presented to Leslie Harvey.* University of Exeter, Exeter.

Hayward, Peter Joseph 1944–
Author of *Seashore* (NN94, 2004).

A marine biologist at the University of Wales, Swansea, who specialises in bryozoa. He is the co-author of the popular *Collins Field Guide to the Sea Shore*.
BOOKS *British Ascophoran Bryozoans* (with John Ryland). Academic Press, London, 1979; *Ctenostome Bryozoans* (with John Ryland). Brill, London, 1985; *Cyclostome Bryozoans* (with John Ryland). Brill, London, 1985; *Animals on Seaweeds* (Naturalists' Handbooks, no. 9). Richmond, London, 1988; *The Marine Fauna of the British Isles and North-West Europe* (editor, with John Ryland). Clarendon Press, Oxford, 1990; *Animals of Sandy Shores* (Naturalists' Handbook, no. 21). Richmond, London, 1994; *Biology and Palaeobiology of Bryozoans* (Editor with J. S. Ryland and P. D. Taylor). Olsen and Olsen, Fredensborg (1994); *Antarctic Cheilostomatous Bryozoa.* Oxford University Press, Oxford, 1995. *Handbook of the Marine Fauna of North-west Europe* (Editor with J. S. Ryland). Clarendon Press, Oxford, revised ed. 1996; *Collins Pocket Guide to the Sea Shore of Britain and Northern Europe* (with Anthony Nelson-Smith and Chris Shields). Collins, London, 1996; *Cheilostomatous Bryozoans, Parts I and II* (with John Ryland). Field Studies Council, Shrewsbury, 1998, 1999.

Hepburn, Ian 1902–74
Author of *Flowers of the Coast* (NN24, 1952).

Ian Hepburn was the science master at Oundle School, Northamptonshire. An early leading amateur ecologist, publishing (in his spare time) scientific papers on coastal vegetation of Cornwall and Norfolk and on the Northamptonshire limestone.
BOOKS *Flowers of the Seaside* (The Country Naturalist series). Collins, London, 1954.

Hewer, Humphrey Robert CBE 1903–74
Author of *British Seals* (NN57, 1974).

An influential mammal zoologist, Hewer spent his academic career at Imperial College, London, latterly as professor and head of department. He was much involved in applied science, including rodent control and animal welfare, as well as in international zoology.

Hodgetts, Nicholas Graham 1959–
Author of *Mosses and Liverworts* (NN97, 2005) with Ron Porley.

He spent the early part of his career in the Nature Conservancy Council, latterly as its specialist on lower plants and their conservation, including the first *Red Data Books* for British and European mosses and liverworts. He now works as a freelance consultant.

Hooper, Maxwell Dorien (Max) 1934–
Author of *Hedges* (NN58, 1974) with Ernie Pollard and Norman Moore.

One of the Monks Wood biologists who studied natural habitats and their management in the 1960s and 1970s, he is best known for 'Hooper's Law' which dates hedges by their constituent species. Most proud of his application of island biogeography theories to conservation, particularly 'Size and Surroundings of Nature Reserves' (11th Symp BES 1970).
BOOKS *Nature through the Seasons* (with Richard Adams). Kestrel Books, London, 1975; *Nature Day and Night* (with Richard Adams). Kestrel Books, London, 1978; *Thomas Tofield of Wilsic, Botanist and Civil Engineer 1730–1779* (with P. Skidmore and M. J. Dolby). Doncaster Museum, 1980; *The Greenhouse Effect* (Editor with M. G. R. Cannell). HMSO, London, 1990.

Hoskins, William George CBE 1908–92
Author of *The Common Lands of England and Wales* (NN45, 1963) with L. Dudley Stamp.

The historian of the British landscape, well known to the public through his television appearances in the 70s. A Devon man, he combined an academic career with writing and service on the government commission for common lands which secured their protection from development.
BIOGRAPHY **Thirsk, J.** In Oxford Dictionary of National Biography.
BOOKS *Midland England.* Batsford, London, 1949; *Essays in Leicestershire History.* Liverpool University Press, Liverpool, 1950; *East Midlands and the Peak.* Collins, London, 1951; *Devon.* David and Charles, Newton Abbot, 1954; *Leicestershire.* Hodder & Stoughton, London, 1955; *The Making of the English Landscape.* Hodder & Stoughton, London, 1955; *The Midland Peasant.* Macmillan, London, 1957; *Local History in England.* Longmans, London, 1959; *Chilterns to the Black Country.* Collins, London, 1959; *Provincial England.* Macmillan, London, 1963; *Rutland.* Faber, London, 1963; *The Making of the English Landscape.* Hodder and Stoughton, London, 1963; *Fieldwork in Local History.* Faber, London, 1967; *Old Devon.* Pan, London, 1971; *English Landscapes.* BBC, London, 1973; *The Age of Plunder: King Henry's England, 1500–47.* Longman, London, 1976; *One Man's England.* BBC, London, 1978.

Imms, August Daniel FRS 1880–1949
Author of Insect Natural History (NN8, 1947).

The leading academic entomologist of his generation, Imms spent much of his career as a university teacher and administrator at home and abroad, specialising in agricultural entomology. Author of the standard university textbook on insects, he was one of the oldest New Naturalist authors, and the first to die, in 1949.

BIOGRAPHY **Wigglesworth, V. B.**, 1949. *Obituary Notices of Fellows of the Royal Society*, 6: 365–384; **Wigglesworth, V. B.** In *Oxford Dictionary of National Biography.*

BOOKS *General Textbook of Entomology.* Methuen, London, 1925; subsequent editions in 1930, 1934, 1938; *Recent Advances in Entomology.* Churchill, London, 1931; 2nd edition 1937; *Social Behaviour in Insects.* Methuen, London, 1931; 2nd edition 1938; *Outlines of Entomology.* Methuen, London, 1942.

Ingram, David Stanley OBE VMH FRSE 1941–
Author of *Plant Disease* (NN85, 1999) with Noel Robertson.

A plant pathologist and university administrator, David Ingram spent the latter part of his career at Cambridge, as regius keeper of the Botanic Gardens and master of St Catherine's College. Outside university life, he was much involved with gardening and conservation matters.

BOOKS *Plant Tissue Culture* (with Dennis Butcher). Edward Arnold, London, 1974; *Tissue Culture Methods for Plant Pathologists* (editor with J. P. Helgeson). Blackwell, Oxford, 1980; *Cambridge Encyclopaedia of Life Sciences* (editor with Adrian Friday). Cambridge University Press, Cambridge, 1985; *Shape and Form in Plants and Fungi* (editor with Andrew Hudson). Academic Press, London, 1994; *Molecular Tools for Screening Biodiversity* (with Angela Karp and Peter Isaac). Chapman & Hall, London, 1998; *Science and the Garden: the Scientific Basis of Horticultural Practice* (with Daphne Vince-Prue and P. J. Gregory). Blackwell and RHS, Oxford, 2002, 2nd ed 2008; *Advances in Plant Pathology.* Vols 1–9. Academic Press, London, 1982–1993.

Johnston, James Laughton 1940–
Author of *The Natural History of Shetland* (NN64, 1980) with R. J. Berry.

A Shetlander, Laughton Johnston served, inter alia, as a schoolmaster before joining the Nature Conservancy Council, serving on Shetland, Rhum and the Highlands. He was the project manager for the team preparing for the Cairngorms National Park. He is also a writer and poet.

BOOKS *A Naturalist's Shetland.* Poyser, London, 1999; *Scotland's Nature in Trust.* Poyser, London, 2000; *Beinn Eighe: the Mountain above the Wood* (with Dick Balharry). Birlinn, Edinburgh, 2001; *A Dream of Silver.* Shetland Times, Lerwick, 2006. *Victorians 60° North: the Story of the Edmondstons and Saxbys of Shetland.* Shetland Times, Lerwick, 2007; *A Kist of Emigrants.* Shetland Times, Lerwick, 2010.

Kington, John Alfred 1930–
Author of *Climate and Weather* (NN115, 2010).

A disciple of Gordon Manley, John Kington worked for the Meteorological Office at home and abroad before embarking on an academic career at Swansea and the climate research unit at the University of East Anglia where he is now a visiting fellow.

BOOKS *World, Weather and Forecasting* (in *The Weather Book*). Michael Joseph, London, 1982; *The Weather of the 1780s over Europe.* Cambridge University Press, Cambridge, 1988; *Observing and Measuring the Weather – a Brief History* (in *Climates of the British Isles: Past, Present and Future*). Routledge, London, 1997; *Even the Birds were Walking: The Story of Wartime Meteorological Reconnaissance* (with Peter Rackliff). Tempus Publishing, Stroud, 2000.

Lack, Andrew John 1953–
Author of *The Natural History of Pollination* (NN83, 1996) with Michael Proctor and Peter Yeo.

A university teacher and botanist, son of the ornithologist David Lack, his wide interests range from population genetics to the philosophy of science and its cultural manifestations; he is the author of cultural anthologies of the robin and skylark, and plays the violin.

BOOKS *Illustrated Flora of Dominica* (with C. Whiteoford, P. Evans, A. James and H. Greenop). Ministry of Tourism, Dominica, 1997; *Instant Notes in Plant Biology* (with David Evans). Taylor & Francis, Abingdon, 2001; *The Museum Swifts* (with R. Overall). University Museum of Natural History, Oxford, 2002; *Redbreast: The Robin in Life and Literature.* SMH Books, Pulborough, 2008.

Lockley, Ronald Mathias
(1903–2000) Author of *Sea Birds* (NN28, 1954) with James Fisher.

The well-known author of nature books on birds and islands, Lockley made his name from his association with Skokholm Island, which he leased and where he lived for a while, raising rabbits and setting up a bird observatory, later establishing another at Orielton. His book on wild rabbits inspired *Watership Down.*

AUTOBIOGRAPHY Lockley did not write a formal autobiography, but many of his books have a significant autobiographical content.

BOOKS *Dream Island.* Witherby, London, 1930; *The Island Dwellers.* Putnam, New York, 1932; *Island Days.* Witherby, London, 1934; *Dream Island Days. A Record of the Simple Life.* Witherby, London, 1934; *I Know an Island.* George Harrap, London, 1938; *Early Morning Island.* George Harrap, London, 1939; *The Way to an Island.* Dent, London, 1941; *Shearwaters.* Dent, London, 1942; *Island Farm.* Witherby, London, 1943; *Birds of the Sea.* King Penguin, London, 1945; *Islands Round Britain* (Britain in Pictures series). Collins, London, 1945; *The Island Farmers.* Witherby, London (1946); *Letters from Skokholm.* Dent, London, 1947; *The Cinnamon Bird.* Staples, London, 1948; *The Birds of Pembrokeshire* (with G. C. S. Ingram and H. M. Salmon). West Wales Field Society, Haverfordwest, 1949; *Island of Skomer* (with John Buxton). Staples, London, 1950; *The Charm of the Channel Islands.* Evans, London (1950); *The Nature-lovers' Anthology* (Ed). Witherby, London, 1951; *Bird Ringing: The Art of Bird Study by Individual Marking* (with Rosemary Russell). Crosby Lockwood, London, 1953; *Puffins.* Dent, London, 1953; *Travels with a Tent in Western Europe.* Odhams, London, 1953; *Gilbert White* (Great Naturalist series). Witherby, London, 1954; *The Seals and the Curragh.* Dent, London, 1954; *Pembrokeshire.* Hale, London, 1957; *The Bird Lover's Bedside Book.* Oxford University Press, London, 1958; *The Private Life of the Rabbit.* Andre Deutsch, London, 1964; *Grey Seal, Common Seal.* Andre Deutsch, London, 1966; *The Island.* Andre Deutsch, London, 1969; *Man Against Nature.* Andre Deutsch, London,

1970; *The Naturalist in Wales*. David & Charles, Newton Abbott, 1970; *Ocean Wanderers: The Migratory Sea Birds of the World*. David & Charles, Newton Abbott, 1974; *Orielton – The human and natural history of a Welsh manor*. Andre Deutsch, London, 1977; *Myself When Young: the Making of a Naturalist*. Andre Deutsch, London, 1979; *Whales, Dolphins and Porpoises*. David & Charles, Newton Abbott, 1979; *New Zealand Endangered Species: Birds, Bats, Reptiles, Fishes, Snails and Insects* (with N.W. Cusa). Cassell, London, 1980; *Voyage through the Antarctic* (with Richard Adams). Allen Lane, London, 1982; *The Flight of the Storm Petrel*. David & Charles, Newton Abbott, 1983; *Eric Hosking's Seabirds*. Croom Helm, London, 1983; *Birds and Islands: Travels in Wild Places*. Victor Gollancz, London, 1991; *Dear Islandman*. Gomer, Llandysul, 1996.

Longfield, Cynthia Evelyn 1896–1991
Author of *Dragonflies* (NN41, 1960) with Philip Corbet and Norman Moore.

'The dragonfly lady', Cynthia Longfield was among a generation of intrepid and independent upper-class women who travelled to remote parts of the world in search of their chosen subject. Her book in the Warne Wayside and Woodland series was the standard field guide on dragonflies for nearly forty years.
BIOGRAPHY **Hayter-Hames, J.** *Madam Dragonfly: the Life and Times of Cynthia Longfield*. Pentland Press, Durham, 1991.
BOOKS *The Dragonflies of the British Isles*. Warne, London, 1937.

Lousley, Job Edward (Ted) 1907–76
Author of *Wild Flowers of Chalk and Limestone* (NN16, 1950).

Ted Lousley was one of the leading field botanists of the mid-twentieth century with an unrivalled knowledge of plants and their localities. He was author of the floras of Scilly and Surrey, and the expert on British docks and knotweeds. By profession he was a bank manager in London.
BOOKS *Study of the Distribution of British Plants* (Ed). Botanical Society of the British Isles, London, 1951; *The Changing Flora of Britain* (Ed).

Botanical Society of the British Isles, London, 1952; *Species Studies on the British Flora* (Ed). Botanical Society of the British Isles, London, 1954; *Progress in the Study of the British Flora* (Ed). Botanical Society of the British Isles, London, 1956; *British Herbaria: an Index to the Location of herbaria of British Plants* (with D. H. Kent and E. B. Bangerter). Botanical Society of the British Isles, London, 1957; *Flowering Plants and Ferns in the Isles of Scilly*. Isles of Scilly Museum, 1967; *Flora of the Isles of Scilly*. David & Charles, Newton Abbott, 1971; *Flora of Surrey*. David & Charles, Newton Abbott, 1976; supplement (with A. C. Leslie) published by A. C. & P. Leslie of Guildford, 1987; *Docks and Knotweeds of the British Isles* (with D. H. Kent and Ann Davies). Botanical Society of the British Isles, London, 1981.

Lunn, Angus 1933–
Author of *Northumberland* (NN95, 2004).

Formerly head of adult education at Newcastle University, Angus Lunn was also chair of the Council of National Parks and its appointee for Northumberland National Park. He is the authority on natural history in that part of the world. Awarded the Royal Society of Wildlife Trusts' Cadbury Medal in 2009, for services to the advancement of nature conservation in the British Isles.
BOOKS *Vegetation of Northumberland: map at 1:200,000*. University of Newcastle, Newcastle, 1976; *A History of Naturalists in North East England* (Ed). University of Newcastle, Newcastle, 1983.

Macan, Thomas Townley (Kit) 1910–85
Author of *Life in Lakes and Rivers* (NN15, 1951) with Barton Worthington.

An entomologist in the Freshwater Biological Association, Kit Macan was an authority on freshwater life, producing a stream of keys and identification guides as well as student's textbooks. Like several New Naturalists, he was a keen promoter of fieldwork. Founding Editor of the journal Freshwater Biology.
BOOKS *The Voyage of* HEMS *Mabahiss, 1933–34*. Two volumes, 1933; *A Key to the British species of Corixidae (Hemiptera Heteroptera), with notes on their ecology*. Freshwater Biological Association,

Ambleside, 1939; *A Key to the British Water Bugs (Hemiptera-Heteroptera, excluding Corixidae), with notes on their ecology*. Freshwater Biological Association, Ambleside, 1941; *A Key to the British Fresh- and Brackish-Water Gastropods, with notes on their ecology*. Freshwater Biological Association, Ambleside, 1969; *A Guide to Freshwater Invertebrate Animals*. Longmans, Green & Co., London, 1959; *A Key to the Nymphs of the British Species of Ephemeroptera, with notes on their ecology*. Freshwater Biological Association, Ambleside, 1961; *Freshwater Ecology*. Longmans, Green & Co., London, 1963; *Biological Studies of the English Lakes*. Longmans, Green & Co., London, 1970; *A Key to the Adults of the British Trichoptera*. Freshwater Biological Association, Ambleside, 1973.

Maitland, Peter Salisbury FRSE 1937–
Author of *Freshwater Fishes* (NN75, 1992) with Niall Campbell.

The authority on freshwater fish and their conservation, Peter Maitland worked at various times at Glasgow and St Andrews Universities, the Nature Conservancy Council (later ITE), and, latterly, as a freelance consultant with a particular interest in salmonids and rare fish.
BOOKS *The Ecology of Scotland's Largest Lochs* (Ed). Junk, The Hague, 1981; *Hamlyn Guide to Freshwater Fishes of Britain and Europe*. Hamlyn, London, 1977, 2006; *Biology of Fresh Waters*. Blackie, Glasgow, 1978; *Conservation Management of Freshwater Habitats* (with Neville Morgan). Chapman & Hall, London, 1997; *Scotland's Freshwater Fish: Ecology, Conservation and Folklore*. Trafford, Oxford, 2007.

Majerus, Michael Eugene Nicholas 1954–2009
Author of *Ladybirds* (NN81, 1994) and *Moths* (NN90, 2002).

Until his tragically early death, Michael Majerus was a reader and later professor of evolution at Cambridge, specialising in moths and ladybirds. Unusually among today's geneticists, he was a field naturalist, and a fervant advocate of Darwinian evolution.
BOOKS *Ladybirds* (*Naturalists Handbooks* series) (with Peter Kearns). Richmond, Cambridge, 1989; *Evolution, the Four Billion Year War* (with Bill

Amos and Greg Hurst). Longmans, London, 1996; *Melanism: Evolution in Action.* Oxford University Press, Oxford, 1998; *Sex Wars. Genes, Bacteria and Biased Sex Ratios.* Princeton University Press, Princeton, 2003.

[signature: Michael Majerus]

Manley, Gordon 1902–80
Author of *Climate and the British Scene* (NN22, 1952).

Perhaps the most celebrated weatherman of his day, Gordon Manley was a pioneer of climate studies in upland and polar regions measuring temperatures and rainfall not by remote census but by lone vigils in cold huts. For the latter half of his career he was professor of geography at Bedford College, London.

BIOGRAPHY Green, C.P. In *Oxford Dictionary of National Biography.*

FESTSCHRIFT Tooley M.J. and Sheail G.M. (Eds), 1985. *The Climatic Scene.* Allen & Unwin, London.

BOOKS *Degrees of Freedom.* Christopher Johnson, London, 1950; *Geography: Our Planet, its Peoples and its Resources* (Ed, with others). MacDonald, London, 1961; *The mean temperature of central England, 1698–1952.* Quarterly Journal of the Royal Meteorological Society, 79: 242–61, 1953; *Central England temperatures: monthly means 1659 to 1973.* Quarterly Journal of the Royal Meteorological Society, 100: 389–405, 1974.

[signature: Gordon Manley]

Marren, Peter Richard 1950–
Author of *The New Naturalists* (NN82, 1995, revised 2005) and *Nature Conservation* (NN91, 2002); also *Art of the New Naturalists* (with Robert Gillmor). Collins, London, 2009.

The unofficial historian and biographer of the New Naturalist library, he worked for the Nature Conservancy Council in Scotland and England before becoming a freelance writer, journalist and consultant. Allowing his interests to lead his life, he is the author of books on woodlands, nature reserves, bugs, mushrooms, flowers and battlefields.

BOOKS *Natural History of Aberdeen.* Callander, Finzean, Aberdeen, 1982; *Woodland Heritage.* David & Charles, Newton Abbot, 1990; *The Wild Woods.* David & Charles, Newton Abbot, 1992; *England's National Nature Reserves.* Poyser Natural History, London, 1994; *Postcards from the Country: Living*

Memories of the British Countryside (with Mike Birkhead). BBC Books, London, 1996; *Rothschild's Reserves: Time and Fragile Nature* (with Miriam Rothschild). Harley Books, Colchester, 1997; *The Observer's Book of Observer's Books.* Peregrine Books, Leeds, 1999; *The Countryside Detective: How to discover, observe and enjoy Britain's wildlife.* Readers Digest, London, 2000; *The Aurelian Legacy* (with Miriam Rothschild, Michael Salmon & Basil Harley). Harley Books, Colchester, 2000. *Britain's Rare Flowers.* Poyser Natural History, London, 1999. Paperback edition published by a&c Black, London, 2001; *The Observer's Book of Wayside and Woodland.* Peregrine Books, Leeds, 2003; *Twitching Through the Swamp* (with David Carstairs). Swamp Publishing, Thatcham, 2004; *Art of the New Naturalists* (with Robert Gillmor). Collins, London, 2009; *Bugs Britannica* (with Richard Mabey). Chatto & Windus, London, 2010; *Mushrooms.* British Wildlife Publishing, Gillingham, 2012.

[signature: Peter Marren]

Matthews, Leonard Harrison (Leo) FRS 1901–86
Author of *British Mammals* (NN21, 1952) and *Mammals in the British Isles* (NN68, 1982).

A leading academic zoologist, Leo Harrison Matthews took part in the last generation of discovery expeditions studying marine mammals. He later became scientific director at London zoo. A born story-teller and populariser through broadcasts and writings, he became a kind of grand old man of British zoology.

AUTOBIOGRAPHY Matthews did not write a formal autobiography, but many of his books have significant autobiographical content.

BIOGRAPHY **Harrison, Richard.** *Leonard Harrison Matthews Biographical Memoirs of Fellows of the Royal Society,* 33: 413–22, 1987; **Bonner, Nigel** In *Oxford Dictionary of National Biography.*

BOOKS *South Georgia: The British Empire's Sub-Antarctic Outpost.* John Wright, Bristol and London, 1931; *Wandering Albatross.* MacGibbon & Kee, London, 1951; *Sea Elephant: The Life and Death of the Elephant Seal.* MacGibbon & Kee, London, 1952; *The British Amphibia and Reptiles.* Methuen, London, 1952; *Beasts of the Field* (The Country Naturalist series). Collins, London, 1954; *The Senses of Animals* (with Maxwell Knight). Museum Press, London, 1963; *The Whale* (Ed). Allen & Unwin, London, 1968; *The Life of Mammals, Volume 1.* Weidenfeld & Nicolson, London, 1969; *The Life of Mammals, Volume 2.* Weidenfeld & Nicolson, London, 1971; *Man and Wildlife.* Croom Helm, London, 1975; *Penguin: Adventures among the Birds, Beasts and Whalers of the Far South.* Peter Owen,

London, 1977; *The Natural History of the Whale.* Weidenfeld & Nicolson, London, 1978; *The Seals and the Scientists.* Peter Owen, London (1979).

[signature: L Harrison Matthews]

Mellanby, Kenneth CBE 1918–93
Author of *Pesticides and Pollution* (NN50, 1967), *The Mole* (M22, 1971) and *Farming and Wildlife* (NN67, 1981). See under Editorial Board.

[signature: Kenneth Mellanby]

Mercer, Ian Dews CBE 1933–
Author of *Dartmoor* (NN111, 2009).

From a background in rural conservation and planning, Ian Mercer was for many years the chief officer of Dartmoor National Park before becoming the first head of the Countryside Council for Wales.

BOOKS *School Projects in Natural History* (Ed). Heinemann Educational, London, 1972; *Nature Guide to the West Country.* Usborne, London, 1981; *Crisis and Opportunity: Devon Foot and Mouth Inquiry 2001.* Devon Books, Tiverton, 2002; MSC *Napoli: Public inquiry into beaching and aftermath.* Exeter, 2008.

[signature: Ian Mercer]

Mitchell, John 1934–
Author of *Loch Lomondside* (NN88, 2001).

John Mitchell was the senior warden of the Loch Lomond area for the Nature Conservancy Council, and played a part in elevating the region as Scotland's first National Park. An all-round naturalist, he also taught further education courses at university. Awarded Honorary MA by the University of Stirling (1993) and Honorary Fellowship of the Royal Zoological Society of Scotland (1994) for significant contributions to nature conservation.

BOOK *The Shielings and Drove Ways of Loch Lomondside.* Jamieson & Munro, Stirling, 2000.

[signature: John Mitchell]

Moore, Henry Ian CBE 1905–76
Author of *Grass and Grassland* (NN48, 1966).

A specialist in agricultural pastures, Ian Moore was the Principal at Seale Hayne Agricultural College, known to a wider public through his books.

BOOKS *Grassland Husbandy*. Allen & Unwin, London, 1944; *Background to Farming*. Allen & Unwin, London, 1947; *Crops and Cropping*. Alllen & Unwin, London, 1949; *Science & Practice of Grassland Farming*. Nelson, London, 1949.

Moore, Norman Winfrid BT 1923–
Author of *Dragonflies* (NN41, 1960) with Philip Corbet and Cynthia Longfield and of *Hedges* (NN58, 1974) with Ernie Pollard and Max Hooper.

One of the best-known conservationists of the twentieth century, Norman Moore was successively involved in conservation in south-west England, the impact of agricultural and modern farming, and as the originator of the Farming and Wildlife Advisory Groups (FWAGS). An all-round naturalist, his first love was, and remains, dragonflies.

AUTOBIOGRAPHY *The Bird of Time: The science and politics of nature conservation*. Cambridge University Press, Cambridge, 1987.
FESTSCHRIFT Norman Winfrid Moore (2003). *Odontatologica*, 32 (1).
BOOKS *Atlas of the Dragonflies of Britain and Ireland* (with R. Merritt and B. C. Eversham). HMSO/NERC, Huntingdon, 1996; *Oaks, Dragonflies and People*. Harley Books, Colchester, 2002.

Moss, Brian 1943–
Author of *The Broads* (NN89, 2001).

A freshwater ecologist with a special interest in algae and limnology, his academic career culminated as professor of botany at Liverpool University. Outside academia, he advises on lake management and conservation.

BOOKS *Ecology of Freshwaters*. Blackwell Science, Oxford, 1980. Fourth Edition, Wiley-Blackwell, Oxford, 2010; *Climate Change and Freshwaters* (Ed, with M. Kernan and Rick Battarbee). Wiley-Blackwell, Oxford, 2010.

Moss, Robert 1941–
Author of *Grouse* (NN107, 2008) with Adam Watson.

A colleague of Adam Watson, and an expert on the grouse family, he worked with ITE at Banchory in Scotland on aspects of their ecology, nutrition and estate management. He now works freelance as a consultant. Currently investigating the effects of human disturbance on capercaillie.

BOOKS *Animal Population Dynamics* (with Adam Watson and John Ollason). Chapman & Hall, London, 1982.

Mullard, Jonathan 1955–
Author of *Gower* (NN99, 2006) and *Brecon Beacons* (NN126, 2014)

An ecologist specialising in the management of protected areas, Jonathan Mullard advised on heritage coasts, AONBs and National Parks, latterly as director at Northumberland National Park authority. He is currently with the Department of Energy advising on climate change issues.

Murton, Ronald Keir (Ron) 1932–78
Author of *Man and Birds* (NN51, 1971) and *The Wood Pigeon* (M20, 1965).

A scientist of distinction, Ron Murton worked for the Ministry of Agriculture on wood pigeon behaviour and control, before joining Kenneth Mellanby's Monks Wood team working on physiology and breeding cycles of farm birds before his untimely death in 1978.

BOOKS *The Problems of Birds as Pests* (with E. N. Wright). Academic Press, London, 1968.

Newton, Ian OBE FRS FRSE 1940–
Author of *Finches* (NN55, 1972), *Bird Migration* (NN113, 2010) and *Bird Populations* (NN124, 2013)

One of the brightest stars of British ornithology, for many years Ian Newton directed the scientific programme at Monks Wood field station. He is an authority on bird behaviour and population ecology, especially of finches, wildfowl and birds of prey, and, most recently, of bird migration. He is author of a celebrated book about the sparrowhawk. Has served as Chairman for the RSPB and is currently Chairman of the BTO.

BOOKS *Population Ecology of Raptors*. Poyser, Berkhamsted, 1979; *The Sparrowhawk*. Poyser, Carlton, 1986; *Lifetime Reproduction in Birds* (Ed). Accademic Press, London, 1989; *Birds of Prey* (Ed). Merehurst Press, London, 1990; *Population Limitation in Birds*. Academic Press, London, 1998; *The Speciation and Biogeography of Birds*. Academic Press, London, 2003; *Bird Ecology and Conservation: a handbook of techniques*. (Ed with W. J. Sutherland and R. E. Green). Oxford University Press, Oxford, 2004; *The Migration Ecology of Birds*. Academic Press, London, 2008.

Nicholson, Edward Max CB CVO 1904–2003
Author of *Birds and Men* (NN17, 1951).

Max Nicholson is famous for his work as a founder of institutions and bird censuses, as a writer on birds, and as the founder and director of the Nature Conservancy, Britain's first official nature conservation body. A brilliant man of legendary energy, passion and independence, he was both a government man and a radical. A biography is long overdue.

BIOGRAPHY **Greenwood, Jeremy J. D.** In *Oxford Dictionary of National Biography*.
BOOKS *Birds in England*. Chapman & Hall, London, 1926; *How Birds Live*. Willliams & Norgate, London, 1927; *Natural History of Selborne* (Ed). Butterworth, London, 1929; *The Study of Birds*. Benn, London, 1929; *The Art of Bird-Watching*. Witherby, London, 1931; *Songs of Wild Birds* (with Ludwig Koch). Witherby, London, 1936; *More Songs of Wild Birds* (with Ludwig Koch). Witherby, London, 1937; *How Britain's Resources are Mobilized*. Clarendon Press, Oxford, 1940; *Britain's Nature Reserves*. Country Life, London, 1957; *Conservation and the Next Renaissance*. University of California, Berkeley, 1964; *British Wild Life*. Hamlyn, London, 1966; *The System: The Misgovernment of Modern Britain*. Hodder & Stoughton, London, 1967; *Handbook to the Conservation Section of the International Biological Programme*. Blackwell Scientific, Oxford, 1968; *The Environmental Revolution: A Guide for the New Masters of the World*. Hodder & Stoughton, London, 1970; *The Big Change*. McGraw-Hill, New York, 1973; *The New Environmental Age*. Cambridge

University Press, Cambridge, 1987; *Bird-watching in London*. London Natural History Society, London, 1995.

North, Frederick John 1889–1968
Author of *Snowdonia* (NN13, 1949) with Bruce Campbell and Richenda Scott.

A geologist and museum curator, North spent his career at the National Museum of Wales where his chief passion was for fossils. He was a founder member of the British Association for Science.

BOOKS *Geological Maps: Their History and Development, with special reference to Wales*. National Museum of Wales, Cardiff, 1928; *The Evolution of the Bristol Channel*. National Museum of Wales, Cardiff, 1929 (revised edition 1955); *Limestones, Their Origins, Distributions and Uses*. Murby, London, 1930; *Mining for Metals in Wales*. National Museum of Wales, Cardiff, 1962; *Sir Charles Lyell: Interpreter of the Principles of Geology*. Arthur Barker, London, 1965.

Page, Christopher Nigel 1942–
Author of *Ferns* (NN74, 1988).

The authority on British ferns and their allies, Christopher Page was based at the Royal Botanic Garden in Edinburgh when not travelling in pursuit of conifers, ferns and other ancient plants around the world.

BOOKS *The Ferns of Britain and Ireland*. Cambridge University Press, Cambridge, 1982 (2nd edition 1997); *The Biology of Pteridophytes, a Symposium* (with A. F. Dyer). Proceedings of The Royal Society of Edinburgh, 1985; *Conifers: Status Survey and Action Plan* (with Aljos Farjon). IUCN, Cambridge, 1999; *Botanical Links in the Atlantic Arc* (with S. J. Leach, Y. Peytoureau and M. N. Sanford). BSBI, London, 2006.

Parslow, Rosemary 1936–
Author of *The Isles of Scilly* (NN103, 2007).

Rosemary Parslow has had a lifelong association with the Isles of Scilly as an all-round naturalist. She worked for the Nature Conservancy Council before becoming the Cambridge Wildlife Trust's director of conservation and, later still, as a freelance consultant. She is currently working on a new flora of Scilly.

BOOKS *Plants and Ferns in the Isles of Scilly*. Isles of Scilly Museum Publication, 2009.

Pearsall, William Harold FRS 1891–1964
Author of *Mountains and Moorlands* (NN11, 1950) and posthumously *The Lake District* (NN53, 1973) with Winifred Pennington.

A botanist and authority on British uplands, W. H. Pearsall made the first comprehensive scientific survey of Britain's lakes, and worked out the relationships between the physical conditions and the plants they support. He held a succession of senior university appointments at Leeds, Sheffield and University College London where he helped to establish its celebrated conservation course.

BIOGRAPHY **Clapham, A. R.** 'William Harold Pearsall 1891–1964'. *Biographical Memoirs of Fellows of the Royal Society*, 17: 511–40, 1971; **Clapham, A. R.**, revised **Prance, G. T.** In *Oxford Dictionary of National Biography*.

BOOKS *Freshwater Biology and Water Supply in Britain* (with A. C. Gardner and F. Greenshields). Freshwater Biological Association, Ambleside, 1946; *Lake District* (Ed). Countryside Commission, London, 1979.

Pennington, Winifred Anne FRS 1915–2007
Author of the *Lake District* (NN53, 1973) with W. H. Pearsall.

Winifred Pennington (Mrs T. G. Tutin) was best-known as a palaeo-botanist who helped to reconstruct Britain's postglacial history from pollen and other fragments buried in peat. She worked in the Lake District as a leading research scientist at the Freshwater Biological Association.

FESTSCHRIFT *Lake Sediments and Environmental History* (edited by Elizabeth Y. Haworth and John W. G. Lund). Leicester University Press, 1984.

BOOKS *The History of British Vegetation*. Hodder & Stoughton/English Universities Press, London, 1969.

Perrins, Christopher Miles LVO FRS 1935–
Author of *British Tits* (NN62, 1979).

A disciple of David Lack, Christopher Perrins was director of Oxford's Edward Grey Institute of Field Ornithology between 1974 and 1992, responsible for the long-term study of tits and other birds in nearby wood as well as the author of a series of well-regarded bird books.

BOOKS *Birds*. Collins, London, 1974; *Bird Life, an Introduction to the World of Birds*. Phaidon, London, 1976; *Avian Ecology* (with Tim Birkhead). Blackie, Glasgow, 1983; *Encyclopaedia of Birds* (edited with Alex Middleton). Allen & Unwin, London, 1985; *The Mute Swan* (with Mike Birkhead). Croom Helm, London, 1986; *New Generation Guide to the Birds of Britain and Europe*. Collins, London, 1987; *New Encyclopaedia of Birds* (Ed). Oxford University Press, Oxford, 2003.

Peterken, George Frederick OBE 1940–
Author of *Wye Valley* (NN105, 2008).

George Peterken is an authority on natural temperate forests and was the main architect of woodland conservation in Britain in the 1970s and 1980s. Now a consultant, he lives in the Wye Valley where, with neighbours, he has set up and runs an ambitious community farming and conservation project.

BOOKS *Woodland Conservation and Management*. Chapman & Hall, London, 1981, second edition 1993; *Natural Woodland: Ecology and Conservation on Northern Temperate Regions*. Cambridge University Press, Cambridge, 1996.

Pollard, Ernest (Ernie) 1939–
Author of *Hedges* (NN58, 1974) with Max Hooper and Norman Moore.

An entomologist at Monks Wood, specialising in farmland insects, Ernie Pollard helped to pioneer 'butterfly transects' by which butterfly numbers are monitored. He retired early to become a farmer and freelance consultant.

BOOKS *Atlas of Butterflies in Britain and Ireland* (with J. Heath and J. A. Thomas). Viking, Harmondsworth, 1984; *Monitoring Butterflies for Ecology and Conservation* (with T. J. Yates). Chapman & Hall, London, 1993.

Porley, Ron 1958–
Author of *Mosses and Liverworts* (NN97, 2005) with Nick Hodgetts.

Ron Poley worked as specialist botanist and bryologist for the Nature Conservancy Council (later English Nature) in southern England before becoming a freelance consultant with a broader, international remit.

BOOKS *Arable Bryophytes. A Field Guide to the Mosses, Liverworts and Hornworts of Cultivated Land in Britain and Ireland*. Wildguides, Old Basing, 2008.

Potter, Stephen Meredith 1900–1969
Author of *Pedigree: Words from Nature* (NN56, 1973) posthumously with Laurens Sargent.

Stephen Potter, who worked as a writer and producer for the BBC in the 1930s and 1940s, is best-known for his humorous and very successful 'self-help' books, *Gamesmanship* ('Or the art of winning games without actually cheating') followed by *One-Upmanship*. His posthumous contribution to the series was as a philologist, prompted also by his interest in birds and friendship with James Fisher.

AUTOBIOGRAPHY *Steps to Immaturity*. Rupert Hart-Davis, London, 1959.

BIOGRAPHIES Jenkins, A., 1980. *Stephen Potter: Inventor of Gamesmanship*. Weidenfeld & Nicolson, London; Potter, J., 2004. *Stephen Potter at the BBC*. Orford Books, Woodbridge; Grenfell, Joyce, revised Taylor, C. L. In *Oxford Dictionary of National Biography*.

Potts, George Richard (Dick) 1939–
Author of *Partridges* (NN121, 2012)

Former head of the Game Conservancy, Dick Potts has studied and monitored the progress of the Grey Partridge over half a lifetime as a 'countryside barometer'. A farmer's son from Yorkshire, he has published papers in an unusually wide range of journals. His book is about 'far more than partridges'; rather it is a study of 'species struggling to cope with modern agriculture'.

BOOKS *The Partridge: Pesticides, Predation and Conservation*. Collins, London, 1986; *Ecology of Temperate Cereal Fields* (Ed. with Leslie Firbank, N. Carter & J. F. Darbyshire). Blackwell Scientific, Oxford, 1991.

Proctor, Michael Charles Faraday 1929–
Author of *The Pollination of Flowers* (NN54, 1973) with Peter Yeo; *The Natural History of Pollination* (NN83, 1996) with Peter Yeo and Andrew Lack; and *Vegetation of Britain and Ireland* (NN122, 2013).

A plant ecologist and photographer, Michael Proctor spent most of his career at Exeter University, latterly as a research fellow. An authority on British plants and vegetation, Michael Proctor is an ecological polymath, at least as much at home in the field as in the lab. His photographs illustrate several of the botanical titles in the series.

BOOKS *Flora and Vegetation: In Exeter and its Regions* (edited by F. Barlow). University of Exeter, Exeter, 1969; *Britain's Green Mantle* (A. G. Tansley, 2nd edition revised by M. C. F. Proctor). George Allen & Unwin, London, 1968; *The Grounds & Gardens of the University of Exeter* (with J. Caldwell). University of Exeter, Exeter, 1969; *Physiological Ecology. In Bryophyte Biology* (edited with B. Goffinet and A. J. Shaw). Cambridge University Press, Cambridge, 2009.

Rackham, Oliver OBE FBA 1939–2015
Author of *Woodlands* (NN100, 2006).

Currently Master of Corpus Christi College, Cambridge, Oliver Rackham is well-known for his meticulously researched yet readable books on the history and ecology of woodlands and landscape. Through his unique literary style and

beautiful maps and drawings, the hidden ancient nature of the landscape has become familiar and understood to a much wider public.

BOOKS *Trees and Woodland in the British Landscape*. Dent, London, 1976, revised edition 1990; *Ancient Woodland, its history, vegetation and uses in England*. Arnold, London, 1980; *The History of the Countryside*. Dent, London, 1986; *The Last Forest: The Story of Hatfield Forest*. Dent, London, 1989; *The Making of the Cretan Landscape*. Manchester University Press, Manchester, 1996; *Trees and Woodland in the British Landscape: the Complete History of Britain's Trees, Woods & Hedgerows*. Phoenix, London, 2001; *The Nature of Mediterranean Europe: An Ecological History* (with A. T. Grove). Yale University Press, New Haven and London, 2003; *The Illustrated History of the Countryside*. Weidenfeld & Nicolson, London, 2003.

Ramsbottom, John OBE 1884–1974
Author of *Mushrooms and Toadstools* (NN7, 1953).

John Ramsbottom spent his career at the Natural History Museum, latterly as keeper of botany, and was the acknowledged expert on British fungi. His interest in the lore and fantasy, as well as the scientific facts, of fungi is showcased in his New Naturalist volume.

BOOKS *A Handbook of the Larger British Fungi*. British Museum (Natural History), London, 1923, 1951; *Fungi – An Introduction to Mycology*. Benn, London, 1929; *A Book of Roses*. King Penguin, London, 1939; *Edible Fungi*. King Penguin, London, 1943; *Poisonous Fungi*. King Penguin, London, 1945.

Ratcliffe, Derek Almey 1929–2005
Author of *Lakeland* (NN92, 2002) and *Galloway and the Borders* (NN101, 2007). See under Editorial Board.

Raven, John 1914–80
Author of *Mountain Flowers* (NN33, 1956) with Max Walters – see under Editorial Board.

A keen amateur botanist and gardener, John Raven's day job was as a classical scholar and teacher at Kings College Cambridge. His work on unmasking the fake plant records of Professor Heslop-Harrison, kept secret for many years, was recently outlined in the book *A Rum Affair* by Karl Sabbagh.

FESTSCHRIFT Lipscomb, J. and David, R.W. (Eds.), 1981. *John Raven, by His Friends*. Docwra's Manor, Royston.

BOOKS *A Botanist's Garden*. Collins, London, 1971. *Plants and Plant Lore in Ancient Greece*. Leopard's Head Press, Oxford, 2000. Raven undertook an investigation into the claims of John Heslop Harrison on the occurrence of unexpected species in the Hebrides. The report was deposited in the Library of King's College, Cambridge and is unpublished, but is the basis of: Sabbagh, K., 1999. *A Rum Affair*. Allen Lane, London.

Redfern, Margaret 1942–
Author of *Plant Galls* (NN117, 2011)

Margaret Redfern has taught and researched the lives of gall-formers since her postgraduate research in thistle galls and the yew gall midge. This research became a long-term project which has now yielded possibly the longest run of data on any insect in the world. She has taught at the Field Studies Council and several universities, latterly at Sheffield University.

BOOKS *British Land Snails* (with R.A.D. Cameron). Synopses of the British Fauna (New Series) no 6. Linnean Society of London and Academic Press, London, 1976; *Insects and Thistles*. Naturalists' Handbook no. 4. Richmond Publishing, Slough, 1995; *Plant Galls* (with R.R. Askew). Naturalists' Handbook no.17. Richmond Publishing, Slough, 1998; *British Plant Galls* (with P.R. Shirley & M.G. Bloxham). Shrewbury, Field Studies Council, 2002, 2011; *De Gallis – On Galls by Marcello Malpighi. Facsimile with Translation and Interpretation* (with A.J. Cameron & K. Down). Ray Society, London, 2008.

Roberts, Peter James 1950–
Author of *Fungi* (NN96, 2005) with Brian Spooner.

Now a consultant and writer, Peter Roberts was a professional mycologist at Kew, the colleague of Brian Spooner. He is an enthusiastic field

mycologist at home and abroad, specialising in coral and jelly fungi.

BOOKS *British Chanterelles and Tooth-fungi* (with D.N. Pegler and B. Spooner). Royal Botanic Gardens, Kew, 1997.

Robertson, Noel Farnie CBE FRSE 1923–99
Author of *Plant Disease* (NN85, 1999) with David Ingram.

A modest but influential and well-regarded plant pathologist, he was professor of botany at Hull (where he taught David Ingram) before returning to his native Scotland as professor of agriculture at Edinburgh University and head of the East of Scotland College of Agriculture.

BOOKS *The Reason for Studying Plant Diseases*. University of Hull, Hull, 1960; *From Dearth to Plenty: The Modern Revolution in Food Production* (with Kenneth Blaxter). Cambridge University Press, Cambridge, 1995.

Roper, Timothy James 1948–
Author of *The Badger* (NN114, 2010).

An expert on the social behaviour of badgers, Tim Roper is Emeritus Professor for Evolution, Behaviour and Environment at the University of Sussex and past chair of the Mammal Society's advisory committee. He regularly advises government on animal management issues.

Russell, Edward John KT FRS 1872–1965
Author of *The World of the Soil* (NN35, 1957).

A distinguished agriculturalist and soil scientist, Sir E. John Russell was director of Rothamsted Research Station for more than thirty years, and helped to promote the scientific approach to farming and food supply around the world through his lecture tours and books. Concerned about the lack of forums for international exchange of ideas, he founded the Imperial (later Commonwealth) Agricultural Bureaux.

AUTOBIOGRAPHY *The Land called Me*. Allen & Unwin, London, 1956.

BIOGRAPHY Thornton, H.G., 1966. *Edward John Russell Biographical Memoirs of Fellows of the Royal Society*, 12: 457–77; Pirie, Norman W. In Oxford Dictionary of National Biography.

BOOKS *Lessons on Soil*. Cambridge University Press, Cambridge, 1911; *Soil Conditions and Plant Growth*. Longmans, London, 1912; *The Fertility of the Soil*. Cambridge University Press, Cambridge, 1913; *A Student's Book on Soils and Manures*. Cambridge University Press, Cambridge, 1915; *Manuring for Higher Crop Protection*. Cambridge University Press, Cambridge, 1916; *Farm Soil and Its Improvements*. Benn, London, 1923; *Microorganisms of the Soil* (with others). Longmans, London, 1923; *Plant Nutrition and Crop Production*. University of California Press, Berkeley, 1926; *The Farm and the Nation*. Allen & Unwin, London, 1933; *English Farming* (Britain in Pictures series). Collins, London, 1943; *World Population and World Food Supplies*. Allen & Unwin, London, 1954; *History of Agricultural Science in Great Britain*. Allen & Unwin, London, 1965.

St. Leger-Gordon, Douglas Francis Edward
1888–1970
Author of Chapters 11 and 12 in *Dartmoor* (NN27, 1953).

A Canadian-born man of Devon who wrote a number of books about the history and rural life of his native county. His wife, Ruth, who wrote a book about the witchcraft and folklore of Dartmoor, may also have contributed to the New Naturalist on which he was co-author.

BOOKS *Wildlife in Devon*. John Murray, London, 1923; *Dartmoor in all its Moods*. John Murray, London, 1931; *Devonshire* (County Books series). Robert Hale, London, 1950; *The Way of the Fox*. John Murray, London, 1951; *Under Dartmoor Hills*. Robert Hale, London, 1954; *Portrait of Devon*. Robert Hale, London, 1963; *Devon*. Robert Hale, London, 1977.

Salisbury, Edward James KT CBE FRS 1886–1978
Author of *Weeds and Aliens* (NN43, 1961).

Sir Edward Salisbury was a distinguished English botanist, director of Kew Gardens during and after the war when he was responsible for their restoration, and knighted for services to botany and agriculture. His work was at first ecological, but later focused on the reproductive biology of weeds and duneland plants.

BIOGRAPHY Clapham, A. R., 1980. Edward James Salisbury. *Biographical Memoirs of Fellows of the Royal Society*, 26: 503–41; Stearn, William T. In *Oxford Dictionary of National Biography*.

BOOKS *An Introduction to the Study of Plants* (with Fritsch, F. E.). Bell, London, 1914; *Elementary Studies in Plant Life* (with Fritsch, F. E.) Bell, London, 1915; *An Introduction to the Structure and Reproduction of Plants* (with Fritsch, F. E.). Bell, London, 1920; *Botany for Students of Medicine and Pharmacy* (with Fritsch, F. E.). Bell, London, 1921; *The Living Garden*. Bell, London, 1935; *Plant Form and Function* (with Fritsch, F. E.). Bell, London, 1938; *The Reproductive Capacity of Plants*. Bell, London, 1942; *Flowers of the Woods*. King Penguin, London, 1946; *Downs and Dunes*. Bell, London, 1952.

Sargent, Laurens C. 1893–1978
Collated notes made by Stephen Potter and co-authored *Pedigree: Words from Nature* (NN56, 1973).

Rector of St Peter's in Thanet, Kent, he was also a keen amateur ornithologist and philologist, and, at James Fisher's request, completed Stephen Potter's book, *Pedigree*, for publication. First President for the Kent Ornithological Society, 1951–56.

BOOKS *Consider the Birds*. University of London Press, Bickley, Kent, 1943.

Scott, Richenda C. 1903–84
Author of *Snowdonia* (NN13, 1949) with F. J. North and Bruce Campbell.

Richenda Scott was an economic historian and Quaker, who wrote several text books and biographies on Nigeria, Wales and aspects of Quaker history.

BOOKS *The Native Economies of Nigeria* (with Daryll Forde). Faber & Faber, London, 1946.

Simms, Eric DFC 1921–2009
Author of *Woodland Birds* (NN52, 1971), *British Thrushes* (NN63, 1978), *British Warblers* (NN71, 1985), and *British Larks, Pipits and Wagtails* (NN78, 1992).

An ornithologist and student of bird song, urban birds and migration, Eric Simms served in the BBC as a sound archivist and film director before turning to writing and looking after protected road verges at home. He is one of the most prolific of New Naturalist writers, producing large volumes on woodland birds, thrushes, wagtails and warblers between 1971 and 1992.

AUTOBIOGRAPHY *Birds of the Air*. Hutchinson, London, 1976.

BOOKS *Bird Migrants*. Cleaver-Hume Press, London, 1952; *Voices of the Wild*. Putnam, London, 1957; *Birds of Town and Suburb*. Collins, London, 1975; *The Public Life of the Street Pigeon*. Hutchinson, London, 1976; *A Natural History of Britain and Ireland*. Dent, London, 1979; *Wild Life Sounds and Their Recordings*. Paul Elek, London, 1979; *Natural History of Birds*. Weidenfeld & Nicolson, London, 1982; *A Natural History of British Birds*. Dent, London, 1983.

Smith, Malcolm Arthur 1875–1958
Author of *The British Amphibians and Reptiles* (NN20, 1951).

Malcolm Smith was an expert on the reptiles and amphibians of India and the Far East where he served as a medical doctor to the British Embassy in Thailand and later to the Siamese court. Founder and first President of the British Herpetological Society, he turned to British 'herptiles' in retirement as an associate of the Natural History Museum.

AUTOBIOGRAPHY *A Physician at the Court of Siam*. Country Life, London, 1947.

BOOKS *A Monograph of the Sea-snakes (Hydophiidae)*. British Museum (Natural History), London, 1926; *Fauna of British India, Ceylon and Burma: Reptilia and Amphibia* (Vols 1 and 2). Ralph Curtis, London, 1931.

Spooner, Brian Martin 1951–
Author of *Fungi* (NN96, 2005) with Peter Roberts.

Brian Spooner is the head of mycology at Kew Gardens where he directs the scientific work.

His personal research has included collecting in various parts of the world, as well as at Esher Common, which he has made one of the best recorded fungal sites in the world. He is also interested in trees, plant galls, insects and general natural history.

BOOKS *Helotiales of Australasia*. Cramer, Berlin, 1987; *Hadleigh Great Wood: The Wildlife and History of Belfairs Nature Reserve* (with J. P Bowdrey). South Essex Natural History Society, 1988; *Mushrooms and Other Fungi* (with T. Laessøe). Hamlyn, London, 1992; *The Mushroom Identifier* (with D. N. Pegler). Quintet Publishing, London, 1992; *British Truffles: a Revison of British Hypogeous Fungi* (with D. N. Pegler and T. W. K. Young). Royal Botanic Gardens, Kew, 1993; *Identifying Mushrooms: The new compact study guide and identifier* (with D. N. Pegler). The Apple Press, London, 1994; *British Puffballs, Earthstars and Stinkhorns* (with D. N. Pegler and T. Laessøe). Royal Botanic Gardens, Kew, 1995; *Mushrooms and Toadstools of Britain and Europe*. HarperCollins, London, 1996; *British Chanterelles and Tooth-fungi*, with D. N. Pegler and P. J. Roberts. Royal Botanic Gardens, Kew, 1997.

Stamp, Laurence Dudley 1896–1966
Author of *Britain's Structure and Scenery* (NN4, 1946), *Man and the Land* (NN31, 1955), *The Common Lands of England and Wales* (NN45, 1963), with W. G. Hoskins and *Nature Conservation in Britain* (NN49, 1969). See under Editorial Board.

Stearn, William Thomas (Willie) CBE 1911–2001
Author of *The Art of Botanical Illustration* (NN14, 1950, new edition outside series 1994) with Wilfrid Blunt.

A bibliophile, scholar and librarian of botany and gardening, Willie Stearn was for many years librarian to the Royal Horticultural Society before taking charge of the herbarium at the Natural History Museum. A natural polymath, he was a master of all cultural aspects of botany including art, language (Botanical Latin), and history. Also involved in British field botany on BSBI mapping schemes.

BOOKS *Botanical Latin: History, Grammar, Syntax, Terminology and Vocabulary*. Nelson, London, 1966; *Culinary Herbs* (with Mary Page). Royal

Horticultural Society, Wisley, 1974; *The Compleat Naturalist: A life of Linnaeus* (with Wilfrid Blunt). Collins, London, 1971; *A Bicentenary History of The Linnean Society of London* (with A. T. Gage). Academic Press, London, 1988; *Flower Artists of Kew: Botanical Paintings by Contemporary Artists*. Herbert Press, Royal Botanic Gardens, Kew, London, 1990; *The Orchid Paintings of Franz Bauer* (with Joyce Stewart). Herbert Press and natural History Museum, London, 1993; *The Art of Botanical Illustration* (with Wilfrid Blunt). Antique Collector's Club and Royal Botanic Gardens, Kew, Woodbridge, 1994.

Steers, James Alfred CBE 1899–1987
Author of *The Sea Coast* (NN25, 1953).

The authority of the geography of the coast, J. A. Steers was author of what was for many years the standard textbook, *The Coastline of England and Wales*. Professor of geography at Cambridge, his work made possible such projects as the National Trust's Project Neptune.
BIOGRAPHY Chisholm, M In *Oxford Dictionary of National Biography*.
FESTSCHRIFT *Orford Ness. A Selection of Maps mainly by John Norden*. Heffer, Cambridge, 1966.
BOOKS *The Unstable Earth*. Methuen, London, 1932; *The Coastline of England and Wales*. Cambridge University Press, Cambridge, 1948; *A Picture Book of the Whole Coast of England and Wales*. Cambridge University Press, Cambridge, 1948; *Physical Geography* (Ed). Cambridge University Press, Cambridge, 1952; *The Coastline of England and Wales in Pictures*. Cambridge University Press, Cambridge, 1960; *An Introduction to the Study of Map Projections*. University of London Press, London, 1962; *Blakeney Point and Scolt Head Island*. National Trust, 1964; *Processes of Coastal Development* (with V. P. Zenkovich). Oliver & Boyd, Edinburgh, 1967; *Coasts and Beaches*. Oliver & Boyd, Edinburgh, 1969; *Introduction to Coastline and Development*. Macmillan, London, 1971; *Applied Coastal Geomorphology*. Macmillan, London, 1971; *The Coastline of Scotland*. Cambridge University Press, Cambridge, 1973; *The Coast of England and Wales in Pictures*. Cambridge University Press, Cambridge, 1978; *Coastal Features of England and Wales*. Oleander Press, Cambridge, 1980.

Summerhayes, Victor Samuel OBE 1897–1974
Author of *Wild Orchids of Britain* (NN19, 1951).

The orchid specialist at Kew, V. S. Summerhayes was an expert on African and Polynesian species as well as those at home. Earlier in his career he was an Oxford ecologist and he served as treasurer of the British Ecological Society for twenty years.
BOOKS *Contributions to the ecology of Spitsbergen and Bear Island* (with Charles Elton). Journal of Ecology, 11: 214–86, 1923 [pioneering study which formed the inspiration for Elton's *Animal Ecology*. London: Sidgwick & Jackson, 1927]; *Flora of Tropical East Africa: Orchidaceae* (part I). Crown Agents, London, 1968.

Swinnerton, Henry Hurd CBE 1875–1966
Author of *Fossils* (NN42, 1960).

H. H. Swinnerton was well-known for his books about fossils, geology and landforms, which he also helped to popularize through his field courses. For most of his career he was lecturer, later professor of geology at what was then University College, Nottingham.
BIOGRAPHY Cleevely, R. J. In *Oxford Dictionary of National Biography*.
BOOKS *Outlines of Palaeontology*. Edward Arnold, London, 1923; *The Growth of the World and Its Inhabitants*. Constable, London, 1929; *Monograph of British Cretaceous Belemnites*. Palaeontographical Society, London, 1936–55; *Solving Earth's Mysteries*. Harrap, London, 1946; *The Earth Beneath Us*. Penguin, London, 1958.

Tubbs, Colin Rodney (1937–97). Author of *The New Forest*, NN 73, 1986, new edition outside series 2001.

Colin Tubbs was the Nature Conservancy's man in the New Forest for thirty years, and a fount of knowledge on the birds and ecology in the Hampshire area. A tireless defender of wild places, he was the foremost authority on the Forest and its management.
BOOKS *The Buzzard*. David and Charles, Newton Abbot, 1974; *The New Forest: An Ecological History*. David and Charles, Newton Abbot, 1968; *The Ecology, Conservation and History of the Solent*.

Pickard, Chichester, 1999; *The New Forest, History, Ecology and Conservation*. New Forest Ninth Centenary Trust, Lyndhurst, 2001.

Turrill, William Bertram OBE VMH FRS 1890–1961
Author of *British Plant Life*, NN 10, 1948.

A botanist and curator based at Kew throughout his career, W. B. Turrill made his name in experimental taxonomy and genetics, concentrating on the British flora (although he was also an authority on the flora of the Balkans).
BIOGRAPHY Hubbard, C. E., 1971. *William Bertram Turrill 1890–1961*. Biographical Memoirs of Fellows of the Royal Society, 17: 689–712; Coote, P. J. In *Oxford Dictionary of National Biography*.
BOOKS *The Plant Life of the Balkan Peninsula*. Clarendon Press, Oxford, 1929; *Pioneer Plant Geography: The Phytogeographical Researches of Sir Joseph Dalton Hooker*. Martinus Nijhoff, The Hague, 1953; *The British Knapweeds: A Study on Synthetic Taxonomy* (with E. M. Marsden-Jones). Ray Society, London, 1954; *The Bladder Campions, Silene maritime and S. vulgaris*. (with E. M. Marsden-Jones). Ray Society, London, 1957; *Royal Botanic Gardens, Kew*. Herbert Jenkins, London, 1959; *Vistas in Botany: A Volume in Honour of the Bicentenary of the Royal Botanic gardens, Kew* (Ed). Pergamon Press, London, 1959; *Joseph Dalton Hooker: Botanist, Explorer and Administrator*. Thomas Nelson, London, 1963.

Vesey-Fitzgerald, Brian Percy Seymour 1900–81
Author of *British Game* (NN2, 1946).

As a writer, broadcaster and editor of *The Field*, Brian Vesey-Fitzgerald was well-known to a wide public for his forthright views and breezy, countryman image. He is perhaps the only New Naturalist author who also wrote Ladybird books.
BOOKS *A Book of British Waders*. Collins, London, 1939; *A Country Chronicle*. Chapman & Hall, London, 1942; *Hedgerow and Field*. Chapman & Hall, London, 1943; *British Countryside in Pictures*. Odhams, London, 1947; *British Bats*. Methuen, London, 1949; *Hampshire and the Isle of Wight* (*County Books* Series), Robert Hale, London, 1949; *Rivermouth*. Eyre and Spottiswoode, London,

1949; *The Hampshire Avon.* Cassell, London, 1950; *British Birds and their Nests* (with Allen Seaby). Wills & Hepworth, Loughborough, 1953; *Nature Lover's Recognition Book.* Odhams, London, 1956; *Ladybird Book of British Wild Flowers.* Wills & Hepworth, Loughborough, 1957; *Ladybird Book of Trees* (with S. R. Badmin). Wills & Hepworth, London, 1963; *Town Fox, Country Fox.* Deutsch, London, 1965; *Portrait of the New Forest.* Robert Hale, London, 1966; *The Vanishing Wildlife of Britain.* MacGibbon & Kee, London, 1969; *The World of Ants, Bees and Wasps.* Pelham Books, London, 1969.

Walker, Norman 1918–1997
Author of *The Soil* (NN77, 1992) with Brian Davis, David Ball and Alastair Fitter.

Norman Walker was a member of the soil microbiology department at Rothamsted, working on the processes of decomposition, before moving to its chemical liaison unit.

Walters, Stuart Max 1920–2005
Author of *Wild Flowers* (NN5, 1954) with John Gilmour, *Mountain Flowers* (NN33, 1956) with John Raven, and *Wild and Garden Plants* (NN80, 1993). See under Editorial Board.

Watson, Adam FRSE 1930–
Author of *Grouse* (NN107, 2008) with Robert Moss.

Adam Watson is Britain's foremost authority on grouse and grouse moor management. Based in northeast Scotland, he is a dedicated ornithologist and hill walker, and an expert on all aspects of the Cairngorms, including its conservation.
AUTOBIOGRAPHY *It's a Fine Day for the Hill.* Paragon, Northampton, 2011.
BOOKS *Grouse Management* (with Gordon R. Miller). Game Conservancy, Fordingbridge, 1970; *The Cairngorms: Their Natural History and Scenery* (with Desmond Nethersole Thompson). Collins, London, 1974 (new edition, Melven Press,

Perth, 1981); *Animal Population Dynamics* (with Robert Moss and John Ollason). Chapman & Hall, London, 1982; *The Cairngorms of Scotland* (with Stuart Rae). Eagle Crag, Aberdeen, 1998; *Cool Britannia* (with Iain Cameron). Paragon, Northampton, 2010; *A Snow Book, Northern Scotland,* Paragon, Northampton, 2011; *Human Impacts on the Northern Cairngorms,* Paragon, Northampton, 2012.

Webb, Nigel Rodney 1942–
Author of *Heathlands* (NN72, 1986).

An animal ecologist, Nigel Webb worked on heathland and soil ecology at Furzebrook Research Station in Dorset, and also became a leading Dorset-based naturalist and conservationist.
BOOKS *The Butterflies of Dorset* (with Jeremy Thomas). Dorset Natural History & Archaeological Society, Dorchester, 1984.

Williams, Carrington Bonser FRS 1889–1981
Author of *Insect Migration* (NN36, 1958).

C. B. Williams worked in the West Indies, then Egypt and Tanganyika on insect pests. He was the first to investigate the phenomenon of insect migration from his base as an agricultural ecologist at Rothamsted. He was also an authority on the impact of climate on insect numbers.
BIOGRAPHY Wigglesworth, V. B., 1982. *Carrington Bonsor Williams.* Biographical Memoirs of Fellows of the Royal Society, 28: 667–84.
BOOKS *The Migration of Butterflies.* Oliver & Boyd, Edinburgh, 1930; *Patterns in the Balance of Nature.* Academic, London and New York, 1964; *Style and Vocabulary: Numerical Studies.* Griffin, London, 1970.

Wooldridge, Sidney William CBE FRS 1900–63
Author of *The Weald* (NN26, 1953) with Frederick Goldring.

Sidney Wooldridge is best remembered for his pioneering work on the geology and

landforms of the Weald, where he regularly took his students from King's College London. Established British geomorphology and was an active promoter of field centres helping to found the first one at Juniper Hall.
BIOGRAPHY Taylor, J. H., 1964. *Sidney William Wooldridge 1900–1963.* Biographical Memoirs of Fellows of the Royal Society, 10: 371–88; Baigent, Elizabeth In *Oxford Dictionary of National Biography*
BOOKS *The Physical Basis of Geography* (with R. S. Morgan). Longmans Green and Co, London, 1937; *London Essays in Geography* (edited with L. Dudley Stamp). Longmans Green for London School of Economics, 1951; *The Spirit and Purpose of Geography* (with W. G. East). Hutchinson, London, 1951; *Railways and Geography* (with Andrew O'Dell and W. G. East). Hutchinson, London, 1956; *The Geographer as Scientist.* Nelson, London, 1956; *London's Countryside* (with Geoffrey Hutchins). Methuen, London, 1957; *Outline of Geomorphology.* Longmans Green and Co. London, 1959.

Worthington, Edgar Barton CBE 1905–2001
Author of *Life in Lakes and Rivers* (NN15, 1951) with T. T. Macan.

A scientific administrator, the early part of Barton Worthington's ecological career alternated between Britain and the then colonies in East Africa, afterwards becoming the first director of the Freshwater Biological Association. Later he directed the science programmes of the Nature Conservancy and the 1960s International Biological Programme.
AUTOBIOGRAPHY *The Ecological Century: a Personal Appraisal.* Clarendon, Oxford, 1983.
BOOKS *Inland Waters of Africa* (with Stella Worthington). Macmillan, London, 1933; *The Evolution of the IBP* (Ed). Cambridge University Press, Cambridge, 1975; *The Nile.* Wayland, Hove, 1978.

Yeo, Peter Frederick 1929–2010
Author of *The Pollination of Flowers* (NN54, 1973) with Michael Proctor and *The Natural History of Pollination* (NN83, 1996) with Michael Proctor and Andrew Lack.

A Cambridge-based botanist, Peter Yeo was a plant taxonomist with a special interest in pollination (as a naturalist he was equally interested in insects). A librarian, he was also interested in horticulture and an authority on geraniums.

BOOKS *Catalogue of Plants in the Cambridge University Botanic Garden.* Cambridge University Botanic Garden, Cambridge, 1981; *Solitary wasps* (with Sally Corbet). Cambridge University Press, Cambridge, 1983; *Hardy Geraniums.* Croom Helm, London, 1985, republished with minor corrections by Batsford, London, 1992.

Peter Yeo

Yonge, Charles Maurice KT CBE FRS 1899–1986
Author of *The Sea Shore*, NN 12, 1949, and *Oysters*, M 18, 1960.

A Scot and a university teacher, Maurice Yonge took part in expeditions to the Great Barrier Reef and elsewhere in the 1920s and 1930s. An authority on bivalves, he was also a f irst-rate administrator, helping to establish marine biology research stations globally and advise government on marine science and fisheries.

BIOGRAPHY Morton, B. (1992). *Charles Maurice Yonge 1899–1986.* Biographical Memoirs of Fellows of the Royal Society, 38: 377–412; Allen, John A. In *Oxford Dictionary of National Biography.*

FESTSCHRIFT Morton, B., 1990. *The Bivalvia. Proceedings of a Memorial Symposium in Honour of Sir Charles Maurice Yonge 1899–1986 at the 1xth International Malacological Congress, 1986.* Hong Kong University Press, Hong Kong, 1990.

BOOKS *Queer Fish: Essays on Marine Science and other Aspects of Biology.* Routledge, London, 1928; *The Seas* (with F. S. Russell). Warne, London, 1928. Completely revised, extended and reset, Warne, London, 1975; *A Year on the Great Barrier Reef: the Story of Coral and the Greatest of their Creations.* Putnam, London and New York, 1930; *The ABC of Biology.* Kegan Paul, London, 1934; *British Marine Life* (Britain in Pictures series). Collins, London, 1944; *Crayfish and Lobsters.* John Murray, London, 1946; *Physiology of Mollusca*, 2 volumes (edited with K. M. Wilbur). Academic Press, London, 1964, 1966; *Pocket Guide to the Sea Shore* (with John H, Barrett). Collins, London, 1958; *Living Marine Molluscs* (with T. E. Thompson). Collins, London, 1976.

C. M. Yonge

Monograph Authors

Armstrong, Edward Allworthy 1900–78
Author of *The Wren* (M3, 1955).
See under Main Series Authors

Brown, Margaret Elizabeth (Peggy) (Mrs George Varley) 1918–2009
Author of *The Trout* (M21, 1967) with W. E. Frost.

Peggy Brown was a fish biologist and university teacher first at Cambridge and later at Oxford, where she was also an Open University tutor. She was active on various bodies of freshwater science as well as the 1960s International Biological Programme.

Buxton, Edward John Mawby 1912–89
Author of *The Redstart* (M2, 1950).

John Buxton's career as an Oxford don specialising in history and literature was interrupted by the Second World War when he was made a prisoner-of-war in Germany. A keen ornithologist, he spent the time studying redstarts. He introduced the mist net to ornithological study. Brother-in-law of Ronald Lockley (co-author of NN28).

BOOKS *Island of Skomer* (editor with Ronald Lockley). Staples, London, 1950; *The Birds of Wiltshire* (Ed). Wiltshire Library & Museum Service, Trowbridge, 1981;

Clay, Theresa (Mrs R. G. Seabright) 1911–95
Author of *Fleas, Flukes and Cuckoos* (M7, 1952) with Miriam Rothschild.

An authority on bird parasites at the Natural History Museum, Theresa Clay is best remembered today as the protégée and companion of Ernest Meinertzhagen, the controversial ornithologist.

BOOKS *A Check List of the General and Species of Mallophaga* (with George Hopkins). British Museum (Natural History), London, 1952.

Fisher, James Maxwell McConnell 1912–70
Author of *The Fulmar* (M6, 1952).
See under Editorial Board

Frost, Winifred Evelyne 1902–79
Author of *The Trout* (M21, 1967) with Margaret Brown.

A fisheries scientist who was also a keen angler, 'W. E. F.' was a senior scientist first in Ireland, later at the Freshwater Biological Association at Windermere working on the food and ecology ecology of charr, pike, eels, trout and minnows. Active member of the Salmon and Trout Association.

Homes, Richard Constantine 1913–78
Author (on behalf of the London Natural History Society) of *The Birds of the London Area since 1900* (M14, 1957).

Richard Homes was a city banker who became much involved with the London Natural History Society and editor of the *London Bird Report.* Served on the Council of the BTO for 26 years and co-founded the Kent Ornithological Society.

BOOKS *The Birds of the North Kent Marshes* (with Eric Gillham). Collins, London, 1950; *London Bird Report: 25 year summary.* London Natural History Society, London, 1974.

Jones, John William (Jack) OBE 1913–83
Author of *The Salmon* (M16, 1959).

A lecturer in zoology at Liverpool University, Jack Jones carried out pioneer work on spawning salmon, as well as other fish studies. Established a field station at Lake Bala and was a joint founder of the Fisheries Society of the British Isles.

Lowe, Frank Aspinall 1904–85
Author of *The Heron* (M11, 1954).

A Lancashire naturalist, Frank Lowe was wildlife correspondent for his local paper for nearly sixty years, and helped to organise local surveys of herons and other birds.

BOOKS *Days with Rarer Birds.* Trefoil, London, 1934.

Markham, Roy FRS 1916–79
Author of *Mumps, Measles and Mosaics* (M10, 1954)
with Kenneth Smith.

Roy Markham was a scientist and colleague of
his co-author Kenneth Smith at the Cambridge
Plant Virus Station, and later director of the John
Innes Institute. He was a pioneer in the use of the
electron microscope.
BIOGRAPHY **Elsden, S.R.** 'Roy Markham',
Biographical Memoirs of Fellows of the Royal Society,
28: 319–45, 1982.

Mellanby, Kenneth CBE 1908–93
Author of *The Mole* (M22, 1971).
See under Editorial Board.

Mountfort, Guy, Reginald OBE 1905–2003
Author of *The Hawfinch* (M15, 1957).

Guy Mountfort became famous overnight
for his groundbreaking field guide to British
and European birds, written with Roger Tory
Peterson. In the 1950s he took part in natural
history expeditions to Spain, Jordan and Pakistan,
and wrote books about them. He helped to found
the World Wildlife Fund and led its campaign to
save the tiger by setting up refuges in India.
AUTOBIOGRAPHY *Memories of Three Lives.*
Merlin, Braunton, Devon, 1991; Several of
Mountfort's other books have significant
autobiographical content.
BOOKS *Portrait of a Wilderness: the story of the Coto
Doñana Expeditions.* Hutchinson, London, 1958;
*Portrait of a River: the wildlife of the Danube from
the Black Sea to Budapest.* Hutchinson, London,
1962; *Portrait of a Desert: the story of an expedition
to Jordan.* Collins, London, 1965; *The Vanishing
Jungle: the story of the World Wildlife Fund Expeditions
to Pakistan.* Collins, London, 1969; *Tigers.* David
& Charles, Newton Abbot, 1973; *So Small a World.*
Hutchinson, London, 1974; *Back from the Brink
– Successes in wildlife conservation.* Hutchinson,
London, 1978; *Saving the Tiger.* Michael Joseph,
London, 1981; *A Field Guide to the Birds of Britain
and Europe* (with Roger Peterson and P. A. D.
Hollom). Collins, London, 1954 (Revised and
enlarged in collaboration with I. J. Ferguson-Lees
and D. I. M. Wallace), 1965); *Rare Birds of the World.*
Collins, London, 1988; *Wild India – The Wildlife
and Landscapes of India* (with Hashim Tyabji and
Gerald Cubitt). New Holland, London, 1991.

Neal Ernest Gordon MBE 1911–98
Author of *The Badger* (M1, 1948).

'The Badger Man', Ernest Neal was a school
biology teacher who devoted much of his spare
time to studying badgers in the field, in time
becoming a pundit, a writer and an advisor on
matters relating to badgers. He was a founder
and sometime president of the Mammal Society.
AUTOBIOGRAPHY *The Badger Man.* Providence
Press, Ely, 1994.
BIOGRAPHY **Baker, Anne P.** In *Oxford Dictionary
of National Biography.*
BOOKS *Exploring Nature with a Camera.*
Paul Elek, London, 1946; *Woodland Ecology.*
Heinemann, London, 1958; *Uganda Quest.* Collins,
London, 1971; *Badgers.* Blandford Press, Poole,
1977; *Biology for Today* (with Keith Neal). Blandford
Press, Poole, 1983; *Natural History of Badgers.*
Croom Helm, London, 1986; *On Safari in East
Africa.* Collins, London, 1991; *Badgers* (with Chris
Cheeseman). Poyser, London, 1996.

Nethersole-Thompson, Desmond 1908–89
Author of *The Greenshank* (M5, 1951).

Desmond Nethersole-Thompson was a passionate
and dedicated nest-finder and field ornithologist,
preferring the birds of the Scottish Highlands.
When not studying birds, he was active in local
politics and stood for Parliament twice.
BOOKS *The Snow Bunting.* Oliver & Boyd,
Edinburgh, 1966 (Second edition with additional
material published by Peregrine Books, Leeds,
1993); *Highland Birds.* Highlands & Islands
Development Board, Inverness. Distributed
by Collins, London, 1971; *The Dotterel.* Collins,
London, 1973; *The Cairngorms: Their Natural History
and Scenery* (with Adam Watson). Collins, London,
1974 (Second enlarged edition, Melven Press, Perth,
1981); *Pine Crossbills.* Poyser, Berkhamsted, 1975;
Greenshanks (with Maimie Nethersole-Thompson).
Poyser, Berkhamsted, 1979; *Waders* (with Maimie
Nethersole-Thompson). Poyser, Calton, 1986; *In
Search of Breeding Birds.* Peregrine, Leeds, 1992.

Prime, Cecil Thomas 1909–79
Author of *Lords and Ladies* (M17, 1960)

A school biology teacher and science master,
Cecil Prime was also a keen field botanist with a
special interest in thistles and primulas, as well
as the arum lily for which he won a doctorate.
BOOKS *Trees and Shrubs. Their Identification in
Summer or Winter.* Heffer, Cambridge, 1935; *The
Shorter British Flora* (with R. J. Deacock). Methuen,
London, 1948; *Experiments for Young Botanists.*
Bell, London, 1971; *Ray's Flora of Cambridgeshire*
(translated and edited, with A. H. Ewen). Weldon
& Wesley, Hitchin, 1973; *Plant Life* (Collins
Countryside Series). Collins, London, 1977.

Rothschild, Miriam Louisa DBE, FRS
(Mrs Charles Lane) 1908–2005
Author (with Theresa Clay) of *Fleas, Flukes and
Cuckoos* (M7, 1952)

Miriam Rothschild was a brilliant, cultured
and protean character whose interests ranged
at different moments from the anatomy and
taxonomy of fleas to animal husbandry, the
chemical basis of insect mimicry and the
restoration of meadows. She was a pioneering
conservationist and President of the Royal
Entomological Society. Her unique personality
lives on in her writings.
BIOGRAPHY **Atkins, Jeannine.** *Girls who Looked
under Rocks. The Lives of Six Pioneering Naturalists.*
Dawn Publications, CA, US, 2000; **Van Emden,
H.F. & Gurdon, J.** 'Dame Miriam Louisa
Rothschild'. *Biographical Memoirs of Fellows of the
Royal Society,* **52**: 315–30, 2006; **Haines, C.M.C.** In
Oxford Dictionary of National Biography
BOOKS *Illustrated Catalogue of the Rothschild
Collection of Fleas* (6 volumes) (with George
Hopkins). British Museum (Natural History),
London, 1953–83; *The Butterfly Gardener* (with
Clive Farrell). Joseph, London, 1983; *Dear
Lord Rothschild: Birds, Butterflies and History.*
Hutchinson, London, 1983; *A Colour Atlas of Insect
Tissues.* Wolfe, London, 1986; *Animals and Man.*
Clarendon, Oxford, 1986; *Butterfly Cooing Like a
Dove.* Doubleday, London, 1991; *The Rothschild
Gardens.* Hodder & Stoughton, London, 1996;
Rothschild's Reserves: Time and Fragile Nature (with
Peter Marren). Harley Books, Colchester, 1997; *A
Diversity of Birds: a personal voyage of discovery* (with
G. Stebbing-Allen, M. Woodcock and S. Lings).
Headstart, London, 1994; *The Rothschild Gardens:
a family tribute to nature* (with K. Garton, Lionel
De Rothschild and A. Lawson). Abrams, London,
1997; *Insect and Bird Interactions* (edited with H. F.
Van Emden). Intercept, Andover, 2004.

Shorten, Monica Ruth (Mrs A. D. Vizoso) 1923–93
Author of *Squirrels* (M12, 1954)

A zoologist, she studied mammals at the Oxford
Bureau of Animal Populations, and later the
Ministry of Agriculture and the Game Conservancy.
Frequent broadcaster on radio and television.
BOOKS *Wonders of Animal Life* (with E. Pinner).
Penguin Books, London, 1945; *The World of
the Grey Squirrel* (with Frederick S. Barkalow).
Lippincott, New York, 1973.

Smith, Kenneth Manley CBE, FRS 1892–1981
Author of *Mumps, Measles and Mosaics* (M10, 1954)
with Roy Markham.

A pioneer of virus research in insects and plants,
Kenneth Smith was the director of the Plant Virus
Research Station at Cambridge. He wrote the then
standard works on agricultural botany and viruses.
BIOGRAPHY **Kassanis, Basil.** 'Kenneth Manley
Smith'. *Biographical Memoirs of Fellows of the Royal
Society,* 28: 451–77, 1982.

BOOKS *Onion, Carrot and Celery Flies* (with J.C.M. Gardiner). Benn, London, 1922; *A Textbook of Agricultural Entomology*. Cambridge University Press, Cambride, 1931; *Recent Advances in the Study of Plant Viruses*. Methuen, London, 1935 (revised editions 1948, 1960, 1968, 1974, 1977); *A Textbook of Plant Virus Diseases*. Churchill, London, 1937 (revised editions 1957, 1972); *The Virus. Life's Enemy*. Cambridge University Press, Cambridge, 1940; *Beyond the Microscope*. Penguin, London, 1943; *Virus Diseases of Farm and Garden Crops*. Littlebury, Worcester, 1945; *An Introduction to the Study of Viruses*. Pitman, London, 1950; *Viruses*. Cambridge University Press, Cambridge, 1962; *The Biology of Viruses*. Oxford University Press, London, 1965; *Insect Virology*. Academic, London, 1967; *Virus-Insect Relationships*. Longman, London, 1976; *Introduction to Virology*. Chapman & Hall, London, 1980.

Smith, Stuart 1906–63
Author of *The Yellow Wagtail* (M4, 1950)

A Manchester textile chemist, he was also a keen photographer and a rare example of an amateur ornithologist with an experimental approach to bird behaviour. Active member of the BTO and founder of Manchester Ornithological Society.
BOOKS *How to Study Birds*. Collins, London, 1945; *Birds Fighting* (with Eric Hosking). Faber, London, 1955.

Summers-Smith, James Denis 1920–
Author of *The House Sparrow* (M19, 1963)

A research engineer, Dennis Summers-Smith has been the world authority on sparrows, at home and abroad, for half a century. At first attracted by their success, his long-term study turned into that of the sparrow's still mysterious decline. Awarded Stamford Raffles Award of the Zoological Society of London in 1992 for world renowned work on sparrows.
AUTOBIOGRAPHY *A Tribology Casebook: a Lifetime in Tribology*. Mechanical Engineering Publications, London, 1997.
BOOKS *An Introduction to Tribology in Industry*. Machinery Publishing, Brighton, 1969; *The Sparrows: A Study of the Genus Passer*. Poyser, Calton, 1988; *In Search of Sparrows*. Poyser, London, 1992; *An Introductory Guide to Tribology*. Mechanical Engineering Publications, London, 1994; *The Tree Sparrow*. Summers-Smith, Guisborough, 1997; *On Sparrows and Man*. Summers-Smith, Guisborough, 2005.

Thompson, Harry Vassie 1918–2003
Author of *The Rabbit* (M13, 1956) with Alastair Worden.

A zoologist at the Ministry of Agriculture, Harry Thompson was the authority on rabbits at the time of the myxomatosis outbreak. He was also much involved in animal welfare and an active member of the Mammal Society.
BOOKS *The European Rabbit. The History and Biology of a Successful Colonizer* (with Carolyn King). Oxford University Press, Oxford, 1994.

Tinbergen, Nikolaas (Niko) FRS 1907–88
Author of *The Herring Gull's World* (M9, 1953)

Niko Tinbergen was the world-renowned animal behaviourist who won the Nobel Prize, with Konrad Lorenz in 1973. Based first at Leiden in his native Holland and later at Oxford, his work on the social behaviour of gulls led to a new discipline of biological research that has been applied to human problems such as autism.
BIOGRAPHY **Hinde, R.A.** 'Nikolaas Tinbergen'. *Biographical Memoirs of Fellows of the Royal Society*, 36: 548–65, 1988; **Kruuk, Hans.** *Niko's Nature. The Life of Niko Tinbergen and his Sciencey of Animal Behaviour*. Oxford University Press, Oxford, 2003; **Burkhardt, R.W.** *Patterns of Behavior. Konrad Lorenz, Niko Tinbergen and the Founding of Ethology*. Chicago University Press, Chicago, 2005; **Hinde, Robert A.** In *Oxford Dictionary of National Biography*.
FESTSCHRIFT **Dawkins, Marian Stamp, Halliday, Tim & Dawkins Richard** (Eds). *The Tinbergen Legacy*. Chapman & Hall, London, 1991.
BOOKS *Kleew: The Story of a Gull*. Oxford University Press, New York, 1947; *The Study of Instinct*. Clarendon, Oxford, 1951; *Social Behaviour in Animals*. Methuen, London, 1953; *Bird Life*. Oxford University Press, London, 1954; *Curious Naturalists*. Country Life, London, 1958; *Animal Behavior* (with the Editors of *Life*). Time Incorporated, New York, 1965; *Signals for Survival* (with Hugh Falkus & Eric Enion). Clarendon Press, Oxford, 1970; *Tracks* (with Eric Ennion). Oxford University Press, Oxford, 1970; *The Animal in its World* (vols 1 & 2). Allen & Unwin, London, 1972 & 1973; *Autistic Children* (with E.A. Tinbergen). Allen & Unwin, London, 1983.

Worden, Alastair Norman 1916–87
Author of *The Rabbit* (M13, 1956) with Harry Thompson.

Alastair Worden was the young professor of animal health at Cardiff, where he specialised in rabbit control, going on to chair the Huntingdon Research Centre. He was a founder and leading light of the Mammal Society.
BOOKS *The UFAW Handbook on the Care and Management of Laboratory Animals* (Ed). Bailliere, Tindall & Cox, London, 1947; *Functional Anatomy of Birds*. Cage Birds, London, 1956.

Wragge Morley, Basil Derek 1920–69
Author of *Ants* (M8, 1953)

From a youthful passion for ants he became a research entomologist interested in insect behaviour and genetics before turning to journalism and consultancy work, including scientific films and early computers.
BOOKS *The Ant World*. Penguin, London, 1953; *The Evolution of an Insect Society*. Allen & Unwin, London, 1954.

Yonge, Charles Morris CBE, KT, FRS 1899–1986
Author of *Oysters* (M18, 1960)
See under Main Series Authors.

Book Dealers, Websites and Other Useful Contacts

BOOK DEALERS

The following is a list of recommended second-hand and new book sellers who frequently hold a good stock of New Naturalist titles:

Acanthophyllum Books
243 Pensby Road, Heswall, Merseyside. CH61 5UA
Tel: 0151 342 8287
Email: a.books@mac.com
Website: www.heswallbooks.co.uk
Contact: John Edmondson

Specialise in second-hand and antiquarian books on botanical art, botany, ecology, gardens, geology, natural history, science, travel and zoology. They keep a good selection of books on the Cheshire, Lancashire and the Lake District and also a more general stock which includes agriculture, antiques, archaeology, architecture, art, biographies, conservation, cooking, equestrian, fiction, genetics, heraldry, history, horticulture, medicine, music, poetry, topography and transport. They also run a book search service.

Birdnet Optics Ltd
5 Trenchard Drive, Harpur Hill, Buxton, Derbyshire, SK17 9JY
Tel: 01298 71844
Email: pflint@birdnet.co.uk
Website: www.birdnet.co.uk
Opening hours: Monday to Saturday, 9.30am–5.30pm
Contact: Paul Flint

Birdnet started as an ornithological paging and information service in 1992 which formed the basis for a business offering binoculars, telescopes and clothing. They also stock several thousand bird books, both new and second-hand, and specialise in New Naturalists, Poyser and 'BB' Watkins Pitchford. Birdnet also supply fine quality reproduction dust jackets of all titles in the New Naturalist library.

Bow Windows Bookshop
175 High Street, Lewes, East Sussex, BN7 1YE
Tel: 01273 480780
Email: rarebooks@bowwindows.com
Website: www.bowwindows.com
Contact: Ric Latham or Jonathan Menezes

Founded in 1964 and deals in good quality general antiquarian books as well as more modern collector's items. Although run by Alan and Jennifer Shelley from 1984 until 2010, Bow Windows is currently owned by Ric Latham and Jonathan Menezes. They have an excellent shop on Lewes High Street as well as issuing printed catalogues and listing much of their stock on their website. They usually have a good selection of natural history books and New Naturalist titles. They are always happy to try to help with either buying or selling books from single volumes to large collections.

Calluna Books
Moor Edge, 2 Bere Road, Wareham, Dorset, BH20 4DD
Tel: 01929 552560
Email: enquiries@callunabooks.co.uk
Website: www.callunabooks.co.uk
Contact: Neil Gartshore

Trading since 1997, Calluna Books are based in Dorset and specialise in buying and selling out of print natural history books. They produce 3 mail order catalogues a year and also attend selected events. Calluna Books maintain a stock list of over 2500 titles covering a wide range of natural history subjects including birds, invertebrates, flora, mammals, wildlife art and general natural history of the UK and worldwide. They also have a good selection of New Naturalist and Poyser titles.

C. Arden (Bookseller)

The Nursery, Forest Road, Hay on Wye, HR3 5DT
Tel: 01497 820 471
Email: ardenbooks@btinternet.com
Website: www.ardenbooks.co.uk
Contact: Darren Bloodworth

Originally established by Chris and Catherine Arden, the famous bookshop in Hay-on-Wye has specialised in New Naturalists for over 30 years. The business is now run by Darren Bloodworth and books can be purchased over the telephone, by appointment, online or through catalogues. Always an excellent stock of second-hand, antiquarian and also new books. Main subjects are natural history, ornithology, botany, gardening, bees and beekeeping. Four catalogues are published every year and mailed free of charge.

G. David Bookseller

16 St. Edward's Passage, Cambridge, Cambridgeshire, CB2 3PJ
Tel: 01223 354619
Email: gdavid.books@gmail.com
Website: www.gdavidbookseller.co.uk
Opening hours: Monday to Saturday, 9am–5pm
Contact: Neil Adams

Established in 1896 and known as 'David's', they deal in antiquarian, second-hand and remaindered books, also maps, prints and engravings. Good selection of natural history books and usually a good stock of New Naturalist titles.

Henry Sotheran Ltd

2–5 Sackville Street, London, W1S 3DP
Tel: 0207 439 6151
Email: chris@sotherans.co.uk
Website: www.sotherans.co.uk
Contact: Chris Saunders

Henry Sotheran Ltd was founded in 1751 and has established itself as a leading dealer of rare, fine and antiquarian books. Books are stocked on all subjects, but there is a dedicated natural history department, one of the last in central London. The Natural History department specialises in finely illustrated bird, botany and zoological books, Darwinism and evolution, earth sciences and, of course, New Naturalists. Catalogues on all subjects are issued throughout the year, with a major Natural History catalogue once a year and subject-specific catalogues appearing periodically.

Isabelline Books

6 Bellevue, Enys, Penryn, Cornwall, TR10 9LB
Tel: 01326 373602
Email: mikann@beakbook.demon.co.uk
Website: antiqbook.com/books/bookseller.phtml/isa
Contact: Michael Whetman

Isabelline Books was launched in 1995, specialising in ornithological books and usually have many of the New Naturalist titles in stock. They published a small range of specialist books on ornithology, all of which are still available. Catalogues appear at irregular intervals, once or twice a year. All books are available online.

Jay Books

Rowll House, Roull Grove, Edinburgh, EH12 7JP
Tel: 0131 467 0309
Email: jaybooks@blueyonder.co.uk
Website: www.jaybooks.co.uk
Contact: David Brayford
Jay Books specialise in out of print and antiquarian books specialising in books on science and technology, natural history, botany and gardening, travel and topography, illustrated books, and most non-fiction. Although they do not have a shop, books can be viewed by appointment.

Loe Books

Landreyne Manor, Coads Green, Launceston, Cornwall, PL15 7LZ
Tel: 01566 782 528
Email: loe@loebooks.co.uk
Website: www.loebooks.co.uk
Contact: Tim and Kate Loe

Loe Books specialise in natural history and related subjects and carry a large stock of New Naturalists, in fact well over a thousand copies. A selection of these is displayed on their website. They can usually offer an excellent selection of fine first edition New Naturalists and also carry a good selection of reprint and paperback copies. Customers are welcome by appointment and they are always happy to offer advice.

McEwan Fine Books
Ballater, Aberdeenshire, AB35 5UB
Tel: 013397 55429
Email: rhod@macewanfinebooks.com
Contact: Rhod McEwan

Mail order business specialising in Scottish non-fiction, country sports and natural history with a good selection of New Naturalists. Catalogues are available on request.

Mike Park Ltd
137 Grand Drive, Raynes Park, London. SW20 9LY
Email: mikeparkbooks@virginmedia.com
Website: mikeparkbooks.com

Specialist booksellers since 1975, their main subject areas are botany, gardening, floras and most branches of natural history. They do not have a shop, but issue several catalogues a year featuring newly-acquired stock in all subjects. These can be sent by post or email. Additions are also made to their website regularly.

NHBS (Natural History Book Service)
1–6 The Stables, Ford Road, Totnes, Devon. TQ9 5LE
Tel: 01803 865913
Email: customer.services@nhbs.co.uk
Website: www.nhbs.com
Founded in 1985 as an ornithological book specialist, NHBS now supplies new books on all natural history subjects including botany, ecology, conservation, environmental science, evolutionary biology, geology and zoology. In 2005 they stopped producing their famous newspaper catalogue and catalogues are now available online and as PDFs. They probably have the world's largest selection of scientific books and also offer an excellent selection of field equipment. There is a standing order service for New Naturalists.

Pemberley Books
18 Bathurst Walk, Iver, Buckinghamshire, SL0 9AZ
Tel: 01753 631114
Email: info@pemberleybooks.com
Website: www.pemberleybooks.com
Contact: Ian Johnson

Established in 1989, Pemberley Books are specialists in natural history (new, second-hand and antiquarian), particularly entomology and related subjects. They usually have a good selection of new and second-hand New Naturalist volumes in stock. Discounts are available on newly published volumes. One or two major printed catalogues are issued a year as well several newsletters highlighting new acquisitions and new publications. Their excellent shop is just to the west of London, near the M25, M4 and M40.

Portland Bird Observatory Bookshop
The Old Lower Light, Portland Bill, Dorset, England, DT5 2JT
Tel: 01305 820553
Website: portlandbirdobs.org.uk
Email: obs@btinternet.com
Contact: Martin Cade

The bookshop was opened in 1998 as a means of fundraising for the observatory and also to provide members of the observatory new natural history books. The bookshop has a huge stock of natural history titles ranging from those currently in print to long out of print and antiquarian titles. Their stock includes many rare and highly collectible titles and they have built up a reputation of being the 'Best Natural History Bookshop in the South West'. There is always a large stock of New Naturalists. The shop is open at weekends and on Wednesdays between 10am and 4pm.

Shearwater Books
78 Harbour Road, Beadnell, Northumberland. NE67 5BE
Tel: 01665 720654
Email: shearwaterbooks@yahooo.co.uk
Contact: John Lumby

Founded in 1975 as John Lumby Natural History Books and changed their name to Shearwater Books in 2000. They concentrate on scarce fine ornithology and New Naturalist first editions. Full stock lists available on request.

Stella & Rose's Books
Monmouth Road, Tintern, Monmouthshire, NP16 6SE
Tel: 01291 689755
Email: enquiry@stellabooks.com
Website: www.stellabooks.com

Two shops in the Wye Valley at Tintern and at Hay-on-Wye, offering a wide selection of rare and out of print books, especially children's and illustrated books. Also has a good selection of second-hand natural history books, including the New Naturalist series.

Sue Lowell Natural History Books
101 Cambridge Gardens, London, W10 6JE
Tel: 020 8960 4382
Email: sue4382@aol.com

Sue Lowell has a large stock of books covering all subjects of natural history including ornithology (including species, Avifaunas home and abroad, and behavioural studies) falconry, New Naturalists, Poysers, entomology, marine biology, bibliography and biography. Visitors are welcome by appointment.

Wildside Books
29 Kings Avenue, Eastbourne, East Sussex, BN21 2PE
Tel: 01323 416 211
Email: wildsidebooks@hotmail.com
Contact: Alan Gibbard

Wildside Books originated in 1982 as St Ann's Books run by Chris and Christine Johnson. They changed the name to Wildside Books in 2000 when a new gallery was opened 'On the Wildside', specialising in natural history art. Alan Gibbard and Lesley Rushton took over the business in 2007 when the Johnsons decided to retire early. They specialise in all natural history books with an emphasis on ornithology. They produce 3 or 4 catalogues a year always with a good stock of New Naturalist titles. Books are available to view by appointment.

WildSounds
Roses Pightle, Cross Street, Salthouse, Norfolk, NR25 7XH
Tel: 01263 741100
Email: isales@wildsounds.com
Website: www.wildsounds.com
Contact: Duncan Macdonald

Publisher, distributor and mail order company covering bird and wildlife sound guides, books, DVDs, atmospheres, PDA software (eGuides) and DVD/CD-Roms for birders and natural history enthusiasts. There is a comprehensive search facility on their website and they produce seasonal newsletters, detailing special offers and new releases. Usually a good selection of the more recent New Naturalist titles in stock.

Wyseby House Books
The Chapter House, Newtown Common, Berkshire, RG20 9DA
Tel: 01635 560009
Email: wyseby@btconnect.com
Website: www.wyseby.co.uk/new-naturalist
Contact: Tim Oldham

Wyseby House Books have been buying and selling old and rare books for over 35 years. They specialise in books on art, architecture, decorative art, gardening, natural history, science and history. Excellent website with over 20,000 rare, out of print and second-hand titles listed. They also have one of the most comprehensive selections of New Naturalist titles available anywhere from fine copies of scarce editions to cheap working copies.

Book Search Specialists
Tel: 07783 824258
Email: enquiries@lostworldbooks.co.uk
Website: www.lostworldbooks.co.uk

Lost World Books: used books and catalogues, rare, out of print, antiquarian and modern. Book searches on request.

WEBSITES

The following is a selection of the many websites which offer new and second hand natural history books for sale, most of which offer book search facilities where New Naturalist titles can be located:

www.abebooks.co.uk
Launched in 1996, AbeBooks is an online marketplace where you can buy new, second hand, rare and out of print books. The website connects with thousands of professional booksellers around the world so that millions of books are listed for sale. AbeBooks is now a subsidiary of Amazon.com.

www.alibris.co.uk
Since launching in November 1998, Alibris have grown to become the Internet's largest independently owned and operated marketplace. The website connects a large number of independent sellers of new, collectible and used books, music, and movies.

www.amazon.co.uk
Amazon is an American company launched in 1995 and based in Seattle. It is one the world's largest online retailers. The company also produces consumer electronics such as Kindle e-book reader.

bookshop.blackwell.co.uk
Blackwell's has been selling books for over 130 years and began their online services in 1995. They are a well respected business both online and in the traditional book selling world.

www.bookfinder.com
BookFinder was launched in 1997 and are one of the most successful resources for bibliophiles online. The search engine covers over 150 million books for sale from new, used, out of print to rare books. Every major catalogue online is searched and the results include which booksellers are offering the best prices and selection. Books can then be purchased directly from the original dealer.

www.ebay.co.uk
Founded in 1995, eBay connects a diverse community of individual buyers and sellers, as well as small businesses. eBay is

possibly the world's largest online marketplace, where it is possible to buy and sell almost anything.

www.newnaturalists.com
This is the official New Naturalists website from the publishers. There are sections on the history of the series, authors, interviews, downloads and features. Exclusive editions are available to buy from signed copies to limited edition leather bound editions. Current in print titles can be ordered as well as the full set of print on demand copies of the earlier volumes.

www.usedbooksearch.co.uk
This website offers a good search engine linked to thousands of book sellers worldwide offering used books and textbooks as well as rare and out of print items. The site offers a wide selection of books together with background information and comparative prices.

www.waterstones.com
A well established business, Waterstones opened its first London store in 1982 and now runs nearly 300 shops throughout the UK including their flagship store in Piccadilly which is the largest bookshop in Europe. Their high street shops offer a place where browsing is encouraged.

www.wildlifebooks.com/
Subbuteo Natural History Books Online has over 20 years of experience and specialise in natural history books. They offer books on avian reference, ecology, field and site guides for birds, insects and invertebrates, flora, mammals, amphibians and reptiles, and regional and country guides. They also stock travel guides and maps.

OTHER USEFUL SERVICES AND CONTACTS

The following is a selection of recommended organisations that provide a wide range of products, materials and advice for book collectors.

The Provincial Booksellers Association (PBFA)
Unit 5, The Old Coach House, 16 Melbourn Street, Royston, Hertfordshire. SG8 7BZ
Tel: 01763 248400
Email: info@pbfa.org
Website: www.pbfa.org

Founded in 1974, the PBFA provide provincial book sellers with a shop window. There are over 500 members that are experienced and reputable booksellers with a wealth of knowledge covering almost every area of antiquarian and second-hand bookselling and collecting. There is a detailed dealer directory available and the PBFA organise around 80 antiquarian and second-hand book fairs a year throughout the UK.

The New Naturalist Collectors' Club
30 Botley Road, Romsey, Hampshire. SO51 5AP
Tel: 01794 830937
Email: tbernhard@btinternet.com
Website: www.thenewnaturalistcollectorsclub.co.uk

The Club was created by Bob Burrow in 1998. Bob's famous shop on Jersey displayed a magnificent collection of New Naturalist titles, probably the greatest stock to be found anywhere at that time. Following Bob's death, the Club was re-launched by Tim Bernhard in 2007 with full colour printed newsletters and a useful website. There is a standing order service for members to receive each New Naturalist title as it is published at a discounted price. The Club offers free advice and book valuations and organises a biannual conference which features lectures by New Naturalist authors. A special sales website is run in association with Wyseby House Books and features one of the most comprehensive selections of New Naturalist titles available anywhere.

The Bookplate Society
Email: secretary@bookplatesociety.org
Website: www.bookplatesociety.org

Founded in 1972, The Bookplate Society is the direct descendant of the world's first such organisation, the Ex Libris Society which began in 1891.The Society encourages the production, use, collecting, and study of bookplates with various publications, lectures, members' auctions, meetings, and exhibitions.

Book Protectors & Company
Protector House, 76 South Grove, Walthamstow, London. E17 7NJ
Tel: 020 8520 0012
Email: enquiries@bookprotectors.co.uk
Website: www.bookprotectors.co.uk

Established in 1969, they offer a comprehensive range of protective covers for books of all sizes, including paperbacks and magazines. Advice is readily available from staff at the Walthamstow office.

D & M Packaging Supplies Limited
5A Knowl Road, Mirfield, West Yorkshire. WF14 8DQ
Tel: 01924 495 768
Email: packaging@dandmbooks.com
Website: www.care4books.com

Launched in 1993, D & M Packaging supply booksellers, libraries, schools and collectors with a wide variety of book jacket covers and book repair materials. They stock a comprehensive range of book protectors, paper repair, book cleaning and book mailing products. Also supply materials and tools for the restoration of books and documents. Catalogues are available on request.

Gresswell Online
Grange House, 2 Geddings Road, Hoddesdon, Hertfordshire. EN11 0NT
Tel: 01992 454512
Email: enquiries@gresswell.co.uk
Website: www.gresswell.co.uk
Orders and Product Advice: Mondays to Fridays, 8.30 am to 5.30 pm.

Gresswell provide a wide range of products such as specialist library supplies, furniture, shelving and other equipment. They are particularly useful for book care and repair materials, book coverings, archival accessories and storage. They offer a same day despatch service and a friendly customer service team. Gresswell are part of the Demco brand.

Preservation Equipment Ltd (PEL)
Vinces Road, Diss, Norfolk, IP22 4HQ, England
Tel: 01379 647400
Email: info@preservationequipment.com;
Website: www.preservationequipment.com.

Suppliers of *Groom Stick,* foam erasers and other book-cleaning materials, archival storage products, and general conservation equipment.

Glossary

Advance copy A copy issued to reviewers, bookshops with displays, authors etc. before the day of publication. Occasionally such copies have different or plain bindings and wrappers.

Arbelave Library Buckram A high-quality, strong & durable, acrylic-coated buckram manufactured by FiberMark Red Bridge International Ltd, of Ainsworth, Bolton, Lancashire. It is produced in over 40 colours, and since 1985 the dark green buckram with the code number '531' has been used as the covering for NN casings.

Arlin An imitation cloth also manufactured by FiberMark and used for the casings of the second states of NN70 *Orkney* and 71 *Warblers*, and the 1986 reprint of no. 64 *Shetland*.

Association Copy A book directly associated with the author, either through ownership or annotation, and if the latter owned by someone directly connected with the author.

Autographed In the hand of the author, hence the term 'autographed by the author', which does not necessarily imply it has been signed by the author; the inscription might read simply 'With the author's compliments' without a signature.

Back A synonym for spine.

Backstrip The spine covering (often paper) – 'backstrip detached' or 'backstrip sunned' etc.

Backing See 'Rounding and backing' and page 73.

Binding Used generically to mean the casing, though strictly speaking bound and cased books are distinct entities. Also used to infer a 'fine binding' i.e. a beautifully and expertly 'bound' book; not generally applicable to NN books, though some authors and collectors have their copies 'done up' in fancy bindings.

Blank A blank leaf i.e. one without any printing, which is an integral part of the book, and usually positioned at the front or rear. They are often simply spare pages, brought about by the necessity of using 16 or 32-page modular units (see gathering); NN82B, the second edition of *The New Naturalists* has two blank leaves at the back.

Blurb A commendatory summary of a book usually found on the front flap of the jacket or, if a paperback, on the rear cover; also used with respect to any statement advertising a specific component of a book e.g. the 'illustrations blurb' on the title page – 'With 56 Colour Plates by John Markham…' etc.

Book-block All the pages of a book, once collected and sewn together, but excluding the casing. Occasionally the term 'text-block' is used as a synonym of book-block.

Bookplate A printed paper plate or label pasted into a book to identify the owner; they are often specifically commissioned, sometimes by notable artists and may be elegantly designed. Bookplates often help to establish provenance and become part of a book's history: unless very crude or mass-produced, they should not be viewed as blemishes.

Buckram A woven, traditionally cotton cloth, starch filled, now often with an acrylic coating, and a particularly strong book-covering material, hence the fact that it is almost unknown for a New Naturalist to split along the joints. Buckram allegedly derives its name from Bukhara in Uzbekistan, where it was first manufactured.

Cancel A replacement leaf, and in the case of New Naturalist titles this is usually concerned with the title-leaf where published under licence by a different imprint, for instance the Philosophical Library edition of *Fleas, Flukes and Cuckoos* substitutes their title leaf for the original Collins leaf, which has been carefully cut out and the new title leaf pasted onto the stub. Cancels are also used where the original integral leaf contained incorrect information e.g. all first edition title pages of no. 2 *British Game* are cancels as the original page referred to 20 distribution maps when in fact there were none, and therefore all 20,000 title leaves had to be replaced.

Case/Casing The outer hard covering of a book to which the book-block is joined. A hardback book is often referred to as a 'cased edition' or case-bound, as against a paperback or softback.

Cockle/cockling Ripples or waves in paper usually caused by damp.

Collation The measure of a book's physical contents.

Colophon Summary of a book's printing details (author, date, printer, place of printing) that appeared at the end of a book and was generally superceded with the introduction of the title page in the early 16th century. Additionally, used to denote a printer's mark or device – what today we might call a trademark, but the term is applied in NN literature to the decorative motifs that embellish some NN monograms.

Concomitant Paperback Used in the context of this book to mean the paperback edition published concurrently with the hardback edition, and bound up from the same sheets, as opposed to paperbacks that are subsequent reprints.

Conjugate leaves Leaves that are joined together; every recto leaf will be joined to a verso leaf e.g. regarding NN13 *Snowdonia* the title page is joined to page xiv and page 4 is joined to page 9. This conjugacy of leaves is derived from both the number of pages per printed sheet and how that sheet is then folded (if a leaf is tipped in, e.g. a cancel title page this will not be the case.)

Contemporary In bibliography contemporary always applies to the era of a book's publication and not to the present, e.g.

if a book is said to have a contemporary inscription, that inscription dates to the time when that book was current.

Copac The merged online catalogues of all the important public and academic libraries in the UK and Ireland to which there is free general internet access. It is an invaluable research tool.

Copy The author's 'raw text' submitted to the publisher, before any editing takes place.

Copy-editing Undertaken by a copy-editor who corrects the author's copy, with regard to spelling and grammar and, depending on the brief, may also restructure sentences and passages to ensure that they are easy to read and unambiguous. A good copy-editor will also try to prevent embarrassing errors of fact, alerts the publisher to points of contention and any possible legal problems.

Copyright page Another, usually US term, for imprint page.

Cover The front (upper) or rear (lower) sides of a bound book or paperback, collectively covers; it does not apply in any respect to a dust jacket.

Dewey number Often used in the book trade in a generic sense to denote the number added to the spine of a library book (regularly in white ink). Derived from the Dewey Decimal Classification system, which organises books on library shelves in a specific and repeatable order, making retrieval simple. First developed by Melvil Dewey in 1876 and now used in 200,000 libraries in at least 135 countries.

Duraseal A proprietary clear plastic (polypropylene) protector fitted to all NN dust jackets between 1971–1985. It folds over the horizontal edges and is fixed to the underside via two beads of adhesive that run parallel with the top and bottom edges.

Dust Jacket The paper jacket that is wrapped round a book, initially designed to protect the binding, but now an integral part of a book's image. Sometimes referred to as the cover – which is both incorrect and confusing, and also the dust wrapper, not incorrect but still with a potential to confuse, as wrappers are the paper covers of a paperback book.

Edition A much abused term: strictly, it is used to identify when a significant change in the text or layout has taken place, and traditionally when a book was reset. In a loose sense, and contrary to its strict bibliographic meaning, it is used as a term to signify a different printing however insignificant the changes to the text and then often qualified numerically, e.g. the book ran to 10 editions.

Endpaper The sheet of paper at the front and back of a book used to join the book-block to the casing; the part that is stuck down to the casing is called the paste-down and the part that moves is the free endpaper, and then distinguished as the front free endpaper and rear free endpaper and so on.

Ephemera As implied, anything not designed to be kept and with regard to a bibliography this will usually be paperwork such as prospectus leaflets, bookmarks, advertising bands, information cards, publisher's catalogues and letters, and calendars. The ephemeral nature of such material means that few examples will have survived, and therefore particularly attractive to the collector.

Epigraph A quotation, phrase or poem positioned at the beginning of a book, often used as a device to set the scene for the following contents or to set a thought in the mind of the reader. Wilfrid Blunt in no. 14 *Botanical Illustration* uses a quote from Ruskin 'If you can paint one leaf you can paint the world'. Occasionally a whole page is dedicated to an epigraph – the epigraph page.

Errata slip A slip of paper inserted or tipped into a book after printing that identifies various errors.

Even working Designing and setting a book so that the contents fit exactly a multiple of a modular 16- or 32-page printers sheet, without any leftover (blank) sheets at the front or back of the book.

First edition The bibliographic meaning is clear and unambiguous: the first appearance of a work in book form. If that first edition has been reprinted, then that reprint is not a first edition – first edition only applies to the first impression of the first edition. The term is often qualified e.g. first trade edition or first illustrated edition, but these are not strictly speaking first editions – see also first edition thus.

First edition thus A euphemistic term favoured by booksellers as it implies first edition status without actually being so; essentially it means that the edition in question is the first appearance of a new production, for instance the Antique Collectors' Club revised edition of *Botanical Illustration*, which was published in 1994 in larger 4to format and with new colour illustrations throughout might be catalogued as 'first edition thus'.

Flap (front and rear) The ends of the dust jacket that fold over the boards and are tucked inside the book, the front flap usually carries the blurb and price and the rear flap advertising and author's biography; also referred to as the wings.

Flat signed Signed by the author to the book itself rather than to a slip of paper pasted-in, and consequently much preferred by the collector.

Flyleaf The front or rear blank, but it is often used (erroneously) to refer to the front free end paper. The term is avoided in this book.

Font Refers to a single set of type characteristics i.e. a precise combination of typeface, style and size. The type design for a set of fonts is the typeface; in the case of the modern New Naturalist it is FF Nexus, and where, for instance, FF Nexus italic 10-point is a font. In practice, font and typeface are often confused and used interchangeably.

Fore-edge The vertical edge of a page, and collectively the vertical edge of the book-block.

Format The size of a book in terms of its horizontal and vertical dimensions (not its thickness), and traditionally determined by the number of times the original printed sheet has been folded – three folds results in eight leaves which is octavo (8vo), that is standard NN size, and two folds results in four leaves which is quarto (4to), that is NN journal size; and so on.

Foxing Disfiguring yellow-brown blotches or small spots on paper, attributed to moulds, often associated with dust and other contaminants, prevalent on acidic paper or paper with impurities, particularly iron particles. Damp conditions are a catalyst.

Frontispiece An illustrated plate that is bound at the front of a book and usually opposite the title page thereby creating an attractive double spread.

Gathering The original printed sheet is folded down to create a gathering (with NN books) of either 16 or 32 pages. These gatherings or sections are gathered together to form the book-block and then trimmed.

G14 The rarest books in the series, published from the mid-1980s to the mid-1990s are often referred to as the *Golden 13*, which is somewhat of a misnomer in that that they are not golden from the collector's perspective (perhaps golden from the seller's perspective); but rather infamous. Furthermore, there are in fact 14 and these are NN70–83. The *gang of 14* might be a more appropriate term, but whether this or the *Golden 14*, the abbreviation 'G14' is the term generally used in this book.

Gang of 14 See G14.

Golden 13 See G14. (*Golden 14* – see also G14).

Ghosting Discoloration or tanning of paper caused by contact with another piece of (usually acidic) paper, often present on endpapers where in contact with the jacket flap, or board.

Half-title The first printed page and positioned immediately before the title page. It usually carries just the book title; occasionally other preliminary material is included here, especially when space is at a premium.

Traditionally the purpose of the half-title page was to identify and protect unbound book-blocks, and then to be jettisoned at the binding stage. But it now assumes the role of *hors d'oeuvres* and psychologically prepares the reader for the meat of the title page.

Head The top of a book, as in head of the spine, or head-margin.

Headband A decorative band fixed to the top edge of the back of the book-block, traditionally manufactured from silk or cotton, but now often synthetic. Evolved from a now-obsolete binding process, and used purely as a decorative accessory. All NN case-bound books since and including NN96 *Fungi* have been fitted with green and white chequered headbands.

Headline The book or section title (including the page number) positioned at the head of a page.

Hinge The internal junction of board and book-block: the internal fulcrum on which the boards are opened (see also joint).

Imitation cloth A paper casing fabric embossed or stamped to look like cloth, but unlike cloth coverings it is not a woven material and not as durable; most trade edition casings use imitation cloth, real cloth fabrics being the preserve of 'top-end' books such as the NN series.

Impression There are a number of different and distinct bibliographic definitions, but is mostly commonly used as synonym of printing (noun), e.g. the second impression or the first impression of the first edition.

Imprint The publisher and specifically the printer's name and address on any printed matter. Often used to denote a subsidiary publisher e.g. 'Collins is an imprint of HarperCollins'.

Imprint page The 'title page verso'; i.e. the reverse of the title page which carries copyright, printing and imprint (publisher) information and usually the ISBN too (referred to in the US as the copyright page, though the two terms are often used interchangeably).

In print A book is said to be in print, when still available from the publisher (see also Out of print).

Integral If a leaf is described as integral then it is an original part of the printed sheet making up a gathering and therefore will be physically joined to another leaf in the book, as opposed to a cancel or disjunct leaf which has been inserted.

ISBN International Standard Book Number; a unique number assigned to virtually every new book published since 1970. Originally consisting of ten digits but since 2007 ISBNs have contained 13 digits.

Joint The external junction of the spine and boards, upon which the boards are 'turned' (see also hinge).

Leaf A single piece of paper made up of two pages. The basic bibliographical unit.

Letterpress Text printed from metal type, but more commonly used to denote text as opposed to illustrations.

Linson A proprietary imitation cloth (see above); the term often used generically to infer imitation cloth rather than a woven cloth, and probably the brand used for a number of bookclub editions published during the 1970s. It is no longer manufactured.

Limpback see Paperback.

Mass-market paperback an inexpensive small format (A-format) paperback of which Penguins are the most famous example; Fontana NN titles are also mass-market paperbacks (see also trade paperback).

Mull An open-weave webbing easily impregnated with glue that lines the book-block and is essentially an apparatus to join the book-block to the casing. When bindings become loose and the original glue breaks down the mull is often visible between the gatherings and also at the hinges.

NN-ophile A lover of the New Naturalist series.

Number line A line of numbers, often 1–10 variously arranged, that identifies a book's print history. Generally, if '1' is present it is a first printing; if '1' is not present but '2' is, it is a second printing; if '1' and '2' are not present, but '3' is, it is a third printing, and so on. Nos 86 *Lichens* and 95 *Northumberland* both have number lines on their imprint pages.

Obi An advertising band that is loosely wrapped round a jacket, also known as a belly-band.

Octavo see Format.

Out of print A book is said to be out of print at the point the publisher's stock is exhausted, though may still be available in shops or from distributors (see also In print).

Out-turn The number of books actually printed rather than the number of books ordered, so for example, the print-order might be for 5,000 copies but 5,093 are actually delivered, and it is that latter number which is the out-turn. The printing industry generally works to a tolerance of +/- 5 per cent of the print-order, but in reality, it nearly always works out that more, rather than fewer books are printed – for which the customer must pay! See also Print-order and page 35.

Pagination System of numbering pages.

Paperback A book cased in paper or flexible card covers.

Panel The front or rear face of a dust jacket.

Paste-down The part of the endpaper that is glued down to the inside of the front or rear board.

Perfect binding One where the leaves are trimmed to all sides and glued together at the spine, not sewn; generally used for mass-market paperbacks.

Plates Additional, usually illustrated leaves, not part of the printed text sheets and either tipped or bound in; invariably printed on different and thicker paper.

Prelims see Preliminaries.

Preliminaries All printed matter before the actual text e.g. half-title, title, dedication, contents and illustrations lists, foreword, preface, etc., and often paginated separately in roman numerals, from the main text; regularly abbreviated to prelims.

Preorder An order received before the book has been published. Publishers will often reduce the price of books preordered as it enables them to recoup their investment more quickly and importantly can give an indication of the print run required.

Print-order The number of books ordered as opposed to actually printed (see also out-turn, p. 35).

Primary binding A term used to distinguish the earliest of any different publisher's binding styles.

Proof A copy of a book, made up from print-outs for the correction of errors. A copy is provided by the printer (or book designer) for the author to make corrections. Often bound in plain paper wrappers, and sought after by the serious collector.

Quarto See Format.

Quire A term with multiple definitions, but used in the Collins sales reports to mean a set of all the sheets in a book, folded and gathered together, but not cased.

Recto The right-hand page. See also Verso.

Remainder copy/Remaindered When a book is selling too slowly for it to be viable, the publisher will remainder the outstanding stock, i.e. sell it off to the highest-bidding wholesaler who, in turn, will sell at greatly reduced prices: such books are remainders.

Reprint A new printing and all but identical to the preceding printing; traditionally a reprint would have been printed from the same typesetting.

Re-set A new edition or a new page to be inserted that requires extensive changes to the text will require the type to be re-set. Most NN new editions are printed from the original blocks, with additional material inserted or the odd page re-set, consequently the layout of type on the majority of pages is unaltered. It used to be an expensive business to re-set type, but now it is easily done electronically.

Review copy A standard trade edition but often stamped 'REVIEW COPY' and distributed before the publication date to chosen reviewers. Occasionally they include the original review slip which notifies the recipient of the publication date and when reviews should be published.

Rounding and backing (R & B) The manufacturing process that gives the spine a pleasing convex shape and ensures the joints are well defined with a pronounced shoulder. As a result the book, when opened, will lie flat (if not designed to be read in the hand).

Rules A continuous straight line e.g. for the first 38 titles of the main series the illustrations blurb to the title page was always positioned between rules.

Section See Gathering.

Signature As a guide to the binder, letters are printed, usually discretely in a small typeface, in the tail margin to at least the first page of each gathering, where the first gathering would be lettered 'A', the second 'B' and so on. These letters are called signatures, and it is for this reason that printers often refer to gatherings (sections) as signatures. With the New Naturalist series the title initials are also incorporated in the signature.

Softback Paperback.

Spine That part of the casing or jacket that is visible when a book is on the shelf; consequently it is the most vulnerable element – and any image provided to show condition must include the spine.

Spotting Areas of disfiguring spots, more prevalent on acidic paper and when books are stored in damp condition; a euphemism for foxing!

Sheets The large sheets of paper on which the pages were originally printed; with NN books there are either 16 or 32 pages per sheet, the sheet then folded down to form a gathering or section. Also know as printer's sheets.

Subscription Subscribing to a book before publication, usually with a down payment of part of the total price, the rest to be paid at publication. But within the context of the New Naturalist series the term is simply used to mean preorders.

Sunning Fading.

Tail The bottom part of a book (see also Head).

Text-block See Book-block.

Tipped-in A leaf, slip of paper, cut-out signature, errata, etc., pasted into a book along one edge only.

Title, (The) Bibliographic convention dictates that the title on the title page is definitive, as often that on the jacket or casing is subtly different, occasionally entirely different.

Title Page The page that carries the title and usually the author too, and often the publisher and publication date.

Trade edition An edition of a book published for distribution to the general public through booksellers.

Trade paperback A larger-sized paperback usually of the same format as the hardback edition and with the same pagination; of better quality than a mass-market paperback, and commonly published after the hardback edition, but in the case of New Naturalist titles trade paperbacks are published concomitantly (see also Mass-market paperback).

Traveller A Travelling Salesman (the term is used in the Collins archive).

Typeface The type design for a set of fonts is the typeface; Baskerville was the predominant typeface used for New Naturalist books until the introduction of FF Nexus with the publication of 96 *Fungi* in 2005 (see also Font).

Verso The left-hand page (see also recto).

Webbing See Mull.

Wing (front and rear) The dust jacket flap; this term appeared at the base of the front flap, in the first few titles in the series, when the blurb on the front flap continued onto the rear flap: 'continued on the rear wing'.

Wrappers The paper covers of a book, i.e. those of a paperback. Often also used in the singular as a synonym of dust jacket though this application is best avoided, as it introduces potential confusion.

Abbreviations and Conventions

[ ] Square brackets denote that the information within them is derived or additional. In the case of page numbering it denotes that those particular pages are present but not numbered.

| Denotes a new line of text.

< Less than

ALS Autographed Letter, Signed

BC Book Club

BCA Book Club Associates

DJ Dust Jacket

Ed. Edition

EP Endpaper

HC HarperCollins

h/b Hardback

HTP Half-title page

inc. Included/including

ISBN International Standard Book Number

G14 'Gang of 14', or 'Golden 14' – referring to NN70–83

GSM Grams per square metre (of paper)

NN New Naturalist

NNC New Naturalist Club

No. Number

o/p out of print

o/s out of stock

over-p. over printed

PA Publisher's Association

p. page (singular)

pp. pages (plural)

Pb, p/b Paperback

pc or p/c Price Clipped (of jackets)

PLT plate

RU Readers' Union

s/b Soft-back (paperback

TP Title page

Acknowledgements

This book was always intended to be a celebration of the New Naturalist library and to incorporate as much information as possible on all aspects of the books, investigating everything from printed ephemera to all of the various editions of the books, from paperbacks to the elusive foreign editions. A project as detailed as this would not have been possible without the help of a great number of enthusiastic people over many years. From its original concept in 2008, I have had the invaluable support from several New Naturalist authors including Professors Sam Berry and Stefan Buczacki, Dr David Allen and especially Peter Marren. Many New Naturalist collectors have been extremely helpful in allowing me to access their libraries, to photograph and describe unusual or rare editions of the books, author correspondence and excessively rare items of New Naturalist ephemera. For this I would like to thank Paul Arnold, Ray Baldwin, John Barber, Ken Davies, David Kings, Ro McConnell, Peter Schofield, Denis Summers-Smith, Tim Sparks and Martin Walters. A number of booksellers have also been very helpful in locating unusual items, many of which are illustrated in this book. I would therefore like to thank Chris Arden, Darren Bloodworth, Paul Fisher, Alan Gibbard, John Lunby, Tim Oldham, Mike Park, Chris Saunders, Jeremy Steeden, Andy Ray and David Wilson.

I am most grateful to the guest writers who contributed a personal account of their connections with and love for these splendid books. These guest writers include such well-known naturalists as Nick Baker, Nigel Marven and Alan Titchmarsh as well as great nature writers such as Mike McCarthy and Stephen Moss. There is also a selection of New Naturalist collectors and bibliophiles including Mildred Davis, Ken Davies, David Kings and John Sykes as well as New Naturalist authors such as David Cabot, Jonathan Mullard and Stefan Buczacki. I am also delighted that Roger Long has contributed to this section, exploring the early days of the New Naturalist Book Club and its founder Bob Burrow.

Grateful thanks also go to the many sources of photographic material. The author and editor bibliography alone took more than a year to research and it became a Herculean task to try to locate a signature of every New Naturalist author and editor. The more barriers I came up against, the more I became determined to complete the task. Many people and organisations were exceptionally helpful in locating rare images and I would especially like to thank the following: Tom Gillmor at the Mary Evans Picture Library, Matthew Bailey at the National Portrait Gallery, National Library of Wales, David Hosking at the Frank Lane Picture Agency, Lianne Smith at King's College Archives, Freshwater Biological Association, Joanna Hopkins at The Royal Society, Julia Buckley at the Royal Botanic Gardens, Kew, Natural History Museum Picture Library, Geological Society, University of Exeter, University of Cambridge, Jamie Owen at the Royal Geographic Society, Lary Shaffer, Robin Easterbrook at the BBC Photo Library, Clem Fisher, Stephen Forge at Oundle School Archive, Liz Allsopp at Rothamsted, Lynne Farrel at the BSBI Archives, The Linnean Society and Jenni Tubbs.

It would be impossible to name every single individual, but I would like to thank every single person who, over the past five years, has helped with the content, design and layout of this book. I would like to thank Jo Foster for correcting parts of the manuscript and for her creative and helpful suggestions and Timothy Loe, my co-author, for his commitment to this project and for all his hard work.

Finally, grateful thanks go to Myles Archibald and Julia Koppitz at HarperCollins for putting up with my numerous requests for information, for allowing me to delve into the Collins archives and for allowing me to become part of the New Naturalist story.

Tim Bernhard, Romsey, November 2014

'No man but a blockhead ever wrote except for money' proclaimed Dr. Johnson. So a blockhead I must be. Albeit one passionate about the New Naturalist series.

Over the last ten years or so I have had the privilege of working with these fine books on an almost daily basis and during this time have been asked many questions relating to the series; some straightforward and some difficult or impossible to answer. It was clear to me that a detailed bibliography was required and in conversation with Tim Bernhard, who had recently taken over the New Naturalist Collectors' Club, it was agreed that we would work on this together. Discussions with Myles Archibald of Collins took place, who then agreed to the proposal, also realising that such a work would be an ideal companion volume to the very successful *Art of the New Naturalists*, and work commenced in 2010.

Naively, I thought it would take around a year to complete the main bibliography section, however, in the event it took nearly three: my apologies to all of you who pre-ordered the book only to see the publication date postponed again and again – and again. But I have argued and believe that it was better to get the book right, rather than to hurry it into print. And even now, there are still unresolved conundrums and a number of unanswered questions. (The protracted nature of this book has led to varying references to the age of the series and the number of books published. But as these do not alter the meaning of the text, they have generally been retained unaltered – a small testimony to the progression of the book.)

It was not until the laborious process of comparison commenced that I began to realise that the position was far more complicated than previously believed; each new discovery required careful verification and by the end of the process, well over 2,000 books have been examined and compared and my reference library, assembled for the purposes of this bibliography, now includes around 900 books, each different, though admittedly, many only slightly so.

What is very clear is that such a book could not have been written before the internet provided a common omniscience – at the click of a mouse, it is possible to instantly locate multiple copies of the same book. Numerous booksellers on numerous occasions have given freely of their time and provided bibliographical details of their books. To all, I offer my wholehearted thanks – and hope that the information contained in this book will go a little way to reward them for their labours.

Achievement of any lasting worth generally requires sacrifice, commitment and support, though even with these ingredients it cannot be guaranteed. It is for you the reader and user of this book, to determine its worth, though I am happy, given the various constraints, not least amongst them my intellectual shortcomings, that it is about the best I can achieve. But what I can say boldly and confidently is that it would not have been possible without the sacrifice, commitment and support of a number of people, and at the top of the pile is my wife and family. Kate has, for long stretches, single-handedly run our business (and looked after the family), freeing me up to work on the bibliography, and by so doing has essentially subsidised this work. She has been unstinting in her support and positive criticism. Simply put: without Kate this book would not be. My daughters Imy and Hattie are owed an apology as they have had to forfeit holidays and outings, and have often been denied the attention they deserve. Of course, to them, why their father spends so much time comparing the little details of the same books, is unfathomable. They accept it, not always politely, and ultimately dismiss it as a nonsense. Lest I take myself too seriously I must acknowledge that they are right, but I have hugely enjoyed the exercise and hope that it will give a little pleasure to others, and if so that is consolation enough.

Innumerable collectors and devotees of the series have offered their help freely and have been happy to consult their collections at the drop of a hat; many have also offered encouragement and support. I would like to thank them all and particularly, Brian Cubbon, John Cunningham, David Kings, John Rudge, Ian Williamson; there are others too who have specifically requested anonymity.

Special mention and thanks must go to Mildred Davis for proofreading my entire 'manuscript'. Not only did she do so quickly and efficiently, but additionally offered invaluable and balanced advice on issues of layout, format and content both from the perspective of a New Naturalist collector (Mildred has also contributed a piece on her own collection) and professional editor.

Finally, an apology to all NN-ophiles: my text, on occasion, may appear a little negative but, as already averred, I am an enthusiastic advocate of the series and any criticism should be viewed within this context. Also, bibliography is preoccupied with blunders, miscalculations and deviation, as it is such errancy that leads, so often, to interesting variation. There will of course be mistakes of my own making and for these I beg your forbearance. However I would be very pleased if you would let me know of them, so they might be corrected for future editions, and for that matter I would be very grateful to receive your views and criticisms generally regarding both the series and this book.

Tim Loe, Landreyne, Cornwall, November 2014

Addendum

TABLE 17A Analysis of the lettering elements to spines of NN first edition casings.

Lettering element to casing spine	Series numbers
TITLE IN CAPITALS	NN1–55, 57–63 & 70–94 and M1–22
Title in lowercase	NN56, 64–66, 67, 69 & 95–120
TITLE IN CAPITALS & lowercase	NN68
Diamond – solid	NN1–4 & 48
Diamond – in outline (in a variety of sizes and shapes)	NN5–12, 14–47, 49–55, 57–60, 62–65 & 67–94 and M1–19, M21 & 22
No Diamond	NN13, 56, 66 & 95–120
Star (instead of a diamond)	NN61 & M20
AUTHOR/S IN CAPITALS	NN1–72, 87, 94 & 96–120 and M1–22
Authors in lowercase	NN73–86, 88–93 & 95
Authors' names omitted	NN13 (B1 variant)
COLLINS IN CAPITALS	NN1–94 and M1–22
Collins in lowercase	NN95–120
With series number	NN66 & 95

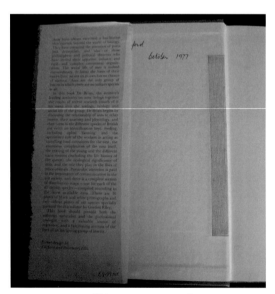

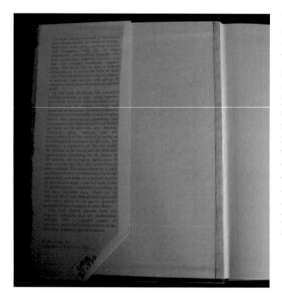

Photographs showing the mull/tape arrangements for NN59 *Ants*. The mull or binding tape is used to attach the book-block to the casing with the end-papers pasted on top. This arrangement is an important diagnostic tool for determining binding variants of a number of NN titles (as described in the text). The variant with the thin strip of tape running the whole length of the hinge nearly always signifies a later binding.

NN59 *Ants*. Internal hinge arrangement for NN59A–B1, Primary Binding Variant. The mull or webbing (here, highlighted in red) is an impression evident under the paste-down paper running only part way along the hinge. Note the inscription in this copy 'October 1977' which dates it to the month of first publication.

NN59 *Ants*. Internal hinge arrangement for NN59A–B2, Second Binding Variant. The binding tape (here, highlighted in red) is an impression evident under the pasted-down paper as a thin strip running the complete length of the hinge. Note the clipped and repriced jacket, which at £7.95 indicates this copy was sold in 1981.

Index